ALSO BY BRAD LEITHAUSER

Novels

A Few Corrections (2001)

The Friends of Freeland (1997)

Seaward (1993)

Hence (1989)

Equal Distance (1985)

Poetry

Curves and Angles (2006)

Darlington's Fall (2003)

The Odd Last Thing She Did (1998)

The Mail from Anywhere (1990)

Cats of the Temple (1986)

Hundreds of Fireflies (1982)

Essays

Penchants and Places (1995)

Light Verse

Toad to a Nightingale (2007)

Lettered Creatures (2004)

The Art Student's War

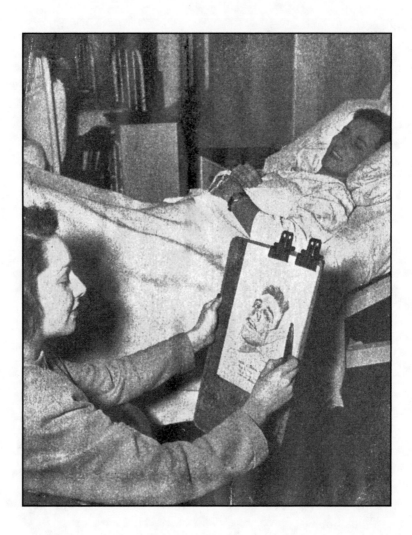

The Art Student's War

BRAD LEITHAUSER

ALFRED A. KNOPF   New York   2009

This is a work of fiction. Names, characters, places, and incidents
either are the product of the author's imagination or are used fictitiously.
Any resemblance to actual persons living or dead, events,
or locales is entirely coincidental.

Library of Congress Cataloguing-in-Publication Data
Leithauser, Brad.
The art student's war / by Brad Leithauser.—1st ed.
p.   cm.
ISBN 978-0-307-27111-2
1. Detroit (Mich.)—History—20th century—Fiction.   2. Domestic fiction.   I. Title.
PS3562.E4623A89 2009
813'.54—dc22   2009019468

Manufactured in the United States of America
Published November 5, 2009
Second Printing, December 2009

FOR FOUR
WHO KNEW BOTH
THE CITY
AND THE WAR:

Lormina Paradise Salter (1924–1983)

Harold Edward Leithauser (1922–1985)

Gladys Garner Leithauser Higbee

Arthur Higbee

From some unimaginably distant corner of the cosmos
a light has come down to illuminate her personally.

A Few Corrections

Colors without objects—colors alone—
wriggle in the tray of my eye,

incubated under the great flat lamp
of the sun . . .

"Colors without Objects"
May Swenson

AUTHOR'S NOTE

While still a teenager, during the Second World War, my mother-in-law began drawing portraits of hospitalized soldiers. I never discussed this with her. By the time I began to contemplate a book set in Detroit during the War, she had been dead some twenty years. But it was a heartening moment when I realized that this vanished woman was offering me, from beyond the grave, with characteristic generosity, another gift: the premise for a novel.

My heroine, Bianca Paradiso, has few connections—of appearance, of character, of family—with my mother-in-law, who was born Lormina Paradise and who composed her soldier-portraits in various places, including New York City. But I retained, as an act of fealty, her surname—going it one better by restoring its original spelling. And I proceeded over the years of the book's writing with a strong sense that it must serve as a tribute—to my mother-in-law, and to my parents, whose Midwest I would seek to capture, and not least to Detroit itself, my beleaguered and beloved hometown, in all its clanking, gorgeous heyday.

My mother-in-law gave the portraits to the soldiers themselves. What I'm left with are, literally, copies of copies of copies. A few of these have been scattered throughout these pages, as well as a solitary photograph: artist, bed-ridden soldier, and the portrait that binds them. It's a small image that seemed to summon me to write a large and grateful book.

PART ONE

The War Comes Home

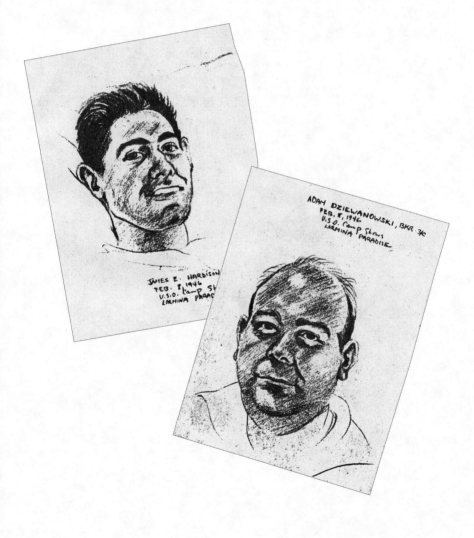

JAMES E. HARDISON
FEB. 8, 1946
V.S.O. Camp Sh
LORMINA PARA

ADAM DZIEWANOWSKI, BKR. 3c
FEB. 8, 1946
V.S.O. Camp Shows
LORMINA PARADISE

PART ONE

The War Comes Home

CHAPTER I

When the streetcar halts at Woodward and Mack, the young soldier who climbs aboard with some difficulty—he looks new to his crutches—is surpassingly handsome. Everybody notices him. His hair, long for a soldier's, is shiny black. His eyes are arrestingly blue. That gaze of his is slightly unnerving and suggests a sizable temper, maybe. Or maybe not, for the crooked grin he releases at seeing himself securely aboard is boyish and winsome. Everybody in this dusty car feels heartened by him. A nation capable of producing soldiers as stirring as this young soldier—how could it possibly lose the War?

Although she doesn't allow herself to stare openly, nobody is more observant of the handsome wounded young soldier than someone called Bea, whose true name is Bianca: Bianca Paradiso. A tall girl wearing a red hat, she stands in the middle of the car. The War has been unfolding for what feels like ages and those tranquil days before the soldiers overran the streets seem to belong to her childhood. The olive drab and navy blue of the boys' uniforms have reconstituted the palette of the city. Bea is an art student. She examines minutely the city's streets and streetcars, parks and store-window displays and billboards, and of course its automobiles. Her teacher last quarter, Professor Evanman, spoke of automobiles as the city's "blood vessels"—this is, after all, the Motor City—and he urged his students to view Detroit as "a living creature." The advice struck powerfully: the city as a living creature. Bea is eighteen.

She cultivates these days an enhanced receptivity to color, including the heavy black of this soldier's hair, and the hovering, weightless, gas-fire blue of his eyes, to say nothing of the emphatic fresh white of the plaster bandage encasing his left leg. Bea is heading home from a two-hour class in still-life painting. Her professor this term is Professor Manhardt, who would never counsel his students to contemplate anything automotive. Professor Manhardt is a purist. He, too, offers inspiring advice. An artist never stops mixing paint . . . That's one of Professor Manhardt's maxims, and while heading home from class Bea typically entertains a drifting armada of colors without objects—big floating swatches and swirls of pigment.

Yes, servicemen's uniforms have colored the city for a long time, but it's only recently, in this sodden late spring of 1943, that you've begun to see many of the wounded. There's a special light attending them, like El Greco's figures. Each glimpse of a wounded soldier forces you into a fearful medical appraisal. *How bad is he hurt?* That's always the first question in everybody's mind. And *Please, God, not too badly* . . . That's the follow-up prayer. *Please, God.* Fortunately, nobody Bea personally knows has been wounded or killed, so far at least, although a high school classmate, Bradley Hake, has long been missing in action in the Philippines.

Well, this one, the very good-looking boy on the Woodward Avenue streetcar, isn't hurt too badly. Though his leg is bandaged all the way above his knee, and though he grimaced on the car step, he exudes a brimming youthful well-being once aboard. It's so good to be home, his grin declares. Good to be alive in a month in which, as the newspapers daily report, American boys by the hundreds are dying overseas. Yes, truly it is wonderful to be back in Detroit, on this last Friday in May, the twenty-eighth of May, after a record-breaking stretch of rainy days, riding a streetcar up Woodward Avenue, the city's central thoroughfare, with a mixed crowd of people who are—men and women, white and colored—heading home for supper.

It's approaching five o'clock and the streetcar is full, with recent arrivals like Bea left standing. Streetcars are always full, ever since the War started. Of course there's not a chance in the world the soldier will be left standing. It's only a matter of who's to have the honor of first catching his eye and offering up a seat.

This privilege falls to a badly shaved, grizzled little man wearing a patched jacket and a tan corduroy cap. His hands, although scrubbed, are still grimed from a day at the factory. Bea observes everything. As he rises from his seat he instinctively doffs his tan cap, revealing a threadbare scalp on which a nasty-looking boil—his own modest wound—gleams painfully. If the young black-haired soldier had been his own flesh and blood, the grizzled little man couldn't regard him with deeper paternal satisfaction. The man with the boil has been granted an opportunity both honorable and precious: the chance for a small but conspicuous display of patriotism.

The young soldier nods obligingly. He has a boy's still-skinny neck, with an outsized, bobbing Adam's apple. It isn't just his crutches that make him gawky. If he weren't so handsome, he might almost be silly-looking. He takes a step forward, on his crutches, halts and glances around the car. Decisively, his eye hooks Bianca Paradiso's attentive eye.

And then—then, to the girl's horror, to her crawling, incredulous, consummate horror—the soldier signals to her. She prays she's mistaken, but there it is, undeniably: the soldier repeats the gesture and lifts a beckoning eyebrow.

No possible doubt what he intends: he means for Bea to occupy the seat vacated by the man with the tan corduroy cap. Instantly, Bea's face blushes so intensely that her nose and forehead actually ache.

Everybody's watching. It's just as though the streetcar has halted. It's as if the whole city has halted and everybody in Detroit is gaping at her, while she, so keenly susceptible to embarrassment, undergoes paralysis. She shakes her head once, vehemently, and with her free hand throws off a jerky motion of dismissal—a helpless, importunate gesture. Is she going to sit while the wounded soldier stands?

Don't, her gesture says. It's all she can say.

But resolution is written on the handsome soldier's face. This boy isn't about to retreat. Retreat? In recent months he has endured far too much to consider *that*. He has been shot at by absolute strangers, people doing their best to kill him, out in unimaginably strange lands. Is he now going to be fended off by a pretty girl in an odd red hat, standing in a Detroit streetcar with a notebook under her arm?

He continues to regard her with his charged blue glance, into which seemingly has entered a beseeching, indeed a vulnerable aspect. He is requesting a favor. *Won't* she oblige him? Please? Or will she refuse him—refuse him a privilege she'd grant unthinkingly if he stood before her whole and unimpaired?

If he stood before her as the boy he used to be, not so very long ago, without crutches or bandages, wouldn't she unhesitatingly take the offered seat?

The ghastly moment unfreezes itself, there is no way out except forward, and, stooping (she's quite a tall girl, who tends to stoop accommodatingly), Bea slips into the empty seat. She plants her gaze on the gritty floor, where a couple of last-drag smokers have, on boarding, pitched cigarette butts. The true painter observes everything, and yet she cannot *bear* to meet anyone's eyes. She vows not to look up again—not once—until her stop is reached.

It's a pity Bea doesn't look up, for the ensuing drama would naturally engage any artist's eye. The delicate, tense pantomime of the handsome wounded soldier and the lanky, dark, strikingly pretty Italian-looking girl serves as a mere prelude. Once Bea has awkwardly swiveled, face aflame, into the offered seat, the rest of the car leaps into motion. Simultaneously, four, five, half a dozen men spring up, each volunteering a place for the soldier. He had their goodwill from the outset, of course, by dint of his uniform and his cheerfully wielded crutches. But something far more potent has been awakened: at the fatigued end of a hot day, and of a long week, he has restored for them the meaning of gallantry. They are abashed and upraised, and they all adore him.

Gaze steadily downcast, Bea holds true to her vow for two more stops. Her red hat is in her lap. She refers to it—a little joke—as her Hungarian beret. It's neither Hungarian nor a beret; it's something she picked up across the river, in Windsor, Canada. It's made of bright red felt, almost scarlet, with a velvet rim of a different red, almost crimson. She'd chosen it after determining that it looked arty without looking *too* arty.

Nagging curiosity soon overcomes her, and she allows herself a few peeks out the window. The storefronts are, if possible, more patriotic than usual, in celebration of Decoration Day, which this year falls on a Sunday, two days from now. A holiday weekend is beginning, and the streetcar passes a movie theater advertising a two a.m. showing for defense workers, whose schedules might not otherwise allow a movie. The War has changed everything.

She permits herself a few darting glances at her fellow passengers. People are still peering at her. The soldier sits on the other side of the car. He has struck up a conversation with the colored woman beside him. Although Bea can't hear what he's saying, she appreciates the unself-conscious way he conducts the conversation. Bea can't hear what the woman is saying either, although the phrase "My boy Hector" lifts into audibility. A moment later it surfaces again, "My boy Hector," and a moment later. The handsome soldier nods attentively and cordially.

Because he seems so engrossed, Bea dares a full appraisal of his face. His eyelashes are long and luxuriant—evident even from here. His nose, prominent but fine-boned, with sharply contoured nostrils, calls out to be painted. (She worries, frequently, that her own nose is too long.) Suddenly, as if having sensed her gaze, the soldier throws her a glance . . . Bea drops her eyes.

This time, she keeps them on the floor for only one stop, and when she peeks upward her demure show of modesty proves sadly superfluous: a fat woman in a preposterous orange coat has posted herself directly between Bea and the soldier. Making the best of her obstructed view, Bea studies the soldier's legs—the good one folded beneath him, the bad bandaged one, which he cannot bend, thrust out into the aisle. He has big feet, to match that big Adam's apple.

The woman in the orange coat shuffles toward the back of the car and across the suddenly cleared vista the black-haired blue-eyed soldier stares straight into Bea's eyes and grins.

So inviting is that smile—so seemingly innocent of the anguish he has inflicted—it seems a pity not to hold his glance. But Bea, flustered, again drops her eyes. She tries to think about the contents of her portfolio, today's sketch of a hairbrush and a glass of soda water, but she cannot bring its reality to mind. And then—

Then something unfolds that she's wholly unprepared for: the soldier stands. He is about to exit the car.

Before he does so, however, he has some unfinished business. Although Bea's eyes are downcast, she feels his approach. And when he speaks—lightly, a little breathlessly—it's as though she has heard that voice before: "Nice ridin' with ya, miss," he says.

Bea peers upward with a guilty frantic quickness, and this time, for a moment that opens into something far more amplitudinous than a mere moment, her eyes hold and negotiate his gaze. And this time, *this* time she uncovers more than genial innocence in his look. She finds hunger, and a wordless understanding. Bea experiences something never felt before—a new chapter in her life. It's almost as though, until this afternoon, she'd never learned the trick of gazing into anybody's eyes. It's vertiginous, truly: her sensation of an instantaneous, fused, fated linkage. It's as though she's melting, but melting in one direction—his direction.

How long do they lock gazes? Once the connection is broken, there's no saying, there's only a belated recognition of his having moved on, and her tardy acknowledgment of gratitude, called out much too faintly: "Thank you, Soldier."

She says nothing further, and once all the clocks on earth recommence, time grinds forward relentlessly: in just a few seconds, the soldier has maneuvered himself off the streetcar. Craning forward, Bea is able to see, as he makes his laborious way down the sidewalk, the crown of his bobbing dark-haired head and his profiled nose. And that's all.

Gone forever: the unreckonable glance that dropped so deeply into her own.

The streetcar clatters forward on its route, the soldier disappears into the bricks and asphalt of the city. The story cannot be finished before it has begun—can it?

"He didn't even hear me thank him," Bea says to herself. Though she's whispering, she can hardly get the words out, for her throat's a knot of aching emotions.

"He didn't even hear me thank him," she sighs once more, and this time, along with her remorse, she locates in the words a bittersweet beauty. Wasn't the encounter perfect in its way? It's one more poignant war story—one among millions of wartime poignancies—and Bea savors this sensation of having been enlisted in a sweeping modern military enterprise: she has shared something beautiful and touching with a handsome, unnamed, wounded soldier. She has plumbed the vulnerable eyes of somebody who just as easily might never have come back.

Everything changes—as it so often does—the moment she climbs down from the enclosure of the streetcar; time itself shifts, shifted. When, in the open air, she spoke the words once more, Bea felt a renewed sense of wistful impoverishment: "He didn't even hear me thank him." This time the phrase sounded dry and matter-of-fact, as though the soldier really did belong to the past tense and their story were over.

Eventually, Bea made her way down the only street she'd ever lived on, which had the oddest name of any street she knew: Inquiry. In all her novel reading, she'd never come upon its like. All the other neighborhood streets had streetlike names: Kercheval, Canton, Lafayette, Helen, Mount Elliott, Sylvester, Gratiot, Goethe, Mack . . . Doubtless there was an explanation, but it seemed no one had made an inquiry about Inquiry; nobody in the neighborhood could explain why she was living on a street that—so she liked to declare—might as well be Question Mark Avenue.

She passed the house of the Sgouroses, who once kept a goat in their backyard, and the Dawkinses, the Whites, the McNamees, and the Higbees, whose boy, Hugh, was in the Navy. She passed the Szots', where Bea's best friend, Maggie Szot, used to live, before getting married at the tender age of seventeen and becoming Maggie Hamm. (As Maggie was the first to point out, she had terrible luck with names.) Maggie lived with her in-laws on the West Side, while her husband, George, was stationed out in Hawaii. George used to have bad teeth but now poor George had no teeth at all. An Army dentist, foreseeing grave problems if any tooth abscessed while George was in combat, decided to yank them, every one, and give him dentures. (As it turned out, George was assigned a desk job.)

A pair of white gulls wheeled overhead, cawing needfully to each other. Inquiry Street lay close enough to the river—the Detroit River— that you often saw seagulls over its rooftops.

Bea passed the home of the "Dutch ladies," two spinster sisters, Miss Slopsema and Miss Slopsema, who maintained the cleanest sidewalk on the East Side of Detroit. They were constantly out front, faces ruddy and resolute over buckets of steaming water. They ignored most every-body, though Bea had been accorded minute nods of recognition ever since the freezing night last winter when her father had restarted their broken furnace and refused all payment. Bea's father—Papa—could fix most anything.

The cobbler's children have no shoes—so the old adage affirmed, which suggested that her own house ought to be dilapidated. In fact, it was the best-kept-up house on Inquiry. Papa was a contractor, though he rarely uttered the word; he tended to keep his English simple. He spoke with an accent, despite having lived in America since he was thir-teen. Bea was relieved that the family's '38 Hudson wasn't parked in front. Her father wasn't home yet. He didn't like it when she arrived after he did.

Bea stepped into the front hall and smelled hamburger and onions. She proceeded warily toward the kitchen, where she found her mother—Mamma—stationed at the table, not doing much of anything. This was a bad sign. Mamma was subject to "moods," sitting immobile over coffee for hours, staring at the kitchen wall calendar, which each month offered a different house built by O'Reilly and Fein, the com-pany Papa worked for.

"I'm home," Bea said.

"Isaac Lustig is dead," her mother replied.

"Isaac Lustig?" Bea could not place the name.

"You know the Lustigs. Up near Charlevoix. Their son."

The Lustigs lived *way* up the street. They had moved in only a month or two ago. Bea hadn't actually laid eyes on any of them yet, but she knew they were Jewish.

"He was a soldier?"

"A student. At Kenyon College in Ohio. Exactly your age, too," Mamma pointed out. "He drove his car into a tree. He planned to be a doctor."

"How terrible. The accident was around here?"

"In Ohio."

"Had you met him?"

Bea's mother took a moment to answer. "N-no." Then she added, on a note of funereal triumph, "And now, I never will."

There was something unseemly and exasperating about this—Mamma's adopting someone else's tragedy. Evidently, in her grief over poor Isaac, Mamma had forgotten her earlier displeasure at seeing another Jewish family on Inquiry. She harbored a dim resentment toward the Jews, who back in Bavaria, where her father's family originated, once swindled an ancestor off his farm. It didn't help matters that one of Papa's bosses, Mr. Fein, was Jewish. The other boss, Mr. O'Reilly, was Irish—another group Mamma disparaged. (Scottish on her mother's side, Mamma saw in Ireland a people whose native ingenuity, as history kept demonstrating, was principally devoted to whining.)

Mamma's appropriation of the Lustigs' tragedy somehow barred Bea from telling her own story—her small but genuine loss today, when the wounded soldier exited the streetcar without being properly thanked.

"What's for dinner?"

"Shipwreck."

It was a recipe drawn from the only cookbook Mamma ever consulted, *The Modern Housewife's Book of Creative Cookery*. Mamma went in for odd dishes with odd names—though almost never Italian food. As she was quick to point out, she was nobody's Italian wife. She drove Papa's car, for one thing. As a rule, Italian wives didn't drive.

Mamma's hair was dark, even darker than Bea's. In the last few years, a few white hairs had crept in—very few, given that she was forty. But the darkness of her hair made each of the white ones—which were of a different, frizzier texture—cry out as interlopers, at least to Bea's painterly eye. "I have a stomachache," Bea said, which though not currently true was often the case. It was a chronic affliction. "I'm going to lie down a few minutes."

Feeling a twinge of guilt, Bea called backward from the living room, "I'm very sorry about Isaac Lustig."

Upstairs, Bea found her little sister knitting a dark blue turtleneck sweater. Edith was twelve. She was working in a room that was and wasn't her bedroom. The house had four bedrooms, one downstairs for the parents and three upstairs for the three children. But since neither Bea nor Edith cared to sleep alone, the usual arrangement was for Edith to spend the night in Bea's upper bunk. Edith was a noisy roommate who often talked in her sleep—sometimes with quite eerie distinctness—but Bea preferred her sister's company to solitude.

Edith's bedroom had become mostly a storage room and workroom. Work was something Edith excelled at. She was an extraordinary child—indeed, she had a testimonial to that effect signed by Madeleine J. Wilton, executive secretary of Needles for Defense, the organization that provided the patterns for the socks and mittens and sweaters Edith so rapidly produced. Most of the knitters for Needles for Defense were grown-up women, and initially Edith had done her knitting under Mamma's name—until Mamma, justifiably proud of her remarkable daughter, had confessed the truth to the women at Needles for Defense. The result, which was headed *A Testimonial,* had been the letter from Mrs. Wilton acknowledging Edith's "extraordinary patriotic contribution, especially for a child."

It was one indication of just *how* extraordinary Edith was that at the age of twelve she knew the word *testimonial.* It was another that she'd assembled a confidently large scrapbook called "My Testimonials." So far, it contained three letters, beginning with Mrs. Wilton's. The second was from a leader of the Detroit Girl Scouts, thanking her for her "skillful salvage." (Edith regularly went around the neighborhood collecting the bacon fat, beef drippings, suet, etc., which all the housewives saved for her—she was a great favorite among them—and which she sold as salvage to the butcher for four cents a pound. She then bought war stamps with her savings.) The third was a letter from her school principal, commending her performance in a school-wide Math-o-Meet. Edith could do complicated multiplications and divisions in her head.

Again Bea hung in the doorway. "I'm home," she said.

"We're having Shipwreck." It was one of Edith's favorite dishes. Edith was plump—the only plump member of the Paradiso family.

"I know."

Edith's hands continued their work as she regarded her sister. Bea, too, knitted for Needles for Defense, but she couldn't match her little sister's output. Bea's hands regularly forgot what they were doing. Edith's didn't, while moving far more rapidly than Bea's daydreamy hands. Though she didn't intend to, Edith continually sharpened Bea's various misgivings about not contributing enough to the war effort. Wasn't there *something* she alone could provide?

Bea was forever reading in the *News* about young women not much older than herself who were running gas stations—their husbands having gone off to war—or driving tractors, or unloading trains. She read such articles with fascination, as well as disbelief, and a little dismay. Was she somehow living the wrong sort of life? Letting down her country? But when she saw the *News* photograph of three California coeds who had learned to ride unicycles in order to reduce wear on their bicycle tires, all she could do was laugh and say to Mamma, "Look at this— it's Edith's next accomplishment." Mamma, too, had laughed nervously. As Bea had recently come to recognize, one peculiarity in the family she'd been born into—one of many—was that its youngest member was often its most intimidating.

What will become of her? Bea sometimes asked herself. Papa joked that Edith's future husband would never discover a sock that needed darning, a shirt missing a button. But it wasn't easy picturing Edith married to anyone. If a girl could be spinsterly at the age of twelve, Edith managed it. Nothing about her seemed twelve. She was stoical beyond her years. It was a rare day when tears marred her clear blue eyes. Brown-eyed Bea, six years her senior, was, mortifyingly, *far* more susceptible to weeping.

"I have a stomachache," Bea said. "I'm going to lie down."

"And apple crisp," Edith called after her.

Bea's bunk bed was a special bed: her father had constructed it for her. You might have supposed she would prefer the airy upper bunk, assigning the lower to Edith, but the sensation of lying within an elaborate wooden nest comforted her. Ever since she was a little girl, nights had been her difficult time and the abashing fact was that she had trouble sleeping at a girlfriend's or a relative's—anywhere but here in this bed of her father's making. Into each of the posts upholding the upper bunk he had carved, totem pole–style, a creature. Whenever Bea lay here, she was surrounded by a lamb, a fish, a stork, and a rabbit.

This was clearly the best place in the world to revive today's valuable gift: the image—unforgettable—of the handsomest soldier in the world, a bandaged boy on crutches, yielding up his seat for her. A boy who had said—casually, but painfully mindful of the moment's poignancy— "Nice ridin' with ya, miss."

Yet Bea had hardly settled down when a great ruckus erupted in the alley.

She knew its source even before clambering out of bed. If in many ways Bea's most treasured place on earth was this bedroom and the bed her father had built for her, the alley was the richest locale for her brother, Stevie. You found him out there in all seasons, sometimes morning till night. Long ago, his games had involved cars and circuses and athletic contests. These days, it was all the War.

Stevie and his friends were forever enacting battles out back of the house. From the rooftops of garages, from the shelters of trash cans and wheelbarrows, they ambushed each other and pitched themselves into headlong advances. Sometimes they took prisoners and tied them up with rope. Bea had even seen the boys, lined up neatly and solemnly, performing a clattering death by firing squad . . .

Just thirteen, Stevie no less than his little sister was tireless in his country's defense. For despite heavy casualties, the finale was always a thoroughgoing rout of the "Krauts" and the "Japs."

Bea had intended to throw open the window and yell at her brother. Instead, she watched intently. The scene captivated her. There must have been a dozen boys—crawling, running, whooping, making explosive noises. She had some trouble locating Stevie, half-hidden behind a barricade of packing crates. Picking him out of a crowd was usually easy, because of his thick glasses. He was all but blind without them.

Those glasses crystallized a family understanding shared by everyone but Stevie. Even Edith, in her mulling clandestine way, had probably guessed that Stevie, who yearned passionately for the day of his future enlistment, never would serve. If—if, unthinkably, the War *were* to continue until 1947, when he would turn seventeen, no branch of the military would likely have him.

The logic behind this disqualification was demonstrated as Bea watched a chaotic battle unfold. Stevie's packing-crate fortress was attacked in a crackling fusillade. One of the crates was toppled and Stevie's glasses fell to the ground . . .

Stevie did not stoop to retrieve them. With a look of crazed determination on his squinting molelike face, an expression of radiant martyrdom, Stevie went on firing his gun at an enemy he could no longer see. It was a haunting face, a haunting moment: *"Rat-a-tat-tat-tat!"* he cried. *"Rat-tat-tat! Rat-a-tat! Rat-a-tat!"*

Fifteen minutes later, it was a subdued and taciturn Stevie at the dinner table. His glasses were restored to his face.

Those glasses made him look studious—a misleading impression. Stevie lagged behind his classmates in reading skills. He lagged in mathematics, too, and here Bea could identify with him, somewhat, though she'd always been an almost perfect student. In grade school, she'd twice been double-promoted, a half-grade each time, and had wound up graduating from Eastern High at the age of seventeen, near the top of the class. Still, math had sometimes kept her from a flawless all-A report card. It was as though Edith, who without even blinking could compute towering sums in her head, had somehow garnered math skills that by rights the Paradiso children should have divided equally.

As was too often the case, tonight's dinner was a lifeless affair. It usually fell on Bea to spark any real conversation. Papa on returning home had repaired immediately to the bathroom. He'd emerged with a bandaged hand, as was fairly common: he often came home with bruises, lacerations, nasty splinters.

He'd done a neat job with the bandage, not surprisingly: he did a neat job with everything.

"You have an injury," Mamma said, over the steaming Shipwreck.

"Not really."

This was untrue on its face—fresh blood had seeped into the white cotton in Papa's palm.

But if Papa declared himself uninjured, this pretty much ended all discussion. He didn't like "fretting." Most of the ministrations he required—the cleaning of wounds, the removing of splinters—he accomplished himself. *I can do it myself* was something of a motto of his.

Mamma said, somewhat defiantly, "I want Dennis to look at that tomorrow."

Papa suspended a forkful of Shipwreck before his mouth. "All right," he replied.

This was the great exception to Papa's motto. Although he would never ordinarily step into a doctor's office, Papa did allow his brother-in-law, Dr. Poppleton—Uncle Dennis—to peer down his throat, to poke into his ears, to eavesdrop with a little cup on his robust heart. Moreover, Papa would confer with Dennis about what sort of mortgage to apply for, which newspaper to subscribe to, whom to support for mayor. Needless to say, Dennis had had to be consulted before Bea could take the peculiar step of enrolling in art school. His approval had helped carry the day.

Uncle Dennis had come by his authority gradually, it seemed. He was the husband of Mamma's sister, Grace—Grace's second husband.

(He had chosen to marry a divorcée.) The Poppletons were childless. Though soft-spoken and seemingly unassertive, Uncle Dennis somehow managed to be the most persuasive person Bea had ever met.

Most Saturdays the seven of them got together—the five Paradisos and the two Poppletons. Years ago, classification-loving Edith had determined that Saturday was American Day and Sunday was Italian Day. The designation, gradually evolving into a little family joke, had stuck. Sundays were reserved for Papa's father, Grandpa Paradiso, who was often called Nonno, and Papa's stepmother, who was sometimes called Grandma and sometimes Nonna but often not called anything. There was no real conversing with her, she spoke so little English.

Bea was waiting for an opportune moment to narrate her affecting story—the Tale of the Handsome Wounded Soldier on the Streetcar. But now the table suddenly turned loquacious. Papa, who rarely said much during supper, began an amusing little story of his own, about Harry, one of his workers, who at the noon lunch break ate a fried-egg sandwich that had been sitting in a lunch box for three days; at the next break, punctually at two-thirty, he vomited it up in the alley. And then the telephone rang—ringing phones at suppertime always irritated Papa—and Mamma chose to answer it, which was a mistake, and she couldn't get the caller (old Mrs. McNamee down the street) off the line. And then Edith launched into a long anecdote about running into Mrs. Marshland at Olsson's Drugs. Who? Mrs. Marshland—*her fourth-grade teacher at Field Elementary*. (Her family's lapses of memory frequently stirred Edith's indignation.) And Mrs. Marshland was buying four hair ribbons, *isn't that strange?*

Bea didn't feel free to begin her story until dessert. It was apple crisp, overcooked. (Mamma had been on a bad streak lately, burning even more dishes than usual.) Papa interrupted Bea's narration to remove from his mouth a bullet of blackened dough and to say, "I'm going to crack a tooth." Though he never visited a dentist, he was rightfully proud of his teeth: white, straight, absolutely unblemished by cavities.

"The oven isn't working right," Mamma replied, sullenly.

Bea resumed her story, rattling along until she reached the punch line, or at least one of the punch lines: "Can you imagine? *Can you imagine? He* offered *me* a seat."

"Well now," Mamma volunteered, "if a young man offers you a seat on the streetcar, you must accept. Decent manners have been dying ever since this war began, I can tell you."

"Take a seat when *he's on crutches*?"

"Crutches? I didn't know he was on crutches," Mamma protested, which only proved she hadn't been listening *at all*.

"That's the whole point. He was a soldier on crutches. He was a wounded soldier."

"Well, that's a whole different kettle of fish," Mamma said in the same authoritative tone, wholly undismayed about reversing herself completely. "For Pete's sake, Bea, you can't take a crippled man's seat!"

"Don't I know it!" Bea cried. "After all, that's the whole point! I was thrust into a *quandary*"—and she saw her mother and father exchange a quick but significant glance. Although the two of them disagreed about many things, in this particular matter they were in tight accord: their oldest child, their elder daughter, was "overemotional." The term had been supplied, years ago, by Uncle Dennis, and Papa in particular had seized upon it, in that characteristic way he sometimes seized on a slangy American phrase. "You are overemotional," he would say, and pause—a long pause. "Overemotional, Bia." Bia—pronounced *be uh*— was his special nickname for her. The other children had no special nicknames.

Bea excused herself as soon as she could and raced upstairs and hurled her body onto her bed. Again a burning lump closed her throat, but she didn't cry—instead, something consoling happened. In her mind's eye, with a clarity vainly wished for ever since she'd stepped off the streetcar, she visualized the handsome soldier. He was staring down at her, into her. She was returned to that blazing moment just before he disembarked, when their glances truly fused.

Bea gazed up into his startlingly blue and yet altogether soothing eyes and found they opened onto unexplored regions—a territory where there was no doubting he understood her essential self. And surely both of them were to be pardoned if they hadn't known how to proceed, given how unlooked for was this one-in-a-million encounter between two young people just possibly made for each other.

There was a knock on the door: Papa's knock. He did this sometimes, when he suspected Bea was feeling sad or overwrought. Usually he made no references to her state, while seeking to supply cheering news.

Bea sat up in bed. Papa took the seat at the desk, sitting backward on the chair, forearms resting on the top. He had freshly bandaged his hand.

"You have an injury," she said.

"Not really." And that was that.

"How's Mr. O'Reilly?"

O'Reilly and Fein built and renovated houses all over the city. The company was widely referred to as Really Fine, a little pun that had represented, in Bea's childhood, a summit of human cleverness. One famous day back when Papa was still new at the firm, big bluff O'Reilly showed up right here on Inquiry Street carrying gifts for each of the children. This was three days after Papa had quit the firm in a huff—or been fired—after refusing to oversee the installation of a cheap brand of copper pipe in a house whose construction he was supervising. Mamma had not stopped crying for three days. Because of Papa's mule-headedness, they were going to lose everything: their home, their automobile, their radio . . . But white-faced, tight-lipped Papa had won that particular battle, in which every material thing the family possessed was jeopardized for an intangible principle. For in the end, red-faced, garrulous O'Reilly had stumbled up the walk, arms laden with gifts.

"The same. Always the same. Drinks too much."

"And Mr. Fein?"

Poor worried-looking Mr. Fein—his only child, a boy, had been born deaf.

"The same. Always the same. Gambles too much."

Mr. Fein liked to play the horses.

Talking with Papa wasn't the easiest thing. He sat there expectantly, as if making conversation were none of his responsibility, and Bea chatted about Professor Manhardt and her art class, until Papa interrupted with the cheering news he'd come to deliver: "Tomorrow, Bia? Maybe we go to the lake."

"The lake!" It would be their first trip this year. They used to go all the time, before the War brought its shortages and restrictions. "And will we swim?"

"Pretty cold."

"Stevie will. *He'll* swim."

Papa chuckled in that way he had—a sort of clucking. "Stevie will go in."

"And you'll go in too."

"Probably so." Papa rose from his chair. "Don't let your brother stay in too long," he said. Papa often departed on a note of solemn advice.

Later that evening, when Edith had climbed into the upper bunk and the lights were extinguished, Bea did at last yield to tears. This time, the lump in her throat wouldn't be swallowed down, for it grew bitterly apparent, in the bedroom darkness, that Bea had encountered and lost her one true love. Never again would she catch sight of him—a burden, itself almost insupportable, rendered all the heavier by the knowledge of not having *thanked him properly.*

Bea lay on her stomach and leaked tears into her pillow, as mutedly as she could, but Edith heard anyway. Edith, who never cried, whispered beseechingly, "Bea, please, *don't.*"

And the shame of once more being the crybaby, of being an eighteen-year-old art student at the Institute Midwest whose twelve-year-old kid sister requested, not reproachfully so much as pleadingly, "Bea, please, *don't*"—this only made Bea sob the harder. She would be all right, she knew, if only she could again summon that soldier's face, with its promise of soulful, wordless exchanges.

But the face materializing in her mind's eye, and refusing to exit from her mind's eye, wasn't the soldier's. No, it was Stevie's—that weird, unsettling glimpse of him from her bedroom window. Stevie was a soldier too, out in the alley, with the other neighborhood boys, transformed into Japs and Krauts. He had lost his glasses. "*Rat-a-tat! Rat-a-tat!*" he hollered in explosive defiance. Firing at an enemy he could not see.

CHAPTER II

Bea woke to a sensation of being summoned: outside her bedroom window, the sky's beauty was so keen it all but called her by name. What a perfect day for a lakeside picnic! Everything was so luminous and lovely, so replete with bounty and promise, it wasn't until she was brushing her teeth—the white sink pulsing with morning light—that she recalled her current state of heartbreak. How could she have failed to thank the wounded soldier properly? Why had her brain been so slow to glimpse what her soul instantly ascertained—that in sitting there like such a dope, with meek downcast eyes, she'd probably lost forever the one person on earth truly meant for her?

Everybody in the family loved going to the lake except Mamma, who complained it was "much too much work." No matter how you helped her, a picnic at the lake was still much too much work. Last year, when the shortages were so severe and Papa fretted about making his tires last for the duration, they'd rarely made the drive. This summer, maybe things would be better.

Bea threw a robe around herself and hurried downstairs, where she found her mother at the kitchen table, sipping coffee. No preparations begun—a bad sign. The gloom Bea had sensed on arriving home yesterday apparently hadn't lifted. This was something everyone in the house silently did: monitored Mamma's state of mind.

Bea got herself a glass of milk. Taped to the side of the refrigerator was a newspaper article entitled THE TEN FOOD COMMANDMENTS. It began, *We shall not use condiments extravagantly.* It ended, *We shall save all food containers made of materials that can be used in war production.* The posting of the article was Edith's doing, who had scattered similar injunctions throughout the house. *Zap the Jap with Scrap!* and *Hit Hitler on HIS Homefront from OUR Homefront!* and *Put War Bonds in your Wallet, not Axis Bonds on your Wrist!* (Edith was fond of puns.) Papa approvingly referred to her as his Salvage Officer, and in fact everyone in the house was a little afraid of Edith's reprimands. Exactitude was another of her passions. When she read in the newspaper that newspapers shouldn't be sent to salvage until reaching a stack five feet high, she went down to the basement with a tape measure and marked the desired height on the wall.

The seventh of the Food Commandments was, *We shall drink only one cup of coffee a day,* but even Edith knew not to challenge her mother in this regard.

Mamma rose from the table and the two of them worked side by side, not saying much. Experience had taught Bea that her mother truly didn't wish to be coaxed out of her moods—she preferred silence. Mamma was prone to melancholy by nature, but what was currently looming was something else again. It happened maybe every three or four months: the arrival of one of "Mamma's moods." And this could well subside into a gloom deeper than gloom, infiltrating every corner of the house.

Bea chopped the celery and peeled the potatoes for the potato salad. Mamma diced onions for the tuna salad. The onions' biting smell and the redness of Mamma's eyes might have served as symbols—symbols of life's prevailing injustice. It was one of her great themes: the world's injustice. She combed the *News* for poignant accounts of crashing unfairness—the young bride drowned on a Florida honeymoon, the boy crippled in an accident while driving to his high school graduation. As Bea worked beside her mother in the incandescent morning sunshine, she was enveloped by something fundamental to her existence and yet ineffable: whenever one of her mother's dark moods impended, she had no suitable vocabulary for her own complicated mixture of feelings, a blending of hot pity and resentment and inseparable guilt, of impatience and weariness and fear. More than anything else, perhaps, fear. At such times, her mother drifted off, and all the calling in the world couldn't fetch her home again.

Stevie clattered downstairs and Mamma set before him a bowl of Cheerioats and an unopened bottle of milk. There was already an open bottle in the Frigidaire—from which Bea had poured her own glass—but Stevie loved the cream at the top, which Mamma saved for her "growing boy." (Papa urged her to reserve the cream for her coffee—she was so bony and thin—but this was advice seldom followed.)

When Bea had all the potatoes peeled and palely resting in a pan of water on the stove, she assembled six grape-jelly-and-cream-cheese sandwiches and sliced them diagonally. Unfortunately, her mother could not or would not break the habit of cutting sandwiches into rectangles rather than triangles. Mamma grumbled sometimes that Aunt Grace's picnic basket always looked more appetizing than her own, as if this were another injustice: Uncle Dennis and Aunt Grace had money for luxuries. What Bea was tempted to point out—but did not point out—was that it cost nothing to cut a sandwich diagonally, to fold a napkin tastefully. Little things . . . So often, it was not a matter of expense but merely of caring how things looked, and Aunt Grace, Mamma's beautiful younger sister, attended tirelessly to the look of things.

When Uncle Dennis and Aunt Grace arrived, the Paradisos were ready to go. Aunt Grace was wearing a straw sun hat, with a lime-green ribbon wound around the crown. Grace, as always, looked wonderful.

"You have a new hat," Mamma said.

Aunt Grace naturally awaited some further observation or appraisal. When nothing followed, she said, "Thank you," and smiled, and called to Edith, standing by the fireplace, "And *you* have a new dress, darling. How lovely you are!"

Lovely had never been the word for Edith, not even as a newborn who arrived on Inquiry Street looking furrowed and highly discriminating. Still, the compliment found its blushing mark: for the first time this morning, Edith glowed.

Edith's yellow jumper, trimmed in forest green, was indeed new. This was another of the girl's singularities: her pudginess. She had *needed* the new dress, having outgrown so much of her wardrobe.

Saturday expeditions followed their own protocol. On the way out, wherever their destination, Bea rode in Uncle Dennis's car—a 1942 royal-blue Packard. On the way home, Stevie and Edith had the privilege. Uncle Dennis had a passion for riddles, and he enjoyed pointing out that his car was perpetually new, always the latest model—one of the few '42s assembled before the automobile companies had briefly closed down to reemerge as airplane and tank and munitions factories. Cartown no longer made cars. There were no 1943 Packards. There would be no '44 Packards either.

Predictably, the children's eagerness to ride with their uncle and aunt irked Mamma. In the old days, there used to be arguments, and lingering bitterness, until Uncle Dennis hit on the system: Bea would ride with the Poppletons going out, Stevie and Edith would ride with them coming back. Over the years, Mamma had indirectly inspired a number of such little systems.

When Bea rode anywhere with her uncle and aunt, Grace usually sat in back. "You with those long legs, you need the room," she would sometimes say. Other times she might say, "The two of you so rarely get a chance to talk."

As a little girl, Bea sometimes had fantasized that her uncle and aunt would adopt her. Perhaps she might be tragically orphaned, forcing the Poppletons to take her in. (Stevie and Edith would be settled elsewhere.) Bea had always felt more comfortable with the Poppletons than with any other couple. For years now, long before she possessed the words to form the thought, Bea had intuited that Mamma was jealous of gorgeous Grace, but only in the last year—after graduating from high school and enrolling in art school and mostly becoming an adult—had Bea come to see just how deep this jealousy ran.

It was a realization that inevitably raised a larger issue: did Grace herself see it? There were moments when Bea felt quite certain that Aunt Grace understood everything and made it her policy to answer her elder sister's coolness with warmth, her suspicion with trust. But there were other occasions when Bea felt certain nothing calculated informed Grace's high-mindedness. It was just her particular nature—the nature of the kindest woman Bea had ever known—to view her surroundings trustingly.

That business with the hat just now—it was typical. "You have a new hat," Mamma had noted—unmistakably an accusation and a lament, one sister saying to another *You get more than I do.* And how had Aunt Grace replied? With a "Thank you." And it may well be that Grace, contentedly settled in the backseat as they drove up Woodward Avenue, now sincerely believed that her sister had praised her hat.

Uncle Dennis lit his pipe. Even when he wasn't smoking, his car smelled of tobacco—a lovely, primordial aroma that tendriled around, as pipe smoke will, so many of Bea's childhood memories.

It was one of the rituals of their drives that Bea ask her uncle about his reading. Uncle Dennis loved science fiction. He subscribed to magazines with names like *Amazing Stories* and *Astounding Science-Fiction.* He was always reading about spaceships and distant planets, about scary trips into the future and futile trips to rewrite the past. They were "silly stories" according to Uncle Dennis. They were "mere relaxation" or "just a way of chasing sleep." They were even "dumb stuff." Nonetheless, his face flushed like a boy's when, in his slow and measured way, he regaled Bea with one more convoluted journey through the coils of time, or one more intricate tale of earth-menacing perils hurtling toward us from the other end of the galaxy.

Years and years ago, Bea's new best friend, who was *still* her best friend, Maggie Szot (now Maggie Hamm), posed a question that made Bea laugh. Having heard so many stories about Bea's beloved uncle Dennis, Maggie had asked, "And is he handsome?" The question was funny because Uncle Dennis was unmistakably meant *not* to be handsome. Being not handsome was so much who he was. Uncle Dennis was plump and round-faced, with thick lips and big, square ears. (He was the only square-eared person Bea had ever met.) Like Stevie, he wore enormously thick glasses, and solely on this basis the two were sometimes taken for father and son. Whereas Bea felt honored whenever mistaken for a Poppleton, Stevie bristled. Stevie was the only son of a man who built houses with his scarred, powerful hands. He idolized his dad.

They were such a unified couple, Uncle Dennis and Aunt Grace, it was as though *he* hardly needed good looks, when *she* possessed them so abundantly. Could anyone imagine a better partnership? Bea could scarcely compass the notion of Aunt Grace's previous marriage. How could she possibly have wed anybody other than square-eared Uncle Dennis? In her entire life, Bea had never heard them quarrel.

Grace's beauty was partly the beauty of Kindness—anybody as nice as she was probably must seem beautiful in time—and partly the beauty of pure Beauty. Had Grace lived in the Renaissance, five hundred years ago, some immortal painter might have asked her to model for the Madonna. She had alabaster skin, vibrant with health, and clever gray eyes, and she had a full and lovely bosom.

They continued up Woodward, past a jeweler's, a locksmith's ("Sleep Tight," the old sign said, which Bea had once thought *extremely* clever), an Olsson's Drugs ("There When You Need Us There"), Honest Abe's Radio, a music store ("Sheet Music—We've Got the Latest"), a tobacconist's, and, on the other side of the street, another Olsson's Drugs.

Uncle Dennis was concluding his story: "So now everything's in his grasp: the kingdom, the beautiful and mysterious princess, the planet itself. The only thing left is to eliminate the young masked man—his rival for the princess and the rocket ship's plunder. Well, the young man doesn't beg. He's quite dignified. He says, You must do what you must do—or words to that effect. And the older man takes out his death ray and declares, You'd do precisely the same thing in my place—words whose irony you'll understand in just a moment, Bea—and then he shoots the young man. And when he does? He feels himself fading away."

"Fading away?" Bea said.

"And well you might ask. Becoming unreal. Just as if he never existed. And how could this be? Good question. Good question. He realizes the brutal truth just before vanishing altogether. You see, he'd gone *backward,* not *forward* in time. You remember the time machine was upside down when he mounted it? Well, because of that, he reversed the direction, and the young masked man was actually himself, back when he was young. By shooting the young man, he's actually committing suicide. And his very last thought, before fading away altogether, is, But then there *was* no enemy and I've been fighting myself . . ."

"I like that," Bea said. "There *was* no enemy."

You could watch, by clear stages, as the inner boy receded from Uncle Dennis's features and the good sober middle-aged doctor assumed his place. "There's a big problem—a big hole in the plot," Uncle Dennis pointed out. "If he shot his younger self with the death ray, how did he live long enough to take the time machine back and shoot himself with the death ray? You see what I'm saying."

"Mostly," Bea said.

"I recognize there's a big problem," she added, struggling to squelch any amusement in her voice. What struck Bea as *funny* was the notion that for Uncle Dennis something so preposterous as an older man shooting his younger self with a death ray could represent a *big problem.*

At the lake—Lady Lake—it was always Papa's job to arrange for the boat and equipment for the men's fishing. While a process seemingly closed to negotiation (the rental prices were posted), Papa invariably turned it into an intricate and protracted business. He was tight with a dollar—even if, or perhaps especially if, Uncle Dennis might ultimately foot the bill. (Papa was forever protecting others from getting swindled.) While this transaction unfolded, Uncle Dennis stood outside the rental shed in a posture of hapless idleness—as if he couldn't begin to assist in any such complex undertaking.

This was another aspect of family life that Bea had only recently come to analyze and appreciate: just how complicated and complementary the dealings of these two men were. Uncle Dennis was a soft, unathletic doctor who spent his off-hours reading about a dizzy, rocketing future. Papa—who read haltingly, not only in English but in his native Italian—was a lean, athletic builder who in his spare time constructed wooden toys and made wine in the cellar and grew roses in the backyard while the rest of the family tended the victory garden. And yet, he and Dennis were not only brothers-in-law but best friends.

Uncle Dennis's show of incompetence was repeated whenever he asked Papa how to fix a leaking faucet, how to pack the crowded trunk of a car, how to trim a shrub. In such moments, if you didn't know better, you might conclude that this man who served the Paradisos so ably as general doctor, financial advisor, political and military analyst, education specialist, legal-affairs consultant, guide to American history, and interpreter of foreign cultures was a bit of a nincompoop.

But roles were completely reversed once the rental had been arranged. "Vico, I need a look at that hand," Uncle Dennis declared, and Papa, meek as any altar boy, sat himself down at a picnic table and unwrapped his bandage. Everybody crowded around. Papa no longer had the authority to shoo them away. He had no authority at all.

"This one's nasty," Uncle Dennis said. Papa had gashed the inside of his palm. "You shoulda come to me yesterday and let me drop a few stitches." Papa mustered an apologetic grin. "Nasty, nasty, nasty," Uncle Dennis chanted as he slathered salve on the wound and redressed the bandage.

"Listen to me, Vico," he began, "you've got a team of men working for you now. You hear me? Let them do the heavy work. Tell *them* what to do. Right?"

Papa nodded eagerly, grateful for such good counsel. It was the same nod he always gave when Uncle Dennis offered this advice.

"*Grazie, dottore, sto bene, sono guarito,*" Papa said when Uncle Dennis had finished rebandaging the wound. He sometimes employed Italian like this—partly as ceremony, partly as solemn joke. Bea only sometimes understood what he said; her Italian was spotty. "I have the best doctor in the world," Papa went on, proudly. "The only one who doesn't like hospitals."

"Now Vico, that isn't quite so," Uncle Dennis corrected, patiently. But it was a matter of steady, unalterable satisfaction for Papa and no clarifications could modify this point: Dennis disliked hospitals. Uncle Dennis went on: "I just don't believe in going unnecessarily—they breed infection. And I certainly don't believe in staying bedridden any longer than you have to."

Uncle Dennis advocated *early ambulation.* It was something of a crusade. To everyone in the Paradiso home, the phrase *early ambulation* was one of those elaborate mouthfuls—like War Production Board or Office of Price Administration—worn smooth by familiarity.

At last the two men had their boat in the lake, which was a milky tan-green color, cloudy with stirred-up sediment. Papa rowed, of course, despite his injured hand. Uncle Dennis wouldn't catch anything. Papa would probably catch something and throw it back. Papa would smoke cigarettes and Uncle Dennis his pipe. They had six bottles of Stroh's between them. They wouldn't return for lunch until the bottles were empty.

Stevie rushed off to swim. There was always something at once comical and depressing in this, because of course he had to remove his glasses. It seemed—poor kid—he could hardly make out the murky water he charged at so excitedly.

Remaining on shore were the "four girls"—Mamma, Aunt Grace, Bea, and Edith. They sat on two blankets. Carefully shielding her fair skin, Aunt Grace had placed her blanket in the shade, with Bea beside her. Having placed hers in the sun, Mamma squinted into the light.

Once Bea had come fully to appreciate the extent of Mamma's jealousy, it was remarkable how many family dealings were freshly illuminated. What was Mamma doing now? She wasn't merely sitting in the sun . . . No, she was registering her disdain for the pampering solicitude Grace showed herself—her disdain, even, for the pretty new sun hat with the lime-green ribbon.

Edith sat beside Mamma in the sun. She had been given a jelly-and-cream-cheese sandwich to "hold her" until lunch. In a patient and exacting process, Edith had set about consuming as much grape jelly as possible without actually biting into the sandwich. Gradually, gently, she squeezed and kneaded the bread, coaxing out little purple seams, which she licked up. Only when satisfied that no more jelly was to be extracted would she bite into the sandwich.

Edith was utterly absorbed in her task, and Mamma was lost to some dangerous foul mood. So it fell upon Bea and Aunt Grace to keep the conversation alive.

Aunt Grace asked about her still-life class and Bea told her about Professor Manhardt, who even on the hottest days wore a vest, which he called a "waistcoat." Aunt Grace's sincere interest facilitated Bea's talk—about her classmates, and even about her bright ambitions for her art. Bea had sold one artwork in her life: a watercolor done on Belle Isle, called *International Waters*, with Detroit lying on the right side and Windsor on the left and the distant Ambassador Bridge, uniting the two countries, in the central background. Aunt Grace had bought it last year, for ten dollars, for Uncle Dennis's forty-fifth birthday. The painting hung in Uncle Dennis's office, behind his desk. *International*

Waters wasn't a very good watercolor—Bea could see that now—and she'd offered a free replacement. But Uncle Dennis wouldn't hear of it.

Then Bea recalled someone and something she couldn't believe she'd forgotten until now: the soldier on the Woodward Avenue street-car yesterday. "Oh, but listen to *this*," she cried. Bea recounted the story at length, and Aunt Grace's little interpolations—"Really?" "Oh my," "You poor thing"—made clear she appreciated its every nuance.

"How mortifying! You must have felt terribly self-conscious," she said.

Oddly, *this* time the story fired Mamma's imagination. "But what did he *say*?" she asked.

"I told you. Just the one remark: Nice ridin' with ya, miss."

"You do know you're not supposed to talk to strangers on streetcars."

"But I didn't. That's the whole point. I don't think he even heard me thank him, for heaven's sake."

Mamma deliberated. "You say he was handsome?"

"He was very handsome." Yes, he *had* been handsome, though in Bea's imagination he'd now become almost the handsomest boy she'd ever seen.

"It's a good way to find trouble. Talking to strangers on streetcars."

"But I didn't, and what trouble was I going to get into? He was a very nice boy, otherwise why would he insist I sit down? Besides, he was on crutches."

"As if that matters! Grace, you remember Pearlie Kulick, and the boy who'd been in the accident."

Pearlie Kulick was a name Bea had never heard. Still, she didn't ask about Pearlie, or the boy, or even the accident—since if she *were* to ask, the story would doubtless prove unsuitable for children's ears. This was another conversational peculiarity of Mamma's, especially in Grace's presence: she was forever alluding darkly to people and anecdotes unfamiliar to Bea and then refusing to elucidate. You might almost suppose, given how many unspeakable stories she knew, that Mamma over the years had encountered nobody who wasn't a dope fiend, a wife beater, a sexual deviant, a shoplifter, a floozy, a confidence man, a heartless seducer—just as you might spend weeks in Aunt Grace's company and conclude that she'd never met anyone who wasn't kindly, generous, sympathetic, well-intentioned. How could the two of them be sisters?

Yet they were and—perhaps more to the point—each was the only lifelong family the other had. Bea's Grandpa and Grandma Schleiermacher had died too long ago for Bea to remember either clearly. There had been no other Schleiermacher children—just the two girls, Sylvia and her eleven-months-younger sister, Grace—and the only Schleier-macher cousins were settled way out in California. Given, also, that Uncle Dennis had no immediate family nearby (only a half brother, in New Jersey), and that Papa was an only child, it was logical that the Pop-pletons and Paradisos got together as often as they did: most every Saturday, and sometimes weekdays as well. Likewise it made sense that Grace had chosen to ignore the whole issue of her older sister's jealousy, blithely fending off an endless series of digs, accusations, slights, complaints.

Yet this was to presuppose that Aunt Grace actually identified them as such. Really, there was no saying how much she understood. Contemplating her now (noting the solemn if sympathetic way Grace shook her head over poor, mysterious Pearlie Kulick), you might swear that here was a woman who embodied the notion that petty sniping cannot exist among those grand enough to surmount it.

After the men returned, empty-handed, and Stevie emerged blue-lipped from the lake, the seven of them settled around the picnic table. This moment was always eagerly awaited: the unveiling of Aunt Grace's picnic basket. She wasn't merely a marvelous cook. Her things always *looked* so pretty.

When Bea was occasionally asked where her passion for art originated, the obvious answer was from the Paradisos. In addition to being a fine builder, Papa was a master craftsman. The wooden pull-toys he'd constructed for his children when they were little—a lamb for Bea, an owl for Edith, and for Stevie a rooster whose wings waggled when you dragged it behind you—were extraordinary. And Papa's father, Grandpa Paradiso, had once been (long ago, back in Italy, before his health broke) a genuine sort of artist who specialized in those trompe l'oeil effects so dear to the Italian imagination. (Bea had seen examples in books.) Grandpa Paradiso had adorned simple houses and he had embellished palazzi. He was a kind of muralist. He'd painted windows opening out of nonexistent rooms, doors leading into nonexistent corridors, shrubs bordering nonexistent gardens. Yes, at one time he'd been a celebrated artist, up and down the coast of Liguria, in Italy, cradle of the greatest art the world has ever seen.

But there was an art-loving side to the Schleiermacher family, too, as embodied in Aunt Grace, whose visual flair surfaced in unexpected byways. Her house brimmed with curiosities that had enchanted Bea's childhood: peacock feathers, a pink blown-glass snail whose shell was revealed as midnight-blue and not black only when held up against the sun, a malachite frog, a dark-skinned strangely melancholy Indian doll from Mexico. There were Asian flourishes as well. Some years ago, Grace had befriended a Japanese woman, Mrs. Nakamura, whose husband, Dr. Nakamura, had worked beside Uncle Dennis. The Nakamuras, like the Poppletons, had no children, though Mrs. Nakamura was indeed as small as a child. Though she spoke even less English than her husband, she had delighted in initiating Aunt Grace into a realm of bewitching oriental tricks: how to use chopsticks, how to fold a simple sheet of paper into a crane or a horse, even how to whittle a humble carrot until it metamorphosed into a flower blossom. In the summer of 1941, a few months before Pearl Harbor, Dr. Nakamura had completed his studies and he and his wife had returned to Tokyo. It was peculiar to think that the Nakamuras were now the enemy. The bombs from General Doolittle's raid could have fallen on them.

Aunt Grace drew from her picnic basket a tray of sticks which she called brochettes, little skewers on which were alternated small cubes of garlicky lamb, pearl onions, pieces of carrot and green pepper: no one cooked like Aunt Grace. And she unearthed from the basket two pies— cherry pies, the fruit so abundant it was popping free of its lattice. "Sylvia's favorite," Aunt Grace announced. "The very first cherries from California. Dennis got them from a patient who works for the railroad."

"California," Mamma said, and her face brightened right up. Gifts wielded a peculiar power over her imagination. That these pies had unexpectedly become *her* pies—it was a notion to cheer Mamma considerably, even while she ate sparingly. She consumed little at mealtimes, despite various urgings—everyone was keen to fatten her up. It wasn't so much that she was picky; rather, food didn't deeply interest her, with the dual exceptions of coffee and candy. She preferred her coffee syrupy thick. Partly because of rationing, she hesitated to throw anything away, heaping new scoops onto the old and exhausted grounds. Hers was a bitter, gritty brew. She didn't understand how people could "mess up" their coffee with milk or sugar, and yet she would snack on sugar all day, in the form of candy. Here, too, her tastes were unusual and off-putting. She didn't much care for chocolate. She favored bright-colored—primary colored—chewy fruit candies. Unusual, too— worrisomely so—was her habit of hiding candy. You'd be poking under the sink for something, or you'd lift the lid of a shoebox, and out would tumble a bag of jawbreakers, a cache of candy corn. This was a practice born with sugar rationing; sly Mamma wasn't going to let anyone take her candy away.

The sight of Mamma's brightened face inspired Uncle Dennis to proclaim, as he so often proclaimed, "Time for a *picture* . . ."

So the two sisters were posed side by side at the picnic table, with a pair of cherry pies before them. Aunt Grace looked lovely in her straw hat with the lime-green ribbon and Mamma's face still wore the radiance of the gift of the pies. Grace set a hand lightly on Mamma's forearm and Mamma, after a moment's hesitation, laid a hand atop Grace's hand. It all came together in a vivid diminished *click:* the comely sisters, the distant sound of children yelling and splashing, the wind purling through the trees, and, above the trees, no louder than a honeybee in your neighbor's yard, an airplane ascending over a city in wartime.

The day at the lake progressed quite well—far better, anyway, than anyone might have predicted—until the swimming after lunch. Mamma was the only one who chose not to enter the water. As Bea had come to understand, she was self-conscious about how bony she was, and about the varicose veins in her legs.

Bea loved these family outings to Lady Lake, where all her observational powers felt heightened—*nothing* escaped her. The folks a couple of picnic tables away must be Polish: they had wide Slavic faces and were eating sausages. The paterfamilias, judging from the way he slumped into himself, was getting drunk. Two picnic tables beyond them sat a white-haired woman who, so the quizzical cant of her head suggested, was half deaf. A boy at the Polish table was eyeing a girl at an adjoining table, and quite a number of boys had noticed *her,* Bea.

This was another of the lake's appeals: she felt especially pretty here. She might be too thin, like Mamma, and she certainly didn't have Aunt Grace's bosom, but rambling about in her new green swimsuit—a happy bargain, purchased for $3.95 at Montgomery Ward's—she felt what Papa must feel in *his* green suit: poised and comfortable.

Papa had a distinctive way of entering the water. He marched forward steadily, arms aswing, like a gunslinger in a Western. Although these days he had a number of men working under him, he continued to throw himself into manual labor and he had maintained his impressive physique: broad shoulders, narrow waist, slender legs, and knotty arms. (He prided himself on his prowess as an arm-wrestler.)

Uncle Dennis, perhaps in unconscious simulation, likewise strode determinedly, arms aswing—though in his case his body betrayed him with little flinches. Uncle Dennis's body was paler and pudgier than you might suppose on seeing him fully dressed. Shockingly white, his skin howled a protest at the sun. Papa's legs were glossed with reddish-brown hair that turned golden in the sunshine. It was hard to believe the two men were roughly the same age.

The sand on the beach was full of little stones. Bea stepped gingerly. The water turned out to be thrillingly cold, as the lake's raspy sand filled the arches of her feet. The breeze riding over her bare shoulders was delicious. She waded in up to her knees and, with that slight nervousness she always felt as water mounted toward her private parts, proceeded more slowly. The icy water embraced her thighs. Her hair was pinned up. She wore no bathing cap, since she planned to keep her head above water. There were boys on this beach who were watching her, and for just a moment, in her mind's eye, she saw herself as they might—a tall girl in a green floral bathing suit, standing in water just high enough to reach her dangling fingertips—then closed her eyes and threw herself forward, outward, letting herself float belly down, while keeping her head above the surface.

The cold water took her breath away, then gave it back in huffing puffs and pants. She swam a jerky breaststroke, head still above the surface. At day's end, traveling home was always more comfortable if she'd kept her hair dry—but it turned out she couldn't resist. After a few more strokes, Bea plunged under, into the turbid lake, and did a few frog kicks below the surface, then came up gasping and flopped upon her back. She loved to float like this, staring straight up into the heavens. The airplane that had wandered into Uncle Dennis's photograph, or another airplane, was humming across the sky . . .

There was a timelessness to such pleasures—floating on her back in cloudy water while contemplating the clouds—though perhaps the real lesson of this excursion to Lady Lake was that, however beautiful the day, some sort of bomb might constantly be ticking and no pleasures were timeless. It was an afternoon to ponder for the rest of her life; she'd never know another quite like it. Today was to be, indeed, the finale of all such beautiful days—for as it turned out, the Poppletons and the Paradisos never again would journey together to Lady Lake.

Stevie had discovered a new game. Immersed in the water, plump Edith was actually light enough for him to pick up in his arms and hurl a little distance. This brought on high squeals of laughter, for Edith, too, delighted in the new game.

"*Look,*" Bea said. She had emerged from the lake and was sitting on a blanket beside her mother. A towel hung over her shoulders. Everybody else was in the water. "Look at Stevie and Edith."

Though so close in age, the two siblings—the quiet plump homebody girl, the noisy militaristic older brother—generally found few pursuits in common. It was marvelous to see them playing together. Mamma laughed aloud . . .

The truth was, Mamma had a wonderful girlish laugh—a bright string of giggles as evenly spaced as beads on a wire. It was hers alone, that round yellowy sound, which sometimes had the power to catapult Bea backward into a sunny room she couldn't place (it wasn't to be found on Inquiry Street), where cooing, volleying voices echoed each other; this was a laugh Bea sometimes registered when floating at the edge of sleep. It was the oldest laugh she knew, and the youngest.

Time and again Edith waded off on her own. Stevie "snuck up" on her—swimming through the murky water and suddenly seizing her by the leg or waist. Edith thrashed and screamed. And Stevie cast her out toward the lake's deeper, colder water.

Given how myopic he was without his glasses, it was surprising the game lasted as long as it did without Stevie's making a mistake.

Once again, he plunged into the water, kicking and racing forward like a human torpedo—but one whose aim was off. This time his grappling hands seized Aunt Grace, who, like Edith, was wearing a powder-blue suit.

It all happened with such suddenness, Bea could make sense of it only later. In their immediate unfolding, the events seemed unreal.

Stevie grabbed his aunt by the waist. There was a struggle. She went down. He brought her up again and hurled her toward the deeper water.

When Aunt Grace rose to her feet, the sight was so *very* strange that, for just a fraction of a second, Bea couldn't isolate its strangeness. The top of Aunt Grace's suit had been yanked from her left shoulder. Her ample white breast above her blue suit was bared for anyone in the world to ogle. The big shocking nipple was dark as a plum.

Aunt Grace didn't realize her shame. As she stood in the waist-deep water, having been assaulted and upended, seized and dunked, shoved and pushed, she didn't know enough to cover herself. She blinked and shook her befuddled, tilted head.

As chance would have it, Papa was wading only a few feet away, holding his bandaged hand above the water. Now both of his hands, the normal, bare hand and the bandaged hand, lunged forward, toward her. Oh, he meant to shelter his poor sister-in-law—shield her from the leering, squalid gazes of a beach full of strangers! But his hands halted. They did not quite touch her.

Only a moment's duration—this surreal little tableau lasted only a moment. Then Grace, in a panicky fluster, yanked up the top of her suit. It flopped back down, baring the left breast once more. The strap had snapped.

Hunching self-protectively, arms crisscrossed over her chest, she beat a retreat toward shore, where Bea greeted her with a waiting towel plucked from her own shoulders. "Angel," Aunt Grace cried, "do you have a safety pin?" and she raced toward the changing cabins.

Full order was reinstated in just a couple of minutes. Once more, Aunt Grace was sitting in the shade, fully dressed, straw hat restored to her head. She appeared as tranquil as ever. It was a simple accident, after all . . .

Yet Mamma's shadowed face suggested otherwise, and an unnamable shame descended over the group. For Bea, there was no erasing the image: Papa waist-deep in water, his good hand and his bandaged hand reaching out toward Aunt Grace's naked breast. And little Edith, eyes bugging out of her head—obviously, she'd witnessed the whole thing. As had Uncle Dennis, who, with a blush on his round cheeks, rattled on about a patient who once got a fishhook lodged in his eye.

Poor half-blind Stevie didn't quite grasp what he'd done, and nobody wanted to inform him. Still, he sensed the unease—how could he not? The air was so dense with it.

Mamma cast a look of fury and revulsion at the lake, at the sunbathers, at the gathering clouds to the south, where the embattled city lay . . .

Aunt Grace's aplomb really was admirable. Pie—would anyone care for more pie? Or cookies? She was particularly solicitous toward Stevie, who no doubt sensed (something purblind Stevie seemed destined to sense throughout his life) that he'd inexplicably misstepped. Hey, Stevie, how's about an oatmeal cookie? Or what about coffee anyone? "Vico, I have a whole nother thermos. I bet it's still hot . . ."

But nobody wanted anything. Clearly the day at the beach was over. According to protocol, Stevie and Edith ought to ride home with

Uncle Dennis and Aunt Grace, and Bea accompany her parents. But Stevie, uneasy and still perplexed, decided to go in his parents' car. Alone in the Packard's big backseat, Edith rode with her uncle and aunt.

On the long drive back, Bea repeatedly tried to initiate a conversation. As did jittery Stevie. Even Papa, who could be so taciturn, worked to get some words flowing. He spoke of the fine house he was renovating in Sherwood Forest. And the promise of rain. And the visit tomorrow from Nonno and Nonna.

But Mamma, hunched darkly in the front seat, lean face tilted toward the window, would have none of it. She wasn't about to be cajoled into conversation. Nothing. Not a word.

CHAPTER III

"You haven't got it right—but it's almost right."

This appraisal of her work—a pencil drawing of a wizened little apple and some long-stemmed onions—ought to have been unwelcome on a number of fronts. Chief among the unwritten rules at the Institute Midwest was a ban on gratuitous criticism: students were to proceed unobstructed by each other's evaluations, unless expressly solicited. In addition, Bea's onions and apple clearly were unfinished—all the more reason to exempt them from judgment. Furthermore, and finally, this particular critic and fellow student was somebody Bea hadn't met yet (though of course she knew who he was). You might think he'd have the common courtesy to forgo criticism until they'd been properly introduced.

Even so, this was somebody she'd been longing to meet: Ronald—Ronny—Olsson, who was not merely extremely handsome but handsome in a fashion guaranteed to fire up Bea's imagination. He looked intensely literary—meaning not so much that he read books as that he belonged *in* one. She'd come across him before, somewhere in her constant novel reading. But which one was he—this pale, tall, dark-haired young man who wore a beautiful camel's hair sports coat and a tawny suede hat? (Not many young men could have gotten away with that hat.) Some disguised prince in exile? Some nineteenth-century consumptive poet on a final pilgrimage?

He always wore cuffed trousers. Cuffs on new trousers had been one of the first casualties of the War—by order of the War Production Board—and Ronny's pants suggested a very deep closet. He dressed beautifully, in pale pastel shirts and bold but subtle neckties.

After letting him stand unanswered for a moment, "What do you mean, *almost?*" Bea replied.

Ronald had done something else odd and theoretically forbidden—he had entered the Institute in the middle of a term. He was a newcomer to Professor Manhardt's class. Yet in just two weeks he'd established himself as its best draftsman—a superiority acknowledged by all eight of the other students, as well as the Professor himself. It was quite remarkable, the speed whereby that pale hand of his could translate an apple or a lemon or a cattail on a tabletop into an apple or a lemon or a cattail on a sheet of paper—in the process losing far less of the thing's tactility than any other student would likely lose. Bea had repeatedly allowed herself to stare, surreptitiously, at those long, quick, shapely, blunt-nailed fingers of Ronny Olsson. They moved more confidently than any fingers Bea had ever watched before. "What do you mean?" she repeated.

As if superior on a social level as well, Ronny chose not to mingle. All the rest of the class went to Nick's Nook for sandwiches; you never saw Ronald Olsson at Nick's. The rest went sometimes to the Run Way for coffee after class; Ronny was never glimpsed at the Run Way. In truth, Bea had already imagined a couple of little quarrels with Ronny Olsson, in which she'd flummoxed him with accusations of snobbery. Still, he was perhaps the most interesting "type" in a class rich in types.

The Institute Midwest was divided into two disciplines, Industrial Arts and Fine Arts. The exclusively male Industrial Arts crowd favored a straitlaced look. Most of them hoped, when the War ended, to go into things like automotive design. The Industrial Arts crowd had few exchanges with Bea's own Fine Arts crowd, where most of the "types" were found.

There was huge Hal Holm, with his big fanning red beard and overalls, who was gaped at wherever he went. And Tatiana Bogoljubov—also gaped at, but in a different way. Tatiana dressed just like a whore (not a word Bea would have voiced to anyone except, perhaps, her best friend, Maggie). Tatiana had dyed her long hair yellow—not blonde, yellow. She wore lengthy gaudy scarves over exceedingly tight blouses. She was a buxom girl who had pierced her ears. And there was Mr. Cooper—David Cooper—far older than the rest of them and perhaps Jewish. He'd come from Poland. He had a long doleful nose and a dark gaze of uncomfortable intensity. The vertical furrows connecting his nose and mouth might have been drawn with a knife. "Art is my only home," Mr. Cooper continually declared, with lugubrious pride. And there was Donald Doobly, Jr., who was a Negro and who studied both Fine Arts and Industrial Arts. Donald always looked neat and dapper but a little comical, since his clothes were mostly a couple of sizes too large. You might have called Donald *slight*, but one day Bea had watched him marching down Woodward against a strong wind that whipped his baggy trousers tight to his thighs, and she'd realized he was slighter than slight: his legs weren't much thicker around than broom handles. Donald drew beautifully, and if glamorous Ronald Olsson hadn't materialized midsemester, Donald might now reign as Professor Manhardt's star pupil.

Ronny, too, took his time in answering. "Might I perhaps?"

And now he moved quickly. Whether or not he *might*, he *did:* before Bea had had time to agree, quite, Ronny Olsson began applying his pencil to her paper. He was a lefty, like her, which somehow cheered her.

His speed was intimidating. A few scratches of shading to the apple's underside, a few smudging strokes of the eraser, and the apple commanded what it had lacked heretofore: the true reserved weight of a terrestrial object. *This* was fruit, however modest in size, to strike a dozing Isaac Newton on the crown of his head and awaken him to a universe bound by gravity . . .

Ronny displayed much the same speed and smoothness in spiriting her away after class. They didn't head to the Run Way. They marched to a little luncheonette a few blocks on, where they were unlikely to encounter classmates. It was called Herk's Snack Shack. They sat in a booth over mugs of watery coffee. Bea was feeling hungry, but she didn't order any food because Ronny didn't. The confident way he'd hustled her here, as though she couldn't possibly have anything better to do, might have been insulting had it not been so suave.

She'd thought Ronny "stuck up." But he spoke warmly and directly—and with a rapid precision comparable to his rapid precision with a pencil. Bea's rushed sentences characteristically went astray. (Maggie was forever teasing her about this, when not mocking her "overflowery vocabulary"; Bea had a weakness for the picturesque and polysyllabic.) Typically, she'd wander off into conversational detours, looping back to establish necessary preconditions, or would leap into parentheses that failed to close. Ronny—impressively—spoke as if dictating to a secretary.

He had mesmerizing eyes. They were mostly green, but mixed with a tempered gold, almost amber. It was a little hard to concentrate when those eyes were upon you.

He called her Bianca, the name she, letter by letter, affixed to her artwork. "Bea," she corrected him, but when he did it a second time, she let it pass. He talked mostly about art. Some of his observations had the pitch and polish of true epigrams. (You had the feeling he might have said them before.) He talked about the Impressionists, whom he didn't much admire ("Human vision is muddy enough without deliberate muddying") and Albert Bierstadt, also unworthy ("I'm afraid I can only deride anyone who would insert a moose into a painting"), and Whistler, whom Ronny applauded somewhat ("He encourages us to examine only parts of his canvas—but usually the right parts"), and Sargent, of whom he mostly approved ("Though you get the feeling, since he really could *draw,* he's often too easy on himself; he trivializes his gift").

No one in Professor Manhardt's class talked this way; indeed, Bea had never heard anyone of roughly her own age talk this way. Dazzling in themselves, the words were also welcome for reasons Ronald Olsson had no way of knowing: at home, on Inquiry Street, things were far, *far* worse than Bea could ever remember. Sitting anxiously across from Ronny Olsson, Bea felt her heart lift—lift and lighten—as it hadn't in weeks.

In retrospect, everything at home had started unraveling nearly three weeks ago, with the trip to Lady Lake and Aunt Grace's little accident. (Though you might say it began the day before, really—the afternoon of the bandaged soldier on the Woodward streetcar, when Bea came home to find Mamma staring blackly at the kitchen calendar.) The mishap at Lady Lake had shaken everybody, but Mamma most: it seemed to fix the hovering darkness over her head.

And then came the night—a Wednesday night, four days after the lake—when everything altered with such swift violence it seemed the family's old peace and happiness might never be revived.

Bea had been lying in bed, nearly asleep, when she heard something peculiar. Her father was raising his voice. He was a man who steadfastly refused to argue. When he became angry, which he did rarely but terribly, his practice was to make forcible, irreversible pronouncements and storm from the room. (At work, a couple of times, he'd resorted to fisticuffs, but that was different. He had to maintain discipline *on his watch*—a favorite phrase of his.) Now, though, he was arguing.

In the darkness Bea crept from bed and noiselessly twisted the doorknob. She stepped out onto the landing. Her parents were downstairs, in the kitchen. Papa's voice dropped away on a peculiar phrase ("Sylvia, you have to clean your mind") and then Mamma, voice honed like a razor, spoke the saddest words Bea had ever heard. When a dark mood was upon her, Mamma had a penchant for hopeless pronouncements, but these were words to rip the heart right out of a person's chest: "But it isn't in *my* mind—it's in *yours*. It's in *yours*, Vico. *It's in yours*. It's true. It's true, it's true. Deep in your soul, Vico, it's Grace you've always loved!"

Once, back in grade school, Bea had seen a boy, Glenn Coney, fall spectacularly out of a tree. This was at Chandler Park. He must have dropped thirty feet, straight down. You could actually hear the leg bone splintering when he crashed to earth. Afterward, Bea had replayed that scene over and over. Far stranger even than hearing a boy's leg—Glenn Coney's leg—cracking into useless fragments was the moment just before impact, while his body was plummeting. Over and over she witnessed the descent, and though it lasted but a second—the interval between the slip and the sickening, shattering thud—still Bea had had time within it to realize that the coming destruction was ineluctable: once Glenn lost his footing, *nothing* could be done. The earth was unforgiving. There was no going back . . .

Now, too, she was confronting something as irreversible as gravity: hearing those low deadly words of Mamma's while standing tiptoe on the landing, Bea had felt similarly unable to undo what cried to be undone. After such a ravaging declaration, how could their neat little home ever be quite the same? Shivering in her pajamas, Bea had heard other things as well—horrible things—but nothing could ever match that most shocking and sad of accusations: *Deep in your soul, Vico, it's Grace you've always loved!*

Bea knew she shouldn't be lingering over coffee in a place called Herk's Snack Shack with a boy named Ronny Olsson; by now, she ought to have boarded a streetcar. Yet she didn't wish to. Although a measure of civility had been restored at home, in other ways life had only degenerated. After words like those, how could things get any better? The desperation and fury could only go underground . . .

So if she heard herself egging Ronny on to deliver still more sweeping and severe judgments, and laughing more recklessly than usual, surely she was to be forgiven. And the truth was, Ronny Olsson hardly needed encouragement. He was something of a performer—actually, an extraordinary performer.

It was a sign of how things stood at home that Papa for the last two Saturdays had put off the Poppletons with excuses. Neither Uncle Dennis nor Aunt Grace had been glimpsed since the outing to Lady Lake. When would normal family life return?

Bea didn't want to go home—she didn't want to think any more about the declaration overheard on the landing. She wanted another cup of coffee. She wanted to listen to Ronny Olsson talk and—almost an equal thrill—she wanted to watch him talk. My goodness, he was handsome!

A crazy notion occurred to her—so outlandish, she momentarily lost the drift of his conversation . . . But *if* she were somehow to marry this Ronny Olsson (about whom, admittedly, she knew next to nothing), she could move out of her bedroom on Inquiry Street. And begin a new life.

So when Ronny said to her, "You'll go with me Saturday to the DIA, won't you?"—meaning the Detroit Institute of Arts—and she replied, "That s-s-sounds just lovely," it wasn't hesitation bringing a rare stammer to her lips. It was sheer bounding eagerness.

After dinner, miraculously, the telephone really freed up. Papa retreated into the living room, to listen to the radio. Edith cajoled Stevie upstairs for a game of rummy, though Stevie typically refused to play card games with Edith, who almost invariably won. And Mamma, who hovered endlessly round the kitchen, decided to take a bath. It seemed a perfect time to call Maggie. Bea longed to discuss handsome, dapper Ronny Olsson.

But if it was hard for Bea to find a private phone in the evenings, it was harder still for Maggie, whose mother-in-law, Mrs. Hamm, seldom left the house, or strayed far when Maggie was on the phone. Still, Bea decided to give it a try.

"And he's *muy splendido*?" Maggie asked, once the conversation really got rolling. The word was pronounced *splen-dee-doe*. Maggie's bright chatter had always been spiced with funny and preposterous slang, often of her own devising. But her talk had grown even more distinctive and peculiar since her move to the Hamms'. These days, she often spoke in a kind of code.

"Very. *Très splendido*."

"And a sharp dresser?" Clothes were a passion the two girls shared— though Bea sometimes wished her friend's taste weren't *quite* so flamboyant.

"The tie he wore the other day?" Bea said. "Blue and gold silk? It would have made the most beautiful scarf you can imagine. And there's a camel's hair coat . . ."

"Sounds like money," Maggie said.

"*Looks* like money. But I don't know. I don't even know where he lives."

"Maybe he's a con man," Maggie suggested.

"I'm thinking a European prince in exile."

"I say a con man."

"Or a Hollywood scout?"

"A con man. You'll be visiting him in jail before you know it."

Maggie wasn't playing along, quite.

Ever since Maggie's wedding, and especially since she'd moved in with her in-laws, conversations about boys had grown complicated—difficult. And it was mostly boys the two girls had always talked about. What else? Certainly not art—a subject Maggie treated with uninterest at best, peevishness at worst. Actually, lots of subjects made her peevish.

Still, there had always been plenty to discuss. For it was of course an inexhaustible subject: the obstinate, proud, uncooperative, thrilling constitution of the male mind. It was the mystery beyond other mysteries: why do boys act the way they do?

"What's he doing studying art?" Maggie went on.

"What am I doing studying art? I suppose he's improving his technique."

"He's a boy, Bea."

"I noticed." There was a pause. "You would too."

This last remark produced its desired effect, eliciting a bright little giggle from the old Maggie—Maggie Szot—as the distance between them on the telephone line shrank away to nothing. "Hard to miss it, huh?" she said.

"Impossible." And they both giggled.

Of course conversations couldn't be the same as before, now that Maggie was a married woman. But often the chief impediment wasn't so much Maggie's married state as her misery at living with her in-laws. Maggie seemed to resent Bea's still being able to look freely at boys, to talk about boys. It was as if Bea, too, was supposed to be married to George, stationed out there at Pearl Harbor. As if Bea, too, were being not merely disloyal but almost unpatriotic in noticing any boy not in uniform.

So it was a little risky, bringing up Ronny Olsson. But if Maggie could be cool and standoffish when Bea spoke of boys, she was also—trapped out there on the West Side with Mrs. Hamm and George's whiny little brother, Herbie—deeply, desperately bored. And it was this desperately bored Maggie, hungry for any stray glimmer of glamour, who began warming to the topic of Ronny Olsson.

"Why isn't he in uniform?"

"Maggie, I can't just ask! Besides, I've only just met him."

"*Only just?* You make it sound like you'll be seeing more of him."

"Maybe. I don't know. I guess so."

"Well, you'd know," Maggie said, and repeated the phrase somberly: "*You'd* know."

This was a long-standing joke between them: Bea had second sight.

"And he's tall?" Maggie went on.

"Nearly six feet, I guess. Maybe he looks taller than he is because he's thin? And because of the cut of his clothes?"

"A tall boy in a camel's hair coat and a beautiful necktie? I can't imagine. When was the last time I saw somebody like that? Don't ask me. Don't ask."

"Well I'm in no hurry to introduce *you* to him . . ."

This, too, was a long-standing joke: Maggie's appeal to men was irresistible. It went beyond her bright good looks. As with second sight, the power was—ultimately—mystical.

Maggie giggled. Bea giggled.

"Bea, surely I'm entitled to a *little* fun."

"Not at my expense you aren't."

"I wish you could see me now," Maggie said. "I'm sticking out my tongue at you."

"It's a scary thought."

And it was. For Maggie could stick out her tongue much farther than the average person could. It was all but lizardlike, the way she could nearly touch the tip of her nose with the tip of her tongue. Maggie was double-jointed—or just weirdly jointed, like a contortionist. Her body was unnervingly loose and elastic.

"It's a gesture you deserve," Maggie said.

"Not yet I don't," Bea replied.

CHAPTER IV

"Bianca, look at those *textures,*" Ronny cried softly. His finger darted and danced in the air, directing Bea's attention toward the satin crown of a hat, a velvety cuff, a crinkly piece of paper, and a scarf that was a different, less brittle kind of crinkly. The painting was called *Young Man Reading a Letter.* It was by a Dutchman, Gerard Ter Borch, whose name evidently rhymed with stork.

Look at the textures! Ronny urged again, with the schooled reverence of an artist attuned to all the pains taken in their replication. If Ronny was the best overall draftsman in Professor Manhardt's class, nowhere was his preeminence more dramatic than in his mastery over textures. He wasn't the best portraitist perhaps, but nobody could equal him when it came to reproducing a coarse, wayworn rag, a swept-together heap of broken glass, a tender pussy willow, a rust-blistered bolt.

The two of them had made it to the museum at last. The trip had begun to look ill-starred. Twice Bea had had to cancel—first for a reason she naturally couldn't explain (terrible cramps) and then because Papa had asked her to attend, in Mamma's stead, the wedding of Jack O'Reilly, the son of his boss Mr. O'Reilly. (Mamma wasn't feeling well, or so she said.)

In the interim, she and Ronny had seen each other alone a handful of times, mostly at Herk's Snack Shack. They'd also had club sandwiches at a luncheonette near the Institute, and a somewhat fancier meal, with a tablecloth, at a place called Luigi's, where Ronny ordered a beer. (Bea was grateful he didn't ask whether she'd like an alcoholic drink. Having earlier determined that he must be twenty-one, she shied at confessing to being only eighteen. Nor, for that matter, was she in any hurry to divulge that she drank wine regularly, that her father *made* wine, in the cellar. She was indeed in no hurry to expose her family background—her mother contemplating the kitchen calendar, her emphysemic grandfather, who hardly spoke English . . . All the more so as Ronny had mentioned, with a glancing assurance, that his father was "a businessman.")

Fortunately, Ronny made it easy to sidestep topics. Bea had never known anyone so easy to talk to about nothing—although none of this felt like nothing, their rapid-fire chatter: oh, it felt like *something,* it felt like life itself. Their first few conversations, Ronny had done most of the talking. But Bea soon learned to leap in—phrase tumbling over phrase—and Ronny had welcomed her arrival in that place where words crowded like exuberant guests at some New Year's fête. Had she ever, *ever* so much enjoyed talking with anyone? She played his words over and over at night, as she lay in bed, and could it be she was falling in love? It could be.

Or was she so eager for Ronny's bright talk because life had turned so dark? Not just at home, though home was the worst of it. There hadn't been another argument, true—and yet Mamma did little but brood over her coffee and candy.

Meanwhile, as if in response to the madness on Inquiry Street, the entire city had gone mad. There had come a night, June the twentieth, when the radio reported that Detroit had broken out into a riot: a race riot. Papa had declared that nobody was leaving home the next day—except of course for him, for he had a job to do.

Yes, it seemed that for some thirty hours the city had gone mad, with terrifying rumors flying everywhere, and President Roosevelt himself ordering soldiers down Woodward Avenue, and some of the rumors turned out to be true: whites had beaten blacks and blacks had beaten whites, including a white doctor named De Horatiis, an Italian, clubbed to death while paying a house call on a little colored girl. Before order was restored, some thirty-four people, nine whites and twenty-five Negroes, lay dead. Mayor Jeffries was quick to explain that full order had been restored, but what in the world was happening to the world? If she hadn't seen the newspaper photographs, Bea wouldn't have believed it. Rioters turning over cars right on Woodward Avenue! It was a true battle—a battle inside a city already at war. The War had been going on forever, but thousands of miles away. Now? *Now?* Dozens of corpses on the streets of Detroit . . .

She needed to talk to Uncle Dennis or Aunt Grace, of course, but they weren't much around. Uncle Dennis had dropped in a couple times, Aunt Grace a couple times—but the Paradisos and the Popple-tons hadn't gotten together for one of their Saturdays in five weeks. When would things return to normal? When would that calendar over Mamma's head, with its dozen new homes constructed by O'Reilly and Fein, brighten at last?

Even away from home, Bea felt the oppressiveness. She'd gone to visit Maggie, who had a reliable knack for cheering her up, but on the long streetcar ride home Bea had felt bluer than ever. Poor Maggie, living way up Grand River with a woman she'd nicknamed the Jailer. Mrs. Hamm made no effort to conceal her distrust of her new daughter-in-law. Meanwhile, George—depending on Maggie's mood—was either doomed soon to die in treacherous Pearl Harbor or living the life of Riley.

No, Bea's mood lifted only in Ronny's company. These days, he alone had the gift of making her laugh. Quickly—remarkably quickly—they'd developed a string of little jokes, as if they'd known each other not for weeks but for years. They often addressed each other by surname. "You know, Paradiso," he might say, "drawing birch bark turns out to be harder than it looks." "I tell you, Olsson," she might reply, "I'd rather draw birch bark than a sponge." And they would exchange looks, and laugh.

She had a taste for irreverence—why else make Maggie your best friend?—but she didn't approve when boys were coarse. Ronny was never coarse, but he *could* be a trifle risqué; he had the sort of sophistication that lifts prurience into repartee. One day at Herk's Snack Shack they were discussing their classmates and Bea mentioned Tatiana, the Russian girl with the yellow hair. "But tell me the truth, Bianca," Ronny interrupted. "Aren't you just *so tired* of Miss Bogoljubov's breasts?" And Bea gaped in amazement, then exploded in grateful giggles, for indeed she was, yes, just *so tired* of those big pale breasts—the cleavage as much a part of Tatiana's daily wardrobe as shoes or a purse.

Standing in front of Brueghel's amazing *Wedding Dance,* with its earthy peasants and their unignorably engorged codpieces, Ronny was capable of dissecting, with perfect equanimity, the distributions of color: "Isn't it something? The reds, the greens—even the colors are dancing." But, in closing, he was also one to remark, of the most flagrantly lusty of the men, "I wonder what's on *his* mind . . ."

Later, seated together in the Kresge Court, Bea had her own observation about distributions of color: "Do you know you have unpaintable eyes?"

"Unpaintable?"

"What color are they?"

"They're green."

"But there's gold in them, too, isn't there?"

And Ronny looked just delighted. "You know what? You're right! Though maybe only a real painter would notice . . ."

Just the sort of talk she'd always imagined having with a dashing young artist! It was as though their remarks were gifts to each other—conversation as an exercise in gift giving. She loved listening to Ronny formulate those all-inclusive, magnificent pronouncements he adored: assertions that initially might sound facetious, or just plain silly, but which subsequently struck her as thought-provoking, and often astute, and sometimes profound. He was frightfully bright. "Facts are tedious," Ronny declared one day. She'd been asking about his high school years, which fascinated her because he was the only young man she'd ever met, outside of a book, who had "gone East" for boarding school. He'd attended Groton, in Massachusetts, the very school that—impossible as it was to imagine—President Roosevelt himself once attended. ("It was my father's idea," Ronny said. "My mother didn't want me to go. I hated it, every minute. I didn't even finish the year.")

How many months, exactly, had he spent there?

"You do know, don't you, Paradiso, that facts distort reality," Ronny replied, and while this particular pronouncement initially sounded grand and impractical, hadn't Ronny crystallized for her a notion long coalescing? Hadn't she always suspected that, beyond life's cluttered aggregations of facts, what counted ultimately were beauty, ingenuity, nobility, iridescence?

When facts about his life did arrive, even significant facts, they often emerged backhandedly, as when Bea happened to mention having had Rocky Mountain spotted fever as a child, and Ronny informed her that *he'd* had scarlet fever. "It left me with what in the movies they always call a *bum ticker*. But I prefer *heart murmur*, it sounds so much more romantic . . ." And here was an answer to the question Bea had so fiercely pondered: Ronny's seeming immunity to the draft.

If facts were tedious, what wasn't tedious? Well, the "mastery of light" in a painting by Gerard Ter Borch in the Detroit Institute of Arts. "What a sense of touch!" Ronny cried in a peculiar squeezed voice that spoke of the ethereality of true artistic aspiration—and yet with these very words about *touch* for the first time he touched her, reached across with his painter's fingers to stroke the back of her hand, her surprised, tremulous thumb, the uncertain open shell of her palm.

Bea recognized immediately that this might be a bolder variety of touch—a more meaningful touch—than anything she had previously experienced . . . Was it perhaps (so she speculated that night, lying in bed, listening to Edith soughing in the upper bunk) her first *adult* touch? Of all the boys she'd ever met, who but Ronny truly appreciated just how beautiful a beautiful painting could be? Who else saw how all of life's fussed-over dailiness (Nonna's precise recipe for risotto marinaro, the price of hair ribbons at Kresge's, the most suitable screws for a banister) paled to nothing before the glittering canvas of some Old Dutch Master whom most people had never heard of, painted when Indian settlements dotted the Detroit River?

But that initial, unlooked-for touch had not been the most remarkable thing about their very remarkable day. No, *that* had occurred before a canvas by Chardin, *Still Life with Dead Hare.* Ronny had gallantly offered his arm as he guided her around the museum. "Now isn't this one lovely?" he asked her, and right through the fabric of his shirt his skin came alive. The goosebumps on his arm were solid as little pellets. She couldn't restrain herself. Lightly, discreetly, Bianca slid her fingertips up his arm: one after another, bump after bump after bump. It was remarkable. No painting had ever stirred *her* quite so dramatically, so physically. Ronny had such eloquence—you could almost say glibness—that a person might suppose he didn't respond freshly to art, but he did. With his whole body, he did.

Those bumps still tingled against her fingertips as she lay in bed—in the elaborate, carved bed where everything she felt was felt with especial keenness. She loved this sensation of pondering life's mysteries while enclosed by the dark silhouettes of her totem-pole bedposts: lamb, fish, stork, rabbit . . . Of course she typically felt uneasy as well, for nights were—nights had always been—her difficult time. That's when the phrases she couldn't get out of her head arrived, or the dopey but insistent melodies whose sheer repetitiveness threatened to drive her mad. Or that's when, sometimes, elaborate tasks coalesced. Most of these made no sense at all. Last year, she'd passed through a period (it had tyrannized her for months, before vanishing almost without a trace) when she'd needed to reconstruct her day in a peculiar, fixed fashion, recalling the precise order in which she'd first laid eyes on her family. Mamma and Papa and Stevie and Edith and (if she'd seen them that day) Uncle Dennis and Aunt Grace or Grandpa Paradiso and Grandma Paradiso—whom had she first clapped eyes on? And second? Third? Fourth? The entire day had to be reenacted around something as arbitrary and meaningless as that . . . There were no words for most of this business, and Bea had no way to think it through, although thinking it through was what she attempted along the seam of sleep, pursuing it in loops and swirls, painterly shapes and also ugly, unimaginative, oppressively repetitive repetitive repetitive shapes, where was the escape and why was sleep so elusive? Defended by its staunch animal quartet, her bed helped keep such forces at bay, and this was the real reason she'd always resisted sleeping over at Maggie's, or at Uncle Dennis and Aunt Grace's.

Were the night thoughts of everybody else so different from their day thoughts? Bea had pondered this a great deal, mostly at night, and while aware of the omnipresent risk of self-delusion, still it did seem to her, to Bianca Paradiso, that she could date precisely the moment when everything turned. She had been twelve—Edith's age. She'd been in church, which was somewhat surprising, given that churches had never figured large in her imagination. She had spent little time in St. Charles Borromeo, or any of the other local Catholic churches. (Papa, relishing his scattering of slang, sometimes called Mass "a load of mumbo jumbo.") And Bea had felt even less affiliated with either the Lutheran or the Presbyterian churches Mamma vacillated between, depending on whether her German or Scottish ancestry called.

For a time, on Sunday afternoons, Bea used to go with Maggie to the MYF, the Methodist Youth Fellowship; it was the church group of the really popular crowd at Barbour Intermediate. Usually it was taught by parents of kids in the group, but on one special occasion Reverend Kakenmaster himself addressed them.

He had a style unlike anything Bea had ever seen in a man of the cloth. He looked right at you and his face burned bright red. He posed a long string of questions, to which the rather puzzling answer always was, *I say yes, I abide by that.* The children chanted the reply. The questions involved choosing good over evil, and God over the Devil, and innocence over depravity.

Through the stained-glass window a beam of golden light from Heaven itself drilled Reverend Kakenmaster's high domed forehead. "It is up to you, boys and girls," the glowing-headed man of God declared. The beam of light added a sort of horn to his head. "You must decide which it will be: purity or filthiness. Jesus Christ instructed you to choose purity, and what do you say to that?"

And it was precisely at this sacred but precarious instant that some impulse *not* originating in Heaven alighted inside Bea's brain.

In her mind's eye she envisioned herself boldly standing up, in the powder-blue dress with white lace collar and white fagoting on the sleeves that Aunt Grace had made for her, and declaring right back at Reverend Kakenmaster, "I say no, I say —— to that," in which the blank word was an unspeakable term. What would they say, yes, and *what would they do*? What would they all *do* if she fearlessly stood up in her lacy blue dress and yelled, "I say —— to that."

It was all somewhat laughable now, so many years later, but at the time the image was so vivid and upsetting that Bea afterward had felt sick, her insides bubbling above the beige toilet bowl in the Methodist ladies' room, and later that evening, in expiation, she had required herself mentally to chant one hundred times, *I say yes, I abide by that.* Only, she could never reach a hundred. No matter how hard she concentrated, a poisoned thought infiltrated (an *I say no to that*, or something far worse), compelling her to start over . . . Had everything changed that day? Well, Bea couldn't be sure her memory was trustworthy, but it certainly *seemed* everything changed on that day when she'd said no to God and, in retribution, an era of bizarre tasks had descended. Or so it might appear while, as now, drifting so near to sleep that nothing could be hauled back to the land of full waking . . .

Facts may distort reality, but the next day Ronny offered a particular factual disclosure so startling, it all but took her breath away; it reordered everything. The two of them were walking up Woodward, just south of the Boulevard. The General Motors Building loomed on the left. Bea pointed to the familiar red-and-yellow sign of the drugstore across the street and said, "Funny, it's the same spelling. As your name."

Olsson's Drugs. They were all over the city.

Although the two of them were not touching, she could feel Ronny's body stiffen. He halted. Even in relaxed moments, his green-gold gaze radiated intensity, but this was more than mere intensity. His eyes were aflame.

He said, "You say it almost like—as if it's a coincidence."

"A coincidence?" Honestly, his eyes had such a feverish look! "What are you trying to—"

"Bianca, I thought you knew," Ronny interrupted. "You didn't know?" He paused. "Really? Truly? I mean, it's my father's. You do know, it's my father's store."

At first Bea couldn't take it all in. Illogically, she thought Ronny must be referring to this particular store, on Woodward just south of the Boulevard. "You mean he—your father runs this place?"

"I mean"—and facts may be tedious, but Ronny Olsson's eyes were burning more brightly than when he rattled on about any Poussin or Fragonard canvas—"he runs them all. He owns them all."

"All? *All?*"

Weeks before she'd ever spoken to the newcomer in class, the wildly good-looking Ronald Olsson, Bea had fantasized, just for fun, that he might be a prince in exile. But to be informed, in the bright no-nonsense light of a Monday afternoon on Woodward Avenue, that her walking companion was the son of the man who owned the leading drugstore chain in Detroit—this was a story more fabulous still. Why, there was even an Olsson's at the end of Inquiry Street; Bea had been living beside Olsson's her whole life!

"Forty-seven stores over three states. I don't know why, but I just thought you knew. Most people just seem to know."

"But I didn't," Bea said. "He's—your father—well, he's *Mr. Olsson.*" Over the years, she'd seen a number of newspaper photographs of Ronny's father and mother. Mr. Olsson led various important organizations for the war effort. The Olssons were among the city's most prominent people.

"I didn't know," Bea repeated, feeling oddly apologetic. But how was she to have known?

Alongside them, automobiles were gliding up and down Woodward. Across the street, people were walking in and out of Olsson's. *There when you need us there.* It was the store's slogan. Bea stared at Ronny Olsson. Unmistakably, everything between the two of them must now stand on a different footing.

Yes, everything had changed and Ronny led her to a new luncheonette, called Big Ben's, and over mugs of watery coffee he regaled her with Olsson family anecdotes. His parents had come together in what was clearly a great love match (though Ronny, in his qualifying way, shrugged off Bea's term). Ronny's grandfather, Grandpa Olsson, founder of Olsson's Drugs, had disapproved of his son's romance and flatly prohibited marriage. Yet Ronny's parents went ahead and married anyway. Ronny's mother was extraordinarily beautiful. (But Bea already knew this, having seen the newspaper photographs.) Mrs. Olsson had grown up in the tiny town of Scarp, North Dakota, but she had found her way to Detroit, and to a party attended by Ronny's father, Charles Olsson, who, the first time he clapped eyes on her, declared her the most gorgeous girl he'd ever seen and vowed to marry her. "Mother is always after me to do her portrait, though she knows I don't do people. I suppose I don't have your gift for it, Bianca."

It was the first genuine compliment Ronny had paid her art, and his words had all the luster—the darting expansive promise—of paint emerged fresh from the tube. Bea immediately blushed. Ronny retracted his approval a little, however, with his next remark: "I'm a still-life artist. Now, does that mean I'm limited and narrow? Is Chardin limited and narrow? Isn't an overreliance on the human element ultimately sentimental?"

Bea responded cleverly: "But still lifes are a comparatively recent phenomenon! If you said to Giotto or Duccio—"

"But there you go again! Always accusing me of being a hidebound reactionary"—of course Bea had never said any such thing; the phrase wasn't even in her vocabulary—"yet I'm now revealed as a progressive! A novelty-lover! Enchanted by that newfangled creation, the still life!"

"I never said—"

"Of course Mother's portrait's been done a number of times, but she doesn't believe they do her justice, and honestly she's right, and I do wish I could oblige, but I don't do people. So you think that's wrong, Bianca? Isn't it enough to aspire to be a still-life artist?"

This was generally the way conversations with Ronny proceeded: a shuttling from personal matters to philosophical questions about the nature of art, back to personal matters, back to art—while he playfully defended himself from accusations Bea had never made, and formulated refutations to objections Bea had never posed. What was so striking, beneath all his banter, was how integrated into Ronny's daily life were these questions about art. Chardin and Ter Borch and Mr. Olsson and Mrs. Olsson—it seemed they all sat at the same table. Meanwhile, her own life on Inquiry Street, with Stevie and his BB guns and Edith and her knitting, with Papa and his scarred builder's hands and Mamma and her cups of sludge—what did such things have to do with Chardin and Ter Borch?

And yet, and yet . . . Here was Ronny Olsson, on another trip to Big Ben's, implying that her own family stories were just as inspiring as any story could be. She happened to mention that Grandpa Paradiso, born two months premature, had been kept alive in the family oven, and instantly Ronny's gaze sharpened. More details, *signorina*—he must have more details . . . And, under his prompting, the tale grew steadily richer.

Nonno had been born on the coast of Liguria, to a very poor teenage girl whose husband had died in a shipyard accident just a week before. The premature baby also appeared destined to die, as did the young widow, who, having delivered her doomed infant, had collapsed into prostrate grief. It was Nonno's grandmother—mother-in-law to the ailing young mother—who fixed on the idea of converting the family stove into an incubator.

This wasn't an electric oven, of course, for nobody on that stretch of coast had electricity yet. No, it was an actual woodstove, whose temperature had to be monitored—day and night, every blessed minute—if the baby wasn't to be cooked alive.

"Paradiso, don't you see? That old woman saved *your* life, too!" Ronny cried, so enthusiastically that a few customers turned and stared. The remark sounded like more of Ronny's far-flung hyperbole—but then Bea got the point, belatedly grasping what she'd somehow never appreciated: yes, that old woman had *saved her life*. And what *could* be odder? Right here in Big Ben's, her own existence broke over her existence; a wash of novel chemicals rippled through her veins. She— Bea—Bianca Paradiso—would not be sitting here, sipping from a chipped white coffee mug, if it weren't for a blood relative who was a stranger, an old Italian peasant woman who had hardly slept for days, who could not sleep, for she was sole nurse to the baby in the family oven.

It was typical of Ronny to wish to hear about her great-great-grandmother; Ronny specialized in peculiar inquiries. What would she choose for her last dinner on earth, and with whom would she eat? ("I'd eat with my family," Bea answered instantly. She added, "Aunt Grace would do the cooking.") And what was her earliest memory? No other boy had ever asked for her earliest memory.

"Well, I was visiting Uncle Dennis and Aunt Grace, who used to live in Corktown—you know, near the Ambassador Bridge. The bridge was just being built. This must have been 1928 or so."

"You would have been—?"

Bea had slipped and almost revealed how young she was. She raced on: "I remember this big muscular man working on the bridge. Silhouetted against the sky. That's my first memory: a man silhouetted against the sky."

"Have you ever tried to paint that?"

"N-no." But why had she never tried to paint that?

She could see him now: the man on the bridge. She would see him forever. High in the metal framework, a muscled silhouette against the sky. Why had she never tried to paint that? (Though, come to think of it—and wasn't this fascinating?—she *had* painted the bridge. It anchored the horizon of her one sold painting, *International Waters,* which she was less pleased with each time she visited Uncle Dennis's office.)

Yes, Ronny was forcing Bea to rethink everything. *Was* it wrong to be nothing but a still-life artist? This was an "ancient debate"—so Professor Manhardt had described it—and yet arguments formulated in ancient times suddenly felt fresh. Bea loved these discussions, the two promising young art students (the boy twenty-one, the girl eighteen) contending back and forth, not always sure what they thought but weighing each thought passionately. (In truth, Ronny was far firmer in his views; she had trouble making up her mind.) There were days when Ronny seemed absolutely correct: it was enough merely to paint a cruet, a daisy, a dead rabbit, a lemon rind. Indeed, more than enough: it was noble, these attempts to place disparate objects in an artful conjunction and capture with near-microscopic exactitude all the intricacies of their interplay. And yet . . . there were times when you had to do something more, or something more direct, about it all.

The *all* was the War, of course—a war bigger than anything else in history. Hitler and Mussolini meeting in the Brenner Pass, Hitler on the Spanish border conferring with Franco, Hitler being cheered as he waved from Prague Castle, Hitler leaning on a balustrade in front of the Eiffel Tower . . . So long as the Nazis had the run of the Louvre, how could you talk dispassionately about a Chardin still life? No, you had to offer some response—something to encompass the soldiers on the Detroit streetcars, the loss of Bataan and Corregidor, Churchill defending his strategies after Tobruk, old Henry Ford ghostly in the newsreels, and the whole throbbing city gearing up as never before. An amphibious vehicle rolled off a GM assembly line, and worlds away its ramp swung down, khaki legs splashed out into a choppy salt surf . . . Those assembly lines were churning out tanks and armored cars, antiaircraft guns and rocket launchers, a whole new alphabet of browns and tans and olives: B-24s, B-29s, M4s, M3s, LCVPs, LCTs, DUKWs, F6Fs, TBFs. Sometimes Bea envisioned herself creating vast tumultuous canvases unlike anything she'd attempted before, streetcars sharing the streets with tanks, wounded soldiers staring out at you with inquisitive, hurt, hopeful eyes, and newspapers tallying the death counts, and whole city blocks darkening in their dim-outs, while dark alarms were wailing—but who in the world could paint such a canvas? It was impossible—and yet to attempt anything less than the impossible seemed tantamount to betrayal . . .

She kept reading about the amazing things girls had learned to do. The articles leaped out from the *News*. Girls were driving tractors through soybean fields, they were manning radar stations in the Arctic, they were riveting armored cars. But to judge from Papa's response when she'd suggested, not very seriously, getting a war-factory job—honestly, he couldn't have been more dumbstruck if she'd proposed joining the circus, or converting to Hinduism. His mouth had fallen open. What would his Bia say next? Wasn't *he* working his fingers to the bone erecting housing for defense workers? Now, in addition, he's asked to send off his daughter, wearing slacks, to work beside a bunch of leering factory rats?

In the face of her anguished perplexities, Ronny Olsson rarely wavered. He was Olympian. It was enough—more than enough—to paint a peony, a pack of playing cards, a guttered candle. "I do my part," he insisted. "Don't I give the maximum amount of blood permitted? Didn't I cart God knows how many tons of salvage from our attic? Don't I serve as a block captain? But no artist should apologize for being an artist." And sometimes Bea hungrily envied him his robust certainty, sensing herself constrained and deficient for its lack. Wasn't Ronny displaying the stylistic confidence of the true artist? And wasn't she showing the churning muddle of the would-be artist, painting bowls of cherries while dreaming of gritty canvases in which turreted armored cars roamed the streets, gun barrels uplifted like the fingers of accusers?

And sometimes she resented Ronny—his confidently declaring, "I don't mean to be callous, but you must take the long view. This is only the latest war. There have been plenty of wars, Bianca." Oh, words easy for him—him with his "romantic" heart murmur! But while Ronny was pondering strategies for committing a tulip to canvas, American boys exactly his age were shipping off to war. The induction notices in the *News* sometimes filled one column and spilled over into a second. Those bare stretches of newsprint terrified and summoned her—the more so, somehow, when appearing opposite the funny pages. On one side, Alley Oop and Rick O'Shay and Superman. On the other, a cold, factual list of hundreds of boys, many of whom would never return. One day she was idly reading "Freckles and His Friends" when her gaze drifted rightward and fell *immediately* upon the name Frederick Rumpelman. This had to be the Fred she knew from Eastern High—

how many Fred Rumpelmans could there be in Detroit?—and the coincidence terrified her. His name leaping out like that—did this mean Fred was destined for a bad end?

Still, it was hard to resent Ronny for long, given how he stretched her preconceptions. Thoughts of him brightened her days, and now more than ever, in this chaotic summer of '43, when rioters were overturning cars on Woodward and American death tolls were exploding overseas, Bea needed brightening. It seemed things at home couldn't get any worse—but they kept getting worse. Having initially shied from divulging to Ronny anything about her family, she soon began to take comfort in discussing how things stood on Inquiry, even if she must censor many details . . .

If Ronny were ever to meet her family, what would he make of them? Picturing Ronny Olsson in his beautiful camel's hair coat, seated in her living room, Bea felt what she rarely felt: a sense of shame at her own family.

When glimpsed through Ronny's projected gaze, Edith was revealed as a plump little old-maid-to-be, Stevie as a gun-crazy boy in oversized glasses, Papa a semiliterate laborer. Mamma—it was almost too painful to consider how an outsider of Ronny's refinement might view the sallow woman who regularly served up burned, blackened dinners. And Uncle Dennis? He was the stereotypical loopy uncle of some Hollywood comedy, the bun-faced man who buttonholed strangers to discuss interstellar space flight.

Only Aunt Grace passed muster, for how could Ronny fail to value Grace's grace—her fair-spoken voice, her authentic empathy and modesty, her long-fingered ivory hands?

In his intuitive way, Ronny sensed just where his deepest interests naturally must lie. Tales about Bea's younger siblings bored him. (Perhaps because he was an only child?) On the other hand, anecdotes about the two sisters, Grace and Sylvia Schleiermacher, captivated Ronny—and this was fine with Bea. No other subject so needed investigation.

"In a way it just gets worse and worse. We saw the Poppletons every week, virtually every Saturday of our lives, and now we haven't had a Saturday together in five weeks!"

Naturally, Ronny wanted to know what had triggered the family rupture. Naturally, Bea couldn't divulge everything she knew, still less everything she suspected.

"I think Mamma's always been jealous of Aunt Grace, and of course she's always been moody—what we call her Dark Spells. Terribly moody sometimes, and in this case everything coincided. I *knew* something was wrong, the day before the last day we all got together. When I came home from school, I felt it in the air."

Sometimes in Bea's mind's eye her mother appeared darker than in life: hair darker, and the circles under her eyes darker, and voice darker, and her coffee black and thick as tar. Meanwhile, as if in compensation, her candies were brighter than in life, almost brighter than colors in life could be: the green of the spearmint leaves, red of the cinnamon chews, orange and yellow and purple of the jelly beans—all crying to be painted, in the cruelest and most heartbreaking portrait anyone ever composed. (Not that Bea would ever paint *that* . . .)

"But when did it start? What exactly happened?"

How could Bea possibly reveal how upset Mamma had become when her little sister, Grace, waist deep in water, stood forth on a public beach with her left breast bared? Or that Papa, with his bandaged hand, had reached forward as if to seize or shelter her?

Clearly, clearly she couldn't tell Ronny about eavesdropping, from the landing, on a voice of abject desolation: "It's *Grace* you've always loved!"

And there was a secret darker still—a secret Bea not only could never disclose but could scarcely bear to think about . . . A week after overhearing that pitiful lamentation, Bea had come home from school and found Mamma alone—in the kitchen, of course, pondering her bare existence.

"Your father and I had an argument last night," Mamma began.

Another argument? Bea had slept through this one.

Mamma's tone was unexpected: informative, dispassionate, remarkably clear-eyed and sane. "I thought I should explain something to you."

"Yes, Mamma."

Something awful was approaching.

"He called me by someone else's name," Mamma said. "By mistake. He called me Grace. There we were in bed, and we were . . . we were, well, in each other's arms"—her whole body shuddered—"and he called me by the wrong name."

"It must have been a mistake."

"A mistake. Yes. I said that already. But you see, mistakes can expose the truth. *That* was his mistake."

"Everybody makes mistakes."

"You're old enough to know the truth, Bea. It's so. The truth. Your father's in love with her. We were in each other's arms—close—and he called me by my sister's name."

"Oh, Mamma—*Mamma*! Papa's not in love with Grace! The whole thing is *ridiculous*."

"He called me by her name," Mamma repeated.

"He was thinking about her! We've all been thinking about her! Good heavens, this is terrible, what's happened between you two. You're *sisters*."

"He called me by her name," Mamma insisted, in the same restrained but immovable tone. "While we were—close. Your father's in love with her. Actually, it's something I've always known, though I pretended to myself I didn't."

It was clear—queerly clear—that Mamma was implying that at the very moment when Papa made his fatal utterance the two of them had been . . . but Bea had no words for such an activity, not where her parents were concerned. Maggie used to talk about hearing her parents, hearing all sorts of things, but never in her life had Bea had any evidence, other than the physical existence of herself and her siblings, that her parents shared physical relations, and it wasn't a possibility she cared to contemplate. But that *was* Mamma's implication . . .

And Mamma was suggesting something further, wasn't she?—the final cessation of such relations? For what she next declared was: "Now, how could I ever again lie close in the arms of a man who wishes I was my own sister?"

Of course nothing of this could be revealed to Ronny, who for all his overflowing curiosity sounded understandably puzzled. "Your mother, is she mentally ill, then?"

"Oh I wouldn't say *that*." The term was deeply offensive.

Yet the nonjudgmental way Ronny spoke the term—as if it were a purely scientific designation—abruptly rendered the idea hideously plausible: *was* that the accurate phrase? Was Mamma *mentally ill*?

"Well, she has her peculiarities," Bea said, and added a little laugh, not altogether successfully.

"Most mentally ill people do."

"And I don't suppose you could call her happy."

"Most mentally ill people aren't."

"Mamma is just Mamma. You'd have to see for yourself," Bea volunteered, but in truth she was in no hurry for Ronny to meet her. Discomfort at the prospect propelled Bea into another profession of concern:

"Well, we've *got* to get together with Aunt Grace and Uncle Dennis this Saturday. It's Aunt Grace's fortieth birthday. Oh, I do hope everything goes all right . . ."

CHAPTER V

Among the many changes at home, perhaps the most puzzling involved the telephone.

The telephone had always played a peculiar role in the house. Papa disliked or distrusted it, often deputizing Mamma or Bea to make his calls. Those calls he did make, he kept short and businesslike. Generally soft-spoken, he tended to yell into the mouthpiece—like some old codger, unaccustomed to this upstart device. Still, as a man who built houses for a living, he could scarcely resist outfitting his own home with "every convenience," and he'd rigged up an easy way to move the phone from the kitchen into his bedroom.

Now Papa found a bedroom phone useful. He spoke behind the closed door, and not in his usual barking telephone voice. Who was he talking to? Of course Bea couldn't ask. It took a couple days to verify who it was—Uncle Dennis—and what they were discussing: Aunt Grace's upcoming birthday.

Tradition held that each sister play hostess for the other's birthday. So Aunt Grace's fortieth should have been celebrated on Inquiry Street. This year, though, the celebration would take place at a restaurant, Chuck's Chop House, up on McNichols.

Who ever heard of a birthday at a restaurant?

Still, given the tight-lipped way Papa broke the news, the matter wasn't open to discussion. Only Edith, as the youngest child, felt it proper to ask, "But *why* a restaurant?"

"It's—Uncle Dennis. He—we wanted a change." Papa followed this with a firm shake of the head.

"Will there be a cake?"

Papa stared blankly. The question of a birthday cake plainly hadn't occurred to him.

"Yes," he said. "There will be cake."

When the Paradiso family arrived at Chuck's Chop House on Saturday, a few minutes before five, Uncle Dennis and Aunt Grace were already there. What Bea had previously suspected now became unmistakable: everything about this unprecedented party had been coordinated by Uncle Dennis. He had chosen well. Although they did not have a private room, the seven of them were settled in an alcove off the main dining room that they could make their own.

Uncle Dennis had determined the seating. Aunt Grace at one end. He himself at the other. Papa and Bea flanking Grace. Stevie beside Papa, Edith beside Bea. Mamma next to Edith, beside Uncle Dennis. Mamma and Aunt Grace sat at opposite ends of the table, then, without actually facing each other.

The tablecloth was red-and-white checkerboard and the glass ashtrays, jumbo-sized, said "Chuck's Chop House—Dine Distinctively" on the bottom. The matchbooks in the ashtrays said the same thing, only with an exclamation point: "Dine Distinctively!"

Chuck's Chop House turned out to be owned by a patient of Uncle Dennis's, who came over and introduced himself, very informally: "Hello, hello, I'm Chuck!" he boomed jubilantly. He slung his arm over Uncle Dennis's shoulder and declared, "Here's the medico keeping me alive!"—which only made a person wish Chuck looked healthier. He was very fat and very red-faced, and Bea suspected he might be a lush. He shook hands with everyone, even Stevie and Edith, and said, "So it's a birthday, huh?" and told a story, actually quite humorous, about picking up the wrong bag at Hudson's and bringing home a Pretty Miss Perfect doll for his son's tenth birthday. Then he said to Aunt Grace, "The birthday girl—you don't watch out, you'll turn *thirty*!" His laughter rang so boisterously, it echoed in the alcove after he'd gone.

But if there was something clownish about Chuck (*buffoonish*, Papa would have said, the Italian *buffone* obviously behind it—there were many such oddities in his English), his departure introduced a sense of letdown. The evening needed a clown, a distraction.

. . . Not that Aunt Grace could have looked more settled and sedate. She was wearing a new cream-colored dress with a pin Bea herself had made, many years ago. And her earrings? Did Mamma notice her earrings? They were the pearl earrings Mamma had given her on her birthday five years before, when Grace turned thirty-five.

Without comment or explanation, Mamma had refused to get dressed up. She was wearing—conspicuous plainness—a brown dress that was really a housedress. Her hair needed brushing. She hadn't said a single word on the drive over.

Uncle Dennis had arranged everything, even what they would eat.

No need for menus. They were all brought bowls of ham and split-pea soup. Mamma tasted exactly two spoonfuls—Bea watched closely—before pushing her bowl aside. The others made a point of exclaiming over the soup, which truly was tasty; why shouldn't a birthday dinner be held at a restaurant? A bread basket circulated. There was pop for the children—today Bea was included among them—and white wine for the grown-ups.

After the last of the soup had been mopped up with the bread, Uncle Dennis announced that the next course would be baked whitefish. It was slow to arrive. Papa eventually asked Uncle Dennis about the War. Uncle Dennis prided himself on seeing through what he called "the propaganda." It was true of our government as well—you shouldn't believe everything they told you. That was just the nature of war.

Now let's see . . . Germany was facing four possible alternatives in Russia. A retreat, which probably made the most sense strategically but would be disastrous psychologically. Two, just dig in, but this, too, might be ruinous for them: nothing's harder than to be an occupying army in only partially occupied territory. Three, they could swing south, toward better weather—but away from the targets they most needed to hit. Four, they could prepare an all-out further attack—though if this push failed, they would be helpless on their eastern front. Meanwhile, the generals in Washington were preparing—count on it, and before the year was out—to open a western front, almost certainly in Belgium. Wherever it was, many American boys would be lost—far greater casualties than anything heretofore.

Far greater casualties . . . far greater casualties . . . The table fell silent. And still the whitefish failed to arrive.

Uncle Dennis continued. We can expect big sacrifices in the Pacific, too. The Japs aren't going down easily. All along, we've underestimated them. There will be no knockout blow. It was a matter of seizing islands one by one. The Japs were prepared to fight to the death.

"The Italians are different," Papa said.

Yes, Uncle Dennis agreed, the Italians were different. Mussolini didn't really command their loyalty (Papa nodded urgently at this), and Italy would be liberated by year's end. There was a sigh of relief around the table. But still no whitefish.

Uncle Dennis's summary was lengthier than usual, and when he finished, an extended and increasingly awkward silence entrenched itself.

Normally, Aunt Grace could have been counted on to stitch any tear in the conversation, with words so apt and sincere they never seemed a mere stopgap. But tonight Grace, though beaming fixedly, seemed in no mood for such talk. The task fell squarely upon Bea, who sought to amuse the table with some eccentricities found at the Institute Midwest—Professor Manhardt in his wool vests on summer's hottest days, and Mr. Cooper, the Polish refugee, declaring, "Art is my only home"—but unfortunately her story seemed to have no *point*. She turned to the reliable subject of Maggie—everybody delighted in Maggie, whose departure for the wastelands of the far West Side had left a big vacancy. "She calls her mother-in-law the Jailer," Bea began. "Mrs. Hamm is this crazy lady who scarcely lets Maggie out of her sight."

But, as the following silence made clear, this was no occasion for an account of a strange, suspicious woman who was a homebody to boot.

Then the subject of race came up—what Mamma called "the colored problem"—which was unfortunate because nobody wanted to discuss this at a birthday celebration. Still, it was hard to ignore a civil uprising which had left dozens of people dead and which, for all the mayor's reassurances that it represented only a few hours of madness, had transformed the city's atmosphere. "Vico, these people have nowhere to live," Uncle Dennis pointed out. "*You* understand better than anyone. Back in April, it's decided none of these federal projects would be integrated, which really meant the Negroes wouldn't get their share, didn't it? They're packed into the few rooms in the few neighborhoods—"

Papa interrupted: "Nobody has places to live."

"That's exactly my point! Who in all Detroit understands this better than you? Heck, Vico, you're working fingers to the bone building places where all these new workers—"

"I've never seen the city like this," Grace interrupted. It seemed she, too, felt jittery. The topic made Bea *very* nervous—especially as debated by these two men. It wasn't so many years ago that Papa had used the word *nigger* in front of Uncle Dennis. This was on an outing to Chandler Park, a picnic, where Papa had been drinking wine. *A couple niggers* was the phrase. And what happened next was extraordinary— Bea had never forgotten it. She would never forget it. Uncle Dennis had walked right up to Papa and said, "Vico, *you* don't talk that way," rebuking him as sharply and dismissively as though he were some schoolboy. And Bea, standing beside her father, this man who prided himself on his arm wrestling, had seen Papa's body tremble all over with fury. He'd gathered his fists together, and Bea had honestly feared Papa would strike Uncle Dennis.

"It's less of a problem Outer Drive way," Mamma observed, which sounded offhand but was actually aggressive. The implication was that the Poppletons, living on Outer Drive near the Grosse Pointe border, were insulated from the Paradisos' legitimate fears. Only a few short blocks separated Inquiry Street from Belle Isle, and when the radio had reported (falsely, it turned out) that Negroes were assembling on Belle Isle and were planning to march on the city, Bea had felt something odd: a social—racial—terror. It was quite unlike anything she'd ever known, this invasive fear of another race.

Uncle Dennis took the topic firmly in hand. "Oh, but it isn't a problem in one neighborhood, it's the whole city's problem. And it has to be a citywide solution. We need more of those Sojourner Truth housing developments. Good heavens, this is America, how can you say to people, Your kind has nowhere to live in the fourth-largest city in the country?" Given Mamma and Papa's attitudes, this wasn't perhaps a wholly rhetorical question. Still, Uncle Dennis proceeded confidently. He was of course a great liberal, as was Aunt Grace, whose heroine was Eleanor Roosevelt. "That's the thing all of us are learning," he declared, and carried on in this vein, his *all of us* shepherding the dinner party safely into a territory where fairness and decency and progress flourished. Uncle Dennis pushed on, delving into some of the specific programs the city needed to adopt, and would adopt, because we remain a *very decent city,* and it soon became evident that at this celebration a potential disaster had been averted.

But still no whitefish. In desperation, Bea said, "Why don't you tell us about your reading, Uncle Dennis?"

"My reading?"

"Your science fiction. You must be reading a science-fiction story."

"Yessss . . ."

Although Uncle Dennis avidly discussed his reading with Bea, he'd never felt quite comfortable sharing such things with the world at large. "Oh, this one's pretty dumb, actually," he said, and his plump bespectacled face looked a little abashed.

Still, he carried on. "The book's called *Lost Planet of the Amazons.* A spaceman from Earth crash-lands on some distant planet and discovers there aren't any other men in sight. No boys. No males anywhere. Only females.

"And at first he's utterly delighted. Jeepers, it's like a harem! I don't mean to suggest the book goes in for hanky-panky. But you can imagine how overjoyed our spaceman is to find himself the only man on a planet overrun by women." Uncle Dennis halted. "That may not sound like heaven to you, but you'll have to trust me on this, Stevie," he said. "Eventually, you'll get it"—which made Stevie blush and everyone else laugh. The laughter felt good. Uncle Dennis was trying so hard, really, to make the party a success . . .

"But then he fell to thinking. Men had to be *somewhere*. Otherwise, where did all the women come from? And he'd caught a few glimpses of pregnant women, and how could they be pregnant without—without the benefit of men?"

Uncle Dennis glanced searchingly around the table. His gaze settled on his wineglass and he took a sip.

Stevie and Edith were staring hard at Uncle Dennis, who only now realized his tale might not be completely appropriate for children.

"But where did the babies come from?" Edith asked in her level, fact-gathering way.

Uncle Dennis was saved by the belated arrival of the whitefish.

Like Chuck, the waitress was very fat and very red-faced. The two of them might almost have been brother and sister, though they didn't otherwise look much alike; it seemed if you were fat enough and red-faced enough, other resemblances scarcely counted.

The fish was covered with bread crumbs—wonderfully crunchy bread crumbs—and it came with buttered carrots and mashed potatoes with dark brown gravy. Uncle Dennis had selected well. They ate in silence. They were going to get through this potentially disastrous celebration. It was merely a matter of everyone's proceeding cautiously—tonight, tomorrow, next week—and letting time do its healing work. They were all one family, the Paradisos and the Poppletons, and they were, besides, all the family each of them had.

The waitress refilled the children's ginger ale, refreshed the grownups' wine. Uncle Dennis was readying himself to make a toast—he was a great one for toasts.

A clinking of knife against glass silenced the alcove. "To the woman at the other end of the table," Uncle Dennis proclaimed, hoisting high his wineglass. "You can't tell me that woman is forty. My God, she looks as fresh as a new bride."

Aunt Grace smiled—beautifully, demurely—and her lips moved in some unspoken message of humility and thanks.

And it was at this precise, exquisite moment that Mamma chose to speak up—opened her mouth to utter something surpassingly blunt and cruel. It was as though all the last few weeks of dark brooding had solidified in a phrase that fell like a butcher's cleaver.

"But she wasn't," Mamma pointed out. "A fresh bride. When you married her. Grace was divorced."

It was a topic rarely mentioned, and *never* mentioned in a public setting.

Mamma, who had pushed her plate aside, now took an interest in her food. She scooped up a large mixed forkful of fish and mashed potatoes and—as everyone at the table, aghast, intently watched—chewed it reflectively.

Mamma swallowed and resumed talking. Almost more upsetting than her words was her matter-of-fact tone. It was all so eerie—her calmly thoughtful and seemingly nonjudgmental mien, as if she wished merely to set the record straight. "In the eyes of the Catholic Church, she's still married to Michael Cullers. Grace is married to a man who isn't even here. I suppose he wasn't invited." Her fork sought out the fish again.

It fell upon Uncle Dennis to speak: "But Sylvia, none of us here *is* a Catholic."

"None of us? Grace and I are a quarter Catholic by blood. And aren't you forgetting Vico? I *married* a Catholic, Dennis. And in the eyes of that church, he is pledged to me forever."

All eyes swung around to Papa, who was leaning forward and squeezing the edge of the table. At times like this, when seriously challenged, he exuded an air of physical forcefulness.

Papa cleared his throat. "The Church," he said. He was visibly searching for something to say.

Papa a Catholic? He did have a soft spot for nuns, particularly the ones collecting for charity. But as for the Church's views on marriage, and its prohibition on divorce, he would certainly dismiss such things with that favorite phrase, a "load of mumbo jumbo." If he believed wholeheartedly in anything, he believed in this marriage between his sister-in-law and his best friend. "Sylvia, we were not married in the Church," he said, slowly. "It was your own wish—"

Uncle Dennis interceded. Behind his thick glasses, his magnified eyes caromed round the table and landed on Edith. Clearly, he scarcely knew what he was saying:

"You were asking about the planet, and where the babies came from, and that's just what our spaceman eventually figured out: they had to come from—seeds, from the male seeds. The women were made pregnant, scientifically impregnated, in laboratories, using the—the seeds stored in the laboratories. And the Amazons want to get rid of the spaceman, but first they needed to get, they were going to collect—" Uncle Dennis halted, thoroughly discombobulated, and his jumpy gaze alighted on Bea. "You *see*," he said. "*You* see."

Just then, providentially, the enormous waitress appeared—large as any Amazon—and Uncle Dennis announced, in an amplified voice not his own, "I think we're all done, very nice, yes, all *done*, you can bring on the cake. My yes. You can bring on the cake." His face swung round the table and he explained, superfluously, "There is going to be a birthday cake for Grace . . ."

"I wanted cake," Edith said.

"And cake you shall have, my dear. Cake you shall have, little Edith," Uncle Dennis all but sang.

But not yet. For when the table had been cleared, as they all sat awaiting the birthday cake, Mamma assumed the floor again: "Have I spoken inappropriately?" she said. "Are we going to ignore certain truths and conditions staring us right in the face?" she said.

"*Sylvia*," Papa called.

"You know what? *I'm* going to have my say." And once again, though her unrestrained words were scary, more frightening still was the inhuman detachment in her voice—she seemed as unstoppable as some machine.

"Sylvia, you shut *up*."

"I'm going to have my say, Vico. Old Sylvia has thought long enough and hard enough and she's going to have her say. There are certain truths and conditions that can be ignored no longer, certain truths and conditions, and one is that Grace *had* a good-looking husband and couldn't hold on to him. Should we all pretend this isn't true? Do you remember what you used to say about him, Grace? About Michael Cullers? You said he looked like a Greek god. Remember? Am I the only one who remembers? A Greek . . . god. And you couldn't hold on to your god." Mamma peered with dark horrible intensity at Aunt Grace, who, with frightened upturned eyes, cowered under her older sister's gaze.

"And that's why you married Dennis, wasn't it? Because you couldn't hold on to a good-looking man? And do you remember how you described Dennis the first time? After your first date? Remember? Come on, Grace, you do remember. Yes, Grace, you said he looked like a *frog*. Beautiful Grace, the most beautiful girl at Eastern High School, the perfect princess, she married a *frog* because she couldn't hold on to a good-looking man."

The cries and protests were universal: everyone was begging her, begging her to stop. But she would not stop. Mamma could not stop. You might as well seek to arrest some allegorical figure in a painting— some streaming-haired Fury, some flying Angel of Death in a plain brown housedress, sowing mayhem and flattened devastation. What could anyone do but sit stunned and motionless, watching the dismembering of a family?

"So what did you do next? You stole Vico's heart. You stole the heart of a good-looking man, that's what you did. Oh I'm not accusing you of any impropriety—because that would be wrong, and our beautiful, perfect Grace *never does anything wrong.* No, you stole Vico's heart. That's all you did. No more than that. You stole my husband's heart, that's all you did. You ruined my marriage, and my life, that's all you did . . ."

Aunt Grace had begun to cry. "How could you—" she began, looking down at her plate. She could hardly find a voice through her sobbing. "How could you think—" She lifted her eyes, beseechingly, toward her older sister.

"What did I ever do to you?" Grace went on. "What did I *do*? Where was the offense? You say I ruined your life, but it's been this way forever, long before you ever met Vico. You're always attacking me, belittling me, attacking me, *attacking* me, and I try to ignore it—I do my level best to ignore it—"

And on this night of catastrophic accusations and revelations, one durable mystery was illuminated: Grace had understood the truth all along. Yes, she had sensed the hostility, and she'd tried to overlook it, or to defuse it, only to discover that it must ultimately declare itself.

Sobbing, pleading, struggling to get the words out, Grace demanded of Mamma, "What did I ever *do* that you treat me this way? On my—my fortieth birthday?"

And Aunt Grace was such a miserable, pitiable, wronged creature that Bea must reach over and place one hand upon the woman's quaking shoulder, the other hand atop Grace's hand, which was wet with tears. "It's all right, it's all right," Bea whispered.

But it was *not* all right and Mamma had some final bitterness to fling

at the world. Nothing could be left intact. Tonight, at this birthday celebration, everything must be irretrievably broken:

"Oh *go* ahead, Bea. Side with her. *Side* with her," Mamma hissed.
"Sure you do. You've always been an unnatural girl. You never loved
your own mother, did you?"

There: the terminating and seemingly inevitable words had been
pronounced, which weirdly seemed to free them all, and Papa and
Uncle Dennis hurried everybody up from their seats. Bea strode blindly
through the restaurant and stepped out into the chill darkness of a driz-
zling rain, a summer night that felt like autumn. The children ranged on
the sidewalk in assorted stunned postures, loosely huddled under the
restaurant's awning, but saying nothing. Papa and Uncle Dennis were
still inside, evidently settling the bill. Mamma stood apart, having edged
out from under the awning into the pattering rain.

Keeping to the awning's protection, Bea wandered on her own
alongside the restaurant. She peered through the rain-struck window.
What she beheld looked remotely familiar, but it took a moment to
focus. This was in the alcove. A quivering nest of bright jewelry, like a
mobile chandelier, floated into it, borne by the enormous waitress, who
apparently had not yet heard the party was over. The quivering jewels?
The candles of Aunt Grace's fortieth-birthday cake.

CHAPTER VI

The woman had set her blazing mark on that kitchen calendar she continually contemplated. She had created a day to go down in Paradiso history.

The rest of the world might not notice, but Mamma had issued a declaration of war. July 10, 1943, would henceforth serve, for the family living at 2753 Inquiry, as the domestic equivalent of December 7, 1941. A day which would live in infamy? A day, anyway, to banish any hope that a truce could be arrived at and wholesale destruction averted . . .

Perhaps the oddest aspect to it all was Mamma's transformation. In the days immediately following the party, she sprang from her kitchen chair and set to work, indefatigably. She emptied the kitchen cabinets and wiped them down, inside and out; she scrubbed the linoleum; she polished the silver; she even took a dust rag to the furnace room. One of the household's long-standing tensions was that Papa always kept up the exterior—paint, shutters, shingles, drainpipes—more meticulously than Mamma kept up the interior. No longer! Everything indoors shone.

No, *she* seemed fine; it was everybody else who stumbled around like numbed survivors of some aerial bombardment. Stevie's toy guns fell silent; Edith retreated upstairs behind her mountains of knitting; Papa was even earlier off to work and later coming home, where he barricaded himself interminably behind the *News*, while the radio played. He smelled of beer and wine. He scarcely spoke, except in stifled telephone conversations, mumbled behind his bedroom door. He looked like somebody suffering the first queasy touches of seasickness. He even walked differently—with the plodding deliberation of a passenger on a pitching ship.

As much as she could, Bea stayed away from home. Merely to step inside the front hall was to feel her throat tighten and burn. Dinners were a horror and bedtimes were worse. Once the lights were out, she felt far more jittery than usual, and soon a truly ridiculous task formulated itself, requiring her to reconstruct childhood classrooms, ages ago, back at Field Elementary. Which pupil had sat where? And what were their names?

What were their names? This was something she generally prided herself on—a better memory for childhood than most people had. (Maggie called her *my memory.* Maggie said, "I don't bother remembering anything—Bea is my memory.") But it was slipping away, wasn't it? Maybe that's what happened when you got older, when you approached twenty: your earliest years silently dissolved away. Until now, this process hadn't seemed so catastrophic; now, it seemed as wrenching as a death in the family.

Bea would clamber out of bed in the middle of the night and tiptoe down to the kitchen in order to assemble lists of old classmates. Sometimes—often—she could recall the face, but the name eluded her. Her failure seemed far, far worse when a boy was involved. The boys might well be shipped overseas by now, and any failure to recall their names invited bad luck, didn't it? Such callous indifference betokened disaster . . . It didn't make any sense, but as she sat in the dim kitchen (she didn't turn on the overhead, preferring the gentler light over the sink), a car might slip down Inquiry, pursuing some cryptic nocturnal errand, and the ghostly probe of its headlights, rifling through the living room, triggered an anxiety she had no words for, and a need—such a need—to make things right.

It was peculiar, but it seemed Bea had commandeered Mamma's chair at the kitchen table. The wall calendar, with its twelve proud O'Reilly and Fein houses, peered down at Bea just as exactingly as it had always peered down at Mamma. Bea recognized her task as a kind of prayer—the setting of names into a litany—and wouldn't merciless calamity follow if she neglected her prayers?

It turned out that the process of pencil sketching some remembered boyish face could sometimes unlock the secret of a missing name. She was sketching just such a face when her mother stepped into the kitchen. Mamma entered so quietly, it was as though Bea had been snuck up on. "Bea, what are you doing?"

Bea's pencil jumped. Her mother was peering over her shoulder. There it was, visible proof of a deep current of lunacy running through another generation of the Paradiso/Schleiermacher family. "Mrs. Nelson, Grade 4B, Field Elementary School" it was titled, followed by a list of student names. "Glenn Havira, Mark Deane, Titus Gardner, Willy Jakiebielski . . ." A few sketched heads floated in the margin.

"I'm—I'm—sketching for class."

And Mamma nodded serenely, as though sketching in the kitchen at two-thirty in the morning were the most sensible thing in the world. She poured herself a glass of milk. (A glass of milk! When was the last time Mamma was seen drinking a glass of milk?) Then she said, "Good night, dear," and retreated from the kitchen.

The next morning, feeling exhausted, to say nothing of desperate and bewildered, Bea went shopping with her mother. They walked down to Kercheval. They stopped in Marcellino's for bread, and in Abajay's for pork chops, and Pukszta's for pork and beans, applesauce, potatoes. On the walk home, Bea proposed a detour to Buttery Creek Park and Mamma, a little surprisingly, agreed. When was the last time they'd gone to a park together? It seemed as if Mamma, too, understood it was time for a heart-to-heart, and that she, too, preferred that it take place anywhere but home.

Though tiny, Buttery Creek Park was laden with memories. Mamma used to bring Bea here to play when she was a little child. Later, she brought Bea and baby Stevie. Later still, Bea and Stevie and baby Edith. Now, Mamma let Bea lead the way. They settled on a park bench near the swings. "Feels good," Mamma said, stretching her legs out. A white seagull had settled on the adjoining bench. He eyed them cheerfully, as if it felt good to him, too, to rest a moment.

A number of little boys were scampering around, aiming fingers and shooting at each other. Had boys always been so combative? Or was this, too, a result of the War? At the other end of the little park, keeping to themselves, a couple of families of Negroes were sitting at two picnic tables, their children playing in the tight space between the tables. In the old days, you didn't see Negroes in Buttery Creek Park.

Closer at hand, a little red-haired girl, who must have been six or seven, was binding up one of the boy soldiers with strips of rag. Playing nurse. She was lanky. Her appearance was heartening; Bea could see herself in that small but lanky creature.

"I am aware, Bea, how much I've upset you," Mamma began. "I've upset everyone, and I'm sorry, but I don't regret it. You see the difference, don't you?"

Mamma had always relished fine distinctions—extremely minute, almost lawyerly distinctions. Papa called it "hairsplitting"—another of his proud English idioms—and he had no patience with it. These distinctions were a reminder that Mamma, though she read little except the *Ladies' Home Journal* and *McCall's,* possessed a fine mind. Like Bea, she'd twice been double-promoted—two semesters—while still in grade school. As she was perhaps a little too quick to announce, *she* had been the better student of the Schleiermacher sisters. Had Grace even once been double-promoted? No . . .

Mamma said, "I can't regret what had to be done. I did have to say something: I couldn't have them thinking I didn't see. And you know what? I feel *better.*"

The truth was queer but inarguable: Mamma looked better, too, in addition to being so much more industrious around the house. The whites of her eyes were whiter, there was vigor in the set of her jaw, she even *sounded* better—a whininess or weariness had dropped from her tone. These days, she spoke so much more forthrightly than she used to.

"Something had to be said, Bea. The truth is, Grace has always envied me. People think she's perfect, but she never stops envying me."

Grace envying *Mamma*? Grace envying *anyone*?

"She envies me my good-looking husband. Do you know the story about Mike, Michael Cullers, her first husband?"

Bea knew a bit, and didn't want to know more. "No, though I'm—" she began, but Mamma pressed on.

"Well *he* was good-looking, with pots of money, too—Grace always marries rich—and they weren't married three years before . . . You know what he did? He got his secretary pregnant."

Pregnant? Mamma rarely talked about physical matters of this sort, except indirectly and disapprovingly, and the unwonted frankness of *pregnant* was startling. But so was the girlish, gossipy way she leaned forward, eyes wide and voice thrillingly hushed, as though they were high school chums, trading scandalous high school stories, rather than mother and daughter, discussing their own family.

But it seemed that Mamma, now that she felt so much *better,* was free to speak with reckless abandon: "As you must know, Grace can't have children, and can you imagine how she felt? Mike's secretary has a bun in the oven?"

Did Mamma just say *bun in the oven*?

"Grace has always envied me my husband. And envied me my children. So what does she do? She sets out deliberately to steal my husband from me, to steal my children from me. Stealing the very things she can't have."

And Mamma, who didn't often touch her children, seized Bea's hand. "But you mustn't let her," she pleaded. "You mustn't, Bea."

And if, just moments ago, Mamma had seemed almost schoolgirlish, there was now—odder yet—something almost old-womanish in this clutched grasping at her daughter's hand, and in her trembling-eyed and importunate look. "Bea, don't let her steal you from your mother."

"Mamma, no one's *stealing* me," Bea cried. *Stealing:* the word was so ugly . . . She withdrew her hand and shifted her gaze toward the red-haired girl, even as she offered her mother a partial reassurance: "No one will ever steal me from . . . all of you."

"You're a good girl," Mamma said. "Yes, a good girl." Then she was launched again: "Do you see why I had to speak out? She *stole* my husband's heart and my husband's loyalty. She's very crafty—Grace. You know the way she always gets her way? It's all done silently, by craftiness. Grace *schemes.* She never stops scheming. She never *rests.* But you're a good girl, Bea. You won't let her steal you away."

This time, Mamma did not clutch Bea's hand but simply patted the top of it. Normally, it was Bea—overemotional Bia, the art student—who was the family "toucher." (Italian families were supposed to go in for touching, but the Paradisos didn't.) Mamma said, "I have *good* children. Yes I do," she insisted, and smiled broadly, a look of authentic joy softening her features. She went on smiling, staring out at this park where, in the olden days, she used to bring her *good* children.

And she looked pretty. (She had always been pretty—a pretty girl with a beautiful sister.) There were occasionally moments, like this one, when you could imagine eighteen-year-old Sylvia Schleiermacher (just Bea's age!) looking irresistibly fetching to Vico Paradiso, who stumbled with his words but was handsome and determined and already making a good living. Yes, Mamma had been just eighteen when she became a bride.

"I am perfectly willing to be civil," Mamma went on. "She may have stolen my husband's heart, but she's my sister after all and I am willing to be perfectly civil. We can proceed on that basis. I only require that she understand she isn't fooling anyone, that the two of them not go around thinking they pulled the wool over old Sylvia's eyes."

The pretty red-haired girl now had a gaggle of wounded soldiers awaiting her ministrations. Mamma smiled at Bea, benignly, and calmly delivered her concluding note: "If Grace and I can only both recognize that she has ruined my life, there is no reason in the world the two of us cannot get along."

What do you say when your mother makes a pronouncement as confident and crackpot and heartbreaking as that? Bea could think of nothing to do but to coax her mother from the bench—"We should get our things into the icebox"—and make their way back down Inquiry. Bea helped put the groceries away and then, as soon as she was able, raced out the door, heading toward the phone booth outside Olsson's Drugs. She slipped a nickel into the slot. Her hands were atremble and her stomach was heaving. She prayed she would raise an answer at the other end . . .

"Hello."

"Aunt Grace," Bea said. "It's—" But her throat had already constricted. For the millionth time, she wished she weren't such a hopeless, hopeless crybaby.

Of course her aunt showed marvelous aplomb. "Bea," she said—she sang—she sighed. There was such a world of welcome in the musical, down-sliding way her aunt spoke her name. "I was so hoping you would call."

Aunt Grace pretended not to realize Bea was on the verge of tears— or a little past the verge—and quickly arranged everything. They would meet tomorrow for lunch, before Bea's class, at Sanders, downtown. At twelve o'clock. Everything was going to be all right—Bea could almost believe this, though there was a hint of more than ruefulness, a touch of true mourning, in Aunt Grace's closing words:

"We'll have an hour anyway, won't we? We'll make do with that."

Usually so pretty, Aunt Grace looked far from her best in the doorway at Sanders. She hadn't slept well for days, obviously. But the quick glint of recognition in her eyes, the eager way she stepped forward and seized Bea by the arm, the gentle, melodious fervor with which she declared, "Bea, I'm *so glad* to see you"—these little flourishes were profoundly reassuring.

Grace was soon launched on the account of a woman on a streetcar this morning who had mislaid her glasses. It was a story that—no doubt deliberately—was far removed from the events at Chuck's Chop House. And it had a happy ending: the glasses, folded up in a newspaper, were spotted by a little colored boy. "But the best part of the story? The boy had a patch over one eye."

"A case of the blind leading the blind," Bea said.

"It *is*, isn't it?"

"And finding the way."

"*Yes*," Grace marveled. "And finding the way."

They had each ordered tuna-fish sandwiches and ice-cream sodas. The sodas were almost obligatory, for Sanders was the establishment— as a sign on the wall proclaimed—where the first ice-cream soda in the world had been concocted, back in 1876.

Sanders, no less than Buttery Creek Park, transported Bea to a domain of potent childhood pleasures. How many times had Grace brought her to one Sanders or another? As a child, Bea used to wear white gloves when she came downtown—the city was such a special place, back then. It remained a special place, of course, but she'd be laughed out of the studio if she appeared in white gloves at the Institute Midwest, where red-bearded Hal Holm lumbered around in overalls and Tatiana Bogoljubov stuffed herself into blouses so tight you could make out the stitching on her brassiere.

It took only a few minutes in Grace's company before Bea began to feel much-needed stirrings of hope. Surely peace in the family could be restored. This was Grace's great gift—her ability to convince you that faith must finally prevail over suspicion, goodwill over rancor.

Aunt Grace allowed Bea to finish her sandwich before addressing the only true topic at hand: "The birthday party didn't work out as we'd figured, did it? I'm so sorry."

"Why, it isn't *your* fault."

"Dear Bea, I'm not sure it's anybody's *fault*—I'm not sure fault can be assigned in a case like this."

"But look who started it all! And the way she wouldn't, wouldn't stop. Why, she said unforgivable things!"

"I'm not sure about unforgivable. Often forgiveness isn't the hardest part, don't you think? It's knowing what to do after. How do we go forward?

"That's the trouble with words," Aunt Grace went on. "Once they're said, they make the situation so much more difficult. Maybe your mother for a long time had been thinking the things she said. Maybe they were constantly in her head. But once they're out, they—they're—"

In her gentle, uninsistent way, Grace often let a sentence languish. She utterly lacked Mamma's determination to see a point to its termination. Bea concluded the sentence: "They change reality." Here was an irony, to be sure, since Bea was often teased—especially by Maggie— for not completing sentences. But in various ways, some easily identifiable and some not, Bea was a different person with her aunt than with anyone else.

"Yes, they change reality, don't they?"

"Yesterday, Mamma said—" But Bea found she couldn't repeat the craziest of all words her mother had ever uttered: *If Grace and I can only both recognize that she has ruined my life, there is no reason in the world the two of us cannot get along.* Bea, too, let a sentence drop.

"Your uncle Dennis believes we need to let things cool off. Avoid all getting together anytime soon. I don't know whether that's a medical opinion, or simple instinct. But I'm afraid I agree."

Bea only nodded. Her eyes were stinging.

"But"—Aunt Grace went on—"you and I can get together, can't we, dear? Without telling your mother?"

Bea nodded rapidly, up and down.

"I don't mean to encourage deception, and I'd understand fully if you don't think we should, but I did want to see you to*day*. Oh, Bea, I wanted so much to see you!

"I don't mean to criticize your mother, but I needed to tell you she's *very wrong* about one thing she said. Bea, your father is not in love with me. I repeat: your father is not in love with me. Oh, I think I'd know! It does happen occasionally, an infatuation. I'll sense that somebody, usually some patient or friend of Dennis's, one of the other doctors, maybe—somebody takes a keen fancy to me. At eighteen, you may think that's very unlikely for a woman just turned forty, but I'll tell you something: these things do happen. And I'll tell you something more: if your father were in love with me, and he's not, but *if* he were, it's nothing I would ever, ever encourage."

"Oh, I know *that* . . ."

"If I could make your mother understand one fact, one fact only, it's that I love Dennis—yes, I really do—and yes I did once, to my everlasting shame, yes I did once, when I first met him, I *did* once say he looked like a frog. Count on your mother to remember. It's his glasses, making his eyes look so big, *you* know. Anyway, if I could take back any remark in my life, I think it would be that.

"And let me pause, dear, to tell you a little story about your uncle. The day after the birthday party, I cried all day. I cried so hard my hands wouldn't stop shaking and I couldn't eat the soup he finally brought me. He had to feed me—I'm not exaggerating—feed me with a spoon, like one of his patients. And while I'm lying in bed having cried my eyes out, he walks up to the mirror over the vanity table, he peers into it, and what does he say? He says, '*I* think I'm quite a handsome frog.' Do you see what I'm saying? I felt so *awful* about his having heard those words, and then he ups and says, '*I* think I'm quite a handsome frog.' " There were tears in Aunt Grace's eyes. "I ask you—how could I not love that man?"

She went on: "It's the strangest thing you'll ever do, I bet—getting married. And I should know. I did it twice." A little smile. "There's no way of knowing what you're in for. How could you know what you're in for, when you say to someone, Yes, I'll share my entire life with you? Bea, maybe someday we'll have this conversation when you're an old married lady like me. And I hope you too will be able to say—"

To say what? Grace interrupted herself: "Oh good heavens, I know that man and he's coming over. He's a Turk. It was his daughter. She was one of Dennis's patients. A hundred years ago. Oh, what *is* his name?"

A little man with steely gray hair materialized beside their table. He looked overjoyed. He talked stumblingly but rapidly in accented English—he appeared to be shaking with excitement. He wore a huge gold watch and a gold tie. "It is the doctor's wife!" he cried.

"Hello—oh hello. So nice to see you again." Aunt Grace was still scrambling after the man's name.

"I want you to see!" he said. "I want you to see! This is my Melek. Doesn't she look big and healthy!"

The wrist with the enormous gold watch made a flourishing sweep toward someone behind him: a homely but indeed quite big and healthy-looking girl of sixteen or so. She was taller than her father. And quite plump. "You tell the doctor how healthy! Not like before, huh?" The glittering little man laughed buoyantly.

"I certainly will. I'll—do that tonight."

"The other doctor said influenza. Dr. Poppleton, he said appendicitis. He was right. He saved her life—my only child. He is a very great man."

"Well, thank you," Aunt Grace replied.

So sharply did the little man peer at Bea, Aunt Grace felt compelled to offer introductions—always an awkward business when a name is missing. Not surprisingly, she pulled it off dexterously. "If I am the doctor's wife, this is the doctor's niece, Bea Paradiso."

"Paradiso?" he said. "Italian name?"

"Yes," Bea said.

"Turk," he said, and thumped himself hard on the chest.

"Yes."

"Two seas to the right. The Adriatic first, the Aegean next," he said, and laughed ebulliently.

"I've never been to Italy," Bea said.

"You come first to Turkey!" the man cried. "First to Turkey! I invite you! Real invitation! The doctor's niece, you are a princess there!"

"That sounds very nice."

He stayed a few minutes by their table, laughing excitedly, again and again calling attention to his daughter's flourishing condition. When he finally departed, Aunt Grace said, "Oh I just *know* I'll think of his name in a minute. He's a Christian, incidentally—a Christian Turk, and there can't be many of those. Now what were we talking about?"

"Uncle Dennis, I guess. You wished Mamma could understand—"

"If I'd paid for it," Aunt Grace interrupted, "could I have arranged a more vivid demonstration? In walks a man whose name I don't even remember, who steps forward to tell me my husband is a great man. But we were talking about loving one's husband. And looks—we were talking about looks. You see, Bea, I had a good-looking husband once—good-looking in the conventional sense. I don't know how much you know about Michael Cullers."

"Not so much." But perhaps more than she should. "A little."

"Well, Mike was a fast one, running with a fast crowd. He was too young to get married. And maybe I was, too. Those friends of his made me nervous, the way they *drank*. Mike could party all night and wake up whistling, but I couldn't live that way.

"Well, you may know he formed an attachment, with his secretary. He was very distraught when we learned I couldn't have children; I sometimes think he took it even harder than I did. Oh, Mike wasn't a *bad* man. He just wasn't a terribly *good* man. And your uncle Dennis? He's the best man I've ever met."

Once more, abruptly, Aunt Grace's eyes reddened. This little lunchtime reunion was continually verging on tears. They were near wrecks, the two of them.

"Oh I know," Bea said. "He's a saint."

"Keep your saints, Bea. And your Greek gods, too, for that matter— I married one once, and once was enough. But Dennis is the best *man* I've ever known. Your mother seems to feel I sacrificed a lot in marrying Dennis but I sacrificed exactly nothing. *Dennis* made the sacrifices. He knew I couldn't have children. *You* understand what a wonderful father he would have been."

"Of course. Why he's the best *uncle* in the world." But something was still rankling Bea, who said, "I think you're being too kind, when you call it nobody's fault."

"Is that what I said? I guess what I meant was, the deeper you look, the harder to assign any blame. You scarcely knew Daddy, he died so young, but he certainly didn't ease your mother's way. *He* wasn't such a bad man either, but the chemistry was all wrong between those two. He couldn't leave poor Sylvia alone. She always disappointed him somehow. He was forever criticizing. So if you could go back, in one of Dennis's time machines, you might conclude it was all Daddy's fault, but if you went back still further, you'd probably turn up someone giving him the problems *he* had."

"She didn't have to say what she said to you."

"Oh I'm all right. At least *now*. It's poor Dennis I'm sorriest for. Summer's here, and you know how he loved summer Saturdays, fishing with your father, taking you kids out for milk shakes."

"We can still see him. Even if Mamma doesn't care to come along."

Aunt Grace paused. Something more than a mere tremor—a jolting spasm—passed over her face. She spoke very carefully: "I think it would upset your mother if she knew the rest of you were seeing us. Your uncle feels strongly that your mother needs to rest, that all those—those tensions we saw on Saturday need a rest."

"She wouldn't have to know. If we saw you. Nobody needs to say."

"But what are we going to do, Bea? Propose to Stevie and Edith that they lie to their mother? Oh, seeing you is one thing. Look at you, you're almost a grown woman. But the others . . . Is that the lesson we want to teach? Can you honestly see your uncle pursuing that line?"

"But things will calm down! Things will come right again and everything will be how it was."

"Precisely. That's everyone's precise hope."

"But what are you saying? *What are you saying?*" Bea felt an inner slithering from chest to stomach—a downward scrambling of pure panic. "Are you telling me I can't see you when I want to?"

Aunt Grace reached over, laid a hand upon her hand. "Oh, darling. I'm not sure what I'm saying. Only, we'll see less of each other. Until things come right."

"But what if they don't? What if this is just the way she'll be now? What are you saying?"

Aunt Grace's eyes tightened. "I suppose I'm saying two contradictory things. That I cannot encourage you to regularly lie to your mother. And that, if you ask to see me, Bea? I can't refuse you." One more pause. "Yusuf Caglayangil," she said.

"What?"

"The Turk's name." Aunt Grace's memory, opening at last, offered up a spilling profusion. "He owns a business called Turk's Trucks. He goes by Joe, or Joseph, but he actually spells it Y-U-S-U-F. And Melek? His daughter's name? It means angel. My husband saved the life of his angel."

"I'm out of cigarettes," Papa said, which was a little surprising. In his apportioned way, he rarely ran out of essentials. "Bia, you come with me," he said, which was more surprising still.

When Papa asked you to go somewhere, you went. Bea threw a sweater over her shoulders and was out the door. She didn't like to keep her father waiting.

"All right now," he said approvingly, and turned left rather than right, though the closest place for cigarettes, Pukszta's, lay to the right.

Papa wasn't completely out of cigarettes. He lit one now, as they walked along. It was a cool, fragrant August night, hazy but clear enough to let a few stars shine through the leaves. Soon it would be fall.

Where were they headed? Bea decided it would be all right to ask. "Where are we going?"

"Olsson's."

The logical place, given their direction. "Olsson's," Bea repeated and, sensing her father's wish that she talk, she said, "One of the boys in my class, his name is Ronny Olsson, and you know what? His father owns Olsson's Drugs."

It was a sign of how very peculiar life at home had become that Bea hadn't yet mentioned this. She'd referred a few times to the Ronny Olsson in her class who drew so well and was so handsome, but she had hoarded to herself the most remarkable fact about him. Usually, she kept her parents abreast of her news. But these past few weeks, given all the upheaval, she'd found comfort in carrying her independent little secret . . .

It was deeply cheering, anyhow, to watch Papa fall into the very same misconception she'd initially stumbled over. Neither of them was used to thinking on so grand a financial scale. "Which one?" he said.

"All of them. Forty-seven stores in three states. Ronny's grandfather started the company. We went out for coffee after class," Bea said— which suggested, misleadingly, but not with outright dishonesty, a single meeting. "I think he's fond of me."

Papa drew pensively on his cigarette. "But what is he doing, this studying art? The son of Olsson's is studying art?"

"He draws beautifully."

"He has older brothers?" Papa was asking whether there was an heir to run the company.

Papa had been thirteen when he came to Detroit from Nervi, Italy—young enough that you might suppose no trace of an accent would linger. But it did, and perhaps more striking still, he spoke English warily. Never in her life had Bea seen him in what might be called a voluble state.

"He's an only child," she told him.

"All of them?" Meaning: Ronny's father owns all of them?

"Every one. Forty-seven stores in three states," she recited again. "His grandfather started the company. I think he intends to ask me out on a date. Ronny."

"The son."

"Yes, the boy in my class. You would admire the way he draws."

True enough. Papa was a craftsman who did beautiful things in wood, and he was the son of a man who had been famous up and down the coast of Liguria. It was one of the few topics where Papa *did* grow almost voluble: how celebrated his father had been as Liguria's master of trompe l'oeil.

"And you think this Olsson boy will call?"

"I think so. Maybe."

Through an exhaled cloud of cigarette smoke, in the light of a street lamp, Papa threw her a glance. Its import was unexpected—and quite sharply hurtful.

He didn't believe her.

He didn't believe her story.

Papa's look wasn't disapproving. No, it was amused and gently pitying. He didn't suspect her of lying but of being misled, of garbling the facts, of letting her imagination run away once more. Yet again, this girl who had read too many books as a child had lost sight of reality. Papa was prepared ultimately to learn that that boy in her class, the one she'd mentioned, wasn't the *son* of the owner of Olsson's Drugs but, say, a nephew . . .

Papa didn't linger in Olsson's. He bought a pack of Old Golds and the two of them turned around. Papa used to smoke Camels. But eventually he'd deferred to Uncle Dennis, who considered Old Golds less harmful. These days, Uncle Dennis was trying to convert Papa to pipe smoking. But Papa would never bend that far.

Bea walked beside her father in silence for a while, and then he opened a new line of conversation: "What she said? It isn't so."

No need to specify who the *she* was. Or what the *what* was, for that matter.

"I know, Papa."

"Never—I never give her reason to talk like that."

"I know."

"It's very bad what she said about me. But worse, what else she said." Meaning: the remarks about Grace.

"That's true."

"Your uncle Dennis, he says it's a problem in her head. What it's like? Like a house with lousy wiring. After a while, you blow the fuse. You turn on a few lights, you plug in the toaster, you blow a fuse." Papa helped himself to another cigarette. Most people halted when they lit a cigarette, but Papa merely slowed.

"Saying that Grace wanted to take me away. Your aunt Grace!"

"I know."

"Would you believe it? Saying such a thing? In front of everybody."

"I know."

"It's not even decent."

"I know."

"And how do I prove it isn't so? That's what I ask her, time and again. Sylvia, Sylvia, how do I prove that I am not—in love with Grace?"

In the light of a street lamp, nearing the corner of Inquiry and Kercheval, her father's handsome features were open and pleading, hopeless and put upon. Yet with just a trembling hint, perhaps, of something shamefaced.

CHAPTER VII

Ronny was forever taking her hands in his. Holding other boys' hands had been nothing like this: the patient, exploratory fingertips sliding over her knuckles and tendons and the almost invisible little hairs, testing one by one the cuticles and the finger pads. Sometimes he stroked so lightly it tickled and she nearly laughed aloud. Sometimes his hands moved deeply, exploring the root workings of her bones, and his touch would ramify up her arms and, in tingling filaments, suffuse her chest.

Those remarkable artist's hands of his that rendered so faithfully a rabbit's-fur glove, a pinecone, a half-dry sponge, seemed to find *her* hands remarkable: Ronny pounced on them eagerly, as if always about to uncover something fresh. While advancing less than other boys had advanced (he hadn't even kissed her yet), Ronny had effectively ventured into further territory. For when he seized her hands and began his explorations, the response was almost unnervingly immediate: Bea's heart pumped harder and her veins coursed with pleasure, as she realized (with a guilty internal lurch, though it seemed ridiculous and unfair to withdraw her hands for this reason) that this must be what, on a grander scale, the sexual act would be—a melting, toppling sensation that extended both inward and outward.

When he took her hands, Ronny often began tentatively. His fingers probed and retreated, probed and retreated, before forging ahead in a kind of verified confidence. And Bea would feel herself reliably succumbing. Sometimes something within her might resist temporarily, but in the end resistance must give way—and she could not regret the giving way.

At home, Bea always tried to be first to answer the phone, which would have been easy if not for Mamma. Papa, Stevie, Edith—they had little interest in what any phone call might bring. But Mamma demonstrated surpassing swiftness—springing out of the bathroom, bounding bonily up the basement stairs—in claiming the receiver. Ronny didn't call often, or unexpectedly, but it was only a matter of time before Mamma got there first.

"Who is Ronny Olsson?" she asked, after letting Bea take a brief call in which a plan was made to meet at Herk's Snack Shack. Apparently, Ronny had introduced himself.

"He's a boy in my art class. I've mentioned him before."

Then Mamma said something unexpected: "He has excellent manners."

This emboldened Bea to say, "His father owns Olsson's Drugs. His grandfather started the company."

This time, Bea was prepared for skepticism—or, worse, for hostility, since Mamma often resented the well-to-do, though perhaps not with the same animus reserved for those, the far-from-well-to-do, who sought to "get above themselves."

Yet Mamma responded cheerfully, if a little absently: "Well, I'll be."

And wasn't this a little unnerving—that Mamma would take her daughter at her word? (That's how strange things had become at home: it seemed *troubling* that Mamma would choose to believe her own daughter.)

From any outsider's point of view, Mamma had flourished since the terrifying explosion at Grace's party. No more kitchen-table brooding. (More likely, you saw her racing round the house with a dust cloth.) No more burned dinners—and no more pushing her own plate aside in favor of candy and coffee. Mamma had begun eating solid, square meals.

This woman who had seldom been heard to attempt a musical note now hummed continually. It turned out she was as rich with melodies as any jukebox, though often switching keys midsong. As she bustled around the house—transporting laundry, mopping floors—one tune melted into another. And on the rare occasions when Aunt Grace's name came up, Mamma's face clouded only slightly, for a moment, before she smiled benignly and resumed her humming.

Yes, to an outsider's eye (in this case, the eye of Ronny Olsson), Mamma might look fine—she did look fine. Though spared the most damning details, Ronny had heard a great deal about Mamma's recent turmoil, and he was naturally surprised when he finally met the mistress of the house. He complimented her china, arranged on the sideboard, and the sideboard as well. Mamma asked whether he'd had any trouble finding the house and complimented him on his camel's hair coat. He praised her Danish crystal vase; she praised his eye for detail. Anyone might suppose she had "beautiful manners" too. The two of them chatted like old friends. And here was an important detail Bea tended to overlook: when she wanted to, this woman who often behaved so peculiarly—hiding little bags of candy all over the house—could be an exemplary hostess.

It was actually Papa, not Mamma, who presented an obstacle for Ronny. Difficult to draw out at the best of times, Papa was rendered all but mute by the arrival of Ronny Olsson. Even if Ronny hadn't pulled up in a convertible, his lovely cream-colored Lincoln Cabriolet, and emerged with the camel's hair coat slung over his arm, the extraordinarily good-looking young man seated on the davenport, wearing tweedy brown slacks—cuffed slacks—and a tan-and-azure tie, could hardly be anyone less than the son and scion of the owner of Olsson's Drugs. Papa was having to absorb the possibility of having wholly misplaced his skepticism: it was accurate, everything his daughter had told him.

Papa grew more comfortable, but not completely comfortable, over coffee and cake, served in the living room. Olsson's Drugs was *not* mentioned. Nor, after the initial introductions, was the name Olsson. Although there were bigger names in Detroit (Bea might have brought home a Ford, a Fisher, a Whitney, a Buhl—one of those families whose daughters' engagement notices she studied so closely in the *News*), none of these names would have resonated so powerfully at 2753 Inquiry Street. Olsson's? Olsson's was the provider of Bayer aspirin for any Paradiso whose head hurt, Alka-Seltzer for victims of heartburn, Pepto-Bismol for their upset stomachs and Ben-Gay for their sore muscles, Pepsodent for the teeth, Brylcreem for the hair, Hill's drops for the nose, Noxzema for the face, Pertussin for the throat . . . and Olsson's was the provider, as well, of products aimed at less mentionable parts. In short, Olsson's Drugs oversaw every aspect of the Paradiso family's health and grooming and hygiene, including their digestive and reproductive tracts, and there was something not quite believable in seeing the drugstore chain's dashing heir perched on their own living-room davenport, commending Mamma on the quality of her coffee. Bea had lured into their home something like an apparition.

But all stiffness vanished when Ronny, with his honed artist's eye, spied the wooden rooster. Other guests might sit on the davenport for months and not notice the solitary bird on its roost above the bookcase; Ronny hadn't been a visitor for fifteen minutes when he cried, "Now what is *that*?"

For just a moment it seemed Stevie might explain. But as someone whose chief business was eliminating Germans in the alley, the boy was abashed by this evidence of having once been the sort of flighty-headed youngster who enjoyed dragging a wooden chicken across the floor. It fell to Papa to take down the bird—according it the same delicacy of touch he showed any well-made thing, whether of his own or someone else's devising.

"Something I built for Steven. For my son's fourth birthday," Papa said. And this head of the family—this man who had overseen the construction of three-story houses in Rosedale Park—carefully deposited the wooden rooster on the living-room floor and gently tugged its string.

The spoked wheels turned, the bird's head bobbed, its beak opened and shut as though cackling a barnyard message.

"But that's wonderful!" Ronny cried, and was down on the floor in a flash. With hands as respectful as Papa's own, he lifted the wooden fowl into his arms. "There must be four different kinds of wood here!"

"Five."

"Five," Ronny marveled. "This is cherry, isn't it?"

Papa nodded happily. "That's right."

"And this is walnut."

"That's right."

"Also mahogany—mahogany for the spokes." And it appeared that Ronny, who knew so much about so much, could make his way confidently around a lumberyard.

"And for the beak too," Papa pointed out.

"Yes and the beak too. And pine for these outer feathers here." Ronny's index and middle fingers darted about. His handling of the bird's wing? Across the room, Bea recognized—less with her eyes than with her awakened body—his feathery, exploratory touch. As Ronny stroked the bird with his artist's hands, her ever-vulnerable stomach went soft.

"And ebony," Papa said. "For the legs."

"Ebony," Ronny repeated. "And no metal anywhere? Nails? Hidden screws holding it together?"

Papa tucked in his chin and lowered his eyebrows—fixing on Ronny an aggrieved, even a censorious look. "No screws in this one, never," he replied. "Wooden pins."

And Ronny nodded vigorously, matching him look for look.

Their gazes burned in agreement—oh, they understood one another! Ronny ceremoniously held out the wooden fowl. Papa took it in his hands and—as if it were a genuine live bird, some prize specimen of his own raising—he ruffled and smoothed the imaginary down on the creature's chest.

A threshold had been happily crossed and talk flowed companionably on all sides; everyone in the family, it turned out, possessed something for this unprecedented visitor to inspect and pass judgment on. Edith fetched her most recent pile of knitted socks. Stevie produced a shapeless little lump of metal which, so he'd been reliably informed, had been extracted from the corpse of a German soldier in the First World War. Bea produced her first "portrait": a stick-figure representation of Papa, completed when she was only four.

Even Mamma had something for Ronny to inspect: a photograph of her prosperous-looking parents, on honeymoon, in Chicago, in 1897.

Although they were strangers to Bea, both having died in her infancy, she had spent enough time with this photograph to feel she knew them well: Grandpa and Grandma Schleiermacher. Yet Ronny had only to examine it for five seconds before he detected something Bea had never noticed: "But they look so alike! Why, they look more like brother and sister than husband and wife."

Bea jumped up to peer over Ronny's shoulder. Yes—yes, they *did* resemble each other. And one of the two daughters these honeymooners would eventually produce, Grace with the wide-set eyes, would resemble them far more closely than would that other daughter, narrow-eyed Sylvia, who now was watching Ronny Olsson so fixedly.

Papa brought forth the wooden lamb he'd made for Bea, the owl for Edith. Again, Ronny assessed the craftsmanship, posed intelligent questions, stroked the animals respectfully—almost lovingly. Bea mentioned that her father had also constructed her bed, carving animals into the very bedposts. A somewhat constrained silence ensued. But naturally this visitor wasn't about to be shown Bea's bed.

There was so much to display, it wasn't easy getting out of the house—Ronny was taking her downtown to the new Gary Cooper picture—but at last they scurried down the sidewalk to his convertible. Bea wasn't quite sure why, but she was laughing—giggling, really—as he held open the car door.

Nor was it easy, a few hours later, when Ronny had dropped her home promptly afterward, to shake off a whole new round of questions. How was the movie? (From Mamma.) Did you have popcorn? (From Edith.) What color is the interior of his car? (From Papa.) Does he play any sports? (From Stevie.) And so on, and so on. Most of the questions would never have arisen if her date had been somebody else. But that bright, too-brief interlude when Ronny Olsson had been a visitor in their home, graciously perched on the davenport with a coffee cup in hand, had left the air aglow, and nobody wanted to see it fade altogether.

So it took Bea longer than she would wish to find herself in bed, with the light off. Once inside the environs of her little four-animal zoo, she could let her thoughts flow freely, at their own pace. She could review the day—everything Ronny had said from the moment he walked through the front door until, after the movie, he dropped her home again, and everything her family had said to him, and said about him later. Two remarks in particular demanded mulling over. The first was Papa's—his final remark of the day: "It's like Italy, isn't it, Bia? The rich folk there. They understand the work."

And what exactly did he mean by this? Did he himself understand everything he meant by this?

Papa rarely spoke Italian, except to his father, on Sundays, and Nonno, like his son, was a man of few words anyway—all the more so because of his emphysema. Papa could easily have made friends among the Italians in the neighborhood (those men you saw in the park, smoking and playing bocce), or he could have hired more of them for his crews, but he chose not to. Yet it seemed that in the background to all his thinking—in some world unsullied by the rise of Mussolini, whom Papa, long before war was declared, had always called a knucklehead— lay the true land of his imagination, his Italia. It was a place where builders "refused to cut corners." In that fabled country, the owners of even the biggest villas esteemed the expertise of the man who, though he might be illiterate, knew how to trim an olive tree, to erect a stone wall, to patch a cracked ceiling—just as Ronny had understood, right away, the care and ingenuity invested in a wooden rooster you pulled with a string. So Papa's praise was high praise indeed.

But what of Mamma's concluding remark? She'd offered it with a cool shake of the head, as if to suggest not malice but admiration tinged with chary recognition. "I've met his type before," she said. But what *could* she mean? When and where had Mamma ever met anyone remotely like Ronny Olsson?

The Olssons did not live where you might expect—but as it turned out almost nothing about the Olsson household conformed to Bea's imaginings. Better than any of her friends, Bea knew the city's finest neighbor-hoods. It had always been one of her father-the-builder's favorite week-end activities—a Sunday morning reconnaissance drive, checking up on which houses were going up where, which were getting added to. Though O'Reilly and Fein had never been in the business of building mansions (even before the War, when there was no five-thousand-dollar ceiling on new homes), Papa adored architectural grandeur, and over the years Bea had peered closely at the city's most splendid residences. Given their money, you might think the Olssons would have migrated to the suburbs, like Henry Ford in Dearborn, or like the other Fords and the Dodges in their Grosse Pointe palaces along the lake. Or, choosing instead to stay in town, they might plausibly have inhabited one of those overgrown structures tucked away in Palmer Woods. And yet they lived in a somewhat older part of the city, in Arden Park, just off Woodward Avenue.

Once, decades ago, these must have been among the city's proudest houses. Now, they looked a little run-down. And the Jews had moved in. (Papa kept careful track of who was moving where.) And though the Olsson house was enormous—the largest house Bea had ever actually stepped inside—it was obscured behind a pair of towering blue spruce. From the outside, it appeared far less imposing than it was.

Ronny had informed her—a number of times—that his mother was quite beautiful, and Bea remembered the occasional glittering glimpses of Mrs. Charles Olsson in the *News* society pages . . . But no such advance signals could have prepared Bea for beauty like this: regal and otherworldly.

Mrs. Olsson was first glimpsed in a room Bea would soon learn to call the music room. (There was a record player in there, though it never seemed to be running.) The music room stood three steps up from the library, from which Bea beheld an elevated figure enthroned in a cone of golden light. Mrs. Olsson was wearing a burgundy-colored dress. Pearls were twined around her ivory throat, and angling lamp-light wove through her tumbles of auburn hair. She held an icy glass in one hand. She was a figure crying out for a master portraitist. Titian himself would have rejoiced to set up his easel before her.

Ronny introduced Bea as Bianca Paradiso.

Mrs. Olsson did not rise from her chair. "I've heard a good deal about you, Miss Paradiso." Her tone expressed less greeting than obser-vation. Bea's would-be-winsome reply—combining the hope that Mrs. Olsson had heard nothing *too* alarming and the wish that she might be called Bea—was thoroughly unintelligible, but fortunately mostly inaudible. Ronny helped her into a seat. He himself had scarcely sat down, however, before Mrs. Olsson said, "Ronny, maybe it's time for a glass of pop."

So there the two of them were and just as quick as *that:* Bea and Ronny's mother. The smallest pearl on Mrs. Olsson's neck was larger than any pearl in Mamma's jewelry box. The glance Bea had fallen under was open, appraising, amused. "You're quite a pretty girl, Bianca Paradiso," Mrs. Olsson noted.

This *was* the type of scene Bea had half expected, similar to glimpses of the formidably rich in old English novels or in Hollywood movies. And her own stammering but verbose reply fit a role too—that of the giddy, gawky ingénue. She tried a second time to clarify her name: "You can call me Bea. Or Bianca. Either. Ronny seems to prefer Bianca. I guess I go by either. Either name. My father calls me Bia. It's a nickname."

The encounter soon wandered into unfamiliar terrain, however. Ronny returned with a bottle of pop and two glasses, and, showing uncharacteristic ungainliness, spilled a sizable puddle on the leather-topped table. He, too, seemed quite nervous. "Oh you *are* a hopeless one," Mrs. Olsson said—and, turning to Bea, asked, with unexpected and almost sisterly warmth, "What *can* be done with this boy?"

Mrs. Olsson drew from her purse a lacy handkerchief and mopped the fizzing pool. She placed the sodden hanky atop a seashell ashtray and declared, "You must tell me about your artwork, Miss Paradiso, Ronny informs me you're quite the talented artist."

Though the request was intimidating, the soft light in Mrs. Olsson's enormous dark eyes appeared genuinely welcoming. And as one question succeeded another (Who were Bea's favorite painters? Had she been born in Detroit? Brothers and sisters? What did her father do?), Mrs. Olsson's tone sounded clement and sustaining.

So Bea sat nervously sipping her drink—Faygo orange, exactly what Mamma had every day at lunchtime—and Mrs. Olsson sipped her glass, and Ronny sat in the chair between them, his quick eyes darting from one to another. Bea talked about her father's job with O'Reilly and Fein. She mentioned Aunt Grace, and mentioned, as a modest claim to social standing, her uncle the doctor. At one point, a man stood in the doorway who could only be a servant, and Mrs. Olsson tapped twice with a fore-finger on the rim of her glass. He took it away and moments later returned with a replacement. All without a word spoken.

Bea was talking about Edith's mountains of socks when another man appeared in the doorway. He was not a servant.

Many times in her life Bea had seen business tycoons—weren't they in half the movies she went to? They were stolidly built men usually hunkered behind stolid desks, barking orders for stock shares into a telephone. None bore the slightest resemblance to Mr. Olsson. He was thin and rangy and blond—or what was left of his clipped hair was blond, for he was mostly bald. His skin was darker than his hair.

With his high, rounded cheekbones and tawny coloring, he reminded Bea of the lynx in her favorite book from childhood, *The World's Most Wonderful Animals.*

Although he stepped forward to shake Bea's hand, he immediately retreated to the doorway, where he asked a number of the same questions Bea had just answered. Mr. Olsson had heard of O'Reilly and Fein. "They turn out good work," he said—a comment Bea happily filed away, to tell Papa later. In answering questions already answered, Bea tried to vary her responses—so as not to bore Mrs. Olsson—and wound up feeling increasingly nonplussed. Mr. Olsson's blue almost-too-close-set eyes were both direct and evasive: they had a way of hitting you and sliding off you.

None of Bea's answers enticed him from his doorway post. He seemed en route elsewhere, so it was something of a surprise when, Mrs. Olsson having suggested that Ronny give Bea "a little tour of the downstairs," Mr. Olsson decided to tag along.

More surprising still, he took on the role of co–tour guide. Ronny's approach might be termed aesthetic—he set out to show Bea the little architectural details and *objets d'art* that most appealed to him. Mr. Olsson's approach might be called anecdotal—he interrupted Ronny with colorful, lengthy stories. He showed Bea the mantel on which, last Thanksgiving, Mrs. Olsson's sister, Betty Marie, had cracked open her head after slipping on the edge of a rug. He pointed out the grandfather clock he'd won in a poker game. ("Unfortunately, I didn't also win the price of shipping. My mistake.") He showed Bea where a huge wind-torn branch had blasted through the ceiling, missing Mrs. Olsson by a few feet. ("We almost lost her to a piece of lumber.") Ronny gradually fell silent. This development scarcely fazed Mr. Olsson, who cheerfully took over as full tour guide. He was—it was already clear—quite a storyteller.

And—apparently—still quite an athlete. As Ronny had mentioned repeatedly, Mr. Olsson had been the track-team captain at the University of Michigan. He ambled through his huge house with a rolling sportsman's gait. To be guided by him was exciting—he radiated pleasure and energy—even as Bea was aware, beside her, of Ronny's stiffening resentment.

Mr. Olsson led them into the basement, which held something Bea had never seen in a house before: a small gymnasium. There were mats on the wood floor, dumbbells and barbells, medicine balls and a punching bag. "I built the place bigger than I needed to," Mr. Olsson said. "I didn't know I'd be the only one using it." And a quick glance between father and son.

Mr. Olsson surely did not need to add anything, but he did: "You see, I was thinking Ronny might want to spend time down here with me."

Bea understood this tension—she felt oddly at home in it, despite the distance from this cavernous palace in Arden Park to her crowded home on crowded Inquiry Street. Notwithstanding Mr. Olsson's ease and geniality, the tensions between Ronny and his father were evidently as labyrinthine and as rich and as difficult to voice as anything between Bea and her mother.

CHAPTER VIII

"Miss Paradiso, may I see you after class?"

So unprecedented was this request, Bea's concentration came utterly undone. Edges of the objects arrayed before her—a halved lemon, a cracked teacup, a rabbit's foot—softened and blurred. What *could* Professor Manhardt want? Was she going to be, as had happened in classrooms before, promoted? (Had he recognized her full bounding potential?) Or maybe demoted—asked to leave class? (Had he discerned her fundamental lack of talent and originality?) There was no saying, really: Professor Manhardt was an impenetrable man.

So at 4:06, six minutes after the official end of class, Bea found herself in the professor's overheated office. The tilted pane of the window was open a crack—enough to admit traffic sounds from Woodward Avenue—but not enough to bring relief. Apparently, the temperature didn't discomfit Professor Manhardt, who wore his usual vest under his tweed sports coat.

Previously so formidable, Professor Manhardt had become, under Ronny's frequent sniping, an almost fatuous figure. Ronny had got the man's number immediately. Though Professor Manhardt was German (a Kraut, Ronny called him, as everybody these days called them—a word to make Bea wince with the knowledge of being a quarter Kraut from her mother's side, and a half Wop from her father's), he'd been educated in London and wanted *desperately* to be taken for English. It wasn't his slight German accent that betrayed him; it was his entire manner. Even Bea, who'd never traveled more than a hundred miles outside Detroit, ascertained in a moment that this was one bogus Englishman.

Sometimes, she did wish Ronny weren't *quite* so scornful. She'd felt vaguely undermined when he pointed out that the name of their school was "laughably pretentious." The Institute Midwest? "Dear God"—Ronny rolled his eyes—"they even inverted the word order . . ." Bea had simply accepted its name as a given.

Yet to have stepped into this overheated office, to be alone with the man, was to feel thoroughly intimidated—suddenly the Professor was his old self. He said, factually, "You may remain standing, or you may take a seat." Anybody else would have turned this into an offer.

Apologetic, as ever, about her height, particularly since Professor Manhardt (a diminutive man anyway) was seated behind his desk, Bea hastened to take the office's one free chair, balancing on its edge by way of compromise, as if prepared to vacate promptly if so requested. The Professor's pale eyes—a soapy blue—contemplated her. His gray hair was so wiry, you could probably have scoured a pan with it.

He said, "You have a family I presume."

It was such an unexpected conversational sortie, and so singular in its phrasing, Bea had no immediate answer. In a near whisper she replied, "Yes. A family, yes I do."

"You have brothers?"

"A brother. Steven."

"He is older, perhaps?"

"He's younger. Thirteen." She added: "Much younger."

"So you have no immediate family in"—the Professor's faint pause suggested distaste—"the military service."

"The military? No."

"Cousins, perhaps?"

"In the military? No." And Bea felt apologetic anew. She quelled a reckless impulse to begin cataloguing some of the Paradisos' war efforts, starting with her father's erecting homes for defense workers.

On the wall behind the Professor hung a pastoral landscape—cows in the foreground, steeple in the background. Unmistakably an English countryside.

"I have a rather personal request to make," the Professor informed her. His eyes tightened their hold. Under the pressure of his steady gaze, Bea felt herself nod unstoppably, while various misgivings bubbled inside her.

"This is all such a damned *peculiar* business, isn't it?" the Professor went on. "They don't know why we're here. They don't see our raison d'être. They do not understand us, do they?"

"I'm sure you're right."

But who was this *they*? And who the *us*?

"The Industrial Arts people—they understand *them*. But you and I? We are Fine Arts people. Obviously, we are a race apart."

Something extremely odd was unfolding, and this word *race*

suggested—unbelievable though it might seem—that Professor Manhardt was about to commit an impropriety. Oh my. Oh *no*. On a handful of other occasions in Bea's life, equally out of nowhere, a preposterous and unthinkable proposition had come her way, often prefaced, like this, by talk of a *we* or an *us,* some unlikely alliance she hardly recognized . . .

"We're a different breed, aren't we?" the Professor said and Bea certainly didn't like the sound of *breed.* Yes: something like this had happened a few times before—wild, misguided words issuing from somebody you'd never in a million years expect to utter them. And each time it happened, it happened afresh; her panic was always the same raw quivery panic.

"We must rise above, don't you suppose?"

And each time it happened, the utter, patent impossibility and *wrongness* of the proposition in no way impeded its delivery. That's how it was, and it did force you to wonder: what *was* the matter with the male mind? Why did they go on thinking unthinkable things?

"I'm not sure I—"

"Yes, a damned peculiar business."

"What business?"

"The War," the professor replied, brusquely.

"Oh." Pause. "Oh."

"It has left us in a very delicate position, hasn't it?"

"A—delicate?"

"It surely will not surprise you to hear that there are administrators at our institution who see no need for classes in still-life painting, or life-drawing, or landscape, at a time like this. Enrollments are *down,* so I'm told. Needless to say, the Industrial Arts faculty are under no similar disparagement."

The dawning blush on Bea's cheeks assumed a new warmth—a private, guilty warmth. Yes, she'd imputed wholly false motivations to the very proper, very English Professor Manhardt! Wherever this conversation was going, it wasn't headed toward anything like an impropriety. She was always letting her imagination run away, and not always in healthy directions . . .

"Yes," she said again. "That's a question we've—I've—" Her impulse to point out that she and Ronny had often discussed this very issue suddenly looked unwise. Bea let it drop. The Professor, in his slow and oblique way, marched on:

"What are we who are 'Fine Arts people' contributing? What is our *contribution*? In this institution, those questions keep arising. Why are we painting still lifes? As if you and I, Miss Paradiso, should be assembling grenades. Or armored *cars*."

If Professor Manhardt hadn't looked so somber, Bea would have allowed herself a smile. Really it was funny to envision the Professor on some factory floor, still wearing tweed jacket and waistcoat. Funny to think of him, with his manicured hands, picking up something so utilitarian, and oily, as a monkey wrench . . .

"But now a peculiar request arrives, and I thought you were perhaps the student best suited to undertake it."

"I am?"

"A peculiar request."

"A—"

"From the USO." Professor Manhardt accorded each of the letters a substantial stress and pause. "The United—"

"United Service Organizations." Bea didn't mean to interrupt the Professor, even if he did talk so laboriously, but she yearned to know where this conversation might be leading. Of all the students in the class, just what sort of task would *she* be "best suited" to undertake?

"According to the USO, there is a need out there, an apparent need, for portrait artists. Not professional portrait artists," the Professor hastened to reassure her.

"Portrait artists?"

"Actually, that is perhaps too grand a phrase . . ."

"Portraitists?"

"Shall we say 'makers of portrait sketches'?"

"All right."

"I've seen a few of your—your caricatures."

"Well, those were hardly—"

"I gather that the emphasis here is not on quality so much as facility. Sheer speed."

What was he saying? And was she being casually insulted? His words were so dizzying, there wasn't time, really, to take offense, even if offense were intended, and it probably wasn't—this was just the Professor's way. He continued: "And it occurred to me, this may be where your particular talent lies. Not perhaps in still lifes," he appended, which Bea again recorded as a possible slight, which must be weighed later—but not now, given how inquisitive and exhilarated she felt. "You recall that I saw you drawing such a portrait sketch. Before class."

"Yes. Of Donald."

"Of Donald Doobly. The Negro."

"Yes."

The portrait was still sitting, unfinished, in the portfolio in her lap. She'd been intending to get back to it, though Ronny hadn't regarded it highly. Bea said, "They're looking for portrait artists?"

"I should perhaps have selected another term. Shall we say portraitists? Young artists with a facility for capturing a quick likeness?"

"These would be portraits of . . . ?" Bea's voice trailed off.

"Portraits of *soldiers*," Professor Manhardt replied. He did sometimes address his students as though they were half-wits. "What are we contributing?—that's the infernal question they keep asking. Why do we need classes in still-life painting? Do you see? There is a war on, they tell me, and I say, Indeed there is and it's being fought right here in this institution. For we in Fine Arts are the besieged. You might think of yourself as a peacemaker."

"I'm not sure I—"

"I am asking you to volunteer."

Hazarding another Manhardt rebuke, Bea asked, point-blank, "So are you asking me to draw portraits of soldiers for the USO?"

"You could regard it as a mission, Miss Paradiso. I gather the subjects would be, in particular, *wounded* soldiers. It may jolly them up, it may lift their spirits, it may fortify the war effort—so goes the thinking I presume. It's what they call morale-building, I believe. And frankly a good thing, from our point of view in Fine Arts, to announce that what you learned at this institution is serving the USO. Let us disregard for the moment that you have been studying still-life drawing rather than—"

It was hardly her style to interrupt the Professor intentionally, but Bea felt an overwhelming desire for outright, air-clearing assertions. "Well," she said. "All right," she said. "Now if you're asking me whether I would volunteer to draw portraits of wounded soldiers, I should be honored." The words felt so stirring and noble, Bea embellished her declaration: "I should consider it a great honor and my patriotic duty."

Bea's pulse was pounding. As happened perhaps all too often, she was experiencing an enhanced, almost surreal sense of her own thumping young heart in her chest—as if this were an organ no longer pink and red but a bright burning gold, throbbing with an almost painful ardor. You would need a Picasso or a Chagall—someone liberated from conventional notions of color—to do it justice.

"It's meant to jolly up the boys and I daresay it will. You're a very attractive girl, Miss Paradiso. We here in Fine Arts, anyway, we needn't disparage the concept, the reality of pure beauty. Do you follow me?"

"I suppose so."

Even now, a few flickerings of wariness revived. Perhaps she should cherish the compliment, yet it unsettled her.

But why should it? Again, again she was being too suspicious—as the look of proud defiant finality on the Professor's face attested. He had established his point. The Professor of Fine Arts had spoken on behalf of the reality of pure beauty, as was not merely his prerogative but his duty.

Professor Manhardt paused and scrutinized her closely, as though seeing her clearly for the first time. Given how high-minded he was being, Bea wished she wasn't feeling her cheeks—again—reddening under his gaze.

Slowly, ever so slowly (the Professor spoke so elliptically!) the various details emerged. For the next three months, *as an experiment,* one morning a week, Bea would donate her talents to the nation's soldiers— especially those in Ferry Hospital. Did she know the place, on the West Side? Yes, she did. Indeed, she did. Indeed—well, actually, she had been born there.

Now it was the Professor's turn to look confused. "You were born there?"

"Yes. Born right there. Right here. In this city. A real Detroit girl. Not that I remember the hospital."

The discovery that she would be drawing soldiers in the very hospital of her birth lent the Professor's proposal, already so promising, a special rightness and richness. It was nothing less than perfect! So long awaited, it had arrived at last: the perfect way to serve her country! How had she failed to glimpse her fate? What else could her destiny be? Obviously, she must at last become the Girl Who Drew Portraits of Soldiers . . .

She would be working in charcoal, the Professor went on. Perhaps one or two portraits per morning? No more than that—this was art, she wouldn't be a sideshow entertainment. (Bea nodded heartily.) The portraits would be given to the soldiers themselves. Each portrait would aspire to be *favorable*—to be *uplifting.* This goal might not always be easy. Some of the soldiers were rather badly wounded, you see. Others might have fallen into dejection—or other psychological problems. It could be something of a sticky wicket. (But what was a sticky wicket?)

Professor Manhardt could advance her the actual cost of supplies. Now did she think she was equal to the task? Did the experiment, as described, interest her?

Invited at last to speak freely, Bea hardly knew what she was saying, her words came tumbling forth . . . This was everything her heart had been craving: not merely to serve her country, but to serve it through her art! What task on earth could be more beautiful and fulfilling than drawing wounded soldiers' portraits? Already she could visualize herself heading by streetcar toward Ferry Hospital, a portfolio under her arm, dressed simply, wearing a plain white blouse and a gray wool skirt perhaps, her hair pulled back in a no-nonsense bun. Or her powder-blue angora turtleneck sweater and a navy skirt and gray-and-white saddle shoes. Or her pink pinstripe blouse and her Hungarian beret? In any event, she would venture up the broad hospital steps into rooms where the poor boys lay, the young who were crippled or maimed. She would acknowledge a debt; in a small way, she would express her country's gratitude.

What offer could be more enthralling? As she headed home, striding down Inquiry, Bea warmed to an imagined opulence under her arm. It was as if her portfolio already held soldiers' portraits, rather than today's mediocre sketches of a lemon, a teacup, and an impossible-to-draw (even Ronny had struggled over it) rabbit's foot. And when she stepped into the front hall she felt—for the first time in weeks—a preoccupation more urgent than Mamma's always precarious state of mind.

Bea managed to hold off telling her story until supper, but the minute the food was on the table she said, Guess what?—and launched into it. A knowing glance passed between Mamma and Papa, a look that said, *She's on a tear* (one more of Papa's proud colloquialisms). Bea didn't care. She had every reason to be excited.

She failed to explain herself well, however, and Papa began muttering reservations. Drawing portraits in a hospital? Over on the West Side? All by herself? He shook his head skeptically. They would need to speak with Uncle Dennis, Bia . . .

Oddly, it was Mamma who came squarely to the rescue. This was the USO, Vico, and their daughter had been asked to serve. These were soldiers, Vico, wounded in service to our country. And it wasn't a strange place—it was the very hospital where the girl was born.

Gradually, Papa came around. And then, bit by bit, everyone at the table succumbed to the romance—surely the most romantic task anyone in the family had ever undertaken. Bea was asked many questions, for most of which she lacked firm answers. (It grew increasingly apparent she didn't fully understand her new duties.) Still, she answered as she could, plausibly filling in the gaps. "Yes," she found herself telling Stevie. "I will be drawing officers, too."

"Officers, too," Mamma marveled.

It had been a long while since this family had shared any promising news, and the conversation buzzed through dessert, which was prune whip with molasses cookies. Edith didn't understand, quite, how the mere drawing of soldiers could serve the war effort. "Oh honestly, it isn't just knitting socks, or recycling tin. It's good to do those things, of course," Bea told her sister. "But it's also building morale." And poor Stevie was almost more excited than he could bear; he couldn't conceive of a place more glamorous than a hospital full of wounded soldiers.

After dinner, Bea telephoned Maggie, who took the news badly. Ever since moving in with the Hamms, Maggie had been much less fun to talk to. Still, the two of them arranged to get together Saturday, if the Jailer would grant Maggie a brief pass.

Bea went to her room and, by way of practice, drew some soldiers inspired by photographs from the Rotogravure Section of the *News*. She was feeling peeved with Maggie, though the longer Bea drew, the more forgiving she became. According to Uncle Dennis, George was in no real danger, out there in Hawaii. But if your husband was stationed anywhere in the Pacific, the image of a hospital full of wounded soldiers might well be unnerving . . .

Bea went to the kitchen for a glass of milk and found her mother seated at the table, a glass of milk before her. Bea said, "Thank you, Mamma."

"Mm?"

"For helping to convince him. About drawing portraits at the hospital."

"You know I wanted to be a nurse."

"I know," Bea said.

"Did I ever tell you what Miss Patterson said? Who taught me biology in high school?"

Instead of saying, "Only a hundred times," Bea said, "I'm not *exactly* sure," which seemed the best compromise between politeness and honesty.

"She said I could be a doctor if I wanted. She said I had the brains for it." And Mamma lifted her chin in that touching way she had, as if both daring and dreading an objection.

"Imagine that," Bea said, and added, as she carried her milk from the room, "Good night, Mamma."

Needing to think everything over, Bea went to bed early, when Edith did, at 9:30. Staring up for the millionth time at the slats in the bunk where her sister lay, Bea calmed down enough to ponder a few misgivings. What had the Professor meant in suggesting her talent might not lie in still lifes? Was she merely in need of more classroom time—or was she really hopeless? And when he'd called her "a very attractive girl" (admittedly, in irreproachable fashion), was he actually telling her she'd been chosen for her looks? Why hadn't Donald Doobly been selected? He also had a flair for portraiture. Was it because he was a boy? Because he was a Negro?

Yet the Professor had recollected the afternoon before class when she had so quickly begun sketching Donald . . . Professor Manhardt had observed, and remembered, the way Donald's bashful, mindful eyes had emerged. He'd seen she could draw.

She *liked* being an attractive girl, particularly in the exalted precincts of the Professor's *reality of pure beauty,* and yet Bea also wanted (was this asking too much?) reassurance that what her heart informed her was true was true: she had a genuine gift for portraiture.

And out of the darkness below her, unbidden but waited for, she began to sense them and to see them, floating up like air bubbles, like white balloons: the faces come to vindicate her. These were the soldiers—the wounded boys—risen pale from their pale hospital beds. They were looking to her, attentively waiting for her . . . At the very border of sleep, Bianca Paradiso catches a collective glance needing no language to convey its importunate privations; yes, she's on the streetcar again, that enclosed and timeless environment where everything that happens happens in present tense, face to the glass, vowing to this city that has become the Arsenal of Democracy that she will not fail them, even as she feels something—her portfolio?—slipping from her lap.

She stoops to retrieve it and her descent enlarges into a cavernous plummeting free fall. The paper faces have scattered upon the filthy floor and she reaches out in every direction, as, one by one, or maybe all at once, the faces dissolve.

The faces dissolve and she's transported miles away, hours away, and deep into the depths of the dark. It's late. She has walked alone to the desolate corner of Day and Midnight, where she takes a left turn and finds herself in bright sidelights marching up the steps of Ferry Hospital, which has a genuine medieval moat encircling its walls. She is here to meet the doctor. Many things happen on her search and yet nothing happens, since these are nothing but tricked-out preliminaries for the moment when she enters the yellow room where the doctor stands with his back turned. The doctor swings round and—it's Mamma.

So flabbergasted is Bea, she cannot speak, though Mamma's cool as cool can be. She hands Bea a waxed paper bag whose fateful heaviness (a wet, packed, sliding heaviness) is ghastly beyond all expression. "We saved everything we could," Mamma says—and the girl wakes, gasping.

In the room's stray streetlight glare, breathing hard, she found in its appointed place the silhouette of the wooden lamb her father had once carved for her, for his little Bia. And then she caught her breath, and, in just a few minutes, she reentered that best of all sleeps wherein all dreams are forgotten.

CHAPTER IX

Standing on the steps of the vast castellated gray structure of Ferry Hospital, Bea felt as though she had stood here before. There was no way in the world she could remember any such thing, of course, but she did have to wonder: had she initially glimpsed this hospital from her mother's arms, carried out into the living world for the first time? A less fanciful explanation was that Uncle Dennis had led her here, years later, on one of his hospital errands. The place's familiarity didn't translate into a sense of comfort, though, and for all her exalted moral purpose, Bea instinctively shrank from its imposingness.

Nor was she put at ease by the menacingly named Mr. Dearth, from the USO, who met her in the lobby. He spoke, as Professor Manhardt spoke, of the need for "cheerful" portraits—adding, while projecting his chin, "This won't always be easy." He was himself an odd study for any portraitist—a tall, bald, stooped, big-chinned man, lipless as a turtle. He added, heavily, "I know what war is like, you see." Nor was she put at ease by Mr. Kronstein, who apparently ran the hospital. The brown pouches underneath his eyes looked large enough to hide a penny in. "One ward has been requisitioned by the military."

"Yes."

"In many ways it's the most difficult ward."

"Yes."

"Some of the boys are downhearted," he told her, mournfully. "Others will be quite—spry," he went on, more mournfully still. "You understand what I'm saying, Miss Paradiso? This isn't a social club."

"Of course," Bea said.

"It's a hospital," he said.

"Of course," Bea said.

Winged creatures were circling inside her—her stomach was absolutely aflutter—by the time she was turned over to a nurse.

Nurse Mildred O'Donnell was a tiny woman—barely reaching Bea's shoulder—with a broad, no-nonsense face. "You're *very* tall," she accused Bea, as the two of them strode along a corridor painted a reptilian green.

"Not *so* tall, maybe?" Bea hugged her portfolio to her chest.

"You must be six feet tall."

"I'm five eight and a half," Bea replied, truthfully. She often "forgot" the half inch, in the interests of both convenience and vanity. But within the walls of Ferry Hospital it seemed imperative to be scrupulous about physical data.

Though mostly content to be tall, Bea would have given a lot to be only half an inch shorter, in which event she wouldn't be classified, under the War Production Board, as a "female of unusual height." Wartime tailoring restrictions did not apply to females of unusual height. Seeing that phrase in the newspaper—*female of unusual height*—Bea had felt cruelly, personally singled out, as if the government itself were calling her a freak. Bea was in the same category with girls who stood six feet tall, seven feet tall, eight feet tall . . .

"My brother Jerry's five foot ten, and you're definitely taller than Jerry," Nurse O'Donnell told her. The fixed expression on her face made plain that while Bea was at liberty to treat the truth as casually as she wished, she shouldn't expect to put anything past Nurse Mildred O'Donnell.

Meanwhile, as the two of them marched purposefully down the corridor, Bea heard a variety of leaked sounds—muffled cries or groans—*male* cries or groans—and was beginning to feel thoroughly frightened. A sharp hospital smell overlay another, human smell: the lingering reek of somebody's having vomited up an assortment of the very worst things inside him. Her own stomach was *very* uneasy and Bea felt as if she were but one touch away—one feather's stroke—from retching up the two strawberry-jelly-and-cream-cheese sandwiches she'd eaten for lunch. Oh my. Oh please. Bea's mind tried, and failed, to mount a suitable prayer.

Perhaps as a result of having seen so many movies, Bea had vividly pictured an enormous barracks-type room: beds to left and right, stretching out for yards and yards. But the first room she was led through contained only a dozen or so beds, some of them empty. Male voices leaped up: "Hello." "Good afternoon, bright eyes." "Well well, hel*lo* hel*lo*." She followed Nurse O'Donnell and did not slow; in truth, she hardly saw the boys on either side.

The next room contained only four beds. Two were empty. In one, a soldier lay motionless, apparently asleep. Only the crown of his blond crew-cut head was visible. He was making a sound between snoring and moaning.

In the other bed lay a ginger-haired young man with a bandaged face, who peered at them groggily.

Nurse O'Donnell said, sharply: "Ya wancher pitcher drawn?"

The soldier's answer, though slow to form, was quite elaborate when it did assemble itself: "Now what's that you're asking, Auntie? Would it be too serious an inconvenience to repeat the question to nephew Michael?"

"None of your nonsense now. It's all explained before. Yes or no—ya wancher pitcher drawn?"

One of the soldier's eyes was covered by a huge white bandage. The uncovered eye swam fully into focus, dragging, as it were, the rest of his features with it. "This another your hard bargains, Auntie?"

"Yes or no?"

"Another your trick questions?"

Bea knew that face, or knew its type. She recognized the appetite for mischief, the antic Irish playfulness. Oh, she'd gone to school with plenty of boys like this one. Who was he? The class clown. At once Bea felt better. She knew where she was, suddenly.

"Yes or no?"

"I would be most delighted" was the soldier's rejoinder. "I'd go so far as to say, enchanted. I will go that far. I am an enchanted youth."

"Enchanted youth my foot. And I'm not your aunt, thank the Lord." Apparently wishing to set the record straight, Nurse O'Donnell added, with satisfaction: "I'm nobody's aunt."

"Oh now just because little Michael is something of a black sheep among certain of our stern kith and—"

Nurse O'Donnell cut him off. "You can start here," she said to Bea. "With this one. You'll be out of the way *here*."

Then the little nurse was gone, and Bea and the red-haired soldier eyed each other across the room. He was sitting up in bed now.

"I've adopted her as my aunt," he said briskly. "Figured I ought to, since we got the same last name. Or almost. Mine's Donnelly. Michael Donnelly at your service, miss. I just hope you won't give me any marching orders."

"Oh no, you stay put."

"Afraid I'm not quite up for the long march, miss."

"That's all right."

With a solemn look on his one-eyed face, Michael Donnelly held out his hand. Still clutching with both hands her portfolio to her chest, Bea crossed the room, removed her right hand, and deposited it in his cool hand. It embarrassed her—her own hand was so clammy.

And what to do next? How exactly to proceed? Although Bea hadn't felt altogether comfortable with Nurse O'Donnell, the woman had disappeared more abruptly than Bea would have wished. Bea needed additional guidance . . . There was a chair in the corner and she dragged it to the foot of the soldier's bed, sat down, portfolio still to her chest. "And yours?" the soldier said, expectantly. But what did he mean?

Oh—of course: her name. "Bea. Really Bianca, but call me Bea. Bea Paradiso."

So bewildering and new was all of this—to be sitting beside the bed of a young man newly met—that only now did Bea discern what must be a stroke of mischief, if not outright malice, on Nurse O'Donnell's part. Bea was here to draw a soldier's portrait, but how was she to proceed with a face nearly engulfed by a white bandage? Was this any place to begin?

"You're an artist," Michael Donnelly said.

"Oh no. Just an art student."

"And I'm just a private. Humble beginnings, huh? I guess we've all got to start somewhere." He grinned. The bandage covered his right eye and eyebrow, most of his nose, his right cheekbone, the right base of his jaw. But his mouth was free to smile at her, free to laugh. An extraordinary amount of jollity was compressed into his visible features. "Let me take a wild guess. Paradiso means Paradise."

"Good guess."

"Italian girl. I like that. As you probably guessed, Donnelly's an old Polish name. From a long line of Battle Creek Poles." Again the flash of a grin, inviting—coaxing—a grin in response. "You know if I may say so, you have a very . . . credulous look."

The pause on *credulous* asked whether she was familiar with the word. He was an entertainer, sounding out his audience.

Bea felt very willing to match vocabularies with any boy her age. "So I look gullible?" she said. "A pushover? Maybe I'm too ingenuous? Should I be wary of you, for instance?"

"Hey, pretty girl like you? Oughta beware everybody. How old are you?"

The veering speed of Private Donnelly's conversation, as well as its presumption of close familiarity, left Bea feeling more comfortable than uncomfortable. She had always enjoyed this sort of boy-girl banter. Oh, she was *quick,* and she could hold her own with any fast-talking Michael Donnelly.

"Old enough to know you certainly ask a lot of questions, Soldier."

"So whatcha gonna do? Draw half my face?"

"I— Well, I—" But what *was* she going to do? What would a real artist do?

"Or you could draw me in profile." Private Donnelly swung his face to the right, his bandage all but hidden from sight, swung back and winked at her—if a one-eyed man may be said to wink. He was a shameless flirt. "I do think that's my better side. Even better than *this.*" He rotated the other way, showing off a face that was nothing but one mammoth bandage, then turned to eye her once more. "Which you think's better?"

"Both have their good points."

This amused him. "Call it a toss-up?"

"I guess."

Then his expression abruptly shifted and he broached a grave topic. "Lately they've been taking pieces of metal out of my face."

"I'm so sorry."

"They've been doing it so careful, you know what kind of metal it must be?"

His expression again altered—became mock-conspiratorial. For someone with so many concealed features, he had a remarkably mobile, expressive face. "*Gold,*" he whispered solemnly. "Got me a face fulla gold, sister. I just want to make sure they give me my cut. Cut's the word, I guess." And again he winked.

"So what *am* I going to do? Do you want me to draw you in profile?" She needed to stay focused. She had come with a job to do.

"Beats me."

"I thought I'd start in pencil, just to get the lines flowing. Then charcoal."

The truth was, she wasn't at all comfortable with charcoal, though she hadn't mentioned this to Professor Manhardt. "I'll do a pencil sketch for me, then a charcoal sketch for you."

"You're the artist, Bobcat. Did you say your name was Bobcat?"

"Bea. I said Bea."

"The other first name."

"Bianca."

"Bianca, Bobcat—what's the difference? If you're the artist," he went on, "does that make me your subject? I thought only queens had subjects. Hey," he cried, "you're the queen Bea!" His conversation moved so fast—he showed all the hectic energy of a young man bedridden for days on end.

"You can be a model, then."

"Me in a nutshell. Michael Donnelly: model soldier." He smiled more broadly still. He looked very pleased with himself.

"Let's see if you can be a good model soldier, Soldier, and hold still while I'm drawing you."

Abruptly, he ventured a new, softer tone: "Nobody has ever drawn my picture before, Bea." And he added: "Maybe you could draw me the way I really look?"

"I'm not sure I follow . . ."

"I mean—before I got my face fulla gold?"

"But—well, good heavens. I can't draw what I can't see. It wouldn't be—" Bea halted just before *honest.* But was honesty what she was here to demonstrate?

Or was it her job, first and foremost, to please the soldiers—to provide something cheerful? She hadn't expected to confront such complicated moral questions, all by herself, on this her first day . . .

Inspiration came to her: "Do you have a picture of yourself? A picture—before you went into the service? That might be helpful."

"Actually I do. In my wallet." But Private Donnelly made no move. "Seem strange to you? Carrying my own picture? My mother sent me a dozen. Told me to give 'em to the girls. Exchange pictures, you see."

"Sounds as if she understands you very well," Bianca said. "Your mother."

"Hey now, Mom's all right. I'll say one thing for the old girl: she knows how to make a person laugh."

"Mama's boy," Bianca said, and laughed herself. "Like mother, like son," she added, and after a moment's thought, Private Donnelly joined her laughter. Then one of his quick hands fished under the pillow he'd propped himself upon and came up with a black leather wallet. He opened it, stared reflectively, then held it out.

But when Bea extended her hand, he recoiled. He was reluctant to let it go. Then, possessively, hesitantly—much the way a shy soldier might tender a portrait of his girl—Private Michael Donnelly at last handed over the precious record of his former face.

For a second, Bea almost didn't recognize him.

To judge from his grave, resolute, would-be-rugged expression, this had to be a high school graduation photo. The Irish face staring up at her was both leaner and solider than she would have imagined. And far handsomer. His hair was unfashionably long—reflecting, no doubt, some well-placed pride in his buoyant curls. He looked a little like an Irish Pan. Notwithstanding its aspirations of solemnity, this was a quick, mischievous, *beautiful* face.

The photograph lay on the left side of the open wallet. On the right, a driver's license listed his birth date: May 16, 1924. This came as a shock. She'd thought this wounded soldier must be a number of years older than she was. In truth, they might have gone to school together. Inside her chest, she felt a heavy wet flop—her heart, going out to him.

Bea kept the wallet open beside her. Private Donnelly unearthed a pack of cigarettes, also hidden under his pillows. "Now Auntie O'Donnell says I mustn't smoke," he confided. "On account of the terrible possibility I may incinerate myself. Or even worse, get ashes on the sheets. This is a woman does hate ashes on the sheets. I tell her, *I'm* not smoking, the cigarette is. I'm just lighting one match. The cigarette does all the rest."

His hands trembled as he lit up. Yes, it rattled him to have his old, intact features scrutinized. Made him far more vulnerable and jumpy, in fact, than to have her looking into a one-eyed face discolored and swollen and decorated with a big stained bandage that needed replacing.

But what tugged most at Bea's emotions was, for all his swelling, how haggard Private Donnelly looked as he pulled on his cigarette. Fretful lines radiated from the corner of his eye, and his mouth seemed to take its shape—as an old man's mouth will, as Grandpa Paradiso's mouth did—from the cigarette inserted into it. To her young artist's eye, the oncoming years melted away and she espied the hard-bitten, hapless middle-aged man Private Donnelly was destined to become. No, it was hard to imagine Time treating any too kindly this Irish class clown, who all so touchingly carried a picture of his old self in his wallet.

"Let's start with a profile," she proposed, and he agreed ("I follow orders"), and for twenty minutes or so she sketched the left side of his face in pencil.

Of course Private Donnelly *didn't* follow orders. She continually asked him to sit still—please!—and keep his glance trained on the wall, but he talked and gestured and was constantly turning to gauge her responses. Bea sketched steadily, but soon had to concede that it wasn't going well, and when at last, in response to his endless beseeching, she allowed him a glance at the work in progress, he, too, showed disappointment. Perhaps this was unavoidable. Private Donnelly wasn't seen to best advantage from the side. His nose came off as beaky, his chin a little weak. More important, the powerful animation in his Irish features was absent.

He said, "Maybe you wouldn't mind drawing my face straight on?"

"But you can't remove—"

"No, but you *could* work from the photograph." Wasn't that what she herself had been proposing, when she'd asked him to open his wallet? "It might help you to . . ." He didn't have a word.

"Project?"

"Exactly."

The request again placed Bea in a dilemma. Was this the sort of thing she was invited here to do—to draw a face that no longer existed, and perhaps would never again exist? Wouldn't they be angry? (This *they* was a vague *they*, but she didn't have time to puzzle it out. Bea knew only that she didn't want to offend *them*.)

"I don't know," Bea confessed.

"You could try."

"I think maybe my job is to draw what I *see*." She recalled Professor Manhardt's habitual injunction ("Look closer, look closer"), as well as the often-quoted words of Goya ("*Yo lo vi*"); could her job conceivably include projecting the half of a face she'd never laid eyes upon?

"You could try," Private Donnelly insisted, mildly, and managed to catch and hold her glance with his one shining, eager, conspiratorial eye. It was like the eye of the Ancient Mariner in the poem. She could not look away. So many emotions in his glance! Including a prostrate look of pure pleading . . .

You could try. Well, she would try.

And Private Donnelly behaved better, now that he wasn't being asked to look aside. He talked less—a *little* less—and gestured less, although he did smoke two more cigarettes. Bea was able, for the first time since walking through Ferry Hospital's imposing entrance, to settle down, to connect what was arranged in front of her to the blank page outspread before her—to use her arm as the conduit it was ideally intended to be.

Not that what she set on paper was good in any meaningful way—

such as Ronny or Professor Manhardt would appreciate. The gap was too great between the big, bandaged, hurt-looking, lively face before her and the neat, pretty Pan in the little photograph. After some initial floundering, she wound up essentially drawing an enlarged version of the photograph—only, a little older-looking, a fuller and more experienced face.

She had arrived at the hospital punctually at ten. Her plan had been to do two portraits on this her first day, but when Nurse O'Donnell came to fetch her at noon, Bea hadn't even moved to charcoal. She was experimenting with pencils of different hardness, still sketching purely for herself. But wasn't the point to do something for *our boys*? "Who's that?" Nurse O'Donnell asked, looking over Bea's shoulder.

It was a cruel remark. Who else in God's name could it be? "It's Private Donnelly," Bea starchily replied.

"Don't look like him."

"I've been working partly from a photograph. And I'm not finished. I'm still finding my way. I'll do it in charcoal after it comes out in pencil."

"Not a very efficient method," Nurse O'Donnell pointed out.

"You can come back tomorrow. Finish then," Private Donnelly suggested.

"I won't be back until next week."

"Next week? I'll have to check my calendar," Private Donnelly went on, in a grand, musing sort of way, "but I don't believe I've got any big travel plans."

"Plenty soldiers in this ward," Nurse O'Donnell informed Bea. "You're not the only face in here," she pointed out to Private Donnelly.

"No, but I sure am the prettiest, Auntie."

Then arrived—no mistaking it—something unforeseen, and wholly welcome: an itch of a smile rumpled the firm horizontal line of Nurse O'Donnell's thin lips.

Private Donnelly, the class clown, had finally accomplished it: he had softened his stern aunt, his forbidding nurse, the old schoolmarm.

No softness crept into her voice, however. "You been smoking again."

"It's the cigarettes. *They* been smoking. No smoke coming outta *me*. Actually, I'm the one puts them *out*." Private Donnelly shifted tacks. "Don't you think Miss Paradiso oughta come back next week? Pretty up my picture?"

Nurse O'Donnell shook her head wearily. "None of my concern," she said. "I got no time for such foolishness. Last thing I heard, this was still a hospital, not a art gallery."

"*Shh.*"

Private Donnelly made a big show of placing an index finger to his lips and whispering, "*I'm* aware of that, Auntie, but you mustn't be disappointing the other boys."

Bea put in a few goodbyes—one or two half-promises were made—then departed from the "wounded ward" with Nurse O'Donnell at her side, or almost at her side. However much Bea slowed, Nurse O'Donnell appeared determined to walk a step behind. Although the nurse said nothing, it was clear that Michael Donnelly's banter had lifted her spirits: the oppressive air of disapprobation had thinned. "I've never met anyone quite like him," Bea said, turning slightly, back to where Nurse O'Donnell padded along.

Nurse O'Donnell looked up at Bianca—the six-foot-tall "artist" who lied about her height—and said, "His injuries are extensive."

"It's a very big bandage."

"Serious wounds."

"Are there many wounded?"

Nurse O'Donnell did not answer, but the upthrust of her jaw signaled assent. "And that's not counting the ones turned a little funny."

"Funny?" Bea said.

Again, Nurse O'Donnell said nothing, merely resetting her jaw.

"Next week, I must be more efficient," Bea said at last, which was surely something even Nurse O'Donnell could not fault.

But Nurse O'Donnell could not approve of it, either, since at some point down this corridor the silent-footed solid little woman had drifted off. Bea Paradiso, at the entrance to the hospital where she was born, stood alone.

CHAPTER X

Ronny was endlessly full of surprises. He took enormous delight in advertisements, and who would have figured this? Given what a purist he was about visual art—visual everything—you'd expect him to regard ads with Professor Manhardt's revulsion, who spoke of a*dver*tisements and who knew of no dismissal more devastating than a comparison to *commercial art*. But ads appealed to Ronny.

More perplexing still, he often found in them hidden humor she didn't see. Oh, she could share his amusement about the little boy holding a dropper to his upraised nostrils while exclaiming, "Gee, Mom, these nose drops are swell!" But what was so funny in the ad for mountain springwater in which a nurse, carrying a glass to her patient, declares, "AND it's good for the kidneys . . ."? Wasn't this what springwater was supposed to be good for? And why did Ronny laugh so hard at the ad that asked, "Are you a rupture SUFFERER?" Or at the clothier who promised "the lowest profit margin known to man"?

With dating, too, he was full of surprises. Bea had thought she understood dating—she'd been going out with boys since she was fourteen—but Ronny Olsson reordered many of her notions. The big and obvious difference was that he had a car—his own car and a beautiful car, the cream-colored Cabriolet. She had sometimes dated boys who could borrow their father's car, but usually she and her date would set out from Inquiry on foot.

The usual date was a movie—maybe the Sheridan on Kercheval, or the Whittier on Jefferson—and a milk shake afterward. Not that money was ever discussed, but on a typical evening Bea knew to a nickel—to a penny, really—what her date had spent. It was twenty cents each at the Whittier, and a nickel for popcorn, and seventeen cents each for milk shakes at Olsson's. Add a total of twenty-four cents for the four streetcar fares if you were wandering farther afield.

But in Ronny's company you had an unnerving feeling of indeterminate sums disbursed—all the more unnerving because he himself didn't appear to notice. Dates with him had a veering, unexpected quality.

(Despite rationing, his car always seemed full of gas.) She and Ronny were heading off to the movies one night when he discovered she didn't know what a taco was—and the next moment they were driving in the opposite direction, toward Mexicantown.

When he learned that she'd always coveted a Winsor & Newton oil paint set—precisely what he himself owned—he showed up at the next date with one under his arm. And when she explained that she couldn't possibly accept anything so extravagant, Ronny grew not only insistent but indignant: "We're both students at the Institute. It isn't *fair* if my equipment's better than yours." Well, Bea surprised herself by accepting the gift. And surprised herself still further by not feeling guilty.

When Ronny took her somewhere really nice—the Fox Theatre, lunch at Hudson's, a piano recital at the Masonic Temple—it was remarkable how often he ran into people he knew. Most were girls—or most who called out greetings were girls. Their dates often looked sheepish and withdrawn. "Ronny!" a happy voice would cry.

Most were college girls. They were home from Ann Arbor or East Lansing for the weekend, or home for longer vacations from those places with really remote names like Bryn Mawr, which Bea knew chiefly through avid reading of the *Detroit News* society pages. These were the sorts of girls whose engagements were "announced on Sunday at a tea given by her aunt." And after their wedding ceremonies, they were the sorts of girls who "for traveling changed to a navy blue suit, white straw hat, and navy accessories." (Imagine having your clothes mentioned in the newspaper!) Some of these girls were cold toward Bea; some were warm, in a distant and at bottom chilly way; and some seemed genuinely, almost alarmingly warm, as if reunited with some distant but beloved cousin. In this range of responses the one constant factor was an intense, open curiosity. Bea was peered at.

Ronny would introduce her as Bianca Paradiso. "Bianca is a talented artist," he would say, and in an instant most of Bea's unease vanished, replaced by a gushing gratitude: in her entire life, nobody else had thought to introduce her in this fashion.

The girls' dates often looked not only sheepish but resentful. The tense, unignorable truth was that the city was populated by pretty college girls who would like nothing better than a phone call from Ronny Olsson.

It would have been troubling had Ronny wished to frequent only places where such girls gathered. And more troubling still had Ronny shied from such places while in Bea's company. But one of the fascinating things about Ronny Olsson was the poised, urbane way he circulated from one world to another. Dating Ronny meant going to hear a tiny, powerful Russian pianist at the Masonic Temple and it meant finding yourself eating a brittle, splintery something called a taco in a room where a man with a colossal silver moustache, dining alone, had dozed off with his head against the wall.

Herk's was another place where you were unlikely to meet a Bryn Mawr girl, and it was at Herk's where Bea finally described for Ronny her visit to Ferry Hospital three days before. (She'd hardly been able to think of anything since.) She felt frustratingly unable, though, to convey the morning's pathos and magic and whirring power. Or perhaps it would be more accurate to say she couldn't overcome Ronny's resistance to her explanation. Before she could finish a thought, he already had it pigeonholed.

"So you're saying the place was depressing . . ."

"Of course, yes, Ronny, it was *depressing*. Good heavens, it's full of these wounded soldiers, and you keep hearing moans and groans off in the distance. You know I've been feeling so fortunate that I don't know anybody yet who's actually died in the War—"

"Yes, you mentioned—"

"Though there was this boy at Eastern, Bradley Hake, who's still missing in action, but I didn't really know him. Though he *did* use to smile at me."

"Let's hope your luck holds."

"But it *isn't* holding for everyone. That's what you see at Ferry. It brought it all home: the scale of the suffering. And there was this strange little nurse, Nurse Mildred O'Donnell—why would anyone name a child Mildred?—who basically accused me of lying when . . ." and Bea felt herself securely under way again. She told him about Nurse O'Donnell's refusal to believe she wasn't six feet tall, and how she'd simply vaporized at day's end, and about the one occasion when she cracked the hint of a smile. And Ronny interrupted again: "So you're saying the soldiers don't receive adequate care?"

"No, that's not it at all. I'm just telling you how strange a place it is, especially knowing I was actually born there, and the feeling of all these bedridden bodies, and all the boys looking hopefully at me . . ." Bea felt some compunction about embroidering events slightly—or at least giving the impression that she'd seen many more soldiers than she actually had when Nurse O'Donnell had rushed her through the ward. But the words were flowing now, with a life of their own and requirements of their own, and their correspondence to the facts was hardly to be questioned. "They honestly seemed to think I could do something for them."

"So you're saying it made you feel appreciated?"

"No—I mean of course, yes, I suppose so, but I just felt their terrible *needs*. They all looked so pitiful." She could feel their intent gazes again—especially the one who'd called, *Good afternoon, bright eyes*. "It's just I guess I never really thought about how it is for the wounded. How *slow* their days are . . ." and she was off and running again, or trying to run.

But it was talk of Michael Donnelly that seemed most to goad Ronny—could it be he was jealous? It was a difficult and delicate notion. It made *her* sound so arrogant, while it made *him* sound so immature to propose that the tall, devilishly handsome son of the owner of the Olsson's drugstore chain was jealous of an Irish boy from Battle Creek with a bandage over his face. But what else could have possessed Ronny to say, "You should see how flushed you've become! Honestly, Bianca, you look *sweet* on him . . ."

"Sweet on him? Ronny, he's got a bandage the size of—of a dinner plate. *On his face.* What you *can* see of his face is bruised and swollen and discolored, and what you can't see is full of metal. I should see *my* face? You should see *his* face."

"Perhaps the lady doth protest too much?"

Bea knew the phrase, of course, but couldn't place the reference, and this sense of her own disadvantaged ignorance—Ronny was so wide-ranging and articulate!—in combination with that superior, skeptical way he had of cocking one eyebrow, sparked a new emotion, not very pretty and yet not wholly regrettable: a slight chafed impatience with that sophisticated, elaboration-loving intellectual's world represented by Ronny Olsson. Why couldn't he be more like other boys?

And yet in ways she couldn't begin to fathom (and, later, in bed that night, could hardly bear to contemplate) it wasn't an hour after their talk, as they took a walk through Palmer Park, that she felt more tightly bound than ever. They were on a little wooded path. No one was about. She was trying again to explain the power of that looming image of Ferry Hospital. Straddling like a mountain range across her mind, it was too large to be envisioned: its borders exceeded her imagination's borders . . . It was an object she couldn't *think* about painting (how could you even start?), and yet every other object in her head—rabbit's feet and pocket watches and nutcrackers and lemons—stood idly in its shadow. In the only canvas that might do it justice, you'd intuit all the soldiers within. Yes, you would look at that gray castle and feel them inside.

She felt the War—it was the largest thing she'd ever felt. She felt it, that is, with a sweep and a complexity burgeoning steadily over time. She absorbed it from every angle—from the newspapers, and the news-reels, and the chatter at the bakery and the butcher's, and in Uncle Dennis's careful, well-researched accounts . . . and yet, for all she absorbed, for all the widening of her vision, Bea occasionally discerned how its true dimensions escaped her. Even the hospital escaped her! It was all so unimaginable: to be sitting before the bed of Private Donnelly, who in the ordinary course of life probably wouldn't have ventured a hundred miles from Battle Creek in ten years, but who had been shipped off to the South Seas, where strange yellow-skinned Japanese soldiers had exploded screaming white-hot metal fragments into his face . . .

Of course she couldn't begin to express her thoughts coherently, which were not really thoughts but images linked to sounds and voices, Roosevelt on the radio and the newsboys calling *Extra* and a whirring projector behind you as an aircraft carrier proudly stretched across the screen of the United Artists, and impossibly remote place names like Singapore and Corregidor and Medjez-el-Bab, and was it any wonder she couldn't express to Ronny everything she longed to express? To make her task all the more formidable, he had halted, and turned and faced her, seizing her hands, and he'd begun to stroke her palms, sending what already felt like a soothingly familiar warmth up her arms.

"Ferry Hospital is where *the war comes home*," she said, and *home* felt unexpectedly right, it resounded in her chest, while the looming gray structure shimmered like some Monet cathedral in the sun.

"It's like this big repair shop," Bea said, feeling her imagination again taking wing. "For broken soldiers. They bring them back to be repaired, only—" Only? Only, some cannot be repaired, is that what she wanted to say? What in heaven did she want to say? Bea felt all but overmastered, as Ronny stoked the fire in her hands—a fire that climbed, as fire naturally will climb, right up the crackling veins in her arms. "All those broken soldiers," she sighed—words that only enhanced the wordless realization that Ronny Olsson, by contrast, stood before her unbroken: intense and gifted and dizzyingly handsome. The heart of this young man with a heart murmur was beating ardently, irrepressibly, and she seemed to glimpse the two of them from slightly above—like a painter who has chosen to expand the view by climbing some knoll. A young woman in a red felt hat and red wool skirt, age eighteen, and a young man, twenty-one, were standing in a Detroit public park one late afternoon in August 1943. Soon the park's greenery would be giving way to autumn colors. Outside the park, encircling it on all sides, stood the city's pluming smokestacks, one after another after another, for this was the greatest manufacturing hub in the world. What had once been the world's automobile capital had become, almost overnight, an outspread and interconnected armamentarium. Everything had been retooled, redesigned, and it was right here, in all of Detroit's beautiful factories, infernally aglow, that the War would be won. Right here began the endless, outbound exodus: Chrysler's tanks and Ford's airplanes and General Motors' amphibious landing craft, rolling off the lines and being hauled away by ship and train, by river and railroad track. And what was returned to the city was a random poor human scatter of wounded soldiers, including one carrot-topped class clown whose face had been splattered with stray metal.

"All those wounded, needy soldiers," Bea sighed again, hardly knowing what she was saying, and it was as if this phrase, in all its flammable imagery, ignited the young man before her. Ronny lunged forward and flattened his lips against hers: their first kiss. And Bea thrilled to an equal answering forward lunging: she fully met the kiss. His arms were lashed round her back, his hips pressed tight enough to hers that she could feel the bulge of his belt buckle.

Before long, his lips parted, as sometimes other boys' lips had parted during a kiss. But this time she did what she resolutely had not done before: she opened her mouth completely to that beckoning male mouth. The stroke of his tongue against her tongue threw a big voluptuous splash of color against the dark of her mind: an orange-gold glow that broke like a wave, tingling like one of those fireworks that die with such high reluctance against the sky's velvet black. His tongue pushed in the other direction, and in the deepest Lascaux-cavern walls of the mind a whole pack of beast-shapes went loping over the rolling hills. Resemblances formed and broke, living things, dreams, colors, colors without objects, pale milky greens and reds with swollen veins of electric blue, and if he'd not continued holding her fevered body firmly in his hands, Bianca could hardly have remained upright: Ronny Olsson alone was keeping her from tumbling disgracefully to the ground.

Ronny wasn't at all keen on the new painters: Picasso and Matisse and Modigliani and Munch and Dufy and Feininger, each represented by a single work at what she still thought of as the Art Institute but what Ronny always called the DIA. (There were other, often still newer painters—Braque and Klimt and Kandinsky and de Chirico and Magritte and Klee and Bonnard and Giacometti—but these were mostly names in catalogues, since she'd never actually seen their work.) He dismissed outright, as "cheap," the Salvador Dalí show whose recent arrival at the DIA had filled Bea with such powerful mixed feelings. (Though it was like Ronny, too, to offer a subsequent qualification: "Paradiso, you do have to admit the man could paint a marvelous loaf of bread.") Ronny was quite convincingly articulate about the painters' various shortcomings, and wickedly humorous, too, and unlike many people who ridiculed modern art, he knew what he was talking about. He had been to New York City any number of times; he had visited the Museum of Modern Art, on Fifty-third Street, in Manhattan. (He saw it as MoMA.) Having so much less firsthand familiarity with the modern painters, Bea was far less confident. And Ronny was so much older. Ronny had seen a number of actual Vermeers—Vermeer was one of his gods. She'd never seen one. He'd seen a number of Brueghels. She'd seen one.

For that matter, she'd seen but one van Gogh, one Chardin, one Velázquez. Of course she had looked at catalogues, and she'd peered hard at magazine articles. But out there, beyond her hometown, and beyond the War that postponed indefinitely all such dream-visions, lay a chain of galleries as distant as the galaxies in Uncle Dennis's science-fiction stories. Galleries in Philadelphia, Washington, London, mythical Paris . . .

Where did she come down on modern art? She knew for certain only that some of it unsettled her stomach—almost as if she'd eaten something strange. That's what happened after she contemplated a magazine reproduction of a Picasso painting of a man and a woman on a beach—only, it wasn't so much a man and a woman as two animate stone beings. They were two living sculptures sprung out of some drunken geometry textbook, with little triangles for heads and big sweeping parabolas, or maybe ellipses, for haunches. It made her feel so *peculiar* . . .

The only thing to which she could compare Picasso's painting was wholly inappropriate—the "pulp art" in Uncle Dennis's goofy and appealing and unnerving science-fiction magazines: *Astounding Tales* and such. Of course Uncle Dennis had no use for Picasso, Matisse, and all the rest, whose bizarre visions were hardly *his* bizarre visions. If asked, Uncle Dennis would doubtless dismiss them as "oddballs" or "goofballs"—a curious dismissal from somebody truly convinced that someday men would pack themselves into rocket ships and steer by the stars; in his universe, it was only a matter of time before "the man in the moon" became a literal man. She'd sometimes tried reading his magazines, but none of the stories ever caught her imagination. The illustrations, though—those were a different matter. They, too, made her queasy. They had populated her childhood with slinking, sliding, darting, levitating aliens: a host of unearthly creatures that nonetheless resembled earthly insects and dinosaurs, snails and great jungle cats. There were also creatures that quivered like Jell-O and creatures that glowed from within like radios and creatures that were, sometimes, queer cousins to Picasso's triangle-headed men and women.

But if Bea didn't know what she felt, finally, about modern art, she knew she loved the Impressionists (Cézanne most of all, but van Gogh, too, even if those greens of his were the strangest, most disquieting greens in all the world). Her taste for Impressionism was something to underplay around Ronny, who saw it as "the beginning of the end of real painting." ("Gauguin," he declared with finality, "was no draftsman." And: "The Impressionists managed some pretty effects, I'll grant you. But we mustn't let them off the hook for what came after.") The only late-nineteenth-century painters he regularly admired were the Pre-Raphaelites ("At least their hearts were in the right place"), with their wide palettes and flattened vistas, gorgeous fabrics and exquisite drowned-looking women. He was far happier in a courtly, long-ago France, the sumptuous allées of Fragonard, Poussin's evenhanded landscapes. (Bea found the former artist a little too frivolous, the latter a bit static.) But Ronny was happiest of all with the Old Dutch Masters: Rembrandt and Vermeer, of course, but also Claesz and Dou and Ter Borch and, sometimes, Ruisdael. He didn't fully share Bea's conviction that nothing in the world was so ravishing as the Italian Renaissance, when some summit in mankind's eternal pursuit of Beauty had been attained, never equaled since. ("Signorina Paradiso," Ronny teased her, "you're such a blood loyalist!") Although she'd seen them only in reproductions, she knew to a glittering certainty that Giovanni Bellini's *Saint Francis in the Desert* and Titian's *Venus with a Mirror* were more beautiful than a whole gallery of Fragonards, even with a roomful of Louis Quatorze furniture thrown in for good measure. And if it wasn't perhaps so beautiful as *Saint Francis in the Desert*, nonetheless the Bellini at the DIA, a Madonna and Child, might just be the most beautiful object Bea had ever beheld. And now there was a gratifying human anecdote attached to its beauty: the occasion when, at her urging, she and Ronny had stood before it for long, long minutes, until he turned and announced, concessively, nobly, "Yes, Paradiso, it's much finer than I ever realized . . ."

It was her passion for Renaissance art that led to one of the oddest afternoons of her life. The episode really began on a Thursday night—the evening after the day when she and Ronny took their memorable walk in Palmer Park. At dinner with Ronny's parents at what she'd begun to think of as the DAC—always formerly known, from afar, as the Detroit Athletic Club—Ronny happened to mention Bea's "passion" for Italian art.

Mrs. Olsson interrupted: "Bianca, you must give me a tour. A tour of the Italian galleries at the art institute." She followed this with a grandly humble yet imposing confession: "*I have always longed to understand the Italian art.*"

Useless to protest—though Bea did of course protest—that she was no fit guide for Mrs. Olsson, who surely could find somebody more knowledgeable. And useless to protest—though Bea did protest—that such a visit ought to be delayed until she could "do a little research." The guided tour was set for Saturday, only two days away.

Naturally, early the next morning, Friday morning, Bea was at the library, where she located a book called *Art in Northern Italy* and a catalogue of the Academy Gallery in Florence and *The Makers of Venice* by a woman named Mrs. Oliphant. There was supposed to be a book by Bernard Berenson, but somebody had checked it out. Bea plunged desperately into the pile, for it grew immediately apparent that, although she frequently referred to the Italian eye and the Italian sensibility, she in fact knew precious little about the Renaissance, which apparently was subdivided into "early" and "high." Giotto, Duccio, the various Bellinis, Leonardo, Perugino, Michelangelo, Piero della Francesca—she would flunk any simple art history quiz about their who, where, when.

But on the dreaded Saturday, little of Bea's crammed research proved useful. Mrs. Olsson tired quickly of the paintings. ("*Another Madonna?* I suppose it's quite beautiful, but wouldn't you think they'd find other things to paint?" "It was a very religious time, I guess." "I guess, but isn't the whole point of being a Renaissance man the ability to *accomplish many things*? It's pretty arrogant of them to call themselves Renaissance men." "I'm not sure they actually—") And Mrs. Olsson tired more quickly still of Bea's commentaries. ("Oh you mustn't give me any more dates, my dear. It's only half the time I can remember Mr. Olsson's birthday.") Having been profusely and graciously thanked (the graciousness truly was imposing; a mere thank-you from Mrs. Olsson descended upon you like some precious gift), Bea found herself seated in the backseat of Mrs. Olsson's car, beside Mrs. Olsson, who was not driving. In the front seat, impressively uniformed, sat a chauffeur. A chauffeur!

"Now we'll go to lunch," Mrs. Olsson said.

They were driven to a place called Pierre's, off Jefferson, not far from the Windsor Tunnel. They were welcomed by Monsieur Pierre himself, who greeted Mrs. Olsson with all but uncontainable warmth. He had a pencil-line-thin moustache, which looked eccentric but which perhaps was to be expected of a restaurateur named Pierre. (Although both men had named establishments for themselves, Pierre and Chuck of Chuck's Chop House probably wouldn't have much to say to each other.) "This is Bianca Paradiso," Mrs. Olsson announced.

Bianca was used to clipping her name—a name that commonly inspired silly jokes or cumbersome gallantries. "Bea Pardiso" was how she often introduced herself, condensing the whole business into four syllables. But Mrs. Olsson strung it out in all its Italianate amplitude: Bi-an-ca Pa-ra-di-so. She might have been introducing a contessa.

Monsieur Pierre lifted Bea's wrist as delicately as though it were a nosegay, and if he did not actually kiss her hand, he brought it near enough to his moustached face to deposit his breath on her flesh. "Enchanted," he sighed, a translation for *enchanté,* which Bea long ago had learned in French class was a standard form of greeting, though until now she'd never quite believed anything so preposterous.

All the tables had beautiful salmon-colored tablecloths.

"Have you been here before?" was the first thing Mrs. Olsson asked Bea once Pierre had seated them.

Now this was a funny question. Only on rare and very special occasions did Bea's family go to a fancy restaurant, and never to a place that looked and felt like Pierre's, where the curtains, too, were a beautiful salmon color. But there was something about this afternoon far stranger and more rarefied still: never in her life had Bea visited a truly fancy restaurant with another woman. (Aunt Grace usually took her to Sanders.)

"I think it's my first time," Bea said.

Pierre and Mrs. Olsson conducted an earnest and somewhat befuddling conversation, in which nothing seemed resolved, and yet within moments a waiter placed a glass before Bea, a different sort of glass before Mrs. Olsson. "I ordered you a glass of wine," Mrs. Olsson said. "You needn't drink it. I don't know whether you drink wine."

"Oh yes. Well, sometimes." Bea had already had occasion to clarify this issue for Mrs. Olsson. Indeed, she had drunk a number of glasses of wine in her presence. But Mrs. Olsson didn't always recall what she'd been told.

"I mean at lunch."

"Oh. Oh yes. Well, Sundays. It's—" She paused briefly. "We always have an Italian Sunday dinner."

"How elegant!"

"I suppose."

"I-ta-ly," Mrs. Olsson intoned, and drank deeply from her glass, which held some clear liquid—vodka? It also held ice cubes, which clinked. The pensive look departed her face and her beautiful dark-brown eyes snapped sharply onto Bea's face. "Should you tell me all about you? Or me tell you all about me? We can talk about whatever we wish."

It was another of those veering conversational gambits from Mrs. Olsson, which, though ostensibly meant to open conversation, inhibited it; they had a way—such remarks—of intimidating Bea to near-paralysis. "Tell me about you," Bea murmured. And added, "Please."

"You ever hear of Scarp, North Dakota?"

"No. Well, yes. I mean I hadn't. Until recently. When Ronny mentioned it. And you—you've mentioned it also." Bea took a deep swallow of her wine. It was quite a dark red, and of a thicker flavor than anything ever tasted at home.

"D'you know what its population was?"

"No, I don't," Bea answered truthfully.

"Five hundred and four living souls. You could argue with that, I suppose. Whether they were actually living."

"It was small."

"And *stupid.* You've heard of 'dirt poor.' That's not so bad. But folks in Scarp were dirt dumb. And dumb enough to be *content* to be dirt dumb, which is *really* dumb. I'm no more than six years old, already I know I must leave Scarp, North Dakota. You see, I knew what I wanted. Let me tell you a story. When I first met Charley—Mr. Olsson—I said to myself, I'm going to get that man to *beg* me to marry him, and you know what? I did. He beseeched me. Implored, down on his knees. And when his parents threatened to cut him off without a red cent if we went ahead? I said to myself, I'll get them to come round. And you know what? I did, they came round, after Ronny was born . . . I had three things working for me. Now can you guess what they were?"

"I—" Bea hesitated, sipped her wine. "Please," she said urgently, a word that covered a lot of ground. It meant, Please tell me. It meant, Please don't put me on the spot like this.

"One: I was very pretty. Am I not supposed to say that? Let me tell you something, Bianca, something that may just save you *heaps* of trouble. In this cold world of ours, being pretty counts a great deal, and a girl isn't pretty, she's lost half the battle before it begins, but you know what counts far more? It's knowing you're pretty. Not in any vain, silly-headed way. Take the men in this place. Talking their little deals?" Bea had dimly observed that, although it was a Saturday, Pierre's seemed full of businessmen. Except for a pair of elderly ladies, tucked into a corner, there were no other women here. "Not one of these men hasn't noticed our presence at the best table in this place. Not one isn't yearning to know who we are. Because you're a very pretty one, too, Bianca. You understand, don't you—that you are?"

But there was no meeting such a question. Even if aware of being pretty, how could she possibly admit as much to the most beautiful woman she'd ever actually spoken to? Truly it was remarkable, beauty like this: Mrs. Olsson's ivory skin, the intricate masses of auburn hair, the imposing cheekbones, the flawless nose with its faint but daring uptilt. And those big brown-black eyes in which, at this very moment, whole candlesticks were dancing . . . In addition, Mrs. Olsson possessed a certain nameless intangible something that Bea associated with a few Hollywood actresses: Paulette Goddard, say, or Gene Tierney, or the tragic war victim Carole Lombard—the sort of larger-than-life beauty that could fill a forty-foot screen. This was the sort of woman for whom, in the movies, men slipped into the boxing ring to challenge the champion, or, falsely accused, shuffled innocently but amenably down to the electric chair. Bea sipped her wine, whose taste she was getting used to. "I don't—" she said. "I hope I'm not—"

Mrs. Olsson cut her off. "Two: I don't give a damn what people think of me. Does my language offend you? Surprise you, Bianca? I'd better warn you: I can do much worse. Because I don't give a *damn.* Just that simple. Charley—Mr. Olsson—my talk drives him crazy. He cares what *every*body thinks and he's got the bleeding ulcer to prove it.

"Three: when I know what I want, I go after it. Not ruthlessly. Never underhandedly. I'm not at all what some people say I am. But I am direct. I'm an honest person." Mrs. Olsson had offered her displays of vanity before—you might even say that her entire carriage and demeanor were an ongoing exhibition of vanity. But this was something else: a plea for understanding. For she really did want Bea to comprehend this, anyway: Gretchen Olsson was an honest woman.

The menu was held together by a tasseled gold string. At the bottom of the first page was a quotation from Louis Pasteur: "Wine is the most healthful and most hygienic of all beverages." Mrs. Olsson finished her clinking drink, dabbed her salmon-colored napkin on her lips, and all at once, as if with a screwing-into-place, fixed her eyes on Bea's face: "And what about you? Do you know what you want, my dear? In your heart of hearts, *what is it you want, Bianca?*"

Bea's response was in a sense perfect—a perfect disaster. Her left hand, reaching for her water glass, recoiled at the question, upsetting her not quite empty wineglass, which instantly, to Bea's horror, sent racing toward her on the beautiful salmon-colored tablecloth a shameful blooded irremediable stain. "*Oh!* Oh I'm so hopeless . . ."

Mrs. Olsson handled the whole matter expertly (which perhaps wasn't surprising, since it seemed she was a woman in whose presence people were forever spilling things). She righted the now-empty glass, said calmly, "Don't give it a thought, dear, don't give it a thought," signaled to a waiter, and suggested to Bea, "Perhaps you want to freshen up?" And by the time Bea returned from the ladies', everything was tranquilly arranged as if no mishap had occurred: a new tablecloth, a refilled wineglass before Bea's chair. Mrs. Olsson had a fresh glass in hand.

Even so, Bea felt as though she'd merely substituted one discomfort for another, for she brought a new problem to the table. In the ladies' room, wearing a pink dress much too tight for her, a big Negro woman had been sitting in a chair beside the row of sinks. After Bea washed her hands, the woman extended a linen towel . . . Was Bea supposed to hand her some coin in return? A nickel? A dime? Of course Bea had met ladies' room attendants before, but never in a fancy restaurant—never under circumstances quite like these. In any case, she had no money; in her dazed fluster, she'd actually fled the table without her purse. "Thank you *very* much," Bea had said, but the woman only grunted in reply.

Resettled in her seat, sipping from her new glass of wine, Bea said, "There was a woman in the ladies' who handed me a towel and I would have tipped her but I had no coin and now I'm wondering if I should perhaps go back—"

"Oh for heaven's sake. Sit still, sweetie." Sweetie? "I'll handle it when I next pay a visit."

"Well," Bea said. "I mean, thank you." And added: "For everything."

And Bea felt oddly at ease . . . Her sense of small excruciating problems all ably surmounted left this afternoon's conversation free to blaze a warmer path. They were having an intimate conversation, Bea and Mrs. Charles Olsson. "You have brothers and sisters," Mrs. Olsson said. "Tell me about them"—which she had requested before. And while Mrs. Olsson didn't appear quite attentive as Bea obediently rattled on about Stevie's worrying that the War wouldn't last until his enlistment and Edith's weird talking in her sleep, she nodded politely throughout. And perceiving how the menu intimidated Bea (the dishes sounded so strange, and they were so expensive!), Mrs. Olsson asked, "May I order for you, dear?"

At once Pierre materialized at Mrs. Olsson's shoulder. She said to him, "Didn't the menu used to have a lady's steak?"

Pierre's wire moustache quivered unhappily. "It's the War," he said. "The supplies aren't what they used to be . . ." Yes, the War was going on, as ever, while Bea reposed with Mrs. Olsson in a restaurant decorated in colors Bea had never seen in a restaurant before—going on in that world where Papa had his own shoes resoled and resoled so that his elder daughter might be given the rationing coupon for a new pair . . . Mrs. Olsson did not actually say a word. She didn't need to. She merely nodded, and smiled at Pierre, who swallowed and said cheerfully, "*Mais oui.* Perfect."

The succeeding talk was light and easy, though Mrs. Olsson did confess at one point, "You know, Charley's not happy about Ronny's studying art." (Somewhere in the course of lunch Mrs. Olsson had stopped referring to her husband as Mr. Olsson.) "Not happy at *all.*"

"What would Mr. Olsson prefer that Ronny study?"

"Accounting? Mortuary science?" Mrs. Olsson then added, light-heartedly and quite shockingly, "What's it matter just so long as it's grim as hell?"

But more shocking still was the line of conversation after their lady's steaks arrived, when Bea—returning the favor—again inquired whether Mrs. Olsson had any brothers or sisters.

"I guess I do," Mrs. Olsson replied. "I suppose you could say . . . yes, I have a sister."

"Is she older? Younger? Your sister."

"She stayed in Scarp. Betty Marie. Good-looking girl. Stayed in Scarp to marry a thug. I don't object to Ed's having mud for brains, but his being a ham-fisted thug's something I do find objectionable. I send her money sometimes. Should I not tell you that? Charley gets the heebie-jeebies whenever I mention money. He's afraid of it—now isn't that peculiar? I suppose that's why he's made so much of it. Myself, I'm not afraid of money. Are you, Bianca?"

"I—well, I don't know."

Again, those vast beautiful brown-nearly-black eyes were full on Bea's face. The expression was vaguely menacing—or simply playful? In any event, the pools of Mrs. Olsson's eyes were deep enough for an eighteen-year-old girl to drown in.

"I wasn't afraid to spell it out to my sister. I said, 'Betty Marie, think of me as offering a bounty to a bounty hunter. Paying a dollar a coyote pelt. Or let's say twenty grand the day you put a slug in Eddie's skull.' " And Mrs. Olsson, looking radiant and cheerful, rose from the table. She was off to the ladies' room. She leaned forward, confidingly, within a low cloud of opulent perfume: "Actually, what I said was, 'It's twenty thousand to you the day you toss that ape out on his ear.' But would she? No . . ."

When Mrs. Olsson returned, she said, pleasantly—as if she hadn't just now been joking about her brother-in-law's murder—"D'you have time for coffee, dear?"

And when, after coffee, Bea herself returned to the ladies' room, it seemed Mrs. Olsson indeed had "handled things" with the formidable Negro woman in the overstuffed pink dress. After Bea washed her hands, the woman offered Bea a fresh towel and said, "Bless you, miss. God bless *you*."

CHAPTER XI

Bea sat once more at the foot of Private Donnelly's bed, sketch pad in hand. So much had unfolded during this past week, it was hard to believe she'd first walked up the steps of Ferry Hospital only last Tuesday. She had prayed for Private Donnelly in the interim and he was indeed much improved. His face was less swollen and discolored. The big fresh bandage on the right side of his face was a somewhat reduced bandage. More of his face greeted the light of day.

In the past week, Bea had gone with Ronny on that memorable walk in Palmer Park; she had attended class; she had met Aunt Grace again for lunch, at Hudson's; she had lunched with Mrs. Olsson at Pierre's; she had sat through a scary Sunday afternoon in which Nonno had suffered another emphysema attack and he and Nonna left before dinner was even served; she had briefly met Maggie, who had coined a new nickname, Ma'am Hamm, for her mother-in-law; and she had accompanied Mamma and Stevie on a shopping expedition to buy Stevie new school clothes. (When she'd suggested knickers—he'd always looked so cute in knickers!—Stevie replied, "I haven't worn knickers for *ages*.") Meanwhile, as Bea was racing about, Private Donnelly had presumably done nothing but lie in this narrow bed, awaiting her return.

"You're looking more like yourself," Bea told him. While this was something she might have said anyway, it heartened her to mean it. The curly-headed Irish boy of the high school graduation portrait was being resurrected. Since last seeing him, maybe her memory had exaggerated how worn he'd become? A week ago, she had detected the middle-aged man inside this boy; today, she beheld the boy again, blessedly restored.

It was a little strange, but on the whole quite comforting, just how at home she felt in Private Donnelly's frenzied presence—how familiar seemed his voice, his gestures, all the tireless flirtations nowise impeded by having nearly half his face under wraps. Truly, she might have known him for years.

Today, as a bandage-free face materialized on the paper before her, Bea felt less like a fabricator than she had last week—less like a liar, you might say. She'd done enough pencil sketching: now she started in on charcoal. She was going to move confidently. In freeing his features from the disfiguring sting of flying metal, she was doing the right thing. Her racing left hand told her so.

His face had changed for the better but his tone was precisely the same: appreciative, impudent, indefatigable, funny. When Nurse O'Donnell stepped in at one point, he called out, "Auntie! Auntie, I dreamed of you last night. I dreamed you brought me a big tin of brownies." "Oh you *hush*." "With *pecans* in them, Auntie. Now how on earth did you know I dote on pecans?" "You've been smoking again. I swear it as a solemn vow: I'm going to steal your cigarettes." "And I didn't know you smoked, Auntie. Looky here, you wanna bum a butt off me some time, just say the—" "Oh you *hush*." And the moment Nurse O'Donnell left the room, he stage-whispered, "Why is every nurse I meet built *exactly* like a fire hydrant?"—which made Bea laugh aloud.

Just the same, too, was his way of rapidly saying absolutely nothing, without ever running out of words. "Bea Paradiso, Bea Paradiso," he chanted. "Gee, I'm so glad your name isn't Bea Paradowsky, because Jake Paradowsky was the biggest meatball at Battle Creek Central. Old Central had *lots* of meatballs, but everyone knew old Jake was the biggest, and . . ." And Private Donnelly embarked on a lengthy anecdote, not exactly proper—but quite amusingly recounted—about how four boys ambushed Jake on the way to school, three of them holding him down while the fourth scrawled MEATBALL on his belly in red lipstick. And when Bea protested that Jake Paradowsky certainly hadn't deserved anything so cruel, Private Donnelly rattled off a catalogue of Meatball Paradowsky's offenses and stupidities. Old Jake had got off *easy* . . .

Meanwhile, Bea's left hand flew—so much more confidently this time around. Private Donnelly's right eye, the one she'd never seen, emerged almost as persuasively as the other. She *stared* into his bandage—she was far less squeamish this week—as if, by pure intensity of sight, she might uncover the hidden pupil and iris.

Of course that was the issue—the question so loaded with hazards she couldn't risk directly asking: was the right eye going to recover? Had the whizzing shrapnel left the eyeball itself intact? Or was she memorializing something gone for good?

Bea had prayed for that eye of Private Donnelly's. She'd meant to do so every night, but—such a busy week—she'd forgotten a couple of times. Now she wished she hadn't. By neglecting her prayers, she enhanced the queerness she felt (all her old jittery superstitiousness coming to the fore) as the tip of her charcoal teased out that hidden eye. To draw him like this—was she asking for trouble? Tempting fate? To draw him might somehow make her personally responsible for Private Donnelly's medical state, muddling his recovery by introducing the blood of her own perplexities and shortcomings—blending her fate with his. And yet—yet her hand held steady, she would see it through to full-bloomed creation: the pale ring of the iris, the sparkling pupil. She was moving forward. And she would posit here, brightly, something which that eye just might accommodate once more: a sharp appetite for approval, and a glowing hint of young, good-hearted tomfoolery.

Yes, he looked so much better! When he smoked, which he did repeatedly, the skin around his eyes betrayed no trace of the haggard old man glimpsed last week. Private Donnelly was nearly a boy again— a boy who admittedly had taken a terrible blow, but a boy even yet.

He talked about Battle Creek Central, and his uncle's cherry orchards way up near Traverse Bay, and his Southern grandmother's sweet-potato pie, and the Halloween night when somebody hoisted a pig ("not a piglet, this was a hefty son-of-a-gun") onto the roof of the fire station—pretty much anything except the War that had landed him in this bed, in a room where the late-morning sun, angling through the green floral curtains, highlighted the animation of his bandaged features.

And then, almost in passing, as one more in a series of trifling jokes, Private Donnelly disclosed the revelation Bea had been praying to hear: "So when the doc this morning announces I'd be able to read with both eyes again, I tell him, Hey that's funny, Doc, I never knew how to read before . . ."

Bea's glance leaped up from her drawing. "Your eye's going to be all right, then?"

"What they tell me. I am seeing better out of it. Though it still *looks* like something the cat dragged in."

"I'm so . . ." What Bea longed to do was to take his hand in hers—no, to cradle against her throat Private Michael Donnelly's discolored and oh-so-very-likable face. Oh, the news elated her! It was as if all her silent hoping, all her superstitious half-formed praying had transported the boy across the seas to safety . . . Things would come right for Private Donnelly, just as the black-and-white sketched face had intimated. Everything would come right.

"You must be overjoyed."

"Well, as the old saying goes, it's better than a sharp stick in the eye," Private Donnelly said. "That's a saying says more to me than it used to, let me tell you."

"Are you eager to go back, then?"

"Go back?"

"Well I . . . Well, if your eye's healing, if your face is going to be all right, I'm assuming you'll eventually . . ." Bea's voice trailed off. "Won't they expect you—"

"To go back?"

Something was *quite* wrong inside this room. Private Donnelly pulled hard on his cigarette, exhaling an expansive plume of smoke toward the green-gold curtains. Then he fixed his single eye glitteringly upon his visitor.

"I mean back to your—your unit," Bea said, and now it was unmistakable, in that eye of his, that she'd committed some grave, overreaching error. "You must have friends," Bea continued, vainly scrambling to extricate herself. "Other soldiers. I'll bet you miss them."

"Back there? To the fighting? But I'm never going back," Private Donnelly declared in a new voice, harsh and flat and contentious—a voice without a trace of irony. "How could I?" he asked her.

Even though his body lay under a blanket, Bea had naturally avoided laying her eyes on the male torso and legs in the bed before her. She had kept her gaze trained on Private Donnelly's face. But now her eyes followed the example of Private Donnelly's burning blue eye, coming to a halt where his eye halted.

The lineaments of his lower body were traceable under the blanket. Near the base of the bed, two pointed mounds should have stood—the projecting bumps of his feet—but only one showed. Under his bedding, Private Donnelly's right leg flatly trailed away, into nothingness. Somewhere below the knee, it had been amputated.

CHAPTER XII

It was hardly as if Bea were unaccustomed to the presence of alcohol. Many of her richest, oldest memories concerned her father's winemaking. As a little girl, she'd yearn and yearn for the day when the magic train pulled in from California. Somehow the news had gotten out—this would be the train loaded with the special winemaking grapes—and a couple of dozen hatted men, mostly Italians like Papa, stood waiting for its clanging arrival. Papa would have removed the car's backseat, so he could load up from floor to roof, and Bea would be driven home in a vehicle that held nothing but her father and herself and the wild scent of a million, million grapes.

Papa drank a beaker of wine every night, when he came home from work, and lately—ever since the terrible mess began—he often arrived home already smelling of beer. Although Mamma generally avoided drink—it didn't agree with her—she'd sip a glass of wine at Sunday dinner, the Italian dinner, when Nonno and Nonna came for their weekly visit. Bea herself drank half a glass on Sundays, and sometimes a whole glass. Papa often poured an inch or so of wine into Stevie's water glass, turning the water pink, and would announce, with his handsome smile, "Put hair on the boy's chest," and thump his own chest—all of which never failed to make Stevie blush. Sometimes Papa even poured a few drops of wine into Edith's water glass—a subtle shift of tint fit for a painter's eye—so that every Paradiso partook of the same bottle. Still, for all her experience, Bea didn't initially understand just how much Ronny's parents were consuming.

At the zoo once, Bea had watched a long-legged bird that maybe was a heron swallowing a fish. It was the strangest sight. The bird flipped the fish over its rigid beak eagerly, greedily—but with a jerky wince, as if the very process of self-nourishment were hurtful. That's precisely the way Mr. Olsson drank. He tossed back the liquor as if he craved it, but with a grimace as if it pained him too (possibly it did, given his ulcers).

Mrs. Olsson drank with no evidence of urgency, slowly and almost absentmindedly, and yet a glass was usually at hand. Ronny said, "If maybe Mother drinks too much, I blame it mostly on Dad. He's always working. Always away. And even when he *is* home, he's off in his little gym, punching at things."

In recent days, Ronny's dealings with his father had soured. Ronny seemed much more openly bitter. Bea couldn't fully explain the change, though in her lunch at Pierre's she'd learned that the Institute Midwest was a source of father-son disagreement. Could she herself—the Italian girl Ronny was now dating, the one whose immigrant father worked with his hands—possibly be another source? Bea kept awaiting some signal that her name and background, or her presumed Catholicism, or her family's modest home within the Boulevard—that such things presented an insuperable problem. But she honestly never received such a signal. Within the cavernous tree-shadowed Olsson home, her presence seemed universally appreciated. In their different ways, all of them greeted her so warmly!

Although he could be remote at times, Mr. Olsson showed her especial warmth. He called her *my dear,* and told her how pretty she looked, and even spoke vaguely of someday—"when things calm down somewhat"—sitting for a portrait. ("But you must promise me, my dear, not to make me look *too* old.") Addressing Ronny and Bea, he also made occasional, excruciating references to their "wish to be alone." This was said with not quite a wink but the unignorable intimation of a wink. Into that lynx's face of his—the round cheekbones slanting upward, the bald tan temples slanting downward—a sort of firelight shone.

In such moments, Mr. Olsson unwittingly touched upon another mystery. Ronny had followed up that unforgettable walk in Palmer Park, the one where he'd kissed Bea so voraciously that she all but swooned, where his tongue against her tongue had sent splashy fireworks fountaining along the inner walls of her brain, with another memorable walk, this one on Belle Isle. They sauntered hand in hand out to the lighthouse at the remote eastern edge of the island, and standing beneath it Ronny said, "Wouldn't you think it was the last thing the world needed? An Art Deco lighthouse designed by a man famous for industrial buildings? This is Albert Kahn's work, and isn't it lovely when an architect gets the proportions right? It's one of Detroit's most beautiful buildings." And *he* was right, indeed it *was,* and the thrill of sharing this discovery covered his body in goose bumps and led naturally to another round of kissing, and fireworks again, only with intenser colors—if that were possible. And the very next day a return to Palmer

Park, and colors brighter still. And Riverside Park, and Waterworks Park, and way out to the lovely fields at Cranbrook School (which Ronny said gave him the "jim-jams"; it reminded him of his brief prep school stint at Groton). The two of them would stand in some field or park for long, long minutes that seemed to unroll into hours, bodies so fiercely locked they might have been—one more of Maggie's vivid phrases—feeding off each other's faces. Afterward, Bea had resolved to speak with him. Weren't things proceeding too quickly? Wasn't this a little dangerous?

And yet it seemed Bea didn't need to speak, after all. The walks suddenly halted and Ronny retreated, which was perhaps his way; he seemed prone to intervals of withdrawal. He was feeling "a bit depressed," and Bea didn't know how to answer such a confession. Oh, she was used to foul states of mind—there were Mamma's Dark Spells, and though Papa was far steadier, every so often ominous states overcame him, when everybody knew not to cross him. But never in a million years would you hear him declare, as Ronny matter-of-factly declared, "I'm feeling a bit depressed." It was all new and perplexing—Ronny was so unlike any other boy.

He didn't look like a rebel, at least as rebellion was envisioned at the Institute Midwest. Unlike Hal Holm, Ronny wasn't about to go around in dungarees and a big red beard. Yet a rebel is what Ronny Olsson was . . . His powerful father didn't want him in art school, but he was in art school. Most of the male students at the Institute were fascinated by industrial design, or at least pretended to be, but Ronny judged it "a terrible bore." He listened closely to Professor Manhardt, but only to hone his objections to the famous professor, who could be a "purblind fool." (Bea had literally felt her jaw drop at that one.)

Like his mother, Ronny spoke his mind. And even when his reckless talk was objectionable (and it made Bea very angry indeed when he'd announce that the War was "the latest in a series of wars"), inwardly she thrilled at his nonconformity. Ronny was forever challenging her. It wasn't just his being remarkably smart. It was his gift for making connections, for constantly demonstrating that in his ruminations he'd surveyed *this* place, too, long before you thought to explore it. Over the years Bea had heard a number of professors talk about art, but none could match Ronny when the right sort of painting—say a painting called *In the Studio*, by a Dutchman named Michael Sweerts—stood before him. There wasn't a single professor who could convey the ardor and the vivacity and the tactile reality Ronny conveyed—who could so light-handedly transport you back to the actual physical process, though it lay submerged under whole centuries, of a bristly brush being freshly dip-dip-dipped into a viscous little pool of pigment. ("You're a born teacher," she told him once, and clasped his hand—something she rarely did, having always been advised that boys don't like your taking the initiative. But while Ronny warmed to the unexpected touch— squeezing her hand in reply—he balked at her message. "But Bianca," he replied, "I don't want to teach. I want to *paint*.")

Yes, she had a little cautionary speech assembled, after all those overheated walks in Detroit's principal parks, but when his ardor suddenly cooled, and it grew apparent her speech was temporarily superfluous, it likewise grew apparent that Bea yearned to be kissed again in Ronny's hell-bent swashbuckling way: his gorgeous mouth open, his hips welded to her hips. Ever since those thrilling walks, it was as though he'd grown even more handsome—resembling more and more, with his longish hair and burning gaze, some Romantic poet of a nineteenth-century portrait, the sort of canvas optimally displayed in a gleaming black lacquer frame.

Those cheap words Maggie tossed off so easily—always finding men so *attractive*, always announcing she was so *attracted* to someone— undeniably applied here. Bea was *attracted*, Ronny was *attractive*. The word had come alive in all its various forms: *attractive, attracted, attraction, attractiveness.* Spoken aloud, to herself, the sounds were quite marvelous—the rupturing second syllable mimicking the expansive, ripped-open feeling in her chest. (The mystery of *attraction* ran so deep that even Stevie was touched by it—in his case, magnetic attraction. Did anyone else understand what Bea understood? That it really was all the same phenomenon? For when Stevie magically set iron filings dancing on a sheet of paper, stroked underneath by a horseshoe magnet, the look on his rapt face was spookily recognizable: it was a wooer's lust enflaming his eyes.)

One morning she woke so shamed from a dream of disrobed abandon that she could scarcely face the bathroom mirror. She was supposed to meet Ronny for coffee at Herk's, but she telephoned and canceled, claiming she had a stomachache.

The following night she went with Ronny and his parents out to dinner at "the club"—the Coral Club, overlooking Lake St. Clair. Drinking started early, before they left the house. Although Mrs. Olsson usually handled liquor well, there were various little signs—like the faintest drag on concluding syllables and a slight indignant lurch when settling into the car—that she was, as Mamma would say, a wee bit pickled. And Mr. Olsson, looking ruddier than usual, was more than a wee bit. And Ronny had had a couple of Manhattans before leaving Arden Park.

For a while, dinner passed smoothly enough. Everyone ordered fresh drinks and a glass of red wine was set before Bea. (Wherever the Olsson party descended, the laws of the State of Michigan went into suspension. That Bea was underage meant nothing.) There was the sound of a singer and a piano in the next room—a woman was sighing her way through "I Don't Want to Walk without You"—and Mr. Olsson invited Bea to dance. Mrs. Olsson glanced meaningfully at Ronny, who asked his mother to dance.

Mr. Olsson turned out to be a first-rate dancer—but what else would you expect? The old track star and fraternity president, the only man Bea had ever heard of whose house boasted a gym, piloted her around the floor with unshowy assurance. He held her a little more closely than she initially was comfortable with, but once she settled in, trusting to the firm splayed hand on her back, they whirled with enviable nimbleness. She felt lightheaded, and giddily grateful.

> I don't want to walk without the sunshine;
> Why'd you have to turn off all that sunshine?

Over dinner, the atmosphere progressively chilled, each new conversational lull icier than its predecessor. Things were in no way helped by an improbable announcement from Mrs. Olsson:

"Bianca, did you know that Ronny and his father are planning a trip together? To Grand Rapids?"

"To Grand Rapids?" This was news to Bea. She looked for clarification first to Ronny, whose features went blank, and then to Mr. Olsson. His face, too, closed up.

"Why don't you explain it to the girl, Charley?" Mrs. Olsson offered in a peppy kind of way—the sort of cheeriness that parades its own falsity.

"Well, I have a few stores out there," Mr. Olsson began, after a moment. "Periodically, I go check on them."

"How long does the drive take?" Bea asked. Grand Rapids was way at the other, the western, side of the state. She'd never been over there.

"Depends how you drive," Mr. Olsson replied, again after a pause.

"Charley goes like a bat out of hell," Mrs. Olsson sang, and sipped her drink. She added, sweetly, "I thought it would be nice for father and son to spend some time together."

Another gruesome pause. Tonight it seemed exclusively Bea's job to relieve these. She said, "How long will you be gone?"

"Just overnight," both Mr. Olsson and Ronny answered simultaneously.

"I was at the Olsson's at Seven and Woodward just yesterday," Bea said, purely in order to say something. "I needed some cold cream and—"

Mr. Olsson interrupted: "You were *buying* something at Olsson's! But my dear girl, you mustn't. No, no, no. You just tell me what you need . . . Here." And with that smooth rapidity which his lean, dapper body always seemed to be tensely holding in check (you felt his athleticism in even the simplest acts—the way he drove a car, or flipped a cigarette into an ash can), he plucked from an inner jacket pocket a little notepad and a pencil. "Here. You just make up a list. I'll have the girl take care of it in the morning. You just make me up a little list right now." As Bea stared, paralyzed, at the blank notepad, Mr. Olsson added, "Cold cream, brushes, tooth powder, cosmetics, Mrs. Olsson gets all her things at Olsson's."

And Mrs. Olsson observed, testily, "Charley, I don't get my cosmetics at Olsson's."

"Go ahead, give me a *list.*" Sometimes, in his pell-mell enthusiasms, Mr. Olsson truly could seem boyish—younger than his son, who, with his qualifying, dicing love of nuances, sometimes seemed never to have lived a boyish day.

The pencil hovered in Bea's hand, stalled. Three Olssons trained their eyes on her. This was so intensely awkward! And then a mischievous, fiendish thought arrived . . . What if she were the sort of girl who would deliberately shock and appall them all? What if she were to name one or two of the most personal things to be bought at Olsson's?

"Hairbrush." Bea wrote in a somewhat larger hand than usual, so all might read. She looked up triumphantly.

"Go on, you gotta make a *list.*"

"Noxzema," Bea wrote and added, in a needless parenthesis: "Face Cleanser."

"Go on."

Bea racked her brain. All those gaudily bright, crowded aisles of entrancing merchandise . . . What did she want? What did she need? She came up with a linked trio of items and wrote eagerly, "Small Scissors, Nail Clippers, Emery Boards." Before Mr. Olsson could urge her further, she passed him the notepad and the pencil and said, "I'm ever so grateful."

A bottle of red wine arrived, and in a couple of swallows Mr. Olsson re-created his winning imitation of a heron flipping a fish across its bill. He set the empty glass down perhaps more loudly than intended and ran a hand tightly over his narrow balding skull. Some sense of calm at last descended over the group.

After dinner, at Mrs. Olsson's suggestion, Ronny asked Bea to dance. The song was "Ev'ry Time We Say Goodbye." He appeared a little morose; he had been shuttered up all evening. "So you're going to Grand Rapids!" Bea said in a cheery voice that—she recognized—parroted his mother's. "I've never been."

"Can you imagine anything worse?"

"It's supposed to be a pretty town . . ."

"I'm not talking about *Grand Rapids*." Ronny's body felt distant. He could be quite a good dancer (though he lacked his father's broad, audacious sweep), but tonight he seemed listless. "You know what I'm saying, Bianca—so why do you sometimes pretend you don't? Why would you want people thinking you understand *less* than you do?"

It was one of those questions that made her so nervous, and made her so thankful for Ronny's company—those powerful, probing questions that jostled her into untested lines of contemplation. He had a marvelously keen eye for veiled hypocrisies. She said, "It isn't immediately clear—"

"I mean riding with *him*. For hours and hours. Battle Creek. Jackson. Kalamazoo. From one Olsson's to the next. There where you need us there."

"It's a nice slogan."

"Slogans . . ." Ronny sighed, and then he said, "Bianca, y'ever think you'd like to get far away from here?"

Far away from here? Whatever did he mean?

Still, at least he was opening his mouth, and Bea said, encouragingly, "I've always wanted to go to Chicago. It's supposed to be ever so wonderful."

"I don't mean *Chicago*, and what is it you're pretending now? I mean *far*. Has it ever occurred to you that maybe you and I could draw the way God meant us to draw, paint the way He meant us to paint, if only we could get away *far*?"

You and I? But what was Ronny saying?

"Just picture it," he went on, "if we went to the Pacific, like Gauguin." And then he added, typically, "Not that I admire his paintings so much." And added, yet more typically, "Though you'd have to say the exotic travel freed whatever talent he had . . ."

"The Pacific?" Bea said. Ronny sometimes treated her so impatiently when she failed to understand him, but wasn't it obvious that in numerous ways he didn't understand himself? "Ronny, Ronny, they're fighting a war out there in Gauguin's Pacific. Those beaches have land mines." And this, too, was one of his fascinations for her: was there another young man in all of Detroit who could, however briefly, overlook the screaming fact of the greatest war in history?

Even so, even if the weight of human civilization endorsed her, Bea had managed to say precisely the wrong thing. She could feel it almost physically: enthusiasm draining from Ronny's body, his heart withdrawing . . .

> There's no love song finer,
> But how strange the change from major to minor,
> Ev'ry time we say goodbye.

When Ronny led her back to the table, Mr. and Mrs. Olsson were having what could only be described as an argument, on the subject, unfortunately, of courage. "Charley, it's simpler than that. The truth about them? They're just *afraid.*" This *them* of Mrs. Olsson's encompassed—so the swing of her hand suggested—all the members of the Coral Club. "Afraid what people think."

"Maybe it isn't fear," Mr. Olsson countered. "Maybe it's something we might call simple politeness. Or quiet decency. You follow me? Respect for certain civilities and time-tested codes of behavior which—"

"Honestly, you can't *smell* it, Charley?" Mrs. Olsson answered her own question: "No-o, course you can't. Fear's got a smell, and like any other smell I suppose after while you get used to it. You honestly can't smell the cowardice in here?"

Mr. Olsson again asked Bea to dance, which seemed an excellent idea. She rose eagerly.

More than ever, she felt sorry for Mr. Olsson, though Bea could never actually confide this to anyone, it sounded so smug and silly . . . An eighteen-year-old girl art student pitying one of Detroit's most successful men? Yet sorry for him was precisely what Bea felt—he was always working so hard, while facing such mutinous opposition at home.

She appreciated the way Mr. Olsson initiated a dance: he sort of drifted you into it, as though dancing required no more thought than walking. They revolved around the floor. Bea very much wished Ronny would try harder to see things from his father's point of view, and she wondered again: was there some way to draw the two of them closer? She wished she had something to give Mr. Olsson. What would he like? What would make him happy? Some bolstering word? Some earnest confession of respect and sympathy? But of course she had nothing to give Mr. Olsson.

A new song began, "Skylark," and she was not at all prepared for the quick tightening urgency of Mr. Olsson's embrace. This might appear—Bea feared—inappropriate. It certainly felt inappropriate: to have their (from a practicing artist's point of view) different-aged bodies pressed so tightly that she could feel her breasts flatten against his chest. Bea tried to pull back, but Mr. Olsson's hold on her, however graceful, was unbudging. "Miss Paradiso, you are so tactful," Mr. Olsson said. Tactful?

"And what an extraordinary name to parade through life with: Miss Bi-an-ca Par-a-di-so." Mr. Olsson's voice, too, was a bit of a mystery, dreamy and purry and seemingly at odds with his vivid physical presence. She did find herself wishing the Olsson family were easier to decipher—though perhaps the Paradisos might appear, to the eyes of an outsider, equally unfathomable . . .

"My father calls me Bia."

"Be a?"

"The first part of my name."

"Oh," Mr. Olsson said. "Right. Your father." After a pause he said, "Works for O'Reilly and Fein, right? They have a good reputation."

"I told him you said that. He was very pleased."

"You told him I said that?" This seemed to quicken Mr. Olsson's interest. "What else did you tell him about me?"

On the one hand, it was odd having this conversation while dancing so close, with Mr. Olsson's thin-lipped mouth lodged right beside her ear. On the other hand, it wasn't odd at all.

"I don't know. I told him you have a gym in your house. After all, Papa's a builder."

"Always looking for a little extra work, I suppose?"

"He has more than he can handle," Bea replied truthfully, and proudly. "You know how it is—the city's booming."

"And will go on booming long after the guns stop," Mr. Olsson said. "Once they start making cars again, all hell's gonna break loose in this town." His voice, especially when uttering the profanity, quivered with excitement; this was a *hell* he was looking forward to. "That's when the real businessman's war will begin."

"I thought the city might slow down," Bea said.

"Slow down?" Mr. Olsson laughed. "My dear little girl, nothing's going to slow down. Ever again. It's a new world. Faster and wilder. Faster and wilder," he chanted, and Bea's head went spinning, off toward a *new world,* and then in a softer voice Mr. Olsson said: "I think courage comes in a hundred different forms."

And what in heaven's name did he mean by *that*?

And when the music stopped, with a final climbing phrase ("Won't you lead me there?"), Mr. Olsson uttered the strangest words of all. He held her even yet, seizing her upper arms, and stared frankly, full-heartedly into her eyes with that queer, arresting face of his—at times a lynx, at times a heron. "You must understand, Bianca, I am not what I seem," he told her. His powerful thumbs pressed into the flesh of her arms.

"No?" Bea said. She could say nothing else.

"Me? I'm searching for purity," Mr. Olsson said.

The agile dancing, and this impenetrable parting declaration, and the lingering print of his thumbs on her upper arms—they all worked to ensure on her return to the table that Bea scarcely heard Mrs. Olsson, who was still expounding on courage and cowardice. No, it took the sound of impermissible words—harsh as a slap to the face—to summon Bea fully: "Kikes," Mrs. Olsson said, distinctly. "Niggers. I'm not afraid of them."

"Gretchen."

"I'm not afraid of the words, itsy-bitsy words, and why am I not afraid? Let me tell you why. It's because I'm not afraid of the people behind the words. Gretchen Olsson is not scared of the Jews. I'm one of the few people in this room who would let them into this club. You know that, Charley. God, it's pathetic. Albert Kahn designs the DAC and they make it clear they don't want him as a member?"

"Did you know he also designed the lighthouse at Belle Isle?" Bea interposed. "Gretchen. It's time to go home," Mr. Olsson said.

"They're all running scared in here. Running scared of people like

Max Fisher and the Bormans, because they're looking to build houses nearly as big as Henry Ford's. The folks in here? They're all afraid they've lost the keys to the bank. D'you honestly not feel the fear in here, Charley? Or is it you're scared, too, Charley—of little two-bit operations like Saperstein's Drugs?"

"That's more than enough. More than enough, Gretchen."

"Charley thinks I'm letting down the team, buying my clothes from the Jews down on Livernois, rather than out in Grosse Pointe where they may know how to dress a horse but certainly not a woman. I say to him, It's a question of justice. I don't want clothes doing me an in*jus*tice. I say, Charley, it's either Livernois or New York."

Ronny inserted himself into the conversation: "Bianca has never been to New York."

Mr. Olsson immediately picked it up: "We must all go to New York. Soon's I get a little time. Gretchen, you'll take Bianca shopping."

But Mrs. Olsson was not about to be diverted from her firm enumeration of principles: "*And* the colored. Jesus, everyone in here, scared to *death*. Of that big black river, big as the Mississippi only it's flowing *north,* from New Orleans to Dee-troit, one godforsaken jalopy after another. The people in here think the lights are going out, the whole damn city turning black as night, but I'm not scared, Charley, and you know why? Because the colored recognize they have a friend in Gretchen Olsson."

"You want to know something, Gretchen?" Mr. Olsson had stood up in order to lean on the table—toward her, over her. Mrs. Olsson did not look cowed. She glared straight back. It was a frozen moment, a tableau right out of a painting. (Later, in her bed that night, Bea would recognize it for a queer sort of painters' allegory: a Contest Between Strength and Beauty.) Mr. Olsson was swaying, obviously ransacking his wits for a suitably ample denunciation. Only now did Bea realize just how much he, like his wife, had drunk tonight.

When Mr. Olsson's utterance arrived, it was unmistakably an anticlimax: "Gretchen, you have, you—you went and really outdid yourself this evening." He tossed his chin, dismissing her, and glanced contemptuously around the room.

Another silence. Then Mrs. Olsson said, "You're not scared of the word 'Wop,' are you, Bianca?" Her dark eyes looked a little bleary, as though peering through fogged glass.

"Scared?" Bea said.

"*Gretchen,*" Mr. Olsson said.

And another voice reentered the fray: "*Mother . . .*"

But with something like self-righteousness—a notion that she would be not only absolved but wholly vindicated if only, if only permitted to have her say—Mrs. Olsson carried on: "Because you know what, Bea? *I don't care.* Dago, Wop, I don't care if your family's hairy as monkeys and reeks of garlic. Doesn't smell as bad as the smell of fear. And I don't care that you're Cat-lick, as we used to say in Scarp, North Dakota. You can pray to the Patron Saint of Lost Handbags, or Laddered Stockings, for all I care . . ."

"Actually, my family's religion—"

"*I don't care,*" Mrs. Olsson repeated, which she clearly meant nobly, though it came off brusquely.

Mr. Olsson had come around the table and placed his hand upon his wife's arm. The imperious way she stared down at that hand was frightening. For just a moment, Bea feared (a horrible fear) that Mrs. Olsson would slap it away. But then the woman rose to her feet, with all her stylistic aplomb, although she had one more remark, or pair of remarks, to bestow. She said to Bea, almost sweetly, "You really are green as grass, aren't you, Bianca?" And added, solicitously, "Oh Christ, Bea, do yourself a favor and never learn a goddamn thing."

Ronny flanked his mother on the other side. Bea took a last sweeping look around the table. In front of Mr. Olsson's coffee cup she saw her list, dutiful and forlorn:

Hairbrush
Noxzema (Face Cream)
Little Scissors
Nail Clippers
Emery Boards

Hardly a word was spoken on the return drive. A soundless rain was falling.

When they reached the Olssons', Ronny disappeared. Mr. Olsson, too, disappeared. Mrs. Olsson sat in her music room, Bea at her side. "We shall have a cup of tea," she announced. She seemed subdued, possibly chastened. She looked smudged, even in this dim light. Bea was aware of rain falling, though she could not see it or hear it.

Bea talked about Professor Manhardt, and Ronny's extraordinary gift for draftsmanship. She felt vaguely complicit in the night's many mortifications. But what ought she to have done differently? Hadn't she herself been blameless?

And Mrs. Olsson looked so *very* tired . . .

Then, rousing herself, Mrs. Olsson interrupted eagerly: "D'you hear that sound?"

"What sound?"

Yes, there it was—like a distant drumming, deep within the bowels of the house.

"Know what that is?" Mrs. Olsson asked, and something about her quickened tone, and the self-satisfied way she canted forward, was disquieting.

"No-o."

"That's Charley? See? D'you see?"

"I'm not sure—"

"Gone down to his gym. And you know what he's doing? Punching his punching bag. And—don't you know?—wishing the whole time it was me. Not that he would ever *dare* lay a finger on me." It was a rain of blows—another sort of rain. With absolutely queenly repose, Mrs. Olsson leaned back in her chair. "But we all can dream, can't we? I mean, it makes you almost feel sorry for old Charley, doesn't it, Bianca? All those forbidden fruits. Things the man wants so desperately—and can never have."

CHAPTER XIII

It was striking just how quickly a new routine established itself. Her portraits were deemed a success, apparently, although nobody in authority said so outright. But Bea's field of operations was steadily expanded. First she was asked to shift from one day to two days a week at Ferry, then she was assigned as well to the USO canteen downtown, in the Hammond Building, where she did *many* portraits. She was much quicker now in moving from pencil to charcoal, but this was still the method—her artistic method as a portraitist. Emotionally, too, her work was easier, because her subjects were largely fresh recruits. They hadn't been wounded, they hadn't turned "a little funny" under the distant unimaginable terrors of world warfare.

But in another way the USO was a harder place to work. These boys seemed even younger than the boys at Ferry: teenagers, like her, and so touchingly innocent! Though just a girl, she had a better sense of what awaited them than they did. Most had never seen anything like the interior of Ferry Hospital.

And the War straggled on. Two years for the Americans; four years now, moving into five, for most of Europe . . . In four more years (could the War possibly drag on another four years?) Stevie's friends, those little boys who dispatched Germans in the alley, might actually be drafted. (In her prayers, though it made her feel funny to do so, she'd sometimes thank God for giving Stevie the myopia that ought to keep him out of harm's way.)

Just how long the War had been dragging on grew clear when old Mrs. McNamee down the street passed away. She was eighty-seven. Edith was asked to help sort out the salvage and Bea came along. (Of course Edith saw nothing peculiar in an arrangement where her big sister trailed along as assistant.) One of the things Mrs. McNamee left behind was a scrapbook of war clippings. Her only grandson was in the Coast Guard and poor Mrs. McNamee had saved only optimistic articles. The earliest headlines, from way back last year, recalled an optimism painful to contemplate: JAPS ADMIT MORALE IS LOW, GERMAN

DESERTIONS CLIMBING, BIG DOUBLE AXIS DEFEAT, NAZI OFFENSE CRUMBLING. Since nobody else wanted it, Bea had brought the scrapbook home. Somehow she couldn't bear to see so much lovingly husbanded naïveté thrown away.

Meanwhile, the hospital's castellated outlines continued to haunt her, looming through the twilight of her dreams, though Bea had a proud, adaptive sense of handling the place. Nurse O'Donnell's air of impregnable disapproval had relented to the extent of a nod in reply to a spoken greeting. Bea would arrive every Tuesday and Thursday at ten and remain until noon. Working quickly, she could finish one soldier portrait, possibly two. (She was no sidewalk artist, knocking off commissions in twenty minutes.)

She'd come to understand that Ferry was like the hub to a wheel. Soldiers arrived and were spun out along the various spokes—home to rest, maybe, or out to the front, if the healing was mostly complete, or, in the saddest cases, out to another hospital or a mental home. The unsettling thing about those who had "turned funny" was how numerous they seemed—not what you'd suspect if you knew the War only through newspapers and newsreels. And still more unsettling: you couldn't always initially identify them.

Bea learned with time not to be surprised, or terribly upset, when a familiar face abruptly vanished. On the day, early on, when she decided to check on Private Donnelly and his bandaged eye, and learned he'd been transferred to another hospital, she'd experienced a surging desperation. She'd immediately felt near tears. Oh, she must *find* him— must write him, visit him! The two of them had shared something significant—a swift but cherished friendship—and she couldn't allow all their amusing, sweet, poignant banter simply to vanish . . . But as the weeks went by, it grew clearer that such vanishings were precisely what the War was all about. Boys were forever being shipped from Point A to Point B. You crossed their paths once, maybe, before they caromed off in unforeseen directions. You met a soldier who knew exactly how to make you laugh—though he had a face peppered with shrapnel and a recently amputated leg—and then he was carted elsewhere, to make some other girl laugh, and in his bunk you encountered a new body, a soldier with a new disability and a new story.

. . . Or one May afternoon you encountered a handsome, blue-eyed soldier on crutches who laboriously boarded a Woodward Avenue streetcar and then insisted on giving up his seat for you, and you exchanged a few glances that etched your soul—and this was the whole of it: the War in essence. You go home that night and throw yourself on your bed and weep with the piercing knowledge that you hadn't properly thanked the one boy meant to be your true love . . . Oh, it made her laugh now! Only a few months ago, that particular incident, but it seemed so much longer! (She'd done so much growing up in the meantime.) She'd learned she must let them go, as they let her go—all those wounded boys, hobbling toward undisclosed destinations. It was one of the things people meant when they spoke of the War *coming home.*

And the hospital also taught her just how devastatingly attractive she could be. Oh, she was quite a pretty girl at the USO canteen downtown, but at Ferry, in the hospital of her own birth, whose hideous green walls eighteen years later housed such wartime despair and desperation, she was an irresistible creature. After a while, there was no *not* seeing it.

A *pretty girl* was customarily how Bea referred to herself to herself—sensing in anything more boastful an invitation to the worst sort of unhealthy and obnoxious vanity. But any *pretty girl* couldn't spend too many afternoons at Ferry without seeing that in the eyes of the wounded and the "funny" she was absolutely the best thing to come along in a *very* long while. Here were big strong men—or men big and strong until recently—unable to recite their names without a shy schoolkid's stammer or a tremor of their powerful, hairy hands.

Some of them she thought of as boys, and some as men, but most were boy-men, something in between . . . They were alike, anyway, in the awakened looks she kindled in their faces: such lit-up, keen, nakedly beseeching looks. One glimpse was often all it took. In truth, it made Bea uneasy, it felt dangerous—to wield *this* much power over strangers. It made her feel exultant and grateful and excited, and also shamefully unworthy. Some of the boys, particularly the farm boys, seemed little older than Stevie, and yet they'd been shipped overseas, sick and scared and lost, to confront horrors outside all her experience. But—but on their return from a hell on earth, they immediately ceded all power and authority to a girl who'd never left Detroit, really. (One of these farm boys, out of the blue, began gently crying as she sketched him. Thinking he soon must stop, Bea halted and took his hand—she didn't know what else to do—but he went on weeping, uninsistently but unquenchably. Her own all-too-frequent tears usually followed a progression, with predictable shiftings of intensity and volume. But this was steady as a leaky faucet. And when at last he spoke, at first she couldn't make him out.

Poor lost soul, he was chanting, over and over, "No one . . . no one . . . no one . . .")

They were transported thousands of miles only to be shipped back thousands of miles, humbled and shaken, jittery eyes pleading for a pretty girl's approving glance, the bright bonus of a smile. Purely by virtue of being who she was, Bea possessed the means to comfort, perhaps even to restore them to themselves. For that's what (so she came to realize, beginning with Private Donnelly) her mission must be: to give them back their carefree boyish prewar faces.

She frequently recalled one of Mrs. Olsson's observations: what counts for more than being pretty is *knowing* you're pretty. Well, Bea knew it. Her job at Ferry seemed designed to impart this knowledge— a situation tailor-made to make the boys fall head over heels. The Army goes and plucks some boy from his family's sugar-beet farm outside Kalamazoo and he doesn't talk to a girl for weeks on end, before he's shipped off to North Africa, where he contracts dysentery and a grenade fragment explodes into his solar plexus . . . Then you ship him back home to Michigan, to the Ferry Hospital, where one day a pretty girl in a blue-and-yellow-plaid skirt and a white cardigan appears and asks if he'd like his portrait drawn. She says, in effect, *Soldier, let me capture your essence on a sheet of paper* . . . Oh, he's half in love before her long-fingered hand has recorded a single hair on his head!

Ever since she was a girl Bea had loved to draw portraits, but at Ferry something new entered the process: a quickened command. This had little to do with how well any individual portrait turned out. It had everything to do with just how vulnerable these boys were—how invested in the business of being drawn. They stared up at her—the artist—with such hopeful and anxious faces . . .

Bea hadn't been visiting Ferry for much more than a month before she infuriated Maggie no end by receiving two earnest marriage proposals. Bea learned to shrug off, with a pert but effective graciousness, even the most preposterous compliments: she was a homecoming queen, a potential Hollywood starlet, the world's most beautiful woman. But she felt a little discombobulated when one clammy-looking Polish kid from Hamtramck stared up out of a distant fever to identify her— the tall dark-haired apparition at his bedside—as the Madonna herself.

When she talked about Ferry Hospital with Maggie, it all sounded charming, or wonderfully flattering, but Ferry was far, far more poignant than charming or flattering. Whenever she thought of the place, particularly while lying in bed, an immovable ache would invade her throat, and on came all the old nightly jitters . . . It was the same ache she experienced on stepping inside the hospital, for she never walked those grim corridors without feeling close to tears.

The boys were constantly wanting to give her something. They couldn't bear to see her depart without placing in her hands a return token—some repayment for the gift of the portrait. At first, she steadfastly refused even the littlest trifle. It seemed improper to accept anything from somebody who had already sacrificed so much for her, and for her country. But Bea soon saw such scruples as overly rigid— ultimately ungenerous. It *pleased* the boys so, to place something in her artist's hands, even if the gift had little material value in the world's eyes: a nickel Sky bar, a pack of Wrigley's Juicy Fruit, a postcard of the Federal Building in San Francisco, a blurry photograph of two boys atop a water tower somewhere in South Dakota, a not-quite-functional kaleidoscope, an actually rather lovely little wooden case in blond wood, which "might be big enough to hold cigarettes," with a Chinese junk and a row of distant conical mountains inlaid in darker wood. Still, she wasn't prepared for the soldier who presented her with a poem he had composed himself.

Henry Vanden Akker had grown up in Pleasant Ridge, out Woodward Avenue, just a couple of miles north of the Detroit city line. Henry's family belonged to the Dutch Reformed Church. He had a very Dutch face. He resembled Vincent van Gogh, or so Bea told him— which wasn't quite true, although Henry did have van Gogh's reddish hair and wild, naked-looking eyes. (Bea was qualified to make such judgments, having spent so much disciple's time before the van Gogh self-portrait at the DIA—the first van Gogh purchased by any museum in the country.)

In actuality, though, for all her badinage, Bea hadn't wandered so far from the truth: for the more she saw of Henry (and she seemed fated to see a fair bit of him), the more he plausibly might have been Vincent's cousin or even brother. Henry had a high forehead—it was possible that, at the age of twenty-two, his red hair was already retreating. His skin was fair. His ears were pink and large.

Bea's only previous exposure to the Dutch Reformed Church had come from the Slopsemas, up Inquiry toward Kercheval—those two impeccable sisters who looked down their pointy Dutch noses at the not always impeccable Paradisos, whose elder daughter was forever being fetched by different boys in different cars, and whose only son had turned Inquiry's alley into a battlefield. (Did they realize, those two dour women, those indefatigable adversaries of dirt and disorder, who—spring, summer, fall—scrubbed their sidewalk every morning, how much delight they brought the neighborhood merely by having a name that began with *Slop*?) Bea had always maintained a wary distance from the Slopsemas.

Evidently, Henry Vanden Akker's family was likewise strict and censorious. They didn't go to the movies, or drink alcohol, or dance. Henry had once spotted his father, alone on a park bench, smoking a cigarette, but the man had looked "absolutely stricken." Furthermore, that was "many years ago," and there was no indication he still succumbed to tobacco . . .

Something changed in the jungle.

This was the phrase that kept surfacing in Henry's talk: *something changed* . . . He was extraordinarily intelligent—he had graduated summa cum laude in mathematics from Calvin College, in Grand Rapids, while still only twenty—and Bea, in studying his lean face, the lovely red hair and pale blue naked eyes, the rust-colored eyebrows and surprisingly red lips, could feel just how intensely he was analyzing, and struggling to understand, this *something* that *changed* for him *in the jungle*.

"It was not a crisis of faith," Henry explained in his careful, distinction-carving way. "I never doubted the reality of God. Or the possibility of divine grace. The truth is, it was more a crisis of outlook—or perhaps a recognition that my previous outlook on the world was inadequate to my radically new situation. I had devoted myself heretofore to mathematics, but now it seemed I must read more widely . . ."

Well, Bea was secretly but potently drawn to any young man who could use a word like *heretofore* unself-consciously: where else was she to locate somebody who might understand her own complicated hunger to draw and paint—all her indefinable hungers? Though Maggie always teased her about her "overflowery vocabulary" (an unvarying phrase—Maggie's own vocabulary, though inventively slangy, was narrow), Bea had a sense of needing every word at her disposal if she were ever to voice even half of the best, oftentimes peculiar, thoughts inside her. And it turned out that Bea had never met anyone, not even Ronny, who read with Henry's speed and intensity and endurance. He had a serious back injury in addition to having contracted a brutal case of malaria out in the

Pacific. ("The truth is, those fevers were amazing. To say nothing of the chills. I must have come very close to dying," he told her in a tone of scientific dispassion. "Can you have fevers like that without lying at death's door? I think not." And were those fevers the *something* that *changed* in the jungle?)

Henry was rapidly consuming the Harvard Classics, having made his way through more than two feet of its "five-foot shelf of books" while chronicling his reading in a series of notebooks. And he was devouring novels by more recent writers whose names Bea loosely associated with those modern painters—Picasso, Matisse, Braque—about whose work she could never fix how she felt. Henry was reading Thomas Mann and Franz Kafka, James Joyce and Knut Hamsun. And he was reading—with enough marginal annotations to create a sort of book-within-a-book—*Fear and Trembling* by Søren Kierkegaard.

"Have you read it?" he asked her.

"Me? No, I'm not really in a regular college. I'm an art student."

"I'm not really in a regular college either. I'm in the U.S. Army."

Henry was fond of clever little reversals of this sort, which evidently tickled the mathematician in him, and since math had always been Bea's one tiny academic vulnerability, this side of him held a special appeal. Presumably, Henry discerned something whose existence she credited more through faith than experience: the exquisite, ethereal beauty of numbers. Beauty, as Ronny liked to point out, was haunting by its very nature. But more haunting still—Bea had come to see—was this notion of a beauty suspected but not quite uncovered. When one of Rubens's sumptuous, sausage-plump nudes failed to stir her, was it the painter's shortcoming—or hers? Had she seen what was displayed on the canvas, and gone beyond it? Or not yet trained herself to assimilate its hidden all-in-all?

Many details of Henry's life were learned a little later—after a few weeks' acquaintance. When she first met him, in Ferry Hospital, it was a grim Thursday in September, and the light was murky and indistinct—as was the pencil portrait she attempted. She didn't dare move to charcoal with Henry. Her drawing failed specifically to capture the fervency of his gaze, while failing generally to fulfill the injunction about cheerful likenesses. (It was difficult, she saw right away, to produce any cheerful portrait of Henry Vanden Akker. Intense, intelligent, soulful, spirited—these she could "do" for him. But *cheerful* she couldn't do.)

While she drew, Henry discoursed, slowly but unstoppably. His words were so fascinating, she could hardly focus on her paper, which partially accounted for the disappointing result.

He told her about his back injury. "For a while, I was semi-paralyzed. The doctors weren't sure I'd walk again. Perhaps I should be ashamed. I simply fell. On a steep little hill in the Solomons, in the New Georgia Islands. Most of the soldiers here are here because of actual wounds. Enemy fire. Me? I slipped and fell."

"It must have been very slippery."

"And of course it's *embarrassing*—a back injury. Nobody believes you. They think you must be goldbricking—shirking. *Ooh my aching back . . .*"

"But the doctors believed you."

"Frankly, I'm not sure all of them did."

"Maybe you weren't feeling well. And that's why you fell." Bea had a sudden inspiration. "Maybe you were dizzy because you were feverish."

"That does seem more than likely."

Nobody she'd ever met before had seemed so capable of viewing himself disinterestedly—as though discussing some separate person. "The truth is, most of the time, I was feverish. That's what makes it so difficult to reconstruct—exactly what happened."

With most soldiers, it scarcely mattered whether her portraits were any good. Beguiled by the mere process of being drawn, they marveled at the rawest resemblance and weren't about to inquire whether Bea had captured vestiges of the soul within. But when she said, apologetically, "I'm afraid it's not a very good likeness," Henry Vanden Akker agreed—though he did append, politely, "I must be a very difficult subject."

"Oh but you're not," Bea protested. "It's all to do with me."

"I don't look like myself, for one thing. I'm eighteen pounds lighter than a year ago." It's true he was *very* thin. "Though saying I don't look like myself is to posit one essential me, and that's precisely the issue, isn't it? The existence of an essential self among multitudes of selves?" His fervid eyes ransacked her face. "Am I making *any* sense?"

"Oh yes." The words leaped from her throat. Bea added, after a pause: "Sort of." And then: "I want to come back and draw you on Tuesday, assuming you'll still be here."

"As far as I know. Among other things, they want to analyze my digestive system, which has become very fussy. It refuses to process many things it once processed. Apparently, I've become a figure of great medical interest." It was surely an unenviable distinction, but Henry looked almost pleased to be the possessor of an unusually fussy digestive system. Not for him conventional food, any more than conventional thinking. "But perhaps I'll be gone." He—Henry—paused, and a new tone, shadowed by a stammer, entered his voice: "But since they may m-m-move me, I would ask for your address now. Provided that's acceptable to you."

Whenever other soldiers had sought her address or telephone number, Bea had managed to sidestep them, but it never occurred to her to refuse Henry's stiffly worded and very adult request. To do so would have seemed disrespectful.

Two days later, on Saturday, an envelope arrived so overloaded it had required six cents in postage. Who was it from? The neat return address told her: H. Vanden Akker. Its length—six dense handwritten pages—sparked immediate misgivings. Surely he was pushing things too fast?

But its actual contents stirred misgivings of another variety . . . Dreading an extravagant mash note, Bea was nonetheless chagrined to find Henry's letter mostly devoted to meditations on Kierkegaard, with a few "random aphorisms" thrown in for good measure.

Random aphorisms? How was she supposed to respond to random aphorisms inspired by some Dutch writer (or was he Danish?) whose name she consciously mumbled, lest her pronunciation be corrected? (Why was there a line through the "o" in his first name?)

Misgivings of a third sort were roused on Monday by a new letter, only one page long. "I'm not a poet," it began, "and I won't pretend to be, but I recently wrote what I suppose might be called a poem. By way of exchange, how about an indifferent poem for an indifferent portrait?" (Was Henry being condescending? Or was he actually showing her respect—figuring she would "savvy," as Maggie would say? So many of Henry's remarks required serious consideration.)

But it wasn't a bad poem, was it? No, whatever it was, Bea felt certain it was far from bad. It was singular, it was *interesting*. Bea lay in bed, the poem held up waveringly overhead. Although she soon had it by heart, she kept reading from the author's own comely hand—an angular, mathematical combination of printing and cursive:

> The life I used to think of as my life
> Was someone else's life.
>
> The lad I once considered my best friend
> Has found another friend.

The girl I used to covet as a wife
Is someone else's wife.

One day it seemed my life had reached its end.
But that was not the end.

Now who was the "lad"? Some actual boyhood friend—or was this what was called poetic license? And more to the point, who was the girl? (Did Henry's past contain violent heartbreak? Bea could well believe it.) And when had his life seemed finished—when he fell on the jungle hillside and nearly paralyzed himself? More to the point, more to the point, when and why had his life recommenced?

CHAPTER XIV

Sometimes, ever so obliquely, Ronny seemed to be proposing marriage, but if so, this was a union grounded in assumptions Bea scarcely recognized. True, he didn't again suggest retreating to some Pacific island (though she still regretted her snippy reply—"Ronny, they're fighting a war out there"). But flight was the common motif of his far-flung hypotheticals: "What if we went away to the north shore of Lake Superior?" Or: "They say the light's beautiful in the Mexican highlands." Or: "Just because there's never been a good painting of the Grand Canyon doesn't mean there couldn't be." This was unmistakably something other than a pretty game of Let's Pretend. Ronny's desire and needfulness were palpable. With all his heart, Ronny Olsson yearned for the one elusive sanctuary where, side by side with his heaven-appointed partner, he might finally paint the pictures he was intended to paint.

In truth, the shortcomings in his art were inexplicable. No other student in Professor Manhardt's class matched Ronny's knowledge of the history of painting, or had seen and assimilated so much art. And no one approached his draftsmanship. And yet—when Bea stood with Ronny before one of his sketches or paintings, she had to accede to his gloomy self-assessment: "Something's missing."

Something was likewise missing, it seemed, in her romance with Ronny, though to confess this even to herself made her feel impossibly spoiled. He could hardly have been handsomer. Or more intelligent. And whatever word might best describe this whole indelicate business, the private truth was that his body wielded a brazen physical authority over her body: at the touch of his hands, at the hot press of his lips, her knees knocked, her stomach flip-flopped. In addition (though she didn't like to think in such terms), Ronny Olsson represented, as the sole son of one of Detroit's leading businessmen, an amazing, a dizzying "catch." Maggie could hardly forgive Bea for dating anyone so glamorous.

Even so, and even though Henry Vanden Akker was nowhere near as good-looking as Ronny Olsson, it wasn't Ronny's "bad paintings" but Henry's "bad poem" Bea found herself obsessively contemplating. "The girl I used to covet as a wife / Is someone else's wife . . ." It was so heartrending! Was it possible to wear your soul in your face? If such a thing were possible, Henry Vanden Akker did it: he wore his soul in his face. And if, by some miracle, she could ever *really* produce Henry's portrait, she might confidently affix her name, Bianca Paradiso, to something that would rightfully hang on a museum wall in a hundred years' time.

Sometimes it seemed most of Ronny's problems were nothing but various facets of the War. All those dismissive remarks of his—weren't they just the defensiveness of somebody whose draft board had classified him 4-F? (Wouldn't everything be different if he had no heart murmur—and who on earth would look more dashing in a uniform?) Wasn't his entire philosophy of the visual arts a response to the War? Truly, there was no way to gauge it or even to think about the War, for it was everywhere, it was bigger than anything—bigger than all else, ever, in human history. And as poor dead Mrs. McNamee's scrapbook attested, the War had dragged on and on—with so many rosy predictions buried in the cold earth.

The scrapbook brought it all back: those inassimilable first months, optimistic headlines competing with terrifying speculations. The Germans might set up Canadian bases from which to bomb Detroit! That, too, had been in the *News*. The Germans were much closer than you thought. A North Pole–centered map showed how nearby they really were. Bomb London first, then Detroit . . . Those were the days when Bea had read in the paper a passage she'd never forget: "The ordinary home has no defense from an incendiary bomb, which will burn through the toughest roof." It was as though the sentence had scorched her very soul, and for weeks she hadn't been able to walk down Inquiry without picturing a metal projectile screaming down out of the sky, sizzling a gaping black hole through one of her neighbors' roofs—the Higbees', the Slopsemas', even the Szots' . . .

Eventually, those bombs had drifted off, into the distance; they were falling now in new places with unfamiliar names. Meanwhile, the Willow Run plant (once the butt of jokes, the Will It Run) was rolling out eight heavy bombers a day, according to Uncle Dennis. We were turning the War around. That was Detroit's job: turning the War around. It was strange, whenever you stepped into a movie house, to know you might discover your own city on the screen, for Detroit was in the national newsreels. You stepped out of the streets of Detroit and sat down in the blue darkness to examine the streets of Detroit. Meanwhile, as the movie projector whirred, the smokestacks outside were belching round the clock, and whether you actually saw the smoke or not, every Detroiter—man, woman, and child—took it right into their lungs: with every inhalation, you breathed the War. It was stamped on your milk bottles; it trimmed your clothes of extraneous material; it lay in the dust of a streetcar floor. Soldiers on the sidewalks, soldiers in Ferry Hospital, soldiers in the newsreels, Roosevelt on the radio, explaining how the soldiers were faring . . .

Placed before the War's immensity, art schools shrank to the size of cereal boxes. What canvas in the world could move her so deeply—so unconditionally—as the reptilian-green walls of Ferry Hospital? *Wars come and go*, Ronny might tell her, and there was genuine insight in his observation, for the world would always need somebody to recall how Raphael and Bellini had been shining for hundreds of years now, bravely, like lamps on an overgrown hillside . . . And yet, it did seem plausible that off in an exploding jungle, where *something changed*, Henry had been granted a vision profounder than anything Ronny would ever know. Bea was haunted, anyway, by that not quite handsome, red-haired, pink-eared, bony Dutch face, wherein some sort of inner light—the soul itself, the soul itself—floated closer to the surface than in other faces. Over the years, when she'd gone fishing with her father, there had been some moments of sheer visual magic after Papa hooked something. It might have been an old boot, a tin can, a silted scarf, but no: when the catch was hauled close enough—up, up through the tannin-brown water—what thrashed into view was a brilliantly jeweled living body. The creature exploded into existence, just the way, when you stare heavenward on a winter day, falling snowflakes (dark silhouettes for all their whiteness) will sometimes spin out of a gray sky, materializing out of nowhere. Silently, for the waiting eye, beautiful things occasionally leap into a crystalline reality. And it was just that way with Henry's soul.

From the start, Bea felt emotionally enmeshed, and the second time she saw him, her drawing hand took to his face as though its every bone and muscle were intimately known. Yes: *this* time the drawing flowed, flowered; *here* was that puzzling certitude without which there was no reason to study art.

Bea knew no sensation in the entire universe finer than this feeling that your hand's far smarter than you are and you can do nothing but follow it appreciatively, seeing where it will lead. She was getting it down, bearing witness to the logic of a pilgrimage whose origins just might be found on the breathless floor of a jungled Pacific island where a shocked, sweating American boy-soldier lay with a shattered back.

"I'm afraid I'm making you look feverish," Bea said, laughing apprehensively—and yet contentedly.

"Then you're doing your job," Henry told her. "I can't tell you how many fevers I've had. Did you know the British in India used to build special malaria beds? The mattress was laid on bricks, so you could stoke a fire underneath, heating the bed when the chills came on."

"I didn't know that."

"It's one of the few things I ever learned in my life that I wish I'd had no occasion to learn."

For all its tone of certainty, Henry's voice was mild. He added, "Though I'm feeling much better. It's amazing how my back's improved. At one point, they thought—well, they thought I might be semi-paralyzed for life."

"Yes. You mentioned."

"Sorry. The truth is, I don't always recall what I've said. Or whether I said it aloud."

"I'm happy to listen more than once . . ."

In the air between them, firm as any handshake, their glances met. Confidently, delicately, Bea said to him, "You must have been so frightened."

"All of us," Henry Vanden Akker said. "Everyone on the whole island. We were all, everybody, so frightened. You know, I'd never seen an ocean before."

"Me neither. Not yet . . ."

"And it was such a little island, really. Look at the Solomons on a map. Dots. Geometric points. The smallness made it much worse, somehow. I couldn't honestly believe how enormous the sea was. Here I am, a trained mathematician. I'm accustomed to thinking about the infinite. And yet I couldn't comprehend the cubic dimensions of the ocean. It bedeviled—" Henry paused. A look of what might have been confusion—might have been fear—shadowed his features. He began anew: "It troubled my imagination."

"It must be very deep," Bea replied—which came out sounding very shallow. "The sea," she appended, by way of explanation.

"And the fear. I couldn't comprehend that either," Henry Vanden Akker continued, with that weird exciting chilly directness of his. "I am a believer after all, a believer in a just and loving God. How could the universe contain anything so fearful to me?"

"Well, the conditions sound positively—"

"The sea made everything else *so small.*" And Henry's voice had grown *so small.* "Even the sky. God's very own Heaven seemed *small.* I'm not making sense, am I," he apologized.

"Neither am I," Bea said, apologizing with him—side by side with him, you might say.

"And most of the men around me, they were believers, too. I asked them. I talked with them about God. But it made no difference: all of us felt that fear. And you know what? It got so I would have sworn to you, absolutely sworn to you, that the vegetation felt it. The palm trees shook all day in perpetual *fear.* The vines were frightened, right down to their muddy roots. The crawling ant-infested earth was frightened silly."

"Well I'd be frightened too, if I thought I might be paralyzed—"

"Oh but the accident came later. Don't you see?" Henry's ears were red as ripe tomatoes. "First came the fear . . ."

This time it was too much to sustain each other's gaze. Henry glanced off, and Bea peered into the half-materialized face of the young man on the white paper before her.

A distant honking of horns vaulted up from the street below. It was odd how, here on the West Side, even the sounds of traffic felt different—they felt yellower, more loosely put together than on her own East Side. "Tell me about the jungle," Bea said. "You know I've never seen jungle."

"It's a very odd place," Henry said. "Especially if you have a Michigan sort of mind. I've concluded I have a Michigan sort of mind."

It was precisely the type of remark that so piqued and attracted her. Was it possible to have a Michigan sort of mind? Did *she* have a Michigan sort of mind?

"Of course I'd been in forests before, but there's always lots of *air* in a Michigan forest. It's not the same desperation. All that choking claustrophobia. You know what it's like? Y'ever look at a drop of swamp water under a microscope?"

"I must have," Bea confidently replied—but when would she have looked at swamp water through a microscope?

"A whole world. It's really a whole world, and everything's just so crowded and crazed, millions of these minuscule creatures—billions, trillions—hunting down even more minuscule creatures. That's . . ." A sizable pause followed, Henry's eyes met hers, he shrugged.

Bea went back to her drawing.

When, some ten mostly silent minutes later, she finally revealed the portrait, Henry scrutinized it narrowly and then—something unexpected, something not seen heretofore—he grinned, broadly. Corporal Henry Vanden Akker had a gorgeous smile.

"Oh I *approve* of this."

"It's nothing like the other soldier portraits I've drawn," Bea hastened to explain. "Behind your head? Those are stars—jungle stars." She had sketched in, lightly, as a sort of joke-tribute to van Gogh, tiny vortices, dense as spiderwebs. "And those are jungle ferns." At the bottom she had supplied, again lightly, some outspread ornamental ferns. Courtesy of Gauguin.

"Am I to keep this?" he asked.

For all the stiffness of his phrasing, Henry resembled a child—a child about to receive a birthday present.

"You are indeed. And I'll take home the previous one and burn it to ash and bury the ashes."

"There's no question this version is much finer. Don't you think it makes me look quite intellectual? Don't I look brainy?"

Brainy? Such a lovely, odd, *funny* thing for Henry to say . . .

"I told you, it makes you look feverish."

"I'll be leaving here soon. Will you come visit me at home, in Pleasant Ridge? You know it's just up Woodward."

"Well . . ." Bea paused judiciously. "The rules are very strict. It's the law as laid down by Mr. Kronstein, he's the administrator here, and also by Nurse O'Donnell. I'm not supposed to—"

"To fraternize with the enemy?"

"How *cruel* you can be, Henry."

Bea's playful words wounded him: his pallid features thickened, his lower lip jutted into a childish pout. "Cruel?" Henry said. "I—but I was only joking."

"But Henry, *I was too,*" Bea answered Corporal Vanden Akker, who, if they were indeed to spend any time together, must learn to appreciate this other facet to her personality: the teasing, the banter.

For a moment Henry's face clouded abstractedly, as if he were pondering the sort of problem you pondered if you were a summa cum laude graduate in mathematics from Calvin College. Then he departed from all that, and did so in the sweetest way imaginable. He grinned at her. Beautifully.

CHAPTER XV

"No. I don't feel sorry for you. Not the least teeniest eentsy bit."

"I wasn't asking you to feel—"

"Like fun you weren't. Jabbering on and on about the burden of having two fascinating men absolutely mad for you."

"I wasn't complaining about *them*. I was merely pointing out how their two mothers—"

"Tell me about it. Do. Go tell me about how hard it is dealing with some boy's crazy mother . . ."

Although Maggie was in her preferred element—stagily tossing off grand-scale lamentations—there was no ignoring how miserable she was at bottom. Poor Maggie! Ma'am Hamm was making life impossible. The irony would have been funny if it weren't so pathetic: having spent the first eighteen years of her life yearning to flee the Szot home on Inquiry, Maggie was spending her nineteenth scheming of ways to return to it. Anything—*anything* other than living with her in-laws.

"She honestly thinks I'm a *slut*," Maggie cried—a word Bea winced at. But Maggie's exasperation was understandable: Ma'am Hamm kept her under round-the-clock surveillance.

To make things worse, the Hamms lived *way* out Grand River—out near Lahser and Fenkell—and Mrs. Hamm didn't approve of her daughter-in-law's riding alone on streetcars or buses. Whenever she wanted to go anywhere, Maggie was dependent on Mrs. Hamm, who insisted that all journeys be planned well in advance and who could be counted on to contrive last-minute scheduling conflicts. Only after lengthy negotiation had Mrs. Hamm agreed to ferry Maggie on today's outing to the zoo.

And of course Maggie hadn't come alone. George's younger brother, Herbie, must come along. Poor Maggie had been reduced to arguing that the afternoon was designed for Herbie's benefit.

Pale, plump, whiny, laggardly—Herbie Hamm was about as unlikable as any eleven-year-old boy who wasn't positively hateful could be. He was forever getting literally underfoot: today, Bea had already twice trod on the boy's heels, each time provoking a wan, contorted expression of pinched resentment. The furrow between his eyebrows was remarkably incisive for someone not yet in his teens.

Bea had lost track of the number of times a pebble got into Herbie's shoe. Also, his knee hurt, and his ankle hurt. The animal smells afflicted him. As did the gnats in the reptile house.

All his complaints turned out to be wheedling maneuvers in pursuit of "treats"—he was a terrible glutton for sugar. Maggie in her seething impatience was determined to provide as few treats as possible; she even threatened Herbie with a *good healthy lunch*.

It was Bea who concocted a jokey counter-notion: "Why don't we stuff him into a stupor?"

In a complete about-face, Maggie seized on the idea. She bought Herbie an ice-cream cone. She bought him a Boston Cooler. She bought him a bag of caramel corn. She bought him a 3 Musketeers and a box of jujubes. She bought him a brownie.

Unlike so many bright-sounding ideas, this one actually succeeded as planned. Herbie asked to sit down and was guided to a bench overlooking a distant pond. He slumped forward in a pacified state, sucking on butterscotch balls. He allowed Maggie and Bea to sit on a different bench, some ways away, where they were free to talk—or where Bea tried to talk and Maggie regularly interrupted.

"But I'm dealing with two of these women. These two very peculiar—"

"Listen, I'll gladly trade you one Ma'am Hamm for any two *peculiar* women of your choice and choosing."

"I mean the contrast couldn't be greater. Have you ever heard of *oliebolle*? They're these revolting Dutch pastries, nothing but grease really, I think they're literally oil balls, topped—"

"Don't get me started on the Jailer's cooking. Don't get me started."

"Meanwhile, Mrs. Olsson is taking me to restaurants where they serve venison—you know, deer. I'm *not* kidding. Appetizers at a dollar a piece—a *dollar*!"

"Don't even ask when's the last time I went to a decent restaurant. Don't even. You didn't bring a picture of him, did you? 'Spite how many times I've asked?"

Maggie simply refused to sit and listen to any comparisons between Mrs. Charles Olsson and Mrs. Horace Vanden Akker. Or to hear about Henry. Ronny, though—the exquisitely handsome young man in the exquisitely tailored clothes, the talented artist who balked at running his family's drugstore empire—was a shining figure. He engaged Maggie's imagination as the gaunt mathematical soldier with that most suspect of all disabilities, an injured back, could not.

These days, Bea saw so little of Maggie that their rare get-togethers were probably destined to disappoint. Maggie's typical habit of interruption, and her eventual monopolization of every conversation, had been less irksome back when she was still single and lived on Inquiry— when they saw each other all the time. But nowadays Bea came to their meetings with such a powerful need of unburdening herself, she couldn't help resenting how all conversations circled back to the Jailer, the Turnkey, the Probation Officer. Bea found herself peevish with Maggie—then guilty at being peevish, when she ought to be commiserating: poor Maggie was so wretched!

It seemed so long ago now that Maggie had been Maggie Szot, the little spitfire, sashaying down Inquiry secure in the knowledge of her sparkly appeal. Even Papa had bent every rule in Maggie's favor. Though her lipstick had been too red, and her skirts too short, though her laughter was too loud and she wore *far* too much perfume, Papa's face brightened on her arrival. Men's faces did. If Maggie was no true beauty, she was something rarer and more precious: a spirit whose fierce vivacity beckoned you irresistibly into her world. Papa forgave Maggie even after he discovered she'd been concealing a pair of high heels under his own front porch—shoes with heels too elevated to get past the fitfully watchful gaze of Mr. Szot. Maggie would step from home in acceptable footwear, saunter down the block to the Paradisos', fish her rain-slicker-wrapped high heels out from under the front porch, and proceed briskly down Inquiry, beaming at everyone she met . . .

What Bea wanted to discuss, at least for the moment, wasn't Ronny, or even Henry, but Ronny's parents, and still more Henry's parents. Henry had gone home from the hospital and Bea, at his urging, had visited him a couple of times in his white stucco house in Pleasant Ridge. It was a perfect mathematician's house, with strict bilateral symmetry. From the front walk, everything was in balance. The trimmed hedges matched each other left to right, the candlesticks in the downstairs windows matched left to right, the arrangement of blue and white vases in the upstairs windows matched left to right.

Henry's father was an accountant, but his real discipline, which he discussed with more enthusiasm than clarity, was church history. Over the years Bea had been exposed to a broad range of Christianity (Catholicism, Lutheranism, Methodism), but nothing had prepared her for the Vanden Akkers' Dutch Reformed Church.

If its guiding principles remained a mystery, this wasn't for Mr. Vanden Akker's lack of trying. He talked about John Calvin, who had spent time in prison, and whose brother was executed, and someone named Zwingli, who evidently believed music was a distraction unsuitable for churches. Mr. Vanden Akker talked about the "beggars," who were apparently not real beggars, and the "five heads," which were not people but some kind of doctrine, and the oppressive Philip, who was the king of Italy. Or possibly Spain. Mr. Vanden Akker would rattle on until abruptly hushed by Mrs. Vanden Akker, who openly commanded the household. When she halted him in midsentence, Mr. Vanden Akker looked apologetic rather than resentful, like a child receiving a deserved reprimand. Henry, too, was a child in Mrs. Vanden Akker's presence. But how strange, and disconcerting, to see this maverick young man lately of Ferry Hospital—so firm in all his pronouncements, so intellectually formidable through all his infirmities—transformed into somebody's deferential and intimidated little boy . . .

Stout without appearing the least bit soft, Mrs. Vanden Akker was blonde and round-faced and fair-skinned. At each visit, she offered Bea a great many strange things to eat: *krakelingen, gebak, poffertjes.* Mrs. Vanden Akker had shown herself so conscientious about Bea's refreshment, and so inquisitive about her family and schooling and ancestry, that Bea didn't initially grasp that Mrs. Horace Vanden Akker deeply disapproved of the sort of Italian-looking girl art student who rode the streetcar with a portfolio of soldiers' faces under her arm.

"You heard from George?" Bea asked.

Maggie hesitated. Her response to this question customarily took one of two sharply divergent paths: imminent death, or paradise on earth. When she took the first path, Maggie could soon turn inconsolable. ("Bea, if the Japs attack, there's nowhere to run. Did you know Hawaii's nothing but an island?") Fortunately, Maggie took the second path:

"George? *George* is fine. Eating pineapples. You know what he wrote and asked me? If I'd ever eaten *fresh* pineapple. He's eating *fresh* pineapple and I'm eating the Jailer's cooking."

"Maybe that helps keep the weight down."

"That's the worst of all. Because it's completely inedible, I eat way too much."

In truth, Maggie looked a little broader than usual. Roundness was part of her charm—her bosomy bounciness—but Maggie, as Mamma often pointed out, would need to watch it when she got older.

It wasn't much of a day for the zoo, damp and chill, the sky a glossy gray through the autumnal trees. The season was nearly over. Not many folks had turned up, and even the animals shared in the listlessness.

Herbie, meanwhile, uncharacteristically reflective, was sitting on his bench, languidly popping butterscotch balls into his face.

"Bea, if I tell you something, promise you won't turn all angry and proper? Or give me any lectures?"

The day's coolness turned a little cooler. Bea knew where this was headed, somehow.

"Tell me what?"

"I've been in touch with Walton. You know—Wally. He goes by Walton now."

"I thought that's what you were going to say."

"You usually do. Know what I'm going to say."

Ages ago, Maggie had embraced this bit of Paradiso family lore: Bea had second sight. With Maggie, though, the notion was a kind of joke. She'd turned it into one more humorous mournful cry of self-deprivation: why oh why had she not been given Bea's gift?

"How do you mean *in touch*?" Bea said.

"We spoke on the phone."

"Does *in touch* include seeing him?"

"How else? We're not supposed to tie up the phone, that's unpatriotic. And only a few times. Only coffee. Obviously I couldn't *see* anyone, not really. What with the Jailer breathing down my neck."

Maggie's *in touch* naturally evoked the first of the two most salient things about Wally: his deformed hand, which he all but invariably kept pocketed. Bea's fleeting glimpses had revealed something less like a hand than—dwindled, twisted, deathly pale—a chicken's wing.

"Coffee where?"

"A diner. Out on Fenkell. He'd meet me anywhere. If I called right now and said, Wally, I'm sitting outside the Chimp Theater at the zoo, he'd say, Sit tight, kid, I'll drop everything and be right there."

"He calls you *kid*?"

"He's still . . ." Maggie paused.

"Still hopelessly, absolutely, doggishly devoted? Still carrying a torch big as the Statue of Liberty's?"

And Maggie laughed—laughed in a bright, throaty, mischievous way

Bea hadn't heard in months. Bea had almost forgotten the sound, though it was one of her favorite sounds in the world. This was laughter that took a bite right out of the air. "Yes," Maggie said, her eyes shining. "I suppose that sums up Wally."

And here was the second striking thing about Wally: his fidelity. It seemed he'd fallen for Maggie back in fourth grade at Field Elementary and had never righted his equilibrium. In the intervening years, all through the Depression, things had gone beautifully for the Waller family (Mr. Waller was the founder of Waller Plate Glass), who had moved first to a pillared house in Indian Village and later to a lakeshore home in Grosse Pointe. Yet it appeared that baby-faced Wally, peering out over Lake St. Clair, pined even yet for a girl immured in a dingy bungalow out at Fenkell and Grand River presided over by a woman called the Jailer.

There should have been something grave about Wally, with his deformed hand and his hopeless passion, but gravity had a way of turning risible around him. It was true of his face—a handsome but boyish face, ideal for embodying puppy love. It was true of his name. So he went by Walton now. Walton Waller. Years ago, at his christening, the family presumably had detected something refined in those echoing similar-but-distinct syllables. But not even Maggie reliably remembered to call him Walton. No, he was destined to go through life with a moniker suitable for a fraternity-house skit: Wally Waller.

"And what if the Jailer were to catch you having coffee in a diner with Wally?"

"Probably will," Maggie assented gloomily. "And that'll be it, won't it? *Finito* to Maggie's life. It'll be solitary confinement, broken only by inedible meals. I wrote George saying I was thinking of moving back home, with my parents . . ."

"Yes, you mentioned."

"And he said I mustn't," Maggie went on, as though informing Bea for the first time. "Ma'am Hamm might be hurt. Obviously, he's as terrified of her as I am."

"I think of you as fearless."

"No. *Terrified* of Ma'am Hamm. Worse than shots."

"Yes, shots," Bea echoed, and laughed happily. Given Bea's nighttime jitters, Maggie's general fearlessness was hugely endearing. Oh, to be so bold! But Maggie's sole phobia was also endearing. She was the only person Bea knew who had actually fainted at the sight of a hypodermic needle.

"Boys and their mothers," Bea went on. "I was talking about Henry's mother and Ronny's mother."

And it seemed Maggie had finally pitched herself into such abject gloom as to be willing to listen without interrupting. Bea told her a little more about Mrs. Olsson—the drinking, the extraordinary clothes, the spats with Mr. Olsson. Bea then turned to Mrs. Vanden Akker: the greasy Dutch pastries and the vats of steaming coffee, the affirmative nodding that masked disapproval . . . but Maggie didn't want to hear about Mrs. Vanden Akker. Or about Mrs. Olsson, except maybe her clothes. Ronny, though—Maggie was keen for more about him.

"You said he's so moody. What do you mean moody?"

"Moody the way anybody's moody. And about—about being romantic. I mean I get into his car, I don't know if he's going to sit and talk about art—or whether he's going to turn into an octopus."

"But you haven't gone to bed with him . . ."

Count on Maggie to say something like that! "No, of course not, but you know there are various degrees."

Bea paused. Who was she to explain such things to Maggie, who was a married woman—who was no virgin? Maggie over the years had always shown a willingness to discuss such matters—far more than Bea herself. But Maggie had had surprisingly little to say about what must be the culmination of all such discussions, and what she *had* said was clipped and self-contradictory. It changes everything, Maggie once remarked, referring to the loss of her virginity. But on another occasion she said, Hey, honey, it's not all it's cracked up to be. Under other circumstances, this *honey* might have seemed annoying—condescending and affected—but Bea had felt too keenly inquisitive to bristle.

Throughout their endless friendship Maggie had always been strikingly insouciant about exposing her body. In the old days, before their builds went such different ways, she was forever coming upstairs to Bea's room to borrow clothes—pausing for long moments in her underwear while narrating another story, initiating a new line of conversation. The same thing happened in the locker room, when they went swimming at the Y: Maggie took on a special glow while chatting, naked as a jaybird, under the covertly appraising eyes of friends and strangers alike. The result was that Bea had a sharper, more painterly feeling for Maggie's body than for anyone's but her own, and what made this a little unsettling, even faintly repulsive, were Maggie's anatomical peculiarities: Maggie was double-jointed; Maggie could wiggle both ears; Maggie could nearly touch the tip of her nose with her tongue. And Maggie openly enjoyed making a naked exhibition of herself, which wasn't the Paradiso way. It was part of Papa's proud propriety that, except at the lake, you never saw him with legs or chest uncovered, and Mamma—Mamma would scramble, almost frantic, when surprised in some state of dishabille. Even Stevie, entering his teens, would glow like a beet on discovering he'd left his fly half zipped.

"So you wouldn't go to bed with him? Under *any* circumstances?"

"Maggie, *stop.*"

"So what's he got to be moody about—Ronny?"

"I don't know. Maybe because he's an artist?"

"Well thank heavens George is no artist. Moody is one thing George isn't."

Though George was quite good-looking in a short, compact, neat-featured way, Bea had trouble picturing him in a romantic setting. She couldn't get past the knowledge that the Army had yanked out all his teeth. She knew she ought to be able to get past it—simple patriotism demanded nothing less—but she couldn't shake the image of George with a caved-in mouth depositing his choppers in a glass. (Sometimes Bea wished she didn't picture things so vividly.)

Maggie went on: "Or you could say he has one mood: he wants it." And Maggie, quite wantonly, ran a hand across her flank.

Just then another hand—Herbie's pale and pudgy hand—pulled on Maggie's sleeve. "I don't feel so hot," he said.

"Oh Herbie, for Pete's sake. Haven't I given you everything you've asked for and more?"

The boy was not only pale but glassy looking. As though his face might shatter if you gave him a slap.

"I don't feel so hot," Herbie repeated stubbornly.

"You *would* do this to me, wouldn't you?"

"I needa go the toilet," the boy said.

"Right," Maggie said. "'Course you do."

The three of them set out in search of a toilet—Herbie in the middle, dragging a bit—but none was to be found. They passed a tiger, looking sleepy, and some lions, also sleepy, and quite a few red-rumped baboons, most of them asleep.

"I needa go the toilet."

"Well you'll just hafta hold it. Or you can do what the animals do . . . You think the zebras have central plumbing? You suppose the giraffes have private rest rooms?"

"I ga go *now,*" Herbie said.

Mysteriously, since Bea would have sworn they'd been mostly following a straight line, they came full circle: here were the very benches they'd been sitting upon. More mysterious still, bathrooms stood right before them. Somehow they'd walked right past them.

Herbie, looking much revived, did not keep them waiting long. Maggie took a new tone: "All right, Herbie honey, whatcha wanna see next? Come to think of it, my stomach's shaky too. All the walking, don't you think? You know, it'd be a shame you mentioned this to your mom, because she might think it was all the treats. She might say I shouldn't buy you *treats*, and we'd be sorry about that, wouldn't we, hon?"

But they didn't get far before Herbie's face turned green and glassy once more. The three of them beat a quick retreat to the restrooms.

This time, Herbie stayed in a *very* long time—so long that Bea said, "Do you think he died?"

"Wishful thinking. Damn the little monster."

After prompting each other, the two of them approached the doorway, and Maggie called in, "Her—bie. Her—bie." No answer. A man exiting with his hands at his waist—he was adjusting his fly—flashed them an interested look. They hurried back to their bench. "She's going to kill me," Maggie sighed, and added, which made Bea laugh, "George is going to be a war widower."

Two boys were nearing the men's room. They looked approachably young—not much older than Stevie—and Bea called to them. "Boys," she said. "Excuse me, boys." Maggie interrupted and made it plain: "Would you go in and see if there's a dead boy named Herbie in there?"

The boys raced inside and returned disappointed a minute later. "Oh he's all right," one of them reported. "He's just been throwing up."

"Throwing up? Oh hell, she's going to kill me."

"Now he's just sort of sitting there," the other boy said.

"If he's thrown up on his clothes, I'm a dead girl."

When Herbie at last emerged, he reeked of vomit. He had indeed thrown up on his jacket.

"Oh hell, oh dear," Maggie said, not knowing which tone to take. "Herbie, honey, better if you sit down. Bea, couldja work on his jacket? Bea?"

Maggie removed the boy's jacket and handed it over. Then she settled her arm around Herbie and said, "Now honey, normally I wouldn't advise anything less than total honesty, but in this case I really think we shouldn't worry your mother. She can be a bit high-strung is how it is."

The only soap available in the ladies' room was an abrasive pink powder. Using first some paper towel and then, feeling desperate, a fine lace handkerchief from her purse, Bea worked and worked on the stained front of Herbie's gray wool jacket. Given how sodden the material soon became, it was difficult to say how successful her efforts were. But she went on scrubbing. It had been her idea, after all, to stuff the boy into a stupor.

When Bea at last left the restroom, she found Maggie and Herbie still on the bench, Maggie's arm extended around the boy. She had bought him a Coca-Cola to soothe his sugar-overloaded stomach. Her conversation had not budged. The first thing Bea heard was: "Naturally, I would never want you to be dishonest with your mother . . ."

CHAPTER XVI

Though almost punitively unappetizing, Mrs. Vanden Akker's deep-fried cooking had its promised recuperative effect on Henry. Each time Bea saw him, he looked healthier and solider. His injured back, too, was mending. He moved slowly, and stiffly, but he was fully ambulatory.

Still, he wasn't venturing often or far from home. Their encounters were restricted to his house in Pleasant Ridge. They sat in the living room. Mrs. Vanden Akker would station herself in either the living room or the adjoining kitchen. She was never out of hearing's range—never so distant that Bea felt that the clink of a spoon against a plate, or the clearing of her throat, went unremarked.

Yet if Henry, like Mr. Vanden Akker, was thoroughly under the woman's thumb, in one regard, anyway, he showed himself defiantly independent: he kept inviting Bea to visit. Nothing could be more apparent, as time went on, than Mrs. Vanden Akker's disapproval of her. Mrs. Vanden Akker once went so far as to say, outright, that Henry would eventually marry "one of us"—somebody from the Dutch Reformed Church. As if Bea were scheming to lead feverish-eyed Henry Vanden Akker to the altar! Whenever Mrs. Vanden Akker issued such a remark, she had a characteristic way of jutting her head sideways and hoisting her chin—just the sort of gesture a fish might make after successfully taking the bait without the hook.

The day when Henry walked her to her bus stop seemed rich with progress, not just physical but psychological: the two of them were liberated, finally, from unshakable presences—from the other wounded soldiers in the bunks beside Henry's, from Nurse O'Donnell, and, more to the point, from Mrs. Horace Vanden Akker.

And what did Henry do and say in their first moments of being utterly alone? He opened up the topic of religious doubt, Kierkegaard's belief that meaningful faith must originate in doubt. And then he talked about Charles Darwin's *Voyage of the Beagle,* which Bea hadn't read. It seemed Darwin had loved the South American jungle more than anything. But Darwin had been unnerved, down at the frigid southern tip of the continent, by the landscape's bleakness and the Stone-Age lives of the Patagonian Indians. Patagonians? Who other than Henry would have heard of them? Or, having heard of them, would think them a suitable topic at such a moment? "I think my response would have been quite the opposite," Henry said. "Starkness is fine." He added: "It's geometric."

When in their slow pace they finally reached Woodward Avenue, Bea said, "Do you like living here, Henry?"

"Living where?"

"Here. In Pleasant Ridge."

"I suppose so. It's very pleasant, to choose the obvious word." Henry gave her a penetrating look. "You wouldn't like living here, Bea?"

"Well, I don't know," she said. "I just think it would be so odd."

"Odd? How so?"

"To live so far from everything."

"Far from what?"

"From the city, I guess."

"We're less than two miles from the city line."

"Oh I know . . . I just think it might feel odd to be living out on the edge of things."

"What edge?" Henry said. "The earth doesn't have an edge. It's a sphere. Roughly."

"Oh I know—"

"If you grew up in New York," Henry went on, "the whole city of Detroit might seem to lie on some edge. Of the Great Plains, I suppose."

Of course Henry's logic was unassailable. And that was part of Henry's problem—for this was a topic, like so many of the world's most interesting topics, where logic wouldn't take a person too far. It was Henry's advantage and disadvantage both: the things that animated his spirit were approachable through the linear analyses he excelled at. It wasn't that way for her, Bea explained—or tried to. There were judgments to be based only on—only on how you felt the light fall. It was sometimes an issue of contending pigments, of complementing and warring distributions of lights and darks.

Ronny would have known what she meant, mostly, but this was nearly inexpressible with Henry. Still, for all the awkwardness, Bea tried to give him some feeling for this feeling that was such a strong feeling within her: this sensation she regularly experienced as she drifted through the outskirts of Detroit. A sense of something not quaint exactly, not cute exactly, though very like quaint and cute: this suburban conviction that fully real lives could be lived out here in Pleasant Ridge, in Royal Oak, in Birmingham and Bloomfield Hills. But how could anyone fail to register a steady diminution of spirit when traveling north up Woodward Avenue—from the heart of the city into its ancillary reaches?

Oh, this was not only an impossible feeling to describe—she also risked insulting Henry and the Vanden Akker family. For it wasn't as though Henry, even if he *had* grown up in a place Bea must finally regard as a stage set, himself was unreal. No, the great irony was that Henry Vanden Akker, although much the most abstruse man she'd ever met, was far "realer" than most everybody she knew.

There were no words for it, but as Bea waited for the bus she gamely struggled on. "I travel to the West Side, the light's different. I'm still in Detroit, but the light's different. Sometimes I think a painter needs to know only two places: a place, and a second place that isn't at all that place. But it's as if there are places where the light's thicker, almost. It isn't any brighter, just thicker, but if your goal is to paint good pictures, you want to go where the light—where the light's thick as cream."

The bus pulled up.

Where the light's thick as cream . . . As Bea rides first a bus and then a streetcar ever deeper into the city, the phrase ricochets internally, it echoes and goes on echoing; she repeats it to herself, silently and then aloud. Her voice is low and quiet and nobody can possibly hear her over the streetcar's racket. Nor the little giggle that follows. Oh, the things Henry's noble gravity inspires her to say!

Or to wish to say. It sounded silly to put it this way, but Henry was unique. It was something she wanted to tell the world: here is one unusual soldier! And when Henry determined that their first outing ought to be a visit to the zoo, just round the corner from his house, Bea didn't mention that she'd visited it recently with Maggie and Herbie. This was actually *perfect*. The two visits would balance each other; they would form a sort of painters' diptych. Surely, the zoo with Henry would be a different zoo.

. . . And different it turned out to be—singular even before leaving the Vanden Akkers'. As if he saw himself heading off on some sort of safari, Henry sported a bizarre hat he must have picked up in the Pacific. It was woven of reeds that tended to fray, so that threadlike curlicues sprang up all over his head. Bea thought it best not to ask about it. (Ronny would have marched to the guillotine before stepping outdoors in such a hat.) Mrs. Vanden Akker, softly sighing disapproval, dropped them at the zoo entrance.

To ease the wear and tear on Henry's back, they rode the little zoo train. "Next stop: *Af-ri-ca!*" the conductor roared. The toylike train inevitably turned children giggly with delight, and today there were many children, but Henry took his seat as somberly and peered out from under his hat every bit as appraisingly as someone riding a real train across the African savannah.

He was far more taciturn than usual. Generally, Henry liked to talk about ideas: about his reading, and about what might be called theological issues. When he encouraged Bea to speak (he did most of the talking), he often solicited her views on visual art, a topic about which, with appealing modesty, he claimed to understand "absolutely nothing." He added: "You *see* so much."

Perhaps because Henry hadn't yet visited her house, most of her family stories left him looking bored—though he asked about Edith, of all people. Her mathematical gift piqued his interest, as did her organizational passions. Henry laughed aloud on hearing of her scrapbook entitled "My Testimonials." And he *loved* the story of how, talking in her sleep, Edith once declared, with the clearest enunciation in the world, "I disagree completely."

"She's a philosopher!" Henry cried, which actually wasn't as fanciful as it first sounded. Whatever else she was, Edith was a deep soul.

Mamma and Aunt Grace didn't ignite his curiosity as they did Ronny's; in that way, Ronny had more imagination. (Bea couldn't stop making such comparisons.) Still, though Bea knew the subject didn't fully engage Henry, she couldn't refrain from mentioning something that had troubled her for days.

"I had lunch this week with my aunt, Aunt Grace. You know I don't mention such meetings to my mother. Anyway, Aunt Grace told me Uncle Dennis wanted to speak to me. Why would he want to speak to me?"

"Maybe he misses you," Henry said. "It seems you don't see much of him anymore."

"But she didn't say he wanted to see me. She said, speak to me. Why would he want to speak to me?"

"The truth is, we won't find out until he does."

And this was deeply typical of Henry. He loved this phrase—*the truth is*—which served him the way others might rely on *you know* or *well, actually.* And when a particular topic's data turned out to be insufficient, all speculation must end. It was futile to pursue what couldn't be solved or clarified.

The truth is? The truth was, Aunt Grace's announcement had only aggravated an already bad situation: Bea had been terribly uneasy for weeks and weeks. Nothing had been the same since the birthday dinner on July tenth, when everything came undone. Maybe the only way to proceed was not to talk too much, forcing your thoughts elsewhere, though it had occurred to Bea that the wild needy intensity of her feelings for Ronny, and more lately for Henry, might ultimately be laid to her troubles at home. These days, her passions felt even less controllable than usual.

Given her feelings for Ronny, how could Henry tug so on her emotions? It didn't make sense—but Henry tugged *hard* on her emotions. Even if, unlike Ronny, he didn't spin her wheels, as Maggie would say, Henry stirred her heart . . . Oh, to see him at the zoo in his preposterous vegetal hat, staring as intently as anyone could possibly stare at a sweet-faced, mild-eyed llama—this little tableau sang to her spirit. And when she saw him emerge from the men's room with one arm folded behind him, propping up what must be an excruciating backache, she was flooded with a sentiment that, although you maybe wouldn't call it longing, did encompass a yearning to see him physically comforted.

Slowly, methodically, the two of them visited the ducks, the bears, the camels. On every creature, Henry fixed the same penetrating glare. "Look at him!" Bea cried, when a bear, suddenly plump as a Buddha, sat up on its hind legs, begging for popcorn. "How cute!"

Yet cuteness evidently wasn't what scowling Henry was seeking in the amiable animal faces around him.

They stopped to rest and Henry bought her a Boston Cooler. "Henry, tell me more about Calvin College. You really enjoyed it?"

Henry's mouth twitched. He was about to establish a fine distinction.

"I think it was absolutely the right place for me, at the right time for me. I learned to love geometry there."

"I liked geometry, too, especially the shapes," Bea replied, though immediately aware of how fatuous this might sound. "Talk about geometry, Henry. If it's not too complicated."

"But it's simple. Which is the greatest mystery of all." Henry went on: "Sometimes the mystery in something—or let's go ahead and call it the miracle in something—simply disappears when you look closely. But this was just the opposite."

"Yes," Bea said.

"I'd always loved the way you can translate some little string of symbols—something as simple as $x = y$, say—into a figure on a plane. And you know what? The closer I looked, the more miraculous it became. Generally, you lose something in translations, but here nothing was lost. In all the universe, there isn't one x that doesn't fall on the line; and there isn't one point on the line that the equation fails to cover. Then you make what appears to be a minor adjustment—you adjust a plus sign to a minus sign, say, or you raise an exponent by one—and the form doesn't merely alter: it transforms, it blossoms, it leaps into another dimension. Your finite ellipse becomes an infinite hyperbola, your circle becomes a sphere. With every step, there's a new sort of blossoming. And I saw—you know what I saw?"

"No, Henry. Tell me what you saw."

"Well, it's like the opening, the very opening verses of the Book of John," Henry said. "You have only the Word, and yet you could say the Word begets everything. You could say, the Word is the world itself. And here was the Word again, this time as a little string of mathematical letters, and you know what? All of Creation happens anew. Do you see what I'm saying, Bea? Every time somebody writes an equation, all Creation is created. I truly believe that. If I write $x = y$ on your napkin, the world is born anew. Yes, math may be *true* in this world, but it also *makes* the world. And so what does that tell us about *truth*?"

"It tells us something," Bea said.

Henry said, "It speaks of God. You remember my telling you I talked to the other soldiers about God? Well one of them was an atheist—he freely admitted it—though actually I think he was an agnostic, since he was open to persuasion."

"I'm sure you're right."

"Anyway, he kept wanting me to talk about theology from the mathematical angle. He'd say, If you added up all the good scientific arguments for God's existence, what *percentage* likelihood would you arrive at? He'd say, And if you added up all the arguments against, what *percentage* would it be? It sounds a little silly, but I eventually realized it wasn't at all. The question maybe was naïve, but it was also brilliant. It's precisely what the greatest, greatest mathematician—the ideal mathematician—would accomplish. He'd find a way to quantify all the arguments and sum it up. If you *believe* in God, and you *believe* in mathematics, I don't see how you can fail to posit the magical point of intersection where—where . . . Oh my—listen to me," Henry said, and he looked both vulnerable and exultant, and Bea felt closer to him than she'd ever felt before. "I'm back in deep water, aren't I?"

"It's a big ocean. So you tell me."

Henry smiled at this. And added, apologetically, "It's all but impossible to express such things without sounding like a blockhead. To say it right, you'd have to be not only a mathematician but a poet."

"But you are! A poet. And I have it by heart." Bea began to recite: " 'The life I used to think of as my life—' "

An anguished look crossed Henry's features and a quelling hand lunged forward, seizing her forearm. Bea paused, unsure why she felt so embarrassed. But Henry, too, was acutely embarrassed. Then a different sort of look dulcified his remarkable features. "You do? You have my poem by heart?" he said.

"I could prove it, Henry. If you'd only let me."

Bea waved her hand at him, imitating his lordly gestures. Henry understood, and took this mockery well. She went on: "Silencing me with a royal wave. Honestly now. Sir Henry of Pleasant Ridge."

Henry said, "Certain things are very hard to say, but I sometimes think they're the only things worth saying." He sipped his ginger ale, or would have done so if any had remained; he rattled the cubes instead. "Do you remember the first time we ever went walking? I walked you to the Woodward bus stop."

" 'Course I do. You make it sound as if it were months ago, Henry."

"Well, that was another of those mystical occasions. Remember, you were talking about art?"

"Not very articulately, I'm afraid."

"And the light thick as cream—remember?"

"Don't remind me."

But Henry shrugged off her levity and self-disparagement. And in the end there was no denying his earnestness, his heavy expectant pauses.

"Yes, Henry," Bea said somberly. "I do remember."

What next emerged was the most roundabout and also the most extraordinary utterance the extraordinary Henry Vanden Akker had managed so far: "Well I realized then, in some objective way that had nothing to do, finally, with my subjective state, or with anything I've been through this past year . . . The truth is, I realized that you are, as a physical presence—you are, as I say, in some absolutely objective, in almost mathematical fashion—well, that you are, Bea, without question, the most beautiful girl in the world."

Her breath couldn't find its way out of her throat. Then it came forward in a headlong rush: "Oh Henry, I don't know what to say . . ."

In fact her words were precisely the sort of demure reply she'd been trained to make when, over the years, lavish and unexpected tributes had dropped into her lap. But this time, they were literally accurate. Up until now, Henry had never offered—not once—a true compliment about her appearance. And when he finally chose to do so, how like him it was—how wonderfully *Henry* it was—to dispense with preliminaries and plunge headlong into the wildest superlatives.

"Bea, have I let my feelings as a male influence my judgment? Perhaps. I don't think so. But perhaps. Still, I'll tell you something where no *perhaps* is admissible. Having watched you draw—having watched you so closely—I can inform you that you have the most beautiful hands in the world. Honestly, they're so perfect, I don't know whether I dare try to hold one of them."

One of Henry's hands, big-knuckled and yellowy pale, twitched on the tabletop. He didn't appear to be joking or exaggerating—no, not the least little bit. And whether now, if given time, Henry would actually have reached across and taken her hand wasn't something Bea would ever know for certain—given the way, oh so naturally, she reached across to slip her hand into his.

Slowly, Bea laced her fingertips through Henry's, interlocking their hands, and when the bases of their fingers conjoined she experienced an internal thud-in-the-blood so potent it made her eyes water. It came with the force of a revelation: who would have guessed that, merely by taking his hand, she would feel this way? But Henry had felt it, too, and who in the world would have guessed that Henry Vanden Akker's raw-looking eyes would well up at a simple touch?

The two of them sat in the zoo refreshment shed in silence a minute or two, sharing a single commanding pulse. When at last Henry withdrew his hand, he said something both typical of him and a little peculiar: "Thank you."

So once more they wandered out into a world recolonized by animals: bears, lions, bison, alligators. The thrill of their hands' coming together continued to daze her. Oh, Bea had peered speculatively at Henry's bony hands at times—rather homely hands, if the truth were told. Likewise, a few times she'd glanced at his thin lips and wondered about kissing him. Mostly, though, she didn't like thinking of Henry in this way. All the more surprising, then, to have such powerful pleasures unlocked with his touch . . . This was all so unlike her experience with Ronny. She'd fully expected it would be marvelous to hold Ronny's hand, to feel his kiss, and marvelous it had turned out to be. She hadn't looked for anything so pleasurable in *Henry's* touch.

It seemed the two of them had crossed an as-yet-unidentified threshold, and Bea was left feeling jittery and giddy and voluble, while Henry appeared inexplicably morose. Perhaps his back was bothering him.

But something more than his back oppressed him in the house of the great apes. Such an extremely peculiar, unforgettably unpleasant thing happened there . . .

They stood and watched a very animated chimpanzee behind a sheet of glass. He swung from a sort of hat rack, he hung upside down, he bounced off a stool on springs. There was a sign on the wall behind him: "Greetings! My name is Custard and I used to play with a spare tire. But I turned it in for salvage, as my part in the War Effort."

Custard, the irrepressible patriot, peered out coyly from behind a wooden crate. Then he stooped low for a drink of water. He must have been ten feet away.

And then (with an altogether astounding accuracy and jetting force) Custard squirted from his mouth a stream of water, directly at the two of them. The water crashed and broke against the glass, sending Henry and Bea leaping backward—it was all so sudden!—and Bea released a little scream. And Henry, too, released a cry—a much higher sound, almost a bleat, than you'd ever expect from his measured throat.

And Custard? Custard threw back his evil skull and howled and howled. He danced—he bounced and leaped with blazing glee. From ear to ear he grinned, grotesquely. The human beings? Their backward stumbling and stunned sheepish looks—these were everything Custard had hoped for . . .

Truly, the creature's joy was insufferable, and Bea and Henry fled the ape house just as quickly as Henry's ailing back would allow. They would put the chimp behind them—but in fact there was no shaking Custard's demented ecstasy: no ridding themselves of that smirking, ferocious, superior, inhuman face. "Well that was something," Bea said, when they reached the outdoors. She felt utterly humiliated, somehow, and this was new: to be *humiliated* by an animal. "I guess he doesn't have enough to do." She waited for Henry to answer but Henry made no reply. "It's the sort of stunt Stevie would pull. Honestly, wouldn't you think a monkey might behave better than my little brother?"

Bea laughed, inviting Henry to join her, but he didn't. Henry refused to make light of the encounter. Under his eccentric hat, he stared forward as thoughtfully as he ever stared—very thoughtfully indeed.

"You can see how deep that sort of pleasure runs," Henry began at last.

"Hm?"

"The pleasure we all take in inspiring fear."

"Well it certainly was very startling," Bea said.

"Bea, admit it. It was more than startling. Think about it. For just a moment, for one split second, we were terrified. And the chimp knew we'd be terrified. *Hoped* we'd be terrified."

"Well, it was all so quick."

"Despite the glass, we were terrified."

Henry Vanden Akker swung his head around and squeezed her hand. "Bea, don't you see? It runs so *deep* in us, inside the primate brain. Even a chimpan*zee* can feel it with extraordinary intensity." Under the brim of his ridiculous hat, Henry's eyes were afire: "I'm talking about the pleasure, the unholy pleasure, of inspiring fear in the heart of a stranger."

CHAPTER XVII

Uncle Dennis seemed so much his old self—affectionate, attentive, solicitous, a little scatterbrained—that Bea immediately forgot all her earlier misgivings about this encounter. Everything would be all right.

He took her to a restaurant on Gratiot, near Eastern Market, called Uncle Danny's. Ever since she was a little kid, Uncle Dennis had been bringing her here, presumably drawn because its name so closely resembled his own. It was the sort of silly coincidence that tickled him. He bought her a clam roll and a chocolate shake. He ordered nothing but coffee for himself. And lit his pipe.

Actually, Bea would have preferred coffee, but the moment they were seated Uncle Dennis had said, "I suppose you'll want a chocolate shake," and she didn't have the heart to disabuse him. He seemed to think he was still dealing with some sort of child—not an eighteen-year-old art student.

"So tell me the latest one you're reading," Bea said.

"Let me see . . . Well in the newest one, I forget the title, the earth's being destroyed by earthquakes. Everything's sort of collapsing and the only escape is outer space. Different groups go up in rocket ships, carrying whatever they most value. You see, they're never returning to earth again."

"How dreadful."

"Yes." Uncle Dennis's huge bespectacled eyes kindled with pleasure. "And there's one old woman who brings some ancient family journal she's never gotten round to reading. It turns out to be a chronicle of her great-great-grandmother's journey by covered wagon across the Rockies. Pioneer stuff. And you know what? She begins to spot all sorts of peculiar coincidences, weird parallels between the wagon-train group and her own rocket-ship group. The same personalities, same problems. In fact, the parallels soon grow so uncanny, she has to wonder whether she's caught in some bizarre reincarnation loop. Either that, or she's going mad."

"Is she?"

"Mm?"

"Going mad?"

"Don't know," Uncle Dennis said. "Haven't finished it yet."

The menu requested customers to limit themselves to one cup of coffee, but Uncle Dennis got around this by ordering a cup for Bea, which he then appropriated. Coffee seemed to be the one phase of wartime rationing no one in Bea's family paid much attention to. When it came to coffee, they hoarded, they wheedled, they bartered with the neighbors.

Uncle Dennis asked about the family and Bea sketched as cheerful a group portrait as she could. Much of what she recounted was familiar information, but because he looked so encouraging, puffing his pipe, she rattled on. O'Reilly and Fein were absolutely flourishing, given the streams of new defense workers, and Papa had more business than he could handle. He'd recently bought Mamma a prewar vacuum cleaner, brand-new and still in its box; Papa had a way of finding such things when new vacuum cleaners were scarce. Stevie was still shooting Japs and Germans in the alley. Edith the Mad Knitter had been asking Mamma to cook the breakfast bacon nearly black, so there would be more fat to salvage. And Mamma—well, she seemed maybe a little calmer. She liked her vacuum cleaner.

"I do worry Papa's working too hard."

"Well you can see why," Uncle Dennis said. "O'Reilly and Fein know what they've got: the man's a genius in his work."

"A genius?"

It was lovely to hear *genius* applied to somebody who struggled while reading the funny pages. Night after night, it pained Bea to see her father make his dutiful way through even the wordiest strips— "Gasoline Alley" or "Vignettes of Life"—until he'd grasped everything but their humor . . .

"I don't use the word lightly," Uncle Dennis said. "Especially now with the War on. There's a lumber shortage? A shortage of nails? Of wire? The man has a genius for making do—for cutting corners without cutting quality. Yes, it's a kind of genius, Bea."

The word heartened Bea so much, she longed to hear Uncle Dennis expand upon it. She prompted him: "Remember the time Mr. O'Reilly showed up with presents for each of us kids?" Of course Uncle Dennis had heard the story a million times . . .

"Your father'd quit the firm because O'Reilly wanted to install defective plumbing."

"Mr. O'Reilly brought me a bracelet, and Edith a doll, and Stevie a huge baseball mitt that wouldn't fit his hand for years."

"He realized he'd lost the best builder in the city," Uncle Dennis said, and sipped contentedly from Bea's cup of coffee.

"Mamma had been crying for three days," Bea went on. "She said we were going to lose the house. It was a notion I'd never contemplated before, it didn't seem possible: we would lose our house. How could a house get *lost*? I was so young, and so confused."

"And scared, I bet."

"You bet I was scared. Our *house* was going to get lost."

"And yet you're still in it."

"We're still in it," Bea said happily.

"Actually," Uncle Dennis said, "speaking of moving, and things like that, I have a new job offer. In Cleveland."

"Cleveland," Bea marveled.

This sort of thing had happened in the past. Uncle Dennis had once been offered a job in Lansing. Another time, it was Grand Rapids. He'd even had an offer in Chicago. Of course he'd stayed put . . . He, too, was still here.

A colleague from medical school days had recently lost his partner to Hodgkin's lymphoma, whatever that was. (Uncle Dennis often seemed to assume everyone had attended medical school.) Cleveland was a lot like Detroit, only smaller.

"You're the very first one I've told," Uncle Dennis said. "In your family, that is. Obviously, I must come over soon and tell the others."

Only now did Bea ascertain that something was radically awry—something was terribly, terribly wrong. She stared sharply at her uncle. "But you don't mean you're taking the job."

Niece and uncle peered searchingly at each other. Then the man's glance wobbled and dropped away. "Actually, yes, I think so," Uncle Dennis mumbled. "Actually, I've already accepted."

"But you're not moving to *Cleveland*?" Bea pointed out.

When her uncle's eyes lifted once more, they wore an importunate look—as if he were begging her permission. "Well that's correct, actually," he said. "We are."

"But you don't *know* anyone in Cleveland."

"Well that's not exactly true. There's Whit Callahan. He's the one who extended the offer."

"But no *family*. You won't have family."

"I'll always have family. Your family."

Uncle Dennis said this so sweetly, Bea knew she ought to return his smile. But she was beginning to feel quite indignant and upset . . .

"But for how long?" she said.

"It's open-ended."

"Well—but what about your house?" Bea asked, almost triumphantly, as though Uncle Dennis had altogether forgotten his lovely home on Outer Drive.

"We're planning to sell it."

"*Selling* it? Your *house*? So you're not planning to come back?"

"We may. Someday. We very well may."

"*Someday?* You know what you sound like? You know what you sound like? You sound like everyone else talking about the War. That's what you sound like! Oh, this will all be over *someday*—or so they keep telling us, but maybe it won't! I'm so sick of it! I'm so sick of it! Maybe it will all go on forever!" And she had begun to cry a little. "You're going to leave us? Oh how *could* you, Uncle Dennis? What about *us*? How *could* you go and leave us, the way things are now?"

And with this last barrage of questions Bea saw, more piercingly than ever before, just how hopelessly dejected and ragged everything was at home. What a pack of lies she'd been selling just minutes ago! There was something dispirited and finally desperate to the way Papa nightly came home so stooped with fatigue, smelling of beer and retreating as soon as possible behind his *News,* just as there was something weird and desperate in Stevie's raging battles, or in Edith's asking for burned bacon. And there was something far, far worse than merely desperate in Mamma's squirreling away candy . . . What hope was there of repairing things if Uncle Dennis and Aunt Grace were no longer on the scene? Their departure would be an admission of how irretrievably broken everything was.

A giddy possibility struck her: "I could go with you! I'm sure there are good art schools in Cleveland. Well, why not? I've never gone anywhere. I could go with you to Cleveland."

Behind his glasses, Uncle Dennis's magnified eyes pondered her closely. "Of course you could, honey."

And now Bea began crying in earnest, for what did his words mean but *Of course you can't, honey . . .* ? How could she leave home, the way things were? The family needed her. She might be a crybaby, and a chatterbox, she might be impetuous and moody and demanding, but they needed her. Who else would initiate conversations? Who else was going to make anyone—maybe—laugh out loud? To picture the remaining four of them, night after night, alone at the dining-room table—it was just heartbreaking . . .

Uncle Dennis said, "Oh look what's happened. I've done what I least wanted to do: I've made my little one cry."

Bea retreated to the ladies', where she rinsed her face with cold water and patted it dry. She reapplied her lipstick and threw a few practice smiles into the mirror.

When she returned to the table, she floated in on a tide of words. "But I haven't even congratulated you, you must think I have *no* manners, really this is so thrilling. You'll see new sights! And you'll be so much closer to all sorts of things!"

"Yes," Uncle Dennis agreed, and then, looking frankly puzzled, he added, "*What* sorts of things?"

"Well." Bea came to a wordless halt. "Pittsburgh—won't you be closer to Pittsburgh? And Dayton. Surely you'll be closer to Dayton?"

"I suppose we will." Uncle Dennis went on, "I think we all need a new start . . ."

"Of course we do," Bea said. "I couldn't agree more."

"I don't think you understand just how hard it's been on Grace. It's been a tremendous strain."

"A terrible strain . . ."

"And on you too, I think." Uncle Dennis eyed her professionally. "You look as if you've lost weight."

"Maybe. Just a little."

"Cleveland's less distant than you might suppose. We're talking under six hours in my good old Packard. Even with wartime speed limits."

"That's not bad at all."

"And there's the overnight ferry. Guess what the ferry costs."

"I don't know."

"Only six dollars. Round-trip."

"Imagine that."

"And these days people fly. It's less than an hour by airplane."

"Isn't that something."

"I know you've never flown, Bea, and I want to make you an offer. Within a year, Grace and I promise to buy you a ticket to fly down and visit. Everyone ought to fly in an airplane once in their life. You see the world differently, afterward. It's an education."

"Why, that's extremely generous."

"Stevie and Edith, too, once they get a little older."

"Stevie would die of excitement."

"I'm afraid I have to run . . ."

Uncle Dennis rose from the booth and Bea rose with him. But when she got to her feet, an unshakable weight dropped squarely across her slender shoulders. She could hardly make her way unassisted out of the restaurant.

The weighted sensation only intensified in the parking lot. As traffic crept by on Gratiot, Bea stooped under the crushing burden of the Poppletons' impending move—the worst of all imaginable abandonments—even while Uncle Dennis, who with all his buoyant, boyish heart adored the very essence of aviation, was chanting, "Yes, you're going to fly, Bea darling. Darling Bea, you are, you are, *you're* going to fly."

On the night when her relationship with Ronny was to change subtly but permanently, he wasn't even there. He was away on another road trip with Mr. Olsson. Father and son were checking up on stores in Ohio and Indiana.

Predictably, Ronny's mood had plummeted as the trip approached. Those last few days, he hadn't been much fun to be with . . .

In truth, he'd been something of a pain in the neck for quite a while. Was he becoming more difficult, or was it simply Bea's having too many other problems? She no longer felt able to give Ronny all the attention he sought. He accused her, a little petulantly, of being "distracted." Well, there were so many problems at home, and Uncle Dennis and Aunt Grace were moving to Cleveland, and there was Henry to consider . . .

Ronny was obsessed with Henry. He wanted to be informed whenever Bea saw him, or whenever he telephoned. Honestly, if she hadn't limited his interrogations, Ronny would have had her confessing each time Henry took her hand.

Things would have been easier if she and Ronny were in a class together. Bea had enrolled in Professor Ravenscroft's Principles of Landscape. But Ronny had refused to sign on. "Manhardt may be a pompous fool, but he can actually draw. Ravenscroft can't."

"But how can you continue without—"

"Without the Institute? Boy, you must not think me much of an artist if I need the Institute Midwest."

Yet it turned out Ronny *did* need Professor Ravenscroft's class—or something like it. His previous role had been a little unusual maybe, but not so unusual that Ronny, in his impeccably stylish way, couldn't pull it off with aplomb: being a twenty-one-year-old male art student of still-life painting in a city engulfed by war. But to be a twenty-one-year-old young man without a job or a schedule, pursuing art on his own—this was an all-but-indefensible role. It certainly left Ronny with no grounds for demurral when a proposal arose of a road trip to Ohio and Indiana with his father.

Ronny was not even in Michigan, but Bea received a phone call anyway from Arden Park. It was Mrs. Olsson, feeling under the weather. She'd begged off an engagement, and now, with nobody to dine with, she was feeling "orphaned." Would Bea come over?

On arrival at the Olssons', Bea was shown upstairs for the first time. Here was the parents' bedroom. Mrs. Olsson was lying on a gigantic four-poster canopy bed, propped upon a mountain of pillows.

It soon grew apparent that this was no terribly sick woman, though her voice bore a faint rasp. Of course it was typical of Mrs. Olsson, in her splendid theatrical way, to exhibit her illness in this fashion. She was apparently wearing no makeup and her hair was piled any which way on her head. She was no longer larger than life, and when she rose from bed, after a few minutes' conversation, Bea glimpsed a Mrs. Olsson never seen before: simply another woman in a robe (even if the robe was an exquisite jade-green silk). Though remarkably beautiful, Mrs. Olsson looked a little puffy-faced, and it seemed her body was beginning to show a small potbelly.

"Where shall we sit? Where shall we sit?" Mrs. Olsson chanted, as Bea followed her down the central staircase. "Don't you think it's a remarkably uncomfortable house?"

Uncomfortable? It wasn't a criterion Bea would have thought to apply to any house that boasted a carriage house in back, where Scottish husband and Irish wife, the driver and the cook, resided. In truth, however, Bea had never felt at ease here, though her discomfort probably wasn't with the house so much as its occupants. Who could feel wholly relaxed in a home where lynx-faced Mr. Olsson padded the dark hallways and Mrs. Olsson was forever issuing explosive declarations?

"Let's try the kitchen. I swear it's the only livable room in this whole monstrosity."

So Bea was guided into another largely unfamiliar portion of the house. The cook, whom Bea could not make herself call Agnes, though everybody else did, was sitting at the table reading a copy of *Look*.

"You can call it a day, Agnes," Mrs. Olsson said.

"You haven't had any dinner, ma'am."

"You know I'm not feeling well."

"Yes, ma'am."

And so it was that Bea wound up sitting companionably at the little kitchen table with a Mrs. Olsson whose hair was still haphazardly piled. "I want to hear more about your family," Mrs. Olsson said. "Italy was once the center of the world, wasn't it. The origin of all culture? You talk and I'll make tea."

"I'll make the tea. You're not feeling well."

"No, I want to. Please, just sit . . ."

So Bea sat and, though naturally uneasy about being waited upon by Mrs. Olsson, offered a few family anecdotes, many of which Mrs. Olsson had heard before. Mrs. Olsson greeted every detail as something new, however. Under her solicitous gaze, Bea rapidly turned to the subject of Uncle Dennis and Aunt Grace and their upcoming move. Bea chatted away, though uncertain whether Mrs. Olsson was listening out of genuine interest or merely showing the polite fatigue of somebody feeling not quite like herself.

"And so last week they put their house up for sale and do you know what? Why, they've already sold it!"

"I'm not surprised. Given the housing shortage. The whole city's gone barking mad." Mrs. Olsson set two cups of tea and a plate of biscuits on the table. "Mr. Olsson suggested we take in a boarder. As a patriotic duty. I said, Fine, he can have my place, Charley, because the day he moves in I'm moving out. As if *we're* not doing enough, putting every cent into war bonds and Charley running every wartime committee in the city."

The next thing Mrs. Olsson did was quite surprising. Although she hardly sought to conceal her drinking, she usually carried it out with an air of refinement. Now, though, she opened a cupboard and removed a brown pint bottle of whiskey, which she placed squarely on the kitchen table. "I have to nurse my throat," she said.

"Yes," Bea said.

Mrs. Olsson poured whiskey into her tea—not a lot, but not such a little, either. "Honey, would you like a little splash?" she said.

"No thank you," Bea said.

"It seems you love your aunt and uncle a lot, Bianca," Mrs. Olsson said.

"Well of course I do. I mean they're both so wonderful. Uncle Dennis is so brilliant and kind, and also eccentric—he's obsessed with science-fiction stories. He truly believes we're all going to fly to the moon someday. Honestly."

"Everybody's got a nutty uncle, Bea."

Bea flinched. Though having described her uncle as eccentric, Bea recoiled at *nutty*. She went on: "And Aunt Grace is so kind, too, and gracious just like her name, and so beautiful, though of course, I mean not . . ."

Bea couldn't quite propel herself to say *not so beautiful as you*. She knew no suitable way to compliment the only woman she'd ever personally known who might reasonably be cast in a movie alongside Gary Cooper or Tyrone Power . . . Nonetheless, if it *were* possible to utter such words, it surely ought to be possible on a night when Mrs. Charles Olsson sat sipping whiskey tea in a dark kitchen, looking disheveled and puffy-eyed.

Mrs. Olsson heard the unspoken compliment. Graciously praising somebody whose graciousness had just been praised, she said, "I can certainly believe she's beautiful. Perhaps you look a little like her?"

"Oh not really."

"You know what? I sometimes think you look a little like me. Tall. Dark hair, dark eyes. Maybe that's why you're Ronny's type."

"Oh well . . . I hardly . . . I mean *you*—" All the blood in Bea's body was clamoring to her face. "Well, that's very kind."

"Kind? Listen to you! You're making me sound conceited."

"I didn't mean . . ."

Bea felt thoroughly outmaneuvered. There were occasional moments when Mrs. Olsson seemed not merely a bold and outrageous but also quite a crafty woman. For somebody who, by her own cheerful admission, had never finished high school, and who apparently thought *reticent* was the same as *reluctant,* and *representative* the same as *representational,* Mrs. Olsson sometimes seemed a not implausible mother for her scholarly, epigram-coining, fine-distinction-loving son.

"Speaking of family," Mrs. Olsson said, "you know I'm worried about Charley. Does that seem incredible to you—that I'd be worrying about Charley?"

"Of course not."

"Well I do worry. And last week I found blood in his handkerchief. That sounds like consumption, but it's not. It's his ulcer. He drives himself to it."

"Well, he's very driven." Bea reached out and took two biscuits. Suddenly, she was feeling almost shaky with hunger. Hadn't she been invited for dinner?

"That's one of the qualities that drew me to him: his exceptional drive. But now I sometimes have to ask: is that such a good idea? Why was I so drawn to that?"

"Isn't it only natural for a woman to be?"

"Bianca, would you say Ronny is driven?"

"Of course," Bea replied. "I mean"—all at once, Mrs. Olsson was watching her *very* closely—"not to a worrisome degree. But yes. Driven as an artist I mean."

"And you do think he's a talented artist?"

"Without question. Oh, he was the best in our class! I mean, he was the best at capturing a thing's likeness. I do wish he'd take more classes . . ."

"*I've* always thought he was talented," Mrs. Olsson declared. "But Charley says, You want a likeness, a camera's far more lifelike. He's not at all sure art like that has a future."

"Oh but it does!" Bea cried, feeling that here at least she could provide Mrs. Olsson with the reassurances the woman seemed to crave tonight. "He's got quite a future. And art does, too," she added.

In the pause that followed, she couldn't resist: she reached out and filched another biscuit.

"Why, you haven't had dinner!" Mrs. Olsson cried. "Agnes just now—she was trying to tell me something, wasn't she? That I ought to see my guest is properly fed! Bianca my dear, you'll have to excuse me: truly I'm not feeling well."

"Oh I'm perfectly—"

"I'll make you some eggs. Would you permit me to make you some eggs?"

"Good grief, there's no need to—"

"Eggs. I'll make us both some *eggs*. And you must promise to sit *right there* . . ."

You might well suppose Mrs. Olsson would be the sort of woman who wouldn't know how to boil water, but as she slid to and fro in her jade-colored robe, it quickly became apparent she was adept in a kitchen. She diced, beat, stirred, and in just a few minutes a tasteful plate was set before Bea: a mound of cottage cheese, toast (sliced on the diagonal), some apple wedges, and half an omelet.

The golden omelet, which enfolded cheddar cheese and finely cut ham and browned onions, turned out to be quite wonderful.

"I can't believe I'm letting a sick woman wait on me. What must you think?"

"Oh but it was good of *you* to drop everything and race over . . . You rescued me when I felt orphaned. You know where I was supposed to be tonight? Another charity 'do.' I swear it's *every night*. You do understand, there's no man in the whole city sitting on more of these war committees than Charley."

"His name is often in the paper."

"He's running one of the biggest drugstore chains in the Midwest, and he's also running half the war committees in Detroit, and where does that leave Ronny?"

The question came out on a high-pitched note—almost as though Bea were being accused of something. "It's damn difficult, isn't it," Mrs. Olsson went on. "Of course, Charley could put him on any number of committees, but Ronny doesn't want that. You know Ronny *is* a block captain."

"Yes."

"And he does far more than he lets on."

"Yes?"

"But it never stops, does it. Tonight's 'do'? They're raising funds for displaced Belgians—or maybe Spaniards? Do I sound cruel?" And though *cruel* wasn't a word Bea would employ, there was a hard unreachable glint to Mrs. Olsson's gaze. "Oh I believe in charity. Did you know I have money in my own name? It's one of the conditions I insisted upon when I married Charley, and I recommend you do the same. He signed over certain properties. And now I drive him crazy by giving away ten percent of the income. To charities. To orphanages. Charley says my philanthropy is disorganized, and I say, Christ, Charley, do you think *Christ* was an organized philanthropist? Do you suppose he kept records of what he gave—ten bucks to the leper, five bucks to the blind woman? I wouldn't help an able-bodied man out of a ditch, my dear, but I'll contribute to the Negro Children's Betterment Fund." And while it was easy to overlook, since it didn't emerge all that frequently, there was this facet, too, to Mrs. Olsson's riddling personality: she could be a woman of moralizing fervor.

"No, it's not the charity I mind, it's that whole damned world where

Charley feels you always have to be climbing another rung. I don't think I'm criticizing myself when I say, Maybe Charley married the wrong woman."

It was too painful a remark to let stand. Bea protested, "Oh but honestly, how could Mr. Olsson have done better?"

"And aren't you the sweetest girl!"

Mrs. Olsson then added—sadly?—"Sometimes maybe almost too sweet?"

"Too sweet for what?"

This was a train of conversation Bea longed to pursue, but Mrs. Olsson had her own ideas. She went on: "And I'm worried about Ronny. Do you think he can ever be happy in this line—this art business?"

"Well I think so. I mean happy sometimes. What I mean is, I don't think he could possibly be happy doing anything else. Do you?"

"Does Ronny seem happy to you?"

"Well he'd be the first to admit it, he can be moody."

"Moody—yes. My son has always been moody. Show me a truly intelligent person who isn't. But overall—do you think you can make him happy?"

"Me? I don't claim—"

"But you're happy with him?"

"I'm not sure when you say *with him* what you're—"

Again, Mrs. Olsson didn't allow her to complete a sentence. "I'm not going to ask whether you're in love with my son, Bianca. I'm not sure that asking you would be appropriate. But surely a mother might justifiably ask whether you understand what all's going on inside his mind right now, studying art while so many boys are in the Army, and living with a father who races off to work and then, after coughing blood into a handkerchief, races off to a meeting attended by Max Fisher and Mayor Jeffries and Henry Ford himself. Surely a mother can ask how much you think you understand."

Bea took her time in answering: "Well, I do think I understand some of the pressures Ronny's feeling. It's a strange time for anybody to be an art student, frankly, but it's especially so for a boy, and yet maybe there's such a thing as artist's hunger, regardless of everything else, including whether you're a boy or a girl? It's as if your hand is hungry—and your hand has never heard of the War. It just wants to draw, to create things. And *that*—well I do think I understand *that* about Ronny."

Mrs. Olsson's attention had begun visibly wandering the instant Bea opened up the topic of art. "No doubt about it," she said vacantly. Then her look and her voice changed. She brought her palms together, in a slow clapping motion, and on this night when she'd introduced so many sides to herself, she came up with an affecting show of glowing maternal gratitude: "Bea, I think you understand my boy!"

Mrs. Olsson carried Bea's plate, on which everything had been eaten, and her own, where the food had been mostly shifted about, over to the sink. "Of course a lot of people can't understand him, can they? Can't understand a boy whose heart is hungry in that way you so vividly describe? What about a boy whose heart wants to draw?"

"Hand, actually. What I said—"

"They want Ronny to be his father and he's not his father."

"That's right."

Mrs. Olsson returned to the kitchen table. "And people leap to conclusions, don't they? In their ignorance. It's the one kind of ignorance I can't abide. You see what I'm saying. Being smart is *knowing* you're smart. And being dumb is knowing you're smart when you're actually dumb. It's different. That's why I left Scarp, though you find it everywhere. You know what they said at Groton? Where they ought to know better? When we sent him off to a fancy boarding school? They didn't understand Ronny at all, did they? Well: they insinuated that my boy is cur."

Cur? For a moment, two moments, Bea hadn't the faintest idea what Mrs. Olsson might be intimating. But this interval was succeeded by different, elongated moments, during which Bea's insides turned all fluttery and queasy.

It was remarkable how many things happened instantaneously inside her. First, a wild, ghastly thought materialized: the strange term, *cur,* was meant to stand for a similar sound, all but unmentionable. Oh, Bea was *used* to having such thoughts—particularly at night, when crazed, unsupervised notions snuck into her brain and wouldn't, just wouldn't, depart. But not here, not in a place like the Olssons' kitchen . . .

Then it grew apparent to Bea—and this was the strangest, strangest thing yet—that she wasn't misinterpreting Mrs. Olsson at all. No, Mrs. Olsson's thoughts were in the very same place as hers: their minds were meeting in the queerest spot imaginable. Mrs. Olsson said, "Obviously, the whole idea's ridiculous. I mean, a mother *knows.*"

While remaining seated at the kitchen table, she drew her spine erect, and her eyes flashed, and for the first time tonight she was absolutely Mrs. Charles Olsson, that legendary figure whose beauty set the *Detroit News* society pages ashimmer. Mrs. Olsson's hand fluttered at her ample bosom—a reflexive gesture at once magnificently self-possessed and coyly vulnerable. "My boy isn't cur. A mother knows such things. And how does she know? How do I know my boy isn't cur? Why, I can see it in the way he looks at me."

CHAPTER XVIII

Perhaps the very worst aspect of the Poppletons' painfully abrupt departure was its effect on Mamma. She watched without visible emotion as a huge moving van, the words "Turk's Trucks" emblazoned in red letters on its side, carted the Poppletons' lives away. (The moving van belonged to that strange, voluble man, Yusuf Caglayangil, whom Bea and Aunt Grace had met at Sanders—the one who claimed Uncle Dennis had saved his daughter's life. Mr. Caglayangil and his daughter Melek—looking healthier, and broader, than ever—personally oversaw the truck's departure, and the two of them, peripheral figures though they were, appeared far more bereft than Mamma.) Three days later, when a postcard from Aunt Grace arrived, Mamma was rosiness itself: "She says their house has two guest rooms—there's room for all of us. And *guess what* . . . there's an actual greenhouse in back!"

There was no ignoring Mamma's conviction that the Poppletons' departure had corroborated every one of her craziest accusations. And no ignoring how she saw herself: a good, gracious winner.

It was as though everything in Bea's life were conspiring to leave her with a blasted sensation of abandonment. Uncle Dennis and Aunt Grace had moved away to Cleveland, Ohio, which might as well have been Buenos Aires or Melbourne to a niece who had never left Michigan (except for jaunts across the river to Windsor, Canada, which scarcely counted, since Windsor was less like a foreign country than an amusement park). And Ronny was no longer a student at the Institute Midwest, and Maggie was effectively imprisoned at the outskirts of the city. And Henry—Henry had been medically examined and judged fit for combat. He was off again to the Pacific, and soon.

There were times, particularly when Ronny swept her into his arms, when Bea could put behind her that very bizarre night in the kitchen with Mrs. Olsson. Ronny was as attractive as ever, he was more attractive than ever, since Bea felt more vulnerable or needy than ever. And yet he'd grown distant—as though he'd drifted off, becoming a soul afloat. Surely, quitting the Institute had been a terrible idea. By dropping out, Ronny had lost that pride-sustaining ability to explain easily, to any stranger, who he was and what he was doing.

Increasingly, Ronny reminisced about shared experiences as if they belonged to some misty past. *Do you remember that first walk we had in Palmer Park?* he might begin, as though Bea could possibly have forgotten—as though it had taken place not months but years ago. Do you remember that unbelievable woman singing "They Didn't Believe Me" under the Kern's clock? Do you remember that night, Bea, when you said the moon over the river resembled the face of a Chinese mandarin?

And—queerer yet—his distancing languor seemed infectious: Bea, too, began feeling as though everything had unfolded ages ago. It was another world—those days when leaves on the trees were still green, when people swam in Lady Lake, when her family felt whole and her aunt and uncle visited weekly.

How many soldiers' faces had she drawn since her first, Private Donnelly—that sweet, touching boy who had made her laugh so gaily and whose mobile features, behind the big stiff bandage over his eye, had all but faded from memory? Since then, there'd been too many boys to remember, drifting off like puppets on strings, wherever the War told them to go. And sometimes the War sent the puppets home, damaged, with strings hopelessly tangled . . .

Her heart wasn't in school—in those dutiful landscapes produced for Dr. Ravenscroft. Nor was her heart in her dealings at home, where poor Papa continued working backbreaking hours. Yes, they were prospering on Inquiry Street. The difficulty wasn't a lack of money but—given the War—a shortage of things to buy. Papa announced one night that the family would have a new car once production started up again, and everybody knew they could depend on his promise: Papa never made a pledge unless he meant to keep it. He brought home a mammoth, gorgeous, all-but-new Philco radio, salvaged from one of his home renovations. And there was the night he came home smelling strongly of beer and said to Bea, as he stood by the kitchen sink eating a dill pickle right out of the jar, "Bia, you know what I made this week?"

At first she thought what he'd *made* must have something to do with houses—something he'd constructed. Papa never talked of money in this way.

"Uh-uh," Bea said.

"I made over a hundred dollars this week."

"A hundred dollars?" An amazing sum . . .

"O'Reilly sold that house we redid on Twelfth Street and I got a bonus. Now not a word to anyone," Papa said darkly, and pressed into her hand a ten-dollar bill. The windfall should have elated her. Why did she feel downcast instead?

Nor was her heart in those portraits she drew at Ferry Hospital, because she'd learned she couldn't afford to bring her heart into that ghost-haunted castle.

It was a lesson perhaps not fully appreciated when she'd met the soldier who offered her an "indifferent poem" for an "indifferent portrait." More than she wanted to admit, more than she knew was wise, Henry's face and voice and darting turns of thought had become a part of her, like the iron and the sugar in her blood. Maybe it was only once a week she rode up Woodward to Pleasant Ridge, but each visit filled her head with words to ponder, images to absorb. Was this what love really was— this finding someone's every remark worth deliberating over?

And now *Henry* was going to leave her.

And there was nobody—truly nobody—to whom Bea could explain how desolating that prospect was. Certainly not Henry himself, to whom she owed a duty to treat his departure positively. And *certainly* not Ronny, though Ronny would have listened eagerly—jealously— enough. And not Maggie, who had no tolerance for such talk when her own husband was forty-four hundred miles away, waiting for the Japs to restrike Pearl Harbor.

And now Henry was leaving—and now Henry was *really* leaving. Though he still walked stiffly, and though Bea was keenly attuned to the precariousness of his recovery, Henry was leaving in four days. In hasty moments, Henry began stealing kisses. Four days! Though he usually seemed such a frugal young man, he took her to lunch at the Book-Cadillac dining room, and he presented her with a silk scarf from Himelhoch's, and he bought her an amethyst locket because (in the sort of endearing skewed logic he lived by) the amethyst was *his* birthstone.

On their last night together, he took her to meet a friend of his, who lived with his parents in Ferndale, a few blocks from the Vanden Akkers'. The friend, whose name was Mitchell Spence, wasn't home. In fact, no one was home. It turned out that Mitchell's mother and father were in Indianapolis. Mitchell had left a key in the milk chute, though.

They sat in Mitchell's house, waiting for Mitchell. It was odd waiting in a total stranger's home, totally alone with Henry. It made Bea uneasy, it made her oddly joyful. Henry suggested they brew up some coffee and she told him she felt peculiar invading a stranger's kitchen and Henry told her that Mitchell not only wouldn't mind, he would insist.

So the two of them wound up sitting in Mitchell's living room, sipping coffee, under the intent gazes of strangers—the room was chockablock with photographs. "That's Mitchell," Henry said, pointing to a tinted photograph, perched on the end table.

The big round face was a little too large for its frame. This wasn't a face Bea would have pictured for any friend of Henry's. Mitchell had an openhearted, plump, friendly face. His hair was combed back in a simple, colossal wave. He looked—truth to tell—not very bright.

Actually, Mitchell's face was everywhere. On the mantel, on top of the radio, on the windowsill.

Bea and Henry sat on the couch, waiting for Mitchell. Henry kissed her and she let him kiss her. This was something she never remembered, except when the actual activity was in progress: the colors were different in Henry's touch, and in Henry's kiss. These weren't those chlorophyll-crazed greens, the detonative reds and yellows and unsoundable blues that Ronny aroused. No, it was a narrower palette of tans and golds and muted oranges—just the colors of Henry's freckled skin, his green-tinted brown eyes, his rusty hair. Ronny's hands had a complete little repertoire of tricks or wiles—the suave way they teased and tested her inner palms, the back of her neck, even her earlobes. Ronny's touch made her feel dizzy and a little frightened, but there was nothing frightening about Henry. There was something so straightforwardly candid in how his hands clenched her hands, his lips pushed up against her lips.

"They tell me I've recovered," Henry said. "It seems I'm fit for service."

"You do seem better, Henry. You *look* better. Your mother succeeded in fattening you up."

"My mother," Henry said.

"I remember when I first laid eyes on you. You were a wraith."

"And I remember when I first laid eyes on you. You were an angel."

"Henry."

"Fit for service? Such a simple phrase. But applied to such a complicated reality."

"I think you're very brave."

"No. Please. Don't say that." Henry looked even more serious than usual. "You see, Bea, I'm very frightened."

"I know you are. And I think you're very brave."

The second time around, the tribute found its mark. Henry flushed with pride, and turned to kiss her . . .

And then she saw him wince—his back had stabbed him—and Bea, riding forward on a tide of sympathy, leaned forward and kissed Henry hard, harder than they usually kissed, and a bright yellow yolk of light ruptured and ran inside her head. When their lips broke apart, Henry's breath lofted into her ear.

The telephone rang.

"We better not answer it," Bea said. She suddenly felt very guilty— virtually criminal—just in being here. But Henry said it might be Mitchell and hauled himself to his feet.

"Hello," Henry said. "Oh hello. Really? All right. All right. I understand. Okay." Henry hung up the phone. "That was Mitchell," he said. "He's delayed. He won't be here for an hour and a half or so."

"Then we ought to leave, Henry."

"I have something I want to say first." Henry sat down and slowly swung round to face her. "Bea, you know how I feel about you," he said.

"I do. Yes. Yes, I do know, Henry."

"Then you know I'm in love with you."

"Well—"

"And I can't express what that does to my thinking, Bea. *All* my thinking. My house is different because I love you. And my parents. *Mathematics* is different because I love you. Do you see where this is going?"

Bea didn't really, for her head was all in a muddle. And Henry's body was so tense—she could feel its internal compression as he leaned toward her, into her, vibrant passion suffusing his face: his eyes were afire. Oh my: was he proposing to her? Is that where this was going?

"And God, too," Henry said. "God is different because I love you. Do you see what I'm saying? I can have no meaningful theology that doesn't include you."

"Henry, please, kiss me," Bea said, but that wasn't at all what she'd intended to say.

Bea hadn't been certain she understood everything he'd meant, but as they kissed, again and again, it grew clearer that she took Henry's measure precisely. And he her. She was a part of his meaningful theology. There were different levels of understanding operating here.

"Do I have to make the conventional pronouncements?" Henry said. "That I've never felt this way before? That I've never told anyone I loved her?"

"No. Because I already know . . ."

"This is all so new to me," Henry said, and—just like that—he placed his hands upon her breasts. "You're . . . you understand all this better than I do."

"No, Henry," Bea whispered. "No."

They kissed again and though his hands were awkwardly placed— they were still settled on her breasts—the colors in her head not only brightened but swirled, the way melted caramel swirls around an apple, hollowing a place for it, enclosing the red and pink skin in a subsiding bed of pure tawny sweetness . . .

"I'm so frightened," Henry said.

"Shh," Bea said.

"You do know."

"Yes. Shh now."

"So frightened it's all going to end before I achieve any clarity."

Clarity: the word threw splinters of light Bea's way, as a cresting wave will, just before its invisible self-supports give way and it goes under. Her mouth was so *hungry* for his mouth. Kissing him seemed the only way to make him stop talking.

"I'm so afraid I won't come back," Henry said.

"No, Henry," Bea said, "no," she repeated, when all at once, as though the visionary wave had awesomely regathered, only to cascade over her head, she was struck by a revelation more overwhelming than any in her life before. It was true—yes, her second sight confirmed it: Henry wouldn't come back. *Henry would not come back.*

Never again would Henry come back and everything so powerfully present before her at this moment—Henry's eyes and Henry's bony hands, Henry's voice, Henry's feverish, wonderful, overburdened brain—was going away forever. She would be abandoned; he would leave her, permanently.

"No, Henry," Bea half whispered and half cried, "no."

"I'm so frightened," Henry said, and he was shaking with his fear. She held him, pulled him toward her, and their mouths locked even more tightly.

Then his hands sprung loose, they were all over her body, and Henry's shaking, or her own shaking, turned into a different type of shaking. "No, Henry," Bea was saying, but what she was denying or protesting was no longer obvious to anyone. Anyone watching—anyone watching from above—wouldn't have known what to make of it. His hand was way up her skirt, her whole body arched forward and backward, and forward. "No, Henry," she said, and everything she did was colored by this horrible, green, glittering metallic certainty: never again, never again after tonight would she enfold poor Henry Vanden Akker in her arms. The brightest mind she'd ever known, maybe . . . the intensest, certainly . . . her one dear Dutch Detroit Vincent . . . this boy would never come back from that jungle that so awed and addled and terrified him. Never. Never.

Everything in the world that Henry longed for would be brutally ripped away and what else was there to do but yield to his hands' hunger? She was aware of fumbling, and uncertainty, and more fumbling, and Henry actually cursing, *Damn,* and pleading, *Please, please.* And then, *Oh dearest God . . .*

It was supposed to hurt and if it had hurt she might have shown the presence of mind to make him stop—only, it did not hurt at all, it merely demanded a deep and a simple and a complicated set of adjustments. The force of him now was almost more than she could bear—his breath was a rasping ransacking gasp down the long tunnel of one of her ears—and she seized him by the shoulders and cried, *"No, Henry!"* as everything at once came distinct, as if seen from above, the absolute *wrongness* of it, and there was a wild, long, quick removing, a sliding free, free into deeper pooled regrets than she could bear, a hot strangled goodbye, and Henry repeatedly shuddering, atop her, and then Henry was still.

And then Henry was talking again but what Henry might say no longer mattered in the slightest. He was speaking of God, he was showering her with apologies, he was telling her he loved her and explaining something about Calvin College and the incalculable size of the sea, and his parents, and a catastrophic fall, which turned out to be his own fall, on a hillside in the jungle, but nothing counted for anything given the crime scene contemplated by Mitchell's big and innocent face from its perch on the end table: there was a spatter of loud bright blood on her thigh and on her stomach and on her blouse and—yes—blood on the couch, too. Bea pushed Henry off of her, completely off of her ("I didn't know," he kept saying, dimly, "I didn't know"), and she gathered her clothes inadequately around her and, whimpering and gasping, she scurried into the bathroom, just the way Aunt Grace had dashed toward the changing room when her bathing suit strap snapped at Lady Lake, and Bea shut and locked the door. She was breathing hard, but she was not crying.

The room's sharper light made everything all that much more coldly horrifying. *What had she done?* At the base of her ribs she found a smear of something altogether alien and then a moment later she knew precisely what it was, this shiny clinging white mud: oh, every cell in her body recognized it in all its concentrated cruelty and selfishness and menace.

Bea removed her blouse, completely removed her blouse, and draped it on the towel rack, and she removed her brassiere too. Her skirt had already fallen to the floor. Henry was speaking from the other side of the door, but she didn't listen. She lowered the rest of her clothing and let it lie piled at her ankles. Bea still wasn't crying, though her breath was coming in sobs. She turned on both the hot and cold taps as far as they would go. Into the tumbling upset tumult of the basin she plunged a washcloth, wrung it out, and applied it to her stomach, her ribs, her breasts. She wrung it out and applied it under her arms, over her arms. Wrung it out and, panting harder than ever now, so that her breathing seemed to get in her way as she bent over, she applied it to her trembling private parts. Lastly, with a second washcloth, Bea rinsed her face, dried herself carefully, and one by one put her garments back on. Then she took the first, soiled washcloth and attended to the bloodstain on her blouse.

When she unlocked the door, Henry was all over her. He was hovering beside her, flailing his hands and talking a mile a minute. Bea all but pushed him away. *"Henry,"* she said. "Don't you see? My God, there's cleaning up to do!"

"Cleaning up," Henry said. "Yes, cleaning up," he echoed. "Of course there's cleaning up."

The phrase seemed to carry great philosophical weight with Henry—he nodded respectfully, as though she'd uttered something terribly profound—but failed to inspire any action. He planted himself beside the end table—beside Mitchell's grinning stupid face—and observed her silently as Bea applied to the couch the same washcloth she'd taken to her blouse. Fortunately the couch's plaid pattern hid the stain a bit.

"How would this look," Bea said, her voice higher than normal by a couple of notches, "if Mitchell came home now? Look at me. Henry, look at this couch."

"I don't think he will," Henry said. "There's still—there's still quite a bit of time."

"Look at me, Henry," Bea cried in anguish, scrubbing and scrubbing at the plaid couch.

Then Henry made a funny sudden cackling sound. He started sobbing and, after a minute or two—unexpectedly—Bea began to feel genuinely sorry for him. She sat Henry down on the half of the couch not wet with her scrubbing and she squeezed in beside him. She placed his face at the base of her neck and held him. Perhaps because she was such a crybaby herself, she could never resist comforting a person in tears.

"It's okay, Henry," she said. "Everything's all right, Henry." It should have been so strange, and yet the whole business followed its own compelling weird logic: on this night when she'd lost her virginity, it was not she, but her partner, who wound up in tears.

"What have I done?" Henry cried. "What have I done?"

"You haven't done anything. *We* did. We did it together."

"You don't see how awful I am."

"You're not awful, Henry. Or no awfuller than I am."

"It's so wonderful of you: it's as if you can't see it, Bea. My God, *you're wonderful*." Henry raised his head from her neck and, eyes red with tears, peered at her intently. "Under any imaginable scrutiny, you're wonderful."

"Shh," she said. "Hush now."

"Bea," he said, "what's the worst color a person could be? What's the very worst, disgustingest color a human being could be?"

"Henry, what in God's name are you *talking* about?"

"You're a painter. What's the very worst color a human skin could be? In theory. Hypothetically." An eager excitement returned to his face. "I mean of all the colors in the whole universe—the whole entire spectrum. The worst-colored skin. Turtle green? Cobalt blue? In all your entire imagination, what's the very worst color any person could be?"

And now—with all the irrepressibility of his eccentric soul—Henry was essentially Henry once more. He had come up with a burning preposterous hypothetical question requiring an immediate answer: "What's the worst, worst color?"

"Any color in the whole spectrum?" Bea asked.

"*Any* color. What's the worst, disgustingest color any human being could be?"

Tonight, Bea had lost her virginity, which made Henry cry, who now was ushering her into some *Astounding Tales* planet of Uncle Dennis's, where a person's skin could be any hue in the spectrum: yes, events were following a logic all their own . . . "Bright shiny plum?" Bea replied, and shuddered, for at once she could see just such a person, aloofly elongated and angular: he was seated in a high chair at a low desk, and his skin, his neatly parted hair, the whites of his eyes were all the same intensely infused, glossy shade of purple.

"Precisely!" Henry crowed. "And it's as if that's me! It's me! It's as if I'm some sort of plum-colored creature—and you? You're color-blind to that particular shade! Do you see what I'm saying? Bea, you've got the best eye of anyone I know, you're constantly pointing out things I didn't see, but *you* can't see the worst, most important fact about me. Whatever the worst shade is, that's the one you can't see. Constitutionally, you can't see it, Bea."

"Henry, *I'm* the one who came up with the color . . ."

"Bea, I have something I must tell you," Henry said.

"Oh Jesus Christ," Bea replied, not meaning to swear. But honestly she couldn't take any more. "Henry, haven't you said enough already?"

When Bea whispered, "Oh you won't believe it, the very *worst thing* has happened," Maggie's face brightened so dramatically, so eagerly, Bea balked at continuing. But she had no choice, really. There was nobody else on earth she could tell . . .

They'd found shelter in a branch library. It was hardly the place for this sort of conversation but Mrs. Hamm didn't approve of luncheonettes (a waste of money), and the Hamm home presumably hid listening devices. Outdoors, the rain was coming down hard. It had taken Bea forever to journey over here—riding the streetcar for miles out Grand River, then walking block after block through the miserable downpour, holding aloft her broken-ribbed umbrella. On her arrival, the Turnkey had eyed her dubiously—no sympathy extended, though Bea must have looked half drowned. But ultimately the two girls were permitted to visit the library. Naturally, Herbie was sent along.

Yet at the library something wonderful occurred. Bea had wisely come equipped: before boarding the streetcar she'd raided one of her mother's candy bowls. She presented Herbie with a little bag of gum-balls and he curled up happily in a chair with a book. He actually seemed to be reading, as he munched his candy. It appeared the two girlfriends might speak in peace.

Quietly they had nudged a couple of armchairs right up to a streaming windowpane. "Tell me," Maggie said.

The rain provided a muffling, tolerant background music, encouraging Bea's confession. She began with some scene-setting. What had unfolded inside Mitchell's house three nights ago obviously couldn't be disclosed right away.

All the preliminary information took some time, partly because Maggie frequently interrupted and partly because Bea shied from divulging the worst. "Oh my God, do you mean you actually lost it?" Maggie said finally, and, when Bea wavered, Maggie asked point-blank: "Your virginity?"

"*Shh*," Bea replied, though Maggie actually was keeping her voice low. And given the rain's drumming against the pane, there was little danger of being overheard.

"Well did you or didn't you?"

"*Shh*. Okay, I suppose I did." To utter even this tentative assent made everything feel fixed and irrevocable as it hadn't quite before. A burning mist filled Bea's eyes.

"I can't believe it," Maggie said. "*You*," she said, shaking her head, and yet her warm touch—she had taken Bea's hand—held far more approval than disapproval. It was from Maggie, as much as anyone, that Bea had learned to be a "toucher."

"My downfall was, I had this sudden *feeling*," Bea said. "Suddenly I had this crazy definite feeling: I just felt completely absolutely certain Henry wasn't coming back. That he was honestly going to die out there."

"You and your *feelings*," Maggie whispered, and the fondness in her voice was almost painfully reassuring. "You and your second sight," she said, and squeezed Bea's hand. Oh, Bea needed this affection! If Maggie all too often made her uneasy, with her keen undisguised appetite for tales of misfortune in Bea's life, still there was no doubting Maggie's steadfast love. No matter what Bea did. Maggie was Bea's best friend, and right now she was the only soul on earth Bea could turn to.

"And he said he loved me. That he'd never loved any girl before."

"Oh, that's what they all—"

"Actually, he said he loved me so much, it changed the way he saw his parents, and mathematics, and even the way he saw God was—" But Maggie was already looking impatient and how in the world was Bea to encapsulate everything Henry had said about God on that cataclysmic evening?

"Do you think he'd marry you?"

Bea hesitated. "Well, he's gone away." It made her feel quite strange to speak of such things, but she went ahead anyway: "But when he comes back, I think he'd want to."

"But do you love him, Bea?"

"Maggie, I don't *know* . . ."

"I thought you loved Ronny."

"Maggie, I don't *know*. I'm feeling so confused! Good grief, what am I going to do *if I'm pregnant*? And Henry across the Pacific!"

"Well, is there any chance Ronny would marry you?"

"Oh but I wouldn't *want* to now, Maggie, even if he would! It wouldn't be fair, under the circumstances—you see that, don't you? Don't you? I've given myself to someone else."

"But you might have to make sacrifices, Bea." Maggie-the-married-woman trained on her a look of worldly wisdom.

"But I couldn't sacrifice somebody completely innocent! You honestly don't think I'm the kind of girl to trick somebody. Do you?"

Maggie delayed just a little too long. "No," she said. "Of course not."

"Well I'm *not*."

"Though it would solve a lot of problems . . ."

This was Maggie being practical, and showing her practicality by biting thoughtfully on her lower lip—but honestly, if she was so practical, how had she wound up living with Herbie in a penitentiary run by Ma'am Hamm?

"But it wouldn't be *fair*. You see that, don't you?"

"What else could you do?"

What else could she do? It hadn't been easy to think logically these last few frenzied, wretched days. After miserable struggling, Bea had formulated a few possibilities, all of them scary and overwhelming. She would move away from home, leaving behind a beautiful candid letter explaining how much she loved them all and how grateful she was to them and this was the reason she couldn't bring her shame down upon them and she would move to New York City and become an artist. Or she'd move to Chicago and support herself drawing fashion ads. Or climb aboard the overnight ferry to Cleveland and throw herself on the dependable mercy of Uncle Dennis and Aunt Grace, who would surely take her in. Or perhaps it was possible that Uncle Dennis, as a doctor, might be able to arrange something, though she wasn't sure she could live with that . . .

"There's really nothing—there's nothing I could do."

"Now tell me what happened. Exactly what happened."

"Well—"

What followed was a conversation unlike any in Bea's life before. It was amazingly intimate, though Maggie herself seemed wholly unflappable. She wanted to know how many times they had done "it" and in exactly what circumstances. She had an all-purpose term for their most intimate parts—his "thing," your "thing"—and it seemed Maggie, while sitting in a public library, saw nothing peculiar or shameful about discussing the "thing" of a man she'd never met.

Admittedly, this branch library offered an especially intimate and comfortable sanctuary on an afternoon like this. The few visitors who had braved the rain looked sleepy and distracted. Even Herbie had drifted off in his armchair, one hand buried possessively in his bag of gumballs. The conversation rolled along . . .

Then an unexpected complication arose. When Maggie eventually discovered that Henry had withdrawn his thing before, in some technical sense, completing the act, she announced, almost indignantly, that Bea hadn't, in fact, lost it: Bea was still a virgin.

Still a virgin? Bea met this conclusion with an indignation far greater than Maggie's, whose remark seemed not only incorrect (surely it was mistaken!) but quite hurtfully dismissive. Having suffered weeping anguish only moments ago, contemplating her lost innocence, Bea felt strangely swindled on being informed that she'd not lost it at all.

"But there was blood!"

"That can happen to you in gym. Or on a playground. Norma Nunnally told me it happened to her riding a horse, when she was all of ten. So are you telling me Norma lost her virginity to a horse at the age of ten?"

"Maggie, stop it."

So that Maggie's judgment could be scientifically, categorically arrived at, she needed to know various excruciatingly personal specifics—matters like how long and how deeply Henry's thing had penetrated. But these were precisely the sorts of questions Bea couldn't answer. Indeed Bea felt—a point she couldn't quite articulate—that her very inability supported her contention: if she hadn't lost her virginity, wouldn't her memories be clearer?

After a torturous grilling, during which Maggie kept asking the same few pointed questions, slightly rephrased, she finally offered her summary: "You haven't lost it yet."

Among other things, this conclusion seemed unfair to poor Henry, who right there on the couch in Mitchell's living room had cried Bea's collar wet, pleading all the while for absolution, and who in the extremity of his guilt and grief had conceived of an altered God and a nightmarish cosmos peopled by high-gloss plum-colored human beings.

"But Maggie—Maggie! What if I'm pregnant?"

"You're not pregnant."

A powerful, stinging rebuttal presented itself: "But what if I am? Good God, Maggie, are you saying this would be a virgin birth?"

Maggie looked at her not only wisely but sadly, as though the gullibility of the world was painful to contemplate. "You don't get pregnant that way."

"That's not what *I* heard."

"That's only what they tell you so you won't misbehave."

"But you can. You *can.*" Bea felt herself on solider ground here. She had read this perhaps. Or heard it definitely somewhere.

"Well *you're* not pregnant and isn't that the point?"

"I didn't know you'd become a clairvoyant," Bea said.

Maggie's reply was quite cutting—cruel, really. "You're the one with the *feelings.* You're the one who knew Henry's not coming back . . ."

A pause opened and it was as if the patter of the rain, previously so soothing, now pricked at the two girls, goading them on.

Bea said, "So are you still seeing Wally?"

Normally, Bea would have uttered this "seeing" more delicately—in deference to the notion that Maggie might be seeing but certainly wasn't *seeing* Wally.

"Walton. I keep telling you that, that that's what he goes by now."

"And I keep forgetting."

"If you want to know, we had coffee this week. Did I tell you he drives a Cadillac?"

"You did."

"They're really getting rich, the Wallers—not just the father but Wally and his two brothers."

"So do you think you're going to sleep with Wally?"

This, too, was a cruel inquiry, to say nothing of being brutally, nastily blunt, and Bea instantly regretted it. What *was* going on inside her—why was she talking this way? She'd have withdrawn the question, if she could, but the words were out . . .

"Bea . . ." was all Maggie offered in sighing answer, and projected her lower lip as if about to cry. There was little danger of that, for Maggie almost never cried. No, this was a long-standing ritual, perhaps originally evolved in response to Bea's perpetual floods of tears. This particular negotiating ploy of Maggie's—a hung lower lip, a flurry of blinks—initially might have surfaced something like ten years ago, when the two girls first became best friends.

Herbie's interruption was almost welcome. "I wanna go home," he said.

"We can't go home," Maggie replied. "See that?" She shrugged at the window. "It's called rain."

"I'm hungry."

"Chew the gumballs Aunt Bea brought you. They're different fruit flavors. You need to try them all."

Bea didn't know quite how she felt about this "Aunt Bea" routine. Though a joke, it acknowledged a stark legal oddity: this sticky-mouthed boy standing beside them truly was Maggie's brother-in-law.

"Already ate 'em."

In truth, Bea felt a little guilty about having brought so many gumballs. Lord knows, she didn't want him sick again, but that was only the start of it. Herbie's teeth were a shocking disaster. You'd think the Hamm family would be more careful. Or at least Maggie would, who had dealt with George's anguished tears when the Army yanked all his teeth. (He'd feared that Maggie would break their engagement, and Bea had often wondered—not a speculation to share with Maggie—whether under different circumstances, if only the Army had left him his teeth, George would have been *quite* so insistent on marrying before shipping out.)

"Christ almighty." Maggie made no effort to watch her language around Herbie. "Kid, jever hear of sugar rationing? Jever hear there's a war on and your brother's fighting it?"

"I'm hungry."

"Oh hell. Bea?"

Bea dug into her purse and found half a roll of cherry Life Savers.

She meant to offer Herbie only one, but Maggie plucked the entire roll from her hand.

"You want to sit with us, I give you one. Or you sit back in your chair, I give you the whole roll."

Herbie shuffled back to his chair.

"Where were we?" Maggie said.

"Discussing virgin births?"

"And you were calling me a slut . . ."

Really, Maggie had grown distressingly coarse. What was happening to the two of them? "Don't," Bea said. "I didn't, Maggie, and you mustn't say I did."

"Sorry."

"You know how I appreciate this. I came through a downpour to see you. You were the only friend I could talk to at a time like this. Maggie, I'm so frightened."

The closing confession rang oddly in this rain-enveloped library, way at the western edge of town, until Bea recognized that the phrase wasn't altogether her own. *I'm so frightened . . .* These were the very words Henry had repeated no end of times at Mitchell's house.

. . . And, with a naked pungency that took Bea's breath away, the whole evening opened up. The feel and fear and smell of it came back. There she was: suddenly she was sitting once more in Mitchell's living room, with Mitchell's big, cheerful face gazing out from its too-tight frame. All Maggie's mortifying questions, all her own descriptions of that living room—no, the audacious words hadn't begun to capture the evening! It was as though, ever since, Bea had been marching around to a hypnotist's orders . . . Only *now* did she remember how she'd *felt,* in her blood and in her face and low in her stomach, the overpowered sense of things gone wrong—wronged—at the very self's center, and how strangely she'd behaved in the bathroom, stripping off her clothes and giving herself a sort of sponge bath while Henry, weeping, stranded on the other side of the locked door, desperately called out to her, and to his Maker.

Then Henry went away. The Army carried him off again. Yes, some facts were facts. Henry was gone. There was no disputing that Henry was gone.

"You're fretting over nothing," Maggie said. "Take it from your friend the old married lady. *Nothing . . .*"

"I'm so sorry," Bea said. "Oh dear, dear *Lord . . .*"

"Sorry for what? It's all nothing, nothing, nothing. Now tell me you feel better." Maggie had again laid a warm hand upon Bea's hand.

"I do," Bea said, which was true. "A little," she added. Which was truer yet.

Her hidden shame—and the entire crushing, incalculable chain of ramifying disasters waiting to emerge from that shame—was a burden Bea carried around everywhere, more closely than her pocketbook. Nothing was untouched by it. The five-minute eggs her mother served in the morning, the damp rising winy smell from the cellar, the dent in her pillow when she first glimpsed her bed at night—these things spoke directly to her body's invaded condition. How in the world could she chat with Ronny in the old way, as though she were the same young woman she'd been last week? Never again would she be that girl. *What if I'm pregnant?* she'd asked Maggie, who asked in reply, *Would Ronny marry you?*

It was a crazy notion—all the crazier because now, and suddenly, Bea recoiled at Ronny's touch. She could hardly bear to kiss him. Under the circumstances, kissing him was *wrong.* And yet this very reluctance turned out to have an unexpected, contrary effect on Ronny.

One of the puzzling things about Ronny was how hot and cold his passions ran. In moments of ardor, there was no questioning the healthy urgency of his desires. The very next day, though, he might turn cool and aloof. Bea had learned to ascribe such changes to his "moods," while also coming around to understanding that, as explanations went, this didn't take her very far. In any case, Ronny wasn't accustomed to Bea's fending off his advances, and her doing so provoked or aroused him. Once again Ronny needed to feel, as he'd constantly needed to feel in the summer, his power to make her swoon—but these days Bea was disinclined to swoon.

Still, Ronny was determined, and he was as skillful as ever, and at times her scrupulous resistance dissolved and she could feel herself almost wholly succumbing. One of Ronny's hands might be drawing circles on her knee, his other stroking lightly, and yet deeply, the back of her neck, while his tongue was formulating its own patterns upon her upper lip, different but harmonious with his hands' patterns, and all the while his body was exuding its wonderful smell—she'd never known a body to smell so good—and in a way Bea wanted him more than ever, while, simultaneously (and this was new), something within her yearned to push him forcibly away and let loose a scream, a scarlet outraged howl from the roots of her throat: Oh *stop* it, *stop* it, *stop* it. Because it was all too much . . .

Bea had even less control than usual over her tears. She cried when she read in the *Free Press* about a Sicilian girl who had lost all four of her brothers in the War. She cried when she read in the *News* about a blind man's offering his Seeing Eye dog to the military. She cried when, in a park, a big Negro woman slapped her little daughter for picking up a piece of chewing gum from the sidewalk—even though the girl hadn't yet put it into her mouth. And she even came close to crying when Edith reprimanded her for throwing away a sheet of paper that should have been salvaged.

At home, they were all circling warily around her. Bea sensed this only dimly, since at the moment most everything was dim, and yet she could tell—and hated herself for being able to tell while being unable to do much about it—that she was perceived as being on what Papa would call "a terrible tear."

What was she doing? Where would it end?

Given all her recent shocks, it seemed impossible that fate had in store any additional upheavals. But it did. In one astounding day, two further revelations arrived. The boundaries of her world were being redrawn, and again redrawn . . .

Exactly eight days after her catastrophic visit to Mitchell's house, and seven days after Henry's departure, she at last received a letter. She took it into her bedroom, settling in her "nest" before allowing herself to open it.

It seemed Henry had been in Illinois—he alluded to the land of Lincoln. The letter ran for eight dense pages, but she didn't read them all, and she never would. Nor would she reply. Instantly, she vowed never again to speak to Henry Vanden Akker.

The first two pages were hard to follow. Henry described his recent thoughts about God, and his parents, and Kierkegaard, and he spoke of "the terrifying jungle, literally and metaphorically." Bea hurried through these passages, figuring she could go back and study them later.

But when she turned to the third page, her every sentiment altered instantly and she had no more intention, ever, of going back and rereading. "But I'm afraid no preamble could ever excuse the confession I now must make," Henry wrote.

I lured you to Mitchell's house under false pretenses. I had no intention of meeting him there. It was all arranged beforehand that you and I would not meet him. Do you remember the phone call? That was Mitchell, calling as arranged. It was meant to look as though he'd been delayed. It was all a ruse I'd worked out to place us alone together at last.

What was I intending would happen at Mitchell's house? As God is my witness, I truly do not know. But one of the possibilities in my mind was what in fact did happen.

I did try to confess that night. You may recall my saying I had something to tell you. And you replied that I'd said enough. Well, perhaps I had said enough. I have no excuse to offer except my love—a love so all-encompassing . . .

At this point Henry's letter reached the bottom of the third page, but what possible reason was there to follow him further? Bea would read no more. It was clear at last: horribly, hideously clear. The whole scheme was exposed in its true underhanded ghastliness. Oh, the effort she'd wasted! All this past week, trying so frantically to find something, *something* noble or beautiful about their last night! But it offered nothing noble or beautiful. It was all slinking ugliness, it was all chicanery and betrayal. She'd been deflowered in some little nasty mathematician's game and so long as she lived she would never again speak to Henry Vanden Akker. Ten, twenty years from now, she might just run into him on the streets of Detroit. It would be raining, and she would lift high a luminous lilac-colored umbrella and saunter right by. Some things couldn't be forgiven.

Bea's hands were shaking so hard, she could scarcely have read further had she wanted to, and she didn't want to—ever. She let the letter drop to the floor.

Oh, she'd tried so hard, really, to give Henry, and their last evening together, the benefit of the doubt! Never, never again . . . She wouldn't do him the favor of reading to the end. Bea sat up on the side of her bed, gathered up the letter, and methodically, patiently tore all eight pages into little bits.

These she did not place in the family salvage. They must be expelled from the house. Bea proceeded very meticulously. First she deposited all the little scraps into her purse and then she put on her coat and a pair of gloves. Then she walked up Inquiry all the way to Mack and down

Mack until she felt she'd traveled a safe and sufficient distance. She dropped some scraps into a trash container on the corner of Bellevue and Mack, walked another couple blocks, to Mount Elliott, and deposited the rest of them. It was like scattering ashes . . .

And later that night, three days early, as if her body yearned to register its own ultimate rejection of Henry, her period arrived, in a flow far heavier than usual and maybe darker than usual too.

For months now, she'd been aware, in the careful arranging of pad and sanitary belt, of a powerful and uncomfortable irony—for these were products purchased at Olsson's Drugs. Though never mentioning it to anyone, she'd come to recognize that there might be something a little peculiar, psychologically, and maybe just a little unseemly, in her reliance on Olsson's for such intimate needs. What mental game was she playing? Was she playing a game?

If so, for God's sake no more . . . Bea suddenly knew with bracing certitude that she was finished with all such games, rituals, symbolic enactments. She wanted nothing to do with Ronny either, who was always talking about psychological "games," who was always so keen to interpret her dreams. No, she wanted nothing more to do with men— especially demanding men. Let Maggie serve as the cautionary tale: before you know it, you wind up married and miserable, with a jailer as a mother-in-law and a whining brat as a brother-in-law, waiting for a man without any teeth to come home and claim you. No, Bea was finished with all that. And—as this newest discharge of muddy blood made clear—she had come through her difficult time safely. And all but pure.

CHAPTER XIX

She'd put it solidly behind her, that evening at Mitchell's house, and yet it continued to spin off various consequences, a few of them actually welcome. In some way the whole extended business—particularly the revelation of Henry's treachery—had freed her. After class one day she discovered a notebook left behind. It belonged to Donald Doobly, the Negro boy who dressed so neatly and drew so neatly too. Normally, Bea would have held on to it until the next class. Now, she decided to telephone him.

Predictably, his full name (Donald Gerald Doobly, Jr.) and address were neatly inscribed on the inside cover. Donald lived on Hastings Street, in a neighborhood most people called Black Bottom but Uncle Dennis and Aunt Grace called Paradise Valley. It surprised Bea a little when the phone directory revealed a Doobly family on Hastings Street—though she felt a flicker of embarrassment at her own surprise. Why shouldn't a Negro family be listed in the phone book? But the discovery scared her a little too, as she realized she truly *was* going to telephone.

Of course she'd never telephoned a Negro's house. Over time, Papa had journeyed quite a distance in his attitudes toward colored people. It was many years since he'd used the word *niggers* in front of Uncle Dennis, who had rebuked him so sternly ("*You* don't talk that way, Vico") that Bea honestly had worried Papa would strike his brother-in-law in retaliation. It wasn't merely that Bea had never again heard Papa use the word. These days, he made a proud point of saying it wasn't allowed *on his watch*. Did Papa recall Uncle Dennis's rebuke? Maybe not. Even so, Bea knew, without anything's being said, that Papa would never approve of her telephoning a Negro boy. He didn't approve of her calling boys at all.

Yet Bea was determined. She'd reached this point partly because she genuinely liked Donald, partly because, after last summer's riot, she felt a heightened sympathy for Negroes. And partly because—the most important part—whether she was still a virgin or not, something had altered inside her and certain conservative, half-nonsensical codes of decorum no longer commanded blind respect.

Still, she wasn't about to call Donald from home, even on some rare occasion when nobody else was there (Mamma left the house less and less these days). Just after dinner, while it was still light outside, she told her parents she needed to buy some deodorant and walked up to the phone booth outside Olsson's. In the orange glow of its neon sign (half her life, it seemed, was unfolding in the light of Olsson's Drugs) she telephoned Donald's number.

A phone rang. Somewhere in Paradise Valley a phone was ringing because she'd dialed it.

"Hello."

She was all but certain it was Donald. Nonetheless, Bea stuck to her plan: "May I please speak with Donald Doobly?"

On the other end, a stunned silence opened. Bea could feel it: just how wholly taken aback Donald was. And then, in a voice thinned almost to a whisper by incredulity and excitement, Donald uttered an astounding question: "Is that you, Tatiana?"

Now it was Bea's turn to halt, dumbstruck. How in the world? Clearly—clearly Donald had recognized her voice as a white girl's voice, but how could he possibly mistake her for Tatiana Bogoljubov? Tatiana spoke with a Russian accent . . .

"No, it's Bea, Bea Paradiso. I just wanted to let you know I found your notebook. You left it. In class. I found it. Your notebook."

"You found it," Donald said, in a still more dwindled voice.

"I thought you might need it."

"I'm glad you found it," Donald said. His voice was fading away altogether.

"I thought you might be worried. That's why I called."

"It's exceedingly kind of you," Donald said, at something like normal volume. "Now I needn't worry."

No matter what, this conversation was probably destined to be stilted. But Donald's initial, bizarre misapprehension couldn't be surmounted, and everything that followed must be excruciating. After some elaborate, ritualistic repetitions, the two of them finally determined that Bea would bring the notebook to Friday's class. "You are most kind," Donald said in closing.

It was on the walk back down Inquiry (Bea was in front of the Slopsemas'—nearly home) when the truth belatedly dawned. Such an obvious thing—she should have seen it right away. And yet a revelation so devastating, Bea immediately turned around and began walking back toward Olsson's. Oh, here was something to ponder.

She could hear Donald's voice so clearly, he might still be speaking into her ear. *Is that you, Tatiana?*

And Donald's tone of voice? It was the yearning sound of somebody on the threshold of a miraculous consummation.

In a couple of seconds, in a mere phrase, Donald had unwittingly disclosed his innermost heart. Oh, Donald was smitten—hopelessly smitten—with the exotic Russian girl, Tatiana Bogoljubov. Ronny and Bea might laugh themselves silly at Tatiana's absurd get-up, her candy-colored yellow hair and sweet little doll's face under its portentous mat of makeup, her devil-may-care scarves and asphyxiating blouses. Ronny might even declare that he was *so tired* of Miss Bogoljubov's breasts. But in another corner of the classroom, where quiet Donald Doobly sat, watching the world through his Negro's vantage, Tatiana embodied everything that was tantalizing and exquisite and unattainably remote.

Poor Donald! As Bea walked back and forth under Inquiry's familiar constellation of just-lit streetlights, this revelation seemed less amusing or touching than purely *sad*. Talk about your hopeless passions . . . Even if they all took classes together until the end of time, Tatiana Bogoljubov would never notice Donald Doobly.

Sad, oh how it was *sad*, and this was lately becoming a much-too-familiar process—this sliding away of facades, revealing life's true, blighting verities. It's what Bea felt more and more at the family dinner table, where dolor turned everything to ash in her mouth. And Ferry Hospital broke her heart whenever she stepped inside . . .

She met a new boy, who was a Jew. He wasn't a soldier, although they met at Ferry Hospital. At the age of only twenty, he was a first-year medical student. His name was Norman Kapp.

They went a couple of times to a luncheonette and twice to afternoon movies. Like Ronny, like Henry, Norman was a great talker, though not so entertaining as either of them. Still, he had a self-disparaging sense of humor Bea found appealing. He also had the heaviest beard of any boy she'd ever dated; by late afternoon, his cheeks looked nearly black. Something inside her recoiled at this, even as the portraitist marveled at skin that in certain lights looked less like flesh than stone—like a sort of wall. This was appropriate, since Bea sensed a sort of wall between them. Norman, too, made her sad.

Norman lived on the West Side, out near Dexter, where many Jewish people lived. He seemed in no hurry to introduce her to his parents, which was quite hurtful—or would have been if Bea hadn't been similarly reluctant to bring a Jewish boy home. She *would* have, though, if she'd really liked him.

One thing had to be said for Norman: he couldn't have been more appreciative. It wasn't merely the incessant compliments; it was his air of being unable to *stop* complimenting her. *You're quite beautiful* he declared more than once, the incredulity in his voice perhaps a comment on his own appearance: by any conventional standards, Norman was no looker. (Maggie would have quickly set him down as one of her LLs—Luckless Losers.) But there was an appealing vivacity to his features, and besides, he was so grateful.

It was this gratitude that induced Bea to allow him to hold her hand, even to kiss her. His touch lit nothing inside her—why couldn't Norman see that? Yet almost as though her languor enhanced her appeal, Norman's hands would grow slick with sweat, his talk accelerate, his eyes pop in his head.

Still, it was easier being with Norman than with Ronny. She'd run out of patience, completely, with Ronny's moods—with the whole delicate and involuted business of trying to discover what, this time, was troubling him, and how best to placate him. And Ronny, doubtless sensing her withdrawal, increasingly adopted a tone of bittersweet retrospection. He even used the phrase "threw me over": she'd thrown him over for a soldier mathematician.

Henry Vanden Akker? Bea had put *him* out of her head, mostly, though it vexed her when a couple of weeks passed without some further word. Perhaps the letter she'd torn up, mostly unread, had been a sort of goodbye? Perhaps it had explained something she now longed to know? But one day she received *three* letters from Henry, two of them thick, and though she didn't tear these up, she didn't read them either. She stored them, unopened, in her bureau's bottom drawer. It felt *good* not to read Henry's letters.

Yes, in many ways she was doing well, despite everything. Her thinking had swung into focus. She had entered a new state of mind, more intimately fused to the city than ever before, and what did it matter if Detroit was the only true metropolis she knew? No other city in the world was so alive. No, nowhere on earth, never before . . . She didn't need the newspapers, or the newsreels, to confirm what the air declared: the whole of Detroit was a single machine. One of the newspapers got it exactly: This was the town where the *Iliad* met Henry Ford. The assembly lines were running twenty-four hours a day, the overburdened railroads were clanking in and out of the city, and she, Bianca Paradiso, portfolio under her arm, was a piece of it all: riding the streetcars to Ferry Hospital, to class, to the USO, observing *everything*. She was sketching more hours per week than ever before.

This new state of mind imposed its own demands and Bea couldn't eat as she used to. Mamma's meals felt too heavy, all those recipes out of *The Modern Housewife's Book of Creative Cookery* weighing Bea down just when her thinking was beginning to lift. She hungered for clarity, for levitation. She rebelled at dishes with names like Shipwreck or Sammy's Sloppy Joes or City Chicken Sticks or Drowned Tuna Loaf. Of course it wouldn't do to malnourish herself and she was careful, when she could get them, to put cream and lots of sugar into her coffee. She ate apples and cucumbers and a great many carrots. This wasn't lack of appetite but an enhancement of appetite, hence it mattered all the more that she eat the right things.

It was Papa, seated at dinner one night, who first remarked on her altered eating habits, in that abrupt way of his. The words came blurting out after a long mulling over. He accused her: "You don't eat."

"Oh I do." She felt herself instantly blush.

And it was Mamma who—surprisingly—came to the rescue. "She eats fine. Tonight isn't so good. I think the meat's off." The meat was calf's liver, which Bea had hardly touched. "That new butcher at Abajay's, I think he's a crook."

Papa said, "That's what you said about the folks at Wrigley's. And A&P. Everyone's a thief."

"Leave the poor girl alone, Vico."

It was an odd reversal of roles. Usually Mamma was the one offering criticism, Papa the one urging leniency. Mamma's support ought to have been comforting, and it would have been—only, there was something disconcerting in having your eating habits defended by somebody who subsisted on candy and black coffee. Mamma's glumness could be unnerving, but even more upsetting were those moments when, as now, gloating triumph suffused her face. Sudden, unexpected mirth creased her features, heightening your awareness of the skull under the skin. It was a skeletal apparition who grinned across the table, encouragingly, at Bea.

. . .

The sadness underneath everything, deep down at the wordless root of things, began darkening even Sundays—the family's Italian Day, when Nonno and Nonna came for dinner.

For all the years Bea had known him, Nonno had been sickly. He'd arrived in America as a shadow of a man, his robust wife beside him—a wife who wouldn't survive transplantation. (She was dead within the year.) To look at him, you'd never suppose he'd once been famous as Liguria's master of trompe l'oeil.

Nonno had never really learned English. Nor, it seemed, had he ever quite learned to converse with Nonna, his second wife, who came originally from a farm near Venice and spoke a remote dialect.

Nonna's lack of English only made her more formidable. Everyone was frightened of her, even Mamma—and Bea took mischievous pleasure in seeing Mamma routed from her own kitchen. Nonna would arrive carrying bags and bags of groceries, since Mamma apparently couldn't be trusted to select even a suitable eggplant or tomato. Nonna brought sausages, cheeses, vegetables, fish, even spices, and she would get busily to work.

Nonno and Nonna lived in a small apartment on Algonquin, so it made sense that Sunday dinners were held on Inquiry—made sense, in its way, that Mamma must wind up a guest in her own home, making distracted conversation in the living room while eavesdropping on the kitchen's thumps and clangs.

It didn't help matters that Nonna was such a marvelous cook. Out of Mamma's kitchen would come steaming lasagnas and veal roasts, rabbit stews and stuffed trout, baked oysters and risotto marinaro. Usually, there wasn't much talk during dinner—only a primitive chorus of sighs and grunts, purred *mms* and guttural *aahs*.

For most of her life, Bea hadn't really minded the languid stretch in the living room after dinner. Nonna might nod off sitting upright on the davenport while the men listened to a Tigers game. Sometimes, if the weather was good and Nonno's emphysema wasn't bothering him, they all walked around the block. On good days, it cheered Bea to see him smoke a cigarette; it meant he was feeling better.

Now, though, the family's Sunday dinners, particularly the long digestive interval after the food was consumed and the kitchen cleaned up, struck Bea as terribly sad. How much of any Tigers game could Nonno actually understand? Why didn't Nonna ask to lie down, instead of napping upright?

One of the recent rituals of Sunday afternoons—a day dense with rituals—had been going on since she started art school. Papa would ask Bea to display for Nonno her recent work. When she'd first begun these exhibitions, Nonno had taken to the task eagerly, with quick nods and gestures. He'd offered evaluations in mixed English and Italian. Sometimes, thrillingly, he even took a pencil in hand.

In recent months, however, he approached the task sluggishly, as though tired of Bea's work, or simply old and weary.

One particular Sunday in November, just before Thanksgiving, seemed particularly sad. A dreary gray rain was splattering against the panes; there would be no walk today. And it was the wrong season for a Tigers game. Bea hadn't been able to eat much dinner, though the main course—risotto marinaro—was something she'd always loved. Things were different today; the flavors jostled aggressively in her mouth, leaving her faintly sick.

After dinner, they all sat in the living room, with the lamps on, though it was early afternoon. This was a dark day. Bea brought out her week's drawing—a tropical atoll with palm trees, based on photographs in *Look*—which Nonno hardly glanced at. For the first time, Bea wondered whether he would even notice if she showed him last week's drawing. Nonno patted her hand and Bea put the drawing away.

The rain went on falling. Nonna had nodded off. Edith knitted furiously, in her tranquil way.

The culminating moment of the afternoon—of a lifetime of such afternoons—arrived when Nonno hauled himself out of his chair and wandered into the kitchen. After a moment, feeling restless, Bea followed him.

The old man, her little Italian grandfather, stood at the sink with his back to her, rinsing his hands in a thin stream of water. "Nonno," Bea called. But he did not turn around.

"Nonno," she called, more loudly. He did not turn around.

It struck her as almost the saddest discovery she'd ever made—though honestly, what difference did it make, since her grandfather hardly communicated with anyone anyway? What difference did it make when, under the best of circumstances, she and he would never hold a real conversation? (But maybe she'd always hoped to—someday? And now she understood that she never, ever would?)

Her grandfather was mostly deaf.

CHAPTER XX

The end of the world arrived with the ringing of a telephone. At the other end, the caller might plausibly have been Ronny, inviting her for coffee, or Maggie, with brand-new complaints about Ma'am Hamm's cooking, or the Jewish medical student, Norman Kapp, proposing another afternoon movie—any number of livable possibilities were still open as Bea sauntered toward the kitchen and the phone.

Bea didn't immediately understand whose voice issued from the other end of the line, though the caller carefully identified herself.

"Hello, this is Mrs. Horace Vanden Akker. I wish to speak to Bea Paradiso."

It was four-thirty in the afternoon and this was one of those rare intervals when nobody else was home. Papa was at work, Stevie was out playing, Mamma had gone with Edith to deposit two turtleneck sweaters with Needles for Defense. The light on Inquiry was always different when Bea was alone in the house. It softened, it deepened—it came into its own, as if it had been waiting to do so, patiently, for her eyes alone.

"This is Bea . . . Hello?"

"Is that Bea Paradiso?"

"Yes," Bea whispered.

"I have some news," Mrs. Vanden Akker announced, in that stolid way of hers. "The Lord has taken our Henry. I thought you would want to know."

For a moment, the caramel light in the kitchen flared up, as though the sun had come out, but the sun was already out. Then things went dark. Bea leaned up against the wall, face flattened against the O'Reilly and Fein calendar.

"I thought you would want to know," Mrs. Vanden Akker repeated.

"He—Henry—" was all Bea managed to say. But this couldn't be. Simply couldn't.

"We received official word two days ago. And then yesterday Mr. Vanden Akker spoke long-distance to an old friend in Washington,

D.C., a member of our church, who was able to provide additional information. You see, Henry's plane went down in a tropical storm."

But this couldn't be. "I—oh I—" Bea said. Elsewhere, on the floor of the mind, it was like prying open some unused cellar door: an exploding blinded frenzy of low creatures scurrying from the light. Inside her head, everything was running away.

"It was about four-thirty in the afternoon. When we received word."

"I'm so sorry," Bea managed to say. "I'm just—I—I just wish I could express—"

"No need for such things," Mrs. Vanden Akker replied, and went on to explain: "You see, our faith is different from yours. Mr. Vanden Akker and I, we understand that God took him for a reason."

"But—oh my *God*—" Bea whispered.

"As Mr. Vanden Akker says, There is no sorrow in the ways of the Lord. Only in the ways of men."

"But oh—oh *please*," Bea begged. Weird, low, dizzying visions were uprising inside her.

"Although I know you and Henry had stopped seeing each other before he left, I still thought you'd wish to know."

Stopped? Stopped seeing each other?

"That the Lord has taken him," Mrs. Vanden Akker added.

But Bea had seen Henry the very night before he left, at Mitchell's. What in the world had Henry told his mother?

Mrs. Vanden Akker was still talking—a service at the church—but Bea could hardly absorb anything. And she didn't need to hear it—since the import was unmistakable. Politely, but firmly, Mrs. Vanden Akker was letting Bea know that her presence would not be required at the service. It was meant for "members of the church."

Of course . . .

It was meant for members of the church, and what about that other one—that inadvisable, ill-suited Italian girl? The one whom their boy Henry had "stopped seeing"? Her presence wouldn't be necessary. No. Not at the service.

There was nothing further Bea needed to do about Henry—ever. This phone call was intended as the end of it: Mrs. Vanden Akker was calling, on behalf of the Vanden Akkers, to bid Bea Paradiso goodbye and farewell.

"I thought you would want to know," Mrs. Vanden Akker said.

"Henry is"—and Bea paused, faltered, but in the end clung loyally to the present tense—"he's so brilliant."

"Yes," Mrs. Vanden Akker said. "A brilliant boy."

"Oh Mrs. Vanden Akker, please accept—"

"We do," Mrs. Vanden Akker interceded. "We certainly do."

"I want you to know that I—" What Bea longed to say, and at the last moment, to her great relief, forewent saying, was, *I loved him.* What emerged instead was, "I'm so sorry."

"Mr. Vanden Akker and I thank you." And then the terminating word: "*Good*bye." And a click at the other end.

Bea hung up the receiver but it slipped from its cradle and cracked its skull against the floor. Bea hung it up once more and drifted with a mounting sense of purpose upstairs to her bed. Where she planned to weep as she'd never wept.

And yet Bea did not weep. Instead, she stared at the rabbit her father had once painstakingly carved into the fine-grained wood of her bedpost. "Henry," she said. "Henry Vanden Akker." As clearly as though Mrs. Vanden Akker were in the room, Bea again heard the mortal pronouncement: *The Lord has taken him.* Bea tried out the words herself, layering her thinned voice directly atop Mrs. Vanden Akker's voice: "The Lord has taken him."

The Vanden Akkers did not want her at the service. Henry's girlfriend—they didn't want Henry's Italian girlfriend there . . . What had Henry confessed to his parents? What did they know? They knew, anyway, they didn't want Bea there. Their unwelcoming God—*He* did not want her. "*Good*bye," Mrs. Vanden Akker had said. *Good*bye.

The watchful rabbit in the bedpost contemplated the hushed girl lying dry-eyed on the bed. Still she did not weep.

Then she heard the clicking of the front door. Mamma and Edith. Instantly Bea sensed that she would not—must not—divulge a thing. Henry's death could *never* become entertainment for the family. She must hold off. She who always delighted in being the family storyteller would be nothing of the kind. She owed Henry silence—the silence of the grave . . .

Yes, she would hold off on the weeping until bedtime. Bea went downstairs step by step and greeted her mother and her sister. Mamma was putting things into the refrigerator. Bea spoke of needing to run up to Olsson's and, hardly awaiting her mother's approval, threw on her coat.

Bea didn't go to Olsson's. She headed over to Buttery Creek Park, where Mamma used to bring her. The hours spent here as a little girl! So much of her life—and yet Henry had never once seen Buttery Creek Park. This was one whole sector of her life Henry would never share. In Henry's personal universe, this park would never exist.

Henry had never seen Inquiry either, the street with the richest name in the whole city. Nor the bed her father had carved, the little menagerie in which she slept each night.

Bea sat on the very bench where she'd sat not so long ago—ages ago—with her mother. "There is no sorrow in the ways of the Lord," Mrs. Vanden Akker had pronounced. Mrs. Vanden Akker would not mourn. She was a heartless woman—it was *terrifying* to contemplate so heartless a woman. Nor would Mr. Vanden Akker mourn. Mourning was solely Bea's responsibility, who would put off all weeping until bedtime. And without a word to anyone . . .

Bea got through dinner all right—in fact, she was a little hungrier than usual. After dinner, she sat in the living room with Papa and listened to Jack Benny and Fred Allen on the radio. She did not mention Henry. Her family had never met Henry and was there anything in the cosmos odder than this: her family had never met the one man to whom Bea had chosen to give herself utterly? Henry was her lover. Henry Vanden Akker had been her lover and she would never have another. The future had grown clear. For her, it was to be just the one occasion, which is why she'd held back nothing from Henry. Yet nobody in her house would pick him out of a crowd. They would never understand. And that's how it was. No one would ever understand what the War had taken from her: her lover.

When she did climb into bed, and lay listening to Edith's steady breathing overhead, the tears finally arrived—but not in the torrential fashion she'd expected and even longed for. Bea had planned to cry all night and meet the dawn with tears streaming down her face. But she was soon asleep.

The real tears didn't arrive until the following morning. She woke to an amazing thought: *the letters!* Of course, of course—the bottom drawer of her bureau contained three letters, unopened. How *could* she have forgotten? Three unopened letters from Henry!

To hold in her fingers those three letters made Bea feel extremely queer . . .

Henry had written them—these letters—just as he was being

shipped to his tragic fate. These were the final testament of a soldier whose plane soon afterward crashed, who burned to death in a hellish tropical storm.

The texture of the paper set her hands atremble. He'd sealed them himself, with those bony, lovely fingers of his. Henry's touch would never again be so close. The letters must be opened carefully, and read in the proper order. Fortunately—*fortunately,* she could do this without possibility of error. The postmarks were different, each a day apart.

The first letter was—it was her own dear bookish Henry all over. He had read the novel *Lord Jim* by Joseph Conrad. It was a tale of shame. It was the story of a man who must purge himself from the taint of a single shameful act, and there were affinities, which not everybody would spot, between Conrad and Kierkegaard . . . Bea read this letter hastily. She would of course return to it. But what was Henry thinking about *her*? Dear boy, why could he never simply say what he needed to say?

The second letter was a different matter altogether. Here was a more intimate voice. Here was the voice she'd been yearning for.

"Yesterday I wrote you a silly letter," it began, and who else spoke this way?

> *I suppose I was afraid to speak directly of what is in my heart. I have wronged you, Bea. In the eyes of God, I have wronged you, Bea, and this is something I must live with, like Conrad's Jim. I do identify the ironies in my circumstances. I too am heading to the Pacific. I could beg your forgiveness; I could plead with you; I could make excuses. But I've already done these things and I will not again do these things. I must change the who-I-am. This is the lesson I learned for the first time when I injured my spine in the jungle. And it's the lesson I learned a second time when I realized the wrong I had done you. I believe in the possibility of human learning. I believe in Resurrection, both divine and human, large and small. I will not trouble you further with my turmoil, at least for a while. Because I don't deserve to write to you again until I know in my heart I'm no longer the man I was. Then I will write. And then I will ask you, Bea, and maybe even deserve, your forgiveness.*
> *Henry*

The third letter wasn't really a letter but a poem, although it began with a brief prose preamble. It said:

Dear Bea,

Don't consider this another letter after I vowed not to write
another letter until I truly purged myself. Consider it a postscript.
Here's another poem from the poet-who-is-not-a-poet:

> *You have invented beauty;*
> *I have invented sorrow.*
> *I show myself unworthy*
> *But a better soul tomorrow.*
>
> *I would take you as my beacon*
> *On the dark seas of Night,*
> *And find my way to landfall*
> *With you as my harbor light.*

"Hen-ry," Bea sighed, and the act of uttering his name instantly materialized him in his ridiculous hat with its trailing vegetal curlicues, somberly scrutinizing all the captive animals scattered before him. Yes, it was as if—on that wonderful, unforgettable day so long ago!—he hadn't comprehended that theirs was no journey through Africa on a real train but a trip through the Detroit Zoo on a toy-sized train, and now Bea's weeping began in grim breathless earnest . . .

It started not so much with tears as with a single desolate cry, a keening howl torn right out of her heart. Henry Vanden Akker was dead and hers was the cry of a soul riven by that mortal recognition from which, henceforward, life must be refigured: the bare, astounding notion that Eternity itself isn't large enough to make good the loss you've suffered. Some cherished, gleaming nonesuch has disappeared from the Earth and it will not come back. No, never in all the celestial unspooling of the ages, century upon century, never will its like return. Never—Bea had glimpsed the true defining *Never* of the human predicament, and a howl was torn right out of the thumping young heart of her . . .

All day in her room Bea wept, sometimes quietly, sometimes tempestuously. She did not step outside. She thought about telephoning somebody—Ronny, Maggie—but she owed Henry solitary grief. Through squalls of tears she explained to Mamma her tragedy, but how could Mamma understand, never having laid eyes on Henry?

Mamma carried upstairs a lunch—a meat loaf sandwich and a glass of milk. Bea drank the milk, most of it, but there was no possibility of eating. Later, in the afternoon, Bea recalled how, in the morning, she'd broken the terrible, terrible news to Mamma. Or had she? Memories of their conversation felt muffled and unreal—as if Bea were recollecting a mere dream, or retrieving one nightmare from a different nightmare.

Bea read and reread Henry's letters, though Henry's final poem made her cry so convulsively she scarcely dared pick it up. He'd called her his harbor light. At some point Bea remembered she was supposed to be in class. What was the chance of that? At various junctures she felt as though she might have slept, but it wasn't sleep so much as a wandering across an enormous baking metallic landscape worse than lifeless—it was all but colorless—while overhead an alien sun raged like a grease fire.

In the afternoon Bea recalled her relief when, three days early, her period had arrived, and only now perceived how unforgivably selfish she'd been, and wept more bitterly than she'd wept all day. Henry would never have children, and yet *she* had felt relief when Henry's one and only chance for children was lost. What had happened to Henry's children? Didn't they, too, perish in that plane crash?

Bea wasn't to be cajoled down to dinner, though Papa tried and Mamma tried and even Edith tried. Eventually Papa brought up a bowl of ham and navy-bean soup. "You have to eat," he said, and sat himself down in the desk chair. She promised she would try if he'd only leave her alone—but Papa wouldn't budge. "I stay until you eat your soup," he announced. He wasn't often like this, but nothing was more characteristic of his inner self: intervals of proud doggedness when he declared himself immovable.

Bea's hands were trembling so pitifully, it wasn't easy getting the soup to her mouth—and, besides, she wasn't hungry. But Papa sat silently, steadfastly, until she'd finished half the bowl, then gave a slow, satisfied nod when she set it down on the bedside table. "That's all," she said. He asked what was the matter.

For a while Bea couldn't get the words out through her sobbing. But Papa was patient and in time she managed to relate much of the story. "I'm sorry you lost your friend," he said.

I'm sorry you lost your friend, her father said.

Lost her *friend?* How could Papa possibly understand, who had never even met Henry? No—no—no: Papa had scarcely *heard* of Henry, partly because Papa was so busy, and partly because lately Bea had chosen to keep things to herself. As far as Papa knew, Henry was just a boy among boys. How could he comprehend that Henry was the one, the chosen unique one, to whom she'd elected to give herself?

After a while Papa went away, downstairs, leaving the soup behind. Edith appeared eventually and asked if she could sleep in the upper bunk. The request started Bea crying anew. Alone—she needed to be alone . . .

Then Bea slept and the next morning she woke up early, feeling much restored, and resolved to clean her room. She changed her sheets and Edith's sheets, and yanked everything out of her bureau and refolded the clothes and tucked them back into the bureau. She was doing much better, but she suffered a serious setback when she found a minuscule scrap of paper, no larger than a quarter, under the bed.

It spoke to her.

Bea's heart knew what it was, though she didn't yet know what it was. But in the assimilating, puzzled interval before recognition, it murmured reassuringly against her fingertips.

Bea examined it closely.

It was Henry's handwriting. This little scrap? It could only be one of those scraps created when she'd spitefully torn up his eight-page letter, so many weeks ago—so long ago. Yes, that's what she'd done. First, he'd tried to apologize in person, and she had rebuked him: *Henry, haven't you said enough?* Then, Henry had composed an eight-page letter, in which he'd laid out the lineaments of his soul, and she had methodically ripped it into angry bits . . . That was the sort of heartless, wretched person she was, and how could he, how could anyone, possibly love her?

Bea had thought she'd discarded every last howling scrap in the two trash bins on Mack, but she hadn't. One fragment, one stubborn little message-laden token of Henry's soul, had survived under the bed.

What was the ultimate message from her Henry?

There was an *ied* and a *th* at the top of the scrap—the tail of one word and the head of another. Below lay a complete word, *rut*, though it, too, was probably a fragment. The word had presumably been *truth*—that pet favorite of Henry's elevated lexicon: he had left her a fragment of the truth. Oh, she could hear him pronouncing it in his distinctive voice—*But the truth is, Bea,* he might begin. Or, *Yet the difficult truth of the matter* . . . And another flood of tears assailed her.

Afterward, Bea felt much better—better even than she'd felt in the morning, and she headed off toward Ferry with her portfolio. But she had no sooner mounted the steps and found herself enclosed by the green corridors than she began trembling with such severity she had to scurry back out into fresh air. She dropped down—all but collapsed— on the front steps, though as far to the side as possible. And there she wept, while people went up and down, up and down. At Ferry Hospital, they were used to such sights.

When she finally tottered off the steps, Bea realized only one destination was possible. Home. Simultaneously, she saw that this plan was unworkable. She couldn't possibly face a streetcar, and it was miles too far to walk. From here, from this hospital where she'd been born, there was simply no getting home.

Though it was an unheard-of extravagance, Bea deposited herself in a taxi and rode all the way home, almost. Obviously, she couldn't arrive on her doorstep in a taxicab. She crawled out in front of Olsson's and straggled down Inquiry and through the front door and, explaining to Mamma as she stumbled upstairs that she wasn't feeling well, finally collapsed on her bed. Where she remained the rest of the day.

When she woke the next morning, Bea knew she couldn't handle Ferry, or the Institute Midwest, and it occurred to her she might be finished with both forever. But what would substitute for them? If she were no longer an art student, the only sensible path was to find a job, but the very thought of getting dressed and heading off into the city—into the humming sleepless madness of wartime Detroit—injected nauseating chemicals into the churning bag of her stomach. What on earth was she to do? Women in slacks were employed in tank factories, they were running gas stations, they were bus conductorettes—but at the moment Bea could hardly imagine even climbing aboard a streetcar. What was she to do?

It was a relief, mostly, when Ronny showed up. (She had telephoned him in the morning, hadn't she? Their conversation, like so many recent conversations, seemed more imagined than real.) Anyway, here was Ronny, on her doorstep. This was sweet. Bea could see that: it was sweet of him to come.

They walked to Buttery Creek Park, where they sat on a bench and she leaned on his shoulder and wept recklessly into the front of his shirt. After a while, once she'd calmed down, Ronny said, "I remember you telling me how lucky you felt because you hadn't known anyone yet who died in the War. Though you did feel it coming closer and closer."

"Yes."

Yes, she'd told him that.

"And then the news arrived. And it would turn out to be *him*, of all people."

"Yes. Though somehow I knew it was going to happen."

"I'm so sorry . . ." Ronny gazed at her, fondly, and maybe a little sadly, and he said, "You really loved him, didn't you."

Oh: and weren't these the perfect words? Oh, it was so *good* of Ronny to say such a thing! Now she could open her heart . . . Yes, of course yes: Yes, she'd *really loved Henry,* and she'd lost her one true love, who had never once heard her declare, and now would never hear her declare, *I love you.*

So Bea wept with renewed anguish on Ronny's shoulder and dried her eyes and confessed again that yes, she had loved Henry. And Ronny looked saddened but also vindicated: he'd thought as much. He'd known how she felt before she herself did.

Oh, it was all so *sweet* of Ronny, so considerate and *good* of Ronny, who held her hand and walked her through the park and took her out for coffee and a cinnamon roll and didn't upbraid her when she ate almost none of it. She drank her cup of coffee and most of Ronny's coffee and then (since Ronny thought more coffee wouldn't be good for her, even if the waiter would have brought it) a cup of tea. The warmth of the drinks was comforting.

Ronny was back the next day and this time he drove her to Belle Isle, where the light inside the green-tiled aquarium somehow made her feel better than she'd felt in—in how long? She couldn't say, really. It was a shame they didn't have some sort of cafeteria set up inside here. The tiles were genuine Pewabic, one of the world's loveliest greens, and Bea, securely enfolded in their unearthly, watery light, could have lingered all day, and her appetite would have returned, the two of them seated at some table overlooking tanks where pike and trout and shy, boldly colored clownfish stared out from one world into another.

It was unexpectedly liberating—the sensation of peering through glass into another world. Yes, this was odd. A strange giddy giggly joy coursed through her veins as she stared at the four-eyed fish, which didn't really have four eyes. They had two, split like bifocals. Half above the surface, half below. She recalled a little game she and Maggie used to play, so long ago. She said to Ronny, "If you put your head right at the surface, and watch them swimming at you, they look just like alligators. You know, the ones in the Tarzan movies. Coming to devour you, chomp, chomp, *chomp* . . ."

The phrase—chomp, chomp, *chomp*—had come swimming straight and fast out of her childhood: Bea saw little pigtailed Maggie Szot, eyes ablaze.

And Ronny tried it, hunched his head level with the water's surface. He stared for quite some time. Then he straightened up and said something at once heartening and a little heartbreaking: "Bianca, I sometimes think you have more imagination than I do. Or at least a wilder imagination."

He looked stricken, and suddenly she wanted to comfort him . . . Yes, in this aquarium, anyway, roles could be reversed and she could comfort Ronny. But of course she couldn't stay indefinitely in the aquarium, and how many days could she possibly expect him to walk her slowly about, like some recovering invalid? What was she going to do now? She had wept herself raw: Bea's throat, her nostrils, her eyes ached all the time. It hurt just to swallow. To blink.

. . . A sense of direction arrived from an unexpected quarter: another telephone call from Mrs. Vanden Akker. The voice was as cold and stiff as ever, and just as unwilling to accept the tiniest offering of condolences, yet it carried an invitation—or maybe a directive. She and Mr. Vanden Akker wished to see Bea again, provided it was convenient. Would there possibly be a convenient time?

Well, what Bea couldn't convey to this terrifying woman, but wished with all her heart to convey, was that nothing significant remained in her life, really, except memories of Henry. In other words, there wasn't a single day when she *couldn't* come. She was basically free every moment for the rest of her life, now that she'd lost the most important thing in it.

Bea arranged to meet in three days' time.

And this appointment, though so deeply dreaded, had a steadying effect—it allowed Bea to get on with her life. She returned to her landscape class, comforted to be a student again, even if unable to focus. And soon she would return—not yet, but soon—to drawing soldiers' portraits. She would get on with her life.

For they had scared her—those days when it seemed she might never return to the Institute, to Ferry Hospital. She had spent a stretch of days peering into an ongoing emptiness. She'd seen a metal landscape, a grease-fire sun. Yes, Mrs. Vanden Akker's request was almost comforting. Bea was grateful for something to dread.

CHAPTER XXI

The woman who opened the door could only be Mrs. Vanden Akker, though for an instant this seemed impossible. How could anyone alter so quickly?

If she hadn't been fat exactly, Mrs. Vanden Akker had been a solid woman—an imposing solidity was her very essence—and yet the woman at the front door was far from solid. It wasn't merely all the weight she'd lost, though she'd dropped a substantial amount of weight. Mrs. Vanden Akker moved differently now. She had turned tentative, and tremulous. This woman who had always served as a domestic drill sergeant, instructing everyone where to sit and when to rise, ushered in her guest with a jerking wave of uncertainty.

Only her voice remained constant—that cool impregnable voice which had convinced Bea, over the telephone, that here was a mother unmoved by her only child's death. Nothing could be further from the truth. No, Mrs. Vanden Akker was being eaten alive by grief.

Mr. Vanden Akker's transformation was less dramatic but no less complete. His silver hair was longer and uncombed; in fact, it stood up in wild patches from his skull, because as he spoke he kept scratching at his scalp—digging at it—with both hands. He had always seemed brilliant but eccentric, with his domed forehead and those jumpy eyes behind constantly drooping spectacles; now, for the first time, hair upthrust as if in flame, he looked, just possibly, mad.

"Would you have—coffee?" asked Mrs. Vanden Akker. Heretofore, a guest had been simply presented with whatever she—Mrs. Vanden Akker—deemed suitable.

Bea adopted the peculiar locution. "I would have coffee—please."

So she was left alone with Mr. Vanden Akker.

Bea swallowed hard and said, "I'm very, very sorry about Henry."

Mr. Vanden Akker flinched, nodded, gouged at his scalp, and said something Mrs. Vanden Akker had already quoted over the telephone: "There is no sorrow in the ways of the Lord."

The three of them sipped coffee in the living room and Mrs. Vanden

Akker passed around some spitefully hard biscuits. Mr. and Mrs. Vanden Akker—those two formerly august presences—seemed so hapless and so routed that Bea felt emboldened to lead the conversation.

"I don't exactly know how it happened . . ."

Mr. and Mrs. Vanden Akker exchanged looks. There was a pause, and a second exchange, during which they evidently agreed that this particular story was Mr. Vanden Akker's.

"Henry's plane went down. Trying to land on an island called Majuro in the Pacific. There was a tropical rainstorm."

"I'm so sorry . . ."

"I telephoned a friend in Washington who is with the government. He belongs to our church. He was able to give me some additional details. I hadn't actually heard of Majuro before."

"No," Bea murmured.

"The plane crashed and burned. It would have been very quick. I could show you where Majuro is," Mr. Vanden Akker suggested. "I have a fine atlas."

"Yes," Bea said, but Mr. Vanden Akker did not rise. She did not expect him to. He simply sat, and tore at his scalp, and went on staring in his matter-of-fact madman's way.

"I hope at least there wasn't much pain in the end," Bea said.

Of course it was the strangest thing in the world to be talking in this fashion—to be sitting in the Vanden Akkers' living room discussing Henry as though Henry could really be dead. Could Henry really be dead? Surely not—yet there was a sense, at the edge of Bea's thinking, that it was only because Henry was dead that the three of them dared attribute to him anything so monstrous as death.

"In the end?" Mrs. Vanden Akker replied, with some of her old forcefulness. "But this isn't the end. Explain it. Explain it to the girl, Horace."

Mr. Vanden Akker took a deep breath. He righted his glasses on his nose and leaned forward. "I would begin this way, Bea," he said. It was perhaps the first time he'd addressed her by name. "My initial premise would be this: heresy is born not through ignorance but through pride."

The pause that followed begged for some response, so Bea replied "Right," and added, "I see," even though she hadn't an inkling, of course, what Mr. Vanden Akker meant. She was struck, again, by a sensation of how remote was this man—how remote this man and woman—from any world she recognized. This was how they talked about their dead son, whose torn-open plane had exploded in flames . . .

"Now, it is a premise of our faith that each of us cannot identify whether we are among the elect—whether we are truly saved. And you can discern the hand of divine wisdom in this arrangement, for what better way to protect us all from the twin vices of pride and complacency?"

"That's true," Bea said.

Mr. Vanden Akker went on: "But just because it is impossible to tell for certain whether you yourself are among the saved, this doesn't necessarily mean it's impossible to make the determination about some other person. It is much like life in the workaday world: we can see others but we can hardly see ourselves."

"That's true."

"The truth is, the workaday world offers us many clues. Things are the way they are for a reason."

"There are signs," Mrs. Vanden Akker eagerly interjected.

Mr. Vanden Akker turned toward his wife. "I'm coming to that," he said and though his voice was mildness itself, this was the first time Bea had ever seen him stand up to her. Mr. Vanden Akker again leaned forward. "And I don't think that's heresy. It's a conclusion I come to quite humbly. You see, Bea, I am a mathematician by trade. Oh I'm nothing like the mathematician our boy was—"

"He was so brilliant."

"Yes, indeed he was. Quite brilliant. You could see it from the very start—"

"Before he spoke his first word," Mrs. Vanden Akker pointed out.

Mr. Vanden Akker weighed his wife's words, then nodded sagely. "Yes, before Henry spoke his first word. You could see he'd been granted a special gift—"

"There were signs," Mrs. Vanden Akker inserted.

"Yes, signs of a gift," Mr. Vanden Akker agreed. "Now, I am no mathematician of that sort, but I have taught myself to observe things closely, to search for clues, and in the case of Henry's death, too, there are signs—"

Mrs. Vanden Akker evidently could not help herself. She interrupted again: "There are signs."

"There are clear signs that Henry is among the elect."

"Henry is in Heaven now," Mrs. Vanden Akker said.

"At the right hand of God," Mr. Vanden Akker said.

"At the right hand of God," Mrs. Vanden Akker intoned.

"I have no doubt," Bea told them.

Of all the many surprises in this household, none was more arresting than husband and wife's reversal of roles. Previously, Mrs. Vanden Akker had made no effort to conceal her impatience with her husband's cloudy theological speculations. And Mr. Vanden Akker would stop midsentence—a flush-faced culprit—whenever she cut him off. But now all conversational authority lay with him alone. Mr. Vanden Akker had become an oracle. For he alone could construe the signs: he alone had the subtlety of mind and the expertise needed to calculate that string of mystical terms by which one arrived at the glittering certainty that Henry was among the eternally elect.

Mrs. Vanden Akker asked after each member of Bea's family—people previously of seemingly little interest. Bea wouldn't have thought Mrs. Vanden Akker actually knew the names of her brother and sister, but she did. "How is Steven?" she asked. "He is thirteen now, correct?" And, more surprising still, "How is little Edith, who has her own mathematical gift?"

Bea talked awhile about her family. It was Mr. Vanden Akker who brought the conversation around again. "You have something you wanted to give the girl," he told his wife.

"*Yes,*" Mrs. Vanden Akker said, and sprang up quickly, almost guiltily. "Excuse me, excuse me. I'll be just a moment."

But what could this "something" possibly be? Bea felt very disconcerted, suddenly. She launched a smile at Mr. Vanden Akker, who scratched at his scalp in reply . . .

And when Mrs. Vanden Akker returned, the "something" turned out to be much, much more unearthly than anything Bea could have imagined.

Holding it carefully before her with both hands, as though it were some platter on which little party snacks were balanced, Mrs. Vanden Akker brought forth the portrait Bea had drawn of Henry so long ago, in Ferry Hospital. It was framed. Henry must have framed it for his parents. Mrs. Vanden Akker stepped toward Bea and, with a lurch, thrust the portrait at her. "We thought you might want your picture back."

From where Bea sat, Henry's face, upside-down, looked oddly asymmetrical. This was the very portrait at which he'd crowed, *Don't I look brainy?*

Although Mrs. Vanden Akker stood awkwardly waiting, Bea simply couldn't lift her arms. Henry's face bobbed up and down—Mrs. Vanden Akker's hands were trembling. But Bea simply could not bring herself to touch the portrait.

"Oh but it's yours," she whispered.

"You drew it," Mrs. Vanden Akker countered.

"But I want you to have it."

Poor Henry continued to bob like a struggling swimmer. Bea had forgotten the mock tribute to van Gogh, the scatter of tropical star clusters . . .

"We thought you should have it," Mr. Vanden Akker said.

"We didn't know what to do," Mrs. Vanden Akker said. "But we prayed and Mr. Vanden Akker received a sign that the picture belonged with you."

"Yes," Bea said.

So, to sit and do nothing ran counter to God's will, then. Bea lifted her arms and accepted the portrait. But before setting it in her lap she swung it around, so that Henry, no longer upside-down, eyed her squarely.

And with this cinching gesture—this final cradling of Henry in her lap—the tears arrived. Bea wiped her eyes, and thanked Mr. and Mrs. Vanden Akker, and half-listened to various reassurances, and wiped her eyes once more, and after five or ten minutes of scarcely hearing what was said, Bea made her way to the door, where she was handed a rectangular object she couldn't at first identify. (It was the portrait of Henry, which she'd evidently at one point handed over and which now was returned, wrapped in brown paper. But which of the Vanden Akkers had stepped out of the room to secure it like this, with tape and twine?)

. . . They ride together, Bea and Henry, artist and subject, first on a bus and then on a streetcar. Although his face is covered, Bea knows it is there. Right through the brown paper wrapping, Henry's gaze blazes. Bea sits in the back of the car and senses his eyes upon her and knows, out at the peripheries of many diffuse sensations, that Henry's glance is still alive, within the portrait she conceived. The artist captured something vital which remains vital. Maybe she failed to conceive everything she might have; maybe her left hand fell short of its noblest extrapolations. Even so, it fixed on something essential about Henry, and no other object on earth captured *this precise facet* of her lover, which, had she not preserved it, would have been lost for good.

Henry's dear face, buried under paper, lies in her lap. Yes, Henry must have framed it for his parents. And it's almost too painful to contemplate—the sort of magnanimity by which Mr. and Mrs. Vanden Akker relinquished the only artist's portrait of their son. Bea weeps a little in the back of the car and gets off at Warren, where she immediately catches another streetcar. It's on the Warren crosstown line that clarity suddenly comes down . . .

Mr. and Mrs. Vanden Akker dislike the portrait. Mrs. Vanden Akker in particular—she'd disliked the portrait from the first. The young man whom Bea had labored so painstakingly to replicate? That feverish-eyed, fiercely freethinking young man, surrounded by van Gogh stars, isn't someone the Vanden Akkers wish daily to contemplate. No, it was a convenient relief when Mr. Vanden Akker received his heavenly "sign" that the portrait must be returned.

The truth is, Bea is utterly dry-eyed and thinking very lucidly. Clarity of this sort always ought to be embraced, even when its light is merciless and raw. Bea has lost nearly everything, and yet she has retained this one indispensable virtue: a sharp-eyed appreciation of exactly where she is.

So it's more painful than it otherwise would be—it all but breaks Bea's spirit entirely—when evidence arrives that she is, in fact, completely muddleheaded . . . Clarity? She's kidding herself—deluding herself. Oh, she can be such a damned little fool! Someone grabs at her sleeve as she's exiting the car. A Negro woman, who evidently has been calling her, lays a hand upon her arm. "Miss," she says, "aren't you forgetting something?"

Yes: she is. Oh my God yes: she's forgetting Henry.

She apparently means to leave Henry on the streetcar.

How could she do such a thing? How could she possibly, *possibly* do such a heartless and indefensible thing? This public exhibition of her deficiencies—her negligence, her unworthiness, her very unfitness for the life she finds herself in—overwhelms her. What would be the point in making excuses? Mere excuses are what they would be. The intense eyes beneath the paper package—they know otherwise. Henry comprehends her every shortcoming. Henry sees it all. He asked her once: in the whole spectrum, what is the worst, the disgustingest color a human being could be? Turtle green? Plum purple? She hadn't fully understood back then—that night at Mitchell's. Now she does. She understands the bottommost degree of self-awfulness Henry was struggling to express. For she's as awful as *he* could ever be. Worse—because Henry had believed, at least, in her purity. And she believes in nothing.

Bea Paradiso carried the head of her lover, shrouded in brown paper, down Inquiry Street toward home.

CHAPTER XXII

Under Henry's steady gaze, her life turned out to be far more manageable. She placed his framed portrait on the right side of her desk, so she could study it from her bed. Henry was the first thing she saw on waking.

His fixed gaze reminded her she must move forward, just as he'd moved forward, toward his recovery, toward his return to the unimaginable Pacific—toward his fiery death on an island called Majuro. Henry understood that the end of everything he held precious might be lying in wait, stranded on some alien shore, but he climbed into the roaring plane nonetheless; it was the only way.

Every day, she wore the amethyst locket he'd given her in those extravagant last days before shipping out. His birthstone. Solemnly, she unfastened it before going to bed; solemnly, she fastened it on rising, while Henry, surrounded by tropical stars, looked on. And so she marched off to the Institute Midwest and sketched meadows and ponds and hillsides for Professor Ravenscroft, who, poor man, wore a toupee. She marched up the steps of Ferry Hospital, whose lizard-green corridors once held the power to sicken her, and pulled out her pencils and her charcoals and drew face after face of young soldiers, some of them fated, like Henry, to die in places nobody had ever heard of.

And people were dying at home. The entire city was besieged by a flu epidemic. Men and women coughed and wheezed on the streetcars on the way to work. The weak, the elderly—they were dying in dreary rooms in a dark city in wartime. Contagion was everywhere. The city was newly under attack. The city would always be under attack. For it was all one war, forever evolving, and the only thing you could do was march forward, past the coughers and the wheezers, to the disabled in their hospital beds: there were wounded soldiers' faces crying out to be drawn.

No one understood how she did it—no one could locate the wellspring of her fortitude. Or grasped that she was, under the circumstances, handling things remarkably well. At home, more than ever, they were tiptoeing around her—Bea sensed that. They feared her taking once more to her bed, they worried she'd weep until her heart actually broke. But Henry's locket would protect her, and Henry's protection was something nobody could understand.

She did try to explain it to Maggie, riding all the way out to what Maggie was now calling the Pig Pen (short for Hamm Penitentiary). Maggie was given a one-hour pass, and the two of them raced around the corner to a luncheonette, where they promptly fell into their biggest argument since junior high school days. Maggie seemed to demand Bea's pity because George *might* get killed, at his desk job in Honolulu. But Bea's true love *had* been killed. But Henry hadn't been Bea's *husband,* Maggie reminded her, and Bea asked what sort of *marriage* it was if Maggie was carrying on with Wally Waller, and Maggie couldn't see how this was *different* from Bea's going out with Ronny Olsson, and Bea pointed out that the difference was that Maggie was a married *woman,* which was how the whole subject of George arose in the first place. The argument only degenerated from there. Maggie was hopelessly, pitifully self-centered. This was a painful truth Bea had actually known for ten years, though never fully confronting it until now.

But not anymore! Striding along Grand River toward a streetcar stop, Bea felt strangely exhilarated. Henry would have admired the savage honesty of her conclusion: her best friend was no true friend. He'd reached various insights before she had, having once composed a poem Bea had by heart:

> The lad I once considered my best friend
> Has found another friend . . .

Likewise it made no sense to continue seeing the medical student Norman Kapp. When Norman had telephoned recently, Bea found herself unable to tell him about Henry—and what was the point in boys with whom she couldn't talk about Henry? After one more afternoon movie (Bea *still* hadn't met Norman's parents), she announced that they must stop seeing each other, and the effect was quite touching, really: Norman gently wept. And she who cried so easily? Dry-eyed, though she almost wished she hadn't been. "I knew this would happen," Norman sniffed, and honked into his handkerchief. "I knew this would happen." And he added, which did give Bea a stab of remorse, "You were so beautiful." (It didn't help matters, his speaking in the past tense. Presumably, she'd already become a remote romance.)

At home on Inquiry, they seemed too preoccupied to notice she was doing better. They all took a negative view of life, which was their main problem, and dinner had become a grave nightly trial. Perhaps because she was hurt at the way Bea toyed with her food, Mamma had gone over to Papa's side: Bea wasn't eating enough. But no one could see it wasn't a lack of appetite, exactly—rather, an inability to procure just what she hungered for. And it made no sense, during a time of shortages, when thousands of young men like Henry needed provisions, to eat what you didn't wish to eat. Later—she could put the weight back on later.

Just how profoundly she had worried her parents became evident when Papa one night made a strange, unprecedented offer. It began with his saying he needed some cigarettes, which had become his usual way of signaling a desire to speak privately.

Whatever was truly on his mind, he gave few hints on the way to Olsson's. But as they stepped out of the store into the night air, Papa lit a cigarette and said, "Bia, I want to give you some money."

It was a peculiar thing to say. This wasn't at all like Papa, usually so circumspect when called upon to open his wallet. He did so now and— right out in the open, in the glare of a street lamp—deposited into her obediently open palm twenty, forty, sixty, eighty, a hundred dollars!

"That's yours to keep. No strings attached." Papa's pride in this choice English idiom was patent. "I wanted you to have the money first. Now you put it away."

"Yes, Papa," Bea said, and folded the bills into her billfold and settled her billfold in her purse.

"I was thinking you might want to visit your Uncle Dennis and Aunt Grace."

"In—Cleveland?"

"You could take the train."

"Alone?"

"Yes. Or the ferry, you just be careful on ferries, the kind of people ride ferries. I know ships." Meaning: I rode in one once, from Italy to America. "But you go visit. Maybe you like to buy things, the things you like with her?" Meaning: maybe you'd like to go clothes shopping with Aunt Grace? "And restaurants. You buy them dinner. You're not begging charity. You just go do whatever they do in Cleveland. They say it's a very nice town."

It was strange how Papa never longed to travel—he who, as a boy, had voyaged alone by ship across the Atlantic to New York, and by train from New York to Detroit. Or perhaps it wasn't so strange. In any case, except for rare day trips across the river into Canada, he hadn't left Michigan in thirty years. And now he was proposing that *she* go to Cleveland—to shop, and dine, and see the sights!

"But what would Mamma say?"

It was one of Mamma's long-standing complaints: she never went anywhere. There was some strangeness here, too, given Mamma's reluctance to leave home. She almost never ventured downtown, which was such an easy trip. She preferred to sit in the kitchen, drinking luke-warm coffee and lamenting a life in which she never went anywhere.

"I can square it with her," Papa said.

"When would I go?"

"Soon, Bia."

"But I couldn't go now! Papa, I've got way too much to do. My classes! And the hospital . . ."

"A little break," Papa said. "And this flu. The city's sick. Everywhere, everywhere, sick people. You go stay with the doctor."

All her life, Bea had dreamed of visiting some other big city—Cleveland, Chicago, even New York. So why didn't she feel giddy and jubilant? Why this wormy fear in the hollow of her stomach? And why this vague resentment toward the man who had just handed her more money than she'd ever held before—a hundred dollars!

"But I couldn't go now." Under the street lamp Bea stared beseech-ingly into her father's eyes. "Papa, you do see I couldn't go now?"

Her father stared right back. His uncomprehending eyes were beseeching too. "I want you think about it. The city's sick, Bia. Now promise me you think about it?"

"I'll think about it," Bea promised her father.

But how could she explain to him all she was contemplating—the things currently running through her brain? Actually, the person who best understood was Ronny, sweeter than ever, who continued to treat her almost as an invalid. This was hardly necessary any longer, though it comforted her to subside into that role. Ronny took her to movies and restaurants but mostly—if the weather was all decent—he took her for walks in various parks: Chandler Park and Balduck Park and Memo-rial Park and Riverside Park. She hadn't known the city held so many parks. As though she were tottering a bit, they walked slowly; in Ronny's company, the whole crazy city blessedly slowed down. His leather-gloved hand held her wool-mittened hand. It was almost as though they were some elderly couple, and one day Bea told him so: "It's as if we're some really old couple, fifty or sixty or something. Sitting on a park bench." They were holding hands on a bench in Palmer Park.

And Ronny's reply was very tender. "I'd like to be sitting on a bench with you in Palmer Park when I'm sixty."

"I'll remember you said that," she said.

"Do. Please. I want you to remember I said that," Ronny said.

She never would have guessed Ronny had it in him to be so self-sacrificing. He made little mention of his own problems, though Bea intermittently grasped that he wasn't doing too well either. Not only had he stopped taking classes, but it seemed he wasn't pursuing art at all. Or anything else, so far as she could determine.

"You'll get back to your art," she told him.

"I don't know." A leery pause. "Know what my mother wants? She wants me to go back to school. Real school. As an academic, not an artist. She wants me to be an art professor."

The notion seemed patently ridiculous. Just imagine Ronny Olsson correcting student papers, running off mimeographs! But only a second later, it made all the sense in the world. Bea could picture it so vividly: the devilishly handsome art professor, in his rakish clothes, striding purposefully across some quadrangle and every girl on campus mesmerized . . .

"I told you the same thing once," Bea said. "That you'd make a great teacher."

"And I told you I don't want to *talk* art. I want to *do* it."

"But who talks more brilliantly than you do?"

"She wants to see you, incidentally."

"Hmm?"

"Mother. You haven't seen my parents in ages. She wants another tour of the DIA."

And this, too—like Papa's proposed trip to Cleveland—instantly roiled Bea's stomach. Yes, she was doing much better, but how was she supposed to progress when people were forever upsetting her? Why couldn't they leave her alone? Under the circumstances, she was doing well.

. . . But these were *such* peculiar circumstances. That very afternoon, after Ronny dropped her home, she went upstairs and sat where she rarely sat, in Edith's bedroom. Bea didn't know what led her there. She sat in the chair where her sister often knitted and her eye fell on an unfamiliar object, suddenly sunlit, on the bedside table.

It was—a homemade dart, obviously of Stevie's construction. Its tip was a sun-glazed knitting needle. It was one more militaristic toy.

Yet when you looked at it closely, it was far more than a mere plaything. This was a little marvel. Stevie had put it together painstakingly, lovingly . . . He had fitted the knitting needle into a piece of wood carved and sanded into a handsome bell-shaped curve. He had outfitted it with gray feathers rimmed in ebony and silver—but where had he acquired such gorgeous feathers?

Maybe he'd found a dead bird? Maybe they'd been supplied by Mr. Glovinsky, the butcher? The point was, this was Stevie's handiwork, and Bea recognized, across an expanse vast enough to make anybody's head spin, that her baby brother, little *Stevie*, knew it too: now and then, Stevie, too, felt a true artist's hunger in his hands. Unmistakably, the boy had stared at this dart as intensely as Bea had ever stared at any of her soldier portraits, and at once Bea grasped how *little* she grasped about her nearest, her most intimate world. You live beside people—strangers. She was so caught up in her life, she couldn't see her life, circumscribed as it was by that most inscrutable of mysteries—a family—where each of us understands everything and nothing at once. She looked still more closely at Stevie's handiwork, and the sunlight dancing angelically on the needle's head was a source of clarification all but blinding.

Mrs. Olsson wasn't someone to be fended off; another trip to the DIA was scheduled. It amused Bea to recall how she'd crammed at the library when last preparing to serve as Mrs. Olsson's museum guide. There was no studying this time.

The morning of the scheduled tour, Bea woke up feeling nauseated. If it weren't for Henry, the sleepless sentinel on her desktop, she wasn't sure she could have dragged herself from bed.

After a bout of diarrhea, Bea examined her face more intently than usual in the bathroom mirror. She'd been aware of losing color these past few weeks—various people had gently pointed it out—but it came as a shock to see her face so thin and ghostly.

And her clothes were beginning to fall off her.

Hoping to disguise the true state of things, Bea put on a baggy black sweater and a baggy gray skirt, and she was more liberal than usual with the rouge, but of course Mrs. Olsson wasn't fooled for an instant. She strolled magnificently across the great lobby of the Detroit Institute of Arts and seized Bea's hands and declared at once, "Oh my poor dear Bianca. You've had such a time." "Hello." "Ronny told me about your friend. My poor dear child," Mrs. Olsson said, "you've had such a time."

The DIA was—as Ronny rightly pointed out—the city's most sacred site, and when previously guiding Mrs. Olsson, Bea had attempted a brief, reverent history of Italian painting. But most of her account had been cut short by Mrs. Olsson, who had hustled them off to lunch. Today, however, Mrs. Olsson wanted to linger—specifically, she wanted to volunteer evaluations. Especially of the portraits.

Mrs. Olsson would have happily conceded that she knew nothing about art history, and yet in her judgments she was, characteristically, opinionated and imposing. They did not intimidate her, those elite faces looking down from the great walls. Leaning confidentially toward Bea, offering pointed little observations, Mrs. Olsson was like a woman at a fête, the belle of the ball, quietly appraising the other, less resplendent partygoers.

Among the French paintings, Mrs. Olsson was particularly drawn toward a pretty aristocrat, a marquise, in a green velvet dress with generous décolletage. "It's hard to say who admired her bosom more," Mrs. Olsson said. "The painter or the lady herself." Then her conversation took an even more indelicate turn, the sort of thing Mamma wouldn't say in a hundred years: "Bianca, you ever ask yourself why God put them there—breasts?"

Mrs. Olsson awaited an answer . . .

"I don't suppose," Bea murmured.

"D'you suppose He liked them Himself? Or was it just His way of turning the tables in a man's world?" Mrs. Olsson laughed and Bea, after a moment, laughed with her.

The two of them found their way to a Flemish painting of the Madonna with two children. Mrs. Olsson said, "No surprise this one's anonymous. That little Christ child is plug-ugly, and the other kid's the ugliest little boy I ever saw."

"That's John the Baptist."

"I should have known," Mrs. Olsson said. "No wonder they cut his head off."

After such an observation, Bea decided to sidestep Bellini's *Madonna and Child*. It was perhaps her favorite painting in the museum, and Mrs. Olsson just might fail to appreciate it . . .

French paintings, English paintings. And then—better yet—a Dutch room. "Ronny's very fond of this one," Bea said. It was a Claesz still life.

"Isn't it too dark?"

"He admires the reflection of the window on the wineglass. It's very subtle. The painting's quite solid, but everything seems afloat."

"Yes . . ."

And Mrs. Olsson, surprisingly, peered long and hard at the painting—as if determined to commune with her son here, within some smoky oak-paneled Dutch interior. Finally she said, "Where do you think Ronny gets it—his talent for art? From me, is it? Or from Mr. Olsson?"

"Maybe both?"

"It has to be me, dear, now doesn't it? Doesn't it? Bea, be candid with me. Suppose I lived to be a hundred. Well maybe, just maybe, I'd paint a painting one day. But let Charley live ten thousand years, he'd still paint no paintings. Can you see him in a little beret, doing a water-color of somebody's poodle?"

Bea laughed again—when was the last time she'd laughed like this? "Mr. Olsson in a little beret? No."

"And now it's time for lunch. You *are* going to let me take you to lunch? We'll go to Pierre's. Have you been to Pierre's?"

The question took Bea aback. It remained among the most memorable meals in her life—that remarkable afternoon when Mrs. Olsson had taken her to Pierre's.

"It's where we went after our last visit here," Bea said gently.

Not even a tad embarrassed, Mrs. Olsson replied, "Silly me. 'Course it is."

So they returned to Pierre's, that dark, cozy, amazingly costly restaurant tucked away off Jefferson not far from the Windsor Tunnel. Once again, the dapper owner, Monsieur Pierre, all but fell over himself at seeing Mrs. Olsson, who again introduced Bea with a flamboyantly elongated enunciation—Bi-an-ca Pa-ra-di-so. And once again Pierre lifted Bea's hand near enough to his mouth that, although he didn't actually kiss it, she could feel his rapturous breathing.

In low, earnest tones Mrs. Olsson consulted with Pierre, who led them to a table different from their previous table. This one, fitted into a corner, was less in the public eye. But the beautiful salmon-colored napkins and tablecloth were exactly the shade Bea remembered. A plump maize-colored candle threw an opulent glow over their table.

It seemed this time there were to be no menus, for scarcely had the two of them been seated when a glass of red wine appeared before Bea, and a clear icy drink before Mrs. Olsson, along with a basket of rolls and a bowl of olives.

Bea sipped her wine, and took another sip.

"You haven't been eating," Mrs. Olsson told her. "I want you to have a roll."

Warily, slowly, Bea selected a roll. Lately, she hadn't done too well when somebody—usually Mamma or Papa—exhorted her to eat. Urgings of this sort turned everything to dust in her mouth.

"*With* butter."

Bea nodded obediently and, more slowly still, buttered the roll, which was warm.

She took a small bite and—and the little roll's condensed flavor opened and ramified on her palate. Its buttery goldenness filled her mouth. She'd never tasted *anything* so delicious. The roll, resting in her hand, was a thing of subtle textures, and she could feel it calling to her, asking to be eaten. Bea took another bite, and another bite.

"And I want you to drink more of your wine. When was the last time you relaxed, darling?"

The wine, too, spoke invitingly to Bea as it went down. As she was consuming a second roll, a new wave of drinks arrived. Who would have supposed she could ever feel so at ease with Mrs. Olsson?

But this was more than ease—it was *gratitude*. This was the perfect place, these rolls were the perfect food, this wine was the perfect glass of wine. It turned out there was nobody in the world whose company she preferred to Mrs. Charles Olsson's—Gretchen Olsson's—and nowhere else she would rather dine than in a restaurant owned by a man named Pierre who wore a pencil-line-thin moustache.

"So you lost someone dear to you," Mrs. Olsson said.

"Yes. Yes I did."

"And was he very dear, Bianca?"

"*Very.*"

Those unreally large and lustrous brown-black eyes of Mrs. Olsson—they were no longer intimidating. It was a wonderful, it was a thrilling experience to stare deep into the eyes of such a beautiful woman—a celebrated beauty. Mrs. Olsson was a celebrated beauty.

I sometimes think you look a little like me, Mrs. Olsson had once told her.

"I'll bet he was very handsome," Mrs. Olsson said.

"Henry? Handsome? I don't know. Maybe. He was brilliantly smart."

"I'm sorry, baby," Mrs. Olsson said. There wasn't another woman of Bea's acquaintance who could successfully deliver a *baby* in quite this way, or that earlier *darling*, lending the endearments such a wry, fluent tenderness.

"It's been very hard," Bea said.

"I can see."

"Is it so obvious?"

"To me it is. You know you can't fool me, Bea."

"I know." And then Bea uttered perhaps the boldest remark she'd ever made to Mrs. Olsson: "But I honestly don't think I've tried to."

It was as though Bea had declared, in perfect candor, *This is really me,* and for a moment their intertwined glances formed a sort of enclosure, wherein each understood the other intimately. Then Mrs. Olsson smiled lightly and said, "Now eat some olives, baby. And a roll. And drink your wine."

Bea needed no encouragement. Without the slightest tincture of self-consciousness, she had cracked open a third crusty roll and had downed most of her second glass of wine. She couldn't remember the last time food had tasted so good. Mrs. Olsson looked amused, perhaps—solicitous, certainly.

"And you felt you couldn't go on?" Mrs. Olsson said.

"For a while."

"You felt you'd lost your one true love?"

Bea took the guidance she was so kindly being offered. "That's right," she confessed. "I did. I wear the locket he gave me. Every day."

The look Mrs. Olsson trained on the locket was disconcertingly cool and appraising. "Garnet?" she said.

"Amethyst," Bea replied. "It's purple."

"Garnets come in purple," Mrs. Olsson said.

"Really? I didn't know. But I wear it every day," Bea said.

"Nice."

"Every day," Bea repeated.

"You know something? I have something for you to ponder." And Mrs. Olsson paused melodramatically.

Bea had long understood just how ardently Mrs. Olsson relished this role of interpreter of life's emotional mysteries. What Bea hadn't understood, until now, was just how much she herself enjoyed playing audience to Mrs. Olsson in this role. She *adored* Mrs. Olsson. "Now, with a very pretty girl," Mrs. Olsson began, "someone like you, Bianca, well, that's the way it has to be."

"The way what? The way *what* has to be?"

"Losing your true love."

What was Mrs. Olsson saying? "You mean Henry was fated to die?"

"Heavens no. But if he hadn't, then he wouldn't have been your true love. You see, for very pretty girls, their one true love's always a lost love."

"Why pretty girls? What's so different about—them?" Bea caught herself just in time. She'd almost said *us.* To clear her head, she took another sip of wine.

"Listen closely. Because this is a difficult thing to talk about, isn't it?"

In the avid way Mrs. Olsson canted forward, with a slight comely turn of the face, Bea was again made aware of just how much Mrs. Olsson was Ronny's mother, or he her son. They shared this eager impulse to talk their way toward the truth. Although Ronny was a bookworm, and Mrs. Olsson freely confessed to not reading much of anything, temperamentally she was no less a philosopher than her son. What linked together all her wayward and inappropriate talk—her jarring observations about money, or Negroes, or Catholics—was this shared probing conversational propulsion. "But I think I can explain. Consider the homely little mouse in your average high school class. She spends a whole lifetime thinking all her achiness and loneliness would magically vanish if she could just nab the heart of the football captain, or the class president. You know, the Charley Olsson of the class. Of course the Charley Olssons don't know she's alive, little mouse. But the Bi-an-ca Pa-ra-di-so of the class, she *can* get the football player, or the class president. Or the Charley Olsson. So let's say she does get him—then what? The ache's still there, isn't it?

"See, it's the one thing she shares with the class mouse. They both need to believe if they could only meet the right boy, the ache would go away. You see? The girl who can *get* the football captain, for her it's *got* to be a lost love. *Got* to be the boy whose family moved away when he was twelve. Or else the one drowned at summer camp. Or the one you exchanged glances with on a bus but never spoke to."

"It's funny you should mention . . . I sometimes feel as though everything in my life really started one Friday afternoon last May on a Woodward streetcar when—"

"Or else the one who goes off to war and doesn't come back."

Lunch arrived on a cloud of inviting aromas. There were steaks and green beans and also long but very thin French fries, which Bea cut with a knife and Mrs. Olsson ate with her fingers. Each flavor was more satisfying than the next. Although Bea naturally wouldn't think of requesting any such thing, and indeed hadn't finished her second glass, a third glass of wine appeared, as well as a new drink for Mrs. Olsson, who talked about her charity work. (She'd recently become active in the War Chest and the Save the Children foundation.) When Mrs. Olsson went off to the ladies' room, Bea ate four quick warm handfuls of French fries. Honestly, she didn't know when she'd last felt so hungry.

Mrs. Olsson, the moment she returned to the table, took up the pressing subject once more. "So now you might say your life's nearly complete, my dear. You have your lost love. And that's something you'll always have. What you *don't* seem to have is some suitable way to live."

"I'm not sure I—"

"And Ronny doesn't either. You know he gets *blue*. Poor sweet boy, it breaks my heart, seeing him so blue. He needs to figure out a future for himself."

Perhaps emboldened by the fancy wine, Bea said, "He tells me you're pressuring him to become an art professor."

"Pressuring? Is that what he says? When I just want to see my boy happy? Is that such a crime?"

"Actually, I'm thinking myself of eventually going back to school. Regular school, not art school. I love literature, and maybe it would enrich my art to study—"

"This Henry of yours. Was he as good-looking as Ronny?"

"Oh no. I mean not in the same—"

"Or as smart?"

You could say that Mrs. Olsson kept interrupting, since so many of Bea's sentences were left unfinished. Or you could say she was facilitating the conversation, given how difficult Bea was finding it to pursue a thought to its end. "Well I think he *was,* though in a different way. Henry was a mathematician."

"Oh mathematics. Charley's a whiz for numbers—he can tell you how many bottles of Hill's nose drops he sold in Grand Rapids last month. But Ronny? Ronny is an *artist.*" Mrs. Olsson offered this with the firm conviction of somebody who had spent the morning in a museum—who had assessed one portrait after another before concluding that, on the whole, her son could have done better.

"I am not pressuring," Mrs. Olsson went on. "I am clarifying. What

I'm saying is, most professors are stuck living in dreary little shoeboxes with bad plumbing. But Ronny wouldn't be. I'd see to that.

"What I'm saying is that if—and again I'm not pressuring, dear, I'm clarifying—that if, just say, if the two of you were ever to decide you actually wanted to tie the knot and get married, I would put up no obstacles. None."

"Well that's hardly what we're—I mean I feel sure Ronny isn't—"

Mrs. Olsson's dumbfounding announcement sparked so many questions and objections that Bea couldn't assemble anything coherent. But Mrs. Olsson quashed all her struggling with one regal wave.

"Do you recall what I asked the last time we lunched here? I asked you: *In your heart of hearts, what is it you want, Bianca?*"

It was one of those typically abrupt turnarounds from Mrs. Olsson. One moment, she couldn't remember having taken you to Pierre's; the next, dark eyes suddenly sharp as tacks, she was reciting verbatim the question she posed at Pierre's three months before.

"Back then, honey? I was thinking maybe you're a bit of a gold digger. You blame me? I wasn't going to blame *you* if you were just a bit of one. I was a bit of one, once upon a time. But I wanted you to understand you couldn't put one over on me.

"Isn't it funny? I worried you were a gold digger and now I'm worrying you're not *enough* of a gold digger—worrying you're so smitten with this idea of a lost love, of becoming some sort of gorgeous starving girl-artist, with such big starving girl-artist eyes, that you don't realize you may accidentally be throwing your life away.

"Do you see what I'm saying? Hell, you can have your lost love, Bea. He was brilliant and he was good-looking and he gave up his life, no less, for you and his country. That's so beautiful. It'll always be so beautiful. But you can also have a life that allows lunches at Pierre's and shopping in New York, all the while married to a husband so handsome you'll be the envy of every woman you meet."

"I better tell you something," Bea began, and then, needing fortification, sipped from her newest tower of wine. She could hardly believe she was going to utter the words she was going to utter: "I gave myself to Henry."

So challengingly sharp was Mrs. Olsson's scrutiny, she obviously expected Bea's glance to curtsy and drop away in shame. Bea flinched—she wavered—but she held steady. She fully met that gaze. It was Henry who steadied her. She was not going to deny Henry.

"You gave yourself?"

"I did."

"To this soldier boy?"

"That's right. The very last night I saw him. Somehow I knew he wasn't coming back."

"And not also to Ronny?"

"To *Ronny*?" Bea said. "Heavens no." What must Mrs. Olsson be thinking of her?

"*Heavens* no?" And yet, Mrs. Olsson seemed faintly offended, rather than what you might expect—relieved.

"Well—no."

"And Ronny knows what you did?"

"I'm not sure."

A long silence fell. "Well, if he does," Mrs. Olsson said, dropping her own eyes to the maize-colored candle beside the ivory-colored ashtray, "it doesn't seem to trouble him. And if he doesn't? I can tell you from experience, it wouldn't be the first time a man mistook his wife."

Apparently, there was nothing on God's green earth that could not be divulged at this corner table in Pierre's. Bea said, "You make it sound like ours to decide—as if Ronny had no say . . ."

"Of course he does. My boy is no milquetoast. Only, I do think you can bring him round. I think you're a young woman of extraordinary powers, my dear. Haven't I made that clear? That I believe in you?"

"I'm so flattered," Bea said. "Nothing could mean more to me than—"

"And"—Mrs. Olsson added, finishing her drink—"I'm so tired. I'm so deathly tired of seeing my boy unhappy."

"I'll be right back," Bea said.

"Yes, you go on," Mrs. Olsson replied, nodding confirmingly, as if she herself had proposed this trip to the ladies'. "You think it over. What I'm saying. *You think it over.*"

But Bea was not in need of anything so high-minded as space to think. She needed a toilet—her tummy suddenly felt very shaky. It had been quite a while since she'd eaten so much, so fast.

What had she been *thinking*? She could no longer eat the way normal people might eat.

One other aspect of Pierre's was unchanged: the same doleful Negro woman served as the ladies' room attendant. Worse yet, she was still wearing the same strained-looking, too-tight pink dress.

Bea recalled how, the last time she was here, some word or coin from

Mrs. Olsson had elicited this woman's blessing. Bea announced, rather nonsensically, "I'm here with the lady who was just in here."

The woman did not look impressed. No, the truth was she looked poised and canny. And amused. Bea felt herself in the wrong somehow. And, flustered by the woman's look, and by Mrs. Olsson's astounding revelations, and by the wine, and flustered, most of all, by her distressed stomach's imminent collapse, Bea had to check herself from additionally blurting out, "And you know what she did? She just proposed to me—on behalf of her son."

CHAPTER XXIII

At home, Edith had a problem—the sort of problem no child on earth except Edith would have.

Months and months ago, she had been given the name of a soldier to write to. Each student in Edith's homeroom had been randomly assigned a soldier, but it seemed safe to say no classmate had a letter in the mail sooner than Edith did—an extremely long and no doubt extremely informative letter. Her soldier's name was Ira Styne.

And surely no classmate would have kept on writing even when no reply materialized. She must have written half a dozen letters in all. Now, miraculously, a letter addressed to Edith Paradiso appeared and, more miraculous still, it enclosed a five-dollar bill.

Bea studied the letter minutely. Everyone in the family studied it minutely. A total stranger had just sent little Edith a five-dollar bill! The soldier's penmanship seemed childish or shy—the letters were *very* small—but the tone and vocabulary were wry and sophisticated.

Private Styne apologized for being so tardy. "All sorts of things came up. To tell you the truth, I had a bit of a time for a while. Anyway, I won't bore you with the details, except to say I'm *very sorry*.

"I was interested to hear that you like mathematics," he went on. "It's very strict, isn't it? I think I like math less than I used to.

"Speaking of math, I enclose five hundred pennies in convenient paper form. Rereading your letters, I was distressed to see that I missed your birthday a few weeks ago. You have become a teenager! This is a very special birthday: thirteen. The gift comes with one strict condition attached: you must spend it on something that makes you *very happy*."

Edith's problem—or at least her larger problem—did not involve the gift itself. She knew precisely what to do with the money. She would buy four dollars' worth of war stamps—she would support our boys—and she would reserve the remaining dollar for treats for herself. No, the problem was what to do with the letter. Specifically, could she legitimately place it in her scrapbook entitled "My Testimonials"?

When Bea eventually realized how much Henry would have enjoyed this story, tears came to her eyes . . . Henry would have understood Edith's quandary. He would have taken it seriously. Edith *couldn't* place it in her scrapbook if it wasn't an authentic testimonial.

The letter had arrived from a stranger, like a testimonial, but in response to mail from Edith, like a regular letter. Would it make sense to compile a new scrapbook, of notable correspondence—or was it a testimonial?

Henry would never have the opportunity to savor this story; Henry would never extend any helpful advice.

Haunted as she was, it was the most haunting thought Bea knew: the sentence that began, *Henry will never* . . . When she stepped off the bus, it was, *Henry will never see Woodward Avenue again.* When she stood in front of the white stucco house, each and every window decoration on the left precisely balancing a twin decoration on the right, it was, *Henry will never see his home again.* Bea was paying another visit to the Vanden Akkers.

Tragedy was the great human reality—Bea grasped this at last—and yet tragedy turned everything else unreal, and to walk up that house's walk was like entering a dream, or a fairy tale, and nothing in Bea's known world could possibly match the queerness of the vision when the front door swung open. It was the same horrible enactment all over again, only worse—far worse. Again Bea knew it must be Mrs. Vanden Akker in the doorway. And again there was a split-second refusal to believe it. In this fairy tale, stolid Mrs. Vanden Akker had been transformed by some curse into a wizened little wraith.

How much weight had she lost? Thirty pounds, forty? Whatever the figure, mere loss of weight could scarcely account for how much shorter she seemed—and how altered in every movement.

To be fair (but why, under these circumstances, be fair?), everything in the spectral Vanden Akker home was being filtered through a haze. Bea had awakened this morning to the realization that she was coming down with something. Or was it all in her mind? She was feeling a little dizzy, and quite achy. And for days now, dreading this visit, she'd been walking around with a knotted stomach.

Bea hadn't expected to hear again from Mrs. Vanden Akker, whose telephone call had stirred up various accusatory resentments. What did the woman *want*? This request for another visit seemed wholly unreasonable . . . *Why* had Bea been summoned again to this ghostly living room, where Mr. Vanden Akker, more woolly-haired than ever, stood waiting to shake her hand? Was it possible to convey a vein of madness in a handshake? If so, this was what Mr. Vanden Akker's trembling hand conveyed.

After a good deal of clumsy fussing, Bea was seated upon the couch. And after a good deal more fussing, coffee was served.

Again Mrs. Vanden Akker asked conscientiously after each Paradiso, in order of age. Her constant nodding at Bea's observations suggested a tremor. Truly, both Vanden Akker parents had aged ten years, twenty years, in just a few weeks . . .

Under these excruciating circumstances, Bea felt it would hardly be suitable to complain of feeling unwell. Was she about to fuss about a little sickness to two people who had lost their only child? Still, she was having trouble answering even simple questions. Her head had floated away.

Mr. Vanden Akker was letting his hair grow—a wild white thicket of curls, somewhat thin on top. Bea didn't understand some of the references at first, but eventually it dawned on her that he'd left his job. Mr. Vanden Akker was unemployed, or he had retired. "I am pursuing my true interest—moral issues in theology," he announced, and Mrs. Vanden Akker, who formerly had treated her husband's abstruse pursuits with undisguised impatience, nodded respectfully—respectfully and, yes, tremulously.

Bea was also served hard little biscuits—they might well have been the same tooth-cracking biscuits she had met when last here, a few weeks ago. She drank deeply from her cup, hoping the coffee would clear her head. In recent days, it had sometimes been very difficult to tell whether she wasn't feeling well or merely thought she ought to be feeling unwell. So there was some reassurance in declaring categorically: *I'm coming down with something.*

After a time, Mrs. Vanden Akker said, "I have consulted with Mr. Vanden Akker, and he informs me that when you last visited I may have committed a significant omission."

Bea drew her spine erect and tried to focus. This must be it: the true, intensely-brooded-upon motive behind this invitation.

"Yes?" Surely they were not going to offer her another portrait of Henry. No, since there were no other portraits of Henry . . .

"Mr. Vanden Akker has examined the issue from all angles, in the light of his scholarship, and he has concluded that I misled you. Not deliberately. I do not lie," Mrs. Vanden Akker declared forthrightly, her projecting chin a poignant throwback to her old forcefulness.

"No of course not," Bea whispered in reply.

"But Mr. Vanden Akker, he made me see that I may have misled you by an act of omission. It is possible to mislead through omission, you see."

"No less possible," Mr. Vanden Akker interjected, and added, "though it's often trickier to analyze."

"Of course," Bea murmured, since some such reply was evidently expected, but what was she agreeing to? Where in the name of heaven was this conversation headed?

"We received a letter from Henry before he passed away."

"Various letters," Mr. Vanden Akker qualified.

"But one in particular."

"One in particular," Mr. Vanden Akker said.

"Henry spoke of you."

"Me?" The word emerged from Bea's throat in a cracked whisper. She found herself blinking rapidly. She couldn't quite bring either Mr. Vanden Akker or Mrs. Vanden Akker wholly into focus.

"Actually, in his letters Henry spoke of you various times," Mr. Vanden Akker said.

"One letter in particular," Mrs. Vanden Akker pointed out.

"One letter in particular," Mr. Vanden Akker concurred.

"Henry said"—and Mrs. Vanden Akker's stalwart manner abandoned her. With fluttery hands she hoisted her coffee cup. Her eyelids didn't blink so much as flap; Bea was aware of the effort involved in brushing back tears.

It was Mr. Vanden Akker who restarted the conversation: "Our son wrote and told us that he was in love with you and that he wished to make you his wife."

"He did? He wrote that to you?"

"It is not such an easy thing for someone in our church to marry someone outside it," Mr. Vanden Akker said. "Though of course it can be done."

"You would need to *convert*," Mrs. Vanden Akker injected fiercely.

"There is no shame in conversion," Mr. Vanden Akker pointed out. "At bottom, and here I'm taking the historical perspective, we are all converts. I explain that to my wife: we are all converts."

"We are all converts," Mrs. Vanden Akker echoed, her head wagging up and down.

"Our Henry wished you to be his wife," Mr. Vanden Akker said. "And we didn't tell you that."

"I had no idea. I'm sure you didn't mean—"

"Our duties are not restricted to our actions," Mrs. Vanden Akker intoned.

"Morally, they are only half the field," Mr. Vanden Akker said, and added, with characteristic, crazy exactitude, "or let's say forty percent."

"Mr. Vanden Akker determined that you ought to have your own copy of the letter. So he has written out a copy for you."

In her rapid new little-womanish way, Mrs. Vanden Akker hastened to the mantel to retrieve an envelope, which she handed to Bea, who said, "I'm so touched," though what she actually experienced was a heavy, body-encompassing dread. She snapped the letter into her purse.

"I'm keeping the original," Mrs. Vanden Akker said.

"That's only right."

"I omitted to mention this letter when you last visited. That was misleading."

"There's more," Mr. Vanden Akker said.

The pause that expanded hinted at a store of resistance—as though Mrs. Vanden Akker were about to contradict her husband. When she spoke, however, they were in complete accord: "There's more," she said.

"In one of his letters," Mr. Vanden Akker went on, "Henry said something highly significant. He said you were the only person, other than his parents, other than us, who truly understood him."

"I omitted to mention that," Mrs. Vanden Akker said.

Deep in the warm swirling mists of Bea's head, deep in a kind of fogged tropical jungle, this last remark from Henry located her. He spoke and she heard. (The sea was whispering in the distance, speaking unimaginable volumes, and she heard that, too.) It was a message even more telling, in its way, than his indirect proposal of marriage. No other girl had understood him—but *she* had. You could see it in the portrait she did. She had known him, soul to soul. She'd known Henry. And here where everything was meant to balance, in this neat, white, mathematically symmetrical house in Pleasant Ridge, Michigan, the three survivors sat—over coffee, over tumultuous revelations: the three people on earth privileged to understand the soul of a brilliant eccentric boy who did not take teasing well and who, back from the War, somberly marched off to the zoo in a laughable hat . . . "He understood me, too," Bea whispered plaintively, and wasn't that all she'd ever asked of life? The living room was overheated—or seemed so because, as she must have been aware for some time now, Bea had a pounding fever coming on.

"There's more," Mr. Vanden Akker prompted, and this time his wife did not hesitate: "There's more," she parroted.

"More," Bea said. In her dizziness and achiness, Bea likewise placed herself in Mr. Vanden Akker's hands. For it was as if, in all his woolly-headedness, the man had achieved true clarity at last: this afternoon, all the sins of conversational omission would be painstakingly, precisely rectified. Together the three of them would say the unsaid.

"My son also reported that he had wronged you greatly. He obviously felt a great deal of remorse and torment over this."

But what was Mr. Vanden Akker saying? How far had he glimpsed into the naked and slippery truth?

Henry had *wronged* her? The words blazed up in Bea's fuzzy, fiery head, illuminating an image of a tall thin girl standing palely in Mitchell's bathroom, without a stitch of clothing on her body, languorously giving herself a sponge bath at the sink while Henry wept on the other side of the door. Elsewhere, on another day, she had walked up to Mack in order to sprinkle paper fragments into two trash containers.

When from the depths of her fever Bea looked Mr. Vanden Akker right in the eye and declared, "Henry did not wrong me," it would have been impossible to say whether she was defending Henry, or herself. But the utterance bolstered her. Just as firmly (just as misleadingly, perhaps—or just as mercifully, perhaps) she glanced into Henry's mother's pale eyes and said, "No, not at all. He was always a complete gentleman. Henry."

It was time to leave and every movement and moment hummed with novel feelings of power. She wasn't the least intimidated by these people. Bea had something she had been longing to announce and would now announce: one remark that would not become an omission. Looking fixedly at Mrs. Vanden Akker, Bea said, "Henry wrote and told you that he *loved* me." The offensive term, startling as any profanity, caused the little old woman to flinch. But Bea was not to be deterred or deflected. "I just want you to know how things stood between us. Because you see, I loved him. I *loved* your son."

It was time to go. Bea felt vindicated—she had been not so misleading after all. Mrs. Vanden Akker urged more coffee, Mr. Vanden Akker volunteered to drive her home, one of them remarked that she was looking tired, one of them told her she would be *welcome* at their church . . . Politely, unstoppably, Bea disentangled herself and escorted her packed, feverish head down the street toward Woodward Avenue.

. . . And later, having in a sense arrived home once more (having seated herself in a streetcar), Bea recalls that she is carrying a letter from Henry. Although she had torn up an earlier letter, it's as if the fragments have miraculously rewoven themselves, all in order to lie within her hands, intact, a second time.

"Dear Mother and Father," the letter begins. It's in Henry's handwriting, which is perplexing.

Actually, it's only *nearly* Henry's handwriting, which is more perplexing still . . . until Bea realizes that son and father—fierce, focused Henry and mild, woolly-headed Mr. Vanden Akker—have nearly identical penmanship:

> *I hope and trust the two of you are well. I am quite remarkably recovered. I still get occasional twinges in my back, but I can hardly complain, especially when I look around at what some of the others have endured. The easing of pain has been a great mercy, largely because it has allowed me to think more lucidly . . .*

Bea doesn't want, doesn't need, to read any further. Enfolded in that last sentence lies the one true note. Henry's yearning pilgrim spirit resides in that voice: "A great mercy, largely because it has allowed me to think . . ."

To think . . . She snaps the letter back in her purse. The streetcar grates in reply. It occurs to Bea just how wonderfully appropriate is her condition as she carries home this unforeseen document in which, so she has been informed, Henry will profess his love: she has a fever, just the way Henry had so many, many fevers. And the fever allows her to think . . .

Down Inquiry Street she is carrying Henry's love. The city is drifting away, into its outskirts, or floating away, up in smoke, but that's all right, since she houses within her the knowledge that she was the only girl ever to commune with Henry's spirit. As he communed with hers. Yes, she understood him before she understood she understood him. And this was the reason, one beautiful, imperishable evening, in the photograph-jammed living room of a complete stranger, eighteen-year-old Bea had chosen to give herself wholly, body no less than soul, to the late Henry Vanden Akker.

CHAPTER XXIV

Long Drive to the City

The book he was reading just before turning off the bedside light was called *The Man Who Chose His World*. In this one, a sort of religious cult moved to the highest Andes. Their religion was really Science, and in their dizzy, thin-aired isolation they began to make unprecedented strides. They began plausibly to envision an Earth free of hunger, menial toil, childhood disease. They mastered the mysteries of genetics, and foresaw new generations of better, brighter, healthier human beings. But with every new advance, the people they'd left behind—the People Down Below—regarded them with increasing suspicion and, eventually, hatred. Down Below, a plot was hatched to exterminate the cult.

It fell upon the book's hero, a young man raised by the scientists, to arrange a compromise. He went down from the mountains and negotiated. The cult would build a rocket ship and fly away. They pledged never to return to Earth. They would take to the stars, those infinite spaces where they could pursue in tranquillity the infinite reaches of Science.

And so it was agreed. Only, now a complication developed. For while visiting the People Down Below, the young man had fallen helplessly in love with one of their young women. Now he faced a choice: abandon his people, and all their unbounded aspirations, or abandon the girl? He must choose his world.

The ringing phone was a call from another planet—or what might just as well have been. A call put through from Detroit. The bedside clock said twenty-five after one. It was Vico calling.

"Dennis, it's Vico."

It was Vico calling from Detroit at one-thirty in the morning and all at once Dennis felt fully, fearfully awake. During nights at home, alone with Grace, this was always the one call above all others to be dreaded: some cry of distress from the Paradisos. He and Grace might have moved from Detroit, but that snug home on Inquiry remained almost more real and precious to the two of them than their own capacious house in Cleveland.

"Vico, what is it?"

A charged pause, during which Dennis sensed that the news must hit in the most vulnerable spot of all.

"It's Bia," Vico said. Of course it was . . . "She's all right, she's all right, but it's a very high fever. I think it may be the influenza."

"How high a fever?"

"One hundred four?"

"For how long now?"

"One hundred four point two, actually."

"Vico, how long has the fever been going on?"

"A day. Maybe a little more than a day. Though not quite so hot before. The influenza can be serious for someone like Bia?"

"Can be."

Dennis knew all about influenza in Detroit. It had been a true epidemic this winter, the worst since '18. It was deadlier than the War. In recent months, the city had suffered more casualties at home, from influenza, than boys lost overseas.

Grace was up and out of bed, standing beside him. Dennis scribbled on the notepad by the phone: *Bea—fever—104°.*

"Vico, you have her at home?"

"At home, right. I know you don't like hospitals."

"Up to a point, Vico. She gets any hotter, take her right away to Ford. Or Ferry. The emergency room. Keep a cool washcloth on her forehead. If she'll drink anything, give her cold water but not ice water. It's one-thirty. I can be there by six-thirty I think."

"You don't have to do that. I just thought you ought to know."

"I'm on my way, Vico."

"I didn't call asking you. I'm not asking you to drive all that—"

"Vico, Vico, I know you didn't. Expect me at six or six-thirty. Sooner, maybe."

"You don't have to come," Vico protested. "There are other doctors in Detroit."

But Vico himself must have heard his own beseeching diffidence. As far as he was concerned, there was but one trustworthy doctor on earth, who happened to be his brother-in-law and best friend, Dennis Poppleton.

"Yes, there are some very good ones, if you need them. Over there at Ford. Or Ferry. Six or six-thirty, Vico. Have some coffee on. Bye now."

Grace—the faithful helpmeet—was already busy in the kitchen. She had the coffee brewing and was assembling a couple of ham-and-cheese sandwiches.

"What do you think it is?" she said.

"I'm guessing influenza."

"How serious?"

"Normally not. I mean statistically. What troubles me is his calling at one-thirty in the morning. You know Vico. He wouldn't do it if he weren't scared silly."

"Oh Dennis . . ."

"Yes," Dennis said.

"You know, Vico played his last card, calling here."

As he often did, Dennis stared at his wife in puzzlement. For a moment, he did not understand. But then he saw that Grace, as was her way—a quicker way than his—had intuited just how things stood in Detroit. Vico never did anything without deliberation. He had weighed the call in his mind, checked on the girl, weighed the call, checked on the girl, weighed the call, checked on the girl . . . And then he'd played the one remaining, desperate card he held: Vico had telephoned Cleveland.

"I could go with you," Grace said.

"I need you here, darling. Call the hospital, tell them what's happened. Reschedule what needs rescheduling. I hope to be back by late afternoon. The girl'll be all right."

"Oh I know she'll be all right."

"She has a strong constitution. They all do—all three of those kids."

"That's right."

Dennis went out to the toolshed, where he kept a five-gallon container of gasoline, and, grunting under its weight, hoisted it into the trunk of his car. In the past year, the gasoline situation had improved for everyone, and as a doctor he'd been given a "C" sticker anyway, all but exempting him from rationing. But at this hour of night you never knew when you'd find an open service station. Being a doctor meant being prepared.

By the time he returned to the house, Grace had fitted his sandwiches in a lunch box, along with an apple, a molasses cookie, and a wedge of spice cake. The big thermos was full of hot coffee. Having asked her once, he had no reason to remind Grace to call the hospital; she was the most competent person he'd ever met. At the front door, he embraced her with one arm (his medical bag was in the other) and pushed his body up against her—his jewel, his pillar of strength.

"You're not too worried, Dennis?"

He confessed the truth. "Normally, I wouldn't be. But Vico clearly is. Calling at one-thirty in the morning from Detroit. The man must be scared out of his wits. You know what she means to him."

"And to you," Grace replied.

"Yep."

"And to me."

"Yep."

Dennis turned and walked toward the dark car, turned once more on his heels, and found Grace where he expected her, surveying him from the lit doorway. "Now don't you worry," he said.

"And you," Grace called, softly. "Don't you worry."

"You're my palm tree," he called, more softly still—a mere whisper. He heard a tremulous "Thank you" as he closed the car door.

It was a doctor's house, their house, with little room for nonsense jokes, and yet the line about the palm tree was a treasured exception.

The phrase had sprung to his lips one evening some fifteen years ago, back in those delirious days when he'd set his sights on the most desirable woman he'd ever laid eyes on, who was somehow all the more unapproachable for being a divorcée. Who was he to aspire to such a creature? He was a pop-eyed frog—he knew it well enough. He was the penniless kid from Alton, Illinois, who had somehow managed to scrounge and scrape his way through medical school, where for one three-week period he'd read his textbooks with one eye, his glasses having lost a lens he couldn't afford to replace. On that vertiginous evening when Grace first allowed him a kiss, Dennis, overwhelmed, so frantic to please her, and to praise her, had proclaimed, "You're my palm tree." The words had popped out from some unvisited, exotic sector in his brain. Of course, back then neither of them had ever seen a palm tree.

And Grace had seized delightedly upon this ludicrous slip, never permitting him to abandon it—until, in time, Dennis, too, cherished its quiet poetry, its lofty and rooted rightness: Grace was indeed his palm tree.

Dennis had later told her, which wasn't quite accurate, that what he'd meant to say was that he wished someday to take her to a land where palm trees grew. In any event, he'd done precisely that, in various spectacular locales. Hadn't he strolled with his beautiful wife along a beach in Key West, Florida, the southernmost tip of the United States?

He picked up Route 6 west of Cleveland and settled his powerful Packard at just under 50 miles per hour. It was 165 miles from his home on Brock Street to Inquiry Street, give or take a few miles. He found an open gas station at Lorain and filled his tank. The poor boy who pumped the gas had a harelip and a stammer. This was something Dennis had observed before: a disproportionate number of stammerers working the night shifts. Coincidence? Or was there, statistically, something to this? Stammerers might naturally gravitate toward lonelier hours and less talk.

Or, alternatively, the bosses might routinely assign the loneliest shifts to those least prepared to protest.

Though Dennis wasn't very hungry, he was feeling extremely nervous, and he had polished off the cookie, the cake, and one of the sandwiches even before reaching Toledo. The car hummed along. In Vico's heart of hearts he must have known Dennis would insist on coming, though perhaps Vico didn't quite realize Dennis had no choice. He simply *couldn't* have stayed home—pacing the floor, awaiting another call. At a time like this, his only comfort was located in the low roar of the engine, the steadily falling mile markers. No, much harder than driving to Detroit in the middle of the night was doing what Grace was doing: waiting at home for news. Once again, she was the strong one.

It was an hour or so later, having just crossed the Michigan state line, when the flashing red light of a police car exploded behind him. Dennis felt very little fear—almost exhilaration, actually. Dennis liked policemen. He'd very rarely met the copper who couldn't be outmaneuvered. The fact was—policemen liked *him.* They seemed instinctively to recognize him as just the sort of person they were put on Earth to aid and protect. Yes, the police car's lights were almost welcome. Though mostly an uncompetitive man, Dennis relished this opportunity to get the better of a cop.

"You Ohio people can't read traffic signs?" the officer began. Dennis had rolled down his window, here on the shoulder of a lightless, flat, totally deserted road. The police lights bled across empty acres and acres of frosty black farmland.

"I'm a Michigan man myself, Officer, despite the license plate. And I'm a doctor."

Dennis handed the officer his driver's license and his hospital ID card.

"Says here Cleveland. Last time I checked, Cleveland was in Ohio."

"The wife and I just moved. But trust me, we're Michiganders through and through."

"You were speeding. I say nearly fifteen over."

"I never argue with a policeman," Dennis said. A pause followed. "Never have, never will." Another pause. Dennis went on: "You see, I'm off to examine a patient in Detroit. My own niece. She's very ill. I got the long-distance telephone call a couple of hours ago and jumped right into my car."

"You say you're a doctor?"

"It's there on the card."

"I can read."

This was a young cop, with much to prove about himself. He wasn't going to bend easily.

"Long night?" Dennis asked.

"Too many speeders," the cop said dryly.

"Deserted roads."

"It's still speeding."

"No argument there. No argument there. Dr. Dennis Poppleton, by the way," Dennis introduced himself, and extended his hand through the open window.

The officer, clearly nonplussed, stared at this hand extended out into the darkness of the night. Finally, reluctantly, he clasped and shook the doctor's hand. "Officer Frank Santovetti."

"Sounds Italian to me. My niece is Italian. Her name is Paradiso. Bianca Paradiso. She has a fever of a hundred and four point two. She's a beautiful girl, and the apple of my eye, incidentally. I don't have any kids myself, but the wife and I think of her as our own."

"You were nearly fifteen over."

"Officer Santovetti, I'm sure you're quite right. You see, it's the girl I'm worried about. She's only eighteen. Younger even than you. She could be your kid sister."

In the shocking oscillating red light thrown by his patrol car, Officer Santovetti looked more puzzled still—as though he didn't quite comprehend how, in these patchily lit negotiations, Dennis and his feverish Italian niece had acquired the upper hand. For there was no chance of a speeding ticket now.

"You were fifteen over."

"It's the girl," Dennis said. "It's the girl. She's the apple of my eye."

"Now listen, Doc," Officer Santovetti said sternly. "I want you to slow down."

"Yes sir," Dennis said. "I plan to do just that."

This note of ready compliance visibly placated the young officer. It allowed him to hold his dignity intact. He patted the top of Dennis's lowered window and said, "You know what? I think I'm going to give you a break."

"I take that as a good omen," Dennis said.

Another pause. The officer seemed younger than ever as he said, "Hey, I hope your niece gets better."

"Yes. I'm going to see to that," Dennis said, and feeling much better himself, he added, "Officer Santovetti, I'll pass along your best wishes."

A moment later, behind him, the red light extinguished itself and Dennis accelerated into the darkness. "I'm the last card," he said aloud, and giggled into the darkness.

Soon he was traveling the same speed as before: fifteen or so over. Perhaps it was only his imagination, but Dennis thought he saw a glow to the northwest, out where the bomber factories of Willow Run lay. Twenty-four hours a day, day in and day out, the rivers of molten steel were flowing. Out on the front lines, military errors were being made all the time, and American boys were dying unnecessarily—it was the nature of war—but here in Michigan it was nothing but pure glory, a technological breakthrough without precedent. Dennis had thought about this and thought about this. No city on earth had ever fought a war the way this city was fighting: it had become democracy's true arsenal. It was bearing the burden of a dream born perhaps in ancient Greece: the governed shall govern. And future historians would recognize that the War's authentic center had lain not in London, or even in Washington, but here in the Midwest, in Michigan, in Detroit. This was where the War's bloodied and beaten victims, the French and the Dutch, the Poles and the Czechs, the Chinese and the Burmese, would be redeemed.

The city's skyline defined the horizon at last, the crowning ball of the Penobscot Building serving as a sort of lighthouse. Detroit as the world's true harbor. The city's familiar stone lineaments inspired such eager impatient nervousness that, though he wasn't at all hungry, Dennis bolted down another ham-and-cheese sandwich and swigged another cup of coffee. He was nearly there . . .

Inquiry Street still lay in darkness when he pulled up before the Paradisos. Back when the city had first begun ordering occasional blackouts, Dennis had paid $1.49 to have the hands of his watch tipped in fluorescent paint—a wise investment. It was now six-ten in the morning.

Vico appeared in the doorway even before Dennis was out of the car.

After the long drive, Dennis was feeling so worried, and so weary, that as he mounted the front steps he forgetfully extended his hand in greeting. Of course Vico would have none of that. He tugged Dennis to him, chest to chest. You felt the man's muscles when he held you.

They whispered to each other in the front hall.

"You didn't have to come, Dennis."

"I had to come, Vico."

"I didn't call asking you to come."

"I had to come, damn it, now enough of that—how's our patient?"

"Sleeping, mostly."

"And her fever?"

"It is about the same."

"And Sylvia?"

"Finally she went to sleep. She was up almost all night."

"And you're up all night too? No sleep at all?"

"It's just sleep," Vico said. "Sleep doesn't matter."

"Now you wait here, Vico. I better go check up on our girl."

Twenty-plus years of visiting the ailing in sickrooms had taught Dennis a solid unflappability. He could usually meet the worst with a professional steadiness. But in Bea's flickery bedroom, illuminated only by a candle on the desk, the pale stripped-away face in the bottom bunk— peaked as a death's head—wrung a loud shivery groan from his chest. On wobbly legs Dennis stumbled to her bedside and lowered his face toward the girl's beloved face. Her eyes were closed.

What he beheld was scarcely the consequence of a few days of fever. Bea had been burning herself up for weeks and weeks now, and a surge of righteous anger welled up inside him: *Why wasn't I called before?* This precious girl—the apple of his eye—was nothing but bones. He laid a palm upon her forehead and felt from deep within her skull the emanations of a dry, angry, indurate heat. He lifted her arm—a mere stick.

"Bea," he said. "Bea, it's Uncle Dennis, honey. Now I'm going to take your temperature."

He placed a thermometer in her mouth and her eyes fluttered open. For a moment she did not appear to see anything. Then a glimmer of recognition. What she seemed to say, however, her lips mumbling around the thermometer he was holding in place, was "Papa."

"No, darling, it's Uncle Dennis."

"Papa," she repeated, nodding her head, and closed her eyes once more. With his free hand Dennis brushed the hair from her face and gently probed the glands in her throat. He drew his face down to the side of her face and inhaled through his nose: that sour-milk smell of high fever.

Dennis carried the thermometer over to the flickering candle. He wasn't about to turn on a light quite yet. It was an Italian touch that ought to be respected—Vico's lighting a candle. The flame wasn't merely illuminating the room; it was serving a vigil.

The girl's temperature was 104.8°.

"Well my darling, you've got yourself quite a fever."

Bea muttered something, though she did not seem to awaken.

"Now I'm going to listen to your heart and look down your throat."

He peeled away the sweaty sheet from her body. She was wearing pajamas and socks. He unbuttoned her pajama top and set his stethoscope over her heart. The skin over her clavicle was stretched taut. His fingers probed at the glands of her stomach. She must be twenty pounds lighter than when he saw her last—and she had been a little too thin even then.

"Now I want you to open your mouth," he said, but Bea didn't seem to hear. His fingers eased open her jaw and he peered down her throat with his otoscope. Her throat was red, but still more telling was the way she winced at being moved, however gently—a deep-in-the-bone achiness he associated with influenza.

"I'm going to try to cool you down a bit, and then I think I'm going to take my girl to the hospital."

He extracted four washcloths from his bag and tiptoed down the hall and into the bathroom, where he soaked them in cold water and, one by one, wrung them out. He carried them back to Bea's room and again closed the door.

He peeled off her socks and began rubbing her feet with one of the cool washcloths. The girl recoiled but did not seem fully to waken. A moment later, she seemed at ease—completely asleep again. He ran a cloth over her bare stomach and shoulders. Her skin was burning. It hurt him to see how rawly her ribs showed, as if the bones longed to break free of the skin.

"I'm going to take you to the hospital and I'm not going to leave until I hear you say, 'Uncle Dennis, bring me a great big breakfast.'" His heart was so sore, his fear so painfully magnified, he hardly knew what he was saying. He repeated the words: "I'm not going to leave until you say, 'Uncle Dennis, bring me a great big breakfast.' "

He ran the cool cloth over the girl's burning forearms, her burning neck, her burning face. "Why didn't they call me?" he asked her, pleadingly. "Was I so far away? Had you forgotten me, I'd moved so far away? Damn it all, why on earth didn't you call me?"

He cradled the crown of her skull in one hand and tenderly wrapped his other hand under her jawbone, so that he was propping her up and leaning toward her, their faces no more than six inches apart. "Now listen carefully, Little One, because now I'm about to say the one most important thing I've ever said to you. Ever in your entire life. Are you listening to me, Bea?" He paused.

She did not stir.

"Bia?"

She did not stir.

"All right, then, here it is. Here it is: you must get better for me," he ordered. Her eyes fluttered open.

Her skull was cradled in his hand: he was seeking through his fingertips to infuse some strength into the girl. Oh good Lord! He might have been some quack faith healer, rather than a true, medical doctor, as he intoned once more, "Bea, now listen, please, now *listen:* you must get better for me . . ."

He restored her socks to her feet and buttoned up her pajama top and stepped out into the hall. Vico was waiting at the bottom of the stairs. "I—" Vico said. He could not speak.

Dennis put a finger to his lips and walked past him, out into the kitchen. Vico followed.

"We're going to take her to the hospital," Dennis said. "In my car."

"Yes, the hospital," Vico said.

"I'm not sure how well she can walk."

Vico's eyes brightened. "Then I'll carry her." The man who prided himself on his arm wrestling had been preparing his whole life for this task . . . "She'll be all right?"

"I think so. She's very ill. She hasn't been eating, has she? For quite some time now."

A twitch rumpled Vico's features. "I tell her all the time, you have to eat."

"She's still a child, Vico. Sometimes you have to make them eat."

"But Bia—you can't tell her. The others, they listen to me. Stevie,

Edith. Them I can tell things to . . ." Vico shrugged hopelessly. "You know how she is."

Dennis did indeed. It was something he'd understood from the very outset, when he first laid eyes upon her. Back then, she was just a slip of a thing, Grace's little niece. But he'd felt it from the start: a spirit to reckon with. *Who is this man?* her wondering gaze demanded, as if she were naturally the judge and he were present only on approval.

"Oh I know," he said.

"The others are different. They will listen."

"I know."

"You told it to me," Vico said, quoting once more, for what now must be the thousandth time, an idle observation Dennis had made a dozen or so years ago: "Bia is overemotional."

It was the solemn respectfulness of Vico's tone, as if citing some diagnosable medical condition, that somehow unexpectedly propelled Dennis over a spiritual threshold. His heart kicked inside his chest and he lunged forward, as though falling, and clutched at his brother-in-law.

Dennis held Vico fiercely, needfully, seeking to conceal what would not be concealed: he had abruptly begun weeping. But Vico could hardly have failed to notice the half-choked sobbing, the violent trembling . . .

In Dennis's entire adulthood this was the first occasion when anyone—anyone other than Grace—had seen him in tears. The only lenitive aspect was that Vico had come along with him: Vico, too, was sobbing, trembling.

Upstairs, the bathroom door clicked shut. Somebody—one of the younger children—had begun to stir. The enfevered city itself was stirring, prodded awake by the peremptory lights of a new day. No repose, no cessation. Coughing, wheezing, the ailing night shift punches out, the ailing day shift punches in. And the War goes on, and will go on, for this is a war to be fought every single day for the duration . . .

Block after block, the city of Detroit was beginning to brighten, while on Inquiry Street the art student's pallid head revolved within the dim and bright derangements of its fever, and the two reunited friends, the two brothers-in-law—the two true brothers—clung to each other, weeping.

PART TWO

Off in the Islands

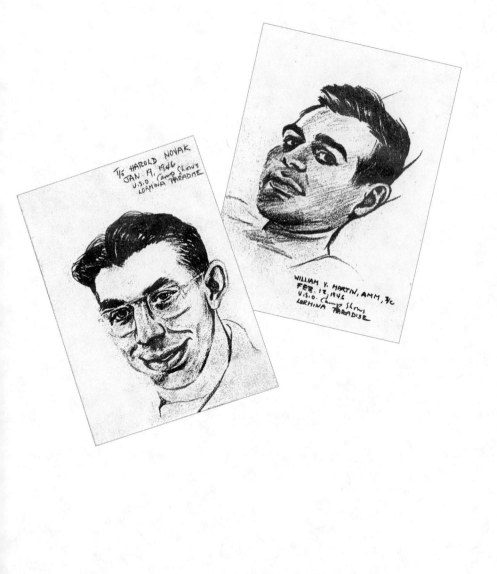

CHAPTER XXV

In the Land of Colors without Objects, learning to read can take a while. There, the pages are less like pages than like teeming microscopic slides, explosive as pondwater. The medium is liquid. And light is everywhere and everything.

In the Land of Colors without Objects, you will find no anchor or hitching post. No compass and no polestar. There is only the outspread where-we-are, and the ever dimming and receding where-we-were, and the projected (the obscure and half erroneous) where-we're-headed in the Land of Colors without Objects.

Entry is often by way of the slimed board on the duckwalk, the missed footing and the backward-sprawling sudden plunging slipping into sleep. But it can be won as well by the steep escarpments of high fever, from whose unchallenged summits the cosmos lies below you as an interlocked, slow-churning, and forever-unblendable spill of waters and oils, pools unspooling within pools, loops overlapping loops.

She's not asleep although it often feels like sleep: she's under a spell, wrapped and rewrapped within a fever like no other fever. It has transported her to this artist's land of colors without objects, where swirls nudge swirls and swing into looser swirls, and lines hunch over into loops; where loops pinch in the middle to become eights and eights divorce themselves into paddles, and paddles thin into spokes, into lines—and lines, inspired, spiral into loops, spools.

Of all colors, blue is the color she most spiritedly loves, since it reaches furthermost, even into the locked heart of the ice cavern, into the whistling heart of the sky-blue gas flame—though when a great sprawling Valentine's Day splotch of red oscillates into view, insolent and irrepressibly amorphous, she recognizes it as the most full-hearted pigment in creation, though naturally this must be just the right bright shocking shade of red: redder than roses, redder than blood, redder than the blood's howl at a forbidden kiss. Red truly has always been her favorite color, or so she'd swear until, there on the other, gentler, purer side of gold—gold into which concentrated gold has been injected—she locates the blazing sum, that high and perfect outpost whose outpourings animate, far so far below, one green extension ladder after another, all the climbing rustling surfs of jungle leaves, the soft mad frothing of flowers, competing blooms budding heads, the garden whereinwhich each primary pigment shatters open like some brashly exotic tropical nut and we are witnesses to lemon blossoms, lilac blossoms, apple-green flowers, apple-red flowers, mauves and peridots, rusts and russets, tourmalines and aquamarines, beryl and blueberry, all of them detonating widely within her head, her poor head.

Her true sleeper's name is White, it is not Bea but Bianca, it is the sun and sanctuary of all colors, which may indeed be the greatest miracle the cosmos encompasses—certainly, it's the greatest of all examples of hiding something in plain sight. Who could ever have divined that Ochre and Olive and Magenta, Chartreuse and Fuchsia and Umber could all lie concealed inside a White that seems, in its illuminated openness, to conceal nothing? This is—no less—the Light of Creation, the trompe l'oeil at the heart of every blessedly extravagant dawn.

She has gone farther than ever into the Highlands of Fever, once the homeland of her own private Vincent, her singular extinct Henry, who found all those crowding leaves so frightening, what with their dark and intratwined whisperings, and yet they scarcely frighten *her*. Why should they, when she knows that no painter ever born, not Turner, not even Vincent himself, beheld pigments purer or brighter than those she now beholds? She has arrived at the land where colors uncouple not only from objects but even from light sources and—allowed to be solely themselves—float atop that sea where the stars are nothing but a wind-tossed scarf of sunlight knotted round an icy ocean wave. Eternity is not commodious enough to exhaust the elated geometry of that sea. When you add a garnet-colored rhombus to an emerald ellipse, what do you get? You get a wan colossal melting pearl the color of tallow with, by way of remainder, a couple of chevrons, robin's-egg blue, arrowing away in cool pursuit of each other.

It is her sister—whose name is Edith, who talks in her sleep, declaring composedly to all the forces of darkness, *I disagree completely*—it is her sister who has the gift for numbered shapes, inside that philosopher's head of hers which, Bea sometimes suspects, with a touch of envious alarm, may be the deepest head in the Paradiso family. She's only a child, Edith, yet she has managed a near-total escape from childhood. She's the solid girl who never cries, the one whose knitter's hands will ultimately topple Berlin and Tokyo, and the occasional provider of observations so much psychologically wiser than her years that, enlightened and unnerved, you recoil. Edith? Whose sister are you, Edith? (Are you Henry's sister? Are you childless Henry's child?) Yet even Edith, perhaps, has never free-fallen quite so head-deep into that ancient well from which numbers siphon all their wit and playfulness. Who would have guessed, there at the bottom of the well, that all the numbers sing like birds?

One day in a blinding tropical rain an overweighted little plane failed to find its runway. Maybe it found palm trees instead. Maybe it found jungle. For a few minutes, the bodies burned. The drumming rain found the earth. And when the skies cleared, palms rustled huskily overhead, those dark leaf-leather voices whispering, *What are we going to do with him? What are we going to do with him?* Bianca has heard that rustling herself, the voices sighing, *What are we going to do with her?* sometimes assuming the cadences of Papa's voice, and sometimes Mamma's, and sometimes the voice of a streetcar's scraping progress, and sometimes the voices of those collusive, long-tongued ancestral creatures in green-walled Ferry Hospital, the lizards' lair where she herself was born and where she returns always with heart in mouth, heart on her sleeve, the crybaby who must learn to control herself, as the others do, boys who have suffered so much and are so much braver than she can steel herself to be. Or it's the world's biggest nestful of baby birds, Ferry Hospital, and each oversized little beak poignantly agape, for they are—everyone is, everywhere they are—clamoring to be fed, and in these strapped times Bianca can hardly bear to feed herself, what with these ever-so-many hungry mouths to which she has become, oddly, accountable.

Step carefully. First you turn pale, and then quite a bit paler, and then paler still, and then your head goes up in flames; her head is up in flames. You stand naked at the sink, proposing to wash yourself by sponge bath, one despoiled limb at a time—but there is always the voice catapulting at you from the other side of the door, beseeching forgiveness, and always the whisper of leaves, wondering *What are we going to do with her?* She learned a poet once, or a poem.

> The life I used to think of as my life
> Was someone else's life.

He was the poet of the resurrection:

> One day it seemed my life had reached its end.
> But that was not the end.

She understood this poem because—because it was her modest ambition to bring a few of the wounded fully back to life. And she understood *everything* better now, since you can't have fevers of this sort without lying at death's door. Death's Door. That's what Henry told her. Henry knocked first, in a pilgrimage memorialized in his eyes. (And later, he walked through that door.) Yes, with more delicacy than you'd need to pick up a single fallen scale from a butterfly's wing, she had reached out and gripped that pilgrimage of his in her left hand, her artist's hand, translating it into Vincent's webby jungle stars, which now stand framed upon her desk, a homemade celestial backdrop for the lamb, fish, stork, rabbit. Sleep carefully.

The young art student, just a girl, not yet twenty, has gone up in flames in a back upper bedroom of a modest house on the East Side of Detroit—a city itself destined to go up in flames. Already the hissing spark races down the evil-minded fuse, like a mouse scurrying along a horizontal pipe, throwing off its occasional sparks just as the streetcars, with their loose and elderly synapses, toss their sparks overhead. The streetcars are doomed. And the city is burning.

Night and day, the factories are burning—burning stones to melt metals, burning souls to feed the foundry flames. There's a whistle in the smokestacks, summoning more and more workers into this overheated metropolis, though there's no place to settle them, even as the new houses spring up like toadstools, even as the old houses are gutted and restored: our beloved city is splitting at the seams. They wander up out of the black night of the South from regions not yet hung with electricity, black faces from black tarpaper shacks, hurt and hungry souls materializing at the rumor of a rumor of a job. The others won't but Mr. Ford will take them in, dark as their faces may be, and he will take in as well the lean white faces, shy and surly, figures gangling out of Appalachian hillsides, who have congregated in this city where the colored folk no longer know their place—where the black people have no place, since most neighborhoods refuse them.

Lodged within its dingy fur, the little mouse racing down the water pipe carries a ruinous plague and in time the entire city will burn with fever. The dead will lie whichways on the sidewalks and the houses burn, in that choking summer of '67, when the fever at last erupts. Some fourteen hundred buildings will blaze, including two whose renovation Ludovico Paradiso once supervised. A bungalow on Euclid, into whose attic he fitted a defense worker's apartment, will roar to the ground, and from a duplex on Twelfth Street, where Vico, with his careful crafts-man's hand, laid in doorjambs and staircases and moldings, outraged choking smoke will stream from the shattered windows. A citywide uprising, forty-three dead, most of them Blacks. They've had enough, it seems, of being thought not good enough—one more demonstration of the confounding notion that the oppressed inevitably resent even their most generous oppressors . . .

The smoke is born long before the fire, though nothing is perceived clearly until the first flame, overheated, sticks out its panting tongue from the crumbling eaves. As the contractor knows in his bones, the houses speak, they tell a tale. And this Detroit journey from pride to rage will sometimes seem to Vico the mystery beyond all others, around which his own fever must be wrapped (were he to have a fever). The man on the ground floor, who envisions doorjambs and staircases, has no notion that a flaming mouse is scurrying along a basement water pipe. In the kitchen on Inquiry Street, Ludovico Paradiso embraces his brother-in-law, Dr. Dennis Poppleton, the two weeping men literally propping each other up—for neither can support alone the prospect looming before them: a world without the girl, a world without their own Bianca.

Other than his wife, nobody has ever seen the adult Dr. Poppleton weep, who will not shed a public tear even on that merciless day, eleven years hence, when he contemplates the slow, tilted descent into the ground of the weighty box that holds his Grace. Over the years of their marriage, she alone has circulated within the inner room where his tears flow freely. But even for that casket being lowered into the chill hacked earth he cannot cry, for she isn't actually to be found within it, Grace is miles from these wind-picked cemetery grounds, she is back home, they have returned home, she's in the kitchen, in the bathroom, in a walk-in closet whose shirts he cannot bear to unbutton, since these are the last of his shirts over whose sleeves Grace's ironing hand has passed. (He will wear one of these shirts on the day he pays a first visit to Edith and her new baby.) Dennis can weep in his kitchen, in his bathroom, in his tidy closet—but not here at Mount Elliott Cemetery, a few blocks from Inquiry Street, because no grace is here.

Yet he's weeping and trembling now, on Inquiry Street, though Grace is far away, still in perfect health, in that other home which can never be their home, in that city whose soil is foreign soil. In the end, for all her adaptability, Grace will shudder at the thought of lying, motionless into eternity, some 165 miles from home. Home forever remains the East Side of Detroit. The ailing woman wishes to go home, and the two of them will pack up and go home. Meanwhile, Dennis is weeping onto Vico's usually sturdy shoulder.

And on one additional occasion Dennis shall weep in public, though on a day of such abrupt astonishments no one will notice his weeping, or any other earthly thing. On July 16, 1969, Dr. Poppleton will stand on a ragged, littered Florida beach, among palm trees shaken by a sudden unnatural wind. Unchecked tears are coursing down his round features. This science-fiction reader has felt the very earth tremble underfoot, as it *should* tremble, for this is the scheduled day on which the planet's most curious species—whose not-so-distant ancestors brachiated through the canopy and took the treetops as their ceiling—forges a path through the inviting vacuum of the universe; this is the day when Homo sapiens embarks for the moon.

On a sudden impulse, this unprepossessing and unimpulsive man has driven day and night to be here, drawn as thousands upon thousands have been suddenly drawn, to a marshy stretch of beach in Brevard County, Florida. Skies are clear. He's a paunchy white-haired pop-eyed round-faced square-eared figure standing among equally unprepossessing figures—for when the single-minded engine lifts, when the seven million tons of aero-engineering scream skyward, we are none of us prepossessing.

The sewing needle lifts and goes on lifting, steadily yanking itself free of all the nagging primeval claims of the planet's core. The needle trails behind it a thread of flame, a thread of rewoven dreams . . . The flashing needle pushes itself into and through the blue, seeking out the blackness behind the blueness, the battered white lantern lost within the blueness, as Dennis never doubted would happen, no, never doubted—though he never expected actually to be present. Yes, here he is, *present,* before the blazing enactment of his highest-flying flights of imagination—who now indeed cannot see much of anything, for the ground trembles underfoot and his eyes stream with tears.

. . . Pause a moment to ponder the numbers in play here, consider the towering improbability of it all. That's what his books have taught him to do: think forward, think backward, think across the generations beyond reckoning, all of them shaken out of the dice-cup womb of time. *Think backward* and *think forward* . . . Think of the wordless pre-hominids, cold and muddy, hunched and shoeless, wandering lost over yet another barren ridge, as real as you and I, and among all those multitudes *he* happens to find himself lodged in the first generation that can stand with its shod feet planted on God's green earth and behold a spacecraft blasting off toward a rendezvous with a heavenly body. What were the odds of any man's being so lucky? This lonely, brokenhearted widower—he is the most blessed of men.

The unremarked man stands on the shore, in Florida's Brevard Country, weeping. He also stands in a kitchen on Inquiry Street, in a neighborhood already beginning to be called blighted, weeping. And looming between these shattering days is the low and overcast day when he will stand dry-eyed in Mount Elliott Cemetery, steadily observing somber, uncomprehending rituals as all that he most loves is locked underground.

Two men are embracing, two souls bathed in the only holy water the earth has ever produced—human tears—and how are we to speak of it, of that other day, more insupportable even than Grace's funeral? Of that catastrophe too near and vast for Dennis to consider, even momentarily? Not even for a moment—Dennis cannot *bear* to think of it. No, the heart of this gentle and accepting man storms and howls at the mere thought . . . But if—*if* the influenza overcomes the girl? He is a doctor, he inhabits a world of pitiless microscopic military campaigns, where even the world's most beloved child may suffer a defeat. And to a doctor, reality must be faced, even when it's far less plausible than the alternative.

Say she *were* to perish, in the city's great flu epidemic of 1943? In that case, there would be no escaping the day he cannot think about. And hundreds of Detroiters have already lost that very battle . . .

If it were to happen? The girl's passing wouldn't make the newspapers. It were to happen, and she becomes a mere statistic in some municipal volume brimming with statistics. It were, and the ripped-open earth becomes a desecration. It were, and father and mother, brother and sister, uncle and aunt—all discover they've lost the one most precious thing they know. The girl's story breaks the heart of anyone whose heart can still be broken, but such losses hardly fit the columned newsprint that bounds our lives. No, it's the novelist's burden: there's scarcely a place for it in the newspapers.

It's a different matter when a singular, earnest young mathematician dies in a plane crash on the Pacific island of Majuro. A mortal fire flares briefly in the rain and his is a death of greater import—yes, it makes the local newspapers—but Henry Vanden Akker is but one of the 2,573 fatalities Michigan will suffer before the rubbled neighborhoods stop smoking in Dresden and Nagasaki. He, too, goes largely unremarked, as the death count is raised by one. It seems the War has taken him, Henry Vanden Akker, whose dream of Heaven was someday to sit with Thoreau and Kierkegaard and Einstein at a colloquium table where every line of argument was pursuable. Henry's simple, stupendous dream was always of some God-given liberty of the mind, the Lord himself having vouchsafed, at the outset, "Feel free to doubt Me, gentlemen, if you must."

Meanwhile, she has gone off to matriculate at that Studio of the Tropics envisioned by Gauguin—where Gauguin and van Gogh and a few prize pupils stand before easels on a tropical slope. Work proceeds brilliantly, alongside burly blooms, and in their company stands the girl's grandfather, her nonno, the Ligurian master of trompe l'oeil. His was the delicate art of verisimilitude in pursuit of illusion: his the hingeless door to nowhere, the open window really a wall.

Bianca has passed through just such a door; she has seen the notional become the negotiable . . . She knew a boy once, so handsome and so gifted he must in time blossom into a great artist—except he could never negotiate that door. Identifying it for what it was—an illusion—he logically concluded that it would never admit him. But the true artist, naïve enough not to discern its illusory nature, saunters right through the plaster wall upon which that door is painted. The true artist walks up the broad stairs of the lizards' womb where she was born, and effectively declares, "Soldier, I want to capture your essence on a sheet of paper." And the soldier answers, *Don't you think I look brainy?* And the soldier answers, *Maybe you could draw me the way I really look?*—as if the metal in his face were merely a disguise.

That near-legendary figure, her young grandfather, in that near-legendary land, Liguria, long ago arranged Bianca's passage through that door. Only a romantic fool would liken the wizened emphysemic man who shows up for Sunday dinners to the immortal Tiziano of the Renaissance, and only a romantic fool would see the matter dead-on right. For they are all the same painter, those figures deployed on the hillside in that visionary Studio of the Tropics, and it is all the same palette and canvas. They will unite the spectrum, the floating red of wind-blown Italian rose petals, the floating blue of Greenland's icebergs, for in the Land of Colors without Objects, all is afloat and there is no land. There is merely the Solidifying Impulse and the Dissolving Impulse, and once you identify these as one and the same, you're ready to embark for the Land of Colors without Objects, where one can never alight for long. The jungle leaves are calling you forward. And those other voices—human voices—call you back. The burning girl hasn't the strength to move in either direction. And yet she can't stay where she is . . .

Fortunately the child is attended (as everyone ought to be attended) by a fairy godmother, whom Bia thinks of as Aunt Grace, but Grace is merely the figure's latest incarnation. Her name was once Immacolata Paradiso, back in the days when she assumed the form of an illiterate peasant who hit upon the idea of keeping her newborn grandson alive in a woodstove. That infant was Bianca's grandfather, Paolo Paradiso, and Immacolata's was a reasonable enough idea, provided you were willing and able, for weeks on end, never to sleep. For weeks on end, Immacolata never slept. How could she? She had a baby in the woodstove.

Tiny Paolo Paradiso lies inside an immense fever inside an overheated wood stove; Paolo Paradiso lies in the Land of Colors without Objects. And in time Paolo is summoned to paint a fictive door through which his granddaughter steps, as she, too, arrives in the Land of Colors without Objects.

Paolo, born two months premature in the year of our Lord 1877, inhabits a woodstove right out of a fairy tale, since it also houses his son, Ludovico Paradiso, and his granddaughter Bianca Paradiso, and (God willing) Bianca's daughter, Maria, and Maria's two daughters, all of them overseen by a woman who has not slept for months—a bustling, obdurate little creature who is descended from brachiating tree shrews, who is descended from plumed angels.

And Bea is attended by a fairy godfather. It is the construction worker of her earliest memory, the powerful man silhouetted on the Ambassador Bridge. (It is Heimdall, god of light and watchman of the Asgard bridge; it is Saint Peter, the gateway's guardian.) Or—nearer at hand—it is the father who built the burning bunk bed she lies in, and who at this moment stands in the kitchen, embracing his weeping brother-in-law. Their huddled, pitiful postures remind us that the riddles of friendship may run deeper than the riddles of romantic love. For these two men, this long embrace is unprecedented. Mostly, they communicate through words—always a challenge for handsome Vico, whose English is halting and whose reading, whether in English or Italian, is uncertain and laborious.

It is his medical-minded daughter Edith who will, twenty-two years hence, finally attach a mysterious term to Vico's lifelong struggles: *dyslexia.* She will be investigating the matter on behalf of her seven-year-old son, who reads more slowly than his classmates. Edith will announce that dyslexia apparently runs through the male side of the Paradiso clan—her father, Vico; her brother, Stevie; her son, Jacob.

And she will later unpack from her medical bag another even more puzzling term, *obsessive-compulsive disorder,* and employ it to explain a few eccentricities that appear to run especially deep in the family's female line—in her candy-hoarding mother, Sylvia; in her sister, Bianca; and in Edith the Mad Knitter herself.

Vico will greet this term, *dyslexia,* suspiciously and shyly and yet in the end eagerly, embellishing its remote Greek overtones with an Italian climb-and-fall. Although he will rarely broach the topic, he'll take comfort in the term's scientific ring, having always suspected that his habitual difficulties with print were not attributable, as others might suppose, to a mere lack of intelligence. Everyone assumes his two brilliant daughters—those all-A students—derive their aptitude from their mother, a woman quick to remind everyone that she, too, was once an exceptional student. There was no arguing with Sylvia's conclusion, since it was perfectly logical. And yet—yet Vico has always believed in his own keenness of mind.

The only person on the planet to whom he feels his true mental capacities have been demonstrated is his brother-in-law, Dennis, in whose slow and measured responses Vico finds his one suitable audience. Dennis has supplied him with something more precious than affection or indulgence—Dennis has given him respect.

It isn't in Vico's nature to dissect his friendships, though in regard to this, his closest friendship, he occasionally suffers an uneasy sense of owing far more than he is owed. After all, Dennis understands the world. Dennis sees into the inner nature of politics and the newspapers, banks and insurance forms, the Germans and the Russians and the Japanese; he understands the War. And yet this man, this doctor, who knows so much about so much, will listen deferentially as Vico sets out his halting observations. What can Vico do in repayment, except see that at the Poppleton home there's no rain gutter not tight and clear; no leaking faucet; no squeaking door? And what in the world can Vico now offer in repayment, since the Poppletons' move to Cleveland?

Vico's not one to write letters, and he's certainly not one to chatter through a long-distance telephone call. When, suddenly, Dennis and Grace packed up and moved to Cleveland, Vico effectively lost his one true friend in the world.

Given his accent, given his name, given his Mediterranean good looks, Vico Paradiso has gone through life stamped as an Italian immigrant, but in the end it's not among his old compatriots he has looked for understanding. The riddles of friendship may run deeper than anything born of romantic love, and the truth is that all those Italian men playing bocce in Chandler Park, drinking coffee while standing at the counter in one of the cafés off Gratiot, conferring in restaurants whose sunny, smoky murals recall a half-forgotten homeland—such people make him uneasy. Vico's heart instinctively searches elsewhere—as it did many years ago when, blindly, needfully, and far less successfully, he went out seeking a wife.

Two men stand weeping in the very room where a brooding woman constructed a view of the world that wound up severing friend from friend, brother from brother. Day after thoughtful day, she hatched her vision. The two men are in love with the same woman—so Sylvia surmised, sitting in her kitchen, all alone but for the oceanic murmur of the wall calendar's pages.

In love with the same woman? The possibility hardly troubles these two brothers, whose shuddering lives, nonetheless, have coalesced around a single dumbfounding revelation: in the end, a fanciful, imagined act of passion can be just as blighting as any consummation. Could Vico have created a deeper schism had he in fact gone ahead and secretly seduced his sister-in-law? The singular tragedy of this particular household, and story, is that a contemplated act and a consummated act may come down to a similar disaster . . .

Dennis is more inclined than Vico to analyze their friendship, and a few times, fumblingly, he has attempted to issue some formal statement of gratitude, which Vico, in bluff embarrassment, has always cut short.

What Dennis has attempted to say, and never quite managed to say, is that he's boundlessly grateful for the numerous ways Vico has welcomed him into the Paradiso family. Vico has shared his children with a man who has no children, encouraging Dennis to be more than an uncle to Bea, to Stevie, to Edith. Vico has sought out Dennis's advice on how to be a father; he has solicited Dennis's approval. It's painfully obvious to Dennis that in this, his closest friendship, he is far more owing than owed . . .

And so, one winter night in wartime, Dennis drops everything on a moment's notice to drive alone up to Detroit. His other patients will have to wait. He finds his niece dwindled into a child, the child's head peaked like a death's head. "Papa," she says.

The two men hold each other. Their daughter has been burning up for weeks and weeks, she is nothing but a smoldering pile of sticks, and their only fit response—the only livable response—is to weep and embrace while they hang over the abyss of what is surely an unendurable life.

Why didn't you call me before now? Dennis is saying, effectively.

You know I couldn't call until I had to call, Vico is saying, effectively.

You did not have to come all this way, Vico is saying.

Of course I had to come, Dennis replies.

Of course you had to come, Vico concedes, and he trembles and gasps in mute male gratitude.

The girl is burning up and for both fathers the prospect of any future without their child, their mercurial Bea-Bia-Bianca, is unendurable. It was something of a miracle from the start—the arrival of this large-eyed changeling, the spirited artist girl—and yet how is life sustainable without miracles? How are they to live without the burning girl who has never known a cool response to anything—who has, from her first day on earth, met every face and flower and flowering cloud with a headlong, vociferous ardor?

How is life to be lived without the soul of this girl who has lost her way and cannot find any means to live?

Her head has gone up in a final fountaining of pyrotechnics, there in the Land of Colors without Objects, and the distant firmament whereupon those fireworks flare and fade, flare and fade, is the deepest and most welcoming blue imaginable—and blue has always been her favorite color. It invites her, it speaks her language, and she now must choose her world . . . Even so, even yet, there are those other, quieter colors, too, the dun hues of human voices, including that of an old peasant woman, any true tale's true hero, muttering prayers and advice in a dialect none of us understand any longer, and those voices likewise have their claims, peripheral and importunate and common as dirt. They are calling her.

PART THREE

All the Lost Houses

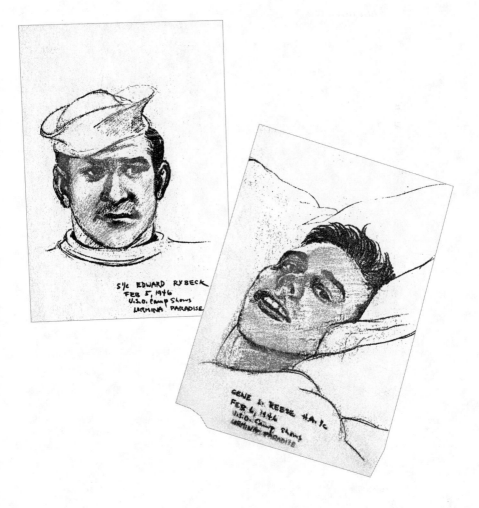

S⅟c EDWARD RYBECK
FEB 5, 1946
U.S.O. Camp Shows
LORMINA PARADISE

GENE L. REESE H.A. ⅟c
FEB 6, 1946
U.S.O. Camp Shows
LORMINA PARADISE

She wakes to a sense of an illicit touch—a male touch—before waking further to find nothing the slightest amiss in this particular contact. Nobody can fault her: she has been sitting on a Woodward streetcar with her head leaned against her husband's shoulder. She's innocent.

"I seem to have drifted off," she says.

"Me too," Grant says. "Or nearly."

"How long was I out?"

"Awhile. You were smiling."

"Was I?" And an unsettled pause. What is she trying to recall? She says, "It's been ages since I rode a streetcar. They seem so comfy."

"They take you back, don't they," Grant says. "Not many left . . ."

What had placed them here was a queer series of coincidences— good luck masquerading as its opposite. Normally, they'd be driving. But as it happens, both cars are in the shop, Grant's Studebaker with transmission problems and her Mercury with what may be a dead sole- noid (whatever that is). Grant initially suggested postponing their little expedition—they're off to lunch at Pierre's. But it turns out to be much more fun, and romantic, *not* to drive. They're celebrating their seventh wedding anniversary.

Bianca was the one to propose the streetcar. Wouldn't that be swell? Yes, just like old times . . . And it was Bianca who proposed Pierre's, a restaurant they've somehow never visited together. Once, it held a sig- nificant place in her life, and lately, for all sorts of reasons, she has been rethinking the old days, before she met Grant, back when the War was still raging, still dragging on.

It seems a shame to lose this disorienting drowse, which links her, as drowses sometimes do, to out-flung memories and perceptions . . . But Grant is cataloguing some frustrations at the office, and his conversa- tional claims are legitimate claims—all the more so on their anniversary. Nonetheless, as Bianca listens she's pursuing someone else or some- thing else: there's an immanence dissolved in the dusty sunlit air of this old streetcar, a someone or a something almost achingly precious and proximate. But who or what is it?

It's the most familiar sensation in the world, and a little dispiriting even so, to disembark from the streetcar. Something—an ongoing process—closes up. All sorts of fluid, wordless feelings recede and Time itself shifts—shifted—the moment the two of them stepped down into the street. (On how many more occasions would she ride a streetcar? All across the city, the lines were being pulled up. Grant was right, of course: the streetcars were dinosaurs.)

They walked down Jefferson, holding hands in the August sunshine. The blue sky looked freshly washed. "I'm so glad you suggested the streetcar," Grant said. "A brilliant idea," Grant declared—something he often wound up declaring. His deference in such matters (which restaurant to dine in, which couch to buy, which color to paint the shutters) was flattering to the point of being faintly alarming. The joke in their house—which wasn't completely a joke—was that Bianca had something more than feminine intuition, she had second sight. What mere male judgment could compete?

"Look! A gull!" Grant pointed upward at a bird flapping south, toward Canada. (This was the only place in the country where you headed *south* toward Canada.) "Now you're happy," he said.

She was touched, anyway, at how excited he became at having a gleaming white gull to point out to his wife. "I do love them," Bianca said.

You often saw gulls in the neighborhoods near the river. They'd been a much more common sight in the skies over her old street, Inquiry, than over her new street, Middleway, seven miles north. She loved her new house, but the move had brought its share of unexpected losses. Gulls were one of many things whose loss she hadn't known she would mourn until they became, abruptly, a symbol of her past.

To step once more into the interior of Pierre's felt quite peculiar, actually. How many years since she was last here?

The man himself, Monsieur Pierre, still presided, though shorter and more peculiar looking—a bit lopsided in his features—than in Bianca's recollection. He still sported the thinnest possible of all moustaches. His hair was darker than it used to be.

The dining rooms had been redecorated. Burgundy and gold had replaced salmon and yellow. In ways that Bianca couldn't quite put her finger on, the place looked shabby.

The moment they were seated, she said, "Tell me the boys are fine. And for once we won't talk about them."

Grant laughed. "Of course they're fine. They're always fine." The boys, the twins Chip and Matt, were home on Middleway with Grant's mother, who could hardly refuse to babysit during an anniversary lunch. Mrs. Ives usually avoided being left alone with her only grandchildren. "Hey, we finally made it to Pierre's. Aren't you glad?"

"Very," Bianca said. "But somehow it makes me feel odd. I haven't been here since I came with Mrs. Olsson."

"I hear she's not doing too well."

"What do you mean—not doing too well?"

Grant shrugged. "Not doing too well."

"I saw her picture in the *Free Press* not long ago. She looked wonderful. Older, of course, but wonderful."

"Maybe my source was no good. It was all very vague."

"Yes . . ."

Generally, though, Grant's sources were good. He worked for Cutting and Fuller, a big law firm in the Guardian Building, the most beautiful office building in the city. Grant wasn't a gossip, but he kept his ears open, and he often brought home intimate news of the city's elite.

"Back then, I think she had a drinking problem." Bianca added, fair-mindedly, "Of course, that may no longer be true."

"Speaking of which," Grant said, "here comes a waiter."

Would they like anything to drink?

"I'd *love* a glass of wine," Bianca said. Grant looked at her questioningly. For some years now, he'd generally restricted himself to one daily drink—though often quite an ample drink—before dinner. "Do, of course," she urged him. "Honey, it's our anniversary lunch."

Grant ordered two glasses of Bordeaux ("Very nice," the waiter said, and went off mumbling, "Very nice, very nice"), and Bianca lit a cigarette and, leaning forward into the sudden confiding intimacy that a restaurant cigarette reliably created, she said, "You know what? Pierre dyes his hair."

"No big surprise," Grant said. "He's an old fruit, honey."

He was? Pierre? The notion had never occurred to her. Bianca tested it now and recognized, immediately, that Grant was correct, and all at once a number of things fell into place.

Actually, the topic of male homosexuality fascinated her—how could anyone interested in art not feel that way?—but she'd repeatedly learned it wasn't for casual conversation. Even among sophisticated people. Grant's fraternity brother Jerry Romeyn, though one of the city's most successful lawyers, and though he stood six feet four and had long scandalized Grosse Pointe society with his womanizing, once stammered himself red-faced at a Christmas party when Bianca broached the subject.

Grant, by comparison, had initially seemed so sane and humane. The topic scarcely discomfited him, probably because it turned out he had an uncle, his father's brother Hughie, who was "an old fruit." Grant always spoke affectionately of Uncle Hughie, a bald, soft-spoken man who owned an antiques shop in Royal Oak specializing in grandfather clocks. It was a detail that Grant, who loved to tell stories, recounted with incredulous delight. *Grandfather clocks?* Grant himself was no more likely to cultivate such an interest than to take up Morris dancing or Japanese calligraphy.

Later, though, after they'd been married a while, Bianca had come to find Grant's easy tolerance objectionable in its way. Her reservations had solidified on the evening when Grant finally met Ronny. For years, Grant had been hearing about Ronny Olsson—perhaps too much about Ronny Olsson—and, though not an overly jealous husband, Grant perhaps had grown to regard Ronny as a rival.

The two couples had met unexpectedly at the symphony. Ronny was with his then-wife, Elizabeth, the former Libby Hubbins. (By a weird coincidence, Bianca had known Libby forever; they'd gone to junior high school together, where Libby, who wore glasses even then, had been a very bright girl absolutely devoid of sparkle.) Whatever else one cared to say about Ronny Olsson, his manners were irreproachable. He could hardly have been more gracious, insisting on taking them out for a drink afterward and displaying a special interest in Grant—who, fifteen seconds after Ronny and wife had driven off, complacently remarked, "So *that's* Ronny Olsson. Why, he's an old fruit, honey." The wife? Poor bespectacled Libby, who was getting a master's degree in Classics at U. of M., who was actually learning to read ancient Greek? She counted for *nothing*. And never again would Grant take seriously any tale of long-ago romantic dates with Ronny Olsson.

Thoughts of Ronny Olsson led naturally back to his mother, and Bianca said, "I do hope Mrs. Olsson's all right. You know, when I wasn't scared to death of her, I was really fond of her. I think."

"Quite the beautiful woman," Grant observed. "In her time. Not that I ever spoke to her. But I saw her out and about, of course."

"Imagine being an eighteen-year-old girl and Mrs. Olsson brings you to this place! I was so young. And so green and hopeless. I was this lanky colt, I suppose I mean filly, I mean this inexperienced horse of a creature, who wasn't here ten minutes before she spilled her glass of wine.

"You can't imagine how imposing this place seemed to an eighteen-year-old girl from inside the Boulevard. It was the most elegant place I'd ever seen. Now it looks almost a little run-down."

"I hear they're not doing very well."

"*Who's* not doing well?"

"Pierre." Grant glanced around. Half the tables were empty. "I'd be surprised to see this place still here in six months . . ."

"Oh, no! Not *this place, too!*"

Her vehemence clearly surprised Grant; it surprised Bianca herself. Still more unaccountable was the sudden burn in her eyes.

"Honey, what's the matter?"

"Well, I don't *know*, Grant. It just strikes me as sad that maybe this is the last time I'll ever have lunch at Pierre's. Having arrived today in one of the city's very last streetcars. Good grief, what's happening to my city?"

"Hey, lots of new restaurants around. The city's thriving!" Grant studied her face and saw that he hadn't said the right thing, quite. Good-naturedly, he tried again. "Listen, this isn't your last time. I promise to bring you back before they close."

"Thank you," she said.

"That's a promise. A solemn vow."

"And I thank you. It's just"—Bianca waved her hand, encompassing with this gesture another room, with salmon-colored napkins and salmon-colored tablecloths—"well, where did it all go?"

"Where did *what* all go?"

The look he gave her was understandably befuddled—she wasn't making much sense—and so very *sweet*: he was concerned. Grant was fearful that this long-awaited anniversary lunch had mysteriously turned wistful and morose.

Touched by that look, and knowing she was again being a little impossible, Bianca said, "Oh, please, darling, don't pay any attention to me. It's just, I've been feeling, I don't know, very emotional lately." Overemotional Bia: again, she felt on the threshold of tears. It was as though, in entering this place, she'd stepped into one of Uncle Dennis's time machines and met that creature she'd mostly put behind her: the wide-eyed eighteen-year-old crybaby.

"Very emotional," she repeated, and added, "I don't know why that is"—though in fact she had a good sense of the *why*. But this was hardly the moment, or the manner, to broach anything so momentous.

"I'll feel better with a little wine," she said.

"And some food," Grant said. "I'm starving."

"Yes, some food," Bianca said, and threw open the menu.

There it was: a lady's steak. The words heartened her and, though she hadn't planned on anything so filling, she announced jubilantly: "I know just what I'm having—I'm having the lady's steak."

Grant studied the menu for all of ten seconds. That he never lingered over menus was something of a point of pride with him. "Then I'll have the porterhouse," he announced. "It's got two advantages. One, it's the most expensive thing on the menu. Two, it's probably the most filling." He laughed. She laughed with him.

It was remarkable how much Grant ate, though you'd never guess it to look at him. He needed to lose, at most, ten pounds. He looked good. He was tall—six feet one—and a little extra weight sat comfortably on his athletic frame.

If Grant were to eat mere man-sized portions, instead of the giant-sized portions he regularly consumed, surely he'd be thin as a rail, for he was almost comically active. Grant was the sort of man who thought nothing of getting up at five on a summer morning in order to fit in three sets of competitive tennis before racing down to the office.

The wine arrived and Grant offered a toast. "Seven years," he said. "My God," he said, "and you're more beautiful now than ever."

"Thank you."

"I really think so," he said.

"I know," she said, which didn't come out sounding right. Bianca stubbed out her cigarette. "I'm very lucky, aren't I?" She sipped her wine.

Was she more beautiful now? Not less so, she'd like to think. Grant certainly was unchanged, other than the thickening around his middle. With his short, direct nose and clear pale blue eyes he remained remarkably boyish. Neither of them had yet found a gray hair. "You do think the kids are all right?"

"They're *fine*. So long as they're not locked indoors, they're *fine*."

The boys, who shared Grant's superhuman reserves of energy, were almost always outdoors. Actually, they shared more than his energy: they were identical twins who, to an almost uncanny degree, in both looks and movements, resembled their father—so much so that people sometimes joked about the "Ives triplets."

But with one important difference. Grant was merely a "decent athlete," as he regularly put it, having lettered in baseball his senior year at State by "out-hustling everybody." The twins were—truly—superb little athletes. Inevitably, kids their own age looked badly assembled by comparison.

Only this past week, Bianca had seen another dumbfounding exhibition of her boys' dexterity. Grant had installed in the backyard a "tightrope," which was really a very long board on its side, half buried in the ground. If you fell off the "rope," you'd fall only two or three inches. A large party of neighborhood boys had tried to walk the rope, but none quite managed it. Then Matt confidently got up and walked it. Chip did the same thing—only he did it backward. Matt then whipped off his T-shirt and draped it over his head—walking the rope blindfolded. Chip was pulling off *his* T-shirt—presumably planning to walk it backward and blindfolded—when Bianca lunged out the back door and called the game to a halt. The twins were almost worrisomely fearless.

Bianca took another sip of wine and felt herself, physically, settling into this place. Yes, she'd chosen well—they were going to have a lovely lunch. She asked Grant about the office and he, obligingly, rattled on.

Three years ago, Grant had gone through a rough period at Cutting and Fuller. He'd gotten into a sorry mess involving a deceased client's estate and the purchase of three lakeside lots. Grant, who really seemed less a wrongdoer than a victim of bad advice from a senior partner, had purchased one of the lots on the cheap—or so the client's outraged heirs had alleged. Suddenly, Grant had been terrified he'd be asked to leave the firm. Bill Hobbema, the senior partner, *was* asked to leave. But Grant's lakeside lot was relinquished and he was retained in his job— and, these days, most of his office stories were harmless tales of others' minor spats or occasional off-hours romantic intrigues.

Their steaks arrived and Grant issued a happy grunt at the crowdedness of his plate, which held a bulging steak, a thicket of green beans, a mountain of French fries. Finding herself less hungry than she'd hoped, Bianca gamely sliced into her steak. The meat was flavorful but tough— tough enough to leave a person wondering whether the eating was worth the effort.

"How's it?"

"Good," she said. "Wonderful. How's yours?"

He crunched on a cluster of French fries. "Just what the doctor ordered."

They ate in silence. Bianca continued struggling with her steak. Memory told her that Pierre's French fries had been marvelous—hot and light and crisp—but these were clumped and greasy.

"Is everything all right?"

This time the question came from Pierre, standing beside their table, who did not look terribly interested in any reply.

"Great," Grant said. "Truly great."

"Excuse me," Bianca said. "You probably don't remember me, but I came here a few times some years ago. With Mrs. Charles Olsson."

"Mrs. Olsson?" Pierre said.

"I bring it up only because I'm wondering whether she still comes in here. I haven't seen her in years."

For just a moment Pierre looked confused, or stricken—his eyes jumped—and then he declared firmly, "Oh yes. Mrs. Olsson is one of our regular customers."

"I'm glad to hear that."

"Of course I remember you," Pierre said, which sounded like a blatant falsehood but, given the penetrating look he fixed upon her, might well have been true. "You came with Mrs. Olsson."

"That's right."

Pierre bustled off, but only a minute later their waiter returned, standing more erect than before. He set before each of them a fresh glass of wine. "Saint Emma Lion," he announced. "Compliments of the house."

"Well I'll be darned," Grant said. "Now isn't that nice."

Grant wouldn't have felt free to order a second glass, but he fell upon it happily: this was a gift sanctioned by the gods. And the truth was, Bianca, too, was ready for another.

"See what happens?" Grant said. "I stick with you, I get the royal treatment."

"You stick with me," Bianca said.

"Seven years," Grant said.

"Seven years . . ."

Bianca broke the thoughtful pause that followed. "Grant, I have a little teeny teeny teeny announcement to make: I'm six days late."

"Late?"

"On the monthly. Let's just say there's some possibility I may be expecting."

"Oh darling," Grant said. "*Oh darling,*" he said, and the look on his face—a handsome and openhearted, proud and avid look— immediately elevated Bianca into the state of mind she'd been seeking all day: a grateful sense that she'd never loved anybody else, and could never love anybody else, the way she loved this good-looking, good-hearted man she'd married seven years ago.

They raised a toast to the baby. They toasted each other. Grant reached across the table and stroked her hand. "This is so *silly,*" Bianca cried. "This whole business might be nothing. I'm only six days late."

"What do your instincts tell you? I trust your instincts." And why not? She had second sight, after all.

Bianca gazed at her husband and, feeling oddly embarrassed, giggled. "Well, my instincts tell me I am. Otherwise, I wouldn't have mentioned it."

"Then I say you are." And they raised another toast to the baby.

Pierre reappeared. "You are enjoying the Saint-Émilion?" he asked.

"Absolutely," Grant said. "It's our anniversary. Married seven years ago this week."

Pierre paused only a second. "Seven years? Then I would say to you, sir, you married a *very* young bride." The mention of Mrs. Olsson's name had seemingly restored him. He was almost the old Pierre again. He added, "I'm not sure it's legal, marrying so young a bride."

Grant's boisterous laugh, warmed with a hint of shared male roguery, pleased Pierre, who smiled, bowed, and strode away.

"*He's* all right," Grant said.

"He kissed my hand," Bianca said. "I'll never forget that. I come in here, an eighteen-year-old girl, and the owner of one of the city's fanciest restaurants kisses my hand."

"I want to know what your instincts tell you about the sex of the child, if I may be so bold as to ask."

Bianca needed think only a moment. "A girl," she stated confidently. "If I'm pregnant, *if* I'm pregnant, I'm carrying a girl."

"And as regards this putative girl-child you are so to speak carrying, have you considered a moniker?"

This was a little joke, or rather a line of jokes, which reliably amused her—it was a routine of his. Grant often spoke in a sham-formal patter, with a generous sprinkling of legalisms, the whole of it vaguely, and perhaps somewhat inaccurately, spun through an Irish brogue; Grant's maternal grandfather had emigrated from Cork.

"Tabatha for the wee lass?" Grant went on. "Agatha? Plethora?"

He got the laugh he was looking for.

"Peppa?" he went on. "Is that a name?"

"I think you mean Pippa, honey. It's a name in English novels." Bianca had a particular fondness for English novels—not that she read enough of anything, ever since the twins' arrival. She'd been taking a course in The Grand Tradition of the English Novel down at Wayne, working toward her B.A., when, to her utter amazement, married just a few months, she became pregnant.

"I'll be the Poppa to a girrrl named Pippa," Grant sang, thickening the brogue—which, in addition to serving him as a raconteur at parties, had a treasured private currency: it often provided him with a language of desire. Bold, sometimes almost too bold, intimacies emerged out of his brogue: declarations that both abashed and amused her. The world was full of wives—Bianca had come to see—who smiled tiredly at their husband's stories and jokes. But Grant had a way about him—he made her laugh, and the laughter was genuine.

He downed his second glass of wine. He'd already finished his steak, and fries, and green beans.

"Boy, you're pretty," he said.

"You're not so bad yourself."

"How will your mother respond?" he asked.

"She's always the great mystery, isn't she?"

It had been something of a surprise, and an enormous relief, when Mamma developed a deep fondness for Grant and the twins. Really, there didn't seem to be anything strained or awkward in her affection. No doubt they had helped matters greatly—those voracious Ives triplets—by being so partial to Mamma's cooking. All those dishes drawn from the worst cookbook in history—*The Modern Housewife's Book of Creative Cookery,* a collection so disastrous that Bianca had come to wonder whether it was assembled as a publisher's joke— pleased them no end: Grant and the boys simply could not get enough Shipwreck, enough Drowned Tuna Loaf and Slumped Pork and Smothered Liver and City Chicken Sticks.

"I'm only six days late, we shouldn't go assuming anything," Bianca said, even as she felt her imagination carrying her off. In a game that might be called How Will So-and-so Greet the News? Grant happily prompted her with names of people they knew and Bianca happily supplied their responses.

Papa would be pleased, of course, hugely pleased, though he wouldn't say much. But he would pull her aside at some point and call her his Bia and surreptitiously slip her a little money. (It didn't matter that she probably had more money in the bank than he did.) And— eventually—he would construct a wonderful wooden pull-toy for the new infant. He'd outdone himself for the twins: a matching pair of tigers, with bold stripes and twitching tails. And the blazing stones in their eye-sockets? Tigereyes, naturally.

And Grant's mother would be positively elated. She'd always wanted a granddaughter—perhaps because, Bianca secretly speculated, she'd mishandled her own two daughters, who lived so far away and returned home so rarely.

Dad Ives would be pleased, too, though the news wouldn't strike deep. Ever since his stroke, two years ago, few topics engaged him except his own health, which wasn't good. Though he had trouble moving and walking, the stroke had left his mind unimpaired—which only increased his frustration. "But he'll be *glad,*" Bianca said. "He's always liked girls."

"All too well," Grant said, and laughed. Girls—grown-up girls— were one of the few things that still pricked Mr. Ives's interest.

"And Stevie?" Grant asked.

"Oh he'll be delighted, truly. But then the next time I see him I'll have to remind him. After all, there's no reality but the Ford Motor Company."

Stevie had taken a job at the Ford plant in Highland Park. He was forever working overtime.

"And Rita?"

Rita, Stevie's wife, presented a more complicated question. The whole issue of pregnancy was an uneasy matter in Stevie and Rita's little house, which lay almost under the shadow of the plant. Stevie had married Rita two years ago, in a panicky hurry—though as it happened they managed to beat, by exactly one week, the arrival of her miscarriage. Back then, Rita had been just-turned-seventeen.

"And Edith?"

"She'll concoct some new health regimen for me. I must henceforth eat only what pregnant Armenian women eat. Or vegetarian Koreans."

Grant laughed. Edith was forever reading about faraway lands, but always—Edith being Edith—with an eye toward improbable, practical applications. "And Aunt Grace and Uncle Dennis?"

Bianca pondered a moment. "They'll make a special trip, won't they, when the baby's born. Aunt Grace in particular—she'll be *so* pleased."

Grace's cancer had appeared four years ago. She might plausibly have turned bitter, having had her right breast removed at the age of forty-five, but the illness had made her, if anything, more generous.

"Priscilla will find it odd," Grant said.

Bianca laughed. "Odd? Yes, she will, won't she. I don't know how or *why*, but she'll find it odd."

Priscilla was a new friend—and much the best-educated woman in Bianca's circle. She'd gone to Mount Holyoke College, in Massachusetts, and then to the University of Michigan for medical school. She found most developments in Bianca's life "rather odd," which was only fitting, since she herself was so odd. Grant didn't much care for her—he said she wasn't a real woman—though her observations amused him.

"And Maggie," Grant said. "She *won't* be pleased."

Lunch was going very well. It was a sign of how much fun they were having, and how secure Grant was feeling, that he would bring up Maggie in this way—a sore subject for a variety of reasons.

"No, she won't be, will she?" Bianca said, and laughed.

"Hey, just *listen* to my girl's mischievous laughter. It's time you admitted it: you don't like her, do you?"

"I like her," Bianca protested.

"But you don't much like spending time with her."

"That's true." And this time Bianca's laughter emerged as an unladylike snort.

"Oh you *girls*," Grant said, and shook his head mock-sternly. "Always complicating everything . . ."

"It isn't that I don't enjoy spending time with her. What I don't enjoy," Bianca began, and saw that, propelled perhaps by the second glass of wine, the distinction she meant to draw was difficult to express. She pushed on anyway. "What I don't enjoy isn't so much how she's always showing off her money. No, it isn't that. It isn't that at all. It's how she fails to understand what a *fluke* her life is. In her eyes, she was *born* to have all this money. She doesn't see how odd it is (and now I know I'm sounding like Priscilla, but I'm going to say it anyway), how *odd* it is she'd wind up filthy rich."

Maggie's marriage to George Hamm had dissolved soon after his return from the Army. Displaying even poorer judgment the second time around, she'd married Peter Schrock, who owned a tavern on Seven Mile and who mistreated her even worse than George had—though Maggie hadn't treated Pete much better. And then, already twice divorced and still in her twenties, Maggie had consented to marry Wally Waller, whose devotion, originating at Field Elementary, remained unwavering. It was one of the greatest of all mysteries of that greatest of all mysteries—love. *Why* was Wally so devoted? He'd become a man of note in the city—a highly eligible bachelor, somebody who could range far and wide in pursuit of a wife. Exempt from military service because of his deformed hand, Wally had done very, very well in business, both during and since the War.

"In any case," Bianca said, "whether I want to or not, I'm seeing her tomorrow."

"Tomorrow?"

Grant could never keep her schedule in his head, no matter how many times she reminded him. "She's coming over for coffee—remember?—while you're at the game."

The Tigers were in town and Grant and the boys would be in the bleachers tomorrow. Cheap seats. When it came to sports, Grant enjoyed slumming it. He was never happier than when playing handball with a factory worker who hadn't bathed in a week.

"That's right."

"She said she wants my advice about something. What'll it be? Whether to buy a yacht? Whether to spend Christmas in Florida, or would California be even nicer?"

The game contentedly petered out over coffee and Bianca's third—and last—cigarette. Grant called for the check. At the door, Pierre, roused to his former magnificence, actually kissed Bianca's hand while murmuring, "À *bientôt*."

"You've got to love the old fruit," Grant said the moment they stepped out into the sun. Having seized her kissed hand in his, he lifted his free hand and pointed: "Look! Another gull."

This one, too, was wheeling toward the river.

"I take that as a good omen," Bianca said.

A couple of years ago, desiring a still bigger house, Grant had proposed a move up to Huntington Woods or even Birmingham. Bianca had resisted, but it had taken a couple of days before her objections crystallized. If she settled any further north, she'd lose all sense of living by the river. "I don't want to move to Birmingham because there aren't enough gulls up there."

It was *precisely* the kind of answer Grant loved her for—loved the artist's eccentricity of it. He broadcast the story everywhere, to everyone. Who was he? He was the sort of man who offered to build his wife a splendid house in Birmingham. And his wife—who was she? She was the sort of woman who refused his offer because there weren't enough gulls up there.

CHAPTER XXVII

Maggie arrived twenty minutes late—which was all right. She breezed in and, without so much as a single question about Grant or the boys, launched into a lament about her impossible new maid—which was a little annoying but mostly all right. But why was she wearing pearls and a cocktail dress?

Bianca was wearing khaki pedal pushers and a yellow cotton blouse from Montgomery Ward. Maggie made a passing but significant reference to having somewhere else to go—clearly prodding Bianca to ask the where and what. She didn't ask.

Maggie shifted topics from her maid to her mother-in-law, whom she called Witch Waller. In appearance, Maggie's life was altogether transformed from the days when she'd shared a cramped bungalow out Grand River with the Jailer, but fundamentally it was the same, and would always be the same. If Maggie were to get married and divorced a hundred times, it was a safe bet that all one hundred mothers-in-law would be insufferable.

Maggie got along fine with Mr. Waller, but no surprise there: men adored Maggie.

Bianca asked whether she'd like tea or coffee, and Maggie wondered whether there might be some beer or wine, and Bianca replied that she had both, and Maggie pointed out that some wine might be nice. So Bianca poured Maggie a glass of wine and, a little guiltily, recalling those two glasses at yesterday's lunch, a half glass for herself. They both lit cigarettes.

When Maggie had called she'd suggested, rather urgently, that she needed Bianca's advice, and it turned out, after a few minutes' conversation, she did indeed have a problem—quite an amazing problem. "Walton wants me to have plastic surgery."

"Plastic surgery!" Here was something completely out of the blue. "Why? On what?"

"On my chin."

"On your *chin*! I don't think they even *do* plastic surgery on chins."

"They do," Maggie said softly, almost meekly. "It's called chin enhancement."

"Chin enhancement! Who ever heard of such a thing? Maggie, do you plan to walk around town with an *enhanced chin*? Are people going to say about you, There goes the lady with the *enhanced chin*? This is absurd."

"I have a weak chin," Maggie said, more meekly still. They were sitting at the kitchen table. Each was on her second cigarette. Maggie was on her second glass of wine. Bianca was on her second half glass.

"You don't have a *weak* chin, Maggie. You have *your* chin."

"I do have a weak chin. Not like yours. You with your bone structure, easy for you to talk. But I'm getting a double chin because my chin is weak."

"You drop five pounds, you'd lose it I'm sure."

"I'm not so sure. I have a weak chin. You don't. You're lucky."

"Maggie, you look great as you are. You're forever turning heads."

"It's very hard to argue with Walton's logic—"

"It always is," Bianca interrupted, though Maggie didn't seem to notice and went right on: "He says, Kid, you're twenty-eight years old. Do you want to spend the next forty, fifty years with a double chin? Or without a double chin? You choose."

"Maggie, is this plastic surgery something *you* want?"

Maggie hesitated. "I think so."

"Maggie, you go tell Walton to have his own chin enhanced."

"Easy for you, giving that advice . . ."

"What do you mean by that?" The conversation had turned a little dicey, all of a sudden.

Maggie again hesitated, then plunged in: "Just that you've got Grant wrapped round your little finger. That's all."

Bianca laughed a little as she protested: "Maggie, I do not."

Maggie proceeded more confidently, with dramatic pauses: "Around . . . your . . . little . . . finger. Look, I say it with envy. What wouldn't I give to have Walton wrapped round my little finger?"

"This is absurd," Bianca protested. "Walton's the most devoted man I know."

"Devotion's different. We're talking about having the say-so. We're talking about having somebody like a bug under your thumb. Honey, believe me, Walton's not the sort of man you have under your thumb."

This pronouncement was vexatious on a variety of fronts: the cinematic way Maggie exhaled a cloud of smoke before uttering it; the *honey*; and, worst of all, the implication that somehow Grant was a victim or a patsy—which manly Walton refused to be. Behind this remark lay an assumption that everybody in the world, except Bianca, now seemed prepared to concede: Walton Waller was a formidable personage. Even Grant, though often tough on the men in their circle, had nothing but respect for Walton, who was "one helluva businessman," who was "easy to underestimate," who was "a gutsy guy." Grant was forever pointing out that having been born into a good thing—his family's plate-glass business—Walton hadn't needed to venture out as he had.

All right, she'd concede this—but what a way to venture! He'd started buying up small businesses, beginning with some car washes. Over each one he'd post a sign: "A Walton J. Waller Establishment." You saw those signs all over town. Grant used to share her laughter at the overweening solemnity of it. But in recent years, as the signs proliferated, he'd stopped laughing. And it had fallen on Bianca to recall that, even were he to become the new Henry Ford, Walton J. Waller was really Wally Waller.

Bianca said: "Look, Maggie, do you want your chin enhanced?"

"Well I think I do," Maggie replied. "Only—"

"Only?"

"Only I'm frightened. Terrified. Of needles, knives. I get the jim-jams. You know how I am."

Bianca did. It was a famous story: Maggie's fainting after a shot in the doctor's office. Here she sat in pearls and cocktail dress, the wife of a helluva businessman, and yet she was still Maggie Szot, of Inquiry Street, that brash young lollapalooza who blanched at the thought of a little needle . . .

Bianca felt an impetuous surge of affection for Maggie. "Speaking of doctors' offices," she said, "I'm hoping to be in one myself. You know, we're trying to have another child."

Maggie didn't respond with the right warmth. "Your idea?" she asked. "Or Grant's?"

Bianca leaned back in her chair. "Both of ours."

"Not that it really matters." Given that she'd been trying for ages to get pregnant herself, Maggie's coolness perhaps was understandable. Still, she might have *pretended* to be nice.

"Maggie, what are you saying?"

"I'm just saying he'll always go along, you've got him under your thumb." Maggie was quite set on establishing this particular point today. "That's all. Look, I'm envious," she said and, irritatingly, smiled. "I envy you."

"One," Bianca said. "I don't have Grant under my thumb. Two, I don't *want* Grant, or any other man, like a bug under my thumb, as you so memorably put it."

"Like fun you don't. Look," Maggie said again, "I'm envious."

The two friends stared at each other. Each drew on her cigarette, exhaled, tapped ash into the ashtray. Then Maggie said, "You know, sometimes I get the feeling you've never forgiven me."

"Forgiven you?"

"You know what I'm talking about."

"Maggie, that was four years ago."

"I know! So why won't you let it go?"

Four years ago, at a Christmas party where everyone had drunk too much, and Grant had typically drunk more than most, Bianca had flicked on the light in an upstairs bathroom and found Maggie Waller, who was then Maggie Schrock—although she'd officially left Pete Schrock a couple of weeks before—passionately entwined with Grant. Yes, they were both fully dressed. But Bianca would never forget, when the light blazed on, the burning expressions mirrored on those ripped-apart faces. The next day, a Monday, after Grant had shuffled sheepishly off to work, Bianca left him a note on the kitchen table and, with one large suitcase and two small two-year-olds in tow, boarded a train to Cleveland.

"I have let it go," Bianca said.

She knew—nobody in the world knew better—the risk of allowing nonexistent dangers to poison your life. Wasn't that Mamma's fate? Accusing Aunt Grace of stealing Papa's affections? Nine years ago now, Mamma's declaration of war, and nine years later, nothing like an armistice.

Yes, you did have to let things go, but you also had to think things through—and that sordid Christmas party had compelled Bianca to rethink a great many things about her friend. She'd felt so sorry for Maggie back in the old War days, married to George and living with her impossible mother-in-law. But wasn't it true that under the Jailer's watchful eye Maggie had remained faithful while George was stationed out in the Pacific? It was only when George returned home, at last moving Maggie out from under his mother's supervision, that Maggie had cheated on George, and George on Maggie, and the marriage rapidly disintegrated. In retrospect, there was another way to think about Ma'am Hamm: she'd taken her new daughter-in-law's measure precisely, and responded accordingly . . . Maggie required watching.

Not that Bianca had lingering fears that Maggie represented any threat to her marriage. Grant wasn't going anywhere—he'd more than learned his lesson—and Maggie had her hands full playing Walton J. Waller's wife. Yes, Bianca was willing to put that Christmas party behind her—but did this mean she must henceforward ignore every one of Maggie's snippy little digs, every one of Maggie's crass little materialistic boasts?

The two of them chatted awhile about this and that—Maggie finally remembering to ask about the twins—and then Maggie said, with significant emphasis, "I really *must* be going."

Again Bianca did not ask where. Presumably, Maggie was meeting some Fords or Hudsons, Chryslers or Buhls; Wally increasingly moved among the city's wealthiest people.

Bianca watched her friend drive off with a feeling of relief—but not so much relief that she could resist the consolations of a second glass of wine. She'd downed half of this when she had another thought: Stevie and Rita. Stevie was rarely home—he worked such long hours—but today was Sunday and he just might be. She'd pay a surprise visit. It would make her feel better . . .

Grant and the boys shouldn't be returning for another hour. Grant had told her not to worry about dinner—he and the boys loved nothing better than ballpark franks. Well, no doubt all three would arrive home stuffed with hot dogs, and no doubt (such were the ravenous males she lived with) they would gobble up the meat loaf and mashed potatoes she'd prepared for their return. If she hurried, she could pay a visit and be back before them.

"Hey, Bea," Stevie said when he opened the front door. Though she rarely showed up unannounced, it was like him to display no surprise— just as it was like him to call her Bea. Most everyone else had long ago acceded to her wish and shifted over to Bianca. (With Edith, it was almost as though Bianca had fed a punch card into her brain; the request was made, it was processed, and Bea would be Bianca forever-more.) When she was young, she'd gone back and forth about her name, an issue that came to a head when she married Grant. Bea Ives? Beehives? It sounded like a joke. Having been christened with almost intimidating grandeur—Bianca Paradiso—she seemed to be marrying into a screwball comedy. As an Ives, she would have to be Bianca henceforward.

"Hey, Stevie."

"You just caught me," Stevie said. "Gotta go see a friend's car's got trouble."

"Well, you let your friend wait five minutes," Bianca said. "Say hello to your sister, whom you so rarely see."

"That's what I say," Rita said, stepping into the doorway behind Stevie. "Let Charley wait all day. Why is it Stevie's always doing Charley favors and Charley's never doing us return favors the other way? Why can't Stevie for five minutes relax for once, that's what I say. Hey, Bea."

Following Stevie's example, Rita also called her Bea, or something close to it. Her Tennessee accent tilted the sound into *Bay*, almost. Bianca was secretly fond of *Bay*, which felt like a nickname. Bianca liked nicknames. She could change her name a hundred times and still her father would call her nothing but Bia.

"For heaven's sake, get out of the doorway, Stevie, let your sister in." Rita laughed and her braces shone.

The three of them took a seat in the cramped living room. Truth be told, Stevie and Rita lived in a pretty miserable little house, but—and this was the amazing thing—it was *their* house. Stevie wasn't going to pay rent to anyone. At the age of twenty-two, he was a homeowner, regularly meeting his monthly mortgage payment.

Stevie was wearing a black T-shirt that showed off his muscles. It sometimes occurred to Bianca that the world saw a far different Stevie than she did. She still viewed him as her little brother. But Stevie was nearly as tall as Grant, and he lifted weights a few times a week in a friend's garage, and his body—far more than Grant's, whose smooth athleticism softened the impression he made—exuded a knotty physical strength.

"Bay," Rita said, "interest you in some ice tea?"

"I'd love some iced tea," Bianca said, and Rita leapt up, in that bustling way she had, and disappeared into the kitchen, leaving brother and sister on opposite ends of the couch.

"So Stevie, how is every little thing?"

Stevie tilted his head and sunlight from the window swept the thick lenses of his glasses. For a moment, his eyes disappeared. "I got Rita a new toaster."

"It's the most wonderful toaster in the whole world!" Rita called from the kitchen.

"I'm sure it is."

Bianca was sure it was. Stevie's keenly mechanical mind subjected every purchase to an exacting scrutiny. This modest house was full of high-quality items: a new Frigidaire, a new washer and dryer, a new floor radio from Grinnell's which—so Grant joked to Bianca—the two of *them* could hardly afford. Step by step, washer by toaster by radio, Stevie was elevating himself out of this somewhat dingy neighborhood.

"How are the boys?" Stevie asked.

"Fine, always the same—just fine. They're off with Grant at the Tigers game."

"That's good," Stevie said. "Real nice."

Yes, it was, but it did raise the question why Grant had so much more time for such pursuits. Stevie was always working. If he wasn't at Ford's, where he welcomed all the overtime he could get, he was moonlighting at a friend's auto shop, where he specialized in "headers"—whatever they were. And if he wasn't at the plant, or at the shop, he was answering, as he was today, some friend's call for assistance. Rita spent many hours at home alone. Still, she kept up a cheerful front, sharing Stevie's conviction that progress was being made—as symbolized by her newly acquired braces. And Rita seemed totally devoted to Stevie, whom she called honeybunch. (Grant found this endlessly amusing. *Honeybunch* wasn't a likely endearment for someone of Stevie's hunched, bespectacled intensity.)

The three of them sat in the living room, drinking iced tea. Rita rattled on about their neighbors the Huckmans, who were really terrible people. Their boy, Rodger, was forever setting off fireworks inside trashcans. ("Sounds like you at that age," Bianca said, but Stevie only looked blank. Did he no longer remember that he'd spent his childhood playing war games?) Bianca talked about Maggie's visit, showing up in pearls and a cocktail dress. Stevie nodded politely. He was eager to be off.

"Hate to go but it's Charley's car." He stood up.

"Before you go," Bianca said, "a quick reminder. This time, I really do think Aunt Grace and Uncle Dennis are coming up." Their visit—originally scheduled to correspond with Grace's birthday in July—had been twice postponed, once because Grace had laryngitis and once because of some medical tests. "Stevie, I'm expecting you and Rita to be there."

"I'll be there."

"Not this Sunday. The weekend after. And I won't stand for any sorry-have-to-work business. Or any Charley-needed-my-help."

"I'll be there," Stevie repeated.

"Isn't that nice," Rita said. She and Stevie adored Aunt Grace and Uncle Dennis. It was Uncle Dennis who had found Rita the dentist and the orthodontist who had transformed her mouth, her looks.

Rita followed Stevie to the door, calling sweetly, "Don'tcha be too long, honeybunch. I'm not holding dinner forever."

But the sweetness in her tone, the smile on her face, vanished as she swung from the door. "I'm worried about Stevie," she said.

"Worried about Stevie? He always seems the same."

"Maybe that's the problem, Bay."

Rita dropped onto the couch in that abrupt style of hers and threw Bianca a piercing look. This was Rita's way, especially when no men were present: very direct. "He's got to get out of that plant," she said.

"He will," Bianca said.

"Bay, it's like it's eating him alive. It's dark in there, it's like he never sees the sun, jever look at those men he works with, the ones been there forever? They don't *look* good, Bay. Pasty. They all look like convicks, you want my honest opinion."

When Rita made remarks like this about "convicks," you couldn't be certain how much she was speaking in metaphors and how much from experience; they were a hard-bitten crowd, the folks she'd grown up with in Appalachia.

"If he's really and truly looking for a new job, Papa would offer him one in a minute."

"But you know he can't do that, Bay."

Yes, Bianca did know this, but still a question remained: why couldn't he?

Oh, it was obvious why Stevie couldn't have done so a few years ago—back when he'd worried the family sick. The minute he'd finished high school, Stevie had lit out, going cross-country, as he put it, with Hal Lepps and Jake Murfree, two good-for-nothings in anybody's book. Stevie was no letter writer and there'd been only a broad scattering of postcards. He was in Sacramento, California. He was in Lincoln City, Oregon. He was away from home for eighteen months, with so little word to anyone, it was almost as if he'd died . . .

And when at last he returned, gaunt and sunburned, what did he do but race out and get a seventeen-year-old girl in trouble, little Rita Comer recently up from Tennessee, whose family clearly were white trash (though no Paradiso wanted to apply the term to future in-laws). A shudder had gone around the table when Edith had asked Rita what brought her family to Detroit and Rita, giggling, replied, "Mamma always wanted a flush toilet."

This was a possible sister-in-law?

Yes, it was apparent why Stevie could not have accepted a job from Papa back then. Papa had been in no mood to extend a helping hand, and Stevie wasn't about to take one anyway. Stevie had first had to prove himself as husband and father. He took a job bagging groceries at Wrigley's, then a job at Hudson Motor, and then he secured the job at Ford's, where he'd done very well, especially with all the overtime.

"I worry about him," Rita said again. "When was the last time you saw him smile?"

"Well, Stevie's not exactly a smiley sort of guy," Bianca said, smiling herself.

Rita wasn't about to be deflected: "Sometimes he just seems so desperate."

Yes, Stevie had had to prove himself, but he'd been back three years now, he'd been at Ford's for nearly two years, and how like Stevie it was that, having proved himself, he'd had to go on proving himself—having proved himself to everyone except, evidently, himself.

But what had Stevie done that Bianca herself hadn't done? *This* was the question that haunted her. Yes, when you looked closely, what had Stevie done that she hadn't done? There had been an interval, as she alone in the family knew, a terrifying stretch of about a week, when she'd feared she herself might be a pregnant teenager. She had given herself to Henry Vanden Akker on the night before Henry went back to the War . . . What would she have done if she'd wound up pregnant? It was hard to believe she would eventually have married Grant and found herself living in luxury in the University District—while Stevie was holed up in a bungalow in the shadow of that Ford plant which, according to Rita, was eating his life.

"And you know he has those nightmares," Rita said.

"Nightmares?"

"Wakes up with such a jolt, it nearly knocks me outta bed."

Bianca paused and then said, "What sort of nightmares?" Her sense of foreboding was all the more unnerving for being familiar. This was common in her dealings with Stevie. She was always taking at face value his ready reassurances ("Going okay," "No serious complaints," "Moving along, moving along"), and suddenly she'd be caught up short, frightened and hopeless, on hearing what sounded very much like a cry from the heart. She had paid this visit hoping for cheer and consolation—Maggie's remarks had disquieted her—but she'd be leaving feeling far more unsettled than when she arrived.

"I don't know," Rita said.

"Well, what does he say?"

"Drowning is in some of them. But he won't talk about it. And sometimes he sweats when he sleeps. *And* grinds his teeth. Bay, I feel so bad for him."

"Oh Stevie will be all right," Bianca said, but wished she could sound more confident. Was Stevie desperate? It was the word Rita had used. *Desperate.*

"Like a little more ice tea?"

It was the Devil talking: "Rita, do you have any wine?"

"Wine? Well no. I do have some bourbon." Rita looked very doubtful. "It's from Tennessee."

"Well then I'll have the smallest possible drop of Tennessee bourbon."

"It's homemade. My uncle makes it." She offered this shyly, but proudly, too.

"Moonshine!" Bianca said.

Rita grinned, her braces agleam. Neither she nor Stevie was anything of a drinker—both had trouble downing even a glass of Papa's wine at family dinners—but Rita clearly relished this *moment*: she was about to sip some moonshine with her grown-up sister-in-law, who was an artist, named Bianca, who lived in a big, gorgeous house in the University District.

It had taken Bianca quite a while to warm toward Rita—quite a while to see bashfulness and intimidation and simple, woeful inexperience behind the girl's remote sullenness. Ironically, Rita's terrible teeth had helped work the transformation. After repeated, gentle prodding from Uncle Dennis, Rita had finally agreed to see a dentist, whose office was way out in Center Line. Bianca gave her a lift. On the drive over, it was revealed that Rita had never been to a dentist. Never? Surely that wasn't possible . . . "A nurse at school, she came and looked in all our mouths. Does that count?"

No, Rita had never been to a dentist. And Bianca had felt much more patient and compassionate after learning that.

The dentist had worked wonders, and his prices—a favor to his friend Dr. Poppleton—were quite reasonable. Rita was so pleased that when Uncle Dennis, on another visit to Detroit, had proposed braces— Rita was badly buck-toothed—she soon agreed, though not without much flustered chatter about being "the oldest girl with braces in all Detroit."

It was almost magic—the change the braces had effected. All that metal in her mouth predictably altered her voice, but nobody could have predicted that it would soften her Southern accent. And who could have foreseen the funny, touching, proud way Rita would respond to her braces? Clearly, they represented all the right virtues in her eyes: progress, education, even civilization. She was the only person Bianca had ever heard of who *loved* her braces.

Rita was growing up fast, and learning fast—the little girl was no dummy—and earlier remarks that had set everybody shuddering were viewed in retrospect as the spunky replies of a seventeen-year-old girl putting on no airs when deposited among grandeur. Yes, to a girl like Rita that's how the house on Inquiry must have appeared—with Mamma's china on the sideboard and Papa's elaborate wooden toys on the bookcase. And Bianca's slate-roofed house on Middleway must have seemed a veritable palace . . .

The bourbon turned out to be ghastly—which Bianca found reassuring. Given her state of mind, the last thing she needed to discover was a taste for bourbon.

But she was still feeling so peculiar—so torn up and strange! What in the world had she been thinking—asking Rita for wine? She knew she ought to be heading home. Instead she said, sipping from her glass, "This stuff is really something."

"It's the hills of home," Rita said, with plucky bravado, though she couldn't like it any better than Bianca did.

"Stevie just needs to work less," Bianca said.

"That's exactly what I tell him."

"But do you ever *tell* him? Ever say, Stevie, I mean it, you've got to cut back?"

Rita's eyes widened. "I don't dare . . ."

The look on Rita's face? It was a look of fear. Rita could cajole with Stevie. She could suggest, and she could wheedle . . . Yet she couldn't stand up to that tense and powerful man in the black T-shirt and say, This won't do.

Bianca sipped thoughtfully from her nasty drink. Was there any comparable reluctance in her own marriage? Nothing, surely—no sentiment she longed to express but didn't *dare.* Rita was scared, and Grant simply didn't scare Bianca in that way. Those troubling remarks of Maggie's came back: "You have him wrapped round your little finger." And—worse—the image of a bug under her thumb. Did Stevie have Rita under his thumb and was that what her look of fear evinced? In any marriage, was it inevitable, or just likely, that one spouse was under the other's thumb? But Grant *wasn't* under her thumb, was he, just because he commonly deferred in various matters of little importance to him?

From out of nowhere, from out of a remote past that glittered like pearls in candlelight, a remark came back: "My boy is no milquetoast." That was Mrs. Olsson. Speaking to Bianca at lunch, at Pierre's. An almost frighteningly obliging and accommodating Mrs. Olsson. A Mrs. Olsson who had all but proposed to her, on her son's behalf.

Everything was so much clearer to Bianca now—back then, her brain had been in such a permanent, passionate muddle. The lunch at Pierre's had taken place not so very long after Henry Vanden Akker's death launched her on that downward spiral which eventually landed her in the hospital, and from the hospital into a long, floating, tranquil convalescence with Aunt Grace and Uncle Dennis in Cleveland. She'd stayed weeks and weeks with the Poppletons before returning home, only to return to them after a couple of months for further weeks and weeks. She'd devoted much of her time to gardening with Aunt Grace, first in the greenhouse and then, as the weather warmed, in the backyard. Very early one morning she'd been cutting peonies when Aunt Grace came out to report the latest off the radio: the Allies had attacked the Germans in Normandy, France. The invasion that Uncle Dennis had so long predicted was beginning. And all over the city, as if the separate neighborhoods had located their common voice at last, church bells began ringing. Standing with rusty scissors in one hand, some big pink peonies in the other, Bianca felt she'd never heard such sweet music— those big resounding bells ringing out broad across the city, across Lake Erie, across the weary and indomitably hopeful United States.

Yes, everything was so much clearer now, when she could easily grasp the undermining panic in the Olssons' mansion. They couldn't agree on anything, Mr. and Mrs. Olsson, but they must have been equally, secretly horrified at the prospect that their handsome only son, who insisted on studying still-life painting, could possibly be "cur." Ronny's girlfriend might be a Wop from within the Boulevard, a girl who wore silly "artistic" clothes and whose father worked with his hands, but the girl was pretty and bright and under the circumstances she looked mighty good . . .

"Oh golly it's so *late*," Bianca said and showily took another, last sip meant to suggest that she'd love to finish her bourbon but simply didn't have time, and then she was up and out the door.

Bianca reached home two or three minutes before Grant and the boys—just time enough to begin warming up the mashed potatoes. She apologized that dinner wasn't quite ready and Grant told her, as she'd known he would, not to fret. They were "stuffed." And then—just as she'd known they would—he and the boys bolted down the meat loaf and mashed potatoes and corn. Mashed potatoes were probably Grant's favorite food in the whole world: mashed potatoes with butter, or with sour cream, or with bacon bits and cheddar cheese melted on top, or with pork and beans, or with sloppy joes, or simply mashed potatoes plain. Although Grant always had his drink of the day when he came home—usually a stiff Scotch-and-soda—he perhaps loved even better a glass of milk, accompanying a big plate of milky mashed potatoes.

Later, the boys finally in bed, Bianca lay down beside her husband. He was nearly asleep. He'd had quite a day, including a pickup basketball game in the morning. Bianca was still troubled by the visit from Maggie, whose face glowed so distinctly in her mind's eye, that look of canny ingenuousness while declaring, "You've got him under your thumb," and adding, "I envy you." Needing reassurance, Bianca reached out and stroked Grant's neck, who in his half sleep received this as a welcome signal of desire. He swung toward her and his tongue swiped the rim of her ear. When he realized, still half asleep, that, tonight anyway, she had other intentions, he rolled onto his back and within moments he was exhaling the heavy, contented breaths of the virtuously exhausted.

The sound wasn't a snore exactly—merely a very heavy breathing—and Bianca typically found it comforting. She usually had no difficulty fitting her own breathing inside it and falling asleep; it was like slipping your hand into a warm and bulky glove. But occasionally the sound kept her awake, as she felt certain it would tonight. Did she have Grant under her thumb? The remark still needled.

Down the hall, the boys were asleep in their bunk bed—the magical bunk bed Papa had built for her so long ago. It surprised people to learn that the boys didn't have a set sleeping arrangement. One night Matt might sleep above and Chip below; the next night, the reverse. Grant had established the policy: whoever went first to bed got first choice of bunks. It was one of many of Grant's ideas which sounded totally unworkable—a recipe for endless squabbling—but it actually worked quite well, getting them into bed sooner than later. He knew his boys . . .

Sometimes, when nobody else was home, Bianca would nap in the lower bunk. She still found it comforting. It occurred to her, lying awake beside Grant, that she could probably fall fast asleep right now, if only she could curl up there, in the world's coziest zoological park.

Did she have Grant under her thumb? If she did, perhaps it had begun with that horrible Christmas party, one of the two big crises in her married life. (The other was the time when Grant nearly got fired over the lakefront properties.) Or it began the day after the Christmas party, when Bianca, after carefully tidying the house, had left Grant a note explaining that she and the twins were going away for a few days. She'd ordered a taxi to the train station.

Knowing how furious she was, Grant left the office early. He must have arrived home only a few hours after her departure. In any event, she'd been at Uncle Dennis and Aunt Grace's only a few minutes, just long enough to cry and dry her tears, when—the arrival itself not wholly unexpected, but far earlier than could have been predicted—Grant pulled up.

She had pictured the argument the two of them would enact, in which she would pose stinging accusations. She had even envisioned herself commanding him to leave her uncle and aunt's home. But none of this was possible when Grant appeared. He was an altered man. Not even in the transports of bedroom passion had she ever seen him so changed, so different from the Grant she knew . . .

He was not only white-faced. His face looked caved in—as if he'd been kicked hard in the head. And he was trembling—not a gentle shiver but a big palsied shaking that would have seemed comically overdone if it hadn't been so terrifying.

Bianca had never doubted—even when, blinking back tears, she'd climbed aboard the train, shepherding the twins with one hand and dragging a suitcase with the other—that Grant loved her. What she hadn't understood, and what Grant no doubt had never contemplated, was that he would become completely incapacitated at the possibility of her abandoning him.

Aunt Grace, with her instinctive good breeding, greeted Grant normally, as if finding nothing out-of-the-way in his arriving on their doorstep. Uncle Dennis, with his doctor's eye, took one look at the miserable, quivering specimen before him and proposed a toast. They wanted to welcome Grant to Cleveland. Four neat glasses were poured. Grant's went down in a gulp. A second, bigger glass was poured for Grant. It, too, went down in a gulp.

Since Aunt Grace longed to spend a little time with the twins, she wondered whether Grant and Bea might wish to see something of the city? Or perhaps they preferred a walk?

Grant didn't make it even to the sidewalk. The two of them had scarcely stepped off the front porch when he clutched his arms around her and issued a howling sob that must have echoed halfway down the block.

Bianca led him to the car, where he collapsed on her breast and in a voice squeezed high by breathless sobbing vowed that if she would only agree to take him back he would never, ever, never, ever do anything like that again . . .

At dinner, after two more hefty shots of whiskey, he'd entered a different phase. He quit trembling. His face wore a politely genial but glazed look. He sat beside Bianca and tightly held her hand under the table. She'd had to unlace his fingers, one by one, to go to the bathroom.

She'd wondered whether this astounding day was meant to end with their making love, which would present a problem, since she obviously hadn't brought her diaphragm. Did they dare risk it? She'd be willing to risk it. But shortly after dinner, while Grace was showing the twins how she could make a bird simply by folding a sheet of paper, Bianca had gone upstairs and Grant had yanked her to the bed, both of them fully dressed, and, tucking his face deep into the hair of her neck, had instantly fallen asleep.

And stayed asleep. Bianca got up a number of times—to tend to the twins, to put on a nightgown, to go to the bathroom—but Grant stayed down, his breathing steady but higher than usual.

And stayed asleep. Bianca got up at six-thirty, at which point Grant had been sleeping for eleven hours—longer than she'd ever seen him sleep before. After thirteen hours, she asked Uncle Dennis whether it might be dangerous for Grant to sleep so long, and Uncle Dennis had laughed and told her this was just what the man needed. When Grant had been asleep for fourteen hours, she began to check on his breathing. Could he have had some sort of stroke? By going away and leaving him, had she killed her husband?

Grant slept for sixteen hours. He got up looking a little sheepish but no more than a little. He was his old self again.

. . . Or so it had seemed, but later it occurred to her that something fundamental in him—in the two of them—forever shifted on the day she boarded that Cleveland train. It was shortly afterward that Grant had adopted his one-drink rule, and though sometimes those drinks were tumbler-sized, he'd stuck by it—stuck by it until it hardly seemed like discipline or deprivation. Wasn't milk his true drink of choice? It was difficult now to remember a time when she'd worried about Grant's drinking.

Still, that pair of remarks from Maggie—especially the "bug under your thumb"—continued to rankle. Admittedly, Maggie had her own reasons for expressing herself aggressively. But this didn't mean she was necessarily wrong.

But Bianca didn't *want* to squash anybody; she didn't want to be *able* to squash anybody.

There was no disputing the degree to which Grant deferred to her. The household's governing assumption was that she was more attuned to the world, and especially to the appearances of things, than he was. You might have thought Grant would concede this resentfully, but the opposite was true: he took authentic pride in her discrimination. And an odd pride in his own indifference. When he traveled away from home on business, which he rarely did, he enjoyed staying in fleabags, eating in greasy spoons . . . "After the Army," he liked to say, "everything else is the Ritz." He liked to play "street basketball" with Negroes. At baseball games, he preferred the bleachers. Though most of his legal work involved trusts and estates, he adored stories of criminals, particularly inept and ridiculous crimes.

Bianca was the house's sole and unquestioned arbiter as to whether a stack of lunch meat had gone bad or a quart of milk had gone sour. It was appalling, really, what Grant would eat if left on his own—things any well-fed dog would turn up its nose at. At parties, he would happily lament the way Bianca had barred him from his favorite restaurant, a Chinese dive on Seven Mile where she'd found a fly in her fried rice.

Pitying once more that sobbing, shaken, shaking man in the car, the one who had pierced her heart when he'd cried out that, if only she would take him back, he would never, ever, never, ever do anything like that again, Bianca reached over and laid a hand on his chest—his powerful heart pulsing slowly and contentedly under her palm—and felt herself, as she did so, subsiding gratefully into sleep.

CHAPTER XXVIII

"Am I speaking to Bianca?"

"Ronny!"

He laughed lightly. "Is my voice so identifiable?"

"Apparently so."

"And how are you?"

"Fine, Ronny. But how are you?"

"I'm all right. Listen, the reason I'm calling—"

"You don't need a reason to call me."

"Thank you. Anyway, the reason I'm calling—"

"You wait for a reason to call me, more than a year goes by. Do you realize it's more than a year since I last heard your voice?"

"The *reason* I'm calling is because I'm coming to town Saturday and I thought we might get together, however briefly, maybe go—"

"Or however *lengthily*. My day looks wide open. I see it right here on the kitchen calendar: SAILING! Grant's befriended somebody who owns a boat and the male members of this household are looking forward to a full day of sunburn and seasickness."

"I thought we might go, *if* you'll let me finish a sentence—"

"Probably not."

"To the DIA."

"Love to. Sign me up."

Yes, more than a year had elapsed since she'd spoken to Ronny, but it was as if the cadences continued to resound and their banter could begin in midflow. To converse with him for only a minute was to be reminded that she'd never known anyone else she so loved to interrupt, or to be interrupted by. There was nobody else she talked to in this particular way—and what better defined true friendship? Oh, she was *glad* he'd telephoned.

She said, "This is so wonderful you'd call now; these last few days, I've been thinking about you often."

"Good things, I trust."

"All good things. Listen, I went to Pierre's."

"Pierre's?"

"The restaurant. You remember. Your mother took me a few times. Pierre has this pencil-thin moustache and he kisses—"

"I remember Pierre."

"Anyway, Grant took me on Saturday."

"Doesn't sound like much fun. Pierre's sort of this embarrassing—"

"It was *lots* of fun. An anniversary lunch—seven years! Anyway—I don't *know*!—I've just been thinking constantly about the old days, your mother taking me to Pierre's, and the Coral Club, and Professor Manhardt and Professor Ravenscroft—"

"He wore a toupee. You remember, I couldn't bring myself to study under somebody who wore a toupee."

"You said it was because he couldn't draw."

"It was the toupee, actually." And Ronny laughed—that wonderful always ever so slightly and unexpectedly nervous laugh of his.

"Anyway, I'm so glad you called." There was a pause. "How *is* your mother?" Bianca asked.

"Mother's all right I guess."

"Your father?"

"Oh he's always the same. Business is tough and getting tougher. Tough and getting tougher. Only the strong survive. The rest of us become art professors."

"Or the mothers of twin boys. Who now are six, I must tell you."

"Six," Ronny said.

So they arranged to meet at eleven, Saturday morning, in the lobby of the DIA.

She was going to meet Ronny Olsson at the DIA.

The plan turned out to be fine with Grant, as she knew it would. He had little interest in museums, and he was all too happy if she and that "old fruit," Ronny Olsson, had a rendezvous at the DIA. This was something actually quite sweet about Grant: he was always encouraging her as an artist. He was glad she wasn't "one of those wives," as he put it. The phrase encompassed half the women they met socially—who were forever talking about their husband's job at GM or Chrysler or Hudson Motor. As Grant often said, with a directness whose simplicity was touching: "You make things interesting."

Of course Grant's attitude toward art was more complicated than she sometimes made out. It would be easy for someone—for Ronny, say— to portray Grant as some sort of philistine. In fact, Grant had the good sense and natural candor to see, when confronted with the DIA's Italian galleries, say, that while their art spoke very little to him, it spoke volumes to his wife, which pleased him deeply. And was this so different, really, from the attraction she'd felt for poor Henry Vanden Akker? Part of Henry's appeal was his air of being linked to another world—in his case, a mathematical world of which she scarcely caught sight.

And Grant had been far more than decent—he'd been admirable, he'd been wonderful —about Henry. It was at Grant's insistence that in the little room off the kitchen she sometimes called her studio Henry's face hung on the wall—the jungle portrait that had made Henry crow (she would never forget it) *It makes me look so brainy!* In Grant's eyes, their duty was clear. Henry, already once wounded, had returned to the Pacific, and sacrificed his life for his country, and the least they could do in tribute was to hang his portrait prominently.

Grant seemed to savor the romance of it, actually, and over time Bianca had divulged a fair amount about Henry—probably more than she should, since Grant sometimes informed visitors that this was a portrait of "Bianca's former fiancé." And inevitably added: "His plane went down in the Pacific." She'd told Grant that Henry hadn't been her fiancé exactly—rather, her "near fiancé" or "almost fiancé"—but in the passion of her storytelling perhaps she hadn't been altogether clear.

Saturday morning, after a few false starts, she donned a turquoise silk blouse from Himelhoch's, a black skirt, and some quite "arty," vaguely Southwestern Indian turquoise and silver earrings. She was meeting Ronny at the DIA.

What she hadn't figured on, however, was that old moodiness of Ronny's: you never knew quite where you stood. Oh, he was gallantry itself from the first moment: "Signorina—surely I can call you that— you're enough to make me take up painting again." She'd never known anyone else so debonair. And Ronny looked almost humorously handsome. She'd forgotten how, the last time she'd seen him, she'd detected a fleck of gray at his temples. Now the gray was unmistakable, and made him look not merely handsome but distinguished, too.

But, as soon became evident, there was an edge to his remarks.

" 'A painter is always mixing colors,' " Bianca quoted. "Now who said that?" They were standing in the white courtyard where the controversial Diego Rivera murals spanned the walls high overhead. The murals had never brought Ronny much pleasure.

"I don't know," he said.

"Professor Manhardt."

"That old fraud."

"I think he helped me. He seemed so imposing. I was only eighteen," Bianca said. "And you were twenty-one."

"Twenty-one," Ronny said.

"I took the advice to heart. I was mixing paint in my head when I went to sleep at night."

"Back when we were going to be painters," Ronny said.

The words felt cruel. Not inaccurate, perhaps—but cruel. Given how busy the twins kept her, and Grant kept her, and how rarely she actually sat down to work in her studio (where, more and more, Henry's penetrating portrait carried a look of reproach), Bianca could hardly talk about pursuing art seriously. She might conceivably claim to be working on a still life in copper and silver—old pans and cutlery, all richly tarnished—since the easel was currently standing in a corner of the studio. But how many weeks had it been since she'd actually broken out the paints? She didn't want to know exactly . . . Even so, why did Ronny seem to relish fatal pronouncements of this sort? Her life still lay ahead of her. She was sure of that: her life still lay ahead of her.

They looked at Jacopo Bassano's *Madonna and Child,* at the incomparable Bellini *Madonna and Child,* at the Botticelli *Resurrected Christ.* Ronny spoke, she listened. He'd always known a great deal. And now he knew a great deal more.

They found their way to the astonishing Breughel *Wedding Dance,* and Bianca said, "How you used to embarrass me with this one! Contemplating it with such composure and sophistication, while all I could see were the outlandish codpieces."

It wasn't merely the codpieces. It was the fact that the men were so obviously, exaggeratedly aroused within them.

Bianca went on: "This was all quite shocking to a girl not long out of Eastern High."

She did not say this flirtatiously—merely, at most, mock flirtatiously—but all the same Ronny's reply seemed overly earnest. "Last year, I went to Vienna and I finally saw Breughel's *Hunters in the Snow* and you know what? It's a complete mess. And you know what else? It really is amazingly beautiful. I concluded that it's the most beautiful mess anyone ever made."

He'd always been a professor, of course, even back in those days when he couldn't find a single professor worthy of his respect, but the process of embodiment now seemed complete. Once, she'd loved to argue with Ronny Olsson. But there was something unchallengeable in his remarks now. The difference was subtle but enormous: he used to make observations, and now he made pronouncements.

They wandered here and there. Ronny went on making pronouncements. Bianca countered with observations. When they reached the medieval sculpture gallery—medieval art had become his specialty— Ronny was especially informative. Who else but Ronny would point out, as they stared at a crucifix, that its Jesus had been carved from a willow tree? After all, Ronny was the one who, on his first-ever visit to her home, had so impressed Papa by identifying the various woods in Stevie's pull-toy rooster. If Ronny was an aesthete, he'd always had a very craftsmanlike grasp of how artworks got made. Still, there didn't seem to be much pleasure today in their wandering. What in the world had happened to those two kids, mad about art, who used to race through this museum like children in Hudson's twelfth-floor "toy kingdom"?

They wound up eventually in the Kresge Court, sipping cups of tea. "We could get some sandwiches," Ronny said.

"That sounds convenient," Bianca said.

"I mentioned *Hunters in the Snow*—have you seen it?"

"Only in reproductions."

"You've never been to Vienna."

"No, Ronny, I've never been to Vienna." Her voice came out sharper-edged than she'd intended.

Ronny looked a little hurt and surprised, and Bianca recognized that look: he'd never taken her rare reproaches well.

"I'm sorry," he said. "I just meant—surely now you could afford to make the trip?"

"Ronny, I have two six-year-old boys. I swear, it would be easier to raise wolves or bears or tiger cubs. You know what Chip did the first *week* of kindergarten? He drilled a hole in a cabinet. With a *hand* drill, no less. I get a call from his school, Your boy drilled a hole in a cabinet. Drilled a *what* in a *what*, I say. And how in the world did Chip get his hands on a hand drill? Well you might ask. But you can be certain, if some janitor leaves a hand drill lying around, Chip's got ahold of it in one minute. And the next minute he's drilled a hole in a cabinet. I go off to Vienna? I'd come back and find there's no *house* left."

Though she still had more to say, somewhere in this spirited rebuttal all sense of indignation drained from her. She felt a little sorry for

Ronny actually, who was watching her with the forbearance of some-body receiving a merited rebuke. Presumably, Ronny would never have children. It was hard to believe he would marry again—though stranger things had happened. (The thing she had yet to say, and chose now not to say, was that she'd never been inside an airplane and—despite various generous offers from Uncle Dennis—probably never would. It seemed her maiden flight had gone down in the Pacific, many years ago, on an island called Majuro.)

"Do you like teaching?" she asked him.

"Well enough."

Ronny now lived in Ann Arbor and taught art history at the Univer-sity. He added: "But I don't much like the writing."

"Then why do it?"

"It would smooth the way to tenure."

As a doctoral student, also at the University, Ronny had raced through his classes in record time, and he'd done brilliantly. But it seemed the completing of a dissertation had been a torturous process.

"It's peculiar," Ronny went on. "I can say things, and believe them wholeheartedly, but more and more the moment I put them down on paper, they no longer look defensible. I suppose I prefer speaking to writing. And—though you'll never believe this, you consider me such a windbag—"

"Ronny, I do *not*."

"I often prefer silence to speaking."

In any case, a silence descended on their little table.

"Getting hungry?" Ronny said.

"If you are. I'll freshen up first." She placed her hands on the table, and stood.

Ronny laid a hand upon her hand, urgently: "Bianca, may I ask you something very personal?" Those unpaintable eyes of his held a glitter she hadn't seen in quite a while.

"Anything you want, Ronny."

"You aren't—forgive me for asking. It's just a wild shot in the dark. Not that you look it or anything. But you aren't by any chance pregnant, are you?"

Her mouth dropped open. For a second or two, she couldn't say any-thing. "Ronald Olsson, how . . . on . . . *earth* did you know? I mean, *I* don't even know—know for sure. That is, I'm seeing the doctor on Tues-day." Bianca sat back down.

"Well—it was the way you moved. The way you got up from the table. As if you were—carrying something delicate?"

"You are—incredible. You do realize that, don't you, Ronny Olsson? That you are—incredible?" He was grinning, and she went on: "A one-of-a-kind? A nonesuch? A nonpareil?"

He was grinning from ear to ear now—jubilant in a way she hadn't seen for ages. His face so rarely opened into a full, unqualified smile. "Maybe it's not so incredible?" he said. "After all, I've known you a long time, Bianca."

But his expression belied his humble words. Oh, he looked exultant. It was possible that not even Grant, on first hearing the news, had exhibited greater pleasure.

"Yes, you have known me a long time, and you know what? You're still amazing. *I'm* supposed to be the one with second sight."

"You know what?" Ronny said, adopting her tone. Suddenly, he was a changed man. "We're not going to eat around here."

"We're not?"

"It isn't good enough for the likes of us amazing folks. I'm going to drive you downtown to Jason's. Have you been to Jason's?"

"I haven't. Grant has. He's always out lunching with clients."

"Who?"

"Grant. My husband."

"Who?"

"Oh never mind. I've never known anyone who's been to Jason's."

"It's actually far more decent than any restaurant named Jason's has any right to be."

There was a moment, on first stepping into Ronny's car (which was a beautiful little foreign sports car, a green convertible), when Bianca's heart misgave her. It was one thing to meet Ronny at the DIA. That was precisely the sort of thing expected of her as an artist, or at least a former art student: meeting an art professor at the city museum. After all, she wasn't "one of those wives." But it was another thing, maybe, to be heading to Jason's. Bianca wasn't in the habit of lunching at fancy restaurants with men other than her husband—particularly with extraordinarily good-looking divorced men who drove green convertibles. But in that moment when Ronny actually helped her into the car, whose door opened backward—hinged on what she thought of as the wrong side—and came around and climbed into the driver's seat, most of her misgivings vanished. This was the most natural thing in the world. The engine started with a tidy, comforting roar. Ronny was driving and she was trying to entertain him, trying to be bright and amusing and complimentary and maybe even insightful.

"Nice green," she said. "The car."

"It's called British racing green."

"The car's an MG?"

"An MGTD. It's a 1950. The year they first got it right."

"I didn't know you had such a taste for cars."

"I have a taste for beauty. As my present company indicates."

"Oh Ronny, honestly," Bianca said, and laughed, fully at ease now. She'd always loved this particular verbal game: a kind of competitively complimentary banter.

Jason's turned out to be not quite what she expected: darker and more masculinely solemn. The maître d' recognized Ronny, or recognized him as the sort of person he ought to recognize, and within moments they were seated in a plush maroon-colored booth. Ronny, who might well have chosen to sit at a reserved distance across the table, sat catercorner. To any stranger who happened into Jason's today, the art professor and the housewife might look very much like two people on a date.

"A glass of wine?" Ronny said.

"I'd love a glass of wine."

"It's all right?" He glanced down at the nonexistent bulge in her belly.

"If I'm correct, or I suppose I should say if *you're* correct, in just a few days I'll find out I'm with child and it'll be no more wine for a year or so. And no more cigarettes. Did you know I smoke?"

"I didn't know you smoke."

"I do. And before this lunch is over, I shall have smoked at least two and probably three cigarettes. These are my last days of vice, Ronny."

"I'm told that's what all the girls say . . ."

"No, really. And I've been terrible all week. Drinking like an absolute fish."

"No you haven't," Ronny said. "Hey, I know fish."

"How are your parents?"

Bianca instantly regretted the question, which sounded tactless. Ronny didn't seem to mind, though. "I think it's been hard for Mother, Bea," he said. Ronny almost never called her Bea and it sounded peculiarly intimate—just as it had sounded intimate when, back in the days when she'd been Bea, he'd insisted on calling her Bianca.

"What's hard?"

"Being the world's most beautiful woman after you've hit fifty. Let's face it. I mean, what are you supposed to *do*, exactly? Other than preserve yourself? Which is a mug's game, as old Professor Manhardt might have said. I mean, you can only lose in the end."

Yes, Mrs. Olsson was in her fifties now. It was hard to picture . . .

When the waiter came over, Ronny ordered a bottle of wine. Bianca didn't hear what it was, but she hadn't a doubt in the world she was going to enjoy it.

"Now tell me about the Middle Ages," Bianca said.

"I like them," Ronny said.

"I mean the art."

"I like it. Not to bring up a painful topic—Vienna—but it occurred to me when I finally went to the Kunsthistorisches: painting was essentially over by the time Breughel got going. He was a sort of last gasp."

This was still Ronny being professorial, but with all the difference in the world. That old sense of fun had entered in, a collusive diversion in which Bianca's task was to goad him into broader and broader, wilder and wilder pronouncements. Ronny was going to look at art—*all* of art, the whole of its history—and redraw its outlines, just the way (he hadn't been able to resist, even back then) he'd corrected a drawing of hers on the very day they first met.

"And Vermeer? Not a real painter?"

"Hey, I'd hang the *View of Delft* on my living-room wall. Gladly. But is it so impossible, in the development of any art form, that things go radically, fundamentally awry? Two roads diverge and everybody takes the wrong one?"

"You used to like the Pre-Raphaelites."

"You know, I think I still *do*. How can you not like an artistic movement that says, Oops, let's start over, because one big colossal mistake was made?"

"And Ingres? You always admired Ingres. You taught me how to pronounce his name."

"Well we can surely agree—can't we?—that it's almost cruel to set an Ingres beside a Renoir, say. Or crueler still, beside a Gauguin. I mean, could anyone deny French painting went downhill in the nineteenth century?"

The wine arrived, a white wine. It was from France and—whatever decline the country had been suffering in general—it was delicious.

Ronny said, "But look—I mean really *look* at a painting by Memling. To say nothing of Rogier van der Weyden, whose *Deposition* in the

Prado has to be the most beautiful painting anybody ever painted. The colors. The brushwork. The proportions, not just large to medium, but medium to small, small to minuscule. The, excuse the expression, grandeur. Isn't it possible that everything else is a falling off?

"I'm not a religious person," Ronny went on, "and I don't suppose you are."

"I guess not. I suppose the test is what you do with your children, and we do very little. It's partly not knowing what I would be if I *were* religious. Mamma's either Presbyterian or Lutheran, depending whether she's feeling more Scottish or German. Papa's Catholic, until they tell his sister-in-law Aunt Grace she can't marry Uncle Dennis, and Mom Ives is Episcopalian, the snootier the better, and—"

Ronny was looking just a little impatient.

"No," Bianca said. "I don't suppose I'm religious."

"Nor am I," Ronny said, "but I've come to the conclusion that the phrase 'secular painting' is self-contradictory. Painting's a holy business, Bianca, or it's nothing."

Bianca almost wished he hadn't spoken this way. The words were a reproach, somehow, to herself, to the dearly beloved (and now defunct) Institute Midwest, even to Donald Doobly, the Negro boy, whose worldly hopes of getting ahead, by way of his art, had been so palpable and so touching.

"But that isn't so, Ronny." She wasn't sure, exactly, what she wanted to say, but she knew it was something her whole soul embraced. "To look at an onion, and see only an onion, and go ahead and paint an onion, no angels hovering in the background, no *anything* in the background, only the layers on layers of onion—that's a noble undertaking."

"That van der Weyden *Deposition*? There's not an extraneous detail. Nine figures, and nothing extraneous. I want purity, Bianca."

The words evoked a distant echo—so faraway that if she hadn't finished most of her glass of wine she might never have retrieved it: "You know who you sound just like? Like your father, Ronny."

"My father?"

Ronny's face registered more than disappointment. He looked unnerved.

"That's exactly what he said to me. Or almost exactly. That night at the Coral Club. Remember? The night when your mother—when she made that extraordinary speech about courage, and Jews and Negroes, although she didn't call them Jews and Negroes—"

"I remember. But what are you saying, Bianca?"

"That's what your father said. 'I believe in purity.' Or words very much like them. We'd been dancing."

"It figures."

"And when the music stopped—I remember the song was 'Skylark,' incidentally—he held me by the upper arms and looked me in the eye and said, 'I believe in purity.' "

"That's quite rich, coming from him. So maybe it's time at last to ask: did he ever proposition you, Bianca?"

"What a thing to say! Of course not."

"Then you're a rarity among the girls I went out with."

"Ronny, you mustn't say such— What are you saying?"

"Look, I don't know, I have no proof the man ever actually"—there was a pregnant pause—"bedded any of them. But he did always have to go and sort of—make his statement."

"But your father isn't *like* that," Bianca protested. "No. Mr. Ives, my father-in-law, he's like that. He's had this terrible stroke, he can't really walk, but still he's got to let you know you're always in his sights. The whole time, in his sights. A little poke here, a pinch there. In comparison, your father's a gentleman. And a pussycat."

But this final observation wasn't right. No, Mr. Olsson was a lynx. At bottom, Mr. Ives's wheelchair-bound appetites were a joke—a feeble joke in extremely bad taste, but a joke nonetheless. But there was nothing humorous in the feral hungers of the man who used to pace that vast shadowed mansion in Arden Park, when he wasn't down in his gym, pummeling a leather punching bag.

"Even poor Elizabeth," Ronny said. "He wouldn't leave her alone."

"Who?"

Ronny looked a little affronted. "My ex-wife."

"Yes. Libby. Of course. You know, I knew her in grade school."

Ronny had pretended, minutes ago, not to recognize Grant's name. But Bianca just now hadn't been pretending. Elizabeth who? Libby who? It made Bianca feel peculiar to think of Ronny actually standing at some altar and solemnly taking this girlhood classmate of hers as his lawfully wedded wife. It hardly seemed *right*—and not for the reasons that someone like Grant might suppose.

"And you found my father attractive," Ronny said.

"*If* I did, it would never have occurred to me to put it in those terms. Not back then."

"But you found him attractive."

"I suppose in a way I did. I mean, he was good-looking, and charming, and gallant, always complimenting me, and he was this great man, running half the war committees in the city."

She'd thought she could get away with this sort of candor with Ronny, who had always allowed her greater forthrightness than other men allowed. But she'd gone a step too far and hurt him. And—a twin realization—she still owed Ronny a duty to lift his mood at such times. It was this duty that induced her to say what she wouldn't otherwise have said: "But I wasn't attracted to him the way I was attracted to this gorgeous boy in my still-life class who was *very* handsome in his camel's hair coat and tawny suede hat and who drew like an angel. My God, do you know how overwhelmed I was? I'd never seen anything like you."

"I wish you hadn't mentioned the hat." He shook his head in feigned dismay.

"Hey, at least you didn't go around in a red Hungarian beret. Boy, was I *young*." And she'd said just the right thing. Feelings were smoothed and their lunch could resume . . .

She loved the wine and she took Ronny's advice in everything. Both ordered duck à l'orange and green salads and they both had a second glass of wine. And Bianca had a cigarette. "Is it a boy or a girl?" Ronny said.

For just a moment her brain played a weird trick and she honestly didn't know what he was talking about. Then she said, "A girl."

"And her name?"

Bianca didn't know she had a name prepared but it turned out she did. She exhaled the lofty syllables on a balmy cloud of cigarette smoke: "Maria."

"Why Maria?"

It turned out, too, she had a solid explanation. "With sons named Matt and Chip? Maybe it's time to pay some Italian dues. And won't Papa be pleased?"

"I think you have the most beautiful name of anyone I've ever met."

"Bea Ives?"

Ronny smiled and ignored her. "I didn't believe it at first. That tall, slim, beautiful girl in Professor Manhardt's class, who nodded so sensibly when he uttered some pseudo-British twaddle, could she really be called Bianca Paradiso?"

Ronny was returning a compliment, but he didn't need to. And probably shouldn't. "Ronny, I think you've had too much wine. Or I have."

"I think *you've* had the perfect amount of wine. You've got a fine flush."

"I think I've had way too much wine or why would I be feeling as if I wanted to cry?"

"There's nothing to cry about."

"Ronny," she said, "I don't know what's the matter with me. Honestly. Listen, please. All this week—a solid week now—I've been feeling as though I'm coming unhinged. As though every other moment I'm going to start crying, or bang my head against the wall, or get in the car and not stop till I reach Mexico. You're smiling but it isn't the least bit funny. For other people it may not be so worrisome when they find themselves feeling strange and disoriented and impulsive, but they don't have a mother who often seems halfway to the loony bin. I do. It scares me. And you may remember I spun out of control myself once and wound up treating my aunt and uncle's home in Cleveland as a private sanitarium. It does something to you. I sometimes think I'm only now beginning to understand what it all did to me. How *burned* I was."

"You're just pregnant, Bianca. That's all it is."

"Do you know I changed my clothes three times this morning?"

"So? I changed my tie."

"You know what's the oddest thing in my life? I don't know what's the oddest thing in your life, but you know what's the oddest thing in my life?"

"Now there's a good question. What's the oddest thing in my life?"

"The oddest thing in my life is that I'm the mother of twins who, so far as I can tell, have absorbed nothing, no genetic whatever-it-is, from me. It isn't merely that the twins look exactly like Grant, though they do—to an extent that actually makes people laugh aloud. Really, I've seen it! I've seen total strangers point and laugh when Grant and the boys walk down the street in their matching Keds. People call them the Ives triplets. The boys tilt their *heads* the same way Grant does when they tie their shoes, they clear their *throats* the same way, they hold their hands the same way when they *yawn.* I'm telling you, my little boys couldn't *learn* this stuff. Not to *this* degree of detail. It's got to be in their blood. But now think about what I'm saying, Ronny: is the way you yawn and walk and clear your throat in your *blood*? And if so, where does that leave you, Ronny? I mean, what are we? What are people?"

Of course there was nobody else in the world with whom Bianca might share a conversation ending with a passionate *What are people?*

And Ronny was there for her. He was weighing her every word. "At this point," he said, "I don't know what's in my blood."

"I don't mean to sound arrogant, but I think of myself as—well, a vivid presence. And so how can I have two kids who don't resemble me in the slightest? Not in the slightest . . . And why does my saying this make me want to cry?"

"I don't know, honey." Honey? "It's just a difficult time."

They had both had two glasses but there was still wine left in the bottle, which Ronny scrupulously divided.

"I don't know if this is such a good idea, Olsson," she said.

"It's a perfectly swell idea, Paradiso," he said. "Propitious, even."

"Ronny," she said. "You know I slept with Henry Vanden Akker?"

"I know," Ronny said.

"How did you know?"

"I just knew."

"But how did you know?"

"I just knew."

"I never told Grant. I never told anyone—except Maggie." Only after the sentence was out did Bianca understand that it wasn't—a realization that made her head spin a little—true. On another restaurant occasion, likewise unsteadied by an Olsson-chosen bottle of wine, she'd made a similar confession. To Ronny's mother. On that astounding afternoon when Mrs. Olsson had all but offered up her son in marriage.

"You could have told me," Ronny said.

"I could have?"

"You could have."

"It was just the one time."

"Really? I didn't know that."

"Yes, just the once, what did you think?" A slight resentment stirred toward the beautiful Ronny Olsson. She let it go.

"It must have been a powerful attraction."

"Not as much as—" Again, she let it go.

She said, "I was always going to tell Grant. I was. I was going to tell him after we got engaged. I was going to tell him the day of our wedding, I was going to tell him at the hotel, the first night of our honeymoon, but you know what happened?"

"No," Ronny said.

"Forgive me for telling you this, I can't believe I'm telling you this, but he'd had way too much champagne, at the reception, and as it hap-

pened, well, I was at the end of my period, you know, and there was a little blood on the sheets, and he was so touchingly *grateful* I'd saved
myself—so it was too late to say anything. Ronny Olsson," she said, "you
are the first person ever to hear the intimate details of that story, and if
you don't say something quick, I really *am* going to cry."

"Let's go for a drive," Ronny said.

Bianca hadn't known it, but this proposal was exactly what she'd
longed to hear. "I'd love to go for a drive with you, Ronny," she said.

They headed west, not the way they would have headed usually, back
in the old days. They weren't so far from Mexicantown and she said,
"Remember the night you taught me what a taco was?"

"Sure I remember."

"There was an old man with an enormous moustache asleep against
the wall."

"The owner."

"The owner?"

"His daughter was the one waiting on us."

"I didn't mention him because I was embarrassed."

"Embarrassed about what, Bianca?"

"Embarrassed that you'd taken me to such a dive? Maybe? Of course
it was thrilling."

"Señorita, if that's the worst dive you've ever been in . . ."

Bianca fished a couple of mints out of her purse, fearing she might
smell of cigarettes. Ronny turned onto the Boulevard, though this was
hardly what she thought of as *the* Boulevard. This was West Grand
Boulevard and for her the Boulevard would always be East Grand
Boulevard. They turned again and came abruptly—powerfully—to a
view of the Ambassador Bridge.

"I've always loved the bridge," Bianca said.

"Of course you have. It's your earliest memory."

"My earliest memory?"

"You told me once. Your earliest memory was looking up at the
bridge, back when it was being built. You were in Corktown, at your
aunt and uncle's, and you saw a workman silhouetted against the sky."

And how on earth was it possible she'd almost forgotten this? How
on earth, how on earth was it possible for Ronny to remember her earliest memory better than she did? And now she really *would* cry. If something didn't happen, soon, she must cry, because otherwise her failure
was insupportable. She was supposed to have a good memory. (Maggie

said it all the time: "I don't have to remember anything, because Bianca remembers everything and she's my memory.") What was happening? *How on earth* had she nearly forgotten the man on the bridge? And it was at this moment that Ronny said, "Bianca, may I kiss you?"

"I don't think that's such a good idea" was what she meant to reply. What in fact she did say was only slightly different—"Do you think that's such a good idea?"—but sufficiently different for Ronny to interpret her words as an assent. Which he did. He leaned across the car, placed one hand on her shoulder and one on the nape of her neck, and—a shockingly simple matter, accomplished merely by inclining toward her—kissed her deeply.

Given her cigarettes, Bianca was glad suddenly for those two mints, though they did raise the question of whether she'd known the kiss was coming. She knew the kiss, anyway. When his mouth came open, invitingly, her mouth opened. She knew nothing at all, really—except this one most fundamental of all truths: no one had ever kissed her as Ronny kissed her. The kiss went on and on. And those colors were still there. It was amazing. (Oh, it was all about color—colors hatching themselves free of their objects . . .) Nine years elapse and it turns out the colors are still there—Ronny's spectrum, and nobody else's spectrum. Nine years fall away and you might be a teenage girl again, necking in Palmer Park with the handsomest boy in the city!

Their lips came reluctantly, adhesively apart and Bianca thought for a moment—feared for a moment—that the kiss had proved what it meant to prove, and there wouldn't be another. But its hunger fed a hunger, and Ronny kissed her again, and yet again.

When they finally stopped for breath, she said, "Oh God."

"Oh God," Ronny said.

And though she'd spoken not so long ago about her lack of religion, she proclaimed now, with something very like religious fervor, "God bless you, Ronny Olsson."

"God bless you, Bianca Paradiso."

"I'm—very surprised," she said.

"Not half so much as I am," Ronny said, with a show of a laugh, though it turned into a sort of gasp at the end.

She went a step further. "You saw the colors?" she said.

"I saw the colors."

"The same ones?"

"The very same, darling."

Darling?

"You know this is madness," Bianca said.

"Total madness."

What could be crazier, three days before you were about to learn you were pregnant, than to go out to lunch with Ronny Olsson and drink half a bottle of wine and ride tipsily around town and then to park before the Ambassador Bridge and wind up necking in a sports car with somebody your husband would call an old fruit?

It wasn't that Grant wouldn't forgive her. (He had no choice, given the way he'd once behaved with Maggie.) But he wouldn't understand—which was no fault of his own, since nobody on earth could ever understand except Ronny and herself. Not even poor Libby, who had once walked down the aisle toward a dream incarnation of a groom at the altar.

It made Bianca very, very uneasy to entertain such comparisons, but there was no possible ignoring how, even if this was only kissing, it was kissing of a different variety than she was used to. With Grant, physical exchanges took place through a code of humor—a warm and often wonderful humor: all the sweet shared silliness of his Irish brogue. *Would the lass be lookin' for some lovin'?* But there was nothing the least bit funny to Ronny's kisses. They were beautiful, and they were desperate—and how could Grant understand?

It was knowledge only she and Ronny shared: just how close they had always been to being the perfect couple. All those hours when they used to neck in the park, hips wedded, the press of what she'd first taken for his belt buckle such an insistent presence against her belly . . . She had aroused him then and this was a condition that went on and on, as they'd kissed and kissed. None of this could be acknowledged back then, not even to each other: the way he'd sometimes stain his trousers with a few drops of leakage, the way she'd come home with what she then called her unders soaked through. The most intimate fluids in their bodies were frantically signaling to each other. They were the truest thing in the world, those luminous fluids, and they understood nothing of the world's mundane demands: some things couldn't be said, could hardly be thought . . .

They were two kids in love with painting, who longed above all to be painters, and the painters within their souls recognized it at a glance: you merely had to strip the clothes away, and body was calling to body, essential form to essential form. And that was why, for all the evidence that could be mounted to the contrary, she could never take fully seriously Grant's talk of old fruits. No, there was a level where Ronny *loved* her—and would always love her. Yes, she was his true *darling*.

. . . There was a level, there was a world . . . Over the years she'd heard enough from Uncle Dennis about alternative worlds for the notion to fertilize her imagination. There existed worlds nearly as real as our own. And on one such world—some hot rapidly spinning ball in space—she and Ronny must always be together. For they were the two most passionate lovers on that planet.

CHAPTER XXIX

The next stop, the next day, was obvious: over to Priscilla's, first thing in the morning. Bianca often joked with Grant about how visits to Priscilla's were trips to the head doctor, but this was no joke: she needed a head doctor.

Priscilla lived alone, in a surprisingly modest ranch house out near Schaeffer and Seven Mile. The first time Bianca had visited, Priscilla said, "It isn't much, but it suits me fine." This phrase, *it isn't much*, turned out to be something of a happy motto for her, if less happy for her guests. "It isn't much," she'd say, pushing toward you a platter of hors d'oeuvres consisting of four pimento-stuffed olives and two wizened radishes, "but we'll make do." Or: "It isn't much," she'd say, having laboriously unearthed a dusty bottle of sherry, less than an inch of liquid sloshing in the bottom, "but I think it will suffice."

Priscilla's wonderful parents had died when she was still in her twenties. Her father, only fifty-two, dropped dead one morning of a heart attack while shaving. Her mother, far too dedicated to her husband to carry on without him, soon succumbed to cancer. Priscilla was much older than Bea—thirty-eight. More imposing still, though, were her educational degrees: Mount Holyoke for college, Ann Arbor for medical school. She was a psychiatrist.

Mount Holyoke was one of those distant institutions Bianca had long read about in the *News*. Its graduates belonged to a social class whose engagements and weddings made the society page. But Priscilla wasn't anything like Bianca's image of a Mount Holyoke graduate. She was frequently disheveled, as if she belonged in the somewhat run-down neighborhood she called home. Priscilla must have money, surely. Her parents once did: Bianca had seen the magnificent house in Indian Village where Priscilla had grown up.

There were a good many peculiarities to Priscilla's story, actually, not the least of which was the extent of her medical practice. Priscilla stayed home a great deal, puttering around in her backyard garden—which, for all the time she spent there, hardly flourished: this wasn't a woman with a green thumb. Grant joked that she was the city's only doctor who had no patients, but Priscilla did have a real—if small—office and occasionally a patient telephoned while Bianca was visiting. Priscilla apparently worked part-time.

She was devoted to her brother, whom she visited almost every day. Michael lived in an institution for retarded adults way out in Farmington. Bianca had gone out there with Priscilla a few times.

Before meeting Michael, Bianca had let her imagination blossom, envisioning a troubled but strikingly handsome and unpredictably shrewd fellow. She'd met instead a bland, plump, genial, middle-aged man identifiable, at a glance, as retarded. Every time Priscilla visited, she brought him a little gift-wrapped present to unwrap: a box of raisins, a pink, rubbery eraser, a campaign button for Adlai Stevenson and John Sparkman. Michael liked unwrapping things.

"I saw Ronny Olsson yesterday," Bianca said, after Priscilla had brought her a cup of tea.

"Ronny Olsson! Imagine that. And how is he?"

One of the things Bianca liked best about Priscilla was how little prompting her memory required. She seemed to hold effortlessly in her head the dense, radiating web of everyone Bianca had ever known.

"Well, I'm not sure," Bianca said. "We went to the art institute, and then downtown for lunch to a fancy place called Jason's."

"Jason's? Never heard of it."

"It's relatively new, and we shared a bottle of wine, and then we went for a drive, out to where my earliest memory is."

"The Ambassador Bridge?"

Did *everybody* know better than she herself what her earliest memory was? Honestly, what was going on?

"And that was the strange thing. I think it was all the wine, or how positively bizarre I've been feeling all week, but when Ronny mentioned my earliest memory, I had no idea what he was talking about."

"The man on the bridge. As images go, it's archetypal."

In response to Priscilla's questioning look, Bianca felt she must show her familiarity with the term. "Archetypal? Not so archetypal that I remembered it yesterday. And then you know what happened? Oh, Priscilla, I'm so mortified: I let him kiss me. Is that so terrible?"

"Maybe not so terrible?" Priscilla said.

Priscilla had quite a distinctive tone of voice. It was little-girlish—at times very close to baby talk.

"Under the circumstances," Priscilla added, and laughed. Her laugh, too, was peculiar. It was the closest thing Bianca had ever heard to the tee-hee-hee of someone laughing in the funny pages: a high, whispery, almost hissing sound, all mouth and no throat, like an infant's laugh.

"You're thinking of that Christmas party when I caught Grant necking with Maggie."

Bianca brought this up partly to excuse her own behavior. The ironic and alarming truth, however, was that yesterday's behavior felt nothing like an act of vengeance. No, it seemingly had little to do with Grant.

"Yes, I was."

The effect of the little-girl voice and babyish laugh was to suggest great innocence, but in conversation Priscilla was the opposite of innocent. Over the course of their friendship, Priscilla had turned out to be far more shocking than shocked—as when she'd happened to mention, with a little whispery tee-hee-hee, that one of her patients, a burly Chrysler foreman, regularly relaxed after work by listening to adventure shows on the radio while wearing nothing but a pair of tight bright-pink women's panties. (Bianca was almost sorry Priscilla had told her this. It was an image—the tight bright pink—she had trouble shaking from her head.) Bianca had assumed that such activities existed only in books, or in New York City. In any case, not in Detroit . . . A genuine *Chrysler* foreman wearing women's underwear while listening to the *Lone Ranger* or the All-American Boy, Jack Armstrong of the SBI?

"I thought Ronny was a homosexual," Priscilla said. She always pronounced it with each vowel distinct—ho-mo-sex-u-al—as though establishing the point that it wasn't a term one ought to mumble. Still, the word was startling enough that Bianca typically felt a jolt in her blood upon hearing it spoken aloud. Priscilla was the only person she knew who regularly uttered it.

In truth, Priscilla talked so often of ho-mo-sex-u-als, and les-bi-ans, that initially Bianca had wondered whether Priscilla herself might be one of the latter—began to wonder, indeed, whether this woman who apparently had little social life besides visits to her retarded brother might have formed some sort of passionate attachment to *her*, Bianca. Later, Bianca had realized how misguided she was. Priscilla had finally introduced the subject of Dr. Cuttwell, and there was no mistaking the flushed, rapturous look on the woman's face: Priscilla was hopelessly smitten.

"I thought he was one, too. Or at least part of me finally did. Agreed with Grant when he called Ronny an old fruit. But there was always contrary evidence."

"Evidence?" The word amused Priscilla, who emitted her little laugh: tee-hee-hee.

"You see, well, Ronny finds me attractive. He always has. I excite him. I did again yesterday. I happened to see."

"He had an erection?"

Oh good Lord. This sort of talk was all so much easier with Maggie—with her slapdash, breezy chatter about "his thing" and "your thing." Priscilla's more medical-sounding language brought home all the disturbing physical reality—Ronny's "thing" suddenly tingled with blood and nerve endings. Still, Bianca pushed on: "Yes, he did. I guess what I'm asking, it's the question I keep asking myself, is, Is it possible?"

"Is what possible?"

"Is it possible for Ronny to be both one of them and still be very attracted to me? I can't put the pieces together."

"Certainly it's possible. The heart is a very . . . disorganized organ." And that high hissing conspiratorial laugh again: tee-hee-hee.

Priscilla said: "It doesn't always go where we choose. At least that's *my* experience." Over the top of her glasses, she gave Bianca a nod of unmistakable meaning.

This was a reference to Dr. Cuttwell, of whom Priscilla often spoke, though usually, like this, in roundabout fashion. Bianca had known Priscilla for many months before the name in all its improbable but magnificent grandeur—Doctor Oliver Cuttwell—had been uttered. But one day, in this kitchen, over soggy Saltines and a half tin of smoked oysters, Priscilla had offered up something of her life story. In addition to a retarded brother, she'd had a hydrocephalic sister, Lois, who died when Priscilla was in medical school. Given her two handicapped siblings, Priscilla had concluded she must never have children and she'd reconciled herself to a single life. She would care for Michael.

She had dated a number of men over the years but nobody who shook her vow to remain single. Then she met Dr. Cuttwell, whom she could not have married but who evoked a tantalizing image of what an ideal partner might be. Dr. Cuttwell was a good deal older, exactly twenty years older than Priscilla. He was now fifty-eight. Dr. Cuttwell's wife had multiple sclerosis and was confined to a wheelchair. They had talked—Priscilla and Dr. Cuttwell—about the tremendous burden of caring for somebody unable to care for himself or herself. It was a topic of great delicacy, of course, but a deep, respectful bond of appreciation had been forged. A conventional romance was, alas, impossible, but the two of them had chastely entered into—Priscilla's quaint phrase—an affair of the heart. In time, Dr. Cuttwell had revealed that Priscilla was the only one who truly understood his life . . .

"I feel very guilty," Bianca went on, "but I can't get yesterday out of my head."

"Which part?"

"All of it."

"In particular, the kissing under the bridge?"

"I suppose."

"And that erection of his?"

"That, too, I suppose. I mean, I'd like to know what it means. Oh, doesn't *that* sound awful."

"Some people would say that what it means is obvious."

"I know. Maggie would."

"But I don't think it's necessarily so obvious."

"What I can tell you is—the whole experience was very, very powerful."

"Of course it was. What did the experience mean for Ronald Olsson? I don't know. But for you?"

There were times when that little-girl voice of Priscilla's, and the evasive old-womanish game she played of looking over and through her glasses, in conjunction with that absurd hissing laugh, made her seem almost painfully antic and eccentric, leaving Bianca to feel like a fool for confiding in her. But then in the midst of her absurd posturing, a wonderfully insightful observation would surface. One of those emerged now.

"Of course it was powerful. No wonder you can't get that erection out of your head. You were encountering your earliest memory: at last you were meeting your man on the bridge."

Bianca would have liked to linger at Priscilla's, discussing further the mistake she'd made in letting her feelings for Ronny run away with her, and for letting him kiss her, and for forgetting her true principles, but she needed to rush home in case he called. Surely he would call. What he would say, how she would reply—these were open questions. But he must call. He would understand the need to acknowledge yesterday's momentous turn.

But Ronny didn't call, not before Bianca and her family finally climbed into the Studebaker and drove to her parents-in-law's. Usually, Bianca would have been hurrying everybody out of the house—punctuality wasn't one of Grant's virtues—but today she was easygoing. Tense but easygoing. She was awaiting a call from Ronny, and he did not call.

The truth was, there was something faintly irritating about the cheerfulness with which Grant visited his parents. He seemed to feel none of the apprehension she regularly experienced before visiting her own parents. Grant never grew pensive as they drove up Waddington, his parents' street in Birmingham, even though the Ives household was usually in a deplorable state. Had Grant wanted to turn morose, he had every excuse.

On this particular Sunday, Grant's cheerfulness was especially annoying, the traffic was especially annoying, the twins' competitive banter in the backseat (they were looking for cars with out-of-state license plates) was especially annoying—and why hadn't Ronny called? And then—almost a relief—she was swallowed up by the various demands of the Ives home.

It had been two years now since Mr. Ives's stroke, and though he could get around with a cane—barely—he was essentially chair-bound. He'd never regained the use of his right side. He was right-handed. Before his stroke, Mr. Ives had been a powerful man—one of the city's leading bankers—and his infirmities galled him.

The twins' actual time inside the house, greeting their grandparents, was probably less than two minutes. Irresistible temptation beckoned. In the backyard of Grandpa and Grandma Ives's house stood a huge oak from which a knotted rope swing dangled.

So the group was reduced to the four adults, plus of course the hired help, since Mrs. Ives couldn't be expected to deal alone with Mr. Ives's disability—though the truth was that Mrs. Ives had employed live-in help years before Mr. Ives's stroke.

This particular visit ran true to form, though Bianca felt far less patient than usual—why hadn't Ronny called? She was greeted with a little kiss from her mother-in-law, who looked pained and overworked—pointedly pained and overworked. Bianca greeted her seated father-in-law with a stooping kiss delivered from a safe distance.

Before his stroke, Mr. Ives had been a tireless womanizer—a mortifying situation that Mrs. Ives had refused to acknowledge. He was flagrant, she was closemouthed. His stroke, ironically, reversed everything: immobilizing Mr. Ives's body, loosening Mrs. Ives's tongue. At any gathering, she could be counted upon to pull Bianca aside and catalogue a numbing list of Mr. Ives's marital offenses, past and present— yes, present as well, for, though largely confined to his wheelchair, he still had wandering hands.

How did Grant manage to remain so cheerful about his parents? Partly by shrugging off every observation Bianca made about his mother's bitterness. While Grant might acknowledge his parents' "ups and downs," he steadfastly refused to see what Bianca saw so clearly: how profoundly, after all her years of humiliation, Mrs. Ives disliked her husband.

Yes, this visit ran true to form, and the dreaded moment arrived when Mrs. Ives motioned Bianca into the den and, with an exasperating broad-gestured theatricality, closed the door behind them. The boys were still out back, swinging on the rope swing, and Grant and his father were swapping jokes and anecdotes out in the family room. They got along famously, Grant and his father.

"I'm going to lose Edna," Mrs. Ives said.

"Edna?"

"One of the nurses and she's seventy-three."

Mr. Ives's nurses came and went with such rapidity that Bianca had trouble distinguishing them. "I'm sorry," she said.

"She told me, 'As a great-grandmother, I'm tired of having to watch my backside.' "

"I'm so very sorry," Bianca said. She was sorry, too, that Mrs. Ives was telling her this. This was no day to hear about illicit passions—not when she was feeling crestfallen that Ronny hadn't called.

"You remember at first I thought I'd be safe with Negroes, since Mr. Ives isn't—isn't all that fond of Negroes."

Mr. Ives was actually quite genial and respectful toward Negroes, except when, as happened only occasionally, he got into his cups. Then he could say quite shocking, virulent things.

"I remember."

"But that didn't stop him. Pinching and poking and squeezing— and the worst of it was, they were willing to put up with it. Well, one of them was."

"Yes."

"So then I figured I'd go with real homeliness. Bianca, I hired some women whose faces would stop a clock."

"I remember the one named Dolores."

"Dolores? Truly, I found it painful to look at her. But did that stop him?"

"No," Bianca inserted into the expectant silence. She could hear the boys outside, ecstatically calling challenges to each other. She could hear Grant and his father, laughing together over one of Grant's jokes. (It was one of the many things Grant did for his father—saved up for the weekend the funny stories he'd heard during the working week.) She wished she were somewhere other than behind closed doors with her mother-in-law. But Mrs. Ives was inescapable.

"So then I figured, age was the only safeguard . . . And now I've got a seventy-three-year-old great-grandmother telling me she's tired of having to watch her backside. I ask you: what am I going to do with that man?"

"I wish I knew . . ."

Here was a gruesome example of everything Bianca had been thinking about these past few days. Having somebody under your thumb? Mr. Ives had had Mrs. Ives under his thumb for forty years, exposing her to every womanly humiliation imaginable, but nowadays he had nobody under his thumb. And only his intense self-preoccupation blinded him to a realization that otherwise must be crushing. What had he harvested in forty years of married life? Didn't the woman hate him? The creased expression etched into her face—it suggested raw hatred.

Still, it was hard to be fully sympathetic with Mrs. Ives when you watched dinner materialize: she'd neither cooked the meal nor would she serve it. She apparently felt it was enough—it was her nature-appointed role—to carp about how it was cooked and served. Even if Bianca didn't say it outright, someone else might: the woman had done all right for herself. Though Grant would deny the accusation—not so much hotly as uncomprehendingly—Mrs. Ives had been a negligent mother. And when Grant had gone off to college, a dozen years ago, her maternal responsibilities had all but come to an end.

Bianca had grown up with the notion that once you'd finished Sunday dinner you must commence a serious cleanup. But not in the Ives household, since the cook and the maid would wordlessly handle it. The rest of them were free. Laughing, kicking at each other's heels, the twins scurried to the backyard. Grant and his father resettled in the family room. Again Grant took up the topic of his law firm, Cutting and Fuller, and of Detroit business scuttlebutt generally. As each new name surfaced, Mr. Ives, in his jovial way, chuckling contentedly, dismissed one man after another: "Oh Danley, yeah, he's a real bastard," and "Isaacson, he's a *real* bastard," and "As for Hutchins, he'd sell his sons for a saw-buck, the bastard." And Smythe? "That son of a bitch? He's a real *bastard.*"

Bianca was led, all too inevitably, back behind the den's closed door. But what happened next was unexpected. "You know, Grant has a big birthday coming up."

"He sure does, Mrs. Ives." Grant would turn thirty on September twenty-eighth.

Some, though perhaps not most, of Bianca's friends called their mothers-in-law by their first names—though Mrs. Ives would certainly never permit that. Some called them "Mom" or "Mamma" plus their last name—but Bianca would never wish to do that. The solution was to insert just a hint of a weary protest when reciting that name, which was also her own name: Mrs. Ives, Mrs. Ives, Mrs. Ives.

"And I want to give him a present, a very special present."

"That's very kind," Bianca said.

"Now, you know Mr. Ives doesn't approve when I do anything lavish for the children. He says they have to make their own way."

Grant's two sisters were usually so distant, and so little spoken of, that they were easily forgotten. The elder, Kate, had married a ne'er-do-well mechanic and lived in Flagstaff, Arizona. The younger, Nancy, had married an actual missionary, a Presbyterian, and lived in Bangkok, Thailand. It seemed safe to say both girls had deliberately settled far from home.

Yes, Mr. Ives believed that children must make their own way—that was one plausible interpretation. Another was that he loved having his hands on the purse strings while they yearningly looked on. It galled him that Nancy, the missionary's wife, wasn't angling for any early slice of an inheritance. And it pleased him, though he railed endlessly, that Kate was always "trying to stick up the old man." To Grant's credit, he honestly didn't look for any financial boon from his father. Still, there was the knowledge that eventually it would be there—and in abundance.

"But I have some money of my own. Which I can spend as I please. I don't need his say-so."

"Not if it's yours . . ."

"For Grant's thirtieth birthday, I want to buy him a car."

"A *car*? Oh, Mrs. Ives."

"A car of his choosing. You can help him pick it out, dear."

"Oh, Mrs. Ives."

"Mr. Ives will *not* be pleased. But I'm going to do it anyway."

It was a wonderful, prodigal, astounding gift, and Grant would naturally be overjoyed. Bianca, too, felt joy—though tempered immediately by something else, a gradually clarifying sense of frustration. Oh, never in a million years would she convince Grant of what had secretly inspired the gift. In all his warmhearted gratitude, Grant would never perceive that cold hostility—Mrs. Ives's decades-long resentment of her husband—was the chief motivation.

Bianca had the house to herself by eight the next morning. Grant was off early to work and the twins had flown outdoors, equipped with two glass jars into whose tin lids she'd poked holes with an awl. One of their friends had seen a frog in a ditch near Hampton School.

It made sense, in retrospect, that Ronny hadn't called yesterday, when everyone was apt to be home. What didn't make sense was his failure to call this morning. What was he thinking?

Another night's sleep had left her feeling less desperate but more resentful. Didn't Ronny feel the need to talk? Hadn't they always understood each other so well? It pained her to think he wasn't trusting in their shared ability to sort things out.

Imagining his call, Bianca saw herself breezily laughing off the entire afternoon: "I guess I *did* have too much wine." Or saw herself speaking with a noble veracity that reproached his craven evasiveness: "I have the very deepest feelings for you, Ronny, and I want to thank you for a day I'll never forget." She read the *Free Press* and waited for his call, tidied the kitchen and waited for his call, took a bath rather than a shower so she would not miss his call. But Ronny did not call.

The twins came home late in the morning and each wolfed down two tuna sandwiches with sweet pickle relish and three glasses of milk. Then they were off again—they loved these summer days. Bianca realized that she'd forgotten to have breakfast and was actually ravenous. She made herself a tuna sandwich and, after only a slight pause, poured herself a glass of her father's wine—something she would normally *never* have done. Not on a weekday, not when eating by herself. "I'm sinking fast," she said aloud. It was all excessively histrionic—the wine, the talking to herself. But hardly so by another light: she *was* feeling anxious, she *was* intensely confused. Tomorrow morning, at ten o'clock, she would see Dr. Stimpson, who would inform her that she was pregnant.

As she poured a second glass of wine, she spoke to herself once more: "I'm not one of those wives," she declared, and then she said, "I'm going to call *him*." The wine would strengthen her resolve. But she didn't call. Instead, having finished the tuna, she made herself a grape-jelly-and-cream-cheese sandwich, something she rarely ate these days. When she'd finished the sandwich, and the wine, she telephoned Ronny.

Ronny wasn't home. He was doing nothing, *nothing* to reach her. She poured herself a half glass of wine. It would serve him right, when he finally thought to call, if he got no answer. She would track down the boys and take them off to a park. It was a beautiful day. Or she would get a sitter, who would be here when the boys returned, and she would visit Maggie, or Priscilla. But she did nothing of the sort. Instead, she telephoned Ronny.

Again, no answer.

By the time Grant got home from work, her mood was poisonous. He seemed in quite a foul mood himself, scowling when informed of dinner's delay. He always came home famished. He poured himself a stiff whiskey. She poured herself a glass of wine. The two of them parked themselves at the kitchen table.

Grant quickly got onto one of his most tiresome hobbyhorses: the need to economize. Usually, he was very good about money. He accepted, gratefully, their happy state. Their married life had begun comfortably, with a tidy inheritance from his little-mourned grandmother Ives, who had conveniently died a week after his college graduation. They had a lovely home. They had two cars. (They would have a third soon—though Grant didn't know about his mother's spectacular plans.) They had money in the bank.

But Grant occasionally got into an aggressive, faintly panicky state about money and absurd economies would be suggested—they were going to start using oleo instead of butter, and why did the boys need haircuts quite so often?

On such occasions, Bianca had learned the wisest course was complaisance. Grocery shopping a week later, Grant would look blank when she proposed buying oleo.

Usually, his suggestions were harmless, but tonight, as he was peering hungrily into the refrigerator, his inspiration took a painful, awful turn. Why did they have a milkman? They no longer needed a milkman. It was silly to have milk delivered when they had two cars. And the boys would enjoy hauling the bottles. It was good exercise.

No milk delivery? But what about Mr. Bootmaker, their milkman, big-black-shoed ever-smiling Roy Bootmaker? Bianca was very fond of Mr. Bootmaker, whose elderly little father always rode in the truck.

"Well, it's one thing to be fond of people. It's another to throw away money."

"But he's a friend. I *like* Mr. Bootmaker."

"I like plenty of people. Doesn't mean I have to line their pockets." Grant was spoiling for a fight.

"He cheers me up in the mornings. He's always got a smile."

"How much do we spend a month with Bootmaker?"

"I don't know, offhand."

"What's our yearly bill with Bootmaker?"

This was one of Grant's most lawyerly, irksome tricks of argumentation: once he heard you admit ignorance to something, he would go on asking you the same question in variant forms.

For a moment, a burning rage welled within Bianca's chest, and it appeared the two of them were about to have one of their rare, terrible, blasting arguments, right here in the kitchen before dinner. Fear prickled her skin all over (though Grant's temper was slow to kindle, when finally ignited his whole big body would shake with rage), as well as a giddy kind of righteous excitement. She wouldn't be bullied. Uh-uh. And then, precipitately, her rage collapsed. What had she done all day but sit over glasses of wine waiting for a call from an old boyfriend, whom she'd kissed many, many times while parked in his green MG? A sense of shamed unworthiness leaked from her very bones. "We'll cancel the milkman," Bianca murmured. "And now I've got to make dinner."

It pleased her to see Grant immediately so flummoxed. She did this to him fairly often: effectively won an argument—won it from a moral standpoint—by abruptly, graciously conceding defeat. "It's the logical thing to do," Grant insisted, but his softening features were already admitting uncertainty.

"I'm sure you're right," Bianca said sweetly.

After dinner, knowing she couldn't confront Mr. Bootmaker face-to-face—it would be disastrous if she started to cry—she wrote him a note, explaining her changed situation and thanking him for his cheerful services. She showed the note to Grant, ostensibly seeking his approval but actually looking to heighten his confusion and remorse. "Oh it's a fine thing, lass," he said. He was wanting to make peace. He was making preliminary amorous overtures. "Thank you," she replied coolly.

She would leave the note in the milk chute. As an afterthought, although the milkman generally wasn't somebody you tipped, she wrote a P.S. explaining that she wanted him to have a very early Christmas gift, and slipped a ten-dollar bill into an envelope, on which she, warming to the task, wrote out his full name with an artful script—Mister Roy Bootmaker—and then drew a little holly wreath. The P.S. wasn't something she showed Grant. Yet even as she was sketching the wreath, embellishing it with little Christmas bells that called out for a bright red pencil, which she would supply, in her heart of hearts Bianca knew this wasn't the end of the matter.

The next day, she found out what she already knew: she was pregnant. The news was almost anticlimactic.

Of course the news changed everything. She was going to have a baby next year, in the middle of May. The baby would come with the spring. She would have to buy new clothes soon. Fashions had changed since she last needed maternity clothes; her tastes had changed. And she would have to decide who was going to be told when. She was going to have a baby, and this time around, the child would bear *some* resemblance to its mother. This time around, she would have a girl . . .

The fight, or near-fight, of the night before belonged to a buried past. Maybe the two of them had been more anxious than they realized, awaiting the official news? But such explanations, too, belonged to a buried past. Had she really sat around all yesterday, soaking up wine like some slatternly housewife and waiting in vain for Ronny to call and waiting, too, to squabble with Grant? How did any of this connect with the quickened, wholesome world she now inhabited?

The following day, Wednesday afternoon, she didn't at first recognize the little man who shuffled hesitantly up her front walk. It was Mr. Bootmaker Senior.

She didn't know him, partly because she never saw him anywhere except behind the wheel of his truck (he did the driving, while his son lugged the deliveries), and partly because he was so much shorter than she'd imagined, and partly because he'd removed his checkered cap. And put on a suit and tie.

"Oh *no*," Bianca groaned, but she wore a smile on opening the door. "Mr. Bootmaker. Very nice to see you."

"Mrs. Ives." He bowed his bare head. She hadn't realized he was mostly bald, and that his face was so lined.

"You've come because I've canceled service."

"Indeed, ma'am." The little man looked just miserable, standing out on her front porch. "Roy has no idea I'm here."

"Please, you must come in." She would have to be courteous, of course. But whatever else, she must stand firm. She'd made such a point of deferring to Grant, who so rarely put his foot down. She would respect Grant's judgment . . .

More hesitantly still, Mr. Bootmaker stepped inside with his hands extended, as though parting veils. He'd been driving up to this house for years, but evidently this was the first time he'd stepped inside. He posted himself beside the mantel.

"Please, you must sit down."

"I never mind standing," Mr. Bootmaker said. Given how diminutive he was, it was odd that his son was so big-boned. In his sweet, beaming way, Roy had more than once complained to Bianca about the burden of finding shoes that fit. He wore a size 12½ EEE.

"Let me get you something, Mr. Bootmaker. A cup of coffee? A bottle of beer?"

"Don't need a thing myself, ma'am. I'll just be a moment of your time. I apologize for disturbing you."

"You're not disturbing me. I'm glad to see you."

Bianca wasn't certain whether she ought to remain standing, given Mr. Bootmaker's refusal of a seat. She sat down on the couch and said, "I've been feeling very bad about this. But we have two cars, you see."

The little man looked down at his hands, which he had linked and knotted at his waist, and said, "Mrs. Ives, I don't know whether you're aware. My boy's health?" He looked up from his hands and stared her straight in the eye. "Roy has epilepsy. He's an epileptic."

"Oh my, oh no, I didn't know. I'm so sorry," Bianca said. "He's never mentioned it."

"He wouldn't, would he? Roy? Nor would he be quick about forgiving me if he knew I'd come tonight. Not our Roy. Oh no. He thinks I'm playing pinochle. But I thought the word might have got round the neighborhood. Some weeks back, he had a little seizure in Mrs. Dahle's kitchen up the street. Do you know Mrs. Dahle?"

"Hardly at all."

"After that, she canceled on us. I thought the word about him might have got round, you see. People don't understand there's no harm in it."

"But Mr. Bootmaker, you honestly don't think I would cancel because . . ." Bianca let the sentence drop. The idea was almost too hurtful for words.

"He can't drive a car, of course. That's why I do the driving."

"I never knew that was the reason."

"But I put it to you, ma'am: what other sort of work are they going to give him, people the way they are? This is something he can do, so long as I drive the truck. I watch over him, you see."

"Of course you do." It was going to be disastrous if she started to cry.

"Mrs. Bootmaker, God bless her, she's been gone a long time, you see. So it's just me now watching over the boy. I'm all the family he's got."

"It's still family," Bianca pointed out, as the shadowy room began to fill with ancestral ghosts, one of whom—another little man—she recognized.

"I say to myself, Dicky, you're seventy-seven and you've got to keep going, you can't retire. And you've got to take care of yourself, because you still have a boy to watch out for. You know what that is. You have two sons yourself."

Something heaved within her and it was all decided in a moment.

"Mr. Bootmaker, I've made a terrible mistake."

"Ma'am?"

"I'd like to start up service again. It was my husband who insisted." But this wasn't fair. This wasn't right. She had to take responsibility. The little man before her was seventy-seven years old, and today he'd finished his long route and gone home and put on his one good suit and, swallowing all his pride, driven over to plead with a woman young enough to be his granddaughter. "What I did was wrong," Bianca said. "I don't know what I was thinking to agree to it," she said, but again this wasn't quite fair. "It was wrong. I made a mistake."

"I don't ask on my own behalf. I don't need a thing myself," Mr. Bootmaker said. "It's my boy. I have to watch over him."

"Of course you do." Of course he did: this little old man had to watch over a grizzled "boy" who wore a size 12½ EEE shoe.

"You won't regret it," Mr. Bootmaker said.

"I know I won't, Mr. Bootmaker."

The old man was looking toward the door. His errand successfully run, he was eager to be on his way.

"Well if that's your decision, Mrs. Ives, I have something for you."

"Something for me?" Bianca couldn't imagine what this might be.

Mr. Bootmaker drew from the inner pocket of his suit coat an envelope, on which was artfully written *Mister Roy Bootmaker*, embellished with a holly wreath and little red bells. "If we have you back, Mrs. Ives, that's all the Christmas present Roy and I would ask."

She accepted the envelope. "Let me be the first to say it, then: merry Christmas, Mr. Bootmaker."

The old man smiled broadly, creasing his face in a hundred radiant lines. For the first time since he'd stepped inside, he looked at ease. Any portrait artist would have glimpsed it in an instant: the old man had a wonderful, luminous face.

"It isn't just the milk and eggs," he explained. "Roy will watch out for you. You go on vacation, he checks up on your house. Makes sure everything's all right. It's good to have someone looking out for you."

"Of course it is," Bianca said.

"Good for the entire neighborhood."

"Of course."

"And not a word about my coming today."

"Heavens no. You've been off playing pinochle."

And the old man actually winked at her. He'd been a charmer, once. He was still a charmer. "You're in good hands," Mr. Bootmaker said.

"Good hands," Bianca said.

The breaking of the news to Grant was something to be done thoughtfully. Not that she *needed* to be cautious—not after the official word of her pregnancy. He was feeling *over the moon,* as he kept announcing to everybody. *It's a wee bairn, is it?* The last few nights, the two of them had been jubilantly, passionately celebrating . . .

Still, she wanted things to go smoothly. Ever since Maggie's remarks about Grant's being under her thumb, Bianca had been feeling misgivings about his authority at home, or lack of it. The truth was, he rarely put his foot down as he had over Mr. Bootmaker, and how had she responded? She'd agreed to follow her husband's advice, then done the very opposite.

She waited until Friday, catching him the moment he came home from work. "Grant, I need to talk to you."

Experience had taught her that a direct approach worked best. The very phrase—*Grant, I need to talk to you*—had a way of turning him jittery and accommodating. She took a seat on the living-room sofa; he took a seat across from her, in the armchair.

"Grant, did you know Roy Bootmaker is epileptic?"

"Who?"

"Our—the milkman. The man who has been delivering our milk ever since we moved here."

"No," Grant said. "How would I know that? Did you know?"

"I didn't, but I had a visitor. Mr. Bootmaker Senior."

"Senior?"

"You know—his father? The little man who drives the truck."

Grant's response came quickly: "Listen, either of them has anything to discuss, they can take it up with me." It was one of his most appealing traits—this unnecessary, chivalrous impulse to protect her even from men who posed no threat or problem.

"Roy-the-son can't drive a car. Now what sort of job is he supposed to get?"

"I haven't the faintest idea . . ." Grant paused a moment—he seemed to take the question seriously—and then his expression clouded. "Bianca, you didn't."

"Didn't what?"

"Start up with them again."

Bianca felt her face flush. "Well, yes—yes, I did."

"After you wrote that note and everything?"

"I didn't know the circumstances at the time . . ."

"And what if old Bootmaker Senior got cancer? Would that be a reason for starting up again? What if Roy's house burned down, would that be a reason for starting up again? What if he got an ulcer, would that be a reason for starting up again?"

"Maybe," Bianca said.

Grant's line of questions veered unexpectedly: "And what if I were absolutely to forbid it?"

"What do you mean?"

"What if I said, You and I came to a solemn agreement, Bianca, and now you're reneging, which is wrong, and I absolutely *forbid* it, we're not having the milkman again—what if that's what I said?"

"But you wouldn't do that, Grant."

"I know. I know, I know. But *what if*? I say, *What if*?"

"You wouldn't do that," Bianca repeated.

"I know, I know, and goddamn it we'll have the goddamn milkman back, of course we will, but what if I were to actually *forbid* it? What if I said, Bianca, we made a solemn deal and *you* can't go back on your word? You'd still have him back, wouldn't you? Damn what anybody says, you'd have him back, wouldn't you? *Wouldn't* you?"

The living room had become a courtroom. The two of them considered each other: the attorney and the woman of the house. Grant's face wore an expression of great intensity, but for the moment Bianca couldn't follow his line of thinking. He looked at her dead-on, demanding an answer, and she said, softly but firmly, "Yes, I would still have taken him back."

A queer moment's pause, then Grant's face broke beautifully into a smile, and Bianca saw that everything was all right. This was a smile of pride. In Grant's eyes, she'd passed some sort of crucial test. She wasn't "one of those wives." He'd married someone else.

He stood up and came eagerly to the sofa, sat down beside her, and took her in his arms. "You do what's right, don't you?"

Instantly, she experienced all the warm radiant well-being her husband's praise dependably stirred. She basked in the feeling, and his words allowed her the freedom of graciousness. "I don't know about what's right, sweetie. I just did what I felt I had to do." Her arms had drifted around his back. Her mouth was at the side of his neck. She was murmuring into his ear.

"My tough, *tough* little girl," Grant said, murmuring into *her* ear. "Damn what anybody said. You'd take him back."

"Tough? Don't I wish. Honey, I had to cave in quickly, otherwise I was going to start crying. You know who he suddenly reminded me of? I felt it very vividly. He reminded me of my *nonno*, back from the grave. I was *helpless*. A total pushover. For these little old men with big hearts . . ."

But this wasn't the direction Grant wanted to take. "Wouldn't matter," he said again. "Wouldn't matter what anybody told you. No, you'd take him back. My girl would take him back."

The muscles in Grant's big shoulders were quivering and she understood, belatedly, what he was referring to. He too was looking into the past. She'd tried to put that distant day behind her, as an insurmountable embarrassment. But Grant had never put it behind him. He never would. Yes, one day she'd left him a note—another of her notes!—and she and his children had gone away on a train. And having left his law firm early, he'd driven down to Cleveland at a hundred miles an hour to plead the case of his life. And his tough, *tough* little girl—the one who did what was right, damn what anybody said? She'd taken him back.

CHAPTER XXX

Having given it all some thought, Bianca concluded that the only place for a family celebration—and there did have to be a celebration—was her own home. No solution was ideal. Stevie's little bungalow was out of the question. While her parents' house could have done in a pinch, it would have *been* a pinch, for they were now eleven: in addition to Grant and herself and the twins, there would be Uncle Dennis and Aunt Grace, Mamma and Papa and Edith, Stevie and Rita. Mamma often seemed resentful about how the family's social life had shifted from Inquiry to Middleway. But she'd be far more aggrieved, surely, if asked to arrange dinner for eleven.

Of course they could go to a restaurant, but they hadn't all chanced a restaurant together since Grace's birthday party at Chuck's Chop House. Restaurants were dangerous. All the more so because this visit, though long postponed, had originally been intended to coincide with Aunt Grace's birthday. She'd turned forty-nine a couple of months ago.

The family dinner was set for Saturday. The Poppletons arrived the night before. On their Detroit visits they always stayed on Middleway, since Bianca had "so much room," though Mamma and Papa's house, now that Bianca and Stevie had moved out, held plenty of space for guests. But—an unspoken agreement—the days were gone forever when Aunt Grace would lodge under her sister's roof.

Aunt Grace arrived looking tired, and pale. Bianca always studied her aunt's appearance closely, nervously. Of course Aunt Grace was cheerful . . .

Uncle Dennis looked mostly unchanged, though perhaps a little heavier. Years ago, it seemed he'd reached a point of near-stability. Yes, the gray was slowly infiltrating his hair—but far more slowly than into Papa's, who recently had grown silver, almost white, at the temples. This, and the limp Papa had developed, because of the plantar wart he could never shake, had seemed to bring the two men closer in age. It was no longer incredible that the two were contemporaries.

The twins adored their great-aunt and great-uncle, who shortly on arrival were dragged into the basement for a display of Ping-Pong prowess, then into the screened porch, to watch a game of catch in the backyard.

Aunt Grace accepted a glass of wine. Grant had already poured his day's drink: a hefty whiskey. Uncle Dennis also had a whiskey. Bianca chose iced tea. The news that she was going to have a baby had turned alcohol, instantly, into a distant memory.

It was amazing how quickly the news had smoothed everything. Less than two weeks ago—it seemed lifetimes ago—she'd met Ronny at the DIA, shared a bottle of wine with him at Jason's, kissed him repeatedly under the Ambassador Bridge, and rushed off the next day, Sunday, to Priscilla the mind doctor's. Sunday had been crazier in its way than the day before, and Monday had been worse still. She'd been nearly mad with frustration, waiting and waiting for Ronny to call . . . Now, just two weeks later, she had to ask herself: what exactly had she wanted him to say? What sort of insane avowal had she craved? Something like "Maybe you're pregnant with your husband's child, but I've just discovered I'm in love with you"? Or: "I want you to abandon your husband and your six-year-old twins and run off with me to Gauguin's Pacific"?

Leaving Dr. Stimpson's office on the following day, Tuesday, she'd thrown into a waste bin her half-full pack of cigarettes. And when she'd telephoned Ronny on Wednesday, in order to confirm his amazing intuition of her pregnancy, she breezed right past his stumbling mixture of apologies and attestations. Ronny wanted to tell her he was sorry about his behavior on Saturday, and also that he wasn't sorry. He wanted to say— She interrupted: "But you mustn't apologize for a *thing*, Ronny." To which she added a sentiment expressible only because, though nakedly revealing, it had become peculiarly irrelevant: "Saturday was the most thrilling day I've had in ever so long . . ."

With regard to the others, she'd considered delaying her announcement until the family celebration. But this had seemed risky, given the tempestuous history of family celebrations. So after calling Ronny, she broke the news wide open: she telephoned Mamma and Papa and Edith, Stevie and Rita, Priscilla, Maggie . . . What lay before her now was the altogether pleasant task of informing Uncle Dennis and Aunt Grace.

It was a gorgeous summer evening, very late summer, for they were into early September now. The four of them were lounging in the screened porch, ice cubes clinking, while the twins played catch in the fading light. To Bianca, the evening felt like early June—as if a capacious summer stretched before her. The world itself stretched before her, and although a number of conversational junctures invited her to break her news, she held off. Everything was in abeyance.

Only after the four of them moved to the dining room—the boys had already been fed—did the impulse strike home. Uncle Dennis, that great toast-maker, hoisted a glass and pointed out how much they had to be thankful for. And Bianca said: "More even than you may know."

A pause opened, with a give-and-take of puzzled looks, and Bianca felt herself blush all over. "It seems I'm going to have a baby."

"Isn't that wonderful!" Grace cried, and Uncle Dennis released a funny, happy, harrumphing sound. He stood up and came over and kissed her on the top of the head, just the way you'd kiss a child, and said, "Now isn't that fine, isn't that something, isn't that *fine*?"

There were many questions, of course: what was the due date? And had she thought about a hospital? And did she think it was a boy, or a girl?

"And if it *is* a girl," Aunt Grace said, "what might you name her?"

"I was thinking Maria. Grant seems to like it."

"Maria Ives," Grant said. "Can't you picture her? We're talking a beauty. A real heartbreaker. Almost pretty as her mother."

Bianca explained that she didn't plan on telling the boys for quite some time. She didn't want to be driven crazy with questions.

That sounded very wise, Aunt Grace said.

Bianca asked everybody to remain seated and went out into the kitchen. She returned with the eggplant casserole and the spinach and blue cheese salad. She had become known, partly through emulation of her aunt, as a versatile cook. "Later, we'll call in the boys for dessert," she told them.

Aunt Grace ate sparingly but Grant and Uncle Dennis tucked in heartily. Everyone complimented Bianca on the food, and talk flowed. Grant, who always had a sound feeling for such matters, told a couple of jokes that were a little racy but hardly inappropriate. (Had they heard that Hollywood was the place where you lie on the sand and look at the stars—or vice versa?) Minute by succeeding minute, Bianca savored a rarefied sense of things being properly in place: her handsome husband across the table, her aunt and uncle on each side, the boys playing catch in the yard, the gentle, conversational slap-slap-slap of the ball against the leather gloves, and the steady blood-whisper of a child inside her . . . After so many turbulent days, she'd come to a graced clemency.

The night, as it turned out, held only a single disappointment.

Bianca had been awaiting a brief opportunity to speak alone with each of her guests, but this wasn't to be. She wanted to ask Grace about her health, but she longed even more for a renewal of that vital connectedness Grace inspired—the woman in whose convalescing hands, back in that cataclysmic winter of '43 to '44, Bianca had placed herself after nearly dying. (Months after she'd fully recovered, Uncle Dennis once began a sentence, "When your temperature hit a hundred and seven, darling, I must admit—" but he hadn't been able to finish.)

She did have a few minutes with Grace in the kitchen, cleaning up after dinner, but this was no occasion for a heart-to-heart. Grace breezed into an anecdote about a man, a patient of Uncle Dennis's, whose daughter, playing in the attic, had been stung by a wasp. Going up to clean out the nest, the man happened upon an old chest in the crawl space, presumably left by one of the house's previous owners. It contained ten antique silver dollars. Grace always had on hand a story of this sort: goodness meeting up with unexpected bounty . . .

"But how are you feeling?" Bianca said. "You look tired."

"Oh. My." Aunt Grace made a face. "Some ups and downs."

In response to Bianca's look of concern, she added, "Oh, I'm *well*. And I'm delighted with your news, darling."

As soon as the kitchen was tidied, Aunt Grace retreated to bed. A few minutes later, Uncle Dennis, yawning cavernously, announced, "I think I'll follow the wife."

Bianca caught him alone at the bottom of the stairs. He stood above her, one step up. On level ground, Bianca was maybe a half inch taller.

"Aunt Grace. Is she feeling all right?"

"Oh I think so. Just tired," Uncle Dennis said. "Now don't you go fretting yourself about anyone but that baby of yours." And once more he kissed her on top of the head.

In the morning, Uncle Dennis and Aunt Grace seemed revitalized. They were looking at a full day—old friends and old patients, and Uncle Dennis wanted to drop in on his old hospital. Having breakfasted heartily—scrambled eggs, pork sausage, toast with marmalade, orange juice, coffee—the two of them were out the door by nine. They promised to return well before the party started, at five.

Bianca asked Grant simply to "get the boys out from underfoot"—a task he embraced. He would take them golfing. They liked to do the caddying, for which they received a quarter apiece, and he sometimes let them get a whack at the ball. Rita arrived at noon to help with the cooking. "What is it we're making?" she asked a number of times.

"Beef bourguignon."

"French, is it?"

"That's right."

"They say *beef*?"

"Actually, *boeuf*."

"Well at least they *almost* got it right."

Rita offered this deadpan, but when Bianca glanced over, the girl was grinning slyly. Rita actually could be quite funny, in a self-mocking way. She understood the situation's humor: the little hillbilly girl receiving an education from her big-city sister-in-law.

And to her credit, Rita left no question unasked.

"How come this fork's like this?" she'd say.

"It's a salad fork."

Or: "What is this fabric called?"

"It's called chamois."

Or: "What do you mean this doesn't go with that?"

"Sweetie, the colors clash."

In many ways, Rita had become Bianca's little sister, more so than Edith, who rarely asked Bianca's advice—or anyone's advice.

Back when she was still fitting herself into the Paradiso family, Rita had regularly criticized Edith in her absence. Even when Rita's complaints were inarguable (Edith did nothing for her appearance, Edith was impatient, Edith didn't understand small talk), Bianca had bristled. It wasn't Rita's place to criticize Edith. But as Rita came around to seeing Edith as everyone else saw Edith, disparagement yielded to a pure marveling. For that's what they all did—they marveled at Edith, who was a breed apart. Count on Edith to enter a family celebration talking about an uprising in some English colony you'd never heard of, or to point out, on leaving a luncheonette, that three days in a row she'd received a bill that was a prime number, and three itself was a prime number—wasn't that funny? Yes, Edith: *funny*.

It was one of life's happy surprises that Bianca would have grown so fond of that sullen little Tennessee girl with the terrible teeth—who had become this sweet young woman hovering so attentively in Bianca's kitchen, intoning, *beef bourguignon, beef bourguignon, beef bourguignon* . . . The girl was steadily remaking herself, and Bianca had a midwife's role in the rebirth.

Though Bianca felt reluctant to turn to the subject, since she already was handling too many worries, eventually she asked after Stevie. It was one of those concerns that wouldn't go away.

Rita's tone shifted. "When'd you ever see him look relaxed? You know what he's like? He's like a clench fist." She clenched her fists in illustration. "I tell you, he's like a clench fist. You know?"

Bianca did. It was one of the great differences between Stevie and his dad. In those times when Papa bore the weight of the world on his shoulders (as when, so long ago, he'd been jobless for three days, until a red-faced O'Reilly marched up the walk bearing children's gifts), he never sped up, he never jerked or scurried, he maintained *la bella figura.* With Stevie, on the other hand, life's tensions wound him agonizingly tight, turning his powerful body twitchy and ungainly.

"He's working too many hours."

"Don't I know it!" Rita cried, almost triumphantly.

"You've got to tell him when to stop."

Rita looked bewildered and repeated something she'd said recently: "Bay, I don't *dare.*"

Yes, the prospect frightened Rita. Did Stevie have Rita under his thumb? For all the physical power he exuded, it was difficult to view Stevie in such terms, given how thoroughly he seemed under the thumb of an unnamed Something Else. *Something* was constantly squelching him. Family expectations? The Ford Motor Company? A society intent on punishing him for impregnating a seventeen-year-old girl who had miscarried long before her shame became apparent to society?

Rita repeated many details from their last conversation. Stevie was so pale. He never smiled. He had nightmares, night sweats. The conversation felt so ominous to Bianca, it was a great relief when Stevie actually materialized. Here he was, simply Stevie, her younger brother. "Hey, Bea," he said. He was the party's first guest.

"H'lo, Stevie. Come on in, can I get you a drink?"

"Jagotta beer?"

This was how he often talked. It was a deliberate choice, and an ironic one, given that Papa, with his unshakable Italian accent, perpetually suffered the fear of being taken for low-class. Papa yearned to speak refinedly, but couldn't; Stevie aspired to sound like Marlon Brando in *The Wild One,* and did a pretty good job of it. The funny thing was, he didn't even like beer.

"Yes, Stevie, I have a beer."

"She been any help? Or she just been getting in the way?"

This, too, was typical of his speech: not *Rita,* but *she.*

"Rita's been loads of help."

"I'm learning how to make beef bourguignon," Rita said.

"French?"

"Right."

"My Italian grampa always said it: French is twice the price at half the quality."

Bianca nodded approvingly. In his taciturn way, that odd ailing little man, once a celebrated artist but dead now for seven years, had left behind a meager supply of quotable remarks. But this was one, which Nonno had always delivered with that sage, slanted shaking of the head, that was his alone—a unique gesture, lost to the grave.

Still, Stevie looked pleased to be married to somebody learning to cook a dish as extravagant as beef bourguignon. Though he made a point of grumbling about the costs, Rita's constant efforts at self-improvement—the braces, the better makeup and clothes—obviously heartened him. If Stevie had no use for Bianca's art museums and concert halls, any more than for Grant's law offices and golf courses, still it was to the house on Middleway he instinctively sent his wife for schooling.

Grant arrived next with the twins, both muddy as hunting dogs; it seemed they'd found their way into a swamp. Grant mentioned in passing that his Studebaker wasn't firing properly, despite recent repairs, and that was enough for Stevie: poor Grant was hauled back outside even before having a chance to greet Rita.

Meanwhile, Bianca ordered Matt and Chip up to the shower and told them their party clothes were laid out on the lower bunk. The twins went upstairs quite docilely. Unlike most boys their age, they were actually good about cleaning up. Grant had somehow instilled the notion that that's what an athlete did at day's end: soaped up from head to foot. Grant called it "building a snowman." Though recently the boys had turned shy about being glimpsed naked by their mother, withdrawing from sight those private parts once her exclusive business to clean and powder, it remained perhaps the most endearing memory she knew: Matt or Chip industriously working himself into an all-encompassing lather. They had such skinny, beautiful bodies, her boys. (It almost embarrassed her—how beautiful she found their bodies.)

Papa and Mamma and Edith arrived next. There was always something a little poignant in Papa's visits. The head of the family became a different sort of man here, oddly diffident when requesting something he would naturally have expected at home. Might he ask for a glass of water? Would it be possible to have a napkin? He had of course brought a jug of Paradiso wine. No family celebration would be complete without it.

Bianca was proud of her home, which had cost $14,800 when she and Grant purchased it three years ago, in June of '49, and yet whenever her parents visited she felt misgivings about its grandeur. What would the house on Inquiry go for today, in an increasingly run-down neighborhood inside the Boulevard? A third of what she and Grant had paid? Bianca knew what Papa was feeling. How had his little Bia wound up in such a home? On sunny weekends before the War, inspecting the best neighborhoods in the city, he had sometimes driven her out here to the University District. It was even possible—really, it was possible—the two of them, father and little daughter, had once stood appraising the very house she would later purchase. What made it all especially painful was that Papa and Mamma could probably afford a home like this one. Papa had always been frugal, and O'Reilly and Fein had prospered over the years. But Mamma refused to budge.

Edith entered with that air of not quite noticing any change in her surroundings. She was in the middle of establishing a point. It seemed there was a tribe in the Pacific, or maybe the Indian Ocean, where the elderly women made the primary decisions, since they were the only ones who could communicate with the dead. Edith was taking a course in anthropology. She'd graduated from Wayne in June but kept taking classes anyway—what else was she to do? Bianca was hardly surprised her sister's eyes had given out over time, or that the glasses she'd selected and wore constantly—imitation tortoiseshell with forbiddingly square frames—were almost comically unattractive.

But where were the Poppletons? Bianca had told them five o'clock, and here it was nearly five-thirty.

Then the Poppletons pulled up, full of good cheer and apologies, and Uncle Dennis shook hands with everyone and marveled at how well they were looking and Aunt Grace kissed everyone and repeatedly apologized: there had been many old friends to see.

And so the party, late in getting started, began in earnest. Papa made the initial toast. He kept it brief, as was his wont: "To friends and family, from near and far." They all drank Paradiso wine; even Bianca, who was no longer drinking, had a sip. Then Grant toasted the wine itself. He always insisted—in utter sincerity, God bless him—no vintages were finer than his father-in-law's. And then Papa lifted his chin and said, a little defiantly, for any talk of Grace's birthday must carry a note of defiance, "And we gather to celebrate Grace's birthday. Better late than never."

Mamma smiled—smiled sweetly. Grace murmured thanks. And then the food was served.

The beef bourguignon was a tremendous hit. Bianca had cooked up a vat holding nearly eight pounds of meat—she'd joked with Rita about eating leftovers for weeks, but nearly all of it was consumed. The Ives triplets asked for seconds, and then thirds, and Stevie also eventually had thirds, and Bianca—having so far skipped all traces of morning sickness—had her own voracious pregnant woman's appetite to appease. Having finished his whiskey, and the splash of wine offered with the toast, Grant before refilling his wineglass had looked to Bianca, who would have preferred less consultation at a time like this: of course he should have a little more wine. The alcohol seemed to do him good, actually, and he did a wonderful hostly job of entertaining the table: he was much the best storyteller among them. Though Grant handled mostly trusts and estates at work, he collected tales of spectacularly bumbling criminals: the blackmailer who printed his return address on the envelopes; the thief who first deposited a sports coat, complete with name and address, before holding up a dry cleaner's; the burglar who, identified by a neighbor despite the mask he was wearing, called out, "No, Harry, it isn't me."

Bianca kept awaiting the arrival of something disastrous, which she must avert, but it never came. While Aunt Grace and Uncle Dennis talked about their lengthy day, Mamma kept saying, encouragingly, "How nice," and "Isn't that nice?" and "How very nice for you"—as though speaking to a well-intentioned but overly talkative stranger on a bus.

There were a few tense or peculiar moments. The subject came up, as it almost invariably did, of moving from Inquiry. The very topic made Mamma fretful. This woman who'd always complained about never going anywhere refused to countenance the idea.

Tonight, Papa teased Mamma ("I tell her, dig yourself in all you want, one day I pry you out with a crowbar"), which wasn't always the wisest course, particularly in a crowd. But Mamma handled the teasing well: "Have I gotten so heavy, you need a crowbar?" Though still too thin, Mamma had managed to put on a little weight these last few years, which everyone agreed was a good idea.

Mamma said: "I tell him, Vico, why is it you don't think a house that used to fit five can now fit three?"

"We can do better . . ." Papa countered.

"And besides," Mamma went on, "I don't want to leave my friends. Isn't that the most important thing?"

"I couldn't agree more," Aunt Grace said, and Uncle Dennis said, "Unquestionably"—and the subject was dropped.

And then Grant happened to mention a fraternity brother who worked for Dow Chemical and Edith perked up in that fact-establishing, party-killing way of hers. "I've been learning about it at school. There are all these new chemicals since the War—in our food, in our paint, even in our furniture polish. And we haven't a clue which ones are carcinogens—which ones cause cancers." A pause naturally ensued, as everybody glanced speculatively around at the food, the painted walls, the polished furniture. Bianca happened to catch the eye of Aunt Grace—the woman who had lost a breast to cancer at the age of forty-five. Poor thing, she looked uneasy.

But the moment passed. Rita and Bianca brought in the peach cobbler and ice cream, and an unforced, festive mood returned. The fruit glistened under the pastry's brown crust.

The final little upset of the dinner came, surprisingly, from Grace herself. She mentioned that she didn't plan to vote for Adlai Stevenson.

Bianca could hardly believe it. She felt almost personally affronted, and said perhaps too sharply, "You're joshing us!" Was Aunt Grace, always the great liberal, whose heroine was Eleanor Roosevelt, actually going to vote for Eisenhower? "What it is," Aunt Grace said, "I just don't like Adlai's face."

"Isn't there something else at stake here? A matter of politics? Of justice? I mean, can you honestly—"

Uncle Dennis gently butted in: "Yes, this will be the first presidential election when Grace and I cancel each other out." He laughed merrily.

"I'm sorry," Aunt Grace said—mildly, but obstinately. "But the fact is, I just don't like the man's face."

And later, after everybody had finished dessert but before Bianca had cleared away the plates, another odd moment arose. This one didn't threaten anything, yet it was disturbing all the same. Bianca was heading toward the kitchen, dishes in hand, when Aunt Grace said to her, tapping her glass, "More wine, dear." Only that brief expectant phrase—but Bianca suddenly felt what Grace so rarely inspired: a surge of resentment. And with it—with it an awakened sympathy for that woman who had lived perpetually in Grace's shadow: Mamma, at the other end of the table, nodding politely, while everyone worried that she might bring this celebration crashing down . . . It was as if Bianca had never quite grasped it before: just how wearing and embittering it might be to have a sister destined—as Nature itself surely intended, bestowing on her beauty and graciousness and an effortless air of soft-spoken command—to be served.

"Everything went so well," Uncle Dennis said.

"The party?"

"Yes, the splendid party."

"Well, thank you."

Here at last was the opportunity to talk with him at length. Aunt Grace had retired early, the other guests had gone home, Grant had promised to put the twins to bed—something he was good at.

"You must be tired," she said.

"*You* must be tired."

Bianca laughed. "This time round, pregnancy doesn't tire me. Maybe because I eat so much." She'd gained 8 pounds already. As of this morning, she weighed 135.

They walked south, toward Six Mile Road. The night was warm but not hot, with a hint in the air—if her pregnant woman's nose could be trusted—of autumn. A bat, and then another bat, swung through the cone of the street lamp in front of Mr. Bickey's house, which seemed appropriate, for he was the neighborhood recluse. Even as a girl, Bianca had been comfortable with most creatures in the animal kingdom—she was fine with bugs, spiders, snakes, mice—but bats were different. It seemed she'd never fully recovered from the hysterical occasion, deep in her childhood, when a bat slipped down the chimney and flapped around and around the living room in dark lunatic fashion. "Bats," Bianca said, and pointed.

"Yes."

"I think I prefer gulls. You remember all the gulls we used to see on Inquiry."

"Yes."

The two of them had the leisure to be gradual, and for a while no grave topics were broached. Uncle Dennis asked after Grant's parents and Bianca told him about Mrs. Ives's plan to buy her son a car for his thirtieth birthday.

"A car," Uncle Dennis said. "Now isn't that splendid?"

"Maybe they're not so car crazy down in Cleveland?"

"Oh they are. It's the whole country. Ever since the War ended. And besides, cars have gotten so pretty."

"I remember your '42 Packard. You used to say it was always the latest model. Because they didn't build any cars the next year."

"And it was a good car," Uncle Dennis said. "It brought me safely up here, one very cold winter night, when a little girl had grown very sick . . ."

Whether he'd intended to or not, Uncle Dennis had offered the perfect transition. Bianca said, "You know, Uncle Dennis, Aunt Grace looks *tired* to me."

There was a pause. Uncle Dennis cleared his throat. He said, "First, I planned to say something. Then I thought I wouldn't. I didn't want to spoil the party. But now I think I will."

"Yes?"

Bianca felt frightened. She knew what was coming.

"The first thing to say is, the prognosis is excellent. These are not empty words. I'm speaking medically. It's an excellent prognosis. You see, your aunt's cancer is back."

It didn't matter if you'd guessed the truth: it hit you flat in the face, all the same. "Oh, Uncle Dennis—I'm so *sorry*."

"I know you are. We all are."

And then came the guilt—always the guilt. This very evening, hadn't she resented Aunt Grace's request for a little more wine?

Uncle Dennis talked in that scientific way he had, almost as if Bianca were another doctor. Some of the terminology was unfamiliar, but the ghastly, ghastly shape of things was unmistakable. Once they returned to Cleveland, Aunt Grace would have her remaining breast, her left breast, removed. And then radiation treatments. And then a slow but— yes—steady convalescence at home.

"It's a terrible disease," Bianca said.

Uncle Dennis thought for a moment. "They have no wish to harm their host—the cancer cells. They merely want to replicate." He offered these words as though there were reassurance in them, but the effect on Bianca was quite the opposite. "But they can be fiendishly clever when you seek to halt their replication," he added.

They had reached Six Mile. They did not cross. The homes on the other side were more modest—some a little seedy. Now and then something happened on Six Mile that gave a person pause—a store was burgled, a car was stolen. It was ironic but true: the city seemed far more crime-ridden since the War ended and real prosperity began.

They turned around, reclaimed by the leafier and more hospitable reaches of her University District.

"That's why we were a little late to your party. I wanted to consult an old friend at Sinai, Dr. Phillips. Joe's a first-class cancer man—really a first-class man."

It was silly to focus on such a niggling thing when so many larger and graver issues loomed, but Bianca, only half listening to the medical talk, kept drifting back to it: after spending the day in discussions about having her remaining breast surgically removed, and radiation treatments, and God knows what else, Aunt Grace had returned to her niece's home and requested another splash of wine, and Bianca had resented her.

Uncle Dennis abruptly halted. "But we need to talk about other things."

"Yes, of course."

"Edith seems well," Uncle Dennis said.

"You'd have to say so," Bianca replied, although she frequently worried about Edith. Maybe because Edith was the baby of the family, nobody else appeared to recognize that she wasn't a child any longer—she was twenty-one. Bianca had a house and two kids, with a third on the way, and even Stevie had a wife and a house and a job, but what did Edith have? What did Edith do? She'd graduated from Wayne but she was still taking classes, not with an eye toward any further degree but simply because it seemed nobody, including Edith, could imagine her doing anything but being in school. Papa used to joke that Edith's husband would never have a missing button or a sock that needed darning, but where was Edith ever to find a husband?

"I do wish she dated more," Bianca said.

"Plenty of time for that," Uncle Dennis said. "Plenty of time for that." He liked to repeat a concluding phrase.

"And when she does go out with a boy? She invariably finds him *silly.*"

"Not so surprising."

"But a little alarming? What does she expect? Silly? They're *boys.*"

"Yes." Uncle Dennis started up again: "Rita seems well."

"You know, she *does*. And she's ever so proud of her braces."

"I suppose she is."

"Although you know *she's* been bending my ear. About Stevie. She's very worried about Stevie."

It probably wasn't fair to introduce this topic tonight, when Uncle Dennis had so much else on his mind. But he'd always been, far more than Papa, who spoke so little and took things so hard, the older man to whom Bianca could bring her troubles. And when would she have another chance?

Bianca went on: "The word Rita uses to describe him? *Desperate.*"

"Desperate?"

"Well, she wants him out of that job. She says he has nightmares. And night sweats. And you know he certainly doesn't *seem* very happy."

"Stevie can be a little hard to read. He's like Edith that way."

"And not like me?"

"They have trouble letting things out. You have trouble keeping them in."

Bianca laughed. "I was always the crybaby."

"You were always the crybaby," Uncle Dennis said fondly.

"With Stevie, I pretend everything's all right, because he tells me everything's all right. But you know what I'm scared of? I wouldn't confess it to anyone but you. You remember when Stevie went 'cross-country,' basically disappearing for eighteen months? I keep thinking everything's going to get to be too much and he'll light out again."

Surely, this was unlikely. But wasn't it also unlikely that Stevie could remain as tightly wound as he was indefinitely? How many more days at the plant could he do? How many more nights of grinding his teeth and sweating through his pajamas and waking up to nightmares of drowning?

Uncle Dennis asked a number of questions (How long had Stevie been working at Ford now? And his hourly salary? And how much overtime? And what had he paid for his house?), which Bianca found comforting: it was a relief to set out the details of her worries.

"Grant seems well," Uncle Dennis finally said.

Bianca paused and then said, "Oh I think he's *fine.*"

She didn't have the heart to mention that lately she'd been worrying about Grant, too. Not that there was anything new, exactly—which perhaps illustrated the problem.

Spurred partly by nasty remarks from Maggie, Bianca felt as though she'd belatedly put two things together. There'd been a pair of crises in her married life—the day she'd boarded the train to Cleveland, and the controversy over Grant's client's lakefront lots—and hadn't his response to both been virtually the same? More than chastened. Each time, he'd come out almost shell-shocked.

There had been a time when Grant had seemed very ambitious at Cutting and Fuller; he'd even talked about breaking off with some younger partners and starting his own firm. But all such talk had died with the crisis over the lakefront lots, and these days he spoke with a sort of resigned spectator's wistfulness about Walton's bold business forays. And surely Grant was too young to have turned resigned and wistful . . .

"And he seemed *very* pleased about your news," Uncle Dennis said.

"Oh yes. Very pleased."

Uncle Dennis appeared deep in thought, and then he opened what was dependably the most difficult topic:

"How does your mother seem?"

Overhead, as if in answer (one of life's typically heavy-handed symbols), another bat zigzagged through the streetlight's glare. "Well, she seemed pretty good tonight. You could feel she was trying. But then you have to ask: why does she have to be *trying*? Why is it an *effort*, when we're talking about a family gathering? And I got a little nervous when Papa mentioned moving."

"She said she didn't want to leave her friends."

"That's what she *said*."

"But there *is* a logic to it, honey." Uncle Dennis was reproaching her, ever so mildly. "At this point, it's the only neighborhood she knows, and she has a role there."

"A role?"

"Yes. A role."

And Uncle Dennis was possibly right. For the peculiar fact was that as the old neighborhood had declined, with people moving in and out much more quickly, and so many homes looking dilapidated, Mamma, the longtime resident, had become an increasingly trusted neighbor. If she couldn't exactly be described as popular, she had become somebody to consult.

"But it's so unfair to *Papa*. Why should he have to live in that house till he dies, when he's spent his whole life dreaming of better, bigger houses? Houses matter so *much* to him."

"Your father hasn't had an easy time of it. But then neither has your mother."

"I keep wondering if there's something we should do. Or should have done. In order for things to turn out differently."

Uncle Dennis thought a moment. "It reminds me of a story I read."

"Tell me."

"Well. There was a man, an ordinary man, but because of the peculiar anatomical structure of his brain, scientists were able to boost his IQ more than a hundred points. He became the smartest man who ever lived. But the side effects were virulent and it turned out he had only a short time to live. And somebody asked him, on his deathbed, what was the *one question*—if he could ask God only *one question,* what would it be? And for a while the smartest man who ever lived cogitated. There were so many good questions to ask: Is there a Heaven? What's the nature of Truth? Does Time have an end? And finally he declared, This is what I would ask God: *Is life more like a movie, or is it more like a play?*"

Even by Uncle Dennis's standards, this was pretty elliptical. "I'm not sure God Himself would understand the question," Bianca observed dryly.

"Well, maybe not. Certainly, all the people were perplexed. So the smartest man in the world explained himself. He said, 'I'd ask God, if You were to start the world over, with each detail just exactly how it was, would everything turn out the same?'

"In other words," Uncle Dennis went on, "is it more like a movie, or more like a play? You start the movie again, it always turns out the same. The play, though, each time's it's different. You see what I'm saying?"

"I'm not sure."

"Really, I'm simply rephrasing your question. I'm saying if you started it all over, you ran it back and here's that young couple on their wedding day, hand in hand, Ludovico Paradiso and Sylvia Schleiermacher, would it all come out the same? Would your mother and your father again wind up so burdened and so put upon? Or was there a possible world where everything turned out just *fine* for Sylvia, for the two of them? That's the one thing we'll never know."

CHAPTER XXXI

She was sitting in the kitchen, over the one cup of coffee she still allowed herself each morning, when the phone rang. She wished it wouldn't. She was enjoying the newfound tranquillity of having Grant at work and the boys at school. The boys were in for the whole day now— they were first graders. She had pressing chores to attend to (she must write another letter to her aunt, who, according to all reports, was doing very well after her surgery) but not quite yet. The light was lovely this morning. And the feeling of privileged aloneness was still novel enough, in this fourth week of September, that a ringing phone felt intrusive.

"Bianca, it's Maggie."

"What is it?"

Something wasn't quite right—this was clear from Maggie's funny pinched tone. Nothing disastrous, maybe—but something wasn't quite right.

"Have you seen today's *Free Press*?"

"It's here on the table. I haven't opened it yet."

"It's Mrs. Charles Olsson—Ronny's mother. She died. I thought you'd want to know . . ."

"Oh *no*. I can't believe it. But this can't be."

Maggie kept talking in her ear as Bianca rifled through the newspaper. The photograph of Mrs. Olsson struck her with a hard *thud*. Dead? The world's most beautiful woman? And meanwhile, at the back of her mind, an absolutely lunatic suspicion: this would never have happened if only she'd been a better person and begun the letter to Aunt Grace she'd been intending to write . . .

"I just thought you'd want to know," Maggie kept saying. She wasn't sure how to proceed. Bianca had encountered this before. The truth was, Maggie was never any good—she was out of her element—in dealing with life-and-death matters. She could be wonderfully funny and acerbic with little or even medium-sized adversities, but tragedy dwindled Maggie's voice; she sounded little-girlish, tentative, and afraid.

Maggie seemed relieved when Bianca cut the conversation short.

Bianca then read the obituary straight through three times. It held few surprises, beyond the stunning surprise of the thing's very existence. Dead at fifty-three. Born March 3, 1899, in Scarp, North Dakota. Active in various charities, including the Vista Maria girls' orphanage. There were many references to Mr. Olsson, of course, and one to Ronny, identified as an art professor at the University of Michigan. And a reference to Mrs. Olsson's sister, Betty Marie Bashaw, of Ferder, North Dakota, whose husband, so Mrs. Olsson had unforgettably proposed one afternoon at Pierre's, ought to be shot. Mrs. Olsson had died of kidney failure.

Placing the obituary carefully on the kitchen table, Bianca retreated to the bathroom and inspected her face. She didn't feel at all like crying. "Mrs. Olsson is dead," she said aloud. "Mrs. Olsson died." Once before, a phone call had brought word of an unexpected death, but under utterly different circumstances. Henry Vanden Akker had been only twenty-two, and in many ways she'd been madly in love, and he was her fiancé, more or less. Mrs. Olsson, on the other hand—Bianca hadn't seen Mrs. Olsson in nearly ten years, and she'd only rarely been able, given the woman's august unpredictability, to muster anything so straightforward as affection for her. It was all right, then, if she didn't feel like crying.

It was all right, then, if she could declare, clearheadedly, "Mrs. Olsson is dead."

But the next moment she realized she wasn't being clearheaded at all. What about Ronny? She must call Ronny!

Ronny had lost his mother. Ronny was an only child who had always had difficulties with his father—and now he'd lost his mother. Bianca returned to the kitchen and dialed Ronny's apartment in Ann Arbor. Her hands were trembling.

She let it ring eleven times before hanging up. What should she do next? There must be something she should *do*—but what? Surely he would call. Who else would he naturally turn to now? She dialed him again—no answer—and after five minutes she dialed again.

Breaking all caffeine restrictions, she gulped down a second cup of coffee, and then a third. She telephoned Ronny, and there was no answer. She made herself a childhood favorite—a cream-cheese-and-jelly sandwich—ate it, and made another. She ate that and called Ronny. This time he answered.

"Ronny, it's Bianca."

"You saw the *Free Press*."

"Yes, I did. I'm so sorry. I'm just *so sorry*."

"Thank you," Ronny said. "Thank you for calling."

"It must have been a terrible, terrible shock. I'm so sorry."

"It wasn't completely surprising, I guess, but yes, it was a terrible shock. I'm not sure how much I believe it even yet. It turns out I don't have much experience with this sort of thing."

"And your poor father."

"That *has* been surprising. He's just a wreck. I would have sworn he didn't much like her—"

"Oh Ronny, you mustn't say such—"

"But he's just a wreck. He'll recover, of course, but for the moment he's fallen apart. And you know what? I think by doing so he's sort of holding me together. I tell you, it's all been very *strange*."

"I'm just so sorry," Bianca said.

"And to make things all the stranger, Mother left very strict instructions about no funeral—no service 'of any sort whatsoever.' Absolutely dead set against. Nothing, she wants *nothing*, and what do you do with that? My father and I, we don't know what to *do*."

"She was always very good to me," Bianca said, which was certainly more true than not.

"She liked you. You know, not to be telling tales, but I think she secretly hoped you and I might someday be together."

"I—well—yes, she did, Ronny. Definitely. I mean, she said as much to me."

"She said so? She really did?" And Ronny's voice had changed. This was that younger Ronny who kept surfacing—that intense, openhearted young man whose parents had required such constant watching, and complicated negotiations, as he sought a path in life.

"At that restaurant, Pierre's."

There was a pause. "I'm coming downtown the day after tomorrow. Thursday. To talk with some lawyers. Perhaps we might meet first? A very early lunch?"

"Ronny, I'd like that very much."

"I enjoyed our time at Jason's. Could we meet at Jason's? At the ridiculous hour of, say, eleven-thirty?"

"I'd like that very much."

They talked a while before hanging up. Ronny sounded remarkably calm and collected.

Yes, once before Bianca had received news by telephone of a death, and in that instance it was as though dying were a family contagion: in the following weeks, Mr. and Mrs. Vanden Akker had withered away like plague victims. Would the same thing happen again, despite how Ronny had sounded? She must have been afraid it would, for there was something hugely reassuring, on Thursday morning, in seeing him looking so splendid. He was seated at a table at Jason's, awaiting her.

Her cheery opening remark was hardly a customary salutation to someone in mourning: "I think that's the most beautiful necktie I've ever seen." These were the first words that popped into her head. Ronny was wearing a solemn black suit—the first time she'd seen him in a black suit—but a bright geometric tie in unusual greens, golds, orange-reds.

Ronny certainly didn't take the compliment amiss. "It's Belgian. I bought it in Brussels, not far from the Musées des Beaux Arts. I didn't even know the Belgians *made* ties. But I saw it and I said, Whoever designed this, he knew the paintings of his countryman Rogier van der Weyden. The same palette."

"How clever of you, Ronny." He was right, of course.

Ronny got up and helped her into a seat. He said, "This time, I wouldn't get any particular credit for guessing you were pregnant."

"I'm twelve pounds heavier than when I saw you last. Or thirteen. It's a little alarming."

"Is it still all right for me to say you look beautiful?"

"More right than ever. I'm beginning to feel like a cow."

This wasn't the conversation she'd envisioned having with somebody who had just lost his mother. But conversations with Ronny rarely followed predictable lines . . .

"I hope your father's doing better," she said.

"You know what? He isn't. I'm not sure how strange death is, but mourning? It's a very strange business. For maybe the first time in my life, I feel quite sorry for him."

"You always make yourself sound much more hard-hearted than you are."

"Do I?" Ronny said. "Actually, I think that's the nicest compliment anyone's paid me in quite some time."

She was ravenous—she confessed—and she ordered the lamb chops. To her surprise, Ronny did, too. "Isn't grief supposed to dull your appetite?" he asked. "That's not what's happening to me." Bianca ordered a glass of milk and Ronny a glass of wine.

"How long had your mother had kidney problems?" Bianca asked.

"You mustn't believe what you read. It was really drink."

"Beg pardon?"

"She did have kidney problems, but drink's what killed her."

"I'm so sorry to hear that . . ."

"And you know what? I think her death's *liberating* in some ways. I'd feel worse about saying this if I didn't believe my mother would understand completely. She wasn't always an easy person to have for a mother—she couldn't stay *out* of anything—but these last few years were difficult in a brand-new way. You know what, Bianca? It ripped me apart to see her drinking the way she did. And the not wanting to go out, because the drinking made her look worn and a little bloated, and sometimes her skin—" He shook his head.

"She had such wonderful skin," Bianca said. "It took all the light in the room and fed it back to you."

Then Ronny said something very unexpected: "Good Lord, I adore you."

"Well—thank you."

"I wouldn't have thought to put it as you just did, but that's exactly how it was with Mother: all the light in the room fed back to you."

"You're going to take up painting again," Bianca said.

"Just as soon as the next world war begins . . ." Ronny lifted his glass, as if in toast, and sipped his wine.

He put down the glass and again took up the subject of his mother: "It became a vicious circle. Not wanting to go out. And if you're not going out, you're home alone, all the more reason to have another drink. I'm telling you, it ripped me apart. And she could see it did. And she didn't want to do that. Whatever else she wanted, she didn't want to rip me apart."

Ronny seemed to be doing quite well, on the whole, but his chin was trembling at the conclusion of this little speech. Bianca launched immediately into a string of reminiscences. The first time she'd laid eyes on Mrs. Olsson, seated in the music room in a cone of light. The evening when Mrs. Olsson made omelets. The wonderfully stylish way she'd introduced an eighteen-year-old girl to Pierre: Bi-an-ca Pa-ra-di-so.

The memories brightened Ronny's face, and even when the lamb chops arrived Bianca went on chattering. The couple of times when Mrs. Olsson demanded a tour of the art museum . . . "And she had such funny, caustic observations, about the portraits especially, the subjects *and* the painters. She was so perceptive. And very tart."

Ronny laughed. "She saw no reason to hold back her opinions."

Bianca remembered something else. "And one day she asked me a fascinating question about you. Did you inherit your artistic talent from your father? Or from her?"

"And what did you say?"

"I'm not sure I answered. But *she* did. She said it came from her."

"Did she now?" Ronny laughed heartily. "Good for her."

"Well, hello."

A sandy-haired young man was loitering beside their table, evidently an acquaintance of Ronny's.

Ronny's reply was surprising, given how faultlessly courteous he usually managed to be: "What are you doing here?"

"We were supposed to meet. Remember?"

Ronny consulted his watch. "Later. After the lawyers."

The young man shrugged. "I got the time wrong."

"And not here. At Haggerty's."

Another shrug. "I got the place wrong." He had a round, appealing, wholesome face, and his shrugs were delivered with the accomplished grin of somebody used to disarming suspicion or censure. "Do you mind if I sit down?" The question was directed, unexpectedly, at Bianca.

"No. Of course not."

Now it was Ronny's turn to shrug, before duly offering introductions. "I'd like you to meet Bianca Ives. We were art students together some years ago. And this is my friend Chris Abendorfer. Chris works in advertising."

"I've heard of *you*," Chris Abendorfer said.

"I think I've heard of you," Bianca replied. She wasn't sure why she said this. It wasn't true.

"Bianca is going to have a baby next May."

"And I can't think of anything more wonderful," Chris Abendorfer said.

"Chris ought to know. He's the eleventh of eleven children," Ronny said.

"Eleventh of eleven!" Bianca said.

"A late arrival. And now Ronny's criticizing me for arriving early . . ."

"Your poor mother," Bianca said.

"Poorer with each child."

"Are you from around here?" Bianca asked him.

"No. But I *am* flattered. I thought the dazzled look in my eyes gave me away. Branded me a hopeless hick. I'm a west Minnesota farm boy originally."

"Not so far from Scarp, North Dakota, actually," Ronny pointed out. "Mother's hometown."

"I'll have to go out there someday," Bianca said.

"Why on *earth* would you do that?" And Chris laughed at her, but quite amiably.

"Did you know Mrs. Olsson?" Bianca asked him.

Chris paused thoughtfully, as though this were a complicated question. "Yes-s-s," he said. He added: "An amazingly beautiful woman." Then added, nodding at Bianca: "But what could be more beautiful than a beautiful woman who is with child?"

"Beware, Bianca. Beware of silver-tongued farm boys. As I say, this one's in advertising."

Ronny offered this warning with a proprietary pride and it was only now, belatedly, that Bianca realized that Chris Abendorfer was Ronny's special friend, or romantic partner, or lover, or whatever you wanted to call it. Never in a million years would Bianca have put the two of them together. When, now and then, she'd tried to envision Ronny with some man (not a direction where her imagination comfortably ventured), she'd pictured somebody much like Ronny himself: extraordinarily good-looking, of course, but also aristocratic, artistic, a little aloof.

While Chris told a long story about a recent business meeting with a soda-pop manufacturer, Bianca gave him a much sharper inspection. The truth was he wasn't really good-looking. The best you could say was he was pleasant-looking or agreeable-looking. Or wholesome-looking.

Still, Chris had a way with him—those big brown eyes so guileless, while his talk rolled puckishly along. "My product's got *sass*," the soda-pop manufacturer had kept repeating. Chris was a skillful mimic. Holding out his arms to indicate a substantial paunch, ballooning his cheeks, he had the manufacturer's gassy pomposity down pat. "My product's got *sass*," Chris boasted once more and all three of them laughed.

Encouraged, Chris went through a gallery of clients. Bianca wasn't used to seeing Ronny serve so willingly as audience, but he seemed not only amused but proudly enthralled. There was the Scottish tool-and-die manufacturer who had asked, in a low simple tone of childlike apprehension, "But what if ad-ver-tising fails to increase my revenues?" The Jewish maker of women's undergarments who had worried that the slogan "There's a better you in you" might be unacceptably racy. The car dealer whom Chris had had to drive home because his car wouldn't start. Each had a different accent, a different repertoire of gestures. At dinner parties on Middleway, Grant could be quite amusing with his Irish brogue, but this was something else again . . .

A pause opened and Bianca said, "Are you interested in art, Chris?"

"I'm *quite* interested in not seeing art."

The remark was a little cryptic, though Chris seemed quite pleased with it.

"I'm not sure I—"

"Ronny takes me to a museum once. And he announces, Okay, Chris, here's the most beautiful painting in the place. And what is it? It's this *cramped* little affair, Adam and Eve and the Serpent, and all three are sort of long and twisted, with these weird, slanted, inhuman eyes. And I say, Okay, Ronny, but which one's the snake? Huh? I mean, this was a painter who couldn't get a job drawing Tootsie Rolls for the firm I work for . . . I don't think Ronny wanted to take me to a museum after that."

Actually, Ronny looked delighted with the story, though he protested, "That's not what happened! Not at all!"

Chris replied, "What you're saying is, Just because something's implausible doesn't mean it's true."

"So that's what I'm saying, is it?"

"Or you're saying, Just because something sounds logical doesn't mean it's incorrect."

"So that's what I'm saying, is it?"

The little exchange left Bianca feeling quite disoriented. Ronny was bantering—but not with *her*. And not in quite the same directing *way* he bantered with her.

Ronny and an advertising man . . . The peculiar truth was that Ronny Olsson had always been fascinated by advertising. This had puzzled Bianca, long ago—the brilliant art student who found nearly all modern art too crass, who was most at home with Fragonard and Poussin and Vermeer and Dou, but who nonetheless pored over advertisements with an absorption that originated in condescension but did not end there. Ronny had constantly found in ads secret meanings that Bianca couldn't see, deep veins of humor underlying the ostensible humor. In truth, he used to make her far more nervous—his spirit seemed more faraway—when chuckling over an ad for deodorant or mouthwash or trusses than when swooning over some refined French canvas that utterly failed to move her.

So there was a kind of logic and rightness to this unorthodox triangle—the former boyfriend and girlfriend taking different sorts of pleasure in a young man who wrote ads for a living—as well as a tension which, though not jealousy exactly, was closer to jealousy than to any other emotion she could name. The tension openly declared itself when, abruptly, Ronny had to leave for his lawyer's appointment. Outside Jason's, Chris was headed one way, Bianca another—toward her car and home. The three of them stood in the doorway. Ronny was visibly torn.

And then he said to Chris, "I'll catch up with you later," and Chris said, "Olsson, I look forward to it"—and Bianca felt a pang of resentment on discovering that Ronny had initiated Chris into this little joke of addressing each other by surnames. Mostly, though, she felt relieved at Ronny's decision to accompany her. Gallantry of course demanded that he walk the pregnant woman to her car. And whatever other turns his circuitous life might take, gallant her gallant Ronny would always be.

"I don't know what to *wear*."

It was one of Grant's jokes—an echoing of something his clotheshorse of a wife might say—but the truth was, neither of them knew what to expect. Stevie and Rita were taking them out to dinner. To a restaurant. And not just any restaurant, but the Tupelo Country House, way out on Telegraph. This was an evening without precedent.

Stevie and Rita were taking them to the Tupelo Country House? Bianca, in her puzzlement, and her fretting over what the bill might come to, had tried to dissuade them, but Rita was adamant. She and Stevie were inviting them to celebrate, belatedly, Grant's birthday. And "something else" as well.

"She's pregnant," Grant declared, for what must be the fourth or fifth time, and for the fourth or fifth time Bianca replied, "No, she made it quite clear she isn't." But what else could *something else* be?

The sitter, Mrs. Hornberger, arrived at 5:45, just when she was supposed to, and Stevie and Rita pulled up at six, just when *they* were supposed to. "Oh dear Lord, Stevie's wearing a suit," Bianca called from the downstairs hall, having glimpsed her brother through the front window. Grant was sitting in the den, reading the *News*. He was wearing khaki slacks and a seersucker sports coat. "Stevie *never* wears a suit. Grant, you've got to race up and change."

Always eager to show how fast he could move, Grant had sprung upstairs even before the doorbell rang. "Hey, don't you look nice," Bianca said to Rita. She was pleased to be able to mean it. Rita was wearing her new blue dress and her new yellow angora cardigan with pearl buttons, both of which Bianca had helped pick out at Hudson's.

"And isn't my little brother quite the Beau Brummell?"

Stevie, stiff and embarrassed, pointed at Rita. "Blame her." He pushed past Bianca into the living room.

"Doesn't he look nice?" Rita said. "That's exactly what I told him: Stevie, you look so nice."

Bianca and Rita followed Stevie into the living room, where he'd already sat down. After a few moments, Stevie called, "Hey, Grant." Grant was descending the stairs in an impeccable charcoal suit complete with gray-and-yellow necktie and white handkerchief in the breast pocket. Grant really could change his clothes at astonishing speed.

"Hey, Stevie."

It would have been more comfortable to go in the Studebaker, but Stevie wanted to drive—or Rita expected Stevie to drive. For as they headed west down Seven Mile, and Rita prattled on, sometimes talking sense (canned peaches weren't worth the expense and it was best to wait for the real thing) and sometimes nonsense (a vote for Ike might not be all that different from a vote for Adlai), it became clear she was conscientiously playing hostess.

For Rita's sake, Bianca was glad they were given an excellent table. This was actually Grant's doing, and all the more commendable for not looking like Grant's doing; he had a warm, easy way with maître d's and waitresses.

Would they care for anything to drink?

Rita asked for a mint julep and Bianca for a glass of milk and Stevie, who didn't usually like to drink, ordered a Manhattan. Grant paused (unsure whether anyone would be drinking tonight, he'd already downed a big Scotch at home), then ordered a Manhattan. Bianca nodded and smiled.

She noticed that Stevie's suit, which was a couple of years old, was tight across the shoulders. He'd bulked up, lifting weights. Grant's suit, which had a black plaid pattern subtly woven through its charcoal gray, fit perfectly. Bianca had selected it for him, at Hughes and Hatcher. She selected his entire wardrobe, with the exception of his athletic wear—admittedly, a large exception.

She wondered how long Rita would wait to reveal the evening's mystery. Not long, it turned out. Rita could hardly contain her news. The moment the drinks arrived, face glowing with excitement, she said, "First of all, we want to wish you a very, very happy birthday, Grant."

"Well, that's so kind," Grant said. "But no need, no need."

"No need," Bianca echoed.

"Second of all, we want to congratulate Stevie. He has a new job."

"You have a new job, Stevie!" Bianca cried, and reached across the table to lay her hand on his. He didn't respond—like the rest of the Paradisos, he was no "toucher"— but he let it remain.

"What sort of job? When do you start?" Grant said.

Again, Stevie looked embarrassed. Like Papa, he never wanted to be "fussed over." But he did not shrink away. He stared his sister straight in the eye and said, "Yes, I have a new job." Then he turned to Grant and said, "I've already started."

"Stevie's already been at it a week!" Rita cried. "I woulda said something, but Stevie kept telling me keep my trap shut. I kept telling him, I'd be keener to listen if you used nicer language." Rita laughed brightly.

"That's right," Bianca said. "Stevie talks like a thug half the time."

"See?" Rita tap-tap-tapped Stevie on the arm. "Your sister's saying just what I say about what you say."

"But who are you working for?" Grant asked.

"I'm working for a trucking company."

"That sounds wonderful," Bianca said, even as her heart wobbled, as it always did when serious alterations came to Stevie's life. Behind his bravado, he was so vulnerable.

"What's the name of the company?" Grant said.

"Turk's Trucks. The owner, he's a Turk. From Turkey," Stevie said.

"Oh I've met him!" Bianca cried, instantly feeling much better.

"You've met him?" Stevie seemed taken aback—crestfallen, somehow.

"Just the one time," Bianca said. "With Aunt Grace. We met by chance. At Sanders. He's a friend of Uncle Dennis."

"That's right."

Actually, Bianca had met him twice, both occasions distant but still vivid. The first encounter had been while lunching with Aunt Grace. Up had stepped the voluble little man with a gold tie and a big gold watch who called Uncle Dennis a great man and adduced as proof his plump daughter, whose name, whatever it was, meant angel in Turkish. The man insisted that Uncle Dennis had saved the girl's life.

And the two of them, father and daughter, had materialized on that teary day when Uncle Dennis and Aunt Grace's earthly belongings had been carted away, bound for Cleveland, in a big truck emblazoned with the words "Turk's Trucks." Father and daughter had waved at it, mournfully.

"What will you be doing?" Grant asked.

"Quite a few things," Stevie replied. "I can repair lots of what goes wrong on trucks. But also there's seeing it's loaded properly, and checking the schedules, and the routes. Lots of things. Making people get along. It's more complicated than it looks," Stevie went on proudly.

"Stevie'll be a sort of foreman," Rita supplied.

"Yeah, it looks like I'm going to be a sort of foreman. Eventually."

"And the pay's so good."

"Better. Better than what I was making at Ford."

"That's just so wonderful, Stevie," Bianca said, and felt herself issuing a sort of prayer of thanksgiving, though channeled not toward God but toward that plump, pop-eyed man down in Cleveland who watched over them all.

Yes, and wasn't it ironic that she'd felt so guilty after her long walk with Uncle Dennis some weeks ago? He'd been so noble, delaying all mention of Grace's cancer so as not to mar the family celebration. And on a night when he was already so burdened, what had Bianca done but drop upon his shoulders her fears about Stevie, who tonight was sitting in Tupelo's Country House in a suit, looking handsome, playing host? It was all so evident what had happened . . . Uncle Dennis had listened that night, and asked her many questions, then changed the subject, as though nothing more were to be done. And the next day he'd driven off to pay a visit to the one man who just might hold the solution. Unexpectedly, quick as a blush, Bianca's eyes welled with tears, and, though they did not spill, Rita spotted them anyway, and in surprise, in delight, she cried, "Bay!" and Bianca, abashed, murmured, "I'm just thrilled for you," and Stevie, who didn't often come up with quips, made everything all right: "We're gonna cut you off at one glass of milk." Gaiety swept the table.

A waitress approached and Stevie, with an authority inspiring to behold, ordered drinks without consulting anyone. "Another mint julep for my wife," he said. "And the boys will have another Manhattan."

Grant looked to Bianca, who nodded at him. "I'm just fine," she told the waitress. Most of her milk was not yet drunk. The truth was, she didn't much like drinking milk.

"And how is Aunt Grace?" Rita asked.

"Hard to say. I got a letter yesterday. She sounded cheerful. Under the circumstances."

Grace had started her radiation treatments.

Bianca went on, "I keep thinking I must go see her. To help out? She was such a help to me once, when I was sick."

But there were huge obstacles to her going. Who would take care of the boys? And she was pregnant. And—in many ways the thorniest problem—Grant was unnerved by the proposal. He was stiffening now. Cleveland had been her destination on that merciless morning when she left a note on the kitchen table.

As an alternative, he kept suggesting they all four drive down . . . But how restful would it be for Grace to have the boys underfoot? Furthermore, Grace truly didn't seem to want visitors—not until she was feeling better. There was no solution, really, other than to feel guilty, and scared—which Bianca did, mostly at night. During the daytime, the whole question of Aunt Grace was surprisingly little on her mind.

When the waitress returned with drinks, they were ready to order. Bianca asked for the baked whitefish and Rita the stuffed pork chop. Stevie ordered the T-bone and, though Bianca winced at the price, Grant did the same.

Again, as soon grew apparent, Grant's instincts were sound. This was Stevie's night, and he was exulting in its lavishness. It *pleased* him that Grant had ordered the T-bone. When had Bianca last seen Stevie, when had she *ever* seen Stevie, talk so freely? He was effusive about trucking, not just Turk's Trucks but, as he put it, the "whole future of the transportation industry."

Stevie discussed the new Interstate Highway System and everyone was cheered to see him so outgoing. He spoke, they nodded and nodded. Trains were outmoded. It's like Nature, they can't adapt fast enough. Did any of them know how many pounds of cargo a good-sized semitrailer can carry? Sixty thousand, easy. And as the roads improve? And the engines improve? Eighty. A hundred thousand pounds . . .

Of course Stevie might conceivably have felt the same way about cars, about his former employer, the Ford Motor Company. But he never had. His job at Ford had never engaged his imagination the way, after only a week, Turk's Trucks had done. It was just lovely: he'd become a part, a real and living part, of something auspicious and vast and challenging.

Bianca had a sudden feeling, disorienting but not unwelcome, that

Stevie was evolving into somebody she didn't intimately know. Who was this man in the brown suit who spouted opinions on any topic under the sun—Mayor Cobo, the proper way to teach shop classes, or the bright future of California, which he alone among them had visited? Tonight she was seeing the emergence of somebody who had long yearned to get out—somebody she hadn't realized was there.

Once the food arrived, which everyone agreed was delicious (though Stevie, establishing himself as unintimidated by such extravagant prices, noted that his steak was "a little tough"), the subject of Grant's golfing arose.

"You've never tried it, you might like it," Grant said, and Stevie said, "I wouldn't mind. Trying it out. At least once. You know, I wouldn't mind."

And why couldn't they all share a world in which Stevie golfed on weekends, and went regularly to Tigers games—did something other than work all the time? Why couldn't a world emerge in which Stevie was recognized as precisely the sort of person Bianca knew he was at bottom: a competent, conscientious man whose virtues were suitably rewarded? Why couldn't the world relent and begin to be fair to Stevie?

It was a sign of his newfound confidence and openness that he introduced over dessert—they all ordered dessert—a subject rarely talked about.

"The first time she"—Rita—"brings up the idea of celebrating Grant's birthday at a restaurant, I say, Uh-uh. I say, No dice. I'm thinking, We don't have such a good family history of restaurant birthdays. You remember, Bea."

"Of course I remember."

Stevie, Rita, Grant—they all turned to her. Everyone knew the story, but even so they awaited some comment, interpretation, illumination.

"Aunt Grace's fortieth birthday," Bianca said. "At Chuck's Chop House on McNichols, now defunct. You could say that's the night when all hell broke loose in the family. Excuse my language, but that really is the word for it."

"She"—meaning Mamma—"just went crazy."

"Mamma just sort of went off her head," Bianca concurred, while softening the phrase a little. "And things have never really recovered. I'm convinced Uncle Dennis and Aunt Grace wouldn't have moved if that night had never happened. I know this sounds—I don't know. Melodramatic? Simplistic? But I'm convinced."

"She went off her head," Stevie pointed out.

"These things are complicated," Grant said, and nodded sagaciously—but of course there were no complications in his own family. Just ask him. Any significance to the fact that the nearer of his two sisters had moved to Flagstaff, Arizona, and the other all the way to Thailand? None at all. Sometimes Grant's refusal to confront such issues exasperated Bianca, but even if you faced them head-on, who could uncover the real underpinnings of any family? Who could isolate its truth? She was seeing tonight a Stevie who wasn't quite any Stevie she knew. And at the close of this inspiriting evening, as they awaited the check, something peculiar and deeply humbling revealed itself.

"I'll never forget that night at Chuck's Chop House," Stevie said. "Suddenly, everybody is marched out of the restaurant, while Dad and Uncle Dennis square up the bill. We're all standing under an awning, and then Mom walks out alone into the falling snow."

"Snow?" Bianca said.

"Snow. It was snowing," Stevie said.

"Stevie, it wasn't snowing. It was raining. It was Grace's birthday. We were celebrating Grace's birthday. This was July."

Stevie sat still, very pensive behind his glasses. Then he picked up a drinking straw, breathed through it, held his index finger over the bottom so he could no longer breathe, and released his finger and inhaled again. "You gotta be right," he concluded, finally. "July. Musta been. So it *had* to be rain."

"It was. It was raining."

"Funny," Stevie said. "But I see it so vivid. I would've sworn. I can *see* the snowflakes. Mom walking out into the snow." Stevie looked very young and vulnerable, suddenly.

"Well, why should you remember? You were just a little kid. You were what—thirteen?"

Stevie ran his index finger around the base of the straw. "Maybe the drink is playing with my head? But it's so funny. Because I see it so vivid: snowflakes. Mom walking off into the swirling snow."

Rain turns to snow . . . And if that evening's eyewitnesses were susceptible to such tricks of memory, what hope was there of arriving together at anything like the truth?

CHAPTER XXXII

At the end of it, putting on her pajamas that night, Bianca said to Grant, "*Quite* some day, don't you think?" It had been a good day, a day of stubborn little problems posed and solved, with one stunning and marvelous revelation . . .

The day had begun in earnest when Matt, whom she thought of as the less observant of the two boys, said to her, "Mom, you have a fat tummy." "Go call your brother," she said to him.

She led the two boys into the den and broke the news that everyone else had known for weeks and weeks. "You know what, boys? You're going to have a little sister or a little brother."

"You're going to have a baby," Chip said, face lighting with pride in his quickness.

"That's right. Daddy and I thought it would be a good idea for you to have a little sister or little brother."

"Which one will it be?" Matt said.

"That's what we don't know. Whether it will be a boy or a girl."

"Who does know?"

"Nobody knows. Or God, I guess."

"If it's a boy, what will you name it?" Chip said.

"We're not sure."

"Will you name it Matt?" Matt said.

"No. Matt is your name."

He nodded, relieved. Chip nodded. Everyone who saw them marveled at how closely they resembled their father, but if you were attentive to small visual details—and Bianca liked to think herself *very* attentive—the similarities were preternatural. Both boys had Grant's exact nod in these moments when great solemnity mixed with perplexity: an outthrusting of the chin while the eyes narrowed into quizzical slits.

How ridiculous she'd been in not telling the boys! She'd thought she would spare herself endless questions. But they weren't going to ask many questions now, or any time before the baby was born. There were a few more issues to clear up (What if the baby was twins? Where would the baby sleep?), but already they were a little overwhelmed; they'd had enough. She had brought them the most momentous news they'd ever heard—an announcement that would transform their lives forever—and they nodded and narrowed their eyes and when she asked if they were glad they replied "Yeah" and "Uh-huh." Five minutes from now, they'd be playing Ping-Pong or scampering around the backyard, and any thought of their new little sister would have flown right out of their heads.

Still, it was a problem solved, a job done—something which, for obscure reasons, she'd turned into a sizable burden. It was time to lift burdens—as of this morning she'd gained twenty-two pounds and this was no time to carry unnecessary weight. She lifted another burden in the afternoon with a short call to Stevie. This was a problem that sounded too implausible to be a problem: she and Grant owned three cars.

Mrs. Ives had made good on her promise. She'd bought Grant a car for his thirtieth birthday. He'd settled on a new red Mercury convertible, which he loved so extravagantly that Bianca joked about feeling jealous—not wholly a joke. "Listen to her *purr*," Grant would say, as they idled before a red light. Or: "Look how the sun lights up her hood." Or: "See the way she responds to the slightest touch."

Grant had given his green Studebaker to her—it would be the "family car." Her own '49 Mercury was now extraneous. Bianca thought she might extend the chain of gift giving to Stevie. Wouldn't it be wonderful for Rita to have a car? Bianca had thought Stevie might actually accept such a gift, now that he was out of the Ford plant and flourishing at Turk's Trucks. But what was she thinking? The offer made him indignant. A car? Rita didn't need a car! And if she did, he could certainly provide one.

So Bianca had considered offering it to Mamma and Papa, but what was the point? Papa had a new Dodge, and Mamma's Hudson was as good as new, she drove it so rarely. (Papa had bought her a car to encourage her to get out more. But while she always made such a point of not being an "Italian wife"—she'd driven since she was sixteen—she seldom climbed behind the wheel.) And Edith drove even less. She preferred the bus. She claimed this was because she liked to read, but in truth she usually got lost when driving anywhere. The girl with the world's most organized mind had no internal compass.

Bianca tried Stevie again. She had taken up P. G. Wodehouse novels a couple of years ago, at Priscilla's suggestion (she found them the perfect books for a mother—so easily picked up and put down), and decided now that it was all a matter, as Jeeves would say, of "the psychology of the individual."

"Stevie," she said, "it's about the car. The old Mercury. You said you might be able to help me out."

"What about it?" He sounded suspicious. "You needa sell it."

"I don't know how to answer all the questions. From potential buyers. How many engines does the thing have?—that sort of thing."

"It's got one, Bea."

"I tell you, I'm in a real fix. I thought maybe you might know somebody to sell it to."

Stevie exhaled into the phone.

"And it's losing value. Every day. Just sitting there. Money's going down the drain."

Silence at the other end.

"They're going to ask me about spark plugs. Does my car have spark plugs?"

Still an unbroken silence, though its nature had changed, she could tell. She'd begun to amuse him.

"It has six," Stevie finally said.

"And a carburetor?"

"*And* a carburetor."

"I tell you, I'm in a real fix. I need help."

He exhaled again.

"Losing money every day . . . Right down the drain."

"All right, all right. We'll come by today. You sign it over to me, I'll sell it when I can, give you the money."

"But I want you to make something. I simply can't let you do it if you don't make something."

"All right, all right. We'll be by today."

And it was as easy as that. Offer Stevie a car as a gift, he'd resent you. But offer it as a chore, a job that needed doing, and after a little huffing and puffing he'd swing by and pick it up that afternoon. It was all just the psychology of the individual.

She was reading a recent issue of *Time,* catching up on the news (the Democrats in despair, Adlai's chances dimming), when Maggie, whom Bianca hadn't seen in ages, dropped by unexpectedly. A new Maggie. A chin-enhanced Maggie.

She was still bruised from the procedure. She was swollen at the cheeks, and purple and yellow up and down her neck—but she was far too excited to sequester herself any longer. And far too pleased. She adored her new look. She was giggling and peering at her reflection in the front window, the mirror over the sofa, the glass of the china cabinet. She'd overcome her mortal fear of needles and knives to become the proud possessor of a new chin, a new face. It was difficult to tell how dramatic the change actually was, given the exultant way she exaggerated the effect by elevating her head and pointing her chin as she talked. But it was a small difference that made a big difference. She did look good, the new Maggie: she looked good.

But new Maggie was in many ways old Maggie, and this, too, was good: Bianca's oldest friend in the world was back. Maggie arrived bearing a gift, a quite tasteful and lovely silver bracelet.

"What's this for?"

"It's for you, silly." Maggie laughed. "Because you're my oldest friend and I haven't seen you in ages."

Yes, the bracelet was beautiful and this was one of Maggie's many puzzles: her gifts were almost always in exquisite taste, though her own clothes and jewelry typically verged on the tawdry. It was as if her gifts declared: *I know good taste but it's not for me.*

They drifted into the kitchen and Maggie said, "Do you have any wine?" and then she answered herself, "You always do," and Bianca said, "It's the Italian in me," and she poured Maggie a glass of red wine and herself a glass of ginger ale. (She'd grown very tired of milk.) And soon they were giggling away, just like the old days, Maggie rattling on about her horrible mother-in-law and Bianca about the latest visit to Mr. and Mrs. Ives. "You look so good," Maggie said, and Bianca said thank you, and Maggie said, "*We* look so good," and they both laughed, and Maggie said, "You're having a new baby and I have a new chin," and Maggie laughed more brightly still and it was suddenly apparent that this was the first occasion—unveiling her new chin to her oldest friend—when Maggie had felt completely comfortable with Bianca's pregnancy.

But Maggie was restless in the kitchen. She sat with legs crossed, upraised foot kicking to and fro. Then she got up and examined herself in the back window.

They wound up in the little room behind the den, which Bianca hesitated to call her studio, since she so rarely attempted art in it. Bianca had never warmed to the space, actually, though uncertain whether she disliked the room itself or the self-reproaches it fostered. "Henry," Maggie said, and pointed.

Yes, here was Henry Vanden Akker, in the portrait with Gauguin's jungle ferns and van Gogh's jungle star clusters. It was the doomed boy who once wrote a poem invoking her as his landfall and harbor light. The portrait hung on the wall, along with one of her landscapes and two of her still lifes.

"Henry," Bianca echoed.

"It's quite good," Maggie said, not knowing what else to say.

"You never met him," Bianca replied. And added: "But it is good," because it was—or because, anyway, it was the best portrait poor Henry would ever have.

Standing side by side, shoulders almost touching, the two old friends contemplated Henry's portrait.

"No, I never met him," Maggie said. "But I heard enough about him."

"Yes, you did," Bianca said. "You sure did."

"Did you ever tell Grant?"

"Tell Grant what?" Bianca said.

Bianca was being coy, and Maggie had every justification for her slightly reedy tone: "About the last night you and Henry spent together."

"No-o." Bianca took a seat in the blue leather chair and motioned Maggie toward the love seat. "But I meant to."

"But you couldn't. Under the circumstances."

"But I really did *mean* to," Bianca protested. Maggie was often far too ready to excuse small deceits, white lies. "It just wasn't possible." Bianca took refuge in Maggie's phrase: "Under the circumstances."

"I know what you mean," Maggie said.

Tensions hovered in the air, but these were the old tensions, far preferable to the new tensions. At the base of the new tensions lay the wasting fear that Bianca really didn't like the person Maggie had become: a woman who, as the wife of a wealthy and important man, accepted wealth and importance as her due. The new Maggie engendered a suspicion that Bianca had stayed in touch with her old friend for merely sentimental reasons—that she was someone Bianca could easily do without. But at the base of the old tensions, which had caused the two girls to squabble and needle each other endlessly, lay the knowledge of Maggie's indispensability. This was the Maggie she had dragged through the rain to a branch library in order to make her confession: *Maggie, the very worst thing has happened . . .*

"I took the portrait down once," Bianca said, "and you know what? Grant insisted I put it back up."

Yes, she'd told Maggie this story before, but she must recall it again, for this was one of Grant's handsomest traits: his heartfelt eagerness to acknowledge heroism wherever it surfaced, whether on the athletic field or on the battlefield . . . Grant had spent the War Stateside, at a flight-training school in Wichita Falls, Texas, but he was quick to acknowledge those who had made "the ultimate sacrifice." He considered himself "one of the lucky ones." He didn't merely *say* this. (It was the sort of thing men felt obliged to say, hoping to look endearingly modest.) No, he *did* consider himself lucky, in most every aspect of his existence. Grant moved through his days—God bless him—grateful for his home, his children, his wife, his life.

"You know, the strangest thing happened," Bianca said. "The other night. I was sort of half awake. I tried to call up Henry's voice, and you know what? I couldn't. Maggie, I couldn't hear it. And suddenly I got this panicky feeling. Something terrible was going to happen to Henry unless I could call up his voice. And I had to remind myself, Henry's been dead for going on ten years. Whatever horrible thing is going to happen to him? It's already happened."

"Ten years," Maggie said.

"And his poor parents! Their only son! Afterward, each time I visited, they were more wasted away. Are they still in Pleasant Ridge? Still alive? I've often wondered."

"You didn't stay in touch."

"They clearly didn't want to. And you remember, I got so sick."

"I remember."

"And maybe I was scared? Uncle Dennis tells me I nearly died . . ."

"You could look them up in the phone book now."

"I could. I've thought many times of doing just that."

"You could do it right now," Maggie said.

"I could. But I'm not going to."

They regarded each other—the pregnant woman and the woman with the newly enhanced chin—and Bianca found it heartening to feel all the old bonds intact. Maggie Szot had always been the one to extend a dare, Bea Paradiso the one to shrink from fears she couldn't quite explain—but still grateful for the dare, *hungry* for the dare . . .

Bianca started—jumped back, really—when the front door opened. It was Grant, home from tennis. Grant hardly seemed to register Maggie's presence, let alone her enhanced chin. His face blazed with excitement. "Bianca, Bianca, ja hear the news? *Ja hear the news?* About Roy Bootmaker?"

"What on earth—"

"It's our milkman," Grant said to Maggie.

"Oh I've met Mr. Bootmaker." In the old days, before she'd married Walton, Maggie had frequently dropped in for morning coffee.

"Bianca, he's a *hero*!" Grant said. "Bianca, I'm telling you! Mr. Bootmaker! He's an honest-to-God hero."

"What on earth are you talking about?"

"You haven't heard the news, obviously. I've just heard it from Mrs. Applegrew." Mrs. Applegrew lived down the block. "I tell you, Roy Bootmaker is a hero."

"Grant, for heaven's sake, sit down and tell us properly. Start at the beginning."

Grant dropped down beside Maggie. He loved delivering stories, and this was just the sort of story he loved best . . .

Yesterday, on his route, Roy Bootmaker had stopped at Mr. Bickey's. (Mr. Bickey lived just down the street, Grant explained to Maggie. He's the neighborhood recluse and a very sour old man, Bianca added. He never goes out, but he replaces his Cadillac every year, Grant said. He has trouble going out, his legs are all swollen, he walks with a cane, Bianca added in fairness.) *Anyway,* yesterday Roy Bootmaker stopped at Mr. Bickey's. He expected a note in the milk chute, Mr. Bickey's usual practice, but there was none. Mr. Bootmaker knocked on the side door and rang the front doorbell, but no answer. The kitchen radio was on, however, which was also odd, since Mr. Bickey wasn't the sort to go out and leave a radio running. The cat was meowing loudly in the kitchen; apparently, it hadn't been fed. Mr. Bootmaker circled back of the house and peered through the garage window. Mr. Bickey's Cadillac was inside, which was odder still . . .

Mr. Bootmaker and his father (his father drives the truck, Bianca explained to Maggie) continued with their milk route, but an hour or so later, going miles out of their way, they returned to Mr. Bickey's and knocked and knocked and rang the doorbell. The radio was still running. The cat was still meowing, hungrier than ever. They knocked on the neighbors' doors. No one had seen Mr. Bickey. The car was still in the garage. Convinced that something might be seriously amiss, Mr.

Bootmaker boosted his father on his shoulders (as you know, the son is quite large, Bianca explained to Maggie, and the father's quite diminutive), and they found a kitchen window not fully closed. The older Mr. Bootmaker (he's seventy-seven years old, Bianca supplied) eased himself through the window and opened the side door for his son, Roy Bootmaker. Roy called and called. And then he thought he heard a voice.

Roy raced upstairs (and Bianca could visualize him doing just that, in his size 12½ EEE black shoes) and looked around. He found Mr. Bickey in the bath.

"In the bath!" Bianca exclaimed.

"In the *bath*. Mr. Bickey had had some sort of stroke. Hours before. He couldn't climb out. The water had grown cold and he was naked and shivering. He wasn't going to live long, an old man like that, lying paralyzed in a cold bath."

"Holy moly," Maggie said. The story had turned very serious indeed.

"And Mr. Bootmaker hauls him out of the bath, wraps him in a robe, and carries him downstairs and into his truck, and they race to the hospital, and the only reason Mr. Bickey is alive today is because of Mr. Bootmaker. He's a hero. He's a genuine hero!"

"And Mr. Bickey's going to be all right?" Bianca asked.

"Apparently. In any case, a helluva lot better off than he woulda been. He woulda been *dead*. I tell you, Roy Bootmaker is a hero."

Grant's eyes were shining. It was a lovely display of everything Bianca had been saying just now: how freely Grant esteemed the heroism of others. The man who had insisted that Henry Vanden Akker's portrait remain on the wall was thrilled—just thrilled—to see Roy Bootmaker, the epileptic milkman, revealed as a hero.

It was also just like Grant to insist on taking the tale one step further: "And you know what, Maggie? Here's the kicker to the story. A month or so ago, I proposed canceling Bootmaker's deliveries. To save a buck or two. And Bianca wouldn't hear of it. I tried to fire a genuine hero, and Bianca wouldn't let me."

"Grant, it's not as if I knew. I just felt sorry for him. After I found out he has epilepsy."

"I didn't know that," Maggie said. "I'm not sure I'd want an epileptic milkman."

"That's the *point*!" Bianca said. "That's the problem! If nobody wants him, he's out of a job, and then what is he—"

Grant was eager to return to the core argument. "Bianca, you had the *instinct,* don't you see? You knew it was wrong. I wanted to fire him. And you knew it was wrong."

"This is absurd. It's not as if I—"

"You were adamant. Absolutely adamant. I tried to fire a man who's a genuine *hero,* and you said no." Grant looked to Maggie for verification: surely they were confronting another demonstration of Bianca's formidable second sight.

"It's not as if—"

"But it *is,* Bianca. It *is.* Don't you see? I said, We're going to cancel Bootmaker. And you said, Are you out of your mind? You basically said, He may not look like it, but that man is a genuine hero."

Grant found the story of Mr. Bickey's rescue so stirring that, over a large whiskey, he recounted it a second time. Maggie—the new, plastically enhanced Maggie—kept pointing her chin at him, but Grant didn't notice. After Grant told the story a third time, Maggie abruptly departed, looking a little nonplussed. "You know," Bianca said, "the way you talked, you were only fueling Maggie. She seems to feel you hold me in too high esteem."

Grant's reply was chivalrously perfect: "But how would that be possible?"

And yet it wasn't mere chivalry. His face still wore its wondering, boyish glow.

And hours later, as she was putting on her pajamas, he continued to throw her wondering, glowing glances. "*Quite* some day, don't you think?" she said.

What reliably accompanied that glow was a neediness, and when they climbed into bed Grant curled his big body around her body and placed one hand on her rounded hipbone and one hand loosely outspread on her collarbone. Soon they were going to make love. He needed to touch her—to touch the body of the woman who, lit with clairvoyance, threw off the glimmerings of another world. "I tried to fire him," Grant said. It was remarkable how deep in him ran this need to believe she communed with mysterious, inestimable forces. Perhaps as deep as her own appetite for a man who felt this need.

CHAPTER XXXIII

She was sitting where she rarely sat, in her studio, when the phone rang. It was Papa. "Bia, can you come? I need you to come."

"Now?" It was eight at night. "Is there—sure, sure I can come. Is there something wrong?"

"Wrong? Yes. Something wrong."

"But is everything all right?" Meaning: is everyone still alive? Has the house burned down?

"It's all right. I need you to come."

She wasn't going to get anything more out of him . . .

Nervous, *very* nervous, but not quite in an absolute panic, Bianca explained everything, or as much as there was *to* explain, to Grant, who said of course she had to go: her father never summoned her like this. He would stay home and look after the boys.

Bianca drove down Woodward to Mack, Mack to Inquiry, all with a heightened visual sense of herself: she was a pregnant woman in a green Studebaker, alone on a gray windy October night, driving home toward some disaster. "Just what I need," she said aloud. "Just what I need."

Papa was waiting for her as she pulled up. "I want to show you something," he said. His face was white with emotion.

Bianca followed him into the kitchen. He was limping on his plantar wart. A peculiar ghastly sound, muffled behind the closed door, issued from her parents' bedroom. It was—unbelievably—it was the sound of Mamma weeping.

Everything was neatly laid out on the kitchen table. Under the harsh overhead light, it seemed internally illuminated, like a dream, but what did it signify? Here were hairnets and bags of hard candy, sunglasses, candles, deodorant and toilet water, handkerchiefs, packs of chewing gum, thumbtacks. Here was a porcelain poodle, a pair of gnomes that served as pepper and salt shakers, a set of bamboo napkin rings, a rabbit's foot key ring dyed emerald green. Here was a far wider array of merchandise than Bianca could absorb all at once. Beside each item, in Mamma's neat handwriting, was a file card with the name of a store (Hudson's, Crowley's, Olsson's), and a price, and a date.

Mamma was sobbing in the bedroom and meanwhile Papa, charged with mysterious intention, was asking Bianca to contemplate a blazing tabletop overrun with cheap, garish merchandise. Once again she had returned home in order to step into a dream. "I don't understand . . . What does this mean?"

"What does it mean?" Papa repeated. He paused. "It means your mother is a thief."

"I don't understand."

Papa's words were stupefying. There was no way to absorb them all at once.

"She did not pay for these."

"I don't understand," Bianca said again.

"It means your mother takes the things and she does not pay."

A dragging sound like Oh-h-h issued from her throat, but it was more grunt than word. The horror was inexpressible. For a few seconds the room appeared to go dark, then to flame into a new spectrum, the merchandise on the kitchen table returning with vibrating intensity. *Your mother is a thief* . . . The horror was inexpressible, and yet even in the midst of it, Bianca recognized a low-lying hungry kind of excitement: surely, now, *something* would have to be done. Surely, now, some long-needed breaking open would break open.

Papa had set everything out neatly, painstakingly—almost proudly, you might suppose, if you didn't know the circumstances. Each shiny item with its file card . . . Things from Hudson's, Crowley's, Cunningham's, but most had come (Bianca began to understand, her eyes jumping here and there) from Olsson's. And now the strongest of all emotions hit her: a wave of insupportable shame. "Shouldn't we put these things away?"

"Better to leave them out," Papa said.

"Who knows about this?" Bianca whispered.

"No one but you and me," Papa said. "And Edith."

"Where's Edith?"

"In there with her." Papa pointed with his elbow at the bedroom. Mamma was still sobbing behind the closed door. "And Uncle Dennis. He knows. He comes tomorrow."

"Uncle Dennis is coming tomorrow?"

"Yes."

"Thank heavens."

But even as she offered these words, Bianca knew the problem was too vast and grave even for Uncle Dennis's healing powers. What could anyone do? She could not take her eyes from the kitchen table. Under the bright light, the stolen items were rioting. They were crying out: *It means your mother is a thief.* Her skin was crawling. There were no words for this sort of horror.

"Tomorrow morning," Papa said. "Tomorrow I don't go to work."

"You stay here," Bianca said.

"I stay home," Papa said.

"So many *things . . . ,*" Bianca said.

There was a pincushion in the shape of an apple. There was an unopened pack of bobby pins. There was a tube of wart-remover cream, which must have been intended for Papa's plantar wart. Yes, Mamma had been tenderly looking out for Papa's welfare, even as she was behaving in a way guaranteed to disgust and desolate him.

Never before in her life had Bianca seen her father so upset. The man who prided himself on his calm was shaking with emotion. His voice, too, was shaking.

"There are extra file cards," Bianca said.

There was a substantial pile of them, nearly of the thickness of a deck of playing cards. The top one, again in Mamma's cramped but neat handwriting, said, "Polident, Olsson's, September 13, 1952, 39¢."

"Those are for the ones she used."

"I don't understand," Bianca said, although this time she did.

"They're gone," Papa said. "She used them up. *We* used them up. I have been brushing my teeth"—and Papa tapped his forefinger against those teeth he took such pride in, still not a cavity in the man's mouth—"with stolen toothpaste. She made these cards as a record."

"I still don't understand. How did you find out about this?"

"It was a box. In her closet."

"You opened a box in her closet and you found all this?"

"Yes."

"And Mamma admits she stole all of it? She confessed?"

"After a while. Yes."

"And there were cards for things that were missing?"

"Yes. Cards for everything. The missing things, too."

So the cards were not something recently compiled. No, they had served all along as the meticulously kept diary of a working thief—and Bianca shuddered once more, for this painstaking process of self-incrimination screamed madness. Would anyone but a madwoman do such a thing?

"No one must know," Bianca whispered.

"No," Papa said. And added: "But we know."

"I feel sick," Bianca said. "Sick to my stomach."

"Sick all over," Papa said. "I've been washing myself with stolen soap. I've been brushing my teeth with stolen toothpaste." Everything about him, body and voice, was shaking.

One of the items from Olsson's was the little pair of porcelain gnomes, presumably a husband and wife. A pepper-and-salt-shaker set. The man was Pepper. He had lifted his hand to his face. He was sneezing. The woman was weeping. Salt tears. Even for gnomes, the two of them were intensely ugly—they had the special grotesquery of objects that fused intended and unwitting ugliness. So it made sense that the gnomes hadn't been removed from their cellophane. But who in their right mind would risk police arrest, public humiliation, and all the gnawing guilt of indelible sin, in order to steal such a pair? What sort of mind could eye them and see temptation and opportunity?

There was no reason to shoplift *any* of these things, of course, but Bianca's attention fixated on the porcelain gnome couple: the sneezer and the weeper. Still in cellophane . . .

"Thank heavens Uncle Dennis is coming," she said, but what could he do for a woman who would shoplift such cheap and useless and *stupid* eyesores? And if Uncle Dennis could do nothing, what on earth could be done? *What could be done?* Bianca knew she hadn't begun to negotiate all the layers of her revulsion, but she also knew, knew to a dead bright trapped certainty, that for days and days and days her problems could only deepen before anything, ever, got any better.

A new day broke, under a sick gray sky, and Uncle Dennis arrived for various surreal consultations and he spent the night on Inquiry Street and returned to Cleveland and then drove back to Detroit the very next day. He had arranged for something. Mamma would be away for a couple days—maybe as long as a week. She would undergo a "thorough examination." She would be staying out near Ann Arbor.

Papa took comfort in the phrase, which he repeated incessantly. Mamma was going for a "thorough examination." This would be both sorts of tests, Uncle Dennis explained to Bianca—as he had no doubt explained to Papa, and to Edith, and to Stevie, though Stevie probably hadn't required much of an explanation. He'd already formulated one. "She's gone off her rocker," he declared with finality, as if this sound medical opinion rendered further discussion superfluous. What was the point? And besides, the whole subject made him very tense—like a clench fist, as Rita would say. Edith, on the other hand, was keen to ana-lyze the whole business, mostly in the light of her anthropology courses. It seemed that in order properly to understand Mamma's behavior you first had to recognize that the very idea of property—and hence, theft—was a culturally created notion. What one culture regarded as "stealing," another might view as sharing . . . In other words, neither Stevie nor Edith was any help at all, and the best thing to do, Bianca realized, was to assign them very specific secondary tasks, like the question of reimbursement.

The money had to be returned, of course. Edith could have quickly summed the numbers in her head, but Stevie, working laboriously, cal-culated everything on paper. The total came to $27.72. It was Edith who pointed out that mere reimbursement would not be sufficient. A num-ber of thefts extended back over a year and an accrual of interest would be required. This, the two of them eventually agreed, should be set at 10 percent, a figure Edith initially considered exorbitant. Stevie may well have been motivated by a wish to keep calculations simple, but he won Edith over with the argument that the stores in question would have "processing costs." He worked for a trucking company, he knew about such things. The actual delivery of the money—in plain envelopes, with a brief and vague anonymous letter of Edith's composing—was left to Stevie, who predictably undertook it with gusto, as an exciting bit of espionage.

It would have been funny, if it weren't all so gruesome and horrible.

Yes, certain problems could be satisfactorily handled, or even dele-gated, but others resisted all mediation. Bianca had just turned onto Woodward, she was heading off to Inquiry to meet Papa and Edith, when a cold perception crept over her: she didn't know where her mother was. Yes, her mother was in Ann Arbor, getting her thorough examination, but Bianca didn't actually know *where*—she couldn't identify the physical site where her mother was spending the night. Never before in her life had she been unable to identify where her mother was passing the night, and this icy recognition, though she was hardly a religious person, sponta-neously prompted a prayer, spoken aloud. It was maybe the shortest meaningful prayer anyone had ever composed, a mere two words, repeated over and over as she drove south on Woodward: *Please, God,* is how it went. *Please, God; please, God; please, God . . .*

And what was to be done about Papa? He wandered around like a lost man. Mamma was away from home six days in all, getting her "thorough examination," getting her "little rest," and Bianca every night was there for her father, sitting beside him in the living room. "You must spend as much time as you can with your father," Uncle Dennis had advised, but what exactly was there to say or do? Bianca tried other subjects, but Papa made no pretense of listening. And when Papa did open his mouth, it was to utter phrases she'd heard dozens of times: "She had plenty of money," or "It doesn't make sense," or—the most touching, because the most helpless—"Why do you think she did it?" And it turned out that Papa—frugal Papa!—had thrown out every toiletry in the house . . . That he might brush his teeth or shampoo his hair or wash his body with illicit goods—the images nauseated him.

So Bianca would come down to Inquiry every night and cook dinner and eat in the kitchen with Edith and Papa and afterward sit with him in the living room and listen to the radio. Mostly, they didn't talk. Sometimes they walked up to a store—*not* Olsson's—and Papa bought cigarettes or some new toiletry. On the walks, too, he said little, and what he did say was so repetitive it frightened her. It was as if her father, too, was coming mentally unwound. "No need to do it," Papa would say, and Bianca would say, "Of course not." And Papa would say, "Don't I give her all the money she wants?" and Bianca would say, "Of course you do."

Papa was drinking far too much and sometimes on their walks this athletic man, who always carried himself in public with a self-possessed flair—*la bella figura*—lurched off a curb or half stumbled over a bump in the sidewalk. And it broke her heart to see her father this way. It broke her heart.

Uncle Dennis had always been the family's trusted advisor, but now it was as though *everything* was placed in his hands. He was back and forth from Cleveland three times in one week. The poor man couldn't be sleeping. He was conferring with doctors, he was "making arrangements." And Papa—helpless, heartbroken—seemed to be only half listening to Uncle Dennis, though taking solace in this or that select phrase. A *thorough examination.* Mamma at last was getting a *thorough examination.* They would *get to the bottom of things.*

And meanwhile Bianca, driving up and down Woodward, took solace in her own phrase: *Please, God; please, God; please, God . . .*

Of course she'd quit smoking and drinking the moment she got official word of her pregnancy, but now she needed whatever assistance could be found. It was all the solitary driving that did it, cranked up her anxiety until she craved a cigarette to the point where she couldn't think of anything else. Up and down Woodward . . . "I'm smoking again and I'm pregnant and I'm talking to myself." And she was chewing mints and jelly beans, to cover the smell of the cigarettes, since nobody must know she'd gone back to smoking, it was all so shameful. "I'm living on candy, I'm becoming my mother, just when my mother's acting"—up jumped the Tenniel illustration from *Alice in Wonderland*—"mad as a March hare."

And then Mamma returned home, smaller than before—it was the strangest, scariest thing. She was always a little too thin, but this wasn't that. While making their thorough examination, the doctors must have removed a couple of vertebrae. And Mamma drifted through her own house uncertainly, and spoke more softly than usual.

Bianca had seen a transformation like this before—but when? What was it? A couple of days had to pass before, lying beside Grant in the middle of the night, it returned to her. Of course. Mrs. Vanden Akker. After the tragic news. Her son had burned up in a tropical rainstorm, and she'd dwindled away to nothing . . . And Bianca, trembling, got out of bed and smoked two quick cigarettes in the downstairs bathroom, blowing the smoke out the open window.

They had entered a new world, where Mamma kept posing questions both painful and unanswerable. "I let everyone down, didn't I?" she would ask, sitting with Bianca at the kitchen table. Or, "I should feel ashamed, shouldn't I?" Or: "What I did was really *crazy*, wasn't it?" The silence after words like these was the saddest silence Bianca had ever known.

Still, it rarely brought Bianca to the edge of tears. Her grief was all too deep for tears. You couldn't cry, but you couldn't laugh either, when, at Abajay's market, your mother lifted a head of lettuce, peered at it as intently as though it were a skull, and said, "What is it inside me that sets out to destroy things?"

Meanwhile, "You must spend as much time as you can with your mother," Uncle Dennis advised, and Bianca seemed to spend half of each day on the road, on Woodward, driving back and forth to Inquiry, often talking to herself, and sometimes talking to herself about talking to herself. "Now I'm talking to myself while driving over to visit my lunatic of a mother."

She'd arrive at her mother's hoping the smell of candy covered up the sour smell of cigarettes, to greet a woman who had always covered up life's sour smells with candy . . .

Actually, food was becoming a general problem. Bianca had lost all appetite for the things she ought to be eating: milk, cheese, salads, meat, fruit. This wasn't anything like her morning sickness with the twins. It was odder, and fiercer. She would crunch almost angrily on a handful of jelly beans after having a cigarette, but to sit down before a moist chicken thigh and a bowl of green beans brought on instant nausea. She who'd been so worried about putting on weight—averaging more than two pounds a week in the first two months of pregnancy!—shied from the scale for a different reason. Was she losing weight? It was the question she couldn't utter aloud: was she starving her baby?

She had journeyed once before—nine years ago now—into a land where she'd lost all appetite and couldn't sleep, and she must not, *would not* return there. The Lord has taken him—those were the words Mrs. Vanden Akker had used to break the news, which was the final stroke, shattering the balance between Heaven and Earth, and Bianca hadn't understood how to move through Life anymore, until she reached a point where the Lord had almost taken her, too. Sometimes—typically when she was driving—those War days came back with such vividness her hands shook convulsively. Sometimes she had to pull the car over and collect herself. *Please God,* she prayed.

This couldn't last—the miserable days bleeding, blurring one by one—but when everything broke, when the flickering light of hope finally appeared on the calendar, she scarcely dared believe it. Could things actually get better? Hope? What was there to hope for?

Papa made the momentous announcement one night at dinner, just the three of them, Edith being away at school. He said: "Uncle Dennis had an idea. And I agree. And now your mother agrees. We need a fresh start. We're going to move. We're going to sell the house."

It hardly seemed possible, some things cannot happen . . . So many emotions crowded Bea's mind, they couldn't be identified, except for one, more powerful than all the rest: yes, it was hopefulness. Oh, the freeing human potentialities of hope! An exit, a respite, a *fresh start* . . . Maybe it could be left behind, it would not follow them: that all-but-visible blackness permeating every room of the house, forming a cloud you could almost see over Mamma's chair in the kitchen. Maybe the family could leave Inquiry Street, and perfect strangers would move into the rooms, shifting the light around, introducing new arrangements of bright and dark—and what on earth could be stranger than that? Well, maybe the house *needed* new people, and what on earth could be stranger than that?

A fresh start. Uncle Dennis was right, of course. They were still young, Mamma and Papa, they could build a new life . . .

The story emerged over days, in bits and pieces. Uncle Dennis was back in town, he never seemed to sleep, he was shuttling incessantly between Cleveland and Detroit, and Bianca had an hour's talk with him at that favorite old restaurant, Uncle Danny's, on Gratiot. This was the place, ironically, where he'd first announced the move to Cleveland. Did he remember that? Probably not.

When she hesitated over the menu, feeling a little queasy, he basically ordered on her behalf: a glass of milk and a tuna sandwich. She was still having trouble eating regular meals. But she managed, under his watchful eye, to get some of it down without retching. "You're looking very pale," he observed.

Uncle Dennis ordered a cheeseburger and a piece of lemon meringue pie for himself. He ate ravenously. Despite all his running back and forth, he seemed to be gaining weight these days.

His conversation today was peppered with phrases like *you know* and *you understand*. Bianca didn't, in fact. But Uncle Dennis was in a rush and she pieced things together. He'd been helping Papa find a house. Free at last to move, Papa was aspiring to something grand. And with all his hard work and economizing, it seemed he could now afford something rather grand. But Uncle Dennis was counseling against it. Mamma "musn't feel overwhelmed." A fresh start, yes—but in a house no bigger than what they had now.

And last week a house had turned up, soundly constructed, on Reston Street, just a couple of blocks west of Indian Village, and this was important, too: it would be a change of neighborhood, but not so distant from Inquiry. Clearly, Uncle Dennis was running everything now. Nobody else had any inkling how to proceed. What do you do when the sky falls in? What else but call on Uncle Dennis, who somehow contrived the means to prop up a fallen sky. He could locate the right doctors, the psychologists and the nerve specialists; and he knew how to mend a shattered household with talk of a fresh start. Without Uncle Dennis, Papa slumped into paralysis, night after night uncomprehendingly shaking his wine-soaked head. With Uncle Dennis at his side, however, he was out tracking down the right new home, arguing price and location, no doubt raising objection after objection to Uncle Dennis's proposals—but listening, always listening to the alluring voice of a *fresh start*. The family had placed themselves in the hands of this man who shuttled back and forth, who tended all his patients in Cleveland before racing up to Detroit, effectively to tend another set of patients. It was like Uncle Dennis now to urge on her the tuna sandwich and the milk, and to ask how Dr. Stimpson, her obstetrician, thought the pregnancy was going. "Honey, you must take care of yourself," he said. "I remember a little girl who didn't take care of herself, and her aunt Grace and I had to nurse her back to health."

A little girl? It was absurd—she stood at least half an inch taller than he did. But it was a comforting absurdity, and under his ministering eye Bianca managed to do what she hadn't done in a couple of weeks: consume a full meal at one sitting.

He was wonderfully capable, but not even Uncle Dennis could anticipate all the ways things could go wrong. The family's problems were like some sort of cancer which, arrested in one location, erupts in another. When the next crisis arrived, it came from a totally unexpected source: Edith. And who would have guessed that *Edith* might fall apart?

Edith had handled the business of Mamma's thievery a little peculiarly perhaps—all that painstaking haggling with Stevie over the interest due in reparation—but this was just the finicky exactitude you'd expect from Edith, and hence was almost reassuring. And Edith had been showing Mamma extra kindnesses—helping more with the cooking and the cleaning, and trying harder to keep up a civil conversation at dinner. Under the circumstances, Edith was handling things reasonably well.

She loved her classes at Wayne. And she was robust with good health, at a time when Bianca was smoking and munching on disgusting candies and suffering from such chronic diarrhea that she'd become familiar with most of the service-station ladies' rooms on Woodward Avenue. Having read in one of her anthropology classes about a tribe of nomadic goatherds in central Asia who live almost forever, Edith had become a great walker, marching purposefully along with great sacks of books under her arms. Somewhere along the way, she'd burned off what apparently had been baby fat. She was solid but no longer pudgy. When exactly had the change taken place? Bianca couldn't say. But one day she'd looked down Inquiry and seen a tallish woman approaching— Edith was almost five-seven—and Bianca had realized with a shock that this was her plump little sister.

Striding easily down the street with all her weighty reading, Edith evoked strength. Even her square-framed imitation tortoiseshell glasses, which she never removed, suggested strength—rationalism, reliability, objectivity. Bianca had once made the mistake of urging Edith toward another pair, something softer and more feminine. It was like trying to give Stevie a car. You met the same bristling stiffness. Evidently, what looked so negligent had been a deliberate fashion choice: Edith *wanted* to resemble (as Maggie once mischievously but memorably put it) an assistant bank manager.

And now the assistant bank manager began falling apart. Edith had handled successfully the catastrophic news of Mamma's crimes, and Mamma's departure for a week of rest, and the almost terrifying transformation when Mamma returned looking dwindled and speaking in an odd, marveling, almost tranquilized way while offering up one devastating observation after another. It was as if Edith didn't notice any alteration. But Edith *did* notice, she was extremely observant, as Bianca realized on the couple of occasions when the two sisters sat down for a chat. "It's as if something has given way inside Mamma, and she may never be her old self again." Edith did not declare this cruelly; she was making a sort of diagnosis. "And Papa's drinking has doubled." "Well," Bianca said, "there's definitely been an increase in—" "Doubled," Edith interrupted, with that fixed mathematical certainty of hers. "He used to drink a beaker of wine a night. Now he drinks two."

Edith saw the difficulties straight on, and her response was to proceed as she'd always proceeded: piling up little unspoken kindnesses, much as she'd piled up sweaters and socks and mittens for the soldiers during the War. It seemed Edith didn't need to draw on one cigarette after another as Bianca did. And Edith didn't drive up and down Woodward Avenue talking to herself.

Who could have foreseen that what would break Edith's spirit was the thought of moving from Inquiry? Surely it was time to go. Wasn't it obvious? In the *Free Press* not so long ago, Bianca had seen all those blocks of the old neighborhood—south of Mack and just west of the Boulevard—described as a slum. A slum!

Moving had never seemed possible because Mamma wouldn't think of it—but even Mamma was mumbling about *a fresh start.* And Edith the good team player? Suddenly she was digging in her heels. She wasn't going to move to Reston Street. She just wasn't.

The two sisters took a walk, though it was cold—a cold and gray December day—and Bianca was wearing an olive-green poncho rather than her black wool coat; she hadn't planned on a walk. They headed down Inquiry to Jefferson, Jefferson over to the Boulevard, across Jefferson to the Belle Isle Bridge, which during the War had been renamed the Douglas MacArthur Bridge, though nobody ever seemed to call it that. Bianca let her little sister guide her. Of course it was even colder out by the river, and colder still on the gusty bridge, the wind throwing up little whitecaps beneath them. It seemed almost self-punishing to walk the bridge today, but Edith kept striding in that defiantly purposeful way of hers. Beyond Belle Isle, across the river, cold Canada lay shivering.

Bianca, pregnant and weak, and desperately craving a cigarette, marched along beside her baby sister. The gray waters were flowing with iron determination beneath them, and by the time they were halfway across the long bridge, Edith was crying.

Edith was crying—all at once. The girl who never wept was weeping. She did not remove her tortoiseshell glasses. Tears flowed down her cheeks, unwiped, and fell to the sidewalk.

"I don't *want* to move," she announced. For all her tears, her words moved purposefully forward—just the way she walked. "Does anyone consult me? Does anyone say, What does Edith want? Do they care about *my* feelings?"

"Oh *sweetie,*" Bianca sighed. Her sympathy ran deep. But fear ran deeper still. The sight of her unflappable sister coming undone was more than she could bear. "Of course they do. We all do."

"Is it the *house's* fault? Is the *house* to blame because Mamma's a thief? Because Papa's a drunk?"

"Papa's not a drunk."

"You know what their logic is? It's the opposite of logic. They don't see that. What's the one thing we have when everything's falling apart? When Mamma's become someone else, and Papa's become someone else—what's the one thing to remain the same? Isn't it the *house,* which no one has a loyal word for except me? Oh it's fine for *you* if we move, you've got your mansion up there on Middleway."

"It's no mansion—"

"You've got your husband and your kids, and it's fine for Stevie, he's moved on, he never liked the house anyway—"

"That's not true."

"Remember when he left us all for a year and a half? It's all Stevie ever talked about when he was a boy: someday he would grow up and leave us."

"I don't remember that . . ."

"But what about me?" And now Edith's crying had altered. The words were not moving purposefully forward. She was choking with emotion. "When does anyone say, What about Edith's welfare?"

"Oh darling, darling, *darling*." Shivering worse than ever, Bianca drew an arm around her little sister. "Of course we do. We think about your welfare all the time."

Edith didn't exactly shrug off the embracing arm, but she began walking resolutely forward once more. Bianca kept her arm around her sister.

Actually, it didn't matter if Mamma and Papa moved—Edith explained—because she herself was about to embark on her own life. One of her professors, Miss Dinney, was a graduate of Barnard College. Edith would enroll in graduate school, she would study biology, she planned to settle in New York City. Or she was moving to Sarasota, Florida. A friend of hers who also wrote for the Wayne *Collegian*, her name was Joanna Mufflin, her family owned a newspaper in Sarasota, and Edith would move down there.

But crazy as these ideas sounded (Edith in New York? Edith in *Florida*?), what she proposed next was crazier still: she would remain on Inquiry. Mamma and Papa would move—that was fine, she wished them all the best, but she needed a place of her own. She would stay put, and pay them rent, and eventually she would buy it outright: the others could do as they wished, but she wasn't about to abandon her home.

Bianca started to say, "*You* know Papa would never permit that." Which was true. Papa move and leave his daughter behind? What was Edith thinking?

Catching herself in time, Bianca said instead, "I think you should talk to Uncle Dennis. He's coming up this weekend. Tell him what you're telling me. He may have an idea." Bianca was shivering so much in her poncho, it was impossible to tell whether, in holding on to her sister, she was offering or seeking warmth. "I'm sure he'll have an idea."

She was smoking again, which in itself maybe wasn't so disturbing. What *was* disturbing was the violence of her hunger for her vile packs of Tareytons—and her lack of hunger for all the foods her baby required. What lesson was she supposed to draw from this? Why was her body telling her, so commandingly it made her limbs tremble, that she needed what she knew she shouldn't have, and didn't need what she knew was essential?

She had been here before, and perhaps most unsettling of all was to see that her recognition of the process in no way prevented its steady devolution. "Everything's falling apart," she declared, any number of times, driving down Woodward Avenue, but the unflinching words were absolutely no protection. *Please, God,* she prayed. *Please, God.* And sometimes her prayer took another form, which would have sounded crazy if anyone had heard her, but no one did, she was talking to herself: *Please, Baby.* And this was a prayer for forgiveness—a prayer to the not-yet born.

There was something almost comforting, actually, when things started coming undone on Middleway. The boys didn't know the full details, of course. They didn't know that their grandma Paradiso was a thief. But they knew Grandma wasn't well. They knew their mother was often away, and wasn't fully present when present. The boys began to squabble and to cry and to ask uncharacteristically jittery questions: "Will Grandma be all right?" And: "Why are you always gone?" And from Chip, with naked puzzlement: "When will it be like before?"

The boys had always seemed so mutually self-reliant . . . And when you linked them up with their father, when they became the Ives triplets, it was hardly surprising if Bianca often felt superfluous, almost like an outsider. So there was some small comfort in discovering that when she was torn away from home, the normally smooth-running household disintegrated.

Some small comfort, yes. But mostly it brought guilt. She'd entered another period of real crisis, and she was mishandling this one, too. She wanted so much to be strong—helpful and good—but it was as though her body wasn't built for such crises. Her nerves were shot, she had diarrhea most days, she couldn't make herself eat enough. She felt so *bad* for the boys, who didn't know what had hit them. They only knew that almost as soon as Mom announced she was pregnant, the world began to crumble. Wasn't she setting them up to resent their little sister bitterly?

She could foresee, with a vision that seemed to open across decades, a new vast network of family problems, a whole new generation of problems, intersecting with other, deeper, ancestral networks of problems . . . It was as though the family wounds, the hurts were independent. Like some cancer, they weren't out to harm their host; they merely wanted to replicate. (Distant words from Uncle Dennis came back to her.) But were fiendishly clever when you sought to halt their replication.

What she couldn't foresee was where this was all heading in Chip's head. Something was happening to the boy. He'd suddenly turned far more nervous than Matt—asking an endless round of trembling-lipped questions. Can blind people see in Heaven? Do dogs go there? What about rats—if you were a *good* rat, could you go there?

And Chip's nervousness only made Matt nervous, and resentful. And it made Grant nervous and resentful too—for he was no more success-ful than Matt at calming the scared little boy. A rift was opening among the triplets.

Only Bianca could offer some small mercy of reassurance, though the boy's jittery questions never stopped. Why did Grandpa have a stroke? How does God choose who will be sick? Why does God let lizards grow back missing limbs, but not people?

The questions were all so bewildering, and unnerving, it took her a little while to see what so obviously linked them: nothing less than Death itself. Chip wasn't too small to find himself abruptly confronting the largest puzzle of human existence. When posing his fearful ques-tions, he sometimes shook his head in a strange new tilted way—it looked like a sort of tic. It was as though he'd gotten a rank whiff of mor-tal decay up his nostrils and couldn't get rid of the smell. He was sud-denly far more burdened than Matt, or even Grant, and how could she, susceptible flesh and blood herself, relieve his distress?

And then Grant tottered and gave way, which in retrospect was inevitable. Why should Grant be immune? She knew how painfully vul-nerable he was underneath. She'd known this ever since the day she left him a note on the kitchen table, and he showed up glassy-eyed at the Poppletons', on whose front walk he'd issued that inhuman howl.

From that first evening when Papa had telephoned—"I need you to come"—Grant had been nothing less than wonderful. She could imag-ine marriages where a wife couldn't confess to her husband that her mother was a thief, where the shame and awfulness would be too great, but never for a moment had she considered not telling Grant. She'd returned home that night and cried and cried and cried, and he'd done nothing but comfort her. Never—there was never a hint of accusation in his tone, no hint of superiority. Bianca must do everything she could for her mother and father now. And he would take care of the boys.

Then came the night when Bianca took Mamma to the movies (more of Uncle Dennis's advice—getting Mamma out of the house) and Grant stayed home with Papa, listening to the radio. When Mamma and Bianca returned, only Edith was home, who reported that Papa and Grant had gone out for a walk.

Out for a walk? Grant and limping Papa?

What on earth for?

Bianca sat with her mother in the kitchen, waiting for the men. Bianca was feeling anxious—the whole business was so odd—and wishing with all her heart for a cigarette. She'd gotten up twice during the movie for a smoke in the ladies', but there was no way to smoke in this house, other than to lock herself in the bathroom, which she did consider . . .

It was after eleven when the men showed up. They were red-faced and disheveled. Papa had been drinking heavily. Grant was flat-out, stumble-down drunk.

Bianca drove Grant's convertible on the way home. Grant sat in the passenger seat and apologized and apologized and apologized. He was slurring his words. "It's not the end of the world," Bianca kept saying.

Grant had tried to keep things within limits—he wanted her to know how hard he'd tried—but Papa was so adamant. Drink up, drink up, he kept saying. "What was I supposed to do? It's so seldom he gets that way, so damn insistent. But when he does . . . Well, you know how he is."

"'Course I do. Look, Grant, it's not the end of the world."

"He just wouldn't take no for an answer."

"It's all right." It was. "It's Papa's way of trying to talk to you—to get close to you. He's been going through hell." Her voice caught in her throat. "Actually, you did the right thing. It's what he wanted. Maybe it's what he needed. You did the right thing, honey."

But there was no convincing Grant. He went on apologizing and repeating over and over that he'd tried to keep things within limits. He didn't understand how things had exceeded the limits. He'd tried to keep to the limits with things, but he'd exceeded them. The limits.

"It's all right," Bianca murmured, but there was no calming him down.

His getting so drunk didn't disturb her so much. But the frantic, unappeasable, abject man revealed by the drink—he made her very nervous.

"You remember when I got into such hot water at the firm?"

"'Course I remember. Those lakeshore properties. It's nothing you need to—"

"And you remember what lake it was."

"It was Lady Lake," Bianca said.

"I knew just what that lake meant to you. You'd told me so many times. About always going out there. As a kid. How much you loved it. I knew what it meant to you. And how it's the last place where your parents and the Poppletons ever really got along."

"That's right . . ."

"I wanted to make things right again," Grant said. "Wasn't that clever? Me and my big ideas, I was going to put things right again."

"I didn't know, quite. Until now," Bianca said. "That that's what you were thinking, Grant. It's very sweet. But darling, I don't think anybody can make things right again."

"Clever, huh? We could buy a cottage and invite everyone to the lake. Start over. And this time people would get along again. Smart, huh?" The bitterness in his voice frightened her.

"You were just trying to help . . ."

"And I only made things worse," Grant said. "That's me: I only made things worse." There was a silence, and then Grant said something that made her want to cry. In the darkness of the car, a small voice from the passenger seat said, "I keep thinking you're going to leave me."

"Oh *honey*," she said. "That's ridiculous. That's absolutely ridiculous."

"I keep thinking you're going to leave me again."

"Grant, darling, listen to me: that's the most preposterous . . . No one's going to leave you."

"You did before."

"Grant, I did not. I went off to Cleveland, for heaven's sake. And you came and got me. Just the way I knew you would. You must have driven a hundred miles an hour. Just the way I knew you would. I hadn't been at Uncle Dennis and Aunt Grace's twenty minutes before you showed up."

"I made a bargain with you then. And part of the bargain was, I wouldn't have more than a drink a day. And I keep telling myself, if I just keep up my end of the bargain, she won't leave me."

"Leave you? For heaven's sake, Grant, I'm going to have your baby. And no one minds if you have an extra—"

"You already had two sons of mine, two little two-year-old boys, and did it stop you from getting on that train? You got right on that train. Bang. Straight out of town. You do what's right. It's like Bootmaker."

The milkman? "Grant, what are you talking about?"

"I tell you you have to fire him and do you? Hell no. You do what's right. And when I make an ass and a fool of myself, chasing after fat little Maggie, when I have *you* for a wife, is it going to stop you that you have two-year-old twins? There isn't any stopping you, Bianca. You made your point."

"Honey, listen to me: I didn't even know what point I was making, only that I was so angry I couldn't see straight. Now hush, darling, enough. Enough, enough—you're getting worked up over nothing. I'm not going *anywhere*. I'm going to stay right here. Carrying your baby. And in May I'm going to present you with a daughter, our Maria, to hold in your hands."

She wanted to cry. It was all too much—Grant's confessions, his dwindled, slurred voice in the car's darkness. She went on driving. The big white castle of Sears was coming up on the left. They were nearly home.

"In any case, I want to say I'm sorry," he mumbled in a different tone of voice. Now he sounded a little lawyerly.

"For what?"

"For getting so emotional just now."

"I like it when you do. It makes me feel less lonely. *Bia is overemotional.* Papa's only said that a million—"

"You're not angry?"

"I'm not angry."

Grant did seem calmer, and dozed off, or nearly did. But once they were home and Bianca had paid the babysitter, and the two of them had climbed into bed, Grant started right up again. He was still slurring his words.

"I keep thinking you're going to leave me."

"Honey, don't. You're working yourself up over nothing."

Bianca put a hand on his shoulder and pulled him toward her. Grant's body seemed bigger and heavier than usual. He was a big man—six feet one, and probably closer at the moment to 210 than to 200 pounds—but his athlete's agility usually made him appear lighter than he was. Because it had been so long since she'd seen him really drunk, she'd forgotten the way alcohol bulked him up. She'd all but forgotten that big man who often drank too much and whose lurching presence seemed to imperil every perishable thing in the house: the china, the crystal glasses, the framed paintings on the walls.

Clumsily, bulkily, his hunching body crawled and slipped down her pregnant body, until his voice emerged below her collarbone: "I had to learn my lesson. But I learned it."

"Honey, you must stop. Please stop. I love you and I'm carrying your baby and now you've got to stop."

"I learned I'm not my father. I don't have to be my father. Chasing anything in a skirt. There I am in a goddamn bathroom, necking with Maggie-the-tramp, and the next thing I know my wife has left me."

It pained Bianca to realize how satisfying it was to hear her best friend in the world described as a tramp, but it didn't pain her too much. She said, "I do think Maggie deserves *some* of the blame. It's the thing that drives me craziest about her: she never has to take the blame." Bianca laughed. "Even Papa couldn't get angry when he discovered that she'd been hiding a pair of shoes under our front—"

Grant interrupted: "The next thing I know? My wife has left me. Gone. An empty house. And I'm standing in the kitchen reading a note in this artful handwriting—even your handwriting is artful, Bianca— and I know suddenly I'm the biggest goddamn fool who ever lived. And yes, I drive all the way to Cleveland at a hundred miles an hour, picking up a speeding ticket on the way. Did you know I got a speeding ticket?"

"I didn't know that . . ."

"Of course you didn't," Grant said, with an unexpected touch of vanity. "I never told you. I'm surprised I didn't get two of them. And my hands are shaking on the steering wheel the whole time."

"But that's what's been happening to me! These last couple of weeks, I'm driving to and from Mamma's and my hands—"

But it was as though Grant couldn't hear her now. He was in the grip of his own story, which perhaps was the central story in his life—the one from which so many other stories constituted an amplification, an after-thought, a consequence, a parenthesis. "And ever since then, I keep thinking you're going to leave me again. I don't mean every minute, but it'll be some day I'm just driving home, and suddenly it hits me: I could arrive home and find a note on the table."

The words hit *her* with such an extraordinary cringing rawness that she felt it all completely: you could be a man named Grant Ives, you could come home and find nothing but a note on the table . . . And in that imagined kitchen a door swung open, and she stepped through it, into an emptied, echoing room wherein it was evident how little she understood this man she was married to—this easygoing, lovable man with all his needless, gnawing fears.

"It's one of the reasons I like taking the boys out," Grant went on. "Because I know you'd never leave without them." All over—his big body—he was trembling just like a little boy. "I know you'd never leave *them.*"

"Oh darling, *please,*" she said. "Oh darling."

CHAPTER XXXIV

Back and forth, back and forth went Uncle Dennis's gray Lincoln, pulling into town out of blizzards and sleet, wind and rain—on top of everything else, it was a messy winter. He would stay with Bianca's parents, briefly, usually just a night, and yet it seemed with each trip something moved forward, something came unstuck or unlocked. A shiny red-and-yellow "For Sale" sign went up on Inquiry. The house Uncle Dennis was so keen on, over on Reston Street near Indian Village, was actually purchased, with a fixed move-in date of February first—less than two months away!

It was shortly after one of his visits that Edith, sitting with Bianca at the old kitchen table, made a peculiar announcement: she was to be "in charge of the move." Edith being Edith, it didn't occur to her that *nobody* need be in charge. "Uncle Dennis asked me to be in charge of the move," she announced, her voice proud but tentative, as though expecting to be challenged. But Bianca saw instantly what a brilliant idea this was—one of Uncle Dennis's finest.

Of course Edith pursued her job with clipped efficiency. Summer clothes? Nobody needed them before the move—into boxes they must go. The silver? The china? Into boxes. The garden tools? The muffin tins? The pewter candleholders? All neatly boxed, all neatly labeled.

Bianca had to stop Edith from packing up the Christmas decorations. "We don't really have time for Christmas this year," Edith actually declared. And Bianca pleaded with her sister: "But you know how Mamma loves Christmas. You know how Mamma loves gifts."

Unfortunately, Edith's decision to undertake the job did not mean she'd accepted the move for herself. Although she no longer talked of remaining on Inquiry—living in the house alone—she was adamantly refusing any transplantation to Reston Street. One of her counterproposals seemed worrisomely plausible: she would find a room in student housing at Wayne. Since she lived by day in the school library, maybe it made sense to live by night on campus . . . But how heartbreaking if Mamma and Papa were to purchase their new house and begin their "fresh start" with none of their children beside them. Somehow, Edith must be made to come around.

Up and down Woodward Avenue went Bianca's Studebaker. She visited her mother every day. They often went to afternoon movies. Or they did their grocery shopping together. Or they even went out to lunch at a soda fountain. This new routine established its own protocol. It soon grew evident that Mamma didn't want a lot of suggestions; too many choices bewildered her. Bianca simply presented her mother with the day's plan—and Mamma, with a touching and sweet and painful docility, went along.

Bianca was especially on the lookout for comedies and the two of them saw pretty much every movie in town that might provide a laugh or two. It was balm for the soul: to hear Mamma chuckling beside her in the blue darkness. She'd always had such a wonderful, girlish laugh—an airborne string of giggles, perfectly spaced.

For all Edith's notions about sacrificing Christmas for efficiency's sake—a return to the spirit of wartime rationing—the coming holidays offered multiple benefits. Gaiety was in the air, particularly downtown, where Hudson's shop windows were even more spectacular than usual, but what else would you expect from the world's tallest department store? And there was the welcome chore of gifts to buy, each requiring much earnest consultation. Christmas shopping took Mamma out of herself.

Still, it was a chore weighted with psychological burdens. Whenever the two of them entered a store, Bianca watched her mother like a hawk, while pretending to be doing no such thing. Bianca was certain— she felt nearly certain—that Mamma had learned her catastrophic lesson and could now be trusted, until the end of time, not to shoplift so much as a stick of gum. But still . . .

Still, after a shopping expedition with Mamma, when Bianca climbed into her car with a groan, she wouldn't make it halfway down the block before lighting a cigarette. Still, she was talking to herself; still, she was getting the shakes, and having trouble eating anything wholesome, and suffering from diarrhea; still, she was having trouble sleeping . . .

There was an old comfort to be derived from the drawing up of lists: to-do lists and grocery lists, lists of Christmas presents bought and needing to be bought, Christmas cards sent and needing to be sent. Some nights, sleepless, she would sit at the kitchen table with pen and paper, putting things in order. "I'm turning into my mother," she declared aloud, not for the first time, but the more likely danger was that she was turning into herself—reverting into that troubled waif of a girl who had sat up nights in the old kitchen on Inquiry, drawing up lists of who'd sat where in her earliest school classrooms, a slave to the ludicrous notion that if she couldn't remember a classmate's name, particularly a boy's name, he might meet a terrible end: his soldier's blood would be on her hands.

Those queer nighttime jitters counted for little most of the time. They faded in the morning sun and left her alone during the day. Lamps sometimes kept them at bay. And yet in the darkness they beckoned like a lit keyhole, opening into the all of her. What mattered most of the time were her boys and her husband, the baby due in May, her mother and father and sister and brother, the circle of her friends and relatives . . . What mattered was her house, and knowing herself pretty, and the paintings at the DIA, and the paintings she herself might paint but hadn't yet painted, and clothes that showed more than good taste— clothes that showed some inner artistry . . . And then would arrive this alternative, nighttime conception of things—corruption of things—and what mattered were the lists to be drawn up, the phrases chanted and the cruel internal tasks to be tended to. Bianca would recognize, at the edge of sleep, that all day long one shape inside her head had been crowding upon another, maybe a baby-blue ungainly trapezoid edging up against a dented olive-gold oval, and what mattered was this precarious business of accommodating all the demands of one's shifting inward geometry. What mattered was getting the colored shapes into some alignment where sleep was possible . . .

Grant usually slept like a log, but at two-thirty one night he came down and found her at the kitchen table, the lists in front of her: a grocery list and a list of necessary or soon-to-be-necessary home repairs. "Honey," he said. "Let it go. You've got to come back to bed."

She did, and she was sleepy enough that somehow it made sense, lying in the dark, to attempt to explain the odd reassurance found in compiling lists, and her sense of various objects pushing at her mind— best warded off by itemized rows. Her sense of shapes, worries, voices emerging from her head at night. And their wanting to claim her. And their insisting that every single aspect of her days was unreal. They were wrong, and yet they were irrefutable.

There was no accommodating them—there was only a constant fending off of intrusions. Nor was there any knowing when the voices might emerge, when the shapes might appear. Or disappear, for when they were gone they were really gone . . . There had been a time, long ago, when she'd needed to figure out, in precise order, which of her family she'd seen first that day, and second, and third, and then one evening it was as though the task had been completed. It was like shoveling snow: once the job was done, there was nothing else to do.

"The funny thing is," Bianca said, still speaking into the bedroom dark, "it's as if I can remember when the whole thing started. Probably my memory's playing tricks, but it's as if the whole thing started when I was eleven, in church, at MYF, the Methodist Youth Fellowship. Reverend Kakenmaster, this huge bald frightening man, he was sort of yelling at us. And a light from a stained-glass window throws this blazing dot on his bald forehead, as if God is pointing him out to us all."

Grant was half asleep—it was three in the morning—and she could feel a slow thickening in the body beside her.

"He says something and all the kids are supposed to answer, 'I say yes, I abide by that.' You know, renouncing sin and selfishness and impurity.

"I'm wearing a powder-blue dress Aunt Grace had made for me, with white faggoting on the sleeves and a white lace collar.

"And Reverend Kakenmaster tells us we must choose between purity and filthiness, and Jesus Christ wants us to choose purity, and what do we say to that?

"And just then, this terrible image pops into my head. I'll stand up in my powder-blue dress with the white lace collar and I'll yell out, I say *blank* to that. Where the *blank* was this unspeakable term.

"And I was just dumbstruck—really terrified, and *shocked,* to find myself thinking this way. I could see it all so vividly. I would stand up and utter this unutterable remark. And you know what the funny thing is? You know what the *blank* was? It wasn't anything so horrible, really, Grant. I mean—well, it wasn't *fuck.* You may be thinking that's what it would be—the most unimaginable word imaginable. But it wasn't."

Grant flinched a little. He didn't like it when she uttered a word like that. Not that she normally ever would—except under circumstances like these, when the word seemed less an obscenity than an illustration of a larger principle. She had thought she could get away with it now, since the story at bottom was so *sweet*: the little girl with the white lace collar who felt as if she'd invented filthiness and sin. Yet Grant had flinched, even though, paradoxically, he relished with his whole soul the notion that, provided he was her partner, she embraced the activity rooted underneath the word. For everything must depend on *his* making it possible.

Bianca went on. "No, the word in my mind was *shit.*" She laughed, which came out brittle sounding. "I saw myself getting up and yelling back at Reverend Kakenmaster, *I say shit to that.* And clearly to think such a thing, at such a time, in such a place, I must be the evilest girl ever born. It was as if my head was infected—invaded. And invaded ever since. And what do you say to that?" she said, and laughed at this echoing of Reverend Kakenmaster, who might well be dead by now, but who survived in his surreal way, with a light from Heaven forever drilling straight into his big bald dome of a forehead.

What did Grant say to that? Nothing, for he had fully drifted off, leaving her alone to face the task of getting through the night, to get through the day, to get through the night, so she might get through the day . . . Surely—she needed desperately to believe this—*surely* things would be better when Mamma and Papa began their fresh start?

Up and down, up and down Woodward she drove, over on Mack, over on the Boulevard, looking for chores and shopping, suitable movies and enticing soda fountains to get Mamma through another day—to edge her one day closer to the move.

So, smoking like a furnace, Bianca drove up and down Woodward, knowing in her heart there were not enough chores and Christmas shopping expeditions, movies and soda fountains to forestall indefinitely the arrival of further heartbreak. There had to come a day—there did indeed come a day—when the two sat alone at the kitchen table and Mamma observed, "It's a bit peculiar, don't you think? That Grace never comes up with Dennis?"

These days, Mamma rarely mentioned Grace and almost never in a context like this—opening up the complex, painful topic of the two Schleiermacher sisters. All at once, Bianca felt very wary.

"Well, he comes for such short periods."

"Granted, but wouldn't you think she might occasionally make the drive? Wouldn't *cost* anything . . ."

Grace hadn't been up to visit since the shattering news of Mamma's thievery. Though nobody had said as much, the truth was obvious: Uncle Dennis and Aunt Grace had made a conscious decision to spare Mamma the burden of confronting her sister while the shamefulness was so fresh.

"And there's her health," Bianca said.

Grace's health was more than a great worry. For Bianca it was additionally a source of tremendous guilt. Mamma's catastrophic collapse had eclipsed everything else. Every attention had naturally focused on Mamma, and on Papa—on keeping the old household functioning. Meanwhile, another battle, almost unremarked, was being bravely fought in another city: Grace was having to surmount, day after day, the misery and the uncertainty and the simple all-out nausea of having her remaining breast removed—the left one, the one so vivid in Bianca's memory, for this was the breast, nipple dark as a plum, Aunt Grace had unwittingly exposed that day at Lady Lake. The prospect of the maiming surgery was one of the things that made Bianca's hands shake as she drove to and from Mamma's, or that kept her up at night: she—Bianca—wasn't doing enough for Grace, she wasn't *thinking* enough about Grace, and by neglecting such duties she was inviting disaster . . .

"Isn't it *peculiar*," Mamma said, clinging to that word, "the way her cancer hasn't affected her looks? The last time I saw her, at your house in August, she looked beautiful."

"She did," Bianca said. "Though she looked tired. Very tired."

"Of course she does dye her hair."

"She doesn't pretend not to. She's actually quite funny on—"

"And who knows what else."

"I'm not sure—"

"You never had a sister like that," Mamma said. "You don't know what it's like having a beautiful, beautiful sister."

The conversation was veering out of control. "Edith's a very pretty girl. You're beautiful too, Mamma."

"I suppose I can't blame your father if he fell in love with Grace."

And here it was again, all at once: the prime, poisonous notion, to which nearly every current family misfortune could be traced.

"Mamma, Mamma, Mamma—you *do* know that's ridiculous. Papa's never been in love with Grace."

It had been years since Mamma had broached this notion directly. But now it was vividly apparent—as vivid as blood—that she'd never abandoned it.

"You know, I would have been all right," Mamma said, "all right in my head, if only he'd loved me."

And Mamma began to cry.

"But he did. He does!" Bianca said. "This is the most ridiculous, ri*dic*ulous—"

An O'Reilly and Fein wall calendar looked down upon the woman slumped at the kitchen table, softly weeping. Of course, this wasn't one of the old-style War calendars; this was a bigger, glossier production, featuring some of the bigger, glossier homes newly constructed in this city that had done so much to win the War. And yet the tears were the old tears . . . "Everything would have been all right, if only he'd loved me."

And Bianca, who had not cried in weeks and weeks, even as the world had collapsed and she'd taken up smoking again and talking to herself, even as every ghost in her brain had awakened and she'd lost the ability to sleep, finally yielded to hot prickling tears, right at the kitchen table, beside her crying mother.

Mamma was crying because she'd come so close in life to authentic happiness, which only one stubborn obstacle had prevented her from achieving: the man she loved with such loyalty had not returned her love.

And Bianca wept because her mother sincerely believed that she'd come so close to happiness and that every shortcoming in her life might have been rectified if only the man to whom she'd given her faithful heart had requited her. Bianca wept because her mother could not begin to see that the original fault lay deeper, deeper, with some fatal wounding in the soul of Sylvia Schleirmacher long, long ago—years before handsome Vico Paradiso ever appeared on the scene.

CHAPTER XXXV

"Sometimes I think I ought to be paying you. For your time. For your counsel."

Bianca offered this as a mere pleasantry, of course. We don't pay our friends for advice. But Priscilla's considered pause suggested that the proposal was hardly outlandish. Could it be—could it be that in Priscilla's eyes Bianca was some sort of freeloader? Somebody who sought professional services but didn't choose to pay?

The idea had never occurred to Bianca. Priscilla's life appeared so depleted, her conversation turning so narrowly from her parents (both dead) to her brother (retarded and institutionalized) to her beloved but necessarily distant Dr. Cuttwell (married to a woman crippled by multiple sclerosis) . . . Surely, Priscilla must embrace a friendly visitor bearing tales of turbulent and unusual encounters, with a colorful, rotating cast of characters?

But there was this aspect, too, to Priscilla: an abiding unease about being taken advantage of. It was the burden of so many of her stories . . . Her neighbors, the landlord from whom she rented her office, her professors at medical school, the other medical students—they were alike in conniving to deceive or defraud her. More than once she'd declared, "The world preys on a single woman," and while this observation was offered dispassionately, as a psychiatrist's assessment of human nature, it bore accusatory overtones. Yes, there was a faint suggestion that Bianca, sheltered on all sides by family, did not grasp the world's nastier realities.

Thoughts were jostling thoughts in Bianca's head as they sat in Priscilla's little living room, a December morning sun playing a feeble game of hide-and-seek among the glass and china knickknacks on Priscilla's mantel. Priscilla had asked her over for tea. There was no sugar, but they were "making do" with raspberry jam. "It gives the tea an excellent flavor," Priscilla noted, "though the seeds can be a little annoying." One of these having apparently lodged between two of her upper teeth, Priscilla was working it free with the nail of a pinky finger. Bianca had chosen to take her tea unsweetened.

It was easy to dismiss Priscilla as a ridiculous figure—in her naked eccentricities, she seemed to court dismissal—but in truth she occasionally offered insights nobody else did. It was Priscilla who had pointed out, as though it were the most obvious thing in the world, a link between Mamma's recent shoplifting and her wartime hoarding of candies: a long-standing appetite for hidden, prohibited treasure. Perhaps this *was* the most obvious thing in the world, but Bianca had never spotted the connection. Likewise, Priscilla had pointed out that there was nothing so remarkable about Mr. Ives's tolerance of his brother Hughie, the old fruit whose antiques shop specialized in grandfather clocks. As a competitive womanizer, Mr. Ives had probably welcomed a brother who presented no rivalry. Again, the logic was compelling, and again Bianca had failed to see it herself. So perhaps it *wasn't* so absurd to conjecture that Priscilla might be paid for her analyses. Wasn't this what a psychiatrist ideally did—point out the obvious, primal connections you somehow failed to see?

But on this morning when Priscilla was perhaps harboring resentments, Bianca wasn't about to discuss Mamma any further. Sipping from her bitter tea, she said, "And so I got a call from Edith this week. Chipper as you please. She announces, *I'm applying to medical school.* And I'm just as obtuse as they come, I say, *But what for?* And she says, *Well, to become a doctor.* My baby sister the doctor, isn't that something?"

"Medical school!"

Priscilla brightened at the news. Though she'd never met Edith—never met any of Bianca's family except Grant and the twins—Priscilla clearly felt affinities with the brainy girl who considered most of the boys she dated too silly.

"And I said . . ."

Bianca paused. For what she'd said to Edith—an impulsive remark, amusing in its stupidity—was hardly something to repeat to Priscilla. She'd said: "But what about getting married?" And Edith—the baby of the family who was, in her way, more philosophical than all of them— had replied: "If I get married, I get married. But I'm going to become a doctor."

Bianca looked at Priscilla, who was canted over in excitement, and said, "And I said, *You'll be a wonderful doctor.*"

"It isn't easy," Priscilla replied. "Being a girl in medical school."

"Oh, Edith's tough," Bianca said. "Like you," she added respectfully.

She was still feeling uneasy about the pause following her joke about payments.

Bianca went on: "You know, it's always been this sort of lost dream of my mother's. *She* could have gone to medical school. That's what the famous Miss Patterson told her, who taught high school biology. I've heard the story a thousand times. Miss Patterson said she had the brains to be a doctor. And now Edith's going to do it."

"Of course it threatens you in some way," Priscilla said.

"What do you mean?"

"You don't even have your B.A."

"I went to art school instead. And I would have gotten a B.A. The twins weren't planned, you know."

"Yes . . ."

A silence fell, and then Priscilla, assuming a vindicated look, remarked, "It does take a certain toughness. A girl in medical school. You have to sacrifice the idea that what you're after is popularity."

"I think Edith sacrificed *that* idea long ago."

"Did I ever tell you about my roommate at Mount Holyoke, Annie McKinney?"

"I don't think so."

"Annie was a most wretched girl, from a large well-to-do Catholic family in Wilmington, Delaware. She wasn't a hunchback, exactly, but she suffered from severe scoliosis. That was neither here nor there, in my eyes, but Annie seemed quite embittered about it. She kept a journal, and one day she left it open, and there it was plain as day: *It doesn't seem to bother Priscilla that she's so unpopular.* I was unpopular? Honestly, the notion had never occurred to me."

Though her claim hardly seemed enviable, Priscilla looked smug as she lifted her teacup.

"Well," Bianca said, "in Edith's case, I knew who was behind the idea."

"What do you mean?"

"I knew who's been guiding her."

"Who?"

"My Uncle Dennis. Isn't it obvious? Can't you picture it? The last time he was here. Saying to Edith, *You might possibly consider medical school.*"

"Maybe she arrived at the decision herself."

"It was Uncle Dennis."

"You don't know that."

For whatever obscure reason—all the more obscure given that she'd never met him—Priscilla resisted notions of Uncle Dennis's enormous behind-the-scenes influence. But Bianca knew that if Priscilla could only meet him—meet that pop-eyed square-eared man who was never happier than when raising a glass, toasting another's accomplishments— he would disarm her.

Yes, Bianca's little sister would enroll in medical school, and like so many startling developments in Edith's life, the decision quickly assumed a logical inevitability. Wasn't this where Edith, marching up and down Inquiry with her overloaded sacks of books, had been trend-ing all along? Didn't it make perfect sense that Bianca would eventually be telephoning Edith when one of the kids got sick?

But could Priscilla possibly be right—did this notion of Edith-the-doctor also *threaten* her? Edith's startling announcement certainly had come at an uneasy and ironic time. It was getting pregnant with the twins that had indefinitely postponed Bianca's pursuit of a B.A., and here she was pregnant again, just as her little sister was announcing plans for medical school. Bianca said, "The best part is, suddenly she's dropped all objections to the move. She'll follow my parents. It's as if she never talked about staying on Inquiry, or moving to Florida."

"Having found a future, she feels ready to move on."

There was this, too, about Priscilla: her knack for sharp summations. After moseying around with circumlocutions—she often seemed the youngest person Bianca had ever met who might be described as doddering—she would abruptly consolidate everything in a phrase.

In her movements, too, Priscilla seemed older than her years. Preg-nancy had heightened Bianca's awareness of other women's bodies, and watching Priscilla set down her teacup and rise from her chair, on her way toward the bathroom, Bianca had a keen sense of her friend's ungainliness: the stiffness in the slow-shifting, ample hips, the breasts uneasily borne, and more sunken than you'd expect in a woman still in her thirties. Was this what Grant had sensed when he declared that Priscilla wasn't a "real woman"? And Bianca had asked him, forthrightly, "Are you saying she's lesbian?" "N-no," Grant had said. "She's not really anything."

But was it possible to be "not really anything"? What did Grant mean? If he meant that Priscilla appeared not quite at home in her body—then Bianca understood him perfectly. It was hard to describe:

this sense some people gave you of living within a body not quite their own. It was like wearing clothes that didn't fit. On the other hand, in some ways Priscilla seemed more at home with the dark and intricate byways of carnality than Bianca ever would be. She was certainly capable of uttering with aplomb words and phrases Bianca would never dare attempt aloud: *fellatio* or *cunnilingus* or *masturbatory fantasies.*

"So Edith's going to cross the bridge after all," Priscilla declared when she returned from the bathroom.

"Beg pardon?"

"Wasn't it on the Belle Isle Bridge that she broke down and cried and declared she wasn't moving from Inquiry Street?"

"That's right," Bianca said. "But I'm not sure I follow . . ."

"And now she's going to cross the bridge after all. She's going to move."

"That's right!"

But Bianca's excitement was immediately tempered by misgivings. Wasn't Priscilla making too much of coincidences? And wasn't there something a little annoying and self-congratulatory in her delivery? Wasn't Priscilla often *deliberately* cloudy and vague—inviting Bianca to play an uncomprehending Watson to Priscilla's cryptic Holmes?

Still—there was something trenchant and attractive to the way Priscilla thought. More than anyone else Bianca knew, Priscilla seemed to filter the world through symbols. She was forever telling you, in that cutting way she had when verbosity suddenly found its destination, that the people in front of you were not really the people in front of you: they were stand-ins for other, earlier figures. The houses were different houses, the streets different streets, the bridges different bridges . . . Everything was always dissolving to reveal a deeper, anterior reality.

"Any further word from Ronny Olsson?" Priscilla asked.

"Not since the time I told you about. When I met what I suppose was his partner."

"Whose appearance and manner surprised you."

"Yes, they did."

"You were disappointed he wasn't more like you?"

"Like me?"

"Yes."

And what in the world did Priscilla mean by *this*? "Disappointed?"

"Yes. He wasn't dark like you, this young man. And not so good-looking. Isn't that what you told me?" And Priscilla laughed her little whispery funny-pages laugh: tee-hee-hee.

"But why should that disappoint me?"

"And not *intense* like you."

"But why should I want Chris to be like me?"

"But isn't it obvious? Isn't it your hope that Ronny Olsson will forever be searching for you, Bianca, in one form or another?"

Bianca paused. "Do you mind if I have a cigarette?"

Other than Priscilla, nobody on earth, not even Maggie, knew she'd resumed smoking.

"Of course you must suit yourself," Priscilla said. "I don't seem to see the ashtray—where did it go?—but you can make do with your saucer. I should add, as a doctor, I cannot recommend cigarettes for anyone in your condition."

"This is only temporary," Bianca said, fishing in her purse for her pack of Tareytons. "But they're better than the alternative, which seems to be a nervous breakdown. I tell you, in the last week I've seen my mother, my husband, and my sister all in tears. Not little tears. Huge rending sobs. And none of these are people who cry. *I'm* the one who cries. I thought I had the crybaby role all sewed up. Anyway, I'm going to quit smoking just as soon as I get through most of this."

Bianca pulled the Tareyton deep into her lungs. These days, it seemed to be the organizing phrase and principle of her life: *as soon as I get through* . . . For a while it had been, *as soon as I get through Thanksgiving* . . . Then it was, *as soon as I get through Christmas* . . . Now it was, *as soon as I get past New Year's,* only a few days away. Then it would no doubt be, *as soon as I get through the move,* scheduled for February first. In the distance, in an unimaginable spring, lay the final and true *as soon as I get through*: the day when she gave birth to her baby, whom she was now poisoning with another Tareyton. "I really am going to put my life in order."

"Let me see . . . Your mother, sister, husband—all in tears. What about your father?"

"Oh no, not very likely."

"I worry about him," Priscilla declared matter-of-factly.

"Do you?"

Did she? Did Priscilla make time to worry about this man she'd never met?

"It must be very hard for him."

"It *is* hard. You know what Mamma was crying about? She was saying that everything in her life would have been all right, if only Papa had loved her."

"And does he?"

"Of course he does."

"That can't be easy."

"Well, I can tell you one thing. He doesn't love Aunt Grace. Not the way Mamma's suggesting."

Bianca drew again on her cigarette. "Something very peculiar happened this week and I immediately thought of you. We've been sorting things at my parents', preparing for the move, and I came across an old photograph. My mother and my aunt. Sitting together. In front of two cherry pies. And I suddenly realized it was taken at the lake, Lady Lake, taken by my uncle, in some of the last calm moments before Mamma declared war on her sister. And you know what? They both look so pretty, the two sisters, and Aunt Grace is wearing a new hat, it was a straw hat with a green ribbon. This was the summer of forty-three. Of course the War was raging full blast, and the city was crazy, but the picture is so tranquil. And beautiful. And sweet. It's another world. The two of them are actually touching each other. I remember it so vividly: Grace laid a hand on Mamma's arm and Mamma paused and then laid a hand on Grace's hand. And looking again at the picture it occurred to me that of course Papa loved Grace—the way I love Grace, we all love Grace. But he didn't *love* her. It's as if Mamma could never understand there can be two kinds of love."

"Two kinds of love?" Priscilla sounded skeptical. "Somebody else then? For your father?"

What was Priscilla implying, and why? Bianca again sucked deeply on her cigarette. She said, "What do you mean?"

"You said it yourself: things have been very hard on your father."

"You mean somebody else romantic?"

"He hasn't had an easy time . . ."

Bianca exhaled a big cloud of smoke and said, "Somebody else? I don't think so. But I'm going to tell you a story I've never told anyone. I was downtown, this was, I don't know, quite a few years ago, the twins weren't born yet. And in the distance I saw this man who resembled my father from behind, only the woman he was walking with wasn't my mother. She had blonde hair. They were walking into the Book-Cadillac Hotel. I was way across the street, the sidewalks were crowded, and it was difficult to see—it was just this time of year, Christmastime—and the whole thing was absurd. It was a weekday, a workday, why would my father be walking with a blonde woman into the Book-Cadillac?"

"What did you do?"

"Well, I went in. To the hotel lobby. Just to make sure. But there was no blonde woman anywhere. And I began to realize just how absurd it was. Everyone's always teasing me about my imagination getting the best of me."

"So you don't think it was he?"

"Oh I'm virtually certain it wasn't. And I'll tell you why. If my father were heading off to some hotel with some blonde woman, which I consider very unlikely, he would *never* choose the Book-Cadillac. Fancy places make him nervous, they make him self-conscious about his accent and all the rest, so what's the chance he'd choose the finest hotel in the city? He'd rather die than step into a place like that and order a room. But it was the man's walk. Whoever the man was, he walked very much the way my father walks, with a slight limp. My father's got a plantar wart."

There was something perhaps a little too overly knowing in Priscilla's look—a skepticism unjust toward various members of Bianca's family, herself included. Bianca retaliated with a sharp question: "And how is Dr. Cuttwell?"

Priscilla stiffened. Though she referred to him with some frequency, it was clearly her own prerogative to broach the delicate topic, in a tone blending wistfulness with a profound respect for human tragedy. The tone acknowledged, tactfully, the plight of the good doctor, tethered to his wheelchair-bound wife, much as Priscilla's life was constrained by Michael, her retarded brother. Cruel fate, combined with a stoical subordination to duty, had kept apart two people otherwise meant for each other.

"I think he is very well."

"And Mrs. Cuttwell?"

"Of course I do not see her. But I hear she is much afflicted."

"I'm sorry."

"The situation is very sad."

Nodding her head up and down, Priscilla had a way of offering such pronouncements instructively—as though Bianca couldn't be trusted to appreciate life's bitter twists of fate. Priscilla often implied that Bianca might be, if not superficial, at least privileged and callow. Or *was* this Priscilla's implication? Alternatively, was Bianca being oversensitive? She certainly wasn't comfortable sitting here—a pregnant woman smoking a second cigarette in the living room of a therapist who, as this morning had revealed, possibly felt taken advantage of.

Bianca was harboring her own small insecurities and resentments then, which perhaps goaded her to press the topic of Dr. Oliver Cutt-well: "He must sometimes get pretty low—quite depressed."

"I think he's very strong," Priscilla said.

"Or angry—angry at life?"

"He's a very gentle man. And I think gentleness is especially won-derful in a man, don't you? And all too rare? Do you know what he told me? The last time we had lunch? He told me he doesn't like fireworks. He actively dislikes them. Isn't that something? This was near the Fourth of July, and he said to me, 'I've never understood why people would choose to celebrate with what sounds like gunfire.' Don't you think that's wise?"

Oh my. For there was something else here—far more noteworthy than Dr. Cuttwell's wisdom. "You haven't had lunch with him since July?" Bianca asked.

Now it was Priscilla's turn to appear defensive. "Dr. Cuttwell is a very busy man. His wife has a paralyzing illness. And I am a busy woman. I am my brother's sole guardian."

Bianca took a final triumphant drag on her cigarette. "But you haven't actually had lunch since July?"

Priscilla paused. "No," she said. "Though I expect we will soon. Per-haps right after the holidays."

A wild thought struck Bianca. "But you've *seen* him since?"

Again Priscilla balked. "At least half a dozen times," she finally replied, and all at once Bianca understood that, whatever the actual details, Priscilla was effectively lying. The number scarcely mattered—it was the nature of the encounters that was a lie. Or call it a pitiful, pregnant delusion. All at once Bianca comprehended how totally one-sided was this "affair of the heart." Had Bianca sometimes been guilty of inflaming her own imagination with visions of an impossible romance? With wild fantasies about the wildly inappropriate Ronny Olsson? Per-haps. But nothing like what Priscilla had done. Oh, Priscilla might, in her knowing and enumerating way, point out the manifold implications of Ronny's being a ho-mo-sex-u-al, but Ronny and Bianca would marry and have a dozen children, Ronny would trade in his British racing green MGTD for a station wagon, he'd settle down and become his sons' Scoutmaster and Little League coach long before Dr. Cuttwell swept Priscilla into his wise and compassionate and gentle embrace.

CHAPTER XXXVI

She was alone in the house. Would she ever again be alone in this house that in many ways felt more like her real home than her real home did? Her legal address might lie on Middleway, with her husband and children, but today she was back on Inquiry, and though most of the household furnishings were in boxes—Edith had packed up ruthlessly once the frivolity of Christmas lay behind them—the late afternoon light was still the same timeless light of old. Nowhere else on earth did sunlight assume quite this quality. The word *beige* suggested blandness to most people, but this light contained a good portion of beige, and it was the richest light in the world. The word *tawny* suggested lushness, and there was a good share of tawniness as well, but in the end it was neither beige nor tawny, there was no term for such a color, and no tube in the world's paint box could replicate it. She was alone in the house in which she'd grown up and which her family, in less than two weeks' time, would abandon permanently, and when again would she ever be alone here? The doorbell sounded.

On the front porch on this cold but bright January afternoon stood a stranger. Bianca peered at him through the glass on the front door. He had long graying hair and was leaning on a cane. Bianca opened the door.

"Is this the Paradiso residence?"

"That's right."

"But you—you're not— Forgive me. This was sort of a spur-of-the-moment decision. I should have telephoned before dropping in. Hey, perhaps I better begin by introducing myself. Sorry. Got off on the wrong foot. Typical. My name is Ira Styne. You see, I remembered the name of your street. Inquiry—who could forget that? Not even me. The number, on the other hand, that was another matter."

He spoke very rapidly. He was nervous. Despite the cane and the graying hair, and a somewhat scratchy voice, he actually wasn't very old—probably not much older than Bianca herself. This was all quite irregular, but she didn't feel the slightest unease. It was impossible to look into the man's long, uncertain face, with its brown puppy-dog eyes, and distrust him.

"You see, I wrote a number of letters to this address," he went on. "Years ago. I remembered the name, Inquiry Street. But you're not— you can't be . . . I wrote to a little schoolgirl. Edith Paradiso."

"That's my sister."

"Then you—you must be Bea."

And everything fell into place. "And you're Ira Styne. She was given your name at school. A soldier to write to. You're Edith's soldier pen pal."

"That's right. But I wasn't much of a pal, sorry to say. I was very bad about writing."

"You sent Edith a five-dollar bill. Five hundred pennies in convenient paper form."

He looked terrifically embarrassed—and pleased, too, to have his little witticism remembered. "For her birthday. Yes. I'd missed her birthday and I felt just awful. She'd written me all these amazing letters, and you can't believe how long and full and mature they were, and you see I hadn't written back, but I was in a bad way, I'd been wounded actually"—he tapped his cane against his leg—"and that was only the start. Oh my, listen to me, boring you like this, forgive me. The point is . . . Do I have a point? You might well ask. But I do, at least I think I have a point. The point is, I happened to be in town today, I remembered the name of the street, and I thought maybe it's time to offer some real thanks. A day of atonement. Better late than never, I thought. Because those letters she wrote, they sure meant a lot to me, even if I was such a deadbeat I couldn't remember a little girl's birthday."

"Edith isn't here."

He paused, confused, and then relief came to his long face. The distance from his lower lip to the base of his chin was remarkable. This was nobody in need of a chin enhancement. "That's all right. You can deliver the message. Just tell her an old soldier came by to thank her. Tell her that her letters meant a lot at a time when—when he was in a bad way. Oh shucks, skip all that. But do give her my thanks, won't you?"

"Why don't you come in? She ought to be home soon."

"Oh I don't think I'd better do that. No. Actually, I'm in something of a hurry. You see, I'm heading back to New Jersey. Where I belong. Sad as that may sound. Woe is me. Better to shut up, huh? I'll shut up. I just wanted to say thanks is all."

"She's at school," Bianca said. "She should be back soon."

"School? She must be in college."

"She graduated last June. These are just extra classes. Things related mostly to medicine."

"She's going to be a nurse!" Ira Styne announced triumphantly.

"A doctor. She's going to start medical school in the fall."

"A doctor," he marveled. "It figures. Very, very smart kid. A friend of mine, I showed him one of her letters, and he says, No little girl wrote that. It must have been her mother, he says."

"Edith wrote it. I can assure you."

"That's what I told him! That's exactly what I said! You could *tell* it was a kid—a terrifically super-smart kid."

"Please come in and wait."

"Oh I don't think I'd better. It's kind of crazy to stop by like this, isn't it? Rude, maybe? All unannounced?"

"I think it's nice. And I'd be happy for the company. Nobody else is here but everyone should be arriving shortly. My mother's just stepped out, she's helping a neighbor, my father's due home from work, and Edith will be back from school."

"Thanks, but you see I better be on my way. Long road." He stuck out his hand in farewell. "Tell Edith I know she'll make a wonderful doctor. She already was a great help to me when I was a patient. No, actually, actually, just tell her an old soldier—"

They did not complete their farewell handshake. "You can tell her yourself. Here she comes now . . ."

Yes, here came Edith, overloaded with books but walking down Inquiry with that strong and purposeful walk. It was wonderful timing, for this was an encounter Bianca wouldn't have missed for the world. Even Edith—unflappable Edith—was surely about to be dumbstruck.

And yet Edith wasn't—quite. Bianca called out "We have a visitor" as Edith reached the front walk, and you could see Edith's eyes, behind those ugly, practical, imitation tortoiseshell glasses she never removed, peering appraisingly at the man on the porch. She marched up the walk. "Hel-lo," she said.

Ira Styne talked even faster than before, again withholding his name: "I should have telephoned first instead of dropping in unannounced but I was in Detroit for the first time in my life and I remembered the name of the street, Inquiry, you see I wrote you a couple of times, when I was in the Army, years ago. I suppose I should begin by identifying myself: I'm Ira Styne."

He extended his hand.

Edith did not immediately take his hand. "Corporal Styne, what on earth are you doing here?" she said. Then she shook his hand and said, "Well, it's way too cold to stand out here, my sister should have invited you in—"

"I did, I did—" Bianca said.

"Ira Styne, come in, come in."

An invitation to enter—such as Bianca had offered—could be refused; but Edith, in her no-nonsense way, converted it into an order and the former Corporal Styne clearly was one to obey orders. Hobbling rapidly on his cane, he followed the two of them into the house. Bianca saw his eyes move to her stomach. He hadn't realized her condition until now.

Even the living room held cardboard boxes, though most were stacked in the bedrooms upstairs.

"Forgive the look of the place," Bianca said. "As you can see, we're moving."

"Yes," Ira said. "I saw the 'For Sale' sign. I guess I got here in the nick of time."

"What they call the eleventh hour," Edith said.

"Please sit down," Bianca said. She made a little joke to put Ira at ease: "Inexplicably, Edith hasn't yet boxed up the couch. You see, she's in charge of the move. And she's *very* efficient."

"I'll bet she is," Ira said, but he did not sit down. Instead, in his scratchy voice, he repeated to Edith much of what he'd already said to Bianca—about how grateful he had been for her letters and how ill-mannered not to answer them and how rude to arrive unexpectedly. Bianca had met a few girls and women who might compete with him, but she'd never met so apologetic a man.

He was in the middle of pointing out, for the tenth time, that he should first have telephoned when Edith interrupted: "I don't know what to call you. I think of you as Corporal Styne."

"Please call me Ira."

"Sit down, Ira."

Ira sat.

He said, rapidly, "You see the thing was, I didn't remember the address, only the street. I thought it was 2753 but I wasn't sure. But I remembered that you'd written that you liked living in a house that was a prime number. So the question was: is 2,753 a prime? So I go round the corner, there's a luncheonette, the—"

"The Red Rose," Bianca supplied.

"That's it. And I get out a piece of paper and I divide 2,753 by every prime up to 60 and everything has a remainder so I figure it *has* to be prime." And Ira actually removed from his pocket a piece of paper and unfolded it and held it up. It was covered, top to bottom, with calculations.

And Edith thought a moment and said, "You didn't have to go higher than 47, Ira. Because 53 squared is 2,809."

Why did Edith always have to say things like that? Why—when the guest in their home was so proudly holding up his page of calculations—did she have to notify him that he'd wasted his time?

But Ira did not seem deflated or resentful. He looked happily dazzled. "I never was much of a one for higher math," he said. And added, "You can do that in your head?"

"Let's have some coffee," Bianca said.

"I'll make it," Edith said.

"*I'll* make it," Bianca said.

She listened in from the kitchen. Ira lived in New Jersey. He had driven all the way to Detroit to look at a house. His aunt—sister of his long-deceased father—herself had recently died and bequeathed him her house, which was in Palmer Woods.

The house, Ira went on, must once have been quite nice. ("I'm sure it is, Palmer Woods is where the swells live," Edith said, which—so often the case when Edith employed slang—rang strangely. Who called them *swells*? And yet, with her fact-establishing tone, she might have been saying, *That's where the Irish live* or *That's a Polish neighborhood*.) Anyway, his aunt, who had died an old maid, had kept twelve cats and the filth and wholesale destruction were indescribable. Having carefully examined the house earlier today, Ira had determined to sell it immediately. He would begin the long drive back to New Jersey tomorrow.

Then Mamma came home. She was often at her suspicious worst with strangers and unexpected events, but from the very first moment she was warm and welcoming. He had turned up at last: the mysterious soldier who had sent her thirteen-year-old daughter five dollars. It was like something out of the movies—first the arrival of the money, then the ultimate arrival of the man—and Mamma loved the movies. Ira began a whole new round of apologies and she cut him off—graciously, wittily. She invited him to supper, and though he declined, he seemed honored (a word he repeated a number of times) by the invitation.

Over coffee, at Mamma's attentive urging, more of Ira Styne's story emerged. He'd grown up in New Jersey. His family was Jewish. He was currently unemployed. He'd been working until October for his father-in-law—or ex-father-in-law, for Ira had become a divorced man in October. He had been separated from his wife, Judy, for more than two years, but he'd continued to work for his father-in-law, who owned a furniture business in Morristown, New Jersey. Ira loved his father-in-law, who had urged him to stay at the job, all the while hoping Ira and Judy might reconcile. But once the divorce became final, Ira had felt the need to move on . . .

"I think the endless drive must have scrambled my wits. I'm not usually such a blabbermouth about myself, especially with complete strangers."

"But we're not strangers," Mamma informed the Jewish stranger in their living room. "We're your friends," she said, and smiled her lovely smile. Who *was* this woman?

And yet in a way Mamma wasn't being merely hospitable—she was acknowledging a sort of truth. For it seemed the Paradisos were not total strangers in Ira's imagination. He had already pointed out, a number of times, that Edith had sent him long letters—but their manifest degree of detail, like the tenacity of Ira's memory, was little short of astonishing. He recalled how Bianca had studied painting under a man who wore a toupee ("You're right, it was Professor Ravenscroft!") and how Uncle Dennis adored science fiction and how Edith had received a testimonial from Needles for Defense. He recalled Mamma's spearmint leaves and Papa and Nonno listening to the Tigers and Stevie playing in the alley. As they sat among cardboard boxes, in a house they would soon be vacating, Ira transported them to a distant and seemingly happier time. "Do you still make Edith's favorite dish, Shipwreck?"

Mamma laughed joyously, and said that, yes, she did. Her laughter ushered in a moment of such pure lambent happiness that not even Edith's obsessive fact-loving need to set all records straight ("Actually, I've grown very partial to Chinese food and my favorite dish is moo goo gai pan, but I still love Shipwreck") could do anything to tarnish it.

And then Papa came home. He, too, was clearly heartened by this unexpected visitor. "You'll stay for supper," he told Ira, who, hardly pausing, nodded.

It wasn't long, naturally, before Papa turned the conversation to the house in Palmer Woods. "You're going to sell?" he asked Ira.

"That's right."

"How much?"

"Beg pardon?"

"You sell the house for how much?"

"The realtor I talked to today, he said I could probably get twenty-four thousand."

"Twenty-four thousand?" Papa said. "How many bedrooms?"

It seemed Ira hadn't bothered to count. "Four," he said. "Or maybe five. What you have to understand is: the filth. You can't *believe* the filth."

Was there an attic?

Yes, with a separate little room, but the cats had been up there, too. The whole place reeked so bad, it was difficult to *breathe.*

What kind of heat? Ira didn't know, but there were radiators. What kind of roof? Ira wasn't sure but—oh yes, it was slate. A garage? Yes, a two-car garage, and it was probably more habitable than the house. And a fireplace? Yes, there was a fireplace—actually two.

"Edith, you go fetch the guest a glass of wine."

This meant two glasses, of course, for Papa obviously would join the visitor.

While Edith was off in the kitchen, a silence dropped over the living room. Papa was ruminating. This was obvious to everyone; it would have been indecorous to speak.

When Edith handed him a glass of wine, Ira said, "Did you make this yourself, Mr. Paradiso? I remember Edith writing me that you made excellent wine in your basement."

Usually this was a topic upon which Papa expatiated eagerly, but he merely nodded. He wasn't about to be sidetracked. He was thinking. He sipped from his glass and said, "Mr. Styne, you are still a young man and the question for you is: do you want to be a fool, or not?"

Ira did not appear to regard this as a rhetorical question. He, too, sipped his wine, deliberating a moment, then said, "I think I'd rather not." And laughed nervously and much too loudly.

"Then you don't sell."

"Don't sell?" Ira said.

"You put four thousand into that house, you sell it for thirty-five thousand. Maybe more. I know the street."

"Thirty-five thousand," Ira said. "But you don't know how filthy and disgusting it is."

"You see the filth, I see the house."

"Well, Mr. Paradiso, I know you do renovations. If you're thinking you could—"

Papa interrupted him not with his voice but with an imperial lifting of his hand. It was a gesture like a traffic cop's, halting oncoming traffic, but for Bianca it always evoked something else: a Roman emperor, as glimpsed in a movie. Ira's voice trailed off.

"You think I'm looking for work?" Papa said. Papa tucked in his chin and lowered his eyebrows. The expression he trained on poor Ira, who was squirming, combined pity and scorn. "I have far more work than time. Far more work than time. No, I give you names of reliable people, good workmen, if that's what you decide. I'm not looking for business from you, a guest in my house. That's not why I give you advice over a glass of my wine. No. You're young and I'm trying to save you from being a fool. A buffoon. "

Another hard silence fell. Ira sipped deeply, uneasily from his wine. "But would you be willing to go look? At the house? Give me some more advice? You see, I don't know what I'm doing," Ira confessed. "I don't know the city. It's as if I've arrived in a foreign land. Would you go over there tomorrow with me? Just tell me what you think?"

Papa deliberated once more. He was enjoying himself, but poor Ira didn't seem to recognize there was mischief in this magisterial sternness.

"I'll go over Saturday morning."

"But I'm leaving tomorrow."

"Saturday morning," Papa repeated. Saturday was three days off.

Ira paused, drained his wineglass, laughed in a way that sounded like a hiccup, and said, "You've got a deal." He added, "Now I do intend to pay you for your time."

"Of course you will," Papa replied.

Ira soon found a motel in Highland Park that rented not by the day but by the week, which was a good thing because, as he pointed out, he might be in town "a couple of weeks."

Clearly, he would be much longer if left to his own devices. It was apparent at once to everyone in the family that Ira Styne was hopelessly incompetent. How had he ever worked successfully in the furniture business?

Somehow, each of them was drafted into serving as helper on one of Ira's ever-growing list of tasks. First, a moving van was needed and of course Stevie—the last family member drawn in—was conscripted:

Turk's Trucks was just the company to haul away the junk inside the Palmer Woods house. According to Papa, this was a heartbreaking business, because Ira's aunt had been a woman of not only expensive but exquisite taste: the house was full of once-gorgeous couches, chairs, rugs, curtains, that the cats had ravaged. Papa identified a few items that might be repaired and sold, perhaps to whoever eventually bought the place, but most were assigned to the junk heap.

Papa found someone to rip up the carpeting. It turned out many floorboards were water damaged and he arranged for someone to fix the plumbing as well as the floors. He'd vowed to stay out of the process, but it was just the sort of project that called him irresistibly: the restoration of a dilapidated but at bottom truly splendid house.

Even if Papa had been far more hard-hearted, it would have been difficult to resist Ira's fumbling pleas for assistance. Ira had confessed it the first day—he'd arrived in a foreign land. He knew nobody in Detroit but the Paradisos, and he was forever dropping in. Nor could Papa fail to notice that Mamma was crazy about Ira, or have failed to appreciate what an unforeseen blessing his arrival was at this particular juncture—the final days before the move from Inquiry to Reston—when Mamma might be expected to fall apart. Ira's gaze was trained forward, and he inspired Mamma to look forward. Because they both faced pressing questions of interior decoration, Ira was happy to escort Mamma to the paint store, the wallpaper store, the hardware store. And given Ira's curiosity about all those interesting-sounding dishes Edith had mentioned in her letters, it was hardly surprising that he sat down to suppers of Shipwreck, Drowned Tuna Loaf, Slumped Pork, Smothered Liver . . . And was it possible that Mamma found it regenerating to open a friendship with someone who hadn't known her on that black day when she'd been revealed as a shoplifter? Wasn't this, too, a *fresh start*?

Because the house in Palmer Woods was so close to Middleway—less than a mile—it was easy for Ira to drop in on Bianca as well. She was the artist of the family, and he wanted her advice about what colors the rooms should be. He drove her to the house one February afternoon while a few irresolute snowflakes dotted the air. In addition to all his other huge expenses—he must have invested a couple of thousand dollars already—Ira had hired teams of people to scrub the house from top to bottom. Even so, the place was musty. "Sorry about the smell," Ira apologized. "Your father says we won't get it out completely until spring, when everything's been repainted and we can open it up completely."

Still, even in the shape it was in, with scraps of old carpet heaped in the corners, and missing floorboards, Bianca could see what Papa had seen before he'd stepped inside the place: the expansive, solid bones of a home that could be truly beautiful.

It was a little odd—in a good way, a sweet way—to wander through this somewhat ghostly house alone with Ira Styne. Outside, snow was in the air. Inside, two burdened people—a pregnant woman and a man on a cane—circulated from room to room. Ira was not handsome but he'd cleaned himself up a bit (he'd looked pretty ratty that afternoon he first showed up shivering on the front porch) or she'd gotten used to his looks. In any event, he had a wonderful face—an invitation to any portraitist. Rembrandt, peering into the mirror on waking, must have daily thanked the Lord for being given something even more precious than a handsome face: a soulful face. Graying Ira, on his cane, had much to be grateful for—and he seemed grateful.

Perhaps it was the cane, or just something about his expression, but Ira powerfully evoked for Bianca those days when she'd hugged her portfolio while walking up the stone stairs to Ferry Hospital, days when the eighteen-year-old girl artist had ridden streetcar after streetcar, always observing, observing. Perhaps that's why, this morning, knowing she would be seeing Ira, she'd put on the amethyst locket that Henry Vanden Akker had proudly offered her before shipping out to the Pacific. Ira seemed to bring her closer to Henry, to whom one night she gave herself, knowing he would never return, and Ira brought her closer to the funny sad boy, Private Donnelly, with the bandaged face and amputated foot. On this gray winter afternoon, the promise of snow lent their desultory conversation a richness, a hidden reserve of lusters, as she followed Ira from room to room in this empty house in which, not so long ago, a dozen cats must have roamed, mewling weakly, ravenously, as their mistress lay dead. Bianca felt oddly jittery: the sharp liveliness she always felt in the company of ghosts. The emptied house was all but calling out to her. And the air contained, as well, the peculiar, not unwelcome tension she felt whenever she and Ira were alone. He studied her so closely. It was as though he couldn't take his eyes off her. Bianca talked about the various colors she might paint the rooms, if this were her own house, and Ira wrote down everything in a little notebook, nodding obligedly.

"Of course what you must think about isn't what would look best, but what would best sell the house." Bianca didn't quite believe this, but she knew what she ought to advise.

And Ira Styne didn't believe it either. "I figure, first make it look best. Then you get the best price."

"A man after my own heart, Ira."

He blushed, as she knew he would. It was hard to resist making Ira blush—he did it so agreeably.

It had occurred to her—a wild inspiration not yet shared with anyone—that perhaps she and Grant might buy this house when the renovations were complete. Grant had wanted to buy her a house in Huntington Woods or Birmingham, but she'd turned him down—"not enough gulls up there." But a house in Palmer Woods, less than a mile north of their home on Middleway—this was plausible. In a weird way, it was near-inevitable, since Palmer Woods had always been, even when she was a little girl accompanying her father on his weekend housing tours, her favorite neighborhood in the city. And besides, having consulted so closely with Ira, she knew in advance she would approve of the color scheme.

"What year was this house built?" she asked Ira.

"Nineteen thirty-one. An act of optimism in the depths of the Depression. Incidentally, it's a prime number, according to Edith."

"You didn't do the calculations yourself this time?"

Again Ira blushed. The two of them were standing in what had been, and what presumably again would be, the dining room. From here you could look upward out the window and see falling snowflakes: the whitest things imaginable, but seemingly dark when, as silhouettes, they first spun out of a gray sky. It was a visual effect she'd always loved: black snow. The subtle winter light had brightened half his face, flushed pink. "I figured she'd know," Ira murmured.

"If anybody would," Bianca said. "Actually, you remind me of a boy I once knew. I met so many soldiers. Did you know I used to draw portraits of soldiers?"

"Yes. Edith wrote me," Ira said.

"She often wrote about me?"

"All the time. You were her chief subject. You were an artist. You wore extraordinary clothes. You were dating a boy named Ronny, who was very handsome. He owned a fancy convertible."

Bianca laughed. "*Someone* has been telling tales."

"From where I was then, it all sounded so far away. Glamorous. A family called Paradiso. Living in this city I'd never seen."

"Back then, I didn't know anyone was reading about us."

"In serial installments. An unknown reader."

"Maybe those are the best kind?"

"Which one do I remind you of?"

"Mm?"

"You said I remind you of a soldier you knew."

"That's what I don't know. Maybe a boy named Henry? He gave me this locket. Before he went off to the Pacific. He never came back."

It was an invitation not even timorous Ira could refuse. He inched over to examine the purple stone between her breasts. Physically, this was the closest they had ever stood. She lifted the stone from her chest and Ira for a few seconds held it in his fingers. "I'm sorry," he said.

Bianca moved away, closer to the window and the falling snow. "And there was a boy on a streetcar once," she said. "We never really spoke, though he said, *Nice ridin' with ya, miss,* but the face, the eyes, stayed with me. I wished I could have drawn him—kept him, somehow—or that he'd reappear. And maybe you remind me of him? He, too, had an injured leg."

Ira reminded her of somebody? Yes, he did, the graying man on the cane summoned her back to those most intense days of her life—and yet Ira was also so vivid a presence, with his rapid, apologetic speech and remarkably long chin and big brown imploring puppy-dog gaze, that it was impossible not to be drawn into the immediacy of the moment. The empty house was speaking to the two of them. Outside, a few lost-seeming snowflakes, so lightweight they appeared to drift rather than fall, wandered the air. Inside, also a little lost-seeming, Ira watched her as, mixing paints in her head, she described interiors only she could see: this room's walls might be painted a subdued terra-cotta, this room's walls a gold softened by caramel, this room's a white tinctured with apple green . . .

If Ira had a gift for ingratiation, or infiltration (he'd inserted himself into the lives of everyone in the family), he was also excessively generous. Not long after the move to Reston Street, Ira showed up not only with champagne but with a handsome and no doubt very expensive set of six champagne glasses from France. Mamma could hardly have been more thrilled! The gift embodied everything the move was intended to effect. She was living in a new neighborhood, in a house with a bay window in the living room and a working fireplace, and why shouldn't she have fine French champagne glasses?

The gift nonplussed Papa, who wanted to be gracious but who had always viewed champagne as an airy swindle—bubbles were a sign of something gone wrong in your winemaking—and saw the existence of special champagne glasses as proof of the shameless ends to which the swindlers will pursue the gullible. This notion that Ira was an easy mark pulled Papa, inexorably, ever deeper into Ira's renovations. A new policy was instituted wherein Ira wrote no checks for the house without first clearing the amount with Papa. How in the world had Ira ever succeeded in the furniture business?

A good deal more of Ira's story emerged eventually from Edith, whose sometimes tactless directness did have its advantages. Bianca and Edith got together for lunch in late February, a couple of weeks after the move. At Bianca's suggestion, they met at Herk's Snack Shack, where she and Ronny used to have coffee after Professor Manhardt's class. Though the Institute Midwest had folded up long ago, Herk's endured, still serving up watery coffee.

"He had a sort of breakdown in the War," Edith said.

Somehow, although it wasn't news she'd actually been told, Bianca knew this already.

Ira had been wounded in North Africa, Edith explained. He was hit in the leg, which is why he carried the cane. But he was also hit in the neck, which rendered him mute for weeks on end. He had naturally supposed he might never speak again.

"How terrible."

"He says his voice has never been the same."

This, too, made sense. There was a faint scratchiness to Ira's voice, as though he perpetually needed to clear his throat.

"Well it's an appealing voice," Bianca said. Which it was.

"And he had another sort of breakdown about two years ago. You know his wife left him?"

"I knew he was divorced."

"She left him for his best friend."

Behind her homely tortoiseshell glasses, Edith gave her sister a hard look. If, according to Edith, boys were too often silly, girls were too often disloyal. Edith had shown no patience with Maggie when she'd gone through her two divorces, and never in a million years could Bianca confess to her sister that, not so long ago, she'd kissed Ronny Olsson under the Ambassador Bridge.

"I didn't know. I'm so sorry."

"He says his father-in-law cried even more than *he* did. They loved each other. His father-in-law declared that he'd lost his only son."

"All of this explains a lot. About how he is."

"What do you mean—*how he is*?"

Edith asked this defensively—as though Bianca had spoken disparagingly of Ira.

Bianca laughed. "Have you ever met a man who apologizes more? Or seems more in need of being taken care of? He's older than I am but he brings out the mother in me. *Ira, tighten your scarf*, I want to tell him. *Ira, eat your peas*. It's hilarious. Papa keeps vowing not to get involved and the next thing you know he's haggling with some carpenter to save Ira twenty dollars. Mamma's sending him home with a tin of brownies under one arm and a pot of Shipwreck under the other. He's got you doing his darning, and yet when I suggest he may not be the most streetwise man who ever came down the pike, you look daggers at me."

"He's extremely intelligent."

"You're defending him and no one's attacking him. Quite the contrary. I think Ira's some sort of godsend. He shows up on our doorstep and everybody's mood immediately lifts. It's as if we all found some stray puppy shivering on our front porch one January day. Isn't he one of the main reasons Mamma's doing so much better than anyone expected? Who ever imagined she'd handle the move this well? And Papa, too. What could be better for him than getting swept up in renovating a beautiful house in Palmer Woods?"

And me, too, Bianca was tempted to add. This sense that her parents' lives were no longer unraveling had brought her a great easing. It was nearly twenty-four hours since her last cigarette. She was going to emerge intact from all this, and get her appetite back, and begin to care properly for the baby inside her.

"But he's very intelligent," Edith repeated.

"I don't doubt that for a minute."

"I keep telling him he ought to teach history. You know he's a real history buff. I don't think he's a businessman."

"He's certainly no businessman. He'd have to go back to school if he wanted to teach."

"He could go back to school."

Not so long ago, at a time when she was floundering, someone had quietly interceded in Edith's life—Uncle Dennis, of course—with the suggestion that she become a doctor, and everything had fallen into place. It was striking, now, the conviction with which Edith argued for the *fresh start* someone else's life ought to take.

"He'd have to finish the house first," Bianca said.

"He'll finish the house."

"Not anytime soon. I remember the day we met him. He'd just come by to deliver a message of thanks. He and I said goodbye on the front porch. He was leaving the next day for New Jersey. Where he belonged, he said."

CHAPTER XXXVII

They rolled up to a stop sign and in the edge of Bianca's vision something green and white flashed in a neighbor's brown garden. A voice inside her head announced, *A crocus!* It was Mr. Bickey's garden—the neighbor who had been rescued by the milkman, Mr. Bootmaker, charging upstairs to haul the old man's body out of a freezing bathtub that had nearly become a casket.

Bianca looked more closely and the crocus metamorphosed into balloon and string, a deflated green balloon and a white string—a woebegone drifter, come to rest in Mr. Bickey's garden. The misapprehension heartened her all the same. Gray as the city was on this overcast March day, the miracle of spring was in the offing.

Spring was in the offing, bringing with it the appearance of someone who, miraculously, would see another spring. Mr. Bickey's front door swung slowly open and the neighborhood recluse emerged—or part of him did. An arm reached out and dropped an envelope into the mailbox for the mailman to pick up.

They were going for a drive in Maggie's new car, a red Nash-Healey convertible. Another gift from Walton. Of course it was far too cold to put the top down, but the car was beautiful, with buttery leather seats, and Bianca, though usually immune to this sort of envy, found herself chafing. (Was there no end to Walton's money?) And laughably out of place. As she entered her seventh month of pregnancy, climbing in and out of nifty little roadsters was laborious.

Maggie was exultant. She turned onto Seven Mile and punched the accelerator. The little car rocketed forward. "I'm thinking about having my nose done," Maggie said.

"*Done?* Maggie, what on earth are you talking about?"

"Straightened. Reshaped a little bit."

"You're going to let them go after your nose with *knives*? Maggie, I don't believe this. I don't believe this!"

"Nothing drastic."

"Maggie, a knife at your nose *is* drastic. And there's nothing wrong with your nose. I'm particularly fond of your nose. It has character."

"Easy for you to say. You with your perfect nose."

"My nose is too long. Maybe."

"But it's straight. Mine's crooked."

"Maggie, was this your idea, or Walton's?"

"Just because he may have thought of it first doesn't mean it wasn't my idea. You never give me credit."

"I just told you you look lovely."

Maggie did. In some mischievous, ignoble corner of her mind, Bianca had been secretly hoping the chin enhancement would prove a failure. It scarcely seemed right—it felt *unfair*—for a person to alter so fundamental a feature. Some things were God-given. But the operation had worked out; pretty Maggie was even prettier with that solid new chin. And in the discomfort of eating after the operation, she'd shed some weight. She looked *good*. And now she was going to have her nose "done."

"Walton put it very well. He said, You can spend the rest of your life with a crooked nose, or the rest of your life with a straight nose, now which do you prefer? Entirely up to me. Though he can be mighty persuasive."

"Oh, tell him to have his own nose straightened, Maggie! Or his ear lobes realigned. Or his—well, I don't know." Bianca had just now recalled Walton's deformed hand.

If this whole business were taken to Priscilla for analysis, she would doubtless spot a connection between Walton's deformity and his pushy eagerness to subject his wife to plastic surgery. Was the connection genuine? Perhaps. Just because something sounds logical doesn't mean it's incorrect, as Ronny's friend Chris Abendorfer would say. In any event, Walton certainly *was* persuasive. Even Bianca had begun to feel slightly daunted. For such a long time, she'd been able to think of him only as Wally Waller, despite his custom-made suits, which he actually bought in New York. (He was the only man Bianca knew who regularly bought his clothes in another city.) But in recent months Bianca, seemingly the last of the holdouts, had begun succumbing to the man's authority. At a couple of recent parties he'd held forth about *the future of the city*. Eyes blazing, he uttered the phrase with proprietary excitement, as if its evolving shape naturally belonged to him, as if he beheld what the rest of them couldn't: a whole new cityscape. Walton's latest undertaking was a sort of shopping center or complex. The largest in the world. It was often mentioned in the newspapers. It was to be called Northland and would be located way out at Eight Mile and Greenfield. Walton was one of the chief investors.

"So where are we going?" Maggie said. They had no destination. They were joyriding in Maggie's snazzy and no doubt very expensive new convertible.

"How about Inquiry?" Bianca said. "The old haunts?"

"Oh that just depresses me. It's so run-*down*. Walton says all those old neighborhoods inside the Boulevard will eventually get bulldozed."

"Maybe they merely need a chin enhancement. Or their nose done?"

"Very funny. Hey, I got an idea. Why don't we drive up Woodward to Henry Vanden Akker's house? You know I've never seen Henry's house."

The story of Bianca's doomed lover, the virginity-stealer who died in the War, had a surprisingly stubborn purchase on Maggie's imagination. Although she'd never met him, and although it was all so long ago, Maggie continually invoked Henry.

Bianca tried fitting Maggie's suggestion into her present mood. Was today at last the day to survey the house of that young man who once, in a poem, called her his *harbor light*—that white stucco house in which everything was perfectly, mathematically balanced? Bianca shuddered. She wasn't ready—no, not even yet. Although she'd passed Henry's street countless times, she'd never once, since the last time she visited the Vanden Akkers, turned off Woodward and driven by the actual house. The very last time she'd seen it, she'd been handed a copy of that letter to his parents in which Henry confessed his wish to make Bea Paradiso his wife. And on that very day she'd started coming down with the influenza that nearly killed her.

"I don't think so," Bianca said. "I think that *would* be depressing. What if the house has burned down? Or been bulldozed? Or worse, maybe, what if it looks exactly the same?"

"Hey, I know. Let's go see Stevie. I haven't seen your brother in ages."

"Stevie's at work."

"Let's go see Stevie at work. I haven't seen him in ages."

"I don't think that's such a good idea either."

"Come on. We'll surprise him."

Maggie wanted to show off her new car. And Bianca, still unnerved, in whose mind the mathematical white house had become a sort of face, like an illustration in a children's book—a quizzical face, a yearning face—suddenly capitulated: "All right. What the heck. Let's go visit Stevie."

The truth was, she'd never visited Stevie at work, though she'd frequently driven by Turk's Trucks. It was on Fenkell. Stevie could be so private and territorial that it had seemed inadvisable to pay a visit.

Turk's Trucks was located in a military-brown building that looked like an armory. It wasn't very welcoming, but Maggie, typically brazen, briskly slotted the car into a space marked "Reserved for Visitors." Bianca experienced a sinking sensation. "I'm not sure this is such a good idea."

"See the sign? Perfect. Visitors? Us."

Having hauled herself out of the car, Bianca felt a good deal better, however, when she spied somebody who was an unmistakable figure, though she hadn't seen him in years. It was a little silver-haired man, hurrying down the street. It was Mr. Caglayangil. The Turk. She didn't hesitate. "Excuse me, excuse me," she called.

The little man turned. His topcoat was open. He was wearing a gold tie, just as when she first met him. He looked puzzled, but he stepped in her direction.

"Hello," Bianca said. "Excuse me. There's no reason why you should remember me, but we've met a few times. I recognized you and just wanted to say hello. My name is Bianca Ives, but I used to be Bea Paradiso. I'm Steve Paradiso's sister."

The years had etched a great many new wrinkles in the little man's rucked face. He was thinking hard, casting his memory backward . . .

Bianca went on: "We met first at a Sanders restaurant, downtown, maybe ten years ago now. I was with my aunt, Grace Poppleton."

"The doctor's wife."

"That's right."

The old man's face eased, and brightened. "You are the doctor's niece."

"That's right."

"He is a great man, Dr. Poppleton."

"Well." Bianca laughed. "We all think so."

"He saved my daughter's life. My only child."

"He's a wonderful doctor," Bianca said.

"I remember you," Mr. Caglayangil said. "I remember everything, though sometimes now, I am old, it takes me moments." This seemed an empty boast, but his next remark demonstrated, amazingly, a vivid recollection of their first meeting. "You told me you never went to Italy. Turkey first, I told you. I told you visit Turkey. I invited you."

"And you know what? I still haven't been to either one." Bianca laughed again.

"You are the doctor's niece and I must not keep you in the cold. Please. You come in. As my guests."

"But you were heading somewhere."

"Please. You come in."

"You must have business—"

"You come in."

So they followed Mr. Caglayangil into a grim lobby and up some stairs and through a room where a secretary was sitting. Mr. Caglayangil opened a door and, the next moment, Bianca and Maggie were sitting in the world's unlikeliest office. They were miles away from the traffic going by on Fenkell; they were miles away from the streets of Detroit. They had crossed a threshold into a sorcerer's chamber.

They sat in plush tawny leather armchairs. Beautiful rugs were hanging on the walls, which were painted gold. Beautiful rugs lay atop beautiful rugs on the floor. There were low, ornate wooden tables on which strange knickknacks were arranged. There were vases overspilling with flowers. The room smelled wonderful. "Wowee," Maggie said. "Shazam!"

Bianca wasn't at all sure this was an appropriate response. Was it even a real word—or just a radio word?

But she needn't have worried. Mr. Caglayangil looked gratified, and he even knew the radio reference. "Captain Marvel," he said.

"My oh my, this is *nice!*" Maggie exclaimed. "Being in here, it's like traveling to a foreign country. It's like some exotic vacation." Mr. Caglayangil grinned broadly. No matter how old they were, men loved Maggie.

"Are most of the things from Turkey?" Bianca asked him.

"Most everything from Turkey."

"That's an extraordinary chest."

Against the wall stood a fantastically ornate cabinet that Papa the woodworker would have knelt to inspect. "It is called a *dolap,*" Mr. Caglayangil said. "More than two hundred years old."

"Well I'll be," Maggie said. "It's so fancy. And look at this paperweight."

"That is a candlestick. We call it a *shamdan,*" Mr. Caglayangil said.

"Well *this* one's a paperweight."

"That is a toothpick holder. We call it *kurdanlik.*"

"And that? That is *quite* an amazing chest," Bianca said. She hardly had a vocabulary to describe it—a wooden chest, painted a weathered green, elaborately done up with constellations of studs and metal fastenings.

"It is a *cheyiz*. A dowry chest. Also antique."

"And that painting," Maggie interposed. "It's like an angel."

"It is an angel. It is Gabriel. And that is Mary. I am a Christian man. Rare in Turkey."

"We're Christians too," Maggie said.

"Yes," Mr. Caglayangil said.

A very dark-skinned woman, though she was not a Negro, brought in a big silver tray on which was resting a vast teapot, some gold-rimmed glasses, a bowl full of ice cubes, and a plate full of pastries. "Baklava?" Mr. Caglayangil said.

"I know it," Bianca said.

"What a lovely teapot," Maggie said.

"*Chaydan*," Mr. Caglayangil said. "Also an antique. This *chaydan* was once used in the court of Abdul Hamid."

"Well I'll be," Maggie said.

"I certainly didn't mean to barge in like this," Bianca said. "I just wanted to see where Steve worked."

"You are welcome any time. Steve is not here until three o'clock, four o'clock. You are welcome to wait right here."

"Oh we can't stay so long," Bianca said. "Though we'd love to. I've never been in a room like this."

Mr. Caglayangil nodded and said, "No, you never."

"I guess I got to Turkey at last. Today."

"Better late than never." And Mr. Caglayangil laughed heartily.

Bianca said, "You know, Steve loves his job. I was so happy when he told me he was working for you."

The dark-skinned woman set before Maggie and Bianca glasses of tea and the plate of Turkish pastries, and placed the ice cubes and what looked like a glass of water before Mr. Caglayangil, then departed from the room, all without saying a word.

"Your uncle, the doctor, he visits me one day. He tells me his nephew looks for a job. I tell the doctor, The boy looks no more, he has a job with me. The doctor says, Joe (he calls me Joe, most people do, but my name is Yusuf), he says, Joe, I want no favors from you. I tell him, Doctor, you saved my only child, my Melek. You are the reason I have two grandsons now. Without you, my family dies out. You ask me any favor, I do it for you.

"The doctor says, No favors, Joe, I accept no favors from you. I say, Doctor, I wait more than ten years to do a favor to you. You ask me give your cat a job, I hire your cat." Mr. Caglayangil laughed heartily. In addition to his gold tie, he was wearing a number of gold rings. He was a sparkling presence. Bianca picked up her gold-rimmed glass of tea, which smelled of flowers she couldn't identify.

Mr. Caglayangil went on: "The doctor says, No favors. So I begin thinking . . ." Mr. Caglayangil illustrated the process by animatedly furrowing his brow. "And then I say, Doctor, will you do *me* a favor? And the doctor says, Of course, Joe. And I say, Okay, do me this favor: let me do *you* a favor. And the doctor says, I accept no favors.

"So I think some more." Mr. Caglayangil again paused to demonstrate. He was enjoying himself hugely. "And then I say, Well then, Doctor, you won't let me do you *one* favor, so I'll do you *two* favors. First, I hire your nephew. Second, I tell you it is no favor."

Mr. Caglayangil was consumed by mirth. At the thought of how he'd outmaneuvered the great doctor, tears of hilarity leaked from his eyes.

Bianca sipped eagerly from her tea, which turned out to be more than wonderful. It was mint and honey and flowers—all the flowers of the Middle East—and with its flavors on her palate the room's beauty intensified. The pigments in the hanging rugs deepened, and the miraculous dowry chest grew yet more miraculous, the filigrees more artfully turned, its colors older and richer and braver. Not even in the movies, perhaps only in dreams, had she ever sat in a room of such color and sumptuosity.

Mr. Caglayangil was still chuckling to himself as Bianca took another, deeper sip from her glass and at once she made a far-flung connection. It might just as well have been Uncle Dennis sitting before her. Yes, it might have been Uncle Dennis, and not a wizened, white-haired, gold-encrusted Turkish immigrant, for the two men were brothers of a sort. Both men saw their acts of kindness as humorous. They shared a kind of cosmic joke: it was ever so funny, it made them *laugh*, to think about engineering some ingenious act of charity.

"And now I will drink a magic drink," Mr. Caglayangil said. "Would you like to see a magic drink?"

"Of course," Bianca said.

"Sure thing," Maggie said.

"It looks like water," Mr. Caglayangil said, holding up the clear glass.

"Yes," Maggie said.

"It certainly does," Bianca said.

"But it isn't. And now I add real water." He poured clear liquid into the clear liquid. Quickly, inexplicably, the mixture turned milky white.

"Shazam!" Maggie said.

"Shazam!" Mr. Caglayangil echoed.

"What is it?" Bianca asked.

"It is raki. Like the Greek ouzo. Only the Greeks do not make it so good. They are a younger culture." Mr. Caglayangil offered this assessment so solemnly, Bianca didn't immediately understand it was another little joke. "Maybe you would try some . . ."

"I'd be willing to try," Maggie said. She was never one for tea.

Bianca glanced down at her domed stomach and said, "I'll stick with the tea. It's wonderfully delicious."

Mr. Caglayangil peered at her. His deep-set eyes were glittering. He said, "Maybe I believe the doctor's niece has her own magic inside her."

Bianca felt herself blush. "Yes . . ."

Mr. Caglayangil lifted his cloudy glass and peered hard into it, as if some stubborn, recondite answer might be divined there. "Someday," he went on, "my grandsons will own this company. They are only six years old and four years old, but already they understand. I explain it to them. They shake hands with Steve. I tell them, You owe your lives to this man's uncle. This is the great doctor's nephew. They understand. As long as he wants it, Steve has a job here—a good job."

"But is he a good worker?" Maggie said. She asked this in a new way she had: her head cocked and her enhanced chin uplifted. No doubt, after she'd had her nose done a whole new repertoire of gestures would surface—and would go on surfacing once she'd had her eyes done, and her forehead done, and her ears done, and her breasts done, and each of these new gestures would turn out to be, from the male point of view, irresistibly winsome. Mr. Caglayangil was enthralled.

Again he furrowed his white eyebrows at her. "A good worker? Steve?" His tone of simulated sternness, as though disdainful of anyone asking so simpleminded a question, was in fact a form of flirtatiousness. "Of course he is. He's the doctor's nephew."

Uncle Dennis had been away for what seemed like ages, since before the move to Reston Street nearly a month ago. He'd given them "time to settle in."

He arrived with two bottles of champagne—which was surprising, since he knew Papa considered it a swindle. But Uncle Dennis must have gotten wind of the new champagne glasses, and the bottles turned out to be the perfect gift: Mamma glowed while leading her guests into her new dining room and offering them champagne from French champagne glasses. The provider of the glasses—Ira—had also been invited, so they were seven in all: Papa, Mamma, Uncle Dennis, Bianca, Grant, Edith, and Ira. Rita and Stevie had their own event to attend—a wedding rehearsal for one of Stevie's co-workers at Turk's Trucks—and this, too, seemed encouraging: the new job was enriching their social life.

Yes, Ira was still in Detroit, still staying in the place in Highland Park that rented rooms by the week. In retrospect, he should have found a more long-term rental; he was into his second month now. The minimal renovations that Papa had recommended if Ira were to get a "fair price" for the house were complete. The carpets had been torn up and the junk hauled away, the floorboards that needed replacing had been replaced, everything had been dusted and scrubbed, and the interior walls repainted. Bathrooms had been retiled, banisters repaired, windows reputtied. The eaves' troughs had been cleaned, new shrubs planted, and the lawn reseeded. But now Ira wished to go a step further. He wanted to renovate the little room on the third floor, which had no proper ceiling. Papa sternly counseled against: it wasn't certain, when Ira sold the house, he would recover the investment. But Ira, in his rapid and roundabout and ever-apologetic way, was also adamant. That room could easily be the most charming room in the entire house. All it needed was a proper ceiling and some built-in bookcases to make a beautiful little library.

"Not every buyer wants a library," Papa told him.

"But the right sort of buyer does."

"The right sort of buyer is the one paying the most."

"The right sort of buyer understands the house."

Papa nodded, not quite able to conceal his pleasure. Ira was learning to stand up to him, at least while echoing Papa's own underlying philosophy.

At dinner, which wasn't Mamma's best (Slumped Pork, greasier than usual), Edith held forth. She'd recently read some articles about tuberculosis, whose infection rates throughout the country were way down. It was possible that we—she spoke of *we*—might eliminate it altogether in the next few years. And Uncle Dennis nodded respectfully, almost gratefully, as though deferring to a medical expert. He would be in for a great deal of this, Bianca foresaw, after Edith began her training in earnest. Meanwhile, Bianca was hoping for some precious time alone with her uncle.

After dinner, the three women went out to the kitchen, to clean up, the four men into the living room, to drink a bit more of Papa's wine. Bianca was cheered to overhear hearty roars of male laughter—Grant was in good form tonight. And Ira, too, was telling stories, in that nervous and rushed way of his. More laughter. And then Papa's voice lifted to say: "We will all go smelt fishing."

This made Bianca laugh. "Can you picture Ira smelt fishing?"

"He was a miler in high school," Edith replied. She seemed to think Bianca was ridiculing Ira, when she was actually speaking fondly. With her unreliable sense of humor, Edith often misunderstood teasing. "He was in the New Jersey state finals," she went on. "He is quite athletic."

"Oh I don't doubt it. It's just I have trouble picturing Papa and Uncle Dennis and Grant and Ira going fishing together. It's what you'd call a motley crew."

"Your father has made a friend," Mamma declared.

Mamma said this with some emphasis and Bianca let the words echo in her head.

She saw, belatedly, that Mamma was correct. It wasn't merely Ira's house in Palmer Woods, with all its engaging challenges, that drew Papa so potently. Nor was it Ira's helplessness, and Papa's gruff but tender-hearted inability to watch somebody getting swindled. No, Papa—who had so few real friends—had come to value Ira as a friend.

On the face of it, this seemed absurdly unlikely: Ira was some twenty years younger than Papa and he was a Jewish boy from New Jersey who spoke ten words to Papa's one. But Papa's friendships had never followed any discernible logic. What did he have in common with Uncle Dennis, who was never more himself than when expatiating on interstellar spaceflight?

"Your father has made a friend," Mamma declared once more, and added, "It's good for him."

And Bianca understood, again belatedly, just how comforting this was for Mamma, who, for all her own troubles these past few months, had been worrying about Papa. About his drinking too much, and nightly barricading himself behind his newspaper. About his slumped posture and repetitiveness. Mamma understood how restorative finding a friend had been, especially a friend of Ira's ineptitude: Papa felt newly helpful and needed. In inviting Ira to dinner so many nights, Mamma had been looking after her husband. Ira's endless renovations were a blessing for everyone. He would be sorely missed, when he returned to New Jersey . . .

Bianca seized on the prerogatives of her pregnancy to uproot Uncle Dennis from the smoky company of men. Could the doctor give her a few minutes? Of course, of course—he was just thinking he needed a trip to the pharmacy.

When they stepped out the front door, it seemed the two of them ought to be walking down Inquiry. But those days were over—forever. This street was called Reston and Bianca felt a little disoriented.

Spring was in the air and this, too, was disorienting, but cheerfully so. Winter had been so protracted and so frightening. Could it really be over? All those cold and dismally dark and scary days were behind her?

"You're feeling all right?" Uncle Dennis began.

"Just fine."

"You're looking much better since I saw you last," Uncle Dennis said.

"Fatter, anyway." Bianca laughed.

"You weren't eating," Uncle Dennis said.

"I was having trouble eating for a while. There was a very difficult stretch."

She was tempted to tell him she'd even taken up smoking—a crime admissible only because she was no longer the secretive, desperate woman who had done so. It had been twelve days since her last cigarette. Tonight, walking down her parents' new street, she felt confident: never in her life would she light another.

The oddest thing about a new neighborhood was the way the houses kept moving around—trading places. By now, she knew this street, but not where the houses stood relationally: half-familiar shapes kept looming unexpectedly out of the March darkness.

"The boys seem fine," Uncle Dennis said.

"I suppose. They're such easy boys, mostly. Like Grant, mostly. Do them the littlest kindness, and they're so grateful. There was a period there, a couple months ago, they were constantly squabbling, and crying, which wasn't at all like them. And I realized it was because I was gone so much, every minute over with Mamma. And actually it was almost reassuring to see them troubled, because they're usually such easy boys I can think they don't need me."

"Maybe it's a sign you've done something right—that they're so easy?"

"But then something got into Chip. He turned very fearful. With terrifying nightmares. He's not fully over it yet. He asks me one day, during the worst of it, with this sort of sick, panicky look on his face, Mom, he says, how many bites would it take for a shark to eat all of me? What does a parent say to a question like that?"

"I'm sure you handled it better than I could have."

"He's better now. Not quite the same, but almost the same. I do wonder how long a full recovery will take."

"I sometimes think it's the most mystical term in the whole universe: recovery. That's a medical opinion." Uncle Dennis laughed.

They were coming up on Jefferson. The sounds of traffic mingled with the rousing wet-soil smells of spring. There was another question that must be asked: "And Aunt Grace. It's been months and months since I saw her. How is she?"

The pause extended a little too long.

"Well of course she's a trouper. But this time has been hard. They took the first breast, four years ago, she bounced right back. But this time has been hard. And we—well, as you know, we're not sure of the prognosis."

"I pray for her," Bianca said.

"And she prays for all of you. These haven't been easy months."

"Easier because of you, though. Uncle Dennis, what would we have done without you? You must have driven up twenty times since—since the day Papa discovered Mamma's crimes."

"Maybe I'm just restless."

"Oh *stop* it." Uncle Dennis had always liked when she pretended to be hard on him—playing a petulant little girl, stamping her foot in indignation. She would never talk this way to Papa; it was a kind of teasing that was theirs alone. "Edith was refusing to move to Reston Street before you gave her the idea of medical school."

Uncle Dennis protested: "Oh but it was *her* idea. She was just a little shy about expressing it."

"And I don't suppose you deserve any credit for the turnaround in Stevie's life? You know he *loves* his job. And where are he and Rita tonight? Out with new friends at a wedding rehearsal. When he was working for Ford, how often did something like that happen?"

"No, no, no—now that *really* isn't a case where I can take credit. They were looking for a young man of Stevie's qualifications."

"That isn't the impression I got from Mr. Caglayangil."

"The Turk? You talked with the Turk?"

"Maggie and I dropped in to visit Stevie. He wasn't there but we talked with Mr. Caglayangil. We had tea. In the inner temple. The Gold Room."

"Extraordinary, isn't it? Apparently some of those artifacts belong in a museum. They're truly that precious."

"Yes, he told us they were rare. Actually he went a step further. He informed us that *he* was a rare man."

The two of them laughed. Then Uncle Dennis said, "I told him I would accept no favors."

"Yes. He told me that's what you told him. And you know what else? He told me he told *you* he was going to do you two favors. One, he was going to hire Stevie. Two, he was going to insist he was doing you no favors."

They were just about to turn onto Jefferson. In the darkness of Reston Street, in the spring air, Uncle Dennis began to laugh again, and this time he kept on laughing. Oh he *liked* being outwitted by a bejeweled little man who spoke broken English. Far away, in an exotic sanctum hidden along an industrial stretch of Fenkell, a rare little gold man in a golden room was laughing to himself, and Uncle Dennis heard, and understood, and joined the laughter.

CHAPTER XXXVIII

"Didn't I promise you I'd get you here before it closed?"

"You did," Bianca said.

As Grant had predicted, Pierre was shutting his doors, after twenty-six years of business.

She went on: "The place is almost as old as I am."

"When it opened, Hoover wasn't yet president."

"Now you're making me feel *old.*"

Loyal customers of many years' standing had turned out today—a crowd large enough to leave you wondering why the place must close at all. But to glance at Pierre, who maintained his pencil-line-thin moustache but who had dyed his hair a darker shade since Bianca was here last summer, was to behold a defeated man.

"Didn't I promise you I'd get you here before it closed?" Grant repeated.

In truth, when Bianca had first heard about the closing, she hadn't wished to return. She'd enjoyed here such a memorable anniversary lunch, where she'd announced the wispy suspicion of her pregnancy over steaks and a farewell abundance of wine—why overlay other memories upon it? Afterward, they'd walked down Jefferson hand in hand, under a rinsed summer sky in which a white gull was wheeling toward the river. That day had been perfect, in its way.

But when Grant had proposed lunch today, it had seemed important to acknowledge his thoughtfulness. And here they were.

She needed to be better toward Grant, who deserved someone better—not that it would ever occur to him to think this way. But she'd been feeling especially tender and solicitous for months now, ever since the night he'd gotten so stinking drunk with Papa and wept on the drive home and confessed his fear of someday coming home to a note on the kitchen table. To look at Grant, seated across this other, very elegant table, you'd never suppose him prey to such fears. He looked so contented, so solid and comfortingly good-looking. It was just that way with the boys, too, who were truly such wonderfully joyful, life-loving children, but who in recent months had constantly drawn her aside to seek reassurances about preposterous terrors: sharks, bears, cobras. Especially Chip. If a toilet's flush were strong enough, could it pull you down inside it? If a rat got into the house, would it eat your eyes while you slept? Only last summer, watching the backyard from the kitchen window, she'd seen Chip walk blindfolded across a wooden "tightrope" Grant had sunk into the ground. And now? Now Chip was scared of toilet seats.

"Tell me the kids are all right," Bianca said.

"The kids are fine." They were home with Grandmother Ives, who was doing one of her rare stints of babysitting. "They're fine and I'm going to have the porterhouse steak."

"And I'm going to have the lady's steak. It's what I had the first time I was here. With Mrs. Olsson."

"She was a beautiful woman."

"And she was alive when we lunched here. Isn't it odd when you phrase it like that? One meal, the woman's alive. The next meal, she isn't. Her death was one of the hundred things that happened this winter. Heaven help us, I'm awfully glad it's finally spring."

"Me too," Grant said. "Me too."

"Most of the time, I felt I was falling apart."

"I think you handled things quite admirably, under the circumstances."

Grant was being lawyerly, though just a little. Still, whenever he got this way—so reasoned and balanced—Bianca felt a wayward impulse to rumple his composure. "Did you know I was smoking for a while? That I took it up again? While pregnant? Because I was feeling so absolutely at wit's end?"

But it turned out *her* composure was about to be rumpled. "Yes," Grant said softly. "I knew."

"You did?"

"Yes, I did. I picked up your coat one day and a pack of Tareytons fell out."

"My coat? But I was always keeping them in my purse."

"Your coat," Grant said firmly.

Bianca pondered a moment. "I guess I'm not surprised. I couldn't keep anything organized, for all the lists I drew up. Incidentally, you didn't say anything."

"I thought about it."

"But you didn't."

"I think I was scared to."

"Scared to?" The phrase scared *her*—sent a little chill skittering into the big dome of her stomach.

"Scared it would make you even more nervous. You were in a real state."

"I *was*, wasn't I?" Bianca tried a laugh, which came out sounding brittle. "Not that I'm out of it exactly. I don't think I'll be out of it until the baby's born."

"Of course not. That's only natural," Grant said. "That's only natural," he repeated, drawing comfort from the phrase.

"Order a glass of wine with your steak," Bianca suggested.

"You're going to have one?"

"No, but I want to drink vicariously. Hell, have a cigarette."

"I think I'll pass." It was a point of pride for Grant that he'd never bought a pack of cigarettes.

"My boyfriend's still in training," she said.

"I suppose."

It was one of Grant's most commendable traits: his athlete's sense of enlightened self-maintenance. Presumably, this was a notion the boys would inherit from their father: your body is something to take care of.

The food arrived and it was wonderful. Last time, the French fries had been greasy. But these were the crisp steaming little sticks Bianca recalled from her visits with Mrs. Olsson. The steaks, the green beans, the bread, everything was delicious. Why did Pierre's need to close?

"So now it's Stevie and Rita," Grant said.

"Mm?"

"Thinking of moving."

"Yes. They're thinking of moving."

This was the latest revelation from Rita. She and Stevie had been "doing a little house hunting."

When Rita, who never could contain her excitement, had dropped the news last weekend, Stevie looked embarrassed—but exultant, too. He and that little Rita Comer, the pregnant seventeen-year-old hillbilly bride with the terrible teeth, were going somewhere.

Bianca said, "I'm beginning to feel like Edith. When she was saying, Let the rest of them move. Anyway, I'm staying put." An image of Ira's house popped into her head. Surely he would finish the renovations soon. "Or not going far," she amended.

"Whatever you want," Grant said. He meant it.

"Hard to believe my baby brother has already bought one house and is thinking of selling to buy bigger. And all without anybody's help."

"Oh I wouldn't say that."

Though Grant generally hesitated to contradict her, this was one area—the cold male world of large-scale finance—where he was quick to highlight her illusions. "He'd still be at Ford's if it weren't for Uncle Dennis."

"True enough," Bianca conceded, and picked up two more French fries. Grant was eyeing them interestedly; he'd already cleared his plate. "Go ahead," she said.

"Thanks." His big hand reached across the table and seized a handful. "And it's not just the job," he said. "I was amazed when Rita told me that the total bill for her braces, I mean everything, was only a hundred dollars."

"A hundred dollars? You're sure?"

Grant grabbed another handful of fries. "Isn't it obvious what happened? It's like the Turk. The orthodontist owes your uncle some huge favor. So he agrees to do everything for a hundred dollars."

"A hundred dollars. That's amazing." This was information to file away and analyze . . .

Grant pilfered still another handful, this time looking just a little apologetic. He said, "I think I'm going to start a little diet soon."

"You look good," Bianca said. "I was just thinking how good you looked. Think about me, the weight I'll have to lose when this is all done. I've gained thirty-four pounds as of this morning. I can't be much fun like this."

Grant seemed a little surprised. "Fun?" he said. "You're all the fun I'll ever need."

Bianca didn't know what to say. Then she looked deeper into his eyes and saw that she needn't say anything. She reached across the table and took his hand. Their fingers interlocked.

Later, over coffee, Bianca said, "Frankly, I'm surprised you didn't mention the cigarettes. You must have been very disapproving. You knew it wasn't good for the baby." She wasn't being exactly logical, but she felt a little resentful. Hadn't it been Grant's duty to intercede?

Grant shrugged. "I knew you were having a very hard time. I didn't want to add to it."

"*You* were having a very hard time. But you didn't take up smoking, or talking to yourself, or half a dozen things I fell into."

"But you're an artist, Bianca."

"An artist? Some artist I turn out to be. I've hardly painted or drawn since we got the news about the baby. And done *nothing* since Mamma went away for her *thorough examination.* Good heavens, I'm still working on that still life with all the tarnished silverware. A cynic might say I keep at the painting so I won't have to polish the silver. Honestly, you give me too much credit, Grant." Although she pointed this out occasionally, it was a message she could never deliver with conviction— partly because she so depended upon his regard, inflated or not, and partly because he clearly didn't *want* his illusions shattered. Still, in deserved self-punishment for having mistreated the baby within her, Bianca went on forcibly: "You *do,* honey. Way too much credit. It's like that business with Mr. Bootmaker. Look at it closely. What is it I do? I merely continue milk deliveries. I merely make things convenient for myself. And what do he and his father do? They break into Mr. Bickey's, they find him shivering in the bath, they haul him out and race to the hospital—they save his life. We're talking about somebody who saves somebody's life versus somebody who's too lazy to go to the store and get her own milk."

"But Bianca, you're not seeing the whole picture." Grant canted forward and narrowed his eyes. He was about to become lawyerly. "You're not making the right distinctions. You're comparing yourself to them, but I'm saying compare yourself to me. And who am I? *I'm* somebody who tries to fire them—I'm doing my best to ensure that people like them go out of business. And then you go behind my back and restart deliveries. And what happens? Not two months later, they go and save somebody's life on our *very own street.* Talk about having your instincts vindicated! Those men are heroes."

These days, Grant was never more endearing than when saluting the milkmen, father and son. "Top of the morning, gentlemen!" he'd cry, with a deep, respectful ducking of his head. It was a wonderful, all too rare example of life making perfect sense: of *course* Grant would come to live in a world with genuine heroes serving as his milkmen.

Grant would scarcely have suffered a pang if you informed him he could never enter another art museum, and yet he loved being married to an artist. He lived in a world of practical—legal and financial— realities, but he longed to believe in his wife's second sight. Why had she resumed milk deliveries? Why else but to contrive, through supernatural agencies he could only dimly discern, that the Bootmakers would save Mr. Bickey's life?

"You give me too much credit," Bianca repeated. "Go and call me an artist after I've actually been doing some art." But she said this mildly. It was all right if he couldn't accept this notion, because she couldn't either, quite. Sometimes her heart took journeys. Certain rare and remote experiences mustn't be denied or discounted, and it was their imperishable value—not mere vanity—that rendered her a little insistent now. By claiming to be something of an artist, she wasn't making a claim solely on her own behalf, was she? Rather, on behalf of art generally—and on behalf of that little man, her nonno, of whom she, pressed so hard by life, too seldom thought, but who had once been celebrated in mythical Liguria . . . And suddenly, preposterously, her eyes welled up.

The little man who had painted trompe l'oeil windows? Dead. Like Mrs. Olsson, like Henry Vanden Akker, her nonno was dead. And she would never again step through the front door of her childhood home, and a particular quality of light was disappearing from this city, her own Detroit—it was disappearing unrecorded, for no canvas in the world, for all the potency of her visions, had managed to capture and preserve it. She must go back—go back to her pencils and her charcoals and her oils.

On the way home, in the passenger seat of Grant's sporty Mercury, Bianca leaned her head against the window. Ahead, an aging streetcar clattered up Woodward. One of the city's few remaining streetcars. There were only four lines left and, according to the newspapers, the Jefferson line would vanish in a couple of months, leaving only the Gratiot, the Michigan, and the Woodward. Already gone was the Grand River line she'd taken through the rain that day—the unforgettable day when she'd confessed, *Maggie, the very worst thing has happened.* It wasn't their leaving she minded, was it? Only her failure to know what to do with their leaving, only this sensation that no one was trying earnestly to record what was being lost . . .

Mrs. Ives looked relieved to see them. Whenever she babysat, which was seldom, she always suggested that—though she wasn't about to go telling tales—the twins had been especially difficult. Nonsense, of course. The boys were out in the yard—where they'd probably spent most of the time since their grandmother's arrival. It was how Mrs. Ives chose to meet the world: *I am so put upon.*

Grant went out to join the boys. He'd recently purchased a tetherball set—a very simple arrangement, just a metal pole with a ball attached to the top by a long cord. Ostensibly, Grant went out to "offer a few pointers." The real reason was to hit the ball himself.

Bianca and Mrs. Ives stood in the screened porch. The minute Grant stepped out the backdoor, her litany began.

"It's like a child. It's like taking care of a child that will never grow up. Day after day after day . . ."

She was speaking of Mr. Ives, whose recovery had stalled long ago. And who continued to pinch and pat and poke any female—irrespective of age, race, body type—who wandered within reach.

"I'm so sorry," Bianca said.

"Your boys will grow up," Mrs. Ives went on. "But Mr. Ives won't. He's frozen the way he is until he dies."

"I'm so sorry," Bianca said.

"It could happen to you," Mrs. Ives went on in a sharpened voice—almost a spiteful voice. "Your husband could have a stroke, and you're left taking care of this wreck of a man for the rest of your life."

Out in the yard, Grant tossed the ball into the air and gave it a solid, resounding whack. He was demonstrating his prowess for his twin boys. Round and round and round, in rapid, ever tightening revolutions, the crimson ball orbited the pole. The soaring ball seemed a more powerful rebuttal to Mrs. Ives's grim imaginings than anything Bianca might say. Legs spread wide, shoulders thrown back, Grant was indomitable.

"It's not that I mind taking care of a child," Mrs. Ives went on. "Honestly, I like children just fine. It's that Mr. Ives is really a big *nasty* child. At bottom, he's a very big *nasty* boy."

She was twelve minutes early but he was too. They met on the great outside stairs of the museum, side by side before they knew it. "Our minds are synchronized," she said.

"Hearts too," he said gallantly, and took her by the arm. Oh, she adored his quick suavity! She'd been feeling like a cow all day—as of this morning she'd gained thirty-six pounds—and yet she turned giddy, almost airborne, as they mounted the steps together.

At the cloakroom, something amusing and actually quite delightful happened. Behind the counter stood one of those gray-haired women of a certain age for whom all pregnancies are an open topic. Nothing like *Are you expecting, my dear?* from her. "When's it due?" she demanded.

"Not for almost two months," Bianca confessed. And felt herself blush.

"This your first?"

"My third, actually."

The woman appraised her admiringly. "You don't look it. I had just the one, but I never did get my looks back."

Bianca started to say *I'm sorry*, but caught herself. "Well—yes."

"Congratulations," the woman called to Ronny, who for a couple of seconds regarded her blankly.

And then he did what he so rarely did: he grinned unreservedly, a full-faced explosion of a smile. "Well, thank you very much," he said.

Fatherhood—even mistakenly attributed—patently agreed with him. His face was aglow as he led Bianca through the great hallway, past the glassed-in suits of armor the twins loved so much. Ronny was even able to glance upward at the murals in the Diego Rivera courtyard with benign approval—something he'd never shown them before.

"How are your boys?"

"Mm?" she said. It was unlike Ronny to ask about her family right away. "They're fine. They went through a rough patch a while back. I had some serious problems with my parents—my mother—and I guess the twins were feeling neglected."

"But when were there no serious problems with your parents?"

The question wasn't posed sarcastically or maliciously. In fact, it was a good question. Bianca pondered and said, "It's just a coincidence, but do you know when the real problems started? About when I first met you. Ten years ago, I guess. You'll have to take my word for it. But there was a time when life seemed quite happy at home." She could confide things to Ronny she could confide to nobody else on earth, but she would never divulge that her mother had once regularly shoplifted from Olsson's, any more than she would tell him about the evening when his mother—sitting in the kitchen in a jade-green robe, drinking whiskey—had raised the possibility that her boy might be "cur."

"I didn't mean to sound flippant," Ronny said.

"You didn't. It was a good question. You always make me think about things, which I appreciate. I remember you once asked me, Why do you want people thinking you understand *less* than you do? I'll never forget that."

"I don't remember the circumstances."

"Neither do I," Bianca said, although she did. It was the disastrous evening at the Coral Club when Mrs. Olsson had spoken of *courage* and *niggers* and *kikes*. "Anyway, the point is that maybe someday I'll piece it all together, but what I can tell you now is that everything changed that summer I met you. The summer of '43. Everybody talks about how hard the Depression was, but that's not my memory. For the most part, I remember my childhood as being so happy. It was the War that really did me in. And how's your father?"

As they conversed, the two of them were not looking at each other. They were both staring upward at the Diego Rivera murals, into the blazing blue and green phantasmagoria that a modernist Mexican had created in response to the greatest industrial city in the world. To confront its packed, elevated inferno somehow made talking easier . . .

"It's the oddest thing," Ronny said. "He's really come undone since Mother died. He's aged ten years at least—you'd be amazed. I would have sworn he didn't really like her. I would have predicted you'd see him two months later with some young honey on his arm. But he's haunted by her."

"She was a haunting woman."

"You're telling me?" Ronny said. And laughed.

They wandered around the museum, halting before the old favorites. Ronny showed little of that instructive impulse he'd displayed on their last visit. His comments were uncharacteristically minute: "I like the handling of the snow," or "Isn't the lining of the robe splendid?" or "He got the dog's fur, didn't he?"

Bianca held her tour guide's arm the whole time. It had been a long while since she'd felt so content—or so content in this particular fashion. Normally, she would not have been wholly comfortable continually holding the arm of someone not her husband in this open and public space. People might come to the conclusion reached by the coat-check woman . . . And yet it felt completely right—walking arm in arm with Ronny here. In some way that Grant himself would have understood, and even approved of, had she only been able to express the point properly, this museum was the one place on earth where she was Ronny's; it was simply appropriate that she take his arm.

After a while, her weight got the better of her. Her lower back began to ache. "I think we better sit a spell." They made their way to the Kresge Court and Ronny fetched her a cup of coffee. "I hope your father finds his bearings again," she said. "It pains me to think of him aging all of a sudden."

"More surprisingly, it pains me. You might think I'd welcome it. You know it wasn't the easiest thing in the world being the son of the former U. of M. track captain."

"I can imagine."

"The weird thing is, I'm actually a pretty good athlete."

"I know. I've danced with you. I've seen you ice-skate."

"Even if I don't feel the slightest desire to go down into a little gym and punch a punching bag."

"I know you don't. How's Chris, by the way?"

She'd meant merely to sound warm and accepting, but Ronny stiffened. "Chris? Who could possibly say how he's doing? He's in advertising."

"But you always liked advertising, Ronny."

"*Liked?* I hope not. I prefer to think I sensed a magical power in it. It's like television. You own a television set?"

"We do. But I don't watch it so much."

"Nobody does. Nobody does, and yet it'll take over the world anyway. Who's going to look at a canvas when you can look at a canvas that moves?"

"Oh Ronny, you're depressing me."

"I don't mean to. It's the painter manqué talking." He looked to see whether she understood the term. She understood the term.

He went on: "I think that's something you and I shared. Neither of us really belonged in art classes. Or you could say we were actually the only two who did belong. The son of the owner of Olsson's Drugs wasn't meant to be studying still life at the Institute Midwest. And neither was this Italian girl from the heart of the city. I always admired that about you, by the way: you didn't play the girl artist. Tatiana Bogoljubov—she did, with the yellow hair and the breasts in everybody's face."

"I didn't have the breasts."

"You were deeper than that. You saw things."

"Saw things?"

"Yes, you saw things."

Such a welcome phrase . . . In their baldness, the words called up dear Grant's repeated declaration, *You make things interesting.*

"Seeing things? Sounds a little cuckoo," Bianca protested. "Which always makes me nervous, given my mother."

"What I'm saying is, our not belonging was a sign we actually belonged."

"I know what you mean," Bianca said, and though his words sounded nonsensical, she did.

"You know what I think of? I think of a conversation we had, I don't know, ten years ago. I said something, and you said, *I'll remember you said that.*"

And it was proof of what soul-intimates they were that she, with so skeletal a clue, was able to say, "I know what you're referring to." Again, she did. "You said to me, *I'd like to be sitting on a park bench with you when I'm sixty . . .*"

Oh, Ronny looked grateful! Had she ever in her life felt closer to him?

"I did!" Ronny said. "That's what I said. And you know what? In thirty years, they're going to tell me I'm right. It's going to come clear— all the peculiarities will come clear, you and me in Manhardt's class, our romantic walks through the park . . ."

Did Ronny himself know what he meant by that? Or was the point only that, in time, he would know what he meant by that?

"We will," she said. "We'll be sitting there together."

"As we're sitting here now," Ronny said.

In thirty years, the baby in her womb would be almost thirty years old—roughly her own age now. No such future seemed possible, though it was almost certain to happen. It was the world Chip and Matt would inherit—a world where one twin would be driving over, with his wife and kids, to visit the other, with *his* wife and kids, and given enough elapsed time this was the very world she, too, would naturally inhabit— but this could hardly be her world. Thirty years—1983? Everything likely was *unimaginable,* and where was her true, her own world? She was feeling quite upended today . . .

"You know what's odd?" she said. "I feel as though the light's chang- ing. Your mother was born in the nineteenth century. I remember see- ing that date in the paper, 1899, and somehow being surprised by it, though I shouldn't have been: I knew exactly how old she was. But I used to feel that that other world, a nineteenth-century world, was so close at hand. You'd see the old G.A.R. veterans parading, straggling along so proudly, and you could still smell the horses in garages that used to be stables. My nonno was born in 1877, and I remember all your wonderful excitement when I told you about his being born so prema- ture and being kept alive in a woodstove. And none of those worlds seemed so far away, and I can't help feeling they feel far away now because the light's changing. That's the biggest historical change there is, and it's the one that only painters know how to record. It changed sometime after the War. Am I making any sense?"

"You always make sense to me. You're the only person I know who makes sense to me even when she isn't making sense."

"May I take that as a compliment?"

"A fond and fair compliment. A deft and memorable compliment."

Bianca laughed.

The sun through the skylight caught the silver at his temples. Good Lord, he was the most beautiful man she'd ever known.

"You're going gray."

Because she said this so approvingly (surely his attractiveness was manifest in her every look and word and gesture, for she'd reached that bedazzled state wherein she could formulate no observation about him that wasn't a compliment), she somehow expected Ronny to welcome her remark. But he looked pained. He said, "You haven't had a single gray hair?"

"Not yet. My mother's hair's mostly dark, and she's fifty. Grant and I have a little bet as to who'll get the first one."

"Who?"

"Grant? My husband, Grant?"

"Who?"

Ronny looked pleased with himself once more. He was going to keep this game going until the end, then.

"Let's go look at more paintings," she said.

"Let's, my dear. Let's."

They were standing before Titian's *Man Holding a Flute* when a male voice—an incredulous voice—inquired, "Bea Paradiso?" Somehow she knew who it was, even before turning around . . .

Years and years ago, she had placed a telephone call to that voice. She had walked over to the phone booth outside Olsson's, deposited her nickel, and reached a voice likewise tinged with incredulity. *Is that you, Tatiana?* the voice had asked—yearningly, touchingly.

"Hello, Donald."

Yes, it was Donald Doobly. The art student, the beautiful draftsman. The skinny Negro boy in the oversized clothes.

Only, he wasn't skinny anymore. He had filled out; in fact, he had grown plump. But it was the same voice, and the same kindly and mindful eyes. She'd drawn his portrait once, or started to. She'd never finished it.

"It is! It's Bea!" Donald announced, and laughed boisterously.

"Yes. So nice to see you, Donald." She turned. "You remember Ronny—Ronny Olsson?"

Donald's eyes seemed to double in size. His glance had already taken in her belly. "The two of you . . . ?" he began, and his voice trailed away. His hands lifted and fell.

For the second time today, Ronny had been mistaken for the father of her child. "Just good friends," Bianca said, and giggled. "I live with my husband out near Seven and Livernois. We already have twin boys."

"Imagine that," Donald said, and shook his head. "Imagine that." Donald made it sound like an impossible feat, but it turned out that he, too, had two sons. They were standing bashfully over near the wall, beside a petite light-skinned Negro woman.

"Step forward," Donald said, and the boys, with downcast eyes, obediently sidled forward.

"Shake hands," Donald said, and both boys simultaneously extended their hands.

"I don't know your last name," Donald admitted.

"Ives."

"This is Mrs. Ives. And this is Donald Junior. He's six." Bianca shook hands with Donald Junior. "And this is Albert. He's five." Bianca shook hands with Albert. "And this is my wife, Rosella. She's a schoolteacher. Bea Ives, Rosella Doobly."

Bianca shook hands with the woman. "I'm pleased to meet you."

"Donald has told me about you," Mrs. Doobly said. Had he? Bianca felt oddly guilty. Had she ever mentioned Donald to Grant?

"I go by Bianca now, actually," she told Donald.

"*Do* you?" This, too, struck him as extraordinary. He was in such high spirits, most anything she might say was at once marvelous and humorous.

Ronny was introduced to Mrs. Doobly and the children. Having successfully negotiated another set of handshakes, the boys retreated to their wall.

"Are you enjoying the museum?" Bianca called over to them. "Yes, ma'am," said the older boy, Donald Junior. "Yes, ma'am," said Albert.

Donald was wearing a beautiful suit of a sober gray wool that held a gossamer shimmer of azure. Dressed like twins, both of his boys were wearing navy-blue suits and red ties. His wife was wearing a lovely black-and-white houndstooth dress. Donald had always been a careful dresser, though in the old days most everything he wore—impeccably clean, scrupulously pressed—had been many sizes too large. He'd grown into his clothes at last.

"I brought the boys to look at the paintings. Never too young to learn about art."

"I'm amazed at how well-behaved they are," Bianca said. "Once when I brought my twins here, they started wrestling in front of that big Delacroix. The battle scene. I guess it inspired them."

"Oh my boys are regular rapscallions," Donald said.

They didn't look it. They looked timid and precise and alert, much the way Donald had always looked, whose voice had deepened and broadened, who had a rowdy new laugh.

"And what about you, Donald? What are you doing?"

"I'm with Ford's. In the design department."

This *with* of Donald's—so blithe, so collegial—was deeply heartening. "Why, that's wonderful!" Bianca cried.

"You remember, at the Institute, I studied both Fine Arts and Industrial Arts."

"That's right, you did!" Bianca marveled. "So, one of us who enrolled at the old Institute Midwest is actually putting something he learned into daily practice? My hat's off to you. Do you really think it helped you—the Institute?"

Donald didn't know how to answer. He regarded her with open amazement and Bianca was able to see, as she hadn't before, the skinny little colored boy within him.

Donald formulated a declaration: "Why, it changed my whole life. It made me what I am today. I knew next to nothing when I arrived there. I was just a little kid with a gift for drawing. You remember Professor Manhardt?"

"Of course." The funny little German man who said things like "sticky wicket."

"You know what he did?" Donald went on. "Do you know what that man did? He gave me my first set of oil paints. *Gave* them to me."

"Now isn't that wonderful."

"I named Albert after him. Albert was Professor Manhardt's name."

"Now isn't that wonderful . . ." The words swelled in her throat—they were almost too big for utterance. Had she not met Donald today, Bianca would never have appreciated how profoundly she still longed to believe in the authenticity and the discernment of the now-defunct Institute Midwest. She would have told anyone who would listen that it was at bottom a silly little school, doomed not to last, with eccentric and mostly laughable instructors and mostly silly students, including an eighteen-year-old girl in a preposterous red Hungarian beret who went around chanting to herself, *An artist never stops mixing paint.* But Bianca still believed in that girl, Bea Paradiso, and it elated her to come upon Donald Doobly, in a gorgeous suit, who had materialized as a reminder that she'd been right all along. She and her classmates hadn't been silly. They had been engaged in the noblest of all undertakings: they were art students.

"And *you* could draw," Donald said, turning to Ronny. "You were the best of us all."

And Ronny, always so gracious, offered a tactless reply: "Maybe that's not saying so much? Given the level of the group?" But he recovered quickly: "Though it's true *you* could draw, too—and you stayed with it. That's the important thing."

"It's how I make my living." Donald paused. "And how about you, Ronny?" It was startling just how much more direct and self-possessed Donald had become.

"I'm an art professor. At U. of M."

"I tell my boys that's where they can go to college. But they gotta work hard."

The boys' mother nodded. The boys, first the elder and then the younger, nodded.

"They can study with Professor Olsson," Ronny said.

"That's an incentive. A genuine incentive." Again, Donald confronted Ronny head to head: "What is your specialty?"

"The medieval period."

"Nothing more beautiful," Donald said. "Nothing more beautiful. The Saint Jerome in here? By Rogier van der Weyden? Nothing more beautiful in this whole place."

Ronny looked sharply at Donald and Ronny's unpaintable eyes were glittering with extravagant intensity. Ronny seemed to be seeing Donald more fully than ever before. "Do you know what?" Ronny marveled. "Why, that may be my very favorite painting in the whole museum."

"Nothing more beautiful," Donald repeated, and he met Ronny's gaze.

Then Donald turned. "You once telephoned me," he said to Bianca. "You remember?"

"I did. I do. You'd lost your notebook and I found it."

"I don't know if I ever thanked you properly."

"You did. You always had impeccable manners . . ."

But the confident look had bled from Donald's gaze. Yes, he was recollecting what she was recollecting: *Is that you, Tatiana?* Donald had been hopelessly infatuated with the yellow-haired Russian doll. But all that was so long ago. Donald had been a boy then, and now he was a man, and he was happy with his wife, and his life, wasn't he? He seemed so happy . . .

"You had impeccable manners," Bianca repeated. "Like your children." Again, she called out to them. "Which do you like better? The paintings? Or the sculptures?"

Another timorous pause. "The armor," Donald Junior said. "The armor," Albert echoed.

"My boys too!" Bianca said. "My boys too!"

"You see what I mean?" Donald said, and laughed conclusively. "You see what I mean? Regular *rapscallions*."

After farewell handshakes, after cries of well-wishing on all sides, she and Ronny parted ways with the Doobly family. The encounter left a lingering burnish, and Bianca took Ronny's arm and exclaimed, "Isn't it wonderful to see Donald doing so well? Isn't it *wonderful*?" The paintings on the walls in this, her favorite building in the world, shone all the more resplendently for having looked out at Donald Doobly, Rosella Doobly, Donald Doobly, Jr., and Albert Doobly.

"You telephoned him," Ronny said.

"I did. From a phone booth in front of an Olsson's Drugs, actually—I didn't dare call from home, isn't that ridiculous? He'd lost his notebook and I found it."

"It was good of you to call."

"I don't think I would have dared, I rarely called *you*, Papa was very fixed on the notion that girls didn't call boys, but I felt so sorry for Donald, and for Negroes generally. You remember—that was the summer of the race riot."

"You're right. It was. I'd forgotten. I guess it got overshadowed."

"Well there was something called the War going on. And isn't it *wonderful* to see Donald doing so well?"

"I didn't know that Ford's hired people like him. In jobs like that."

"Times are changing."

"He's got to be one of the first . . ."

It was all so hopeful and inspiring. Someone like Donald really could work hard and get a good job at Ford's—and why couldn't he and his wife eventually send their two boys to U. of M.? And why couldn't those boys study medieval art with Professor Olsson? One of those boys was named after a pompous German would-be Brit who, nonetheless, had given the gift of art itself, and with it a solid livelihood, to a skinny boy who had grown up in Black Bottom. Bianca didn't quite have the words to crystallize this feeling of having glimpsed, here in Detroit's true palace of marvels, something more wondrous yet: the brilliant blueprint of a just commonwealth, a better city. "Isn't it *wonderful*?" she said, but it was clear that Ronny—always so moody, so prone to a sudden plummeting melancholy—wasn't sharing her elation.

Well, she knew how to handle this. Over the years, she'd had a great deal of experience hauling Ronny out of his moods. You didn't ask him about them, or acknowledge them. You simply kept on—you wore down his despondency.

She thought about telling Ronny the true story behind her phone call. *Is that you, Tatiana?* But she found she couldn't do that. She could have done it to the Donald she'd seen today—so substantial, so prosperous-looking—but not to the resolute colored boy whose legs were thin as broomsticks.

Instead, she said, "We have a new friend in the family." She told him about Ira Styne. About the strange way he'd materialized, after ten years—this soldier who once memorably sent Edith a five-dollar bill for her birthday. About how Mamma liked cooking for him, and Papa was overseeing his checking account. About how this man who originally came for a few minutes had stayed in town a couple of months already.

But the story did nothing to lift Ronny's mood—as she should have realized it wouldn't. She was plunged back into those heady days when she was the girl-artist at Ferry Hospital, talking so excitedly about the poor Irish kid with the patch on his eye and the amputated foot, Private Donnelly, and finding Ronny chilly to her talk. Jealousy. He could never brook her speaking warmly about any other man.

"Did you see the way Donald's eyes bugged when he saw us? That was the second time today somebody mistook you for the baby's father."

This did cheer Ronny. Always so attentive to visual impressions, he was keenly aware that the two of them were catching glances and drawing surmises: the tall fine-looking man in the tan linen suit, a distinguished flicker of gray at his temples, and the tall, pretty young woman who was so exorbitantly pregnant.

She went on: "What a summer that was! First my mother gets it into her head that my father's in love with my aunt, and our entire family explodes as a result, and then the city itself explodes, the radio actually reports that the Negroes are assembling on Belle Isle, they're going to march on the city, and my family's living three blocks from the Belle Isle Bridge . . . And all the while there's the War, the War, the War, the whole city's in a perpetual frenzy, and the wounded soldiers returning by the hundreds, and what is Bea Paradiso doing? She's trying to do art. She's trying to learn still-life painting."

Bianca paused, then pushed ahead: "She's trying to do art? How could she concentrate, when one day the handsomest boy she'd ever seen, who was also the most beautifully dressed, steps into her classroom? And tells her her drawing isn't right and asks if he can show her how it's done?"

Ronny laughed. "Did I really do that?"

"You certainly did."

"My god I was *insufferable*," Ronny said, and he was restored: he was fully happy once more. Yes, she'd done it—she'd brought Ronny Olsson back where he was supposed to be. "How *did* you bear me?" he asked.

"Very easily," Bianca said. "All too easily."

They had paused before her cherished Bellini. Madonna and Christ. Mother and Child. The two sacred figures looked not toward each other but outward—two spirits partaking in a human covenant of divine mercy. Behind them lay a gently hilly terraced landscape where lambs and rabbits gamboled, where fruit trees sweetened and Italian was spoken, the alternative world, the true *paradiso* of heaven on earth.

"Do you realize it was ten years ago we first looked at this painting together?" she said.

"And here we are," Ronny said. "Still standing here."

This time, Bianca had the last word: "It's because we've been here all along. We never left."

CHAPTER XXXIX

Long Walk through the City

"Here we are at last," Uncle Dennis said. "You're sure it's not too late?"

"No, no, no," Bianca said. "This is a fine idea."

"Really not too late?"

"Perfect timing."

They stepped off the front porch together. It was a warm, beautiful May night. Uncle Dennis was carrying his pipe, unlit.

"I need some air," she said. "Even if I do move like a tortoise."

"You know this really will all end."

"You mean the pregnancy? I don't think so. No. I'm going to carry this baby forever."

She would carry her baby until the end of time. That was all right. It was Thursday, the twenty-eighth of May, and she was nearly two weeks overdue. As of this morning, she weighed 168 pounds. Was she actually heading past 170? And was it possible that only last summer she'd weighed 127? It wasn't possible. But that, too, was all right. She had been different people along the way. Or else she hadn't—she'd dreamed them all. Actually, she was very tired.

They turned right, toward Six Mile. The night had taken on that special ballasted quietness of late spring—a newly leafy quietness. Soon it would be summer.

"Grant seems well," Uncle Dennis said.

"You know, I think he is. He went through a rough patch for a while."

"I know."

"With everything. But maybe the worst wasn't that his mother-in-law turned out to be a thief. Maybe the worst was that his wife went crazy because her mother turned out to be a thief. I went through a rough patch, too."

"I know you did," Uncle Dennis said.

"And *I* knew *you* knew. I keep using that phrase, *rough patch,* but it was all much scarier than that suggests. And you sensed it. You'd drive up for a day or two, back when you were arranging the move and everything else, and you kept urging me to take care of myself."

"You were very pale."

"I could hardly eat. I was losing weight, which is quite ironic. This morning I weighed one sixty-eight."

"I've been gaining weight, too. The difference is, it doesn't improve my appearance any. *You* look wonderful. I don't think I've ever seen a more beautiful pregnant woman."

"Is that a medical opinion?"

"Certainly," Uncle Dennis said. "Certainly." The air was heavy—heavy and light at once—with the fragrance of blossoming trees. In the distance—also heavy and light—came a rumbling sound of explosives, and a pause, and another rumble.

"Fireworks," she said. "Someone's celebrating Memorial Day a little early."

"I'm old enough to think of it as Decoration Day."

Memorial Day fell on Saturday this year. Aunt Grace and Uncle Dennis had driven up for the holiday weekend. They had long planned this trip around the baby's birth, which would surely have arrived by Memorial Day. Was it possible they were going to drive home without glimpsing the baby? Possible. Likely.

They had arrived at noon today, and Mamma and Papa and Edith, Stevie and Rita had all come over for an early supper. The dinner guests had just now departed, and Aunt Grace, pleading tiredness, had gone up to bed. Bianca had been waiting weeks to have this walk with Uncle Dennis.

"Your boys? They seem *very* fine."

"I guess so. They had their own rough patches."

Formulaic questions, ritualistic and repetitive answers . . . The two of them had been here before, so many times. And yet their conversation was—Bianca sensed eagerly—moving forward.

"Especially Chip," she went on. "He had all these fears, and Grant couldn't seem to reassure him—only I could reassure him. But he seems better, which I guess means less dependent on me. You know what I was thinking? I can tell you because you're someone who truly understands I wouldn't change a hair on either boy's head, I love them with all my heart. But I keep thinking *this* child, the one I'm carrying, which my intuition tells me is a girl—*this* child will be *my* child. You're a doctor. Have you ever seen sons who look more like their father? Or act more like their father?"

"It is remarkable." Uncle Dennis chuckled. But having been asked a medical question, he must answer in medical fashion. "I can honestly report I've never seen a closer resemblance."

"Down to the least littlest gesture," Bianca said. "You know Edith keeps talking about anthropology, she uses words like *socialization,* she talks about how cultures perpetuate themselves, and I keep thinking they should send a team of anthropologists to study Matt and Chip. How do they *learn* these things? Did you know the boys open a straw exactly the way Grant does?"

"A straw?"

"A drinking straw. They each tear the paper at the bottom and then give the top three little taps with an index finger. Always three: tap tap tap."

"How extraordinary!"

"Isn't it? As I say, Where do they learn these things?"

"I mean extraordinary that you'd *notice.* You're remarkably observant."

"I am observant," Bianca declared, relishing her immodesty. She could talk this way to her uncle. "It was something I consciously culti-vated, when I was studying art."

"And this other child. This daughter you're carrying. Is she going to be an artist?"

"I'm not sure. A novelist? Or, better yet, a poet? In any case, I guar-antee she'll be a beautifully dressed little girl. I'll buy her white gloves and take her down for a soda at Sanders, just the way Aunt Grace took me." There was a pause. "Grace looked tired tonight."

"You know she's not well."

"I know," Bianca said. She halted, considered, then plunged ahead: "How bad is it, really?"

More fireworks rumbled in the distance, expanding and subsiding— like a collective city heartbeat—and all the while a sleeping woman's life hung in the balance. "I don't lose hope," Uncle Dennis said finally. "But it seems they didn't get it all. The cancer. It's spread."

"Oh *no,*" Bianca moaned, but she already knew this. Maybe she'd known it for weeks now. "But there's hope?" There *had* to be. The alter-native wasn't imaginable.

"Of course," Uncle Dennis said. "Always hope. Plenty of hope."

It was all too grim and terrifying to contemplate, especially when she was so tired. Later, in her brooding insomniac's way, she would think about it and think about it. She would find a suitable prayer . . . In the meantime, she would cling to her uncle's encouragement: *Always hope.*

He talked awhile in his medical way, introducing terms and procedures she didn't understand, as if she were a medical colleague. Well, Edith would become one.

The problem, you see, was a lack of selectivity in the treatment. It wasn't that the scientists didn't know how to kill the cancer cells. The problem was that the chemicals and the radiation destroyed so much with it. But the science was improving by the day. There was a good deal of hope . . .

They had reached Six Mile. The houses across the street were smaller, denser, a bit run-down. On evening walks, Bianca rarely ventured across Six Mile. They turned around.

"Stevie and Rita seem fine," Uncle Dennis said. He desired a change of subject, clearly.

"Now *they* really do. Buying a bigger house? Little Stevie buying a bigger house? It was a godsend, your getting him out of Ford's."

"Didn't have much to do with me."

"No—no—no," Bianca half said and half sang. "'Course not, 'course not," she went on in a gruff mock-male voice. She was teasing her uncle in a way he enjoyed. She was raising his spirits. "Which reminds me of something else." Oh, she'd been longing to bring up *this* for weeks. "You know what Rita told Grant her braces cost?"

"I haven't the faintest idea what Rita told Grant."

"She told him the total cost, *everything,* I mean years of orthodontics, and you remember what her teeth looked like—the total cost is one hundred dollars. Doesn't that seem a *very* good price to you?"

"Well Dr. Ropinsky, the orthodontist, he's a particular friend of mine."

"Right. And so he's willing to do your nephew and his wife a huge favor. That's what Grant figured. But the more I thought about it, the more it didn't add up. Only a hundred dollars? Just the equipment must cost more than that. So you know what I think? You know what *I* think?"

There was a silence and then a little laugh. This wasn't Uncle Dennis's usual laugh, which was bright and boisterous—it was a kind of low giggle, which rolled outward in an unloosed fashion. Among the people she was closest to, there were many laughs Bianca cherished: there was Mamma's rare, unexpectedly lovely, evenly spaced girlish laughter; there was Grant's bluff triumphant rumble when, playing the storyteller at a party, he "got off a good one"; there was Priscilla's funny-pages tee-hee-hee and Maggie's bright bite of mischief. But this was the laugh Bianca loved perhaps best in the world. For this laugh was grafted to the very taproot of human charity. This was the mischievous hilarity, shared with Yusuf the Turk, of the soul that perceives its own acts of kindness as funny.

Uncle Dennis's laughter confirmed everything. Bianca went on: "Now this is just a wild surmise, but you know what I think? I think you arranged with Dr. Ropinsky that Stevie, who's an absolute mule, as we all know, and who won't take charity from anybody, that Stevie would pay a hundred dollars up front and you would surreptitiously make up the difference. That's what *I* think."

The low nervous happy chortle rolled on. Then Uncle Dennis collected himself. "Well, we all said it since you were just a tot. Little Bea has second sight."

"Second sight my eye," Bianca said. "Good heavens, what a terrible poker player you'd make! *One* hundred dollars. Couldn't you have done better than that?"

"But Stevie and Rita don't know . . ."

"No, *they* don't. Your terrible secret is safe with me." And they both laughed.

"But Stevie and Rita are doing well," Uncle Dennis said again. Tonight he was seeking encouragement.

"I think they're doing very well," Bianca said. But what was she herself seeking tonight? She wasn't sure, she only knew she'd been waiting weeks and weeks for this opportunity. Things were always so rushed when Uncle Dennis dropped into town; there never seemed time for a real palaver.

"I haven't seen Maggie in ages," Bianca said. Uncle Dennis had always adored Maggie. "She's lying low after getting her nose done. Did I tell you she'd had plastic surgery on her nose?"

"I think you said chin."

"That, too. First chin, then nose. She'll show up any day now, bright as you please, with a sharp little nose high up in the air."

"Little Maggie Szot," Uncle Dennis said. "She was a breech birth."

"I didn't know that."

"Mrs. Szot told me. More than once. Maggie almost died at birth."

Bianca drew a hand protectively around her outspread waist. Her best friend had almost died at birth? Had things fallen out just a little differently, Bianca would never have met Maggie. The universe would have held no Maggie Szot Hamm Schrock Waller. It was an unassimilable notion . . .

Bianca said: "You remember Nonno was so premature, they kept him in a woodstove."

Uncle Dennis said, "I've thought of her many, many times—your father's great-grandmother. Of course I never met her. But she was a better doctor than I am." The thought pleased him—he repeated it in heightened form: "A much, much better doctor. You talk about being observant? You wonder where you get it? Well, she looked right into the wrinkled little face of a premature infant and she saw *everything*. She understood him. I don't mean to sound like a mystic, but I do believe that. She *had* to understand. Otherwise, you see, she couldn't have kept him alive—not under those conditions."

Uncle Dennis had a special fondness for this sort of remark. The man who never stopped reading science fiction was forever planting an assertion backward a century, forward a century.

Bianca said, "Maggie's husband, Walton, he's deeply involved in that big shopping whatever-it-is they're building out at Eight and Greenfield."

"I've read about it."

"Walton's one of the big investors. Grant seems to think Walton's going to make oodles of money."

Uncle Dennis pondered. "I can't believe it's going to work. Not in the long run."

"You honestly don't think so?"

It wasn't so much that she wished Grant to be wrong. It wasn't even that the thought of Maggie's having *more* money was distasteful. But Bianca very much wanted to believe in the wisdom of Uncle Dennis's pronouncement. For Uncle Dennis, like Walton, had a vision of the city—and his was a city, unlike Walton's, she wanted to live in.

Uncle Dennis said, "You spoke earlier of buying your daughter white gloves and taking her downtown for a soda at Sanders. Is any mother going to buy her daughter white gloves to take her to a super plaza, or whatever they're calling it, at Eight and Greenfield?"

"A shopping complex, I think it is."

"It's like putting white gloves on your daughter to take her to a parking lot. Oh, it may succeed for a while. As a novelty. But how is a shopping complex going to compete with a real downtown? It doesn't make any sense."

"No, it doesn't."

Physically, these were far from comfortable days—it had been ages since Bianca had been able to lie on her stomach—but she felt more comfortable than she'd felt in a long while, strolling on Middleway beside her uncle on this beautiful evening. She'd been quite tired when they set out, but the May night had revivified her.

With all the weight Uncle Dennis had been steadily putting on these past few harrowing months, he wasn't merely chubby, he was looking positively fat. As they walked side by side, they filled the sidewalk. Tonight it felt good to fill a sidewalk.

"And your mother—she seems well?"

It was the same rhetorical formula he'd been using, only this time it surfaced as a question.

"I think so. I do. You did the right thing, insisting they move."

Uncle Dennis made a confession: "Oh, how I worried over that one . . ."

It was an uncharacteristic thing for him to say—at least to her. No doubt he opened his heart about such fears to Aunt Grace. But with his niece, he generally played the confident counselor. He was the voice of optimism, advancement, the growth of slow but unstoppable enlightenment.

He went on: "It seems I've done nothing but worry for months and months. And eat. You see I've put on weight."

"Not that I've noticed," Bianca said.

"You remember last fall? When your mother went away for a week? You know why I did that?"

"She went away for a *thorough examination.* Papa repeated the phrase a hundred times."

Uncle Dennis studied the unlit pipe in his hand. "Well—yes. A thorough examination. But I also wanted to make sure your mother didn't jump off the Belle Isle Bridge."

In the gorgeous night air, Bianca's skin crawled. "You weren't genuinely worried she'd—?"

"I knew it was extremely unlikely. But I needed to be sure. The poor woman felt so worthless. So terribly ashamed."

"But why put yourself in such a position? I mean, why do you think she did it—stole all those things? Why would anyone do something guaranteed to make them so miserable?"

"I wish I knew . . ."

"Self-punishment?"

"Yes, but for what?"

"You know what my friend Priscilla says? You remember, the psychiatrist? She says it's no coincidence that most of what Mamma stole came from Olsson's."

"Meaning?"

"Meaning that Mamma was angry with Ronny Olsson—or just plain angry with life. Because maybe Mamma had dreamed someday I'd marry some millionaire's son. When Priscilla proposed this, I told her she couldn't be right, because if there's one thing infuriates Mamma, it's people trying to get above themselves. But Priscilla said that that's the whole point. The ones who hate people getting above themselves are the very ones who dream of doing exactly that. And Priscilla looked so shrewd, I didn't dare question her. Anyway, does that sound plausible?"

"It sounds plausible."

"And there's another thing. I remember the first time Mamma ever met Ronny Olsson—he drove up in his cream-colored convertible, and when he left, Mamma said something peculiar. She said, I've met his type before. What could she mean by that?"

Uncle Dennis thought for quite a while. Then he said, "Long before your father ever came on the scene, I gather that your mother—well, she'd set her cap for some very well-to-do, good-looking boy at her high school. But it didn't work out."

"A boy? What do you know about him?"

"Nothing."

"Do you even know his name?"

"I must have once. Grace could tell you."

A good-looking boy without a name? Some other man in Mamma's life besides Papa? The thought made Bianca feel very queer . . .

She said, "And I suppose Priscilla would say that it's one more reason Mamma stole from Olsson's."

"It sounds plausible."

"You don't sound convinced."

"Maybe it's plausible but not convincing?" Again, Uncle Dennis reflected. "I suppose I have the medical doctor's skepticism of the psychologist. I don't know what a *cure* means for them."

Bianca laughed. "You're saying you don't believe in psychology but you honestly believe we'll travel to the moon? We'll travel to Mars?"

"Oh we will," Uncle Dennis said, in a different, breathy voice. "Maybe your boys. Maybe the child within you. Walking on another planet. *Some* mother's child will do just that."

It was a clear night and a few stars were visible through the still-thin leaves of the elms overhead. Bianca had a feeling (the return of a dizzying, bizarre feeling) that the stars over her uncle's head were different stars from the stars over her own; his heaven was a different heaven. For her, the night sky was a kind of shield. For him—oh, she was perched at the brink of dreams!—it was an open labyrinth. Beckoning pathways. For him, the sky's boundaries were arbitrary—they were negotiable—and he was ready to launch the baby inside her into the firmament.

The two of them strolled along the brink of dreams. He had brought her back, years ago he'd brought her back. He had held her enfevered skull in his cupped hand and said, Now I'm going to tell you the most important thing I've ever told you . . . He'd sought to summon her, to understand her. She scarcely remembered this; she did not remember this. But he felt it too, yes, another mind was at work beside hers, and he'd brought her back, just as her great-great-grandmother brought her grandfather back, in the ark of a woodstove, by way of the only human claim that ultimately has counted for anything over the faltering centuries, the one that says, *No, little one, I will not let you go.* One night, in the dead of winter, the scientific man embarked on his long drive to the city in order to deliver his mystic's message, and now they were taking their long walk through the city, the plump middle-aged doctor and the pregnant young woman, and she marveled at the two different heavens over their heads, which are the same heaven.

"Your father seems well," Uncle Dennis said, resuming his ritual formulation.

Bianca took it up. They were earthbound once more. "Yes, he does. He, too, was floundering for a while. He was drinking too much—"

"I was eating too much—"

"And he just looked so—defeated. But he seems quite happy, and proud, in the new house. And speaking of houses, he's having so much fun with Ira's house. It's the unlikeliest thing. Papa has found a new . . . friend."

At the last moment, Bianca tendered the word warily, fearing that Uncle Dennis, Papa's best friend, might meet it with jealousy. But just the opposite. Uncle Dennis nodded vigorously and she was struck by how little she understood about—her father? About male friendship? "Indeed he has," Uncle Dennis concurred. "A new friend. And a good friend."

"Have you seen the house? Ira's house?"

"No—no, I haven't."

"Would you like to see it? It's just past Seven—just a little ways into Palmer Woods."

"Can you walk that far? Aren't you tired, dear?"

It did seem a long way. But she took a special, almost proprietary interest in Ira's house. In the darkness, its spacious contours were calling her. "My new plan is, I won't stop walking until this baby's born."

"All right, then. Let's. Let's go have a look at Ira's house. And then I'll deliver the baby." Uncle Dennis laughed. She joined his laughter.

They continued on Middleway, past her own house. Lights were off in the boys' room: Grant had gotten them down for the night. He was so good at that. It was a comical, lovable scene right out of some illustration to a children's book: the three of them so much alike, Grant in the chair by the window, talking like a coach ("Tomorrow, if the weather's good, maybe we should hit a few"), and one twin or the other in the top bunk, and the other in the other, you never knew which would be where, and all so much alike as they nodded wordlessly, knowingly at each other: Grant a little boy, the boys two grown-up men.

It filled her with love, the image of that mute trio in the room, nodding male reassurances, just as it filled her with a different sort of love to be out in the open air, on the street, pregnant and purposeful, waddling alongside her uncle, a big baby girl upside-down inside her . . .

A thought came out of the blue. "Do you remember the time Papa used the word *nigger* in front of you?"

Uncle Dennis's reply was immediate: "Your father doesn't talk like that."

"Oh but he did. And that's exactly what you said to him. We were at a family picnic. Do you remember? Don't you remember? You went up and said, quite sternly, you said, Vico, *you* don't talk that way. Do you remember?"

Uncle Dennis sucked on his plump lower lip. He was searching his memory. "You know, I guess I do . . ."

"I was just a little girl, but I remember it vividly. You said, Vico, *you* don't talk that way. And Papa clenched his fists. Boy, did he clench his fists. The veins in his arms were bulging. I don't think you saw that. Oh he was furious! And I honestly thought he was going to hit you."

Sudden, hearty laughter erupted—clearly, Uncle Dennis had never heard anything so preposterous. "Oh darling, listen to you. *Listen* to you. You always did have the wildest imagination of any child I ever—"

"But he *did*."

"Your father *hitting* me . . ."

"But he did. He came very close."

"Of all the most ridiculous . . . Honestly, your father hitting *me*." And laughter exploded out of Uncle Dennis once more. Had he once publicly rebuked his brother-in-law at a family picnic? If he had, he'd done so in absolute safety. How could his brother-in-law resist him? For on his side he'd had rightness—dignity, justice, the prospect of a fairer brotherhood of man.

They crossed Seven Mile. Immediately, the houses grew grander—the streets more expansive and winding. Here were wider yards, looping contours. It was in this neighborhood that Ira's aunt had holed up in a house almost destroyed by a dozen cats. And it was here that Papa used to bring his daughter, just a little girl, when he was still a brown-haired man, and the two of them would examine the houses one by one—some of the finest houses in the city. One by one, he would ask her opinions. And he would listen to what she said. He, too, had been teaching her, his little Bia, to observe.

"So what have you been reading?" Bianca said.

"Well—this one's *really* dumb."

"Good," she said happily.

"This one's a time-travel story. A man builds a time machine because his wife has an incurable disease and he wants to see if future scientists have developed a cure. Well, it turns out they *have*, and he brings it back, along with a box of newspapers. He saves his wife. But when he reads the newspapers, he discovers that in the original world, the one where there was no cure, he'd eventually married another woman, after his wife died, and he'd had three children. Which means that by curing his wife and not marrying this second woman, he'd effectively murdered his children. Are you following me?"

"Mostly."

"It's a bit tricky. Anyway, having cured his wife, he decides he'll divorce her—she's a bit of a pill, actually—and marry the other woman, so he can still have the children he would have had. But when he travels again into the future, he discovers that his third child's child—his grandchild—is destined to become a terrible tyrant. A sort of Hitler. What should he do? Should he not have that third child? Or go ahead and have that child, but then travel again into the future and somehow stop his grandchild from becoming a tyrant? I suppose the lesson of the story is the terrible danger of meddling. If so, it's not a lesson I've taken to heart. It seems I'm forever interfering in all your lives."

"You answer cries for help," Bianca said. "That's a different matter."

"Well, thank you." And Bianca saw she'd said exactly the right thing. "Well, thank you.

"Here's the house," she announced. "The one that Ira planned to sell for twenty-four thousand, before Papa talked him out of it."

In the darkness, the place looked particularly inviting. Ira had left a few lights on. The foyer glowed through the front door's tinted panes. Upstairs, the room with the big bay window also glowed.

"Beautiful house," Uncle Dennis said. He lit the pipe he'd been carrying all this time. He inhaled his first breath of smoke with a grunt of pleasure. To stand beside him was as near to smoking as she would ever come again—the intricate and primordial aroma of her uncle's pipe.

"Absolutely beautiful," she said. "Papa's advice was sound. Ira's going to make a tidy sum. And that's only fair."

Even in the darkness, the house exuded a sense of careful, loving husbandry. It had all taken place under Papa's watchful eye: the new gutters, the new shrubbery. A light had also been left on at the top of the house, in the room Ira was converting into a library. Over that little room, the slate roof shone, as if with moonlight, though no moon was visible.

"Big place," Uncle Dennis said.

"Big enough for a batty old woman and a dozen cats," Bianca said.

"Or a growing family," Uncle Dennis suggested.

"I suppose."

The two of them turned around, heading at last toward home. "And Edith," Uncle Dennis resumed. "She seems well."

"Very well. Getting into medical school cheered her up remarkably."

"Now I had *nothing* to do with that."

"I'm not saying you did." Surely, Edith had needed no help in getting admitted. The lowest grade she'd ever received at Wayne was an A–. "But the *idea* of applying . . ."

"It was already in her head."

"Actually, I do worry about her decision, though."

Bianca felt a little guilty bringing up this topic. Tonight, Uncle Dennis so clearly yearned for reassuring news. But she'd been waiting such a long time to open her heart to him . . . "You know, she almost never dates. And now medical school? I worry Edith's going to wind up an old maid."

"Edith an old maid?" Evidently, this particular worry didn't trouble Uncle Dennis. No, it tickled him. "What an idea!"

"But she says she's going to become a doctor."

"So what? She'll be a married doctor," Uncle Dennis said. "I don't know if you've happened to notice, but when she takes her glasses off, your baby sister has grown into quite a beautiful young woman."

"She never *does* take them off. And she won't listen when I tell her they're the world's least flattering design."

"She's beautiful with them on, for that matter."

Edith a beautiful young woman? She'd lost her baby fat, somewhere along the line, and grown taller. Though she hadn't the slightest interest in clothes—as a shopper, Edith showed a positive *knack* for the unbecoming—there was no way fully to disguise that she'd developed quite a fine, shapely figure.

"Think about the boys at medical school," Uncle Dennis said. "Now what's going to happen when they see someone as pretty and brilliant and competent as that? They'll be lining up six deep behind her. Not that—my guess is—she'll be wholly unattached come fall."

"Uncle Dennis, what on earth are you talking about?"

"Mm?" He pulled tranquilly on his pipe.

"What are you talking about?"

"Why, Ira Styne, of course."

"Now you're ribbing me! I don't think I get the joke! What are you talking about?"

"I'm talking about Ira and Edith."

"Ira? Ira Styne?"

Ira Styne? Ira Styne? The self-described "old soldier," who had appeared on their doorstep one day in January? The gray-haired young man on a cane, talking so fast and so nervously that Bianca had hardly understood him? *Edith and Ira?* "You're talking about them as some sort of twosome?"

Uncle Dennis paused dramatically. Again he drew on his pipe. He was about to deliver one of his pronouncements. "I'm talking about the fact, my dear girl, that Ira Styne is so mad for your little sister that he can hardly see straight when she enters a room. His heart palpitates. He gets short of breath and words die in his throat. He forgets what he was going to say. As a medical man, I'd hazard a guess the boy's in love."

"Uncle Dennis, you *can't* be serious . . ."

"Couldn't be more so."

"But he must be thirty years old."

"As a medical man, I've heard tell of men as old as forty falling in love . . ."

"But you *can't* be serious."

"For somebody with second sight, my dear, you sure missed a lot this time around."

Bianca let the words sink in. *Was* it possible? Ira and Edith? Yes—she supposed—it was possible. And there was something else as well: an unexpected *delight* in realizing she'd been an utter fool.

But if it were possible . . . Well, the delicate truth of the matter (something she could never tell anybody) was that she'd harbored flattering suspicions that shy, blushing, stammering Ira Styne was susceptible to her own charms, pregnancy and all. And all this time he was dreaming of her sister? *Was* it possible she'd been such an utter fool? Yes, it was possible.

"Let me tell you another little story," Uncle Dennis said. "Would you mind another story?"

"I'd love another story."

It was the perfect place for a story. They were on Wellesley Drive, and these were some of the very largest, the most enchanting houses in the city. These were Papa's mythical palaces.

"Once there was a young athletic Jewish boy who went off to fight people who were dead-set on exterminating his entire race. And he was gravely wounded—shrapnel in the leg—which meant he would never walk smoothly again, though he'd once been quite a runner. And shrapnel in his esophagus, which traumatized the vocal cords and rendered him mute for a couple of weeks. This very shy young man didn't know whether he'd ever talk again.

"And he had some sort of mental breakdown and then he recovered, and after the war he went home and married his high school sweetheart, to whom he was devoted, and in time she left him for his best friend, and he had another catastrophic breakdown.

"And one day he happened to find himself in a distant city where a girl lived who once had written him amazingly precocious letters while he lay in a hospital, unable to walk and talk. The girl is unfinished business, and all these years later he decides to go thank her properly. Sure, he'd been shot in the leg, and in the throat, but that hardly justified not answering a little girl's letters. He remembers the name of her street but not the house number, though the girl had told him it was a prime number, and so he does calculation after calculation, and the number he thought he remembered is indeed a prime number. Of course he could have looked the family up in the phone book, but that wouldn't have been the same, would it? No, that wouldn't have been a signal from Heaven. This is a somewhat fragile young man, and he needs nothing less than a signal from Heaven. And then, after all sorts of agonized hesitations—for he's very, very shy—he climbs up the front porch and rings the doorbell. And while he's standing out there, she comes down the street, carrying a satchel full of books."

"My goodness, how do you *know* all this?"

"Simple. Let's just say it's my story. I was that boy."

"Uncle Dennis, what are you talking about?"

"It's my story, sweetie. It's only all the details that are different."

"I think you're trying to give *me* a nervous breakdown. Now you must tell me: what are you talking about?"

"Put it another way: one frog recognizes another frog a mile off."

"Come on, please! Now you're just torturing me. Even by your standards, you're talking in riddles tonight . . ."

"I mean, I recognize all the symptoms. Do you remember the night at Chuck's Chop House? Your aunt's fortieth—"

"How could I forget?"

"And your mother revealed how your Aunt Grace came home after our first date and told your mother I looked like a frog?"

"Oh, Aunt Grace obviously didn't mean—"

"But she obviously *did*. It's all right, sweetie. Hey, it's all right. On our very first date—you know how quick and intuitive Grace is—she saw how the land lay: I was a frog who'd found his princess. And Ira? Christ, honey, I recognize all the symptoms! I know what it's like to feel that way. You can't *believe* her, you can't *breathe* near her. One amazing day, Ira beheld his princess, walking down the street with a satchel full of books: this pretty girl who happens to be kind and unselfish and so intelligent it's positively scary."

"But what about Edith?" Bianca said. "What about Edith?"

"What *about* Edith? What's been Edith's primary complaint about boys? They're silly. Well, Ira couldn't say 'boo' to a rabbit, maybe he's someone who's going to go through life bullied by bellhops and elevator operators, but heaven knows he isn't silly. I think he's going to wind up a history teacher."

"Yes . . ." Yes, Edith herself had mentioned something of the sort. "But what about her feelings?"

"What *about* her feelings? If Edith commits to him, which I suspect she will, which I suspect she already has, she'll never waver. She's got the loyalest heart I've ever seen."

Bianca stiffened—she wasn't accustomed to hearing her uncle promote some other girl ahead of her. But in the end there was no arguing with this remark. Once Edith joined your team—once she'd agreed to supervise your family's move, or to knit sweaters for your country's soldiers—her commitment was absolute.

"But he's a Jew," Bianca pointed out.

"That's right," Uncle Dennis said contentedly. "He's a Jew."

"And how would Mamma like that?"

"She'll like it just fine. We grow, honey. We grow as we go.

"The real question," Uncle Dennis went on, "the question your father and I keep wondering, is, How many rooms is Ira going to renovate in that big house before he finds the courage to pop the question?"

"You're telling me that *Papa* knows? Everybody knows but me?" And this, too, delighted her.

"Of *course* he knows. Your dad's the father of two pretty girls. You don't think he sees why Ira's over every other night? You don't think he notices when Edith's darning one of Ira's socks, or when Ira's talking about putting up a wall or tearing down a wall, reflooring the basement, renovating the attic? Sweetie, Ira can't stay away from Edith. And the question is, Is Ira going to build a solarium, or a bowling alley, or a tennis court, before he screws up his nerve?"

Bianca said, "I'm just—amazed."

She was—and yet she wasn't. For this was how momentous turns in Edith's life typically unfolded. Some dumbfounding improbability would emerge—and very soon it took on an air of rightness and inevitability. Of *course* Edith was going to marry Ira. The nuptials were set back when Ira sent his earnest schoolgirl correspondent "five hundred pennies in convenient paper form," and oh how his cleverness had enchanted the—actually—hopelessly romantic heart of our little coolly calculating Edith . . .

"So you're saying Edith's knight in shining armor is a cripple?"

"They're the best kind. They're stronger."

"Another of your riddles?"

"Honey, look at the facts. Ira's been to Hell and back. And it toughens you. He came back from Hell for Edith."

"I suppose what you're saying is obvious. Now it's just so *obvious.*

But I didn't know. I guess my thoughts were elsewhere. The things I didn't know . . ." Bianca said.

"That's okay. He didn't know it either."

Her pronouncement echoed pleasingly in her head, and she repeated it: "The things I didn't know . . ."

But Uncle Dennis wasn't through. He said, "You mentioned Ira's making a profit on the house? What profit? No, no. He's never going to sell. Because that's the house he and Edith are going to live in, after they're married. He's building his princess her palace. Do you honestly suppose the upstairs library is intended for him?"

"Well I'll be," Bianca said.

She'd fantasized that she and Grant would buy Ira's house once the renovations were complete. Now she needed to ponder a moment— reordering things, moving things. And as she walked along, it silently slipped away, her claim to the house in Palmer Woods whose renovations her father was overseeing.

The neighborhood was transfiguring itself, even as she walked through it.

And it was strange, but even here in Palmer Woods, the most magical neighborhood in the world's most magical city, you could still hear the pulsed detonations of fireworks. Ever the patriot, Grant was planning to take the boys to the downtown parade on Saturday. It was dear Grant, after she'd removed it from the wall, who had insisted on restoring Henry's portrait. And wouldn't it be something if she had her baby on Memorial Day? It came now as a sharp intuition: her body had been waiting, all along, to deliver a Memorial Day baby . . .

"I'm sorry you can't stay through till Sunday," Bianca said. Uncle Dennis and Aunt Grace were planning to drive back to Cleveland on Saturday morning. His hospital beckoned. "We don't see enough of you. And we never see Grace."

"Well—we may be seeing more of you. It's one of the things I wanted to discuss. Now please don't say anything to anybody yet. Not even your father."

"Yes . . ."

Bianca did not know where this chain of revelations was headed, but with every cell in her body—again, with her soul's second sight—she grasped that this was news she'd been yearning for.

"As a medical man, I would have to say that your aunt's long-term prognosis looks doubtful. But as I say, there's always room for hope. And

I'm hopeful. I remain hopeful. Even so, Grace feels—your aunt feels that if we're looking at the worst, well, she wants to do that at home."

"You're saying—"

"She wants to move back. Now not a word to anybody. But I'm telling you tonight, I'm telling you first, because I think maybe over the years it's been hardest of all on you: you do get so emotional, Bia. But yes, we're moving back to Detroit. Where Grace was born. We're going to look at a few houses tomorrow."

"Oh Uncle Dennis . . . Oh *Uncle Dennis* . . ."

Bianca didn't know the words—but she didn't need the words, which would in time take their own shape, they were as voluminous as the child within her. There were so many questions to ask—to ask Uncle Dennis, to ask Aunt Grace. There was so much wonderful talk ahead, and, beyond all the talk, such wonderful prospects! And if it was the worst for Aunt Grace, well, Bianca would *be* there for her aunt, as her aunt had been there once for her.

Then the words spilled out of her. She said: "Does that mean it's over? Could it really be over? Really? Really all over? It's as if Mamma declared war, so long ago, and everything was torn apart, it never has been the same, and could it really all be over? I don't even know why it started."

The man who had always served as the family's military analyst drew on the remaining embers in the belly of his pipe. Then he said, within a sweet cloud of smoke, "That's how it is with most wars. The origin is usually a mystery. What matters is that it comes to an end, darling. And this war's over."

A NOTE ABOUT THE AUTHOR

Brad Leithauser was born in Detroit and graduated from Harvard College and Harvard Law School. He is the author of five previous novels, five volumes of poetry, a novel in verse, two collections of light verse, and a book of essays. Among the many awards and honors he has received are a Guggenheim Fellowship, an Ingram Merrill grant, and a MacArthur Fellowship. He served for a year as *Time* magazine's theater critic. He is a professor in the Writing Seminars at Johns Hopkins University. He and his wife, the poet Mary Jo Salter, divide their time between Amherst, Massachusetts, and Baltimore, Maryland. In 2005, Leithauser was inducted into the Order of the Falcon by the president of Iceland for his writings about Nordic literature.

A NOTE ON THE TYPE

This book was set in Caledonia, a Linotype face designed by W. A. Dwiggins (1880–1956). It belongs to the family of printing types called "modern face" by printers—a term used to mark the change in style of the type letters that occurred around 1800. Caledonia borders on the general design of Scotch Roman but it is more freely drawn than that letter.

Composed by North Market Street Graphics
Lancaster, Pennsylvania
Printed and bound by Berryville Graphics
Berryville, Virginia